SAILING ACROSS THE RED STORM

JOHN XIAO ZHANG

Copyright © 2020 John Xiao Zhang

The moral right of the author has been asserted.

Apart from any fair dealing for the purposes of research or private study, or criticism or review, as permitted under the Copyright, Designs and Patents Act 1988, this publication may only be reproduced, stored or transmitted, in any form or by any means, with the prior permission in writing of the publishers, or in the case of reprographic reproduction in accordance with the terms of licences issued by the Copyright Licensing Agency. Enquiries concerning reproduction outside those terms should be sent to the publishers.

This is a work of fiction. Names, characters, businesses, places, events and incidents are either the products of the author's imagination or used in a fictitious manner. Any resemblance to actual persons, living or dead, or actual events is purely coincidental.

Matador
9 Priory Business Park,
Wistow Road, Kibworth Beauchamp,
Leicestershire, LE8 0RX
Tel: 0116 279 2299
Email: books@troubador.co.uk
Web: www.troubador.co.uk/matador
Twitter: @matadorbooks

ISBN 978 1838592 547

British Library Cataloguing in Publication Data.
A catalogue record for this book is available from the British Library.

Printed and bound in the UK by TJ International, Padstow, Cornwall
Typeset in 11pt Adobe Garamond Pro by Troubador Publishing Ltd, Leicester, UK

Matador is an imprint of Troubador Publishing Ltd

To the innocent people who died during the social and political upheaval: you did not die in vain. Your sacrifice stirred the conscience of an entire nation. It held up the historical mirror to the survivors, allowing them to learn from the past, preventing any recurrence of this historical tragedy, and beckoning them to find a new way towards a brighter future.

CONTENTS

CONTENTS		VII
LIST OF CHARACTERS		XI
PROLOGUE		XVII
PART I	**FLOWERS BLOOMING IN THE LIGHT OF THE FULL MOON**	1
CHAPTER I	ENCOUNTER ON A BUS RIDE	3
CHAPTER II	THE HERO SAVES A BEAUTY	12
CHAPTER III	CHARMING PRINCE ON WHITE HORSE	24
CHAPTER IV	AT THE RIVER BANK	39
CHAPTER V	HUMILIATION IN A DISTINGUISHED GUEST HOUSE	48
CHAPTER VI	A SWEET HOLIDAY	62

PART II	**THE RED STORM**	**71**
CHAPTER I	THE RED SEA	73
CHAPTER II	WHAT CRIME HAS HE COMMITTED?	84
CHAPTER III	THE RED AND BLACK	94
CHAPTER IV	HOME SEARCH AND CONFISCATION	102
CHAPTER V	A RED HORROR	113
CHAPTER VI	A FARCE IN THE PROVINCIAL PARTY COMMITTEE COMPOUND	126
CHAPTER VII	I WANT TO ACCOMPANY MY MOTHER	135
PART III	**THE RED FLOOD**	**149**
CHAPTER I	TRAIN ENCOUNTER	151
CHAPTER II	THE CRAZY SQUARE	165
CHAPTER III	THE QUARREL IN THE WARD	173
PART IV	**JANUARY STORM**	**195**
CHAPTER I	TO FIND THE BIGGEST CAPITALIST ROADER OUT	197
CHAPTER II	ON THE EDGE OF THE CLIFF	206
CHAPTER III	I AM POLITICALLY BLACKER THAN YOU	215
CHAPTER IV	WE CAN NO LONGER REGARD FRIENDS AS THE ENEMY	228

PART V	**A BLOODY STORM SWEEPS THE DIVINE LAND**	**241**
CHAPTER I	FINDING THE CAPITALIST ROADER HIDING BEHIND THE ARMY	243
CHAPTER II	BACK TO THE ANCIENT BATTLEFIELD	258
CHAPTER III	IN THE RAIN OF BULLETS	270
CHAPTER IV	A TALL FIGURE IN THE SMOKE	281
PART VI	**SWEEP AWAY ALL MONSTERS AND DEMONS**	**305**
CHAPTER I	CLEAN UP THE RANKS OF THE CLASS – THE HORRIFYING RED TERROR	307
CHAPTER II	IN THE DARK JAIL	322
CHAPTER III	ON THE WAY TO THE EXECUTION GROUND	346
CHAPTER IV	AT THE GATES OF HELL	368
CHAPTER V	THE MAGICAL HERB	383
PART VII	**IN THE DAYS OF EXILE**	**395**
CHAPTER I	IN THE BACKCOUNTRY	397
CHAPTER II	PEASANTS WEEDING AT NOON, SWEAT DOWN THE FIELD SOON (FROM AN ANCIENT CHINESE POEM)	412
CHAPTER III	IN THE HARVEST SEASON	429
CHAPTER IV	IN THE BLIZZARD AND CHILLINESS	445

PART VIII	**'ESCAPE TO VICTORY'**	**463**
CHAPTER I	A POLITICAL EVENT THAT SHOCKED THE WHOLE COUNTRY	465
CHAPTER II	WHY CAN'T HE GO TO UNIVERSITY?	481
CHAPTER III	LIFE IN THE CHEMICAL FACTORY	500
CHAPTER IV	A TEAR-SHEDDING WEDDING	513
PART IX	**FINALLY THE STORM HAS PASSED**	**533**
CHAPTER I	DAWN ON THE HORIZON	535
CHAPTER II	WALKING OUT OF THE UNDERCLASS	548
CHAPTER III	HISTORY HAS PROVED YOU ARE INNOCENT	573
CHAPTER IV	AT THE FUNERAL	591
EPILOGUE		**607**

LIST OF CHARACTERS

Main Characters

I. Zhang Feng, *the main hero in the story. A handsome and talented young man. He is also called Brother Feng by his lovers and friends. Elder Brother by his close friends. Xiao Feng or Xiao Zhang by his family and people around him who are older than him.*

II. His close friends: Wang Hai and Li He

III. His lovers:

    A) Yu Mei, *daughter of a high ranking officer. (Her name means plum blossom. Her full name is Li Yu Mei.) She is also called Xiao Mei or Mei Mei by her family and lovers.*

- B) Dan Dan, *a girl from the neighbors of Zhang Feng. (Her name means peony and her full name is Liu DanDan.)*
- C) Qing Lian, *a classmate of Zhang Feng and an active Red Guard. (Her name means lotus and her full name is Liu Qing Lian.)*

IV. His rival: Chang Zheng, *son of a military commander of the province, an active Red Guard. (His full name is Zhao Chang Zheng.)*

V. His personal and political enemies:
- A) Cai Wenge, *a classmate of Zhang Feng and an active Red Guard. (He is called Cai Desheng before the Cultural Revolution. His new name Wenge means Cultura Revolution.)*
- B) Hei Tou, *a local hooligan and an active Red Guard. (His name means a person with a dark coloured head.)*

VI. Parents of the main characters:
- A) Zhang Wenbo, *Zhang Feng's father, a well known scholar and professor, but was denounced as a Rightist in 1957. Hu Yun, Zhang Feng's mother, an university lecturer.*
- B) Li Jiangguo, *Yu Mei's father. A high ranking official, first secretary of the provincial party committee. Song Lihua, Yu Mei's mother*
- C) Zhao Wu, *Chang Zheng's father, a general, the commander of the military area of the province.*

    (The above three fathers used to be university classmates before the liberation in the 1940's)

Characters by Alphabet

Cai Wenge, *an ambitious villain, enemy to Zhang Feng. Also called Cai Desheng before the Cultural Revolution.*

Chang Zheng, *rival of Zhang Feng, a Red Guard, son of general Zhao Wu.*

Chang Jingyu, *a principal of a senior middle school, also called 'old principal' by his students.*

Chen Xing, *the youngest of the Four Talents of The River City.*

Chen Hao, *director of the workshop in the chemical factory.*

Dan Dan, *Zhang Feng's lover, a beautiful and talented girl.*

Du Zhongqing, *a commissioner from the central Cultural Revolution Group. Called 'a man in black'.*

Fan, Director, *a wicked officer who followed the Cultural Revolution Group closely.*

Hai Jing, Master, *a Taoist who teaches Zhang Feng martial arts; with a secret identity.*

He Hua, *a younger girl in the countryside where Zhang Feng and his friends worked as 'Educated youth'.*

He Qiang, *the general director of the general headquarters of the workers' revolutionary rebellion.*

Hei Tou, *a local hooligan, later becomes an active Red Guard.*

Huo, Deputy Director, *an officer in the public security bureau who used to be a subordinate of Li Jianguo.*

Hu Yun, *Zhang Feng's mother.*

Jiang Qing, *wife of Chairman Mao.*

Lao Hou, *the foreman of the production team in the village.*

Li He, *a close friend to Zhang Feng.*

Li Jianguo, *the first secretary of the Province Party Committee. Yu Mei's father.*

Li Li, *a Red Guard, university student, Xu Jianguo's girlfriend.*

Li Yue, *The third elder brother of the Four Talents of The River City.*

Li Yulan, *Zhang Feng's classmate, in the same collective household during his time working in the countryside.*

Liu Jianqiang, *a chief of staff in the provincial military area.*

Liu Tian, *The eldest of the Four Talents of The River City, a talented student in Beijing University.*

Liu Zhongguo, *a persecuted rightist, Dan Dan's father, disguised as a Taoist priest named Hai Jing Master.*

Liu, Director, *a director of a government department, a subordinate of Li Jianguo.*

Liu Ming, *the commander of the rebel army of the Normal University.*

Li Xiaogang, *Yu Mei's younger brother.*

Mao Hongxing, *a factory worker; a wicked man who harasses other people.*

Qing Lian, *an active Red Guard who loves the main hero Zhang Feng.*

Song Lihau, *Yu Mei's mother.*

Sun, Teacher, *a violin teacher of Zhang Feng.*

Wang Hai, *a close friend to the main hero Zhang Feng.*

Wang Hui, *Dan Dan's mother.*

Wang, Lieutenant, *works for the militiaman platoon in the village.*

Wang Weimin, *the director of the Propaganda Department of the Provincial Party Committee. A sucordinate of Li Jianguo.*

Wang Xiaohong, *Zhang Feng's classmate, lives together with him while living in the countryside.*

Wang Yang, *one of the Four Talents of the River City, a talented student of Qinghua University.*

Wu Xiaoli, *a Red Guard, Chang Zhang's girlfriend.*

Xiao Fang, *a friend of Yu Mei. Her university classmate.*

Xiao Sun, *a young worker in the factory, friend to Zhang Feng.*

Xu Jianguo, *a university student, Red Guard and leader of a rebel fraction, Zhang Feng's friend.*

Ye, Teacher, *a music teacher.*

Yu Mei, *Zhang Feng's lover. Daughter of the party secretary of the province.*

Zhang, Doctor, *a medical doctor, friend of Dan Dan's mother.*

Zhang Feng, *the main hero in the story. A handsome and talented young man.*

Zhang Lin, *Zhang Feng's younger sister.*

Zhang Qiang, *a political commissar in the military area.*

Zhang Wenbo, *Zhang Feng's father, a professor and a famous scholar.*

PROLOGUE

In Northeast China, the Songhua River zigzags through thousands of kilometres, passing through two provinces before making its way into the sea at the Russian border. Upstream of the river lies an artificial lake over 100 kilometres long, called the Songhua Lake; it was formed when the huge dam of a hydropower station was built on the river. About 10 kilometres downstream from the hydropower station lies Jili City, a large provincial capital known by locals as the River City. The clear Songhua River runs through the city and flows quietly into the distance. A bustling bridge called the South Bank Bridge spreads like a huge dragon across the banks of the river, connecting two city districts together. On the southern bank of the bridge is the beautiful South Bank Park, the university Campus Area, and high-level officials residential area (where provincial and city-level leading officials live). On the Northern bank are the business area, industrial area, and residential area. At the river bay on the northern side of the river, there stands the green Northern Mountain. The rushing river bursts as huge white waves onto the steep cliffs of the mountain. On the top of the mountain, an ancient majestic Taoist temple named Wangjiang Temple overlooks the river and looks far at the distant mountains. Our story unfolds in this ancient city.

Chinese society in the 1950s was peaceful; following the brutal civil war, the Communist Party defeated the Nationalist Party and built a new socialist China. After eradicating the corruption and suppression of the old society, the new society was formed as essentially an equal, clean and stable one. Though life was simple, a strong sense of happiness was pervasive. People trusted each other, the party and government. However, the Anti-Rightist movement that took place in 1957 marked more than half a million intellectuals who gave advice to the Communist Party as "rightists". Some of them were expelled from the party and from public office. Some were sent for labor reform at remote labor camps. After that, nobody dared to give advice to the Communist Party. Mao Zedong hurried to create economic miracles and started the 'Great Leap Forward' and 'People's Commune' in 1958, which violated the basic laws of economics and brought great disaster to Chinese society along with three consecutive years of natural disasters. Under the dissatisfaction and pressure of the party's cadres, Mao Zedong had to confess his mistakes and relinquish his power of managing the nation to Chairman Liu Shaoqi. Leaders like Liu Shaoqi, Zhou Enlai and Deng Xiaoping summed up the lessons learned and corrected the flawed policies of the past. By 1964 and 1965, industrial and agricultural production had gradually recovered and people's livelihood had improved, ushering in what seemed to be a new period of vitality for society. However, the good times were not to last; despite hopes of a period of peaceful, long and stable life, thick and dark clouds began to gather on the horizon. A dark, fierce and disastrous red political storm was about to sweep across the entire nation of China. Our story unfolds on the eve of the storm.

As spring blooms in the year of 1965, a delicious spring breeze teases the willows on the Songhua riverside. The entire River City is shrouded in greenery. On a Sunday afternoon, on the mountain road leading to the Wangjiang Temple on the top of the Northern Mountain, three young men talked and laughed as they paced together. One of them, Zhang Feng, is tall and handsome; he is the hero of this book. His two companions were named Wang Hai and Li He. They were all second-year students in the Second Senior Middle School of the city, and today was their well-deserved break from their intense studies; a hike through the beautiful scenery and landscapes on the path to the Northern Mountain.

The spring scenery of the Northern Mountain was indeed beautiful, with green pines and verdant cypresses, green willows and red flowers.

On reaching the mountain top, Wang Hai paused and turned to Zhang Feng.

"Tell me, elder brother", he said, referring to his friend as though a sworn brother, "is your martial arts teacher Master Hai Jing a Taoist in the Taoist temple on the Northern Mountain? Can we see him?" Zhang Feng gazed for a moment at the temple before turning to his friend.

"No, he's been away for a few weeks now, visiting his family back home. And anyway, he never lets me see him except during our lessons." Zhang Feng paused for a moment, puzzled at the sensation that there was some important memory that his subconscious was trying to remind him of.

"Ah, since you mention him, I remember now. Master Hai Jing mentioned before he left that a roaming Taoist recently arrived at the temple. Apparently he is a renowned fortune teller who has been very accurate at predicting the fates of those who come to see him. How about we go and pay him a visit?"

"Great idea!" replied Wang Hai and Li He; they both had an interest in the supernatural and the chance to see a fortune teller piqued their curiosity. Their teachers had predictably instructed them to stay away from superstition, but what harm would it cause if they just went to listen without believing?

Wangjiang Temple was a Taoist temple with a history spanning hundreds of years. It was said that once a roaming Taoist master from Wudang Mountain had found some incredibly rare herbs here and had decided to stay. These herbs, under the correct method, could produce an elixir so powerful that it could raise a dying person; as such it was named the "soul returning elixir". Later on, the Taoist master and his disciples built this majestic temple. Over the centuries the secret recipe of the elixir had been lost and no one could reproduce the mythical properties that were spoken about in the legends of the temple.

By the time the sun had passed its zenith, the three boys had reached the hall of the Taoist temple. Before them stood a marvellous structure, red and golden and shimmering in the midday sun. Pagoda towers encircled the temple like dragon claws. Enormous and foreboding, two stone lions stood guard at the entrance. Wang Hai reached out his arm to touch one of the heads, but found the gentle grip of Zhang Feng stopping him.

"Master Hai Jing once told me that things at the Taoist Temple are all sacred and clean. The hands of mortals will only stain them." Quietly, they proceeded into the main hall. They heard the gentle murmuring of drone-like speech, and as their eyes followed the sounds they saw various Taoist monks seated around the hall, eyes closed, deeply engrossed in meditation. Zhang Feng told the two companions not to disturb them. The three companions sneaked around one side of the hall, making their way to the inner courtyard. In the distance they could see the sun illuminating the square of the courtyard, sharply contrasting against the dim and incense-obscured light of the hall. As they approached, they saw that an old man with a long white beard was sitting behind a table, eyes closed and deep in thought. Zhang Feng recognised him immediately; his appearance matched exactly the fortune teller that his master had described. He carefully approached the old master, and as he came to face him across the table he stopped and bent forward in a deep bow.

"Revered master, forgive me for my intrusion, but my master has told me of your renowned mastery of reading the future."

The old man opened his eyes and studied them for a moment, his ancient eyes flickering across every feature and aspect of their puzzled faces. After a brief pause his thin mouth opened into a wide smile and he gestured with his hand at the temple around them.

"Tell me, my young friends, do you believe in feudal superstitions?".

"Taoism advocates nature, so it is materialistic, right?" Zhang Feng replied quickly.

"No, no", the old Taoist retorted, waving his hands impatiently but continuing to meet Zhang Feng's look with a kind gaze.

"If I were destined to meet someone, then I would certainly guess his future." The old Taoist said slowly and carefully. Wang Hai though had become impatient and immediately replied,

"My brother is studying martial arts with a Master in your temple. Is this destined?"

"Are you studying with Master Hai Jing?" the Taoist asked.

"Yes, I am", Zhang Feng replied.

"Fine, if that is the case, I will tell your fortune, but the other two must wait outside."

"We are all friends and there is nothing to hide!" Wang Hai muttered, and reluctantly walked out of the hall with Li He.

The two waited outside for what seemed like an eternity, though in reality it had only been a little over ten minutes. Wang Hai was starting to become a little anxious and wanted to go in and have a look. Li He was much calmer by temperament; he persuaded Wang Hai to wait. "Be patient, and don't bother them. Maybe this old Taoist master is really accurate in telling the future." A few minutes later, Zhang Feng emerged with a confused look on his face, holding a piece of paper in his hand.

"How did it go, what happened?" Wang Hai asked eagerly.

"Have a look for yourself." Zhang Feng handed the paper to them. Wang Hai and Li He took the paper and studied it closely. What they saw before them was a very old and somewhat yellowed piece of rice paper, roughly the size of two pages of an ordinary book. Its condition made it impossible to guess how old it was. There was something on the paper that was scribbled like an ink painting. In the middle was a mountain, flanked on both sides by smaller mountains. There were three small flowers at the foot of the mountain peak. On the mountainside was a plant that resembled a vine. On the lower right corner was an obscure number which seemed to be thirteen, or fifteen.

"What do all of these mean?" Wang Hai shook his head and asked.

"I don't know either." Zhang Feng replied. "The old Taoist master talked with me for about five minutes and then went back to his room. Then he gave me this painting. I asked him whether this was my future fate and he nodded his head. I asked how to I could understand the things in this painting. He told me that I must find this out by myself. If I believe it, it will become true; if I do not, then I should just throw it away."

Wang Hai looked at the painting and said, "This tall mountain must be you and the two mountains on the sides are me and Li He. That is to say, we will be life and death brothers like those in the Oath of the Peach Garden? Yes, I can do whatever I can for my friends. How about you, Li He?"

"No problem for me." Li He replied.

"Then how about these three flowers? Our elder brother is handsome and attractive. Would this mean that he will have three women in his life?".

"Nonsense!" Zhang Feng retorted, "Monogamy has been enshrined in law ever since the formation of the Republic of China. What three women?" Li He thought for a moment before replying,

"Maybe it refers to three women who are related to him, for example, his mother, wife, and daughter."

"This makes sense." Zhang Feng said.

"What about the vines that are wrapped around the mountainside?" Wang Hai wanted to guess further.

"This is a bit like a snake. So it means our elder brother will be troubled by a villain?" Li He said.

"No, surely this could never happen." Wang Hai quickly replied. "Our elder brother is bold and generous, courteous and humble. How could he offend anyone?"

"Enough." Zhang Feng said impatiently. "I think this old Taoist is just guessing and painting arbitrarily. There's no meaning at all. Just throw it away." After this, he was just about to throw the paper into the garbage bin on the side of the road.

"Don't do that," Wang Hai hurriedly pulled him back, saying, "Keep it, maybe it will become true a few years later."

"Fine, I will keep it. I can ask Master Hai Jing about it later. Anyway, if the old Taoist died, this paper would become a cultural relic." Zhang Feng said half-jokingly.

"I will find a good place to hide it." Wang Hai said, He ran to the wall of the Taoist temple, and stuffed the painting into a gap where the mortar had fallen away between two bricks.

After leaving the Taoist Temple, the three young people ventured on and enjoyed the scenery of the pine forest along the cliffs of the Northern Mountain and slowly descended back to the city. In a few days, Zhang Feng forgot about the fortune-telling incident. But what he had not expected was that the content of this painting would affect his whole life.

PART I

Flowers Blooming in the Light of the Full Moon

CHAPTER I

Encounter on a Bus Ride

A bus stop in South Bank teemed with the bustle of people going to work and students headed for school. Zhang Feng and Wang Hai were also among the crowd. The bus was late today. Zhang Feng was worried about being late, while Wang Hai seemed not to care. He touched Zhang Feng with his hand.

"Elder brother, you should watch yourself. You're a popular guy – chairman of the Students' Union, outstanding in your studies, captain of the music band, and captain of the sports team. You are becoming quite the heart breaker. Did you know that when you were giving that speech at the union meeting last time, I saw several girls wide-eyed, mesmerised by you? Even when you finished talking they just stood there frozen like statues, gawking at you. I can tell you there are plenty of pretty girls out there tossing and turning at night, unable to sleep, with you on their minds…Ow, what did you do that for?!" Wang Hai winced, kneading his shoulder, warily eyeing Zhang Feng's finger which had stabbed him a moment earlier.

"You, my friend, are talking nonsense. Do you even realise we have our university entrance exams next year? And here you are, focusing on rubbish like this instead of your studies! You're the one yearning for love," said Zhang Feng.

At that moment the bus arrived, and they got on. Wang Hai turned to Zhang Feng and said mysteriously,

"Elder brother, I know you have your head in the clouds sometimes, so I'm going to tell you something. An amazingly beautiful girl has started to take this bus recently – some celestial goddess not from our realm of mortal men. Have you seen her? She always gets on at the next stop. She might be a student from the First Senior Middle School. It's said that no one who sees her can resist staring at her."

"You're making up another story," said Zhang Feng absently, looking at rows of green willows dancing in the wind outside the South Bank Park. Then the bus stopped slowly at the South Bank Park stop.

"Hey, look, here comes our goddess!" Wang Hai nudged Zhang Feng and pointed to the back door. The two looked over their shoulder and saw almost all the seated men standing up. A young girl walked onto the bus airily. Zhang Feng felt that all other passengers held their breath just as he did, watching the girl with undivided attention. Zhang Feng had never seen such a beautiful girl. She really did look divine in her perfection; curving willow leaf-like eyebrows, bright and watery eyes and a fair-skinned face as white and smooth as ivory. She wore her pitch black hair in a long braid. Her plain blue dress accentuated her slender and graceful body. For a few seconds time stood still; even the air in the bus seemed to stop flowing. Then all of a sudden time unwound in a frenzy of activity; all the men near her jolted upright, falling over themselves to offer her their seat.

"Please take my seat! Sit here! No, over here, take my seat!" A few even tried to reach out to pull her over. A slight flush came over her face, like a crimson rose in the white snow. She politely declined all of them and continued on her way further into the bus. The expressions on the men who were willing to offer their seat changed from excitement and expectation to disappointment as she passed by. She came closer and closer to Zhang Feng and Wang Hai. For a moment they both had no idea what to do because they were standing there with no seat to offer. Wang Hai was a clever boy, he knew that the girl preferred standing to sitting down, so he gave up his hanging rail to her politely. She thanked him with a smile, before taking it in her hand, standing shoulder to shoulder with Zhang Feng. The other men sat down sullenly, eyeing Zhang Feng with envy. They could not help but wonder though at what a natural match the two made. Zhang Feng with a handsome face and a strong build and the girl with a fairy-like figure were like copies of Handsome Fan Li and Beauty Xi Shi, in an ancient Chinese legend. Zhang Feng felt his heart throbbing. He was at a loss until Wang Hai gave him a nudge. Then he realized that he should say something to the girl.

"Going to school?" Zheng Feng could normally speak for hours and was not known for being shy, but now found that he had lost his tongue. It took him quite a while to force the few words out. He felt that his face was burning.

"Right," answered the girl naturally.

"From First Senior Middle School?" added Zhang Feng.

"Yeah, are you in Second Senior Middle School? Are you also acting as a leader in the Students' Union?" The girl's voice was soft and beautiful, like dulcet tones from a Chinese lute.

"Yes, he is chairman of our Students' Union, captain of the music band, captain of the sports team as well as a math and physics competition champion!" shot Wang Hai.

"Oh, how accomplished!" said the girl half seriously and half-jokingly. Zhang Feng was somewhat embarrassed at being spoken highly of in front of others. He said in a hurry,

"Don't pay attention to his nonsense!" After a brief pause, he asked another question. "Have we seen each other somewhere?"

The girl said, "I saw you organizing the group from your school weeks ago when we had a spring outing to the North Mountain. Thank you for making way for us."

Wang Hai cut in, "But your leader with a shoehorn-like face was impolite. We waited for a long time to let your group by, without even a simple thank you from him." At the mention of shoehorn, the girl giggled with her hand covering her mouth. Zhang Feng recalled it. Weeks ago, students from the Second Senior Middle School went to the North Mountain for a spring outing, paying their respects for the dead at the martyr's cemetery. They encountered students from the First Senior Middle School on a bridge across one of the ravines on the mountain pass leading to the cemetery. Most of the students in the First Senior Middle School were officers' children and relatively arrogant, while most of the students in the Second Senior Middle School were children of intellectuals and common citizens. The two middle schools were the best schools in the province and had competed fiercely with each other. At that encounter it felt like two ancient foes had come face to face. The two groups of students had met, each at one end of the bridge. The bridge had a narrow deck only allowing one group to pass. The deadlock lasted several minutes. Seeing that the other had no intention to go second, Zhang Feng said to Mr. Li, the teacher in charge,

"Give way to them, OK?" Mr. Li nodded. Zhang Feng shouted, "Fellow students, stand aside and let them go." All the students moved away toward the roadside to allow the other group to pass, although many students muttered, "Why they go first!" The group leader from the First Senior Middle School was a tall boy, who had a long face with an air of dignity like a general. He walked by without giving Zhang Feng and his group a glance.

"What a big man!" Zhang Feng heard Wang Hai mumble with anger.

While Zhang Feng was recalling, the bus stopped slowly. The stop for First Senior Middle School was already here. Why did the bus run so quickly today? There was so much more that he had wanted to say to her. She seemed to be willing to listen to him. But he was completely lost for words.

"Oh, are we at your stop already?… See you."

"See you." The girl smiled. Zhang Feng's eyes blankly followed her every step of her journey from the bus door until she disappeared into the crowd.

"Ah," said Wang Hai in a low voice, giving Zhang Feng a nudge, "Fascinated? Am I right? She's worth nine points out of ten at the very least. Why didn't you seize the opportunity to catch her? Look, the fish is gone!"

"Fishing! She is only a student." Zhang Feng said, He regretted not talking more with the girl. At that moment, he overheard a group of people beside them talking about the girl.

"It is said that she is the daughter of the secretary of the municipal party committee."

"Is it possible that the daughter of the secretary goes to school by bus?" Zhang Feng wanted to get more information from them, but the bus had arrived at the school gates. He and Wang Hai jumped off the bus and rushed to school; he didn't want to be late this morning because the principal had asked him to come to school half an hour earlier to talk about the student's union.

The school was situated at the edge of the city in a tranquil environment, not far from the edge of the North Mountain. The main building was a two-story structure built during the Japanese occupation. The students, all selected by examination, were clever and well-mannered. When Zhang Feng and Wang Hai walked through the gate, they saw the old principal was already standing there, as usual, greeting his students like a loving father looking after his children. All the students saluted him and said,

"Morning, Principal!" Principal Chang was in his fifties this year and only had a daughter. However, he always said that he had hundreds of daughters and sons whom he was proud of. Because the Second Senior Middle School was a key school at the provincial level, it was the first in the provincial rankings in respect of the percentage of students admitted to university every year.

Zhang Feng always felt a tinge of sadness whenever he saw the hint of white hair on the principal's head. He was always the first to arrive and the last to leave, and his devotion left him exhausted.

"Hi, Zhang Feng, hurry up, let's talk in my office." Upon seeing Zhang Feng, the old principal's face brightened. Zhang Feng was his favourite student. He had always regarded him as the best of the best and the most talented of the talented. He was sure that whatever profession he chose, he would excel and be distinguished amongst his peers. He had a feeling that he would also make a highly successful artist. The old principal was very strict with his students. He nurtured all of them and took every care of their health and wellbeing, but if someone made a mistake, he would be sure to criticize them rigorously. He held the firm belief that a capable student is trained by a strict teacher. Nevertheless, he treated Zhang Feng with favour. If Zhang Feng made a mistake, he would never blame him in public but would tell him privately. He knew that Zhang Feng was responsible and understanding of any feedback and would correct himself. After about 20 minutes of discussion around union matters in the principal's office, Zhang Feng went back to his classroom.

Zhang Feng was not himself the whole day at school. The girl's smile reappeared before his eyes constantly. During Mr Liu's Physics lesson he was so distracted that it took him several attempts before he could answer a question. Mr. Liu asked with surprise,

"Zhang Feng, what happened to you today? Your brain seems to be stuck in slow gear.",

"I went to bed late last night." Zhang Feng said in embarrassment

"Well, you should have a good rest tonight. Go to bed early!" Zhang Feng pinched his hand forcefully, warning himself not to lose himself in his daydreaming. He finally managed to control his mind in class in the afternoon.

At night, the voice and the smiling face appeared to him over and over again as he lay sleepless in bed. He could not figure out why none of the girls around him, many of whom were very beautiful, had never really aroused his interest. A long time ago, his father had told him that a man should establish his career before thinking about having a family. Zhang Feng was aware of his attraction to girls, but he was always able to maintain control of himself. He simply regarded them as ordinary friends and classmates. However, this girl's charm seemed irresistible to him. Beauty radiated from her in such a natural and intimate way. Zhang Feng tossed and turned in bed and could not fall asleep. He blamed himself and felt stupid for becoming so engrossed. Such a beautiful girl must have a boyfriend. And anyway, if she really was the daughter of the secretary of the municipal party committee, she would be far out of his league. At long last, he fell into a deep sleep.

Zhang Feng got up early the next morning. Although he could have gone to school at the usual time instead of arriving at school half an hour early, he got to the bus stop at the same time as yesterday in spite of himself. Despite his hopes of seeing the girl that he had met yesterday, he could not shake the feeling of ridicule and scorn. When the bus finally arrived, he boarded and found that there were vacant seats on the bus. All of sudden he remembered that the girl would not take a seat, so he stood up from the seat and chose the best position opposite the back door with his hand holding the rail. He noticed that quite a few men sitting at the door were those who offered seats to the girl yesterday. He smirked. Surely they were just waiting for a hare under the tree, as the ancient proverb went – describing those who had witnessed a hare crashing into a tree by accident and waiting for it to happen again. It did not take long for his smirk to vanish, as it occurred to him that he was also exactly what he was doing. After a short drive the bus reached South Bank Park. Zhang Feng felt his heart beating faster. The men in the front stretched their heads and stared at the door. When the door opened, the few men closest to the door raised their hips and were ready to offer their seat. The first to get on the bus was a pupil, and the second a middle-aged woman. Seven or eight passengers got on the bus in succession, but the girl was not among them. When the door closed, all those men sighed and heavily seated themselves again. A chill rose from Zhang Feng's heart. But he brushed his feeling aside and asked himself why her absence should have anything to do with him.

He met Wang Hai in the corridor before class. Wang Hai said in a mysterious tone,

"You shouldn't have taken the early bus. Weren't you waiting for your fairy? How is it going? You are a perfect match, a hero and a beauty!"

"You are talking nonsense again" Zhang Feng rolled his eyes. "I really had something to deal with this morning. Besides, that girl didn't take the bus."

Throughout the rest of the day, Zhang Feng tried to forget that girl to focus on his studies and the work with the student union. Over the following few days, Zhang Feng tried taking a bus at a different time every morning, having to find various excuses to satisfy Wang Hai every day. Of course, Wang Hai saw through it. He sometimes blinked his eyes and said in an amused tone,

"Good luck!"

However, the girl evaporated from the world as if the Seven Fairies had returned to their heavenly palace. Day by day, her image gradually faded away from Zhang Feng's memory.

CHAPTER II

The Hero Saves a Beauty

With the onset of spring, the River City became a green ocean. The weeping willows kissed the clear river. On a particular Wednesday morning, Zhang Feng got up early and went to the North Mountain Taoist temple to observe and practice martial arts with master Hai Jing. He came back in high spirits; his master had praised him, saying that his "Pili" fist technique showed great progress. Zhang Feng had started studying martial arts two years ago. Aside from his love of martial arts, there was a darker motivation. The neighbourhood where he lived was plagued by frequent attacks and fights caused by hooligans and street gangs. One particular incident stood out in his mind. A few years earlier, Zhang Feng and the children in his neighbourhood had made pole vaults from bamboo sticks and were playing high jump. However the hooligans approached them and began to push and shove them, calling them names. Zhang Feng was neither tall nor strong at that time. Although he was the leader of the children, he did not have the physical presence to challenge them. He knew the leader of the hooligans, a boy named Hei Tou (which means a boy with a dark face). He tried to reason with him, but Hei Tou smashed the bamboo poles into smithereens, throwing them at Zhang Feng before leaving with the other hooligans. Zhang Feng felt anger and frustration at being so helpless, but there was nothing he could do.

It was about a year after this incident, when Zhang Feng was jogging through the paths on the North Mountain, that he happened upon a Taoist practicing punches in the woods. The Taoist look middle aged, around 40 years old, weather beaten and seasoned but sure of his technique. He exuded confidence. Zhang Feng was so fascinated that he stopped, awestruck by this martial artist's immense skill; enthralled, he suddenly burst into rapturous applause. Alarmed, the Taoist stopped and stared. He was visibly annoyed but held back his displeasure when he saw Zhang Feng was just a child.

"Master, what form of martial arts are you practising?" Zhang Feng had found the courage to speak.

"The name of this form is not to be mentioned to the foreigners or outsiders. Only the learned ones of our order may know its name."

Zhang Feng paused to consider these words. "Master, is this martial art capable of fighting against bad people?"

The Taoist smiled and asked, "What bad people do you want to fight?"

Zhang Feng described the bullying of the hooligans. The master waved his hand in dismissal. "You can ask the police for help."

"But master, the police can't arrest them unless they kill or commit a serious crime." A sudden solemnness came over his voice. "Master, can you accept me as an apprentice? I will worship you as a teacher." Before the master could react, Zhang Feng fell upon his knees, laying his head upon the ground performing a kowtow.

"There now, don't do that. Get up. Look, you seem like a good and decent boy. But practicing martial arts is very bitter. You have to rise early, practice hard and sustain your studies for many years. You won't be able to take it."

Zhang Feng stood up, defiant. "I am not afraid. I'm very good at sports … I'm a member of the school sports team. I can take suffering."

The Taoist master stopped and thought for a moment. "What do your parents do?"

"They are all university lecturers."

"Which university is it?"

"The Normal University".

The Taoist looked suddenly interested. "Which department?"

"My father teaches Chinese, my mother Chemistry. Master, do you know anyone at the university?"

"No, no, no, no." After considering for a few moments, the Taoist spoke again. "Fine. If you are really sure of your commitment. I ask you to meet me at five o'clock in the morning for three consecutive days. If you can do this, I will consider it."

"Of course master, I will do as you say." Zhang Feng knew what it was to be trustworthy and to do as he had promised; his father had drilled into him the importance of being sincere ever since he was a child.

For three consecutive days, he went to the North Mountain Temple at five o'clock to see the Taoist master doing martial arts.

By the end of the third day, the Taoist smiled and asked him, "Young man, have you ever practiced any martial arts before?"

Zhang Feng replied, "I have only ever practiced Tai Chi and Long Boxing".

"Very well, show me."

After Zhang Feng had demonstrated his ability, the Taoist master nodded. "Your foundations are good, speed and strength are also good, just a little soft. It seems that you do have potential. So, I will pledge to teach you once a week, starting from the basics, working from the simple to the complex. But we have to follow three rules. First, you must never tell any other about the details of this boxing method. Second, do not fight with others unless you have to defend yourself. Third, never mention who your master is."

From this time on, every Wednesday morning without fail, he would wake up early in the morning, proceed to the temple and train with his master. Over the next two years, Zhang Feng grew taller, his body became stronger, and his boxing skills improved dramatically. The master had finally revealed to him the real name of this form of boxing was Pili (thunderbolt) boxing. It was a very powerful form of boxing, requiring skilful coordination of both fists and feet. It was especially designed and suited to fighting against a group of people. He also taught Zhang Feng Qi Gong as exercises to build up his internal strength. This internal strength, once applied to the fists and feet, magnified the effectiveness of fist and foot, making a lethal combination. Zhang Feng had grown physically and mentally, confident and a skilled martial artist, and these two years were to prepare him for what was to come. But somehow, despite his initial curiosity, the master never again mentioned the University and the Chinese department.

So it was that on this particular Wednesday morning, Zhang Feng found himself walking down the mountain, in high spirits, singing as he walked. The crisp morning mountain air made the echo especially vibrant. He still had another two months before the school art festival where he was due to sing; but his tenor solo was due to be one of the highlights and the principal urged him to practice hard.

After some time, Zhang Feng arrived at the pine forest at the foot of the mountain. Up ahead, the path split; one route lead to the middle school in the city, and the other lead to the bridge on the river. As he approached the fork, he suddenly heard a noise not far from him. He took a few quick steps and saw a group of people hanging around in the open space in the forest. Moving closer, he saw the scene more clearly; it turned out to be a group of men surrounding a girl. The girl was clasping her bicycle handle with both hands. A stout man was trying to snatch her bicycle.

"What are you doing? This is robbery in broad daylight!" The girl shouted in a trembling voice.

"Hey, little beauty, don't say it like that. I just want borrow it for a few days. I'll give it back to you." With a hard yank, he broke her hold on the bicycle. "Ha, flying pigeon brand, good bike."

The girl cried out in fury. "What? Give it back to me!'" At that moment she turned around, and Zhang Feng recognised her in a moment of shock – she was the girl that he had met on the bus. Even in this moment of panic and anger, her face pale and troubled, she was still as beautiful as he had remembered her to be. Zhang Feng did not have much time to admire her; almost immediately after she turned around, Zhang Feng also saw the face of her attacker – it was Hei Tou, the bully who had tormented him and his friends those years ago. It was unmistakable; Zhang Feng remembered clearly the fleshy, round and dark face and the fierce eyes. Zhang Feng felt the flush of hot blood flowing through his face.

Hei Tou looked at the bicycle for a few moments, then leaned over and tried to ride it. It was not designed for his size though and after a few minutes of awkward manoeuvring, he gave up. He blinked. A suggestive grin crept across his face as his expression darkened.

"Tell you what, little beauty, I'll return the bike to you. But there is a condition … you have to let me kiss your little tender mouth. Or no, it would be much better if I could touch your little tits!" The other hooligans began laughing wildly.

"Stop it! You worthless piece of slime!" Zhang Feng could not help himself any more. Overcome with anger, he jumped out from where he was hiding and leapt towards them. Hei Tou spun round but did not recognise him; several years of hard physical training had left Zhang Feng taller and stronger than the small boy that he had taunted and pushed those years ago. Hei Tou was caught by surprise and momentarily lost his focus, but he quickly recovered his fearlessness.

"Well well, what do we have here? A noble hero come to save his little girl?" Hei Tou looked up and down at Zhang Feng, trying to gauge the strength of his opponent. Seeing that Zhang Feng was dressed like a student, he became confident and angry.

"Well, let's see if you can take a few punches from a real man. Maybe then I will return the bike to the girl." He handed the bicycle to one of the men next to him and walked towards Zhang Feng. By this time, Zhang Feng had calmed and remembered his master's instructions not to fight with others.

"I don't want to fight with you. You are bullying a weak girl. What kind of man are you? Give the bike back to her immediately!"

Hei Tou sneered. "Afraid are you? Too late, my little friend. It's time that you learned a lesson to respect your elders." Hei Tou had no formal martial arts training, but his experience through years of street fights and his strong physical physique made a brutal combination. Nevertheless, as Hei Tou swung his first punch, Zhang Feng deftly stepped aside with ease. Hei Tou, undeterred, lunged and delivered a second punch. Again, Zhang Feng dodged his fist with a twist of his torso. He could not attack, but could he win through self-defence? When Hei Tou threw his third punch, Zhang Feng dodged like a flash and, in one smooth but swift movement, grabbed Hei Tou's arm and followed through, tipping him off balance. This manoeuvre was called 'turning the boat' and was in fact one of the simplest defensive techniques taught by his master. Hei Tou, however, was not prepared at all. As a result of his excessive force, he tripped over and fell hard, landing square against the hard bark of a nearby tree. He screamed, not just through physical agony, but through the shock of a defeat the size of which he had never known before.

It did not take more than a few seconds for him to issue the command to his henchmen.

"Get him!" The girl looked on in horror as three hooligans surrounded Zhang Feng in semicircle. Two of their timid brethren stood slightly behind. Zhang Feng recognised his good fortune; it would have been a much tougher battle if all of them had come forward.

The girl turned to Zhang Feng in horror.

"Run! You have to run away as quickly as you can! These people mean to hurt you and there are too many of them." Zhang

Feng drew in a calming breath, focusing his mind. He knew that there was no retreat. He could run, but the girl would be left helpless. Sorry master, he thought to himself. Today I have no choice but to attack. I cannot let these gangsters bully this girl. Zhang Feng recalled that his Pili form was specifically designed to combat groups of rivals. In his heart, he was confident. So when they had approached to about one and a half meters away from him, his strike was decisive. With a scream he launched his legs sweeping from left to right, like two flying columns of iron, landing heavy blows on two of his unsuspecting foes, sending them flying into the dirt. With a quick flick he recovered his poise and smashed his fists into the third, sending him crashing into the two behind him. The group of thugs rolled on the ground, screaming in pain. Through the deafening beating of his heart, Zhang Feng could hear the girl shouting excitedly.

"Amazing! You really showed them!"

Zhang Feng smiled as he reminded himself that he had only used a fraction of his strength; his master had instructed him to exercise maximum restraint, saving the bulk of his force, to prevent serious injury.

Hei Tou witnessed the obliteration of his gang and was shocked to silence. How could he have anticipated this? He hurriedly shouted to his fellows to escape, and ran off as they stumbled away. But as he left he could not bear the wound to his pride without a final riposte.

"Just you wait, you little man. I will have my revenge." And with that he was gone.

Zhang Feng lifted the bicycle off the ground and handed it to the girl.

"Thank you so much." The girl's soft voice was full of gratitude.

"You're welcome. It's nothing. This group of thugs have had it coming for a long time, and this was long overdue." As he looked at her, the girl's face had turned from an ashen grey back to the vitality that he had remembered on that bus. He leaned in and whispered.

"Be careful not to walk or ride on this path again." Zhang Feng wanted to say more, but did not want to give the impression that he would ask for something in return. So he said:

"Time is getting on, I think we need to hurry if we are to get to school without being late." The girl anxiously looked into the distance at the long tree-lined path ahead. Zhang Feng understood and said:

"I will send you to school. It is not much of a diversion for me." The girl was visibly relieved.

"Thank you!"

They walked side by side in as they meandered through the forest. The early morning carried the refreshing fragrance of blooming flowers, and the air was filled with morning birdsong. Walking alongside the angel that Zhang Feng had missed day and night since that bus ride, Zhang Feng felt like he was in a dream. A sense of happiness that he had never felt before settled in his heart. Whenever the girl's shoulders brushed against his, intentionally or unintentionally, his heart felt like it had skipped a beat. Keen not to miss this opportunity in the same way that he had on the bus, he began to ask about her.

"Why is it that you don't go to school by bus anymore?".

"Because the bus is too irritating…ah no, what I meant was, my aunt in Guangzhou bought this bike for me. It's very convenient for me to ride to school."

"But you should be careful, especially riding through the forest on this path."

"I thought the air here would be fresher than riding on the big roads. I didn't expect to encounter these thugs."

"You don't know how horrible these hooligans are. They often bully people and do many bad things. Even the police can't control them." Zhang Feng suddenly realised that he still didn't know the girl's name, and he said, "My name is Zhang Feng, how about you?"

"Ah, my name is Li Yu Mei. This year is my second year in my school."

"I am also a sophomore."

Yu Mei turned to him. "I heard that you are the chairman of the student union, and you have many extracurricular jobs. You must be very busy?" Listening to Yu Mei's question, Zhang Feng was secretly pleased. It seemed that the girl was impressed with him, and that she had remembered him from their previous short bus journey, even though it was quite some time ago.

"Well, it is quite intense, but I do like the challenge."

"I would have never guessed from your appearance that you would have been so strong in the martial arts. I never knew one person could fight against so many people. I used to watch it in the movies but I always thought it was just made up. I only realised today that there are real martial arts heroes." When she finished, she turned and looked at Zhang Feng. Zhang Feng felt that there was something other than gratitude in her wide eyes.

"Ah, it's nothing. I only learn it as a form of self-defence, not with the intention of going out and fighting others. You know, my martial arts master doesn't even allow me to fight with others."

"Oh, I'm sorry that you had to break that rule for me."

"Don't worry, it was worth doing it to save you from those thugs." Zhang Feng suddenly realized that he had spent too much time talking about himself, and immediately changed the topics, talking to Yu Mei about his and her schools.

Zhang Feng was used to walking this path, but on this day the path felt much shorter than usual. Even though he had deliberately been walking at a slow pace, it was not long before they had reached the crossing. The beautiful and ornate school gates of the First Senior Middle School were just a short distance in front of them. He knew that he should have said goodbye to the girl, but he couldn't bring himself to leave. The girl had also kept quiet and had not asked him to go. They reached the gates. Just as he was about to speak, a tall male student wearing an old military uniform appeared and shouted at them.

"Mei Mei, why are you so late?" Zhang Feng felt that this person looked a bit familiar. The male student strode over, took the bicycle from Yu Mei in one hand, and put his arm around her shoulder.

"Go ahead, class is about to start". At the same time, he threw a hostile glare at Zhang Feng. Yu Mei quickly explained:

"This is Zhang Feng. I'd like to thank him today for..." Before she could finish, the young man had pulled her away. Yu Mei could only wave apologetically.

On the way to the school, Zhang Feng felt strange. Only moments ago he had been living as if in a perfect dream, but in an instant everything had changed. "Who is that man? Her boyfriend? He acted like he was her husband." In a flash of recognition, Zhang Feng suddenly remembered that he was that arrogant student leader who had given him and his class the cold shoulder when the two schools had met at the bridge.

"Just my luck. Of all the people I would run into again. I suppose this means that his dad must be a military commander". Zhang Feng began to laugh at himself. How could a civilian like him ever hope to be friends with these high ranking officer's children? Yu Mei's parents must also be high ranking officers. These thoughts preoccupied him as he made his way to class.

CHAPTER III

Charming Prince on White Horse

As late May approached the River City, the scent of midsummer accompanied the gradual onset of the hot noon sun and balmy evenings. Just after noon on a particular Saturday, Zhang Feng hurried excitedly down the steps of the City Youth Palace. He had just taken part in the annual middle school maths contest, and he had turned in a confident attempt; he had been champion for the last three years and he held secret hopes to take first place again this year.

"Hey, Zhang Feng, wait." He paused mid step as he heard the girl's voice behind him. Looking back, he saw his schoolmate and neighbour Liu Dan Dan. Dan Dan studied in the same school as Zhang Feng, one grade ahead of him. Her mother was the doctor in the Normal University school infirmary. Her father died many years ago from what had been explained to him as caused by a sudden illness when working outdoors. She had her suspicions about this story, but no one ever seemed willing to talk about it. Zhang Feng only knew that her father was one of his father's students and had worked as a teaching assistant when he was at the university. Zhang Feng's father was a well-known classical Chinese literature expert, working as a professor at the Normal University before the year 1957. However, in 1957, he had made a suggestion to the government about improving the well-being and living conditions of the general populace; as a result of this, he was labelled as a rightist, discharged from his position and demoted to the position of librarian in university library. This was also the time that Dan Dan's father had disappeared. Zhang Feng regarded Dan Dan as his older sister and the two were like siblings from childhood. Zhang Feng always came forward to protect Dan Dan if she encountered bullies, while Dan Dan spared no effort to help Zhang Feng when difficulty came. Dan Dan's mother treated Zhang Feng like her own child. The two visited and stayed at each other's home regularly. Dan Dan was a smart and beautiful girl, a recognized bluestocking at her school. She was good at both art and science, as well as poetry and painting. Influenced by his father, Zhang Feng was also interested in classical literature and poetry. Therefore, the two often studied calligraphy and painting together.

"Dan Dan, you aced the contest right?"

"I think I did pretty well. If we win the first prize this time again, we should celebrate!"

"No problem". Dan Dan was flushed with excitement and from the hot weather, looking like a blooming peony against white snow. She looked mature and fully-grown, even though she was only 18 years old. Wang Hai had said she possessed the same beauty as the Consort Yang, the legendary beauty from the Tang Dynasty. Li He believed Dan Dan was the goddess Athena in human form. Dan Dan was the only girl Zhang Feng felt comfortable opening his heart to.

"Xiao Feng, how about going back by boat?"

"Great idea!" Zhang Feng loved to take the steel cable boat across the river. He always preferred to cross by boat as long as time permitted. They took the bus to the riverside pier. There stood two steel cable towers supporting a thick steel cable hanging above the river. A large wooden boat floated on the river. The mooring rope at the bow was attached to a large iron ring which was placed over the cable. Once ready to leave, the boatman pushed his pole against the pier step and the boat launched into a 45° angle against the river flow. The momentum of the water flow and the tension of the cable made the boat head slowly to the opposite shore. There were few people returning back to the South Bank at noon except an old couple sitting in the middle of the boat. Zhang Feng and Dan Dan sat at the stern. As the boat glided quietly towards the opposite bank, there was only the sound of the flowing river and iron rings sliding on the rope. In the breeze, the weeping willows on both banks looked like a dancing green screen. The mountains in the distance were bathed in bright sunshine. Both Zhang Feng and Dan Dan were immersed in this picturesque scenery.

Two months later, on a warm weekend, the auditorium of the Jili Cultural Palace was filled with bustle. The city student's art performance was in full swing. All of the performers were the best students in literature and art of their respective schools. The principals of each school were each secretly vying against each other to see which of their schools would win the most prizes and awards, especially for key schools such as the First and Second Senior Middle Schools which always took the top two positions each year. Also present were the leaders of the Municipal Cultural Bureau and the provincial and municipal art schools. They were essentially talent scouts for the brightest young successors in music and art and hoped to enlist the best to their institutions.

Zhang Feng kept busy in the rehearsal room backstage. His private violin teacher, Mr. Sun from the Provincial Academy of Art, was giving him some final guidance. Zhang Feng had a lot of shows to perform today, including violin solo, vocal solo, and folk music ensemble. Zhang Feng had been coached by Mr. Sun for four years. Mr. Sun was once the student of a famous Russian violinist, and was the best violinist in the province. He was a quirky and serious man, over 40 years old but still single, with few friends. But he was a very earnest and skilful teacher. Zhang Feng's performance piece was the well-known violin concerto called the Butterfly Lovers; this was a beautiful piece of music based upon the legend of two lovers who, unable to be together in life, could only wait until after death to be reunited, reincarnated as two butterflies. Today Zhang Feng would be accompanied on the piano by Miss Ye. As Sun listened to his last play through, he nodded without expression. Zhang Feng knew that it meant he was satisfied; Sun never said well done or gave any praise. "What a weird man." Ye whispered. She was Zhang Feng's vocal instructor and also Sun's colleague. She was over 30 but also single. It was rumoured that she had once declared her love to Sun, but had been refused by his indifference. Ye on the other hand was warm and outgoing. She always encouraged and praised Zhang Feng whenever he sang. After Zhang Feng finished singing Gada Melin, a Mongolia song, and a Russian song Troika, she applauded and said, "Good job, the first prize is yours today."

After leaving Sun and Ye, Zhang Feng hurried to his school's traditional instrument orchestra, for which he was the bandmaster. He wanted to rehearse one last time before the performance. While the orchestra was tuning, Zhang Feng frowned; he could hear that an Erhu and a Chinese lute were out of tune. He said to the Erhu player, "Cai Desheng, tune your strings." Cai Desheng was Zhang Feng's classmate. He had an oddly triangular face, with a few untidy hairs on his chin. He wanted to compete with Zhang Feng in all aspects, though the reality was that he was both ugly and incapable. For example, he had fawned on the teaching director to let him work as the commissary in charge of subsistence in the students' union, only because Zhang Feng worked as the chairman. The job actually involved merely arranging for students to sweep the snow when winter came. He also managed to join the band, again by currying favour with the teaching director, even though he had no particular talent with the Erhu; his skill in fact was so bad that both Zhang Feng and the music teacher thought he would negatively affect the whole band. In sports, he jostled to participate in long-distance running, always coming last or second last. In all of these lacklustre attempts, his real motive for participation was to attract the attention of girls that he liked, because that was exactly what Zhang Feng achieved. Zhang Feng then turned to a delicate girl playing the Chinese lute called Qing Lian, another classmate of Zhang Feng. Her lute was deliberately out of tune. She was unwilling to tune it until Zhang Feng explicitly reminded her; the reason she did this was known to all the students in the class except Zhang Feng. Like other girls, she had once fallen in love with Zhang Feng and worked up the courage to write a love letter, secretly placing it in his desk. Unfortunately for her, the letter was found by

Wang Hai, and he stuck it on the wall in the classroom on a day that Zhang Feng was absent. Qing Lian had become the laughing stock of the class, especially amongst the prettier girls. Qing Lian had no idea that Zhang Feng had nothing to do with it. Her deep shame turned to anger, and she resolved herself to become his enemy since that day, trying her best to sabotage him at every turn. So it was that on this particular performance day, she was reluctant to tune her strings when warned by Zhang Feng. Zhang Feng, wary of the time, hastened the orchestra through two runs of each of their two performance pieces, the famous Cantonese tunes "A Moonlit River Bank with Flowers in Spring" and "Colourful Clouds Chasing the Moon".

The actual art performance started well. Zhang Feng's performance was particularly successful; his violin solo was perfect and smooth, winning an ecstatic round of applause, even gaining a rare smile from Teacher Sun, sitting in the corner. After Zhang Feng finished his amazing vocal solo, the representatives from the various art schools crowded round principal Chang, enquiring whether Zhang Feng had any interest in applying for their schools. The principal could only reply proudly, "He is a talent in both the arts and the sciences. And the first prize winner in the maths contest. He is destined to become a Qian Xuesen or a Hua Luogeng (both famous Chinese scientists); art is only his hobby", upon which their collective faces fell in unison. The performance reached a climax with the instrumental ensemble's inspiring renditions with Zhang Feng at the helm. Principal Chang was sure that his school would win at least 3 prizes. His counterpart at the First Senior Middle School sat nearby, dejected.

Backstage, Zhang Feng and his fellow musicians were in high spirits. They were packing up their instruments and preparing to watch the rest of the shows from the hall. Just then, Principal Chang and the Principal of First Senior Middle School hurried backstage. Principal Chang looked around the room for a few moments, before catching sight of Zhang Feng and coming over.

"Zhang Feng, we have a bit of a situation. One of the solo dancers from the First Senior Middle School is about to perform on stage, but there is a technical fault with the backing music tape and it cannot be used. The music she has chosen is "A Moonlit River Bank with Flowers in Spring", exactly the piece that your band just played. Their principal has requested the band to provide the accompaniment for the dance. Would you be able to help them?" Principal Chang was concerned that they wouldn't help because of the rivalry between the two schools. His counterpart was on the verge of begging for help. Zhang Feng, being a warm-hearted person, agreed to negotiate with his band members; he hoped their respect for him would sway them. He went back to the band and briefly described the situation. Most members agreed to help, except Cai Desheng and Qing Lian.

"If their school won another award, we would stand to lose a lot," Cai said.

"Why should we help them anyway? Just because the dancer is a pretty girl?" Qing Lian retorted loudly.

Zhang Feng was unwilling to argue with these two demanding individuals. "Those who want to help, please stay. Those who do not, you are free to leave." Cai and Qing Lian left in a huff with their instruments. Behind the curtain, Zhang Feng wanted to discuss the accompaniment with the girl who would dance the solo. He saw a slim girl in an ancient costume standing uneasily. When he walked over, the girl turned around. Both of them gasped as if jolted by lightning; there before him stood Yu Mei, the girl whom Zhang Feng had rescued in the forest. Wearing a pink traditional dress, Yu Mei looked particularly beautiful, almost celestial. Zhang Feng could feel his heart beating faster. Yu Mei smiled and thanked him for accompanying her solo; with him there she felt more confident. There was little time left and they were not allowed to talk any further. Zhang Feng quickly returned to the band and prepared. As the beautiful melody of "A Moonlit River Bank with Flowers in Spring" played, the curtain rose slowly. Yu Mei's dance steps were soft and gentle, and she started her solo dance with immense grace. The whole audience was stunned to silence by her grace and beauty. Zhang Feng could not help but sneak a glance as he directed the ensemble, and was similarly enchanted. It was as if he was watching Chang E, the goddess of the moon, singing and dancing as she prepared to fly to heaven. All too soon Yu Mei's performance ended, greeted by warm applause; Zhang Feng blinked as if waking from a dream. Yu Mei's dance received praise from the judges and won second prize. Her principal rushed over and thanked Zhang Feng and his band. After receiving his thanks, Zhang Feng immediately left and went to find Yu Mei. She was in the backstage dressing room removing her makeup. When she saw Zhang Feng coming, she stopped what she was doing and stood up, looking at him with gratitude and affection.

"You danced very well, congratulations."

"Your performance was better. Your voice and your violin both … fascinated me." Her last two words were wistful. A look of shyness came over her face. Zhang Feng was about to say something more, when suddenly two people with bouquets came over and interrupted their conversation. The person who presented the flowers to Yu Mei was the tall boy who wore a military uniform waiting for her at the school gate. He handed the flowers to Yu Mei attentively and congratulated her on her success. It was Dan Dan who gave flowers to Zhang Feng. Zhang Feng took the flowers but could not stop himself from staring at Yu Mei. Yu Mei also looked at Dan Dan and Zhang Feng with a hint of disappointment. Then, the two pairs left the backstage.

A few weeks later, shortly before the summer vacation, Jili Province held its Middle School Sports day. This was also an opportunity for each school to show its strength in the field of sports; it went without saying that each school's sports team had been carefully prepared and intensively trained. Zhang Feng, the captain of the Second Senior Middle School team, was under pressure because over the last few years, the First Senior Middle School and Second Senior Middle School were always in the top two rankings. Principal Chang said that this year their school must defeat all other schools to ensure they took first place. This year saw a particularly good attendance at the 10,000-capacity City Stadium; the sound of thousands of people singing and chatting excitedly hovered over the stadium. The thunder of rapturous applause shook the very ground. The first competition Zhang Feng took part in was the high jump. As soon as he entered the filed, he met the arrogant young man from First Senior Middle School, who seemed to be Yu Mei's 'protector'. This young man stretched out his hand and introduced himself, in a show of magnanimity.

"I'm Chang Zheng from First Senior Middle School."

"My name is Zhang Feng. Second Senior Middle School." Zhang Feng politely shook hands with him.

"You want to win a prize?" Chang Zheng asked with an air of arrogant incredulity, as if Zhang Feng had come here only for fun. Zhang Feng smiled.

"I would be happy winning first or second prize."

Chang Zheng glanced at Zhang Feng. "Don't brag. Let's have a competition and see."

Zhang Feng and Chang Zheng were both tall, about 180 centimetres, which gave both of them an advantage in the high jump competition. There were more than a dozen people participating in the competition. After two rounds, only six people were left to participate in the finals. Their scores were all above one metre seventy. After two more rounds, there were only Zhang Feng and Chang Zheng left. They had all jumped over the height of one metre eighty. The loudspeaker announced that the final high jump battle would be contested between Chang Zheng from the First Senior Middle School and Zhang Feng from the Second Senior Middle School. The whole stadium was abuzz. All eyes were focused on the high jump venue. Yu Mei, sitting in the crowd, heard the loudspeaker and felt a little excited. She told her friend that she would go to cheer Chang Zheng. In fact, the real person she wanted to see was Zhang Feng. Generally, outsiders were not allowed to enter the competition area. However, because this was the final round and many students had squeezed into the venue, the staff turned a blind eye. Yu Mei made her way through the crowd and saw Zhang Feng and Chang Zheng making their final preparations. Suddenly, Yu Mei saw a familiar face in the crowd. She looked carefully and realized that it was the beautiful girl who had presented flowers to Zhang Feng at the end of the art performance festival. Yu Mei felt a little uneasy, but soon forgot her concerns in the heat of the fierce competition. The crossbar rose to one metre eighty-five. Zhang Feng was the first to make the trial jump. He steadied himself, eyes fixed straight ahead, and began to run. He gathered speed, pounding towards the crossbar. Yu Mei's heart jumped into her mouth. With an almighty leap, Zhang Feng sprang high into the air, his jump bringing him clean over the crossbar like an eagle in flight. The audience burst into thunderous applause. Yu Mei was so happy that she clapped her hands and applauded. She was interrupted by a girl standing next to her

"He is from the Second Senior Middle School, not from our school."

"Oh, my mistake." She immediately left, finding a spot where there were no students from her school. Chang Zheng also jumped over one metre eighty-five for his second jump. The atmosphere became tense. The crossbar was moved up to one metre ninety. Chang Zheng made three attempts at this height, but none of his three trial attempts saw him beat the crossbar. Disappointed, he hung his head and left the competition area. Zhang Feng made two attempts, but did no better and failed to clear this level, hitting the crossbar both times. The students from his school and Yu Mei watched, disappointment slowly creeping into their nervous and hopeful faces. Finally, it was the time for his last jump. Zhang Feng took a deep breath. He closed his eyes with intense concentration. In that moment, as all sound stopped except the pounding of his heart; he visualised himself in the mountainous forest, cold air and hot blood coursing through his body. His eyes opened. With a jolt he launched himself forward, foot upon foot crunching into the dirt, running faster and faster. Time seemed to slow to a crawl. He reached the end of the track and leapt into the air; he could feel and see the earth falling away from him. With barely a passing moment, he saw his legs clear the crossbar as he fell back into the sand. He saw the joy and elation in the faces of those around him, jumping and clapping, as it dawned upon him that he had succeeded. The entire stadium erupted with applause. Yu Mei jumped up, clapping her hands. Such was her joy that it took several seconds for her to realise that the flower girl had walked over to Zhang Feng and was wiping the sweat from his face. Yu Mei wondered who she was – perhaps she was a girlfriend – and walked back to the auditorium in disappointment.

Back in the dressing room, Zhang Feng was changing his clothes. Chang Zheng entered the room, saw Zhang Feng and walked over. "Humph. If it hadn't been so cold, I would have never let you win. Enjoy your triumph while it lasts, but don't get used to it. See you in the 100 metres final." He knew Zhang Feng was running in the 100 metres final. He took out a big piece of chocolate and put it into his mouth while looking at Zhang Feng. During that time, only the children of high-ranking officials were allowed and could afford chocolate; it was well out of the reach of common people. Chang Zheng was showing off his social status. Zhang Feng thought, "So what. Nothing extraordinary. I can win the race without chocolate." He despised the arrogant and spoilt children of high-ranking officials the most. He quietly took out a steamed bun from his bag and ate it. The steamed bun was made from sticky rice flour and was stuffed with sweetened bean paste; his mother had told him that it can keep him from hunger for a long time.

Yu Mei was a little uncomfortable under the heat of the sun. Suddenly the loudspeaker announced that the last event was about to begin; the men's and women's 100 metres finals. This was the most anticipated and exciting event of the games so far; all the cheerleader squads were lively and preparing for action. Hearing that Zhang Feng was in the final list, Yu Mei was excited and forgot all about the flower-presenting girl. The starting gun went off. Six strong athletes shot off the start line like arrows from a bow, running at full speed to the finishing line. The stadium reverberated with cheers and the rolling of drums. Yu Mei could clearly see that Zhang Feng and Chang Zheng had left the others far behind in the last 30 metres and that they were practically running neck to neck. All the students from their two schools stood up shouting and cheering their own athletes at the top of their voices. Yu Mei stood and cheered with them, though unknown to her schoolmates, she secretly hoped Zhang Feng would be the winner. The last ten metres approached. Zhang Feng gathered all his strength and suddenly pounced a half-body ahead of Chang Zheng, perfectly breasting the tape. "Zhang Feng! The winner of men's 100 metres is Zhang Feng from Second Senior Middle School!" The reporter excitedly shouted. "He has just broken the games' record with his result of 11.2 seconds!" Yu Mei shouted with joy when she saw that Zhang Feng had won, a clear juxtaposition against her schoolmates who were sighing in despair. She abruptly stopped when she saw the startled looks of her schoolmates; feigning confusion she asked, "Chang Zheng didn't win the race?"

The games were drawing to a conclusion. Yu Mei could not help the urge to find and talk to Zhang Feng. She wanted to congratulate him on the good results, and she also wanted to explain to him about her relationship with Chang Zheng. She waited at the exit for the athletes for a while and saw Zhang Feng was coming out with Wang Hai. Wang Hai had come fourth in the 100 meters final. Yu Mei approached them as they rounded a corner. Zhang Feng and Wang Hai were both stunned when they saw her. Wang Hai quickly realised what was happening and said to Zhang Feng, "The Bus Fairy, she wants to talk to you." Then he walked away.

"Congratulations to you! Your results were outstanding. I didn't expect you to be so good not just in the arts but also at sports. It's quite rare."

"It's nothing. I just happen to like arts and sports at the same time." Zhang Feng immediately replied. Yu Mei looked into Zhang Feng's eyes, and her eyes were full of tenderness. Just as she wanted to explain her relationship with Chang Zheng to him, a flattering voice rang out. "Zhang Feng, congratulations! You won so many first prizes. I really must try harder." Zhang Feng turned and realised that it was the ever irritating Cai Desheng, who had come last in the 800 metres. Cai turned to Yu Mei and spoke in a particularly sleazy tone. "Isn't this the beautiful lady dancer from First Senior Middle School? It's my honour to meet you." He even tried to shake hands with Yu Mei.

"Sorry, I don't know you." Yu Mei felt physically sick. She turned and walked away immediately. Zhang Feng did not want to talk to Cai either and walked away after a few reluctant replies to his attempt at conversation. In his heart, Zhang Feng cursed him. "This jinx, he always shows up at the worst time whenever he is not welcome. Extremely annoying."

Having not been able say much to Zhang Feng, Yu Mei was a little disappointed. As she was walking out of the stadium, she overheard some girls talking about something.

"He is really handsome, good-looking, strong, and chic." One girl said.

"I heard he is the chairman of the student's union in the Second Senior Middle School." Replied another. Yu Mei immediately realised that they were talking about Zhang Feng. A beautiful girl said, "Don't you remember? A few days ago, he sang a solo, played the violin and conducted the band in the theatrical festival."

"Really?"

"He stole my heart when he was singing."

One of the taller girls laughed. "You say that he stole your heart? He is quite the Mr. Perfect, endowed with both beauty and talent. There are few women in Jili City who can attract his attention." The other girls agreed. The beautiful girl sighed. "Well, he can be our Prince Charming, but only in our dreams."

The Prince Charming in our dreams. These last few words lingered in Yu Mei's mind. That night, she could not sleep.

CHAPTER IV

At the River Bank

It was now mid-July, the onset of the summer vacation. In addition to doing his daily summer homework and reading reference books, Zhang Feng also borrowed some advanced mathematics books from the library. He believed in the old adage: 'The higher you stand, the farther you can see.' His dream was to dedicate himself to science. When he had time, he would play the violin, swim with Wang Hai and Li He or discuss painting with Dan Dan. He also went to the North Mountain to practice Kung Fu once a week. Life seemed to be very fulfilling. However, the stunning beauty of Yu Mei always lingered in his mind. Her attractive eyes made his heart beat faster. What was she going to say to me when we met at the end of the sports day? If only we had had five more minutes. That damned Cai always follows me like a ghost. How can I have another chance to meet her? These thoughts persisted in Zhang Feng's mind. Suddenly, it occurred to him that on the day when he rescued Yu Mei from the hooligans, Yu Mei had said that she liked to walk on the riverside, especially on Sunday mornings.

The next day was a Sunday, and at 6 o'clock in the morning, Zhang Feng set off with a drawing board. His plan was this: if he couldn't meet Yu Mei, he would sketch on the riverside. Thus, it would not be a totally useless trip. Starting from home, Zhang Feng jogged to the South Bank Park. After running for a while, he went to the river. From here, the view on the right was of the South Bank Bridge. On the left, there was grass and forest. On the opposite side of the river was the urban area. Zhang Feng used to come here frequently; amidst the tranquillity and desolation, he could practice painting or reading or whatever he wished without disturbance.

About forty metres away from the river was an old poplar tree serving as a cool shelter during the sweltering summer, graceful like a rich canopy with its thick trunks and luxuriant branches. When Zhang Feng and his friends came here to play, Wang Hai said that this old tree was like the matchmaker in the Chinese fairy tale of the Seven Fairies and Dong Yong. He also said that according to his research, this fairy tale actually happened in northern China, not in the south of China, which made Zhang Feng and others laugh for a long time.

Zhang Feng put his backpack under the tree, practiced Kung Fu before singing for a while. After looking at a few passers-by, he opened the easel and prepared to begin painting. Deep down in his heart, he was afraid that he wouldn't get to meet Yu Mei because she perhaps did not go for a walk every Sunday. As he adjusted the colours and began to conceive the picture, he was deeply attracted by the beautiful scenery in front of him. On the surface of the river, the limpid water drifted away out of sight. Along the opposite shore was a line of swaying willows standing as a green promenade. The majestic South Bank Bridge and the magnificent North Mountain both added charm to the splendid scene. As he gazed at the water rolling away while painting, Zhang Feng thought of Confucius's saying: "Time passes quickly like flowing water." Gradually absorbed by the view, Zhang Feng forgot his original purpose and became intoxicated in the picturesque paradise.

On Zhang Feng's drawing board, a beautiful landscape painting had already been completed. A breeze blew, waking him from his reverie, reminding him of the main purpose of the day. He stood up and looked around. There were only a few elderly people in the distance practising Tai Chi. He sat down again and began to make additions to his painting. As he was doing this, the graceful dance of Yu Mei suddenly occurred to him. The poetry of 'A Moonlit Riverbank with Flower in Spring' was just like the beauty in front of him. 'The spring river links the ocean, the moon rises softly from the tides…' Zhang Feng recited this famous Tang poem while working away. He first added a bright moon over the river bank and painted the colour of the night sky. Then, he began to carefully draw a beautiful woman dressed in costume and dancing. He was so absorbed that he did not hear a light footstep behind him. Just as he finished the final stroke, a soft and familiar voice rang behind him.

"Who is confusing black and white?!" Zhang Feng was shocked and jumped, and the brush fell to the ground. This was exactly what he was waiting for, but he did not expect it to come so suddenly. Yu Mei stood behind him, wearing a set of blue sportswear, with a black scorpion hairpiece behind her head. Her beautiful pink cheeks showed a faint blush, and the eyes suggested surprise and gentleness. Compared with the ease of Yu Mei, Zhang Feng was very nervous. He didn't know what to say because his paintings had revealed his ideas. Yu Mei first said:

"Do you often paint? You paint really well."

"No, no, it's just a hobby. Are you going for a walk?"

"Yes, the air in the morning is very fresh." Yu Mei said with a smile. Beautiful women often had confidence in front of men; even without using her own charm, she found it easy to control the situation.

"May I sit and watch you paint for a while?" Yu Mei wanted Zhang Feng to relax.

"Of course, of course," Zhang Feng said quickly. The two sat almost side by side.

"You are painting the beauty of the Tang Dynasty?" Yu Mei asked even though she knew the answer. Zhang Feng became more relaxed. With no one else around, he felt more comfortable expressing his feelings to Yu Mei; after a short moment he plucked up his courage.

"I did a sketch of a living painting. The scenery here reminds me of the poem 'A Moonlit Riverbank with Flower in Spring', and I remembered the dreamy and intoxicating dance of a beautiful girl from the First Senior Middle School jumping in the middle of the painting. "

"You are bad!" Yu Mei said softly, while gently touching Zhang Feng with her shoulders; her hair almost touched his face. "How can I compare with the girl in your painting?" Yu Mei asked. But the faintness on her face belied the happiness in her heart. She knew her position in Zhang Feng's heart.

Zhang Feng added: "Li Yu Mei…"

"Call me Yu Mei", Yu Mei said with affection. Zhang Feng felt a hot stream rushing to his heart, letting him call her with such an intimate name, which clearly showed that Yu Mei liked him.

"Yu Mei, to be honest, I was accompanying you on the stage that day. When I watched you dance, I hoped that time would stand still because at that moment, poetry, painting, beautiful music and dance, and the spirit of ancient Chinese art all mixed together. It was a wonderful expression of ancient people's love and sorrow as well as the idea that life is like a dream. You were like a lady living on the moon, dancing with joy."

"Don't be silly. I am not the lady in the moon. Although, there were times when I was sad, when I thought about how calm it would be on the moon!"

"Really?" Zhang Feng smiled. "You have also had times of sadness? Is your life not very happy? Yu Mei, is your father a high-ranking official?"

"No, he is just working for the government." Yu Mei seemed to be unwilling to talk about her father and immediately changed the topic. "Hey, Zhang Feng, your friend said that you are versatile. After the arts performance, your singing and violin melody kept replaying in my mind over and over. When you saved me from the hooligans, you were so brave. And then there was that exciting time when you competed in the high jump and sprinted in the sports event. You know, there were moments then when it seemed like my heart beats had almost stopped…"

The sports meeting! Zhang Feng suddenly thought of Chang Zheng. There was a pang of pain in his heart. What am I doing here today? Isn't it just to find out about her situation and what she is thinking? Yu Mei must have had something important to say to me on the day of the sports meeting. If Chang Zheng is really her boyfriend, isn't this a waste of time? When a breeze blew, Zhang Feng calmed down. Turning around and looking at Yu Mei, he asked in a cold tone:

"But Chang Zheng lost to me, don't you feel sad?"

"Why do I have to feel sad? I will only feel sorry… I know what you want to ask. You have seen several times that Chang Zheng cares about me and guessed that we might be in love. In fact, I wanted to tell you at the sports meeting that it was not as you imagined, but I was interrupted by your classmate. Fine, then I will talk to you today." Yu Mei seemed a little bit unhappy and the red blush on her face was like the red glow on the white snow. Zhang Feng's heart softened.

"Yu Mei, don't be angry." At the same time, he felt relieved, or in the words of the Chinese proverb, like a falling stone at last reaching the ground.

Yu Mei flicked her hair off her forehead and began to speak. "Chang Zheng's father and my father are old army comrades. The Provincial Party Committee and the Military District Courtyard are separated by a wall. So we are like neighbours. Since we were young, we have always played together. Later, we studied in the same elementary school and middle school. Because I don't have an elder brother, rather only a younger brother, he always protected me like a big brother. I also treat him as a brother. I am used to it."

"I understand," Zhang Feng said. But he was still worried: "You were like brother and sister when you were children; but now that you both have grown up, is he still just regarding you as a sister?"

"I don't know," Yu Mei said, "I just care about and respect him like a brother anyway. In the past two years, I can feel that when I was with other boys, he was a little unhappy. I didn't talk about it with him."

"This is the problem." Zhang Feng whispered.

"What are you talking about?" Yu Mei asked.

"Nothing". Zhang Feng replied. He thought, in any case, Yu Mei was not interested in Chang Zhang. He was happy again. Yu Mei said:

"Zhang Feng, I want to ask you a question. Who is the beautiful girl who always follows you?"

"Who are you talking about?" Zhang Feng was confused.

"The girl who gave you flowers and wiped your sweat. Is she your sister?"

"Ah, you mean Dan Dan!" Zhang Feng smiled. "As you regard Chang Zheng as your brother, then equally Dan Dan is my sister."

"Sister?" Yu Mei asked with a hint of doubt. "Are you inventing a story to match mine?"

"I am not making a story." Zhang Feng said. "I never tell lies. Dan Dan has been my neighbour for many years and my schoolmate. But she is one year older than me. So she always takes care of me like a sister. Everyone knows this in our school."

"Is it true?" Yu Mei was suspicious. "But I have noticed the expression in her eyes when she looks at you; it is not the look of a sister, but a look like the ones other pretty girls give you when they are around you."

"How can you see it?" Zhang Feng asked, puzzled.

"Because of my woman's intuition." Yu Mei said.

"No, no" Zhang Feng said, repeatedly shaking his head. "Everyone knows that women can't love men who are younger than themselves. Dan Dan is a clever girl. How can she not know?"

"That's not true if you really like someone; age is not an obstacle. You are so handsome and versatile and any woman would fall in love with you…" Yu Mei's voice became quieter and quieter, becoming almost like a soliloquy. Her sweet voice was mixed with jealousy and happiness.

"Let it go and don't worry." Zhang Feng said with a smile. "It is our fate to be together, and maybe it's a good thing. See how we ran into each other today. Can we talk about something else?"

"Okay." Yu Mei said softly. The confusion in their hearts was solved. Both of them were intoxicated by happiness, talking about family, school, learning, and hobbies. They seemed to have countless topics to talk about. In a blink of an eye, the river had become tinted with the sunrise and was shimmering in the sunshine. The number of tourists walking the riverside had also begun to increase. Both of them suddenly realised that they should end the conversation and go home. But they were a little reluctant, and neither of them wanted to say goodbye. Finally, Zhang Feng said:

"Yu Mei, your family must be waiting for you to have breakfast?" And then he tried to ask: "Can we see each other often in the future?" Yu Mei nodded her head.

They walked back and forth side by side. Zhang Feng wanted to send Yu Mei home and accompanied her on her way to the South Bank Park. The provincial and municipal party committee officials' residential area was just behind there. They first crossed the grove in the river and followed a small road into the north gate of the park. There was a vibrant lilac tree not far from the back door of the park. "This smells so good", they said together at the same time. As they passed through the tall lilac bushes, both of them slowed down and enjoyed the rich aromas and love. Zhang Feng suddenly thought of the words of Shakespeare's "Twelfth Night" in The Duke's Acacia,

"Away before me to sweet beds of flowers: Love-thoughts lie rich when canopied with bowers." But he reminded himself that the relationship with Yu Mei had just begun. He should behave himself. It was not yet time to talk about love. So he calmed down. Looking at Yu Mei, he asked carefully:

"Yu Mei, can we meet under the big poplar tree on the river next Sunday morning?"

Yu Mei said happily: "Sure. Now I am really enjoying the beauty of the river and the breath of fresh air. And what's more, I am doing this with someone whom…" She wanted to say "whom I love" but shied away. Instead, she said: "All right. See you next week. Don't make me wait too long for you."

"Of course I won't." Then the two reluctantly parted.

CHAPTER V

Humiliation in a Distinguished Guest House

Over the next few weeks, Zhang Feng and Yu Mei met on the riverside every Sunday morning. On one occasion, Yu Mei said to Zhang Feng:

"Do you have time to visit my house?"

"Well, I have never been to the senior officials' area. Your home must be a large Western-style house with security and servants, right? "

For the ordinary citizens, the senior officials' area is a mysterious place isolated from the rest of the world, where the senior officials of the Communist Party and government lived. During the revolutionary period, they had lived amongst ordinary people. But now they had become a privileged stratum, enjoying a much better standard of living. Yu Mei said:

"It's not as special as you think – there's not much difference from other neighbourhoods except for the bigger houses and better greenery. Anyone can visit. My parents are not at home this afternoon. I will tell you the address; come to my house at 4 o'clock, okay?" Zhang Feng nodded.

At 4 o'clock in the afternoon, Zhang Feng passed through the South Bank Park and entered the senior officials' area. This was a block with neat streets and vibrant greenery. There were nice houses on both sides of the street, many of them were built by the Japanese during World War II. Following the address given by Yu Mei, Zhang Feng came to two beautiful houses with yards that were much larger than the other houses. Zhang Feng hesitated, wondering whether this was her home. A young man with the look of an officer came out of the big house on the left.

"Who are you looking for?" he asked Zhang Feng, noticing that he was searching for something.

"Is Li Yu Mei's home here?" Zhang Feng asked.

"Do you mean the daughter of secretary Li of the provincial party committee? That house is his home." He pointed to the big house on the right. 'Provincial Party Committee secretary Li?' Zhang Feng thought. 'Yu Mei's father is the first secretary of the Provincial Party CommitteeLi Jianguo? He is the highest ranking official in the province!' His hesitation increased as he thought more about it. Originally he thought that Yu Mei's father was only a director-level officer, and didn't expect him to be such a senior official. His own father was just a librarian. The social status of the two families was so different. Just as he hesitated, Yu Mei came out of the courtyard of another house.

"Hey, why are you so late? I have waited for you for a long time!" Yu Mei pretended to be unhappy, but the blush on her face could not conceal her excitement at seeing Zhang Feng.

"I…" Zhang Feng wanted to explain, but he couldn't say anything.

"Let`s go." Yu Mei took his hand and went to the yard. There were many flowers and trees in the yard. Entering the gate, the first thing Zhang Feng saw was the entrance hall with a cloakroom. A door on the left was open; through it he noticed a large living room inside. Yu Mei took Zhang Feng into the living room and let him sit on a soft leather sofa. Zhang Feng curiously looked at the precious antiques and tourist souvenirs in the glass cabinet.

"These were all brought back from when my father went abroad on official business. Some are gifts from friends."

"Your house is really luxurious!" Zhang Feng thought of his own home and the humble dwellings of ordinary citizens, as a sudden, strange feeling of imbalance began to form. "Are there a lot of rooms?"

"Yeah… There are several rooms." Yu Mei saw the strange look in Zhang Feng's eyes and stammered. "Here, have an apple." She quickly changed the topic. She took a big apple from the plate on the table, started to peel it with a knife and asked Zhang Feng about the university entrance exam that would soon take place. Zhang Feng was listening to Yu Mei absent-mindedly. He felt more and more uncomfortable staying here.

At that moment, a middle-aged woman came in and asked Yu Mei about arrangements for dinner. Yu Mei asked Zhang Feng to wait a minute before heading to the kitchen with this woman, who seemed like she was a housekeeper. Several minutes had passed without her return. Suddenly, Zhang Feng heard the sound the door opening behind him. He stood up quickly and waited to see who was entering; he stood very still, feeling very self-conscious given that he was not a member of this family. He heard two men's voices, moving closer; one of them was harsh and familiar. When two people walked through the living room door, Zhang Feng was suddenly stunned; one of the two people was Zhang Feng's old rival Chang Zheng. The other looked around 50 years old, with some slight greying on the temples. Zhang Feng thought that he might be the father of Yu Mei. As soon as Chang Zheng saw Zhang Feng, he jumped as though seeing an enemy:

"Why are you here? Who let you in?" Zhang Feng did not expect that he would meet his rival in love here, whom Yu Mei only treated him as a brother. But from a man's point of view, Zhang Feng knew that Chang Zheng had always regarded Yu Mei as his own girlfriend. Zhang Feng suddenly woke up from the sense of loss and recovered his self-esteem. He calmly replied:

"Li Yu Mei invited me. Hello Uncle!" he added, realising that Yu Mei's father was still there and should be addressed with the politeness afforded to elders.

Just at that moment, Yu Mei returned. Sensing the tense and awkward atmosphere, she walked over immediately and introduced them to each other. "Dad, this is Zhang Feng. He is the president of the student union of the Second Senior Middle School. He is very multi-talented; he is also the band captain of the school and the captain of the sports team. The soundtrack backing tape broke when I danced in the last art festival, and it was he who directed his band to accompany me. I owe my prize to him."

Then she looked at Chang Zheng and added naughtily: "At the middle school student sports meeting, he beat Chang Zheng in the high jump and 100 metres race." She followed with a laugh. Chang Zheng's face turned red and white, and he mumbled:

"If I didn't have a stomach ache, I wouldn't have lost to him." Then he said loudly: "Wait and see, I will certainly beat you next year!"

Zhang Feng relaxed a little. He smiled and said: "I look forward to it."

Yu Mei's father smiled after hearing Yu Mei's introduction. He looked at Zhang Feng with kindness and patted him on the shoulder and said, "Ah, great. Young talent. You must be a man with a promising future."

Yu Mei pulled her father's arm and said, "I haven't finished yet. He is also my saviour. I was hassled by some hooligans a few months ago, and he saved me. He beat the gangsters to the ground."

"Really? Thank you so much. You are also a martial arts master." Yu Mei's father said. Suddenly he frowned and said: "This gang of rascals are too much. I have mentioned it to director Li of the Public Security Bureau several times. Why can't they control these people?" Then he paused for a moment and said, "How about staying for dinner tonight? One must learn to express gratitude."

Yu Mei immediately took Zhang Feng's hand and said, "Stay, please. There is stewed pork with soy sauce and yellow croaker tonight. Aunt's cooking is very good." At that time, ordinary people could only afford stewed pork with soy sauce and yellow croaker once a year during the Spring Festival. Zhang Feng certainly wanted to eat, but he was also wise. He understood that he was just a middle school student from an ordinary family. It was not appropriate to stay for dinner when he came to the home of the Provincial Party Committee secretary for the first time. Moreover, Chang Zheng was also here. The atmosphere would definitely be awkward. So he said,

"Thank you, uncle. Maybe next time. A distant relative will visit my home tonight, so I have to go back." With that, he politely said goodbye. Yu Mei's eyes showed her disappointment. But she also knew that Zhang Feng and Chang Zheng were not on friendly terms and they would be both uncomfortable if they had dinner together. So she had no choice but to send Zhang Feng away reluctantly.

A few days later, Zhang Feng heard on the radio that a North Korean national leader was coming to visit. This leader had once fought side by side with the Northeast Anti-Japanese Alliance United Army during the Anti-Japanese War, so it was equivalent to revisiting his homeland. Provincial and municipal leaders were all preparing to warmly welcome him. The next day, at school Zhang Feng received a letter from Yu Mei (they agreed to write to each other if they had something to do before their Sunday meetings). In the letter, she said that in order to welcome the North Korean guests, provincial and municipal leaders would hold a welcome ball at the South Lake Distinguished Guest House on Friday night. Family members could enter the venue with a ticket. She had an extra ticket, so she wanted to invite Zhang Feng to attend the ball with her. She would wait for him outside the guest house gate at 6.30pm on Friday. Zhang Feng was very excited after reading the letter. First, this would be an opportunity to see the legendary North Korean leader with his own eyes. Second, he could see what it looked like inside the Distinguished Guest house. This luxury hotel was a mysterious place, a high-class hotel that only senior officials and foreign guests could enter. Wang Hai had once had the chance to visit the hotel when delivering food there. According to what he said, it was "extraordinary luxury".

At 6 o'clock on Friday, Zhang Feng came to the gate of the guest house. Two guards with guns stood at the door and checked all visitors and their vehicles. There were more fully armed soldiers by the door. Perhaps due of the arrival of North Korean guests, the level of security was much higher than normal. As Zhang Feng looked around, he suddenly saw Yu Mei coming out of the gate, wearing a white skirt. As soon as she saw Zhang Feng, she waved to him.

"You are so beautiful today," Zhang Feng said.

"Well, it is an official ball for foreign guests after all. My dad asked me to dress appropriately." The guards were obviously familiar with Yu Mei. They waved them through without even checking the tickets. Zhang Feng was astounded; it was like a paradise with a wide spacious boulevard and flowers, pines, and cypresses as far as they eye could see. In the distance, a beautiful building could be seen, flanked by a myriad of smaller service buildings. Walking into the hotel, Zhang Feng was overwhelmed by beautiful objects all around him. It was a truly luxurious setting, with red carpet, marble columns and huge chandeliers. Ordinary citizens had never seen such a marvellous place.

At that moment, Yu Mei touched Zhang Feng's arm and whispered, "Look, the foreign guests are coming." Zhang Feng looked behind him and saw a large group of people entering the hallway. There were three people walking at the front; one was the Yu Mei's father and the other was the national leader of North Korea, who Zhang Feng had only ever seen a photo of in the newspaper. There was also an army officer who wore the rank of major general. The three people, like old friends, talked and laughed while walking, followed by a large number of cadres, security personnel, waiters, and reporters. Two waiters greeted them and guided them into the party hall. "Let's go and have a look." Yu Mei said. Upon entering the hall, they saw many people waiting; the beautiful actresses of the provincial song and dance troupe were on the side of the hall, waiting to dance with foreign guests and provincial and municipal officials. There were also people who looked like family members of officials. Yu Mei's father gave a brief speech and welcomed the arrival of the Korean guests. Then the North Korean leader also gave a speech expressing his thanks for the hospitality. Following the speeches, the dancing began. The atmosphere in the hall became light and warm. The waiters began to serve drinks to the guests. Suddenly Zhang Feng saw Yu Mei's father waving to her. Zhang Feng quickly hid behind her. It turned out that Yu Mei's father wanted to introduce her to the North Korean guests. Yu Mei walked over and greeted them. The guests seemed to be complimenting her; Zhang Feng guessed that they would be complimenting her beauty. Suddenly Zhang Feng saw Chang Zheng also walking towards the guests. The general introduced him to the guests. Zhang Feng now understood that Chang Zheng was the son of the provincial military commander. No wonder he was so defiant and no wonder he was so familiar with the Yu Mei family.

Just then, the cheerful music began. The North Korean guests first invited Yu Mei to dance the waltz. Other foreign guests and provincial and municipal officials also choose their own dance partners to dance. Zhang Feng felt that he was an outsider here. It was not convenient for him to participate, so he slowly slipped to the door of the hall and stood there watching the fun. Among the dancing crowds, Yu Mei was particularly attractive, standing out due to her beautiful face, slim body, and light movements. Her white skirt was like a fluttering butterfly. She was more youthful, brighter and more elegant than the actresses of the provincial song and dance troupe. She was undoubtedly the queen of the party. Zhang Feng was fascinated. Yu Mei's dance performance as a fairy in the dream dance sequence of "Moonlight flowering of the Spring River" appeared before his eyes again.

Just as Zhang Feng was immersed in the beautiful illusion, suddenly someone slammed his back rudely. At the same time, he heard the familiar and hoarse voice.

"Why are you here?" Zhang Feng looked back and saw that Chang Zheng was standing behind him. There were also a few children of officials next to him. They were all his buddies.

"Li Yu Mei invited me to come here."

"I knew you would say that!" Chang Zheng raised his voice. "She doesn't know the rules of the provincial authority. This is a diplomatic occasion. Not just anyone can attend!" Zhang Feng was afraid that the quarrel with Chang Zheng would affect the party, so he said:

"Shall we talk about this outside?" After going into the hallway, Chang Zheng continued to say boldly:

"Do you know that only the families of provincial and municipal leaders can attend? Even the children of the departmental-level officials don't have this opportunity. What is your father's level?" He clearly knew that Zhang Feng's father was not an official, but he still asked this question deliberately. His buddies also kicked up a fuss and asked: "How high is your father's position?"

Zhang Feng and his classmates from the Second Senior Middle School had always been very disgusted with the children of the officials of the First Senior Middle School. Facing these arrogant guys, Zhang Feng really wanted to teach them a lesson. However, it was not suitable for this occasion. Just as they were in a stalemate, an army officer came over. Chang Zheng said to him:

"Secretary Lin, this guy broke into the party. You take him out right away!" The army officer was polite to Zhang Feng. After asking about the situation, he said to Zhang Feng:

"This is a bit difficult. You are brought in by Secretary Li's daughter, but today is an important diplomatic occasion. We must be responsible for the safety of the heads and foreign guests. How about…?" Zhang Feng still felt uncomfortable in his heart, but there was no choice. So he said,

"Don't worry, I will go." And he turned back to Chang Zheng and his fellows, and said to them: "Your arrogance is worthless." Then he strode out without looking back. As he approached the door, he could hear the sounds of the guys screaming behind him.

After coming back home, Zhang Feng fumed the whole night. He had always believed in equality. It seemed wrong to be discriminated against simply because of family and social status. The respect that people receive should be earned, and dependent upon your ability and contribution to society instead of your privilege. What made him feel even more uncomfortable was that now it seemed that there was an invisible wall between him and Yu Mei. Although he loved Yu Mei deeply, this wall may well have been insurmountable. His mother and sister were very concerned about him and asked him what happened. Zhang Feng said that he had a slight cold and was not feeling very comfortable.

The next day after coming back from school, Zhang Feng wanted to ease his depressed mood, so he walked into the woods in front of the house to relax. When he was a child, he often climbed trees here and used slingshots to shoot birds. He was a good shot and usually hit his target. During the time of "Eliminating Four Pests", when the government mandated the culling of sparrows, he shot the most sparrows and was praised by the teacher. It was not until later that he realised that the sparrow was a beneficial bird, and he regretted having killed so many birds. From then on, whenever he saw other children shooting birds, he would stop it. Zhang Feng sat down against a tree, closed his eyes, listening to the rustling sound of the breeze blowing the leaves and the sound of the birds. He felt much calmer in his heart. Suddenly he heard light footsteps behind him. Looking back, it was Dan Dan. She was wearing a blue lapelled top. The white jade-like face was slightly light pink, just like a blooming peony flower.

"Why are you sitting here alone?" Dan Dan asked while sitting next to Zhang Feng. The moment Zhang Feng saw Dan Dan, he immediately felt at peace.

"Nothing, I just wanted to be alone." Dan Dan gazed at Zhang Feng's face and asked with the tone of an elder sister:

"Xiao Feng, what is on your mind recently?" Zhang Feng took a look at Dan Dan. There was a feeling of warmth in his heart. Whenever there was something unhappy in the past, especially something that was embarrassing to say, he would always talk to Dan Dan. These days, there were too many things on his mind and it was hard to keep them quiet about them all, but he felt embarrassed talking to his parents. He felt solace in talking to Dan Dan because he always regarded her as his elder sister. He told Dan Dan all about his relationship with Yu Mei and his worries about the problems that may arise from their different social status. He told his story intently and did not notice the change in Dan Dan's facial expression. In the beginning, there was a slight blush on her face. Her eyes hade also dimmed. However, she soon recovered her calm. When Zhang Feng mentioned his loss when he was at Yu Mei's home, especially the humiliation he suffered at the hotel, her beautiful big eyes were filled with sympathy. After Zhang Feng finished telling the story, he turned and looked at Dan Dan.

"Dan Dan, is it possible for me and Yu Mei to be together despite the different social status of our families?"

"Is it that dancing girl? She is really beautiful."

"It doesn't matter if one person is beautiful or not. You are beautiful, too?"

Hearing his words, Dan Dan was very happy, and touched Zhang Feng's shoulder. "What are you talking about!" Dan Dan then asked:

"Do you really like her?" Zhang Feng nodded.

"Does she like you, too?" Zhang Feng nodded again.

"Then it all depends on whether her family can accept you," Dan Dan said. "Families of senior officials especially pay attention to the equal social status of families in terms of marriage. It can make things impracticable even if a slight difference exists. The children of senior officials also like to look down on ordinary people."

"Yu Mei is not that kind of person. She is a very easy-going girl and down to earth, just like the children of ordinary people." Dan Dan pondered for a while and said,

"You have to think about it. Affection is affected by many external factors."

"Yes, affection is very complex and sometimes it cannot be analysed and judged by reason." After a while, he asked Dan Dan:

"Dan Dan, have you ever liked anyone?"

Dan Dan gave a bitter smile and said: "I like a man. He is an amazing person. But there are complicated factors at play, so I can't tell him about my feelings. I can only bury my feelings in my heart."

"Doesn't that make you feel uncomfortable? Tell me who he is. I will tell him."

Dan Dan glanced at him mysteriously and said, "No, no, that would make it even worse."

After talking with him for some time, eventually she left. Zhang Feng remained there, pondering the question in his mind; why couldn't she confess to that person?

Sunday had arrived. Ever since waking up, Zhang Feng had been in two minds as to whether or not he should see Yu Mei today. Every time he thought of Yu Mei's luxurious house and being driven out from the hotel, his self-esteem would tell him, forget it, why should I be so humbled? But every time he thought of her beautiful appearance and amorous eyes, he could not help but wonder what Yu Mei thought. In the end, he decided that he would still go. He ran to the river, watching from a distance instead of waiting under the big poplar tree. It was 7 o'clock. Yu Mei had not yet appeared. Zhang Feng thought that perhaps she would not come, having also considered the social status of his family. A few minutes later, just as Zhang Feng was about to leave, he suddenly saw Yu Mei rushing over. She looked very anxious at not having seen anyone by the tree. Zhang Feng cheered up immediately and walked over at once, pretending to be unhappy.

"I'm sorry for being late. I had some family issues to deal with. Zhang Feng, I'm sorry that I didn't take care of you on the day of the party. It's all Chang Zheng's fault. I had a big row with him after discovering that he drove you off. I won't talk to him anymore."

"It's not all his fault. The reality is that our social status is too different. It seems that you live in another world that is completely different from us civilians. Yu Mei, we should think about it carefully. Although the traditional concept of marriage is not completely right, this difference in family background will cause problems in our future relationship." Yu Mei was a little anxious, and for a moment it seemed like tears were poised to flow

"Are you going to break up with me?"

"No, I hope that we can think calmly. Come to see me if you still think we have a chance. I am going to the Fengman Power Station to visit my uncle during the summer vacation, he is the chief engineer there. So, maybe we can see each other only when the new term begins. If you regret it, don't come to see me anymore." After saying that, he left firmly, leaving Yu Mei alone in a daze under the tree.

CHAPTER VI

A Sweet Holiday

Three days had passed since Zhang Feng had arrived at Fengman Power Station. Aside from parties, dinner with his uncle's family or chatting with his cousins, his favourite activity so far had been swimming in the Songhua Lake. On this particular morning, after having had breakfast at a little past 8 a.m., he packed a pair of swimming trunks, a towel and the Chinese version of Dickens' David Copperfield in his backpack; he was very fond of western literature, English and French literature in particular. He headed towards the hill from the power station's residential area and soon reached the top of the hydropower station dam. Into sight came two beautiful vistas. Seen from above, water from the surging Songhua Lake was pouring down through ten huge gates, converging into the clear Songhua River and flowing to a faraway place. Seen from below, it was the mountain surrounding Songhua Lake with boundless green stretches. The views were breathtaking; Zhang Feng gasped in admiration. He walked along the road running over the dam top to the marina by the lake. The road along the lake was built half way up the mountain. Looking down, you could see cargo ships and passenger ships entering the marina from time to time. Whistles echoed in the mountains. Zhang Feng preferred to stay in a quiet place for swimming and reading. He stopped at a turning of the road a kilometre away from the marina. The full view of the grand dam and the Songhua Lake extending into the distance unfolded before his eyes. He descended the road hidden in green plants, passed through thick grass, and reached the lake. Here the mid of July was the hottest month of the year. The sun was burning like a fireball. Zhang Feng sweated on account of the walking. He put down his backpack, put on his swimming trunks and touched the clear warm water with his hand. Zhang Feng could not wait to jump into the water and began a good swim. He changed swimming strokes once in a while: backstroke, butterfly stroke, and freestyle. The spray stirred up the clear water surface.

Having swum for half an hour, he climbed onto the bank for a rest. He was sunbathing while reading his novel. After a while, his body became warm in the sunshine. He felt very comfortable, lay on the grass with his eyes closed and took a nap. Suddenly he felt something like a worm crawling on his face, which made his face itchy. He wiped his face with his hand and returned to his nap. However, the worm climbed onto his face once again after a few minutes. "Nuisance!" Zhang Feng muttered as he made a hard grab. Unexpectedly, he caught hold of a soft small hand.

"Little Sister – stop being so naughty!" Zhang Feng had thought it was his female cousin, calling him back home for lunch as she knew he was swimming here. "I'm not going back for lunch. I've brought some bread. You go back first," he said with his eyes still closed. But this small hand kept rubbing his face with something. The itch was a little beyond his endurance. He said as he sat up,

"Little Sister, why you are so naughty?!" When he sat up and opened his eyes, he was shocked. It was not his female cousin but Yu Mei in a blue dress, who, wearing a broad smile, was preparing to rub his face again with a Setaria Viridis grass blade. Zhang Feng had thought that he was in a daydream. He rubbed his eyes and looked carefully. Yes, it was Yu Mei.

"It's only been a few days since we last saw each other. You've forgotten me already?" She gave a sweet smile.

Zhang Feng could not hide the surprise from his voice. "Why are you here? How did you come here?"

"Why can't I be here?" Yu Mei said, pretending to act like a spoiled girl. Then she added with a mock jealous tone, "Who's your Little Sister? Is she a charming girl?"

"She's just my female cousin, a little girl."

Yu Mei teased him on purpose. "Why is your face red? Are you feeling guilty?"

Zhang Feng came to his sense and said jokingly: "I'm excited to see you."

"Nobody knows whether you're really excited or not," said Yu Mei happily at hearing this, and sat down beside Zhang Feng. All at once, it occurred to Zhang Feng that he only wore a pair of swimming trunks. Immediately he pulled his shirt over his thighs.

"Ah, you're quite conservative," said Yu Mei with a smile. "Your strong muscles can compete with those of a god of war in ancient Greece," she added in an adoring tone. A series of naked images of gods of war in Greek mythology flashed through her mind, and she flushed with embarrassment. She hastily said, "No wonder you are able to beat up a flock of hooligans by yourself."

Both of them calmed down from excitement. Yu Mei told him of why and how she came here. There was a sanatorium for provincial officials by the Songhua Lake not far from the town where Fengman Power Station was located. On the second day after Zhang Feng left, an old subordinate of Yu Mei's father's was going to the sanatorium for recuperation for a period of time. There was a vacant room for his family, but his wife had passed away, and his children worked in other places, so he asked Yu Mei's father whether his children would like to go. Yu Mei was immensely glad to hear the news. She insisted that she was the right person rather than her younger brother who was also willing to go. Therefore, she came to Fengman with his father's subordinate in his car.

"How did you find me?" asked Zhang Feng.

"That's easy," said Yu Mei jauntily. "This old subordinate of my father's is the director in charge of the electricity power department. He called Fengman Power Station and got your uncle's address. This morning I visited your uncle's house and your male cousin told me where you were swimming." Looking at Yu Mei, Zhang Feng said attentively,

"You've covered such a long distance. Are you tired?"

"Tiredness is all gone when I see you," said Yu Mei shyly.

Zhang Feng put on his clothes. The two seated themselves under a tree by the lake, enjoying the inviting scenery before them, reveling in the fragrance of wildflowers and swimming in the crystal and warm lake. They sat in silence as if lingering in some intoxicating dream. This was a period of time when boys and girls were rather simple and adhered to tradition and etiquette; bodily touching was not allowed before marriage. They had to control themselves even though the desire was there. Previously whenever they had met each other by the river on one of their rendezvous, there had always been people doing exercises or taking a walk around them. They had kept their distance the whole time. But here there was nothing except the lake, mountains, and vehicles passing from distance now and them. Around the lake were thick trees, so no one could see them. They felt like they were Adam and Eve in the Garden of Eden without any worries. Zhang Feng looked around and saw no one; gathering his courage, he reached out and held Yu Mei's hand. Instinctively she had wanted to draw her hand back, but after a moment of hesitation, she held his hand in hers. With Yu Mei's smooth and pure white hand in his hand, Zhang Feng sensed his heart beating faster. Yu Mei also looked around, before leaning shyly against Zhang Feng's shoulder. Hand in hand, and side by side, the two were overwhelmed with happiness. After a while, Yu Mei whispered,

"Brother Feng, will you always love me?"

"Sure," answered Zhang Feng, his hands fondling hers.

"Will you still love me when I'm old?"

"You'll remain young."

"Why?"

"Because you're a fairy!"

"Behave! You're not telling the truth,"

After a few seconds, Zhang Feng turned to her and spoke seriously. "Yu Mei, for our future, I'll work hard, go to a good university, and become a scientist. Then your family won't look down on me."

"You're so excellent, and Qinghua University and Peking University will admit you for sure. I like children and hope to be a teacher. So Beijing Normal University will be my dream school. We can be together then. "

After a few seconds of silence, Yu Mei asked another question,

"Brother Feng, when did you fall in love with me?"

"When I first saw you on the bus," said Zhang Feng. "Yu Mei, do you know you're a peerless beauty in a man's eyes."

"Well, you're no different from other men who judge women by their appearance only." said Yu Mei, pretending to be angry.

"I judge a person not solely by their appearance. Love at first sight is the starting point of love. Love will go deeper when you find more merits in the other."

"What merits have you found in me?"

"Too many; tenderness, kindness, intelligence, artistic culture. Whenever I think of you, I see the dance of the haunting beautiful deity Chang E in my mind."

"You always know what to say." Yu Mei gave Zhang Feng a nudge on the shoulder.

Somehow Zhang Feng thought of what had happened in the Distinguished Guest House.

"I feel your father seems inclined towards Chang Zheng. Although Chang Zheng has a rough look, he is masculine like a soldier. He takes after his father. Moreover, his father and your father are old comrades. Is it possible that they arranged your marriage when you were very young merely without speaking out?

Yu Mei became a little angry. "Impossible. My parents treat him well only because as kids, we often played together. Let me say this again: I have no feelings for him at all. I only see him as a big brother." Seeing that Yu Mei was offended, Zhang Feng quickly tried to cheer her up. "Well alright, let's forget it."

Their topics turned to more light hearted topics, such as their friends and features of their schools. They stayed there until over 4 p.m. Having sent Yu Mei to the sanatorium, Zhang Feng went back to his uncle's house.

His uncle's family lived in a Japanese style bungalow; the power station was built when the Northeast was occupied by the Japanese. Upon entering the door, his aunt and male cousin asked him whether that beautiful girl had found him. His female cousin raced to ask,

"They say she looks like a fairy. Could you bring her home another day?" Zhang Feng lost no time in explaining that she was a girl he had met at an art performance and was just a friend. However, his aunt and his cousins winked at each other. They suspected that she was more than an ordinary friend of his.

Over the following week, Zhang Feng and Yu Mei met each other for a date at the lake every day, where they were embraced by nature and escaped from the noisy outside world. Yu Mei also went to Zhang Feng's uncle twice. His uncle's family all liked her. Free from the worries of the reality of daily life, they were immersed in that pure love between a boy and a girl. They both knew that this would be one of their happiest periods in their lifetimes.

One evening, Zhang Feng noticed his uncle sitting by the radio and paying full attention to the CCTV News broadcast. The sonorous voice of an announcer came over the radio. It seemed that an editorial from the People's Daily was being broadcast on the air. In general, that meant the Central Committee of the Communist Party would make a significant policy announcement. Zhang Feng sat down as well. He heard the words "the Cultural Revolution" repeated in the editorial over and over again. It reminded him of the criticisms against some writers and works not long ago. He thought that another political movement might take place. After the editorial, Uncle turned off the radio, and said to Zhang Feng,

"Probably a powerful political movement is coming near."

"Does it mean criticisms will involve more writers and works with political problems?" asked Zhang Feng.

"I'm afraid that it's not only about a couple of writers and a few works, but rather a much wider range of people." At that time Zhang Feng knew very little about politics and sincerely believed in communism just as most young people did. He believed that the Communist Party and Chairman Mao would lead the Chinese people to a prosperous and happy society.

His uncle pondered for a while and said: "You can ask your father about it when you're back. Your father is experienced in politics, and capable of foreseeing what movement it might be. "

The next morning, he had just finished breakfast when someone knocked at the door. His female cousin opened the door.

"Wow, fairy is here!" she cried. Zhang Feng came to her in haste. Right at the door stood Yu Mei. She was not in a good mood, judging from her expression. She spoke to Zhang Feng in a low voice.

"Uncle Liu, the old subordinate of my father, told me yesterday evening that all the recuperating officials are required to go back without delay, according to a notification from the department at the provincial level. Maybe a great event is about to happen. My father also called me to go home at once. Would you like to go back with us?"

"No problem, I'll go with you. I also miss my family. Sister had asked me to spare some time to instruct her in math." Seeing Yu Mei was nervous, Zhang Feng comforted her. "It doesn't sound like anything serious. I listened to the radio yesterday. Chances are, some people and culturally questionable works will be cleared out. "

At about 11 a.m., Yu Mei, Zhang Feng, and others headed to the provincial capital, the River City, in Director Liu's car. That was the first time that Zhang Feng had ever taken a car before; ordinary citizens could not dream of owning a private car, the bus was their only means of transport. Cars were reserved only for senior officials and they were really comfortable, fast and steady. Zhang Feng and Yu Mei sat at the back. Director Liu and the driver took the front seats. Zhang Feng did not sleep well the night before, so he was dozing off for most of the journey. He held Yu Mei's hand stealthily, enjoying the scenery, absorbed in the air of this sweet holiday. As they drove, he noticed a roaring river running besides the boulevards, towards the distance. Looking out of the window, Yu Mei whispered in melancholy,

"Brother Feng, why do I always get the feeling that something will happen? I mean something that will affect us." Zhang Feng fondled her hand gently, and comforted her. "Nothing will happen. We are both young students loving our country and the party. What could happen to us?"

PART II

The Red Storm

CHAPTER I

The Red Sea

Noon. The car drove into the suburbs. The rainstorm had stopped. The dark clouds had dispersed and the sun shone again on the earth. Zhang Feng and Yu Mei were feeling relaxed. Because she hadn't slept well last night, Yu Mei was a little sleepy, resting on Zhang Feng's shoulders.

The car suddenly slowed down. There were many people in the street. It seemed that they were all going to the city centre.

"What is going on?" Director Liu asked the driver.

"It seems that a revolutionary organisation has been established by the students of the school. In response to Chairman Mao's call, the Cultural Revolution was carried out."

"What?" Zhang Feng and Yu Mei were fully awake and looked outside the car hurriedly. When the car drove to the widest pedestrian street in the city, the road ahead was crowded with citizens.

Director Liu said, "Let's get out and see what's happened." They got out of the car. Zhang Feng and Yu Mei squeezed into the crowd. They could hear raised voices and see slogans in the distance. They saw a mighty parade holding red flags and banners with slogans, walking towards them. When the parade approached, it was clear that the banner read, "Long Live the Great Proletarian Culture Revolution!" and "The revolution is not guilty; rebellion is justified! We are Chairman Mao's Red Guards."

At the forefront of the parade were students from the Jili University directly governed by the Ministry of Education, followed by five other universities. Many students wore yellow military uniforms and red armbands. The words "Red Guard" were printed on the armband. As they walked, they sang "The sea is sailed by the helmsman" and "We are Chairman Mao's Red Guard" and other songs. And they shouted slogans, "Breaking four old institutions, erecting four new ones!", "Sweeping away all the ghosts and snakes!". As young students, Zhang Feng and Yu Mei also felt very excited but at the same time very confused. They didn't know what these slogans meant.

Director Liu looked a little anxious because with the tradition of party leadership, this group of students, who were not afraid of anything, could suddenly become a disaster for all party and government officials. While he was urging Zhang Feng and Yu Mei to go, Zhang Feng suddenly saw the school banner of the First Senior Middle School.

Immediately, he turned to Yu Mei and said, "Look, your school is here." Yu Mei looked forward and indeed saw a large red flag which read "Red Rebel Army from First Senior Middle School." On the front line of the parade was Chang Zheng. He was wearing a brand-new grass green army uniform and the Red

Guard armband. Yu Mei just wanted to wave to him. But she suddenly remembered that Zhang Feng was still nearby, so she gave up that idea immediately. Zhang Feng thought that if the First Senior Middle School was here then the Second Senior Middle School must be here too.

Just then, Yu Mei touched his shoulder and said,

"Look, your school's parade is coming." Zhang Feng took a closer look. It was true, the red flag waving in the wind said "Red Rebel Army of Second Senior Middle School" and the figures in the forefront turned out to be Wang Hai, Li He, Cai Desheng and Qing Lian. They were all dressed in old-fashioned military uniforms and wearing red armbands. In order to steal the limelight of the First Senior Middle School, their voices reached an earth-shattering volume. Just as Zhang Feng wanted to greet them, Director Liu was somewhat impatient.

"We have to go quickly," he urged. "Otherwise, we will not be home until dark."

"Uncle Liu, let me see where they are going. Then we will go." Zhang Feng said. He looked forward. He saw the parade like a red torrent flowing into the wide People's Square. Seen from afar, it was like a red sea. Zhang Feng could still faintly hear the voice from the loudspeaker in the Square.

"Red Guard comrades, now is the time for us to take revolutionary action. We are going to sweep away all the muddy waters of feudalism, capitalism and revisionism. We are going to build an utterly new red proletariat culture!"

Zhang Feng still wanted to hear more. However, Director Liu urged more intensely. Zhang Feng had to go back to the car with Yu Mei. But he was still figuring out what those words from the loudspeaker – "take revolutionary action" – really meant. There were still too many people in the street. The car went very slowly. Zhang Feng wanted to get out, take the tram home. But the tram seemed to be blocked by traffic too. After more than half an hour, the car had only moved 500 metres. At this time, Director Liu said:

"You are all hungry, aren't you? Let's stop and get some food. Wait until the crowd is gone."

So they got out of the car. There was a dumpling restaurant nearby. Director Liu said that this dumpling restaurant had been here since before the liberation and was very famous. As they walked into the restaurant, there were not many people eating. There were empty seats. Zhang Feng was not willing to let Director Liu pay, so he said he wanted to choose the flavour himself. He chose the pork and leek stuffing. Yu Mei and Director Liu chose beef and mutton stuffing. The three sat down to eat their dumplings. After more than an hour, it seemed that there were fewer people outside, and they returned to the car, continued their drive toward the city centre. However, the road ahead was blocked by the Red Guards. Maybe their rally was over.

The driver said, "Let's take a detour." So they drove towards the city centre from the road that ran alongside the river.

When the car was about to arrive at the Provincial Art Gallery they saw a lot of people gathered in front of the gallery. The outside was surrounded by the public. Inside were the Red Guards wearing yellow uniforms. The Red Guards seemed to be busy moving things out of the Gallery. Once moved out, they were piled up and then ignited and burned. Zhang Feng thought, 'Is this their revolutionary action?' He said to Director Liu:

"Uncle Liu, we can't leave. So let's go and check it out." The three of them got out of the car together, squeezed into the crowd and looked inside the building.

Suddenly Yu Mei said: "Hey, this is someone from the Second Senior Middle School." Zhang Feng quickly glanced in the direction Yu Mei indicated. Sure enough, the flag of the Second Senior Middle School's Red Guard was inserted on the steps of the gallery. Looking more closely, they saw it was Wang Hai, Li He, Cai Desheng and Qing Lian who were commanding the action at the door. Other students were moving various Chinese paintings, oil paintings and watercolours for Wang Hai to decide if they were going to be burned. Wang Hai often seemed hesitant but Cai Desheng and Qing Lian resolutely waved their hands and cried,

"Burn! Burn!"

Cai Desheng said loudly to the onlookers,

"The revolutionary masses. The collections and exhibits here are all products of feudalism, capitalism, and revisionism. They are the Four Poisonous Old Institutions. We must completely destroy them!"

The other Red Guards were also shouting slogans: "Rebellion is righteous! Rebellion is righteous!" Cai Desheng pointed to a person standing next to him, the sullen curator, and said,

"This is the person in charge of this dirty place. Everyone, what punishment should he receive?"

Several Red Guards shouted,

"Bow down and plead guilty! Bow down and plead guilty!" Then they forced him down. On his chest they hung a big plate with the words 'An anti-revolutionary propagating feudalism, capitalism, and revisionism.' Seeing this, Zhang Feng and Yu Mei were both stunned, thinking, 'What is going on here? The collections in the art gallery are all ancient and modern art treasures. How can you destroy them at will?' Zhang Feng wanted to rush out of the crowd to stop them but was dragged back by Director Liu who whispered,

"Stop! This may be directed by the new policy of the Party Central Committee."

At this point, several students came past carrying a few large oil paintings from inside, all of which were female nude portraits, saying,

"Look, so ridiculous. They were all hidden in the storage room."

Qing Lian waved his hand and said, "Burn them!" She turned around to the curator, who was squatting on the ground, and gave him two big slaps.

"Rogue!" she cried, and added the words 'Great Rogue' to the sign that he was hanging. The curator argued,

"This is what the Central Academy of Fine Arts gave us!" But no one cared about him. Yu Mei saw the nude portraits and shyly turned away. Director Liu then took the opportunity to say to them,

"Let's go back and ask Secretary Li to find out what is going on."

At first their car managed to pass through the crowds but after just 20 minutes, the way was blocked again. Zhang Feng thought to himself, 'Have the Red Guards taken any other action? But this is a commercial street, right?' They got out of the car and saw that many people were in front of the largest barber shop in the city, Wei Mei Xiu, where a group of Red Guards were doing something. Looking closely, it turned out that the Red Guard, Chang Zheng, was taking off the nameplate of the barber shop. The owner of the barber shop was standing to one side, looking scared. Chang Zheng waved his fist and shouted,

"Comrades, Red Guard comrades, see – this shop name is reactionary. Wei Mei Xiu means to support US imperialism and revisionism. What do you say?"

Other Red Guards shouted together, "Smash it! Smash it!" Then a few Red Guards swarmed forward and used big hammers to smash it until the nameplate was totally destroyed. Chang Zheng turned back to the female owner and asked,

"What social class are you from, landlord or rich peasant?" The owner just said with great fear,

"I, I…" Then fell into a faint. Several barbers rushed to save her. Chang Zheng had no sympathy, saying,

"Coward, playing dead? Wait until I come back and settle with you!" Then he waved his hand and led his team to search the next shop. Zhang Feng, Yu Mei and Director Liu were all stunned. They whispered,

"What's wrong with this shop? This shop has been here for more than ten years. Many provincial and municipal leaders have come here before to get a haircut. How can the name of the shop have political problems?" Because Chang Zheng was there, Yu Mei did not say much.

Seeing that the road ahead was still blocked, Zhang Feng said, "I will take the tram home."

Yu Mei looked at the tram on the roadside and said,

"It's been a long time since the last tram came. Is it out of service?" A passer-by heard their exchange and pointed to the tram station across the road and said to them,

"Look at what is posted on there!" The three men looked up and saw a notice on the pole of the tram station, "Bastards of the tram company, you must limit your driving to the left side within 24 hours. If you drive on the right side, you are the rightist, the reactionary!"

Director Liu whispered, "What's this? Everything is so messed up."

Zhang Feng wanted to go home and said,

"I am going home, which is not far from the South Bank Bridge. You two should drive slowly." Then he said goodbye to Yu Mei and Director Liu. Yu Mei reminded Zhang Feng, "Don't forget. Sunday morning".

Zhang Feng walked along the street, puzzled. Fear, chaos and noise shrouded the entire city. Many shops had closed early, people were at a loss, rushing home. Only the courageous continued to stay in the street to watch the excitement. There were very few cars on South Bank Bridge. Zhang Feng soon crossed it. Close to the university district, there seemed to be a checkpoint on the roadside. Some Red Guards were checking the people passing along the road. Next to them was a red flag reading 'Red Guards from Thirtieth Middle School.' When he came closer, Zhang Feng saw something curious. The Red Guards were forcing the people on the road to take off their shoes and they were checking them. Among the Red Guards, a man was arguing with a girl. Zhang Feng felt that this Red Guard was familiar to him. He took a look again; the guy turned out to be the notorious hooligan Hei Tou who had been punished by Zhang Feng a few months ago. 'How can he be a Red Guard?' Zhang Feng thought. He looked at the girl again, who turned out to be Dan Dan. Zhang Feng was furious. He strode up to protect Dan Dan, and sternly questioned Hei Tou,

"What are you doing? Are you bullying someone again?"

Hei Tou looked at Zhang Feng and instinctively stepped back.

"You, you…," he stuttered. "Mind your own business. We… we're taking revolutionary action."

Zhang Feng turned back and asked Dan Dan what was going on. She said that the word 'People' was printed in a pattern on the plastic soles of the shoes that she wore. The Red Guards said that this was deliberately designed by the counter-revolutionaries, meaning to trample the people under their feet. So she must take off her shoes. Zhang Feng thought this was absurd because the purpose of the design was to increase the friction of the sole.

Dan Dan added, "My feet were swollen for two days because of a mosquito bite. If I didn't wear shoes, it would still hurt. I asked them if I could wear my shoes and go home first. They refused."

Then a group of about thirty other Red Guards came over. When Hei Tou saw that he had his own people there to support him, he said,

"I can tell you that the technician who designed these shoes has already been arrested by the Public Security Bureau. So whoever continues to wear these shoes is his accomplice!" Zhang Feng was not afraid of Hei Tou. But he didn't know what the current situation was; even little hooligans like Hei Tou had become Red Guards. He glanced at Hei Tou and offered Dan Dan his arm.

"Let's go!" When they walked away, Hei Tou and the group of people jeered at them. After they had walked for more than 50 metres, Zhang Feng said,

"Dan Dan, may I carry you on my back?"

Dan Dan said with embarrassment, "You will be very tired!"

"It doesn't matter, I can carry 200 kg of hemp bags, how many kilograms are you?" Zhang Feng said. Then he squatted, let Dan Dan wrap her arms around his neck and lifted her up. Dan Dan couldn't bear to tire him, but as she gently pressed against Zhang Feng's broad and powerful shoulders her face showed a happy glow.

While Zhang Feng was walking, he asked Dan Dan why there were so many strange and chaotic things happening. Dan Dan told him that Chairman Mao had launched the Cultural Revolution to eradicate the ideas and culture left by the old society and to establish a new culture of the proletariat. The action of the Red Guard in the city was called "breaking four old institutions." They believe that the things that have been shattered and burned are harmful to our new society. Zhang Feng asked,

"Who can be a Red Guard?"

"You must be born into a good family, that is, a descendant of a poor peasant, a worker or revolutionary officials," Dan Dan explained. "Wang Hai, Li He, Cai Desheng, Qing Lian, they are all descendants of workers, poor peasants, and they have all become Red Guards. More than that, they have all become heads of the school's Red Guards organisation, especially Cai Desheng. He is most active and arrogant. In order to show his loyalty to Chairman Mao, he has been renamed as Cai Wenge (which means Cultural Revolution in Chinese). Those who are descendants of intellectuals, or rich landlords and businessmen, generally cannot be Red Guards." She was silent for a moment, and then said,

"Zhang Feng, you have to be careful. I see Cai Wenge is jealous of you. He may persecute you. These days I've heard people say that he was collecting your remarks. Now all the schools and companies are beginning to put up big writing posters, exposing counter-revolutionaries and bad elements. Teachers and faculty are fearful and afraid of being persecuted."

After Zhang Feng had taken Dan Dan home, he returned to his house. As soon as he entered he felt that the atmosphere was weird. His parents were sitting in the big room and talking nervously. His sister sat next to them and said nothing. Seeing that Zhang Feng had come in, his parents did not greet him happily as they usually did, but just faintly asked,

"You're back? Oh, is your uncle all right?" Dad told Zhang Feng to sit next to him and asked if he already knew the change in the political situation. Dad said,

"I have never told you about 1957 but I want to tell you now. In 1957, I did not do anything wrong. I only gave the provincial and municipal leaders a little advice on how to improve people's lives and I was tagged as a rightist. I was not allowed to teach. In 1961, I got rid of the right-wing hat, but I was still seen as a "rightist with a hat removed" and did not get back to my professor position. Now the movement we're experiencing is very strong. I guess we, as people with historically political problems, can't hide. My charge is likely to involve you also. You must be psychologically prepared. But no matter what happens, you have to believe that your Dad has never done anything to damage the Communist Party or harm the country and its people."

Zhang Feng felt very down after listening to his father. He believed that his father was an honest and kind person, not just a knowledgeable intellectual.

CHAPTER II

What Crime Has He Committed?

Zhang Feng didn't sleep well that night, and he kept dreaming. For a while, it was a sweet dream with Yu Mei, and later, it was a nightmare of him being chased by a group of people. After getting up in the morning, he rushed to school to see what had happened. When he first entered the school, he met many familiar students. He greeted them as usual, but they were hiding from him. Even the pretty girls who usually came up to talk to him pretended not to see him and quickly walked away. Zhang Feng felt very strange. He saw many students and faculty members going to the gymnasium and he followed. When he walked in, he was shocked. The four walls were all covered with big paper posters. The most striking thing was the large Chinese character posters on the front wall with the headlines talking about the old principal. These headlines read,

"Overthrow the executor of the bourgeois education route, Chang Jingyu!" and "If Chang Jingyu does not surrender, he will be destroyed." Zhang Feng was shocked. 'What happened to the old principal? Has he not worked conscientiously for the party and the country for decades? What mistake did he make?' Almost the entire wall were paper posters that lodged complaints against the old principal. But Zhang Feng did not understand why everything the old principal did was to "restore capitalism." Suddenly someone touched his arm. Zhang Feng looked back and it turned out to be Li He. Li He looked around and whispered to Zhang Feng, "There is also yours over there. But don't be afraid, they can't do anything to you." Then he left.

Zhang Feng went to the corner where Li He had pointed and saw a few large paper posters, on which were written in brush pen "The black seedling of the bourgeoisie, Zhang Feng" and "The son of big rightist Zhang Feng and Chang Jingyu bullied the children of workers and peasants together" and many more. Zhang Feng was astonished. How did they know that his father was a rightist? He suddenly remembered that it must be the teaching director. The teaching director was usually very cold to him. Once in a political class, the teacher had said a bourgeois rightist is a reactionary while watching Zhang Feng, as if to remind him that his father was also a rightist. Zhang Feng's application to join the Communist Youth League had been rejected several times. Zhang Feng guessed it was because the director was a member of the party branch and had the power to veto applications.

Zhang Feng was looking at a few other large-character posters, and suddenly heard a loud noise outside, as if it came from the school auditorium. Five minutes later, two Red Guards ran in and said to him very seriously, "The Red Guards Corps ask you go to the auditorium!"

As soon as he entered the auditorium, Zhang Feng saw that it was crowded with people. Under the stage were students and faculty. On one side of the stage stood the old principal, and on the other side, several people were sitting and questioning him. Zhang Feng took a closer look and saw Wang Hai, Li He, Qing Lian, Cai Wenge and the teaching director. Cai Wenge pounded the table and stood up.

"Chang Jingyu, you have to be honest and tell us how you have implemented the bourgeois education route!" he shouted loudly.

"You always encourage the students to become famous and an expert, not to be politically red and special," said Wang Hai, in a very low voice.

Qing Lian suddenly stood up.

"You poison us with feudalism, capitalism, and revisionism, let us sing Russian revisionism songs, and play feudal music. We must completely eradicate these cultural wastes!" she shouted.

Afterwards, she picked up the pipa (a four-stringed Chinese lute) that she used to play, threw it hard on the ground and smashed it. The Red Guards under the stage applauded her. Then she shouted to the crowd under the stage, "Let us sing the revolutionary songs!" Then she directed everyone to sing "The Sea Is Sailed by the Helmsman". Just as the song ended, the teaching director also criticised the old principal and commanded him to admit the crimes he had committed.

"I have worked for the party and the country for decades," the old principal said calmly. "I have never done anything wrong to the party and to the people. I don't know what mistakes I have made."

Before he had finished speaking, Cai Wenge, Qing Lian and the teaching director jumped up.

"You were a stubborn capitalist, you still don't confess!" they shouted.

They immediately led the students and teachers in the audience to shout out their slogans, "Leniency to those who confess, severity to those who resist. If Chang Jingyu does not surrender, we will let him perish!" Then two Red Guards hung a big sign on him with the words "Overthrow the capitalist roader Chang Jingyu" and made a big red cross on his name, putting on his head a big hat made of paper. Two Red Guards stood next to him, treating him like a criminal; each guard grabbed one of his arms and push his head down, forcing him to bow his head and plead guilty to the masses.

Zhang Feng was confused and worried about the old principal. He suddenly heard the director say:

"Another crime of Chang Jingyu is that he heavily uses students from families from the Five Black Categories (a general designation of landlord, rich peasant, counter-revolutionary, bad element and rightist) and suppresses students from families of workers and peasants like Cai Wenge. Everyone knows that the most popular student lauded by Chang Jingyu is Zhang Feng, but you know what? His father was the major rightist in our province in 1957."

Here, all the people turned back, looking at Zhang Feng, who suddenly felt hot, his heart pounding. The teaching director looked at him and called:

"Zhang Feng, come on stage!" Zhang Feng was in a state of shock and went slowly to the stage. The girls looked at him sympathetically. The boys who were usually naughty and jealous of him were excited and kept shouting "Confess! Confess!" The director asked Zhang Feng to stand next to the old principal and said:

"You are a seedling of revisionism cultivated by Chang Jingyu, a typical example of the white special road (do one's own professional work well, but do not care for politics), you must expose the crime of Chang Jingyu of taking the capitalist road."

Zhang Feng did not know what to say, and he really could not think of bad things done by the old principal. Moreover, Zhang Feng had always been honest and would not do anything contrary to his conscience. Therefore, he whispered:

"The principal usually lets us listen to Chairman Mao's words, study hard, and improve every day." The director immediately was angry and loudly announced,

"It seems that Zhang Feng has no understanding of the crimes of Chang Jingyu. I announce the withdrawal of his position as student union chairman and all other positions and urge him to stop and reflect on himself. If he doesn't change his position, he will receive further punishment."

Wang Hai looked at Zhang Feng sympathetically and said,

"You'd better draw a line with Chang Jingyu."

Cai Wenge said strangely, "It will not be easy, will it?" Then he winked toward his footmen. One of them, who usually did not study much, went to the front of the stage and said:

"Zhang Feng does not only sway the power of Chang Jingyu, but also makes a fuss, bullying the students from workers' and peasants' families. He also seduces girls everywhere, relying on his handsome appearance."

Wang Hai immediately said, "You can't talk nonsense, do you have evidence?"

The Red Guard said, "How could I not have? What is the relationship between Liu Dandan and you?"

"You are framing a case against him!" Suddenly, the angry voice of Dan Dan came from the crowd. Zhang Feng had never seen her so angry.

"We have been neighbours since we were young. I am older than him. I always take care of him. We are like brother and sister. What's wrong with that?" The Red Guard had nothing to say. But then Cai Wenge whispered something to the guard. He immediately came back and said:

"What about Li Yu Mei in the First Senior Middle School? Is this also a relationship between a sister and a younger brother?" Their group immediately stirred up the atmosphere.

Zhang Feng calmed down at this time and said loudly, "We met each other at the art performance. Then we saw each other at a sports meeting and nothing happened."

Dan Dan immediately said, "Yes, I know, that's it."

Wang Hai said, "I also know this." The teaching director saw that they could not go on accusing Zhang Feng so he said to Zhang Feng,

"That's enough, go home and write a self-criticism letter." He thought more about knocking down the old principal in order to replace him.

He walked to the old principal, who was bent over, and said:

"Chang Jingyu, you don't admit you are guilty, do you?" The old principal must have been exhausted by then.

"I… I… have committed no crime," he gasped.

Cai Wenge and Qing Lian jumped up all of a sudden, shouting to the crowd,

"Chang Jingyu is stubborn and refuses to plead guilty. What shall we do?"

The activists in the Red Guards shouted, "If he doesn't surrender, let him die!" Then a horrible scene took place. A

Red Guard first hit the old principal with two big slaps. After that, it seemed that Cai Wenge kicked him from behind, and the old principal fell face-down onto the floor. Then a group of Red Guards came swarming up, kicking and smashing him. Wang Hai tried to stop them from behind, but couldn't. Zhang Feng and those who were sympathetic to the old principal could only watch these atrocities, and no one else dared to stop the perpetrators, because, after all, whoever sympathizes with the counter-revolutionary is a counter-revolutionary himself. The old principal held his head in his hands, and his body twitched with pain. Slowly, his hands were released, spread out on the floor, and his body did not move.

"He's dead!" Zhang Feng heard a scream in the crowd. That was the voice of Dan Dan.

The teaching director announced loudly without fear,

"The stubborn capitalist roader Chang Jingyu deserves to be found guilty of the crime. If he has died, he deserved to die. If he has faked death, he cannot hide from the criticism of the revolutionary masses."

Cai Wenge went on to say, "Red Guards, rebel comrades, the unrepentant capitalist roader Chang Jingyu was defeated. The first stage of our Second Senior Middle School Cultural Revolution has achieved a great victory, and we must continue to sweep all the ghosts and monsters!"

Then he announced that today's public condemnation conference was over. Under the command of Qing Lian, all of them sang the song "Rebellion is Justified" and exited the auditorium, leaving the old principal on the stage motionless.

In the auditorium, only Zhang Feng remained, while Dan Dan stood at the exit, with dozens of students and teachers who were sympathetic to the old principal. Zhang Feng's fear gradually turned into anger, thinking, 'Is there any law at all? In broad daylight, people can be killed, who have contributed to the education of the motherland. What revolution is this?' He forgot that he was also involved with the old principal. He ran to the stage in tears and picked up the old principal. He called him,

"Old principal! Old principal!" Dan Dan also ran up, crying with tears. The old principal did not respond at all. Dan Dan's mother was a doctor, so Dan Dan also had some medical knowledge. She asked Zhang Feng to lie the old principal down so she could give him first aid. After Dan Dan touched the old principal's neck artery, she said excitedly,

"He is still alive!" Then she raised his head slightly and made his breathing easier. She said to Zhang Feng,

"He has a prostration. He is old and weak. He cannot withstand such violent torture and may also have internal injuries. How can these people be so cruel? We should get him to a hospital quickly."

Zhang Feng slowly picked the old principal up and walked out of the auditorium. More than a dozen people standing at the door came forward to ask how the old principal was. Outside the auditorium, Zhang Feng saw Wang Hai standing on the steps, looking apologetic. He came over to Zhang Feng and asked how the old principal was.

Zhang Feng said angrily, "You have done such a good job, haven't you?"

Wang Hai defended himself, "Elder brother, you have just come back and you don't understand the situation. This Cultural Revolution led by Chairman Mao is to create a new world. So many people have to be involved, it is going a bit too far to beat people. Cai Wenge led a group of Red Guards who were very fierce. I don't have control over them. Elder brother, you have to mind your own business."

Zhang Feng was still angry, so he said:

"I'm fed up with it. I don't have time to listen to you. I have to get him to hospital quickly."

Wang Hai asked if he could help. Zhang Feng was a loyal person. He said:

"Forget it. You are the head of the Red Guards. I am a child of the Black Five Categories. At worst, I will be blacker but I don't want to affect your future."

Wang Hai was moved and said, "Elder brother, let me know if you have any trouble, and take care."

Zhang Feng and Dan Dan rushed to the nearby district hospital and went to the emergency room. He placed the old principal on the bench and let Dan Dan go and find the doctor. A few minutes later, Dan Dan came back with a middle-aged male doctor. The doctor asked about the situation and leaned over to check the principal. When he saw the face of the old principal, he was shocked.

"Isn't he the principal of the Second Senior Middle School? How is his face hurt so badly?"

Zhang Feng said that he was injured by the Red Guards, thinking that this would make the doctor sympathise with him. But Zhang Feng didn't expect the doctor to retreat, as if he had seen a ghost. "No, no, I can't treat him. I shall ask the director." He ran away immediately. Five minutes later, he came back with a doctor in his fifties and introduced him as the director of the emergency department. The director explained very politely that the hospital's rebel faction had informed them that all counter-revolutionaries, bad elements, and capitalists were not allowed to be treated, or they would be punished themselves.

"Doctor, he is so old, the injury is so bad, if it is not treated, he will be in danger," Zhang Feng begged.

The director said helplessly, "Young man, we have no way. If I treat him, I will end up like him. You should send him home, let him rest and rely on his vitality to recover."

After that, he looked around. No one was there, so he took from his pocket a few bags of medicine, saying, "Here are some tranquilisers and painkillers. You can go back and give them to him. They will help." Then he hurried away.

At this time, Dan Dan said, "Let's take him home, I will go and ask my mother to come and see him."

Zhang Feng said, "Well, that's good. His home is not far from our university campus."

Half an hour later, Zhang Feng took the old principal on the No.4 bus and went back to South Bank, and walked for another ten minutes to bring the old principal home. The old principal's daughter opened the door and burst into tears as soon as she saw her father. Zhang Feng advised her not to be upset, while talking about the details of the matter and putting the old principal on the bed. After ten minutes, Dan Dan and her mother also arrived. Dan Dan's mother gave the principal an injection and fed him a little medicine. She said that the kicking of the Red Guard may have caused a coma, internal bleeding and other traumas as a result of a concussion, which needed time to heal. The old principal's daughter said that the elementary school where she taught was also suspended. She could take care of her father at home. Seeing that the old principal's breathing and pulse were smoother, Zhang Feng and Dan Dan left.

CHAPTER III

The Red and Black

Over the next few days, Zhang Feng went to see the old principal every day. The old principal had been awake but was still very weak. He knew from his daughter that Zhang Feng had saved him. He held Zhang Feng's hand with tearful eyes. He murmured,

"Thank you. I was right. You are a child of affection and righteousness. But I'm sorry I got you into trouble."

Zhang Feng shook his head and said, "It wasn't you that got me into trouble, my father already had historical issues – ."

The old principal interrupted him, "No, don't complain about your father. I know him. He is a loyal patriot and a profound scholar. It is because of his integrity and honesty that he suffers misfortune. What is this…?" He wanted to say, "What is this world coming to?" But the words were stopped from his mouth.

Zhang Feng went back to school. The campus was cold and clear. Occasionally he saw a few students, and wanted to ask what was going on. However, as they saw Zhang Feng, they quickly dodged him as if he was already a class enemy. Later, he met Li He who told him that the Red Guards had gone into society to start the revolution. Zhang Feng said to him,

"Tell Wang Hai that the old principal has already passed the dangerous period and is still recovering. If Cai Wenge asks, just say that the old principal is already paralysed in bed, so the Red Guards will not come to persecute him again." Li He agreed.

The things that had happened in the last few days had left Zhang Feng very confused, depressed and exhausted. Those who had been kind, honest and conscientious suddenly became class enemies, and those who had been mischievous, misbehaving, insidious and sinister had suddenly become revolutionaries. His parents at home reminded him to check his diary and see if there was anything that did not conform to the current revolution and that could violate Mao Zedong Thought. When he opened the drawer, he suddenly saw the handkerchief embroidered with plum blossoms that Yu Mei had given him. He suddenly remembered. Damn! He had forgotten to meet Yu Mei on Sunday morning, because that day was the second day following the old principal's incident. Zhang Feng had been taking care of the old principal at his house all day. What should he do? Zhang Feng knew that Yu Mei was a very loyal girl; no matter what happened, she would not have broken the appointment. If she didn't see Zhang Feng, she would be anxious. Thinking of his current situation, Zhang Feng felt very depressed. Both the family and he were 'black,' and the Yu Mei family was red, of senior officials. Their social statuses were too different. However, Zhang Feng was a trustworthy person. Since he and Yu Mei had vowed, they must have a confession to make to each other. 'If I go to Yu Mei's home, it will be too abrupt. If I walk around her house, maybe I can run into her.' While thinking about this, Zhang Feng left home and walked to the high-ranking officials' district.

There was a small bridge not far from Yu Mei's house, which was the only way for Yu Mei to get home. Zhang Feng thought, 'If I wait here, maybe Yu Mei will pass through here.' He waited from 10:00 in the morning until noon, but he still did not see any trace of Yu Mei. Yu Mei would go home for lunch. Zhang Feng thought, 'I will count from one to a hundred; if I still don't see Yu Mei by then, I'll leave.' One hundred counts were over. Yu Mei did not appear. He thought, 'I will count a hundred more'. After this count was over, he still hadn't seen Yu Mei.

In this way, he counted a total of five times. Zhang Feng leaned against a big tree by the bridge and thought, 'People often say that one can sense another person's mind. So I will count a hundred more in the end. If I don't see her, I will give up.' So he faced the big tree, closed his eyes, and counted while thinking about the image of Yu Mei. Halfway through, there was no movement; he thought, I will count slowly. He slowed down the speed, 90, 91, 92. . . 99, Zhang Feng thought, 'Is it God who does not allow me to see my beloved?' When he finally got to 100, he felt a hand gently patting him on the back, making him jump. He looked round. It was Yu Mei! She was dressed in a grass-green military uniform, wearing a Red Guard armband, and she was as cool as an angel descending from heaven. They hadn't seen each other for a week, and there were so many things happening. Both of them seemed to have thousands of words to say to each other. Yu Mei said,

"Come to our house, my parents are not there. I just bought a Shanghai camera. You can take a few photos of me."

Zhang Feng was very confused; he had no interest in thinking about photography. While he was walking, he kept talking about what had happened to him, his home and school last week. He told Yu Mei seriously that he was now a 'black five category' descendant. He was no longer a youth who had a promising future and whom everyone admired. He said,

"Yu Mei, now you are red, I am black. Red and black are incompatible. It is impossible for us to be together. Chang Zheng has been so good to you; you two are the most suitable."

Zhang Feng thought that Yu Mei would tacitly approve his words or indirectly imply that their relationship was no longer sustainable. But what he didn't expect was that Yu Mei became so angry that her cheeks turned bright red, making her look even more beautiful.

"What are you saying? I love you, not your social status, not what your family does, nor what political mistakes your father has made. I don't care. What are red and black? That is the opinion of others. You are still you, nothing has changed. What I like is that you're handsome, generous, honest and kind, versatile; I'm not interested your political achievement, nor your being an official or not."

Zhang Feng was speechless. Yes, there was no need to add a condition to love someone. But reason reminded him that social pressure was irresistible. So he changed his perspective to persuade Yu Mei.

"I know that you are a loyal girl, but your father is a senior official, and my father is a rightist. Your family will not accept me." But Yu Mei still ignored his words, taking his hand and dragging him towards her home.

When they arrived at Yu Mei's home, Yu Mei happily took out the camera and let Zhang Feng take a photo of her. She also took a few photos of Zhang Feng, and finally took out a tripod and asked if they could take a photo together. Zhang Feng was hesitant. Yu Mei said,

"I am afraid of nothing; my family won't say anything." Zhang Feng just dressed in his black shirt, while Yu Mei wore a Red Guard's grass green uniform and a striking red armband. This red and black lover's photo was thus fixed at the moment when the great turmoil in Chinese history began. The face of Yu Mei was full of joy, whereas Zhang Feng's handsome face was shrouded in depression.

Just after the photo had been taken, he heard a movement at the door. It turned out that Yu Mei's parents were back. Yu Mei's father walked into the living room, looking very tired. He reluctantly greeted Zhang Feng and asked about the Cultural Revolution in the Second Senior Middle School. When he suddenly remembered that Zhang Feng's home was in the Normal University, he asked,

"Are your father and neighbours affected?"

Zhang Feng said, "They're okay now…" Yu Mei's father then asked,

"What is your father's name?"

"His name is Zhang Wenbo."

"Zhang Wenbo?" Yu Mei's father's face suddenly twitched, as if he was scared. His face also became very ugly. He stood up from the sofa and said,

"I'll let you talk." He hurried out of the living room. A few minutes later, the secretary of Yu Mei's father came in and called Yu Mei out very mysteriously. After that, Zhang Feng could vaguely hear Yu Mei's voice arguing with her father upstairs. Zhang Feng suddenly realized that his arrival might have brought trouble to Yu Mei. He stood up, intending to leave. He walked to the corridor and saw the secretary coming towards him. He said to Zhang Feng very seriously,

"Please don't see Li Yu Mei again. Your father's political problem is very serious. He was the major rightist in our province in 1957. This time, the revolutionists will surely investigate him again. You must know your own position."

When he finished speaking, he pointed to the door. Zhang Feng knew that he had no room for excuses and went out silently.

Zhang Feng left Yu Mei's home with a leaden heart. Although he had expected such a result, he was still very sad. On the one hand, he had to part from his beloved one, and on the other hand he was also worried about his father. Deep in thought, he walked to the bridge without knowing it. When he saw the big tree on one side of the bridge, he felt even more disheartened. He stopped and sat down under the big tree. Suddenly he heard Yu Mei's shouting. He had never heard Yu Mei sound so desperate. He looked round and saw Yu Mei running to him from her home. Her face was full of tears and her hair was messed up. Zhang Feng stopped, quickly stood up, and did not know if he should run away or wait for her. Yu Mei saw Zhang Feng under the tree, ran to him, and plunged into his arms. Zhang Feng could feel that Yu Mei was shaking and crying. He felt as if a knife were being twisted in his heart, but he really didn't know what to say, only gently patting Yu Mei's shoulder to comfort her. Yu Mei cried and said brokenly,

"No, no, I will not leave you, because I can't live without you!"

A gust of wind blew over them, and Zhang Feng suddenly felt wide awake. He knew that facing family, social and political pressure, his relationship with Yu Mei could not continue. Long pain was worse than a short one. He raised Yu Mei's shoulder and said to her:

"Yu Mei, we have vowed to love one another, but the current situation is that if we continue our love, your future will be ruined, and your family won't approve of our relationship. Really, our love will not have any result." Yu Mei was still crying, and she stubbornly shook her head and said,

"No! No!"

Zhang Feng couldn't convince her, so he had to come up with a reason to refuse Yu Mei.

"Yu Mei, I haven't told you that Dan Dan has been with me and has been comforting me recently. Her mother also has a political problem because she is one of those who had joined the Kuomintang party before. We are all children of the Black Five Categories. I think, since she has been caring for me for so many years, we are the most suitable,"

Yu Mei listened to him, suddenly stopped crying, and asked in surprise,

"What are you talking about? You and Dan Dan are in love? This is impossible! You are lying to me. Isn't she your sister?"

Zhang Feng said, "I have got over that. I don't believe in those superstitious things that a woman older than me should not be my wife. I think, as long as two people really love each other, age is not a problem."

Yu Mei looked furious; her face turned rose-red.

"I don't believe it. You are lying to me!"

Zhang Feng suddenly thought of Dan Dan's handkerchief in his pocket, so he took it out and presented to Yu Mei.

"Look, this is the handkerchief Dan Dan gave me." Yu Mei looked at it, and indeed, several white peony flowers were embroidered on it. She was dumbfounded. Zhang Feng immediately took Yu Mei's handkerchief from another pocket and handed it to her with a trembling hand. He said:

"Your handkerchief is returned to you. Let's not meet again in the future. Chang Zheng will take care of you."

Yu Mei was not willing to take the handkerchief. So Zhang Feng put his hand back into his pocket. After that, he turned around and strode away. He wanted to walk away as soon as possible so as to end this torture, but his heart still stayed with Yu Mei, and his ear still listened to what was happening behind his back. Only after a dozen steps, he heard Yu Mei slap the big tree and give a heart-breaking cry. Zhang Feng couldn't go on. When he just wanted to turn and go back to persuade Yu Mei, she raged at him in a hoarse voice,

"You are so ruthless. Well, well, I am going to find my brother Chang Zheng!"

When he looked back, Yu Mei had already run back to her house. Zhang Feng, whose heart was being twisted by a knife, walked heavily all the way home. He felt that his world had gone dark; he had neither future nor love anymore. But he did not know that this was just the beginning. Ahead lay many more catastrophes of his own, and of his family and his society.

CHAPTER IV

Home Search and Confiscation

A week later, panicked messages began to spread throughout the university area that the actions of the Red Guards had expanded from the city to the residential areas. They were going from house to house, searching and destroying anything to do with feudalism, capitalism, revisionism and counter-revolution, such as paintings, literary works, antiques, monuments, even personal diaries and letters. Whoever showed the slightest hint of rebellion would be treated as a counter-revolutionary.

When getting up in the morning, the whole family would have to go to the neighbourhood committee to participate in the 'morning request and evening report.' At that time, all the people had to participate in this activity of learning Chairman Mao's quotations. Everyone must have a red booklet entitled 'Quotations from Chairman Mao' and they had to study

Chairman Mao's 'highest instructions' together. They also had to chant the slogan of "Long Live Chairman Mao, Long Live Chairman Mao, and Long Live Chairman Mao" to show loyalty. If they didn't show loyalty to Mao, they were in danger. On the street, people even danced the 'loyalty dance.'

After attending the morning request, Zhang Wenbo was busy in the study checking the books on the bookshelf to see if there were any that did not meet the 'new culture of the proletarian' standard. Mom checked the calligraphy and paintings in another room. Zhang Feng was flipping through drawers in his own room to check his diary and letters. When he heard his father calling him, he walked over and saw that the table and chairs in his father's study were full of books. Dad sat on a small stool with a sweaty and frowning face. When he saw Zhang Feng, he sighed and said:

"Hey, these books are the essence of Chinese and world culture. How can they be cleared and treated as cultural waste overnight? Xiao Feng, could you help me see which books may be illegal?"

Zhang Feng looked at his father's books and said:

"The newspaper said that, in the traditional culture, the works that advocate emperors, generals and ministers, gifted scholars and beautiful ladies, and romantic matters were of the old culture. Only works that extol the workers and peasants and the labouring public will be preserved. The exceptions are some poems written by Du Fu and Bai Juyi, the novel Water Margin which writes about rebels against the royal court, and Heroes on Liangshan (a mountain in eastern China). Most other classical works do not meet the new standard either."

Zhang Wenbo said, "The most valuable books have to be hidden. Otherwise, I will be sorry for our ancestors."

Zhang Feng said, "Isn't there a small storage room under the floor of our house? How about putting them there?"

Zhang Wenbo said, "We have no choice but to put them there."

While they were busy they heard Mom's voice:

"Dan Dan. You are here, come in, Xiao Feng and his father are busy." The family saw Dan Dan as their own member and hid nothing from her. Dan Dan hurried in and said to Zhang Feng and his father:

"It's not good. There are several teams of Red Guards who have entered the faculty's residential area. They are searching from house to house! Any Four Old things that are found on the spot are burned." Seeing that Zhang Feng and his father had too much to do on their own, Dan Dan helped them organise and hide those valuable books and calligraphy.

Ten minutes later, they heard a loud knocking on the door. Zhang Feng, Zhang Wenbo and Dan Dan looked at each other. Zhang Wenbo and Dan Dan looked nervous and overwhelmed. Zhang Feng calmly said:

"Don't worry, I'll open the door." When he went to the door and looked outside, he gave a surprised "Ah!" Dan Dan and Zhang Wenbo went running to join him at the door. The Red Guards at the door turned out to be led by Chang Zheng and Yu Mei. Chang Zheng and Yu Mei looked at Zhang Feng and Dan Dan with surprise. In Yu Mei's eyes Zhang Feng saw a look of sadness and envy, probably because Dan Dan was standing by his side. 'What a coincidence!' Zhang Feng thought, 'Yu Mei does not know my address, maybe Chang Zheng told her.' Suddenly he heard Chang Zheng speak:

"Hey, we are the rebel group from the First Senior Middle School. You have a complicated 'class struggle' in the university area. There are many political monsters and ghosts, and many things of the Four Olds. We have to check your house to see if there is anything of feudalism, capitalism and revisionism."

Then he glanced at Zhang Feng with a scornful look as if to say 'You must wait for me to kick your ass this time.' Zhang Feng knew that under the pressure of the political movement, people had to bow their heads. But when he saw his domineering old rival, he said with conviction,

"Check your own home first. I don't believe that there are no old things in your house."

"You!" Chang Zheng did not expect Zhang Feng to say this, and for a moment, he didn't know what to say. Yu Mei pulled Chang Zheng's sleeve and whispered,

"Chang Zheng brother, we're all acquaintances. Forget it. Let's search another home!"

Chang Zheng hesitated for a moment. Then he turned back and said to the Red Guards behind him,

"Some intelligence said that there was a black painter nearby. There were a lot of Four Old things in his house. Let's go there first in case it was robbed by other rebels."

He then turned back to Zhang Feng and said:

"You guys wait. When I come back, I will search your house."

Then he followed the other Red Guards and hurried away. Looking at them walking away, they all breathed a sigh of relief. However, Zhang Feng saw Yu Mei looking back at him, with her eyes showing nostalgia and sadness. He felt very uncomfortable. Dan Dan saw this scene and gently asked Zhang Feng,

"Can't forget her?" Zhang Feng had already told her that he and Yu Mei broke up. Zhang Feng did not answer but just walked back into his room silently

The family was relieved and thought they had escaped. Dan Dan began to ask Zhang Feng's mother Hu Yun about how to knit a sweater. However, after ten minutes, there was another knock on the door outside.

"What's happening?" Hu Yun asked in a panic, "Has Chang Zheng come back?" Everyone was a little panicked. Since the valuable books were almost hidden, Zhang Feng said to everyone,

"Don't panic, let me open the door to see." After opening the door, he once again gave a cry of surprise. Dan Dan thought Chang Zheng had come back but it was Cai Wenge and Qing Lian leading the Red Guards from the Second Senior Middle School. The Red Guards looked at Zhang Feng in surprise. Although he was not the man of the past whom everyone admired, his influence still remained amongst these students. They all looked at Cai Wenge, as if waiting for his order to retreat. However, Cai blinked at them and sneered, saying,

"Chairman Mao said that the revolution is not inviting somebody for dinner, neither is it painting or embroidery. We must not forget his teachings. Class struggle cannot be empathetic!" He turned back again and said to Zhang Feng sarcastically,

"I'm sorry, Comrade Zhang Feng, former student union chairman. Now is the hour of your test. Are you going with Chairman Mao's revolutionary route and making a clear distinction between you and your reactionary family, or fighting the Cultural Revolution? The Four Old things in your home are probably many in number. We have to check today."

Qing Lian looked at Dan Dan standing next to Zhang Feng. Then her eyes flashed with a strange look. She waved at the other Red Guards, saying,

"What are you looking at? Search, now!" Then the group swarmed into Zhang Feng's home.

They went into Zhang Wenbo's study, but they found nothing. When they reported to Cai and Qing Lian, Cai stared and took two books from the bookshelf, Tang Poetry and Song Poetry, and said,

"What are these? Aren't they either the extolling of the emperor, generals and ministers, or the moaning and groaning of gifted scholars and beautiful ladies? Are they not of the Four Old? Burn them!"

Zhang Wenbo looked anxious and said, "Students, they are the reference books I used to teach in class!"

Cai Wenge said scornfully, "Do you still want to use this feudal culture to poison young students? Chairman Mao said the fact that bourgeois intellectuals rule our school can no longer continue."

Dan Dan had been disdaining Cai's 'villain holding sway' posture, so she couldn't help but interject and said, "Chairman Mao often quotes Tang poetry and Song poetry!"

Cai did not know how to refute her at that moment, so said arrogantly, "There's no room for your speech here. You are also a typical 'white special.' Transform yourself first!" Then he threw these books to a Red Guard. Zhang Wenbo was so angry that he could not speak.

Cai went into Zhang Feng's room and looked around. When he saw the painting of 'A Moonlit Riverbank with Flower in Spring' on the wall, he suddenly seemed to think of something. He sneered at Zhang Feng who followed him,

"Is this painting about a beautiful woman in the First Senior Middle School? Did you win her heart by deception?" Zhang Feng saw Cai's look, and could not wait to beat him. But he suppressed his anger and said:

"This is an ordinary ink painting, nothing special."

Cai said coldly, "I am sorry. This is a typical example of feudal culture and cannot be kept." Then he was about to take it off the wall. Zhang Feng was about to block him when he suddenly heard Dan Dan's shouting.

"Oh no, uncle is ill!" Zhang Wenbo had coronary heart disease, and it was dangerous when he fell ill. Zhang Feng abandoned the painting. He quickly ran back to the other room and saw his father leaning on the chair, his face pale and struggling to breathe. Zhang Feng quickly picked up the blood vessel dilation emergency medicine on the table. After serving the medicine, he and Dan Dan helped Zhang Wenbo to lie down on the bed. Just as they watched his condition anxiously, Cai and Qing Lian took out a lot of 'trophies' and walked out of Zhang Feng's home. They piled up these 'trophies' together with the books and paintings found in other houses and prepared them for burning. Next to them, a group of people was watching. There was a female Red Guard from another school who seemed to pay special attention to what they'd found from Zhang Feng's home. After telling the crowd about Chairman Mao's quotations about Four Olds, Cai left the two Red Guards to ignite the books and led the team to continue their home search. Just as the fire started to burn, a shadow flashed by the fire and disappeared into the crowd.

Once his father's condition was stable, Zhang Feng remembered that he hadn't seen Master Hai Jing for a long time. He wondered if this wave of destroying the Four Olds could affect his Taoist temple. Confucianism had been criticised as a toxin of feudalism, and it was not known whether Taoism would also be implicated. He felt the urgent need to go see his master. After getting up the next morning, he entrusted his sister with their parents and walked all the way to North Mountain. The Taoist temple, overlooked by trees, looked peaceful. Zhang Feng hoped nothing had happened. He went directly to where he always practised martial arts with the master, behind the temple. Before he even reached the back door, he heard the sound of clapping hands and stomping feet. Zhang Feng knew that the master was practising martial arts. Going to the back door, he saw the master and several other young Taoists practising martial arts on the lawn outside the back door.

The master saw Zhang Feng and immediately came over and began asking him all sorts of questions. It seemed that he knew something about what was happening outside. Listening to Zhang Feng recounting the situation about the provincial and national Cultural Revolution over the past few weeks, he frowned. When he heard that many teachers in the university were being attacked, his face looked even more solemn. He said to Zhang Feng,

"This is just the beginning. Worse things are yet to come!"

Astonished, Zhang Feng asked, "Master, how do you know? You are a Taoist, how do you still understand politics?" The master pondered and wanted to say something. Suddenly a young Taoist acolyte ran over, a panicked look on his face.

"A large team of Red Guards is at the door, saying that they need to check for foreign agents."

"What foreign agents?" Zhang Feng and the master were puzzled. Zhang Feng suddenly remembered that there was an anti-agent story called 'Bell in an Ancient Temple' which contained an old monk who was a foreign agent. 'They are really catching the shadows,' Zhang Feng thought, 'as if there were enemies everywhere.'

Zhang Feng and the master went to the front of the temple and they saw a large group of Red Guards standing in front of the door. The leader was shouting at the Taoists. Zhang Feng took a closer look and saw it was Hei Tou. Zhang Feng thought, 'Smashing and robbing is what they do. The little hooligans are all cocky.' When Hei Tou saw Zhang Feng, he instinctively stepped back two steps and stuttered,

"You – you! What are you doing here? We are here to check the special agents, don't meddle in this!"

Zhang Feng said to him bluntly, "Which special agents? They are all monks, who are even afraid to step on ants, how can they commit murder and arson?"

Hei Tou stammered again and said,

"Yes, there are! Some people have reported it. I heard the sound on the radio station."

"The sound of the radio station?" All the Taoists looked at each other. Zhang Feng thought for a moment and said,

"What is this sound that you heard on the radio station like; is the sound something like 'Qiu Qiu'?"

Hei Tou said, "Yes, yes, you heard it too?" Zhang Feng smiled and said to everyone,

"Let's listen carefully. Listen!" Everyone listened. Gradually, they noticed a distant chirping sound coming from the trees.

"Isn't that a cicada chirp?" said a Red Guard.

"Yes," everyone nodded. Zhang Feng looked at Hei Tou and said ironically,

"Hey, the special agent is in the grass, go and grab him!" Hei Tou instantly realised he was being mocked. So he said anxiously,

"Search, search inside, there must be special agents inside!" Zhang Feng wanted to stop them, but Master Hai Jing said,

"Let them search. We have no special agents and are afraid of nothing."

Hei Tou and the Red Guards under him rushed into the

Taoist temple and began turning the whole place upside down. Zhang Feng was very angry. Suddenly among the Red Guards he saw a boy, a former neighbour of his, with whom he used to play and had a good relationship. Zhang Feng stopped the boy and whispered a few words to him. The boy immediately left and ran down the mountain. Hei Tou and his Red Guards searched the Taoist temple for more than an hour but did not find anything. They then asked the Taoists whether there was a cellar, because the special agents in the story 'Bell in an Ancient Temple' were hiding in the cellar. Master Hai Jing said:

"The cellar is used to store winter vegetables. It is empty now." Hei Tou was happy and immediately ordered the guards to search the cellar, but specifically to see whether there was a double wall which may have hidden a radio station.

The Red Guards searched for a long time in the cellar behind the Taoist temple, but they still found nothing. Several people said to Hei Tou,

"Commander, we've found nothing, shall we retreat?" Hei Tou was still unwilling to leave; he walked around and around the temple. Then he walked to the stone lion in front of the temple and asked the Red Guards around him,

"There are lions at the ancient office gates, right? This lion is a symbol of the feudal society's ruling class oppressing the people, and should not be kept!"

He then asked if anyone had a hammer. There was a Red Guard who said,

"I have a sledgehammer." Hei Tou took the sledgehammer and aimed it at the lion. Zhang Feng screamed,

"Stop!"

Hei Tou was scared. The hammer didn't hit the target. A small piece dropped off the lion's foot. He glanced at Zhang

Feng and raised his hammer again. Suddenly he heard a shout in the distance,

"Stop!"

The group looked back and turned out to see Wang Hai, Li He and a group of Red Guards from the Second Senior Middle School running towards them. Hei Tou was displeased.

"What are you doing here? You want to rob us of the credits for destroying Four Olds?"

Wang Hai looked down with disdain on the hooligans like Hei Tou. He said loudly,

"We have already asked the leaders of the Cultural Relics Bureau. They called the relevant department of the central government. They said that this Taoist temple was a place where North Korean leading comrades hid and secretly contacted each other during the Japanese War. Therefore it should be protected as a revolutionary cultural heritage. So you should immediately stop. Go and search somewhere else!"

Zhang Feng and master Hai Jing were happy. This was the work of the Red Guard that Zhang Feng had sent, who had found Wang Hai. Wang Hai had hurried to get instructions from the authority in central government, which helped to save the Taoist temple from being destroyed by the Red Guards. Hei Tou reluctantly withdrew his Red Guards and descended back down the mountain. Zhang Feng patted Wang Hai's shoulder and said:

"Good job, thank you!"

Master Hai Jing caressed the wrecked place on the lion's foot and said with distress,

"It's a disaster," he said to Wang Hai. "But fortunately you were here, otherwise, the loss would have been even bigger."

CHAPTER V

A Red Horror

With the advent of summer, a more terrible red horror began to shroud the River City. Not only did the Five Black Categories feel precarious; ordinary people became cautious, afraid to talk or comment about the current situation. If people had been reported to have done things against the Communist Party in the past, or if anyone had ever said that they had been dissatisfied with the Cultural Revolution, they would be immediately arrested, beaten and paraded on the street wearing tall hats. Some would be killed on the spot. A son would report his father, a wife would report her husband, and even best friends could not tell their true feelings to one another.

One day, Zhang Feng met Wang Hai on the street. Wang Hai was still hospitable towards Zhang Feng. He told Zhang Feng to pay attention to what he said and that Qing Lian had publicly announced that she had severed her relations with her parents in order to express herself as a true revolutionary because her parents were found to have a small historical problem. Zhang Feng listened and shook his head, saying,

"Wang Hai, you are the head of the Red Guards; you can be part of the revolution, but don't do things that hurt people or that will make you sorry and will be on your conscience forever."

Wang Hai said that he was very careful not to let his Red Guards beat people. Zhang Feng nodded.

Zhang Feng's own family atmosphere was very tense. His father had been quarantined for his rightist status in 1957 and for once being a prisoner in the Kuomintang prison before the liberation. He could only go home on weekends. Because his mother had studied in Japan and was suspected of being a Japanese special agent, she went to the rebel group every day to write confession materials. The home was cold and quiet only Zhang Feng's younger sister Zhang Lin was at home. When she first entered junior middle school, she encountered the revolution. Seeing her parents' situation and the horror surrounding her, she often sat silently in tears. Zhang Feng constantly tried to comfort her by saying that all of this would pass. His cousin in the Fengman Power Station had written a letter to him saying that because his uncle had studied in Japan, he was also quarantined and was suspected as a Japanese special agent.

The fortunes of Dan Dan's family were not good either. Originally, mother and daughter were living together. Dan Dan's mother Wang Hui had joined the Kuomintang Party in the past and had studied in Japan so she was censored. She was the deputy director of the university hospital. She had often criticised people who were not good at their work. Now they had the opportunity to take revenge. They punched and kicked her in the public condemnation conference, and shaved her head. Wang Hui was a stubborn person, and did not accept the crime imposed on her. One day, Dan Dan ran to Zhang Feng's house when no one was at home. When she saw Zhang Feng, she couldn't help but burst into tears. She suddenly rushed into Zhang Feng's arms.

"Xiao Feng, my Mom, she… I can't stand this anymore!" she sobbed. Zhang Feng was worried; Dan Dan's warm and full body made him feel the arousal of his youthful passions. But when he thought of Yu Mei, he calmed down, gently patted Dan Dan's back and said,

"Don't be afraid. I know that auntie has been suffering in the hospital. So many honest and kind people were persecuted. It's not normal, not at all. It won't always be like this. Hang on."

Resting her head on Zhang Feng's broad and powerful shoulders, Dan Dan felt comforted. She began to calm down. She used to help Zhang Feng in a sisterly way, but now she showed her weak side. She told Zhang Feng about her own fear that her mother's obstinate personality would lead her towards suicide. There were too many people who had committed suicide as they could not stand the torture. She told Zhang Feng that when she passed South Bank Park a few days ago, she was horrified to see that three people had hanged themselves in the woods. Zhang Feng sighed, but he immediately realised that he could not lose his strength as a man, so he continued to comfort Dan Dan for a while.

Suddenly Zhang Feng remembered that he needed to take neighbour Aunt Li to the train station so he sent Dan Dan away. Aunt Li was Zhang Feng's former neighbour. Her son was a young teacher of the Chinese Department and was being quarantined and censored for criticising the Cultural Revolution. Her daughter-in-law was teaching in the middle school of another county, and their registered residences were not transferred to the provincial capital, so they had been living in two places. Aunt Li had been widowed for many years. Her family used to be landlords. She was found by the rebels on the street a few weeks ago. She was punished by being paraded through the streets as a landlord wife with a group of Black Five categories. She would be sent back to her home town and asked to leave the provincial capital within three days. Today there were several trains that were specifically for taking these landlords and rich peasants to the remote rural areas.

Zhang Feng knocked on Aunt Li's door and saw that she had been waiting for him on the stool at the door, holding a cloth bag in her hand and with a shabby small box on the ground next to her. Zhang Feng felt very sad. Aunt Li was a very kind rural woman; she would come to help anyone who was in trouble. When Zhang Feng was a child and came back home with his sister, if their parents had not returned, Aunt Li would bring them to her home and cook for them. Such a kind woman! Simply because her family had owned modest acreage farmland before the liberation, she had become a criminal and was not accepted by society.

Aunt Li cried when she left her home with Zhang Feng, and took the tram to the train station.

There were a lot of people in the square in front of the train station. Zhang Feng wondered why, since today was not a holiday. There were also many flags of the Red Guards. Suddenly Zhang Feng heard the sounds of kicking, screaming and crying. He felt a little odd, so he told Aunt Li to wait for him under a tree and went to see what had happened. Squeezing into the crowd, Zhang Feng saw an appalling scene.

At the entrance of the station, a group of old people were queuing, but near the entrance, a group of Red Guards were punching and kicking the old men on both sides of the line, whipping them with a leather whip, and screaming loudly,

"I hit you, landlord thug!"

Some old people were knocked down to the ground, groaning, struggling to get up, some twitching, unable to get up. An old lady was vomiting blood and lying on the ground motionless. Her family squatted on the ground, trying to wake her up. The people hitting people most fiercely in this group of Red Guards were Hei Tou, Cai Wenge and Qing Lian. Zhang Feng also saw Chang Zheng who simply advised people to walk away quickly, and did not beat them. These poor old people were waiting in line for the train. Obviously, they could see that people in front were being beaten, but they still moved forward helplessly because they had no choice and no way to retreat.

Seeing all this, Zhang Feng felt chilled, and suddenly recalled in his mind a picture of Germans shooting Jews in the past: a group of unarmed Jews lined up before a big pit. Standing at the pithead were the German soldiers, shooting at the Jews who came up. The dead bodies fell into the pit. But the people behind were still walking forward, waiting quietly for their death. 'How could this be? These damn thugs!' Zhang Feng thought with anger. At the same time, he also began to worry, 'What should Aunt Li do?'

While Zhang Feng was at a loss, someone pulled his arm from behind him. He instinctively turned and entered a self-defence crouch, with both palms protecting his chest. However, he was surprised to see that the one standing in front of him was Yu Mei, whom he still missed day and night. She was as beautiful as ever, but her face looked haggard.

"What are you doing? I know that you are a master of martial arts. But we're still friends. Relax," Yu Mei said to him half-pettishly. Zhang Feng was shocked and happy, but he did not know what to say. Yu Mei asked with envy,

"Where's your Dan Dan? Why isn't she here with you?"

Zhang Feng quickly told her why he had come to the train station and explained his difficulties. Unexpectedly, Yu Mei said,

"I have a way. There is also an entrance for insiders at the train station. I know the Red Guards there. Let's go through there."

Zhang Feng and Yu Mei found Aunt Li. Zhang Feng told her that Yu Mei could help her to enter the station. Aunt Li thanked her very much.

"Beautiful girl, thank you!"

Yu Mei took them to the west side of the train station. In those short five minutes, Zhang Feng and Yu Mei had so many words that they wanted to say to each other, but in the end all they could muster were the same words.

"Are you alright?"

Zhang Feng asked Yu Mei about her current situation and eagerly asked her whether the provincial and municipal leaders knew that the actions of the Red Guards were so destructive and so terrible. Yu Mei said that her father and other leaders had now lost their power and could only stand by and watch. Everything was commanded by the rebel factions of the provincial and municipal committees, and several people sent by the Central Cultural Revolution Group. The instructions of the Cultural Revolution Group were to ruthlessly attack class enemies, so that those who killed the Black Five Categories and other enemies were not only innocent but also meritorious. But she could not stand this cruel behaviour, leading many Red Guards to say that her class position was wrong. Zhang Feng couldn't help asking,

"How about Chang Zheng, is he fierce?"

Yu Mei said, "I always remind him not to beat anyone."

Zhang Feng hesitated and asked, "Is he good to you?"

"Good, but only the type of good from a brother to a sister!" Yu Mei said angrily. Zhang Feng did not dare to ask more.

At a small entrance on the west side of the train station, there were a few Red Guards standing there. Yu Mei went up and whispered a few words to them. They opened the door and let Zhang Feng and Aunt Li go in. After seeing Aunt Li safely onto her train, Zhang Feng walked out of the station and saw Yu Mei still waiting for him under a tree. Zhang Feng wanted to say a few words to her, but suddenly he saw Chang Zheng running from a distance and shouting at Yu Mei. Zhang Feng quickly left.

Wang Hai had been annoyed by differences within the Red Guards of the Second Senior Middle School. The main reason was that Cai Wenge and Qing Lian had got new ideas from the Central Cultural Revolution Group from somewhere, and they wanted to lead the Cultural Revolution in a new direction. At the same time, they thought that Wang Hai was too conservative and was not cruel enough against the enemies. Therefore, they were planning to set up a rebel army organisation, and to separate from Wang Hai and the other Red Guards. If this happened, Wang Hai would have only two hundred people left.

In the morning, Wang Hai and Li He went to the Red Guard organisations of the other middle schools and universities to discuss the possibility of a coalition, because they had heard that many Red Guard rebel organisations in the provinces and cities had united and set up provincial and municipal headquarters.

While they walked to the Provincial Art Academy, they suddenly saw a large group of people on the road shouting slogans and pushing along a person who was tied up. The man was probably in his 40s. His head was shaved into a 'ghost head' and behind him was a big plate with the words "The active counter-revolutionary Sun Cheng." When Wang Hai saw this person's face, he realised it was very familiar to him. This was Zhang Feng's violin teacher. Wang Hai had seen him in the youth Palace. He also heard Zhang Feng say that someone else had once introduced a girlfriend to this teacher. Zhang Feng said that this teacher Sun was very serious about his teaching, but his temper was a bit strange, and often offended people. 'Maybe someone he had offended informed against him?' Wang Hai thought. Since the beginning of the Cultural Revolution, many people had used this opportunity to take personal revenge. Wang Hai asked a Red Guard in the team why this person was forced to be condemned. The man said that this man was a teacher, and he usually had a bad relationship with the young teachers in the same dormitory. Yesterday, he had been accused of saying bad things about the Cultural Revolution in his dormitory. What was more serious was that he had broken the plaster statue of Chairman Mao in the room. He himself said that he had accidentally knocked it to the ground, but the Red Guards said he was a capitalist; he must hate the revolution and the great leader. Wang Hai listened, thinking that this problem was serious, and Sun's fate would be very miserable. But his instinct was that Sun was not a bad person. What to do? It was impossible to stop these Red Guards, but it was best to let Zhang Feng know because he had always been very respectful and concerned about his teacher. Wang Hai told Li He to hurry to Zhang Feng's home and tell him that Mr. Sun was in trouble.

Half an hour later, Zhang Feng rushed to the art academy. When he got to the location Li He gave him, he couldn't see the crowd but only the corner of the road where a person was lying on the side of the pavement. Another person was kneeling on the ground, as if trying to wake him up. A woman standing nearby was crying. Zhang Feng walked over and saw that the kneeling person was the old man of the art academy who managed the faculty dormitory. In the past when Zhang Feng went to Teacher Sun to study the violin he had often met this old man, called Uncle Wang. The relationship between Uncle Wang and the teacher Sun was very good because Sun's father used to work for the Kuomintang government and was suppressed after the liberation. His mother was a White Russian, who had returned to the Soviet Union. Therefore, the teacher Sun was alone in China. Uncle Wang had no children, so he regarded Sun as his own child. They would drink and chat together from time to time. Uncle Wang also liked Zhang Feng very much. He always said that Zhang Feng was a handsome and talented young man. The woman standing nearby, crying, was the teacher Ye who tutored Zhang Feng in singing.

Seeing Uncle Wang and Teacher Ye, Zhang Feng felt that the situation was not good. Then he looked at the person lying on the ground, whose face was covered in blood, his head shaved; his was wearing the black jacket that the teacher Sun often wore. The body was still twitching slightly. Zhang Feng gently patted Uncle Wang and eagerly asked,

"Is it teacher Sun? How is he?" Uncle Wang looked up and saw Zhang Feng, and immediately his tears started to fall.

"How evil it is!" he said sadly. He and teacher Ye, choked with tears, began to relate how Mr. Sun had been beaten. When Sun was dragged out by the rebel faction to the parade, Uncle Wang had been following behind. Originally, the Red Guards of the Art Academy planned to arrest Sun and put him into the temporary detention centre. But they encountered a team of Red Guards from the 30th Middle School. When the leader of the group, who was dark and rude, heard that Sun had broken the statue of Chairman Mao, he began to beat Sun and shouted that the Red Guards of the Art Academy were too soft on the class enemy. Sun was beaten to the ground. Finally, the dark guy hit Sun's head with a big wooden stick until Teacher Sun stopped moving.

'Hei Tou, you are a bastard! One day, sooner or later, you will meet retribution.' Zhang Feng clenched his fists. He leaned down, supporting Sun's head. Searching through his pockets, he found the handkerchief that Dan Dan had given him. He hesitated briefly before using it to dry the blood on Sun's face.

"Teacher Sun! Teacher Sun!" he cried softly. A minute later, Teacher Sun opened his eyes slightly and looked at Zhang Feng. He said in a weak voice,

"It is you...You came..." A weak smile appeared on his face. This was the second smile that Zhang Feng had seen since he met Teacher Sun six years ago. The last time was when Zhang Feng played the violin in the provincial middle school student art performance and won a prize. Zhang Feng said through his tears,

"Teacher, I will take you to the hospital."

Teacher Sun shook his head gently. "It's useless... I... I'm going to see my father..." Then he drooped his head.

"Teacher! Teacher!" Zhang Feng shouted brokenheartedly. He said to Uncle Wang,

"Uncle, go find a trolley. Let us take Sun to the hospital."

After a minute, Teacher Sun opened his eyes again and said in a weak voice,

"Let me be buried on the riverside. My violin…I leave it to you." After that, he struggled to breathe out his last few breaths and did not move again.

Zhang Feng held the body of Teacher Sun and burst into tears. Teacher Ye wept beside him. Ten minutes later, Uncle Wang came rushing back pushing a trolley. He saw Zhang Feng and teacher Ye crying, and knew that Teacher Sun was dead. His legs became weak and he dropped down next to Zhang Feng. He shed tears and comforted Zhang Feng. The two men carefully examined Sun's breathing and pulse and confirmed that he was dead. They discussed how to deal with his funeral. At that time, people in the city had been practising cremation, and there were also grave burials in the countryside. Uncle Wang said,

"Go to the crematorium first."

Then they put Sun's body on the trolley and bid farewell to Teacher Ye. Uncle Wang returned to teacher Sun's dormitory and found a piece of clothing that he only wore during the New Year. It was left to him by his father. There was also a hat to cover his shaved head. They dressed him, wiped his face and hands with a towel, and pushed the trolley to the crematorium in the suburbs. Pedestrians on the road saw them and crossed over to the other side. The crematorium was far away, so they took turns to push the trolley. Zhang Feng was pushing and looking at Teacher Sun's face from time to time. He sadly remembered his strict training and the practice regimens that had given him such skill with the violin; but all this had changed now. It no longer mattered. Both Western music and Chinese classical music were criticised as cultural waste which no one dared to play. Professional musicians like Teacher Sun were also persecuted if they were found to have opposed the Cultural Revolution.

After an hour and a half, they came to the crematorium. The unpleasant smell was unbearable. They found the assistant at the gate and explained their intentions. They did not expect to be told that for cremation one must have a death certificate and a company reference letter because the Black Five categories and counter-revolutionaries that had recently been killed or who had committed suicide were particularly numerous. None of them mattered to the crematorium employees. The assistant pointed to the dozen or so bodies piled up in the yard and said,

"Look, these were the suicides and people who had been killed collected by the city's cleaners from the streets and parks. They all wore the Black Five category bands or were shaved like ghosts. We did not dare to deal with them. The leader said that we would use a big truck to transport them to a large pit in the wild and bury them there."

Zhang Feng could smell the stench from the pile of bodies and could see maggots crawling on them. He felt sick and about to vomit, so he quickly left with Uncle Wang.

When the sun set, the sparkling Songhua River was dyed with a bleak blood red. In a small wood at the corner of the river, Zhang Feng and Uncle Wang buried teacher Sun under a big willow tree. Zhang Feng piled up a small grave with a shovel and drove a piece of wood into the ground. He and Uncle Wang felt that they should not write the name of Teacher Sun because they were afraid that the rebel faction would dig up the grave. Zhang Feng used a knife to engrave a violin pattern instead. After that, he and Uncle Wang knelt in front of the grave and kowtowed three times. Weeping, they recited the words of farewell to the dead.

Teacher Sun's relics were very simple. Apart from a violin, there were only some simple mementos. Zhang Feng wanted to bury this precious violin with Teacher Sun. But Uncle Wang disagreed and told Zhang Feng to keep it. Even if he didn't dare to use it, it would be a souvenir. Uncle Wang kept Teacher Sun's other relics, for if Sun's mother returned from the Soviet Union, these things would be reminders for her.

That night, after Uncle Wang left, Zhang Feng sat by the grave of Teacher Sun until sunset. He hugged the violin and looked at the river, remembering his teacher. He knew that Teacher Sun's favourite music was related to rivers, like the Blue Danube waltz. He muttered to the grave, "Teacher, I know that you suffered a wrong. You were innocent! You have been a person of integrity your whole life, dedicated to art. I will right the wrongs for you. Now you can listen to the sound of the river day and night. Rest in peace!"

CHAPTER IV

A Farce in the Provincial Party Committee Compound

Yu Mei's attitude during these months had turned from initial excitement to confusion. If the Cultural Revolution was really about getting rid of bad things in society and creating things that were good for the people and the country, then it should be a good thing. Chairman Mao was wise. He was far-sighted. He had said that some leaders who followed the capitalism road had already seized power in the party and the country. The Red Guards rose up and rebelled to defend Chairman Mao and to regain the regime of the proletariat. But why were these things happening in front of her; bad people doing bad things and good people being persecuted? People had lost basic trust, and there were whistle-blowers everywhere. Family and friends didn't even dare to tell the truth among themselves. Zhang Feng, such a good young man, suddenly became a problematic youngster that everyone was afraid to approach, and Hei Tou, a former hooligan, had become a hero.

She took out the painting of Zhang Feng that she had saved from the fire and looked at it for a long time. Thinking of the happy moments she had shared with him, bittersweet tears flowed down her cheek.

"Xiao Mei, Xiao Mei!" There came the voice of Chang Zheng. Every time he came to Yu Mei's home, he never knocked on the door. Contrary to Yu Mei, he was very active and even excited about the Cultural Revolution. He acted as if he were a hero who had found a place to use his power. He took the Red Guards all over the place, trying to catch the Five Black Categories and the capitalist roaders. He also showed Yu Mei that he was now the commander of the Red Guards, like his father, a military region commander. However, Yu Mei was not interested in these things. Before entering the living room, he deliberately puffed up his chest, re-arranged his grass-green military uniform, tightened the wide belt, and tried to look like a mighty general.

"Today, the rebel faction at the Provincial Party Committee compound will condemn Wang Weimin. When he presided over the Propaganda Department, he carried out a lot of revisionism. The Red Guards of the Culture and Education Department will all go there, so it will be overwhelming," he said after entering the living room. Yu Mei turned around and quickly wiped her tears. She said with confusion,

"What? They want to condemn Uncle Wang? What problems does he have? He worked so hard even when his child was sick. How can he be a capitalist roader?"

Chang Zheng said sternly, "Xiao Mei, don't take up the wrong class position. I know that Wang Weimin has a good relationship with your family. He is your father's old subordinate, but Chairman Mao said that the revolution was not about fun and games. Class enemies are sometimes hidden in our revolutionary ranks. We can know whether one is a capitalist roader by exposing him."

Yu Mei did not want to go because she knew the horror that would await her. However, she suddenly remembered that her father had been nervous when he left that morning. He had whispered a few words to her mother. It seemed he mentioned the name of Uncle Wang. She was concerned that her father would be implicated, so she agreed to go with Chang Zheng.

The Provincial Party Committee Compound was in the city centre, and it took twenty minutes to get there by bus. Before they had even reached the compound, they could hear the sound of the big loudspeaker and loud slogans. They could also see that the Red Guards teams were entering the compound one after another. Yu Mei walked in with the Red Guards from the First Senior Middle School, and saw that the compound was full of Red Guards and rebel groups. In front of the Provincial Party Committee building, a platform was set up with a large banner slogan that read, "Completely Liquidate the Bourgeoisie Route that Wang Weimin Implemented in the Cultural and Educational Propaganda Department." A rebel leader with a microphone was pointing to Wang Weimin, who was standing on the stage, and was criticising him for his crimes in the Propaganda Department of the Provincial Party Committee that had taken place over more than a decade. Yu Mei's father and other provincial and municipal leaders were also sitting on the stage. Then, several staff members in Wang Weimin's office also stepped onto the stage to expose his words and deeds against Chairman Mao's revolutionary route. What surprised

Yu Mei was that these people had previously been the most loyal and friendly to Wang Weimin. Yu Mei sometimes saw them when she went to Wang Weimin's home. The exposure of Wang Weimin's issues also involved his personal life, saying that he pursued personal privileges, rode a high-class car, and used special-supply daily necessities and foods, watched foreign movies, danced with young actresses, and so on. These of course caused dissatisfaction among the people present because the living conditions of ordinary citizens were very poor; they lived in overcrowded conditions, without enough food, and they could eat meat only once a month. They also needed special shopping coupons to buy cloth, cotton and daily necessities.

When Yu Mei heard these accusations of Wang Weimin, she felt very scared because her father and other provincial and municipal leaders also had special privileges. She looked at her father sitting on the stage and felt an inexplicable fear in her heart. A young female secretary also revealed that Wang Weimin often had sexually harassed her. This led people to start chanting "Overthrow the Rogue Wang Weimin." Yu Mei had heard that some leading cadres had had problems to do with lifestyle before. But Uncle Wang looked like a serious and decent person on the surface. However, Yu Mei remembered seeing this female secretary at Uncle Wang's home. Her relationship with Uncle Wang indeed seemed to be a bit too intimate.

Yu Mei wanted to talk about this with Chang Zheng, but she looked sideways and Chang Zheng was no longer there. Suddenly she heard a loud noise on the stage. It was Chang Zheng jumping up and seizing the microphone. He pointed to Wang Weimin's face and said,

"Wang Weimin, you often boast about how great Lu Dingyi is [the Minister of Central Propaganda Department, who had been overthrown] and about how some articles in Chairman Mao's Excerption were modified by him. What do you mean? You are too reactionary!"

He gave Wang a slap in the face. Wang Weimin had also had a good relationship with Chang Zheng. He did not expect Chang Zheng to treat him like this, so he stood in confusion. At this time, the rebel factions at the stage began to shout:

"Overthrow Wang Weimin! If he does not surrender, let him perish!" Two Red Guards forced him to wear a big hat made of paper and hung a big sign board on him, on which was written "Capitalist Roader Wang Weimin," with a red cross. Then they push his head down and forced him to bow 90 degrees and plead guilty to the revolutionary masses.

At this time, the head of the rebel group who presided over the conference told everyone to calm down, saying that Du Zhongqing, a special commissioner from the Central Cultural Revolution Group, wanted to give a speech. The Red Guards were very excited when they heard that he was from the Central Cultural Revolution Group, because this group had been receiving their instructions directly from Chairman Mao since the beginning of the Cultural Revolution. They saw a man with medium build, wearing a black coat and a black hat, coming out of the background. His hat was so low that they could barely see his face. The man waved at the crowd who applauded and then spoke in a low voice. On behalf of the Central Cultural Revolution Group, he first paid tribute to the Red Guards and rebels in Jili Province, praising them for acting in response to Chairman Mao's call to fight against the party's capitalist roaders and various ghosts and monsters and defending Chairman Mao's proletarian headquarters. Then he said that the leadership of the culture and education front had been dominated by the capitalist roaders for many years. He pointed to Wang Weimin and said that the capitalist roaders like Wang Weimin who actively advocated the bourgeois route must be resolutely defeated. At this time, the crowd again broke out with chants about defeating Wang Weimin.

The man in the black coat suddenly turned to Yu Mei's father and said,

"Secretary Li, Wang Weimin's propaganda department is under your leadership. Can you be without any responsibility for this?" Yu Mei was shocked and quickly stepped back, afraid that others would notice her. When she saw no one looking at her, she worriedly looked at the stage to see if her father would be implicated. Yu Mei's father was a man who had experienced war and political movements. He seemed calm. He slowly stood up and said to the man,

"Comrade Commissioner, Wang Weimin has made many mistakes indeed, but he has been blinded by Lu Dingyi from the Central Propaganda Department. It is not that he himself wants to oppose Chairman Mao's revolutionary route."

The words of Yu Mei's father sent the place into uproar, because what he was saying was obviously an attempt to excuse Wang Weimin. The man sneered and said,

"According to Secretary Li, Wang Weimin just executed the bourgeoisie route and he is not a capitalist roader?"

Yu Mei's father immediately said, "I have made no final conclusion; let the revolutionary people test him."

The man was silent for half a minute. Finally, he raised his voice and said to the masses,

"Well, Red Guards, revolutionary masses of the rebel factions, let us expose Wang Weimin's crime of taking the capitalist road in the Cultural and Educational Propaganda

Department in this province! At the same time, we have to dig up his sinister backstage supporter." When he had finished, he looked at Yu Mei's father coldly. Yu Mei's father pretended not to see his gaze and sat back in his seat. Yu Mei suddenly remembered that her father had said a few days ago that the Central Cultural Revolution Group had sent a special commissioner named Du Zhongqing to encourage the Red Guards and the rebels to further promote the movement. The main goal was to destroy the local party and government organisations. Her father also said that this person was well-known in the party specialised in persecuting people. During the rectification of incorrect styles of work in Yan'an, her father had come close to being labelled as a counter-revolutionary by him. His coming this time could be a disaster more than a blessing.

Yu Mei began to feel overwhelmed by the continued criticism and noisy chanting, so she quietly left the Provincial Party Committee Compound. As she passed through the door, she felt that someone was following her. Looking back, she saw a Red Guard who was not tall, and seemed older than his real age, calling her 'Little Fairy' in a sarcastic voice. He squinted his eyes and smiled at Yu Mei. This smile made Yu Mei feel very uncomfortable. Yu Mei remembered this person was Zhang Feng's classmate, called Cai… He had no ability compared with Zhang Feng. At the sports meeting, he had deliberately hindered her conversation with Zhang Feng. Now he was the head of the Red Guards in the Second Senior Middle School. According to Zhang Feng, this man was ruthless and arrogant, and took part in everything bad including beating, smashing and looting.

"My name is Cai Wenge." While introducing himself, he stretched out his sweaty hand to shake hands with Yu Mei. Yu Mei felt disgusted, but still politely asked,

"Do you have anything to ask me?"

Cai said with a smile, "I meet you again, little fairy. I know that you and Zhang Feng were lovers before, but now you have broken up? He is an offspring of the Black Five Categories, a typical white special. He cannot be your Prince Charming, right? Now I am the commander of the Second Senior Middle School Red Guards and my future is boundless." He looked around and saw no one. He leered at her and said:

"Be my girlfriend. I can protect your father from attack. He is the backstage supporter of Wang Weimin, and he will soon be in trouble."

Yu Mei was flushed by his rogue words, but she didn't know what to say.

"You, you… no," She wanted to say 'Shame on you' but couldn't. Cai saw that Yu Mei was blushing and so laughed more wretchedly. He said,

"Oh, sorry." He reached out and tried to touch Yu Mei's face. Yu Mei instinctively raised her hand to stop him. At this moment, she heard Chang Zheng at the gate shouting at her. As if finding her saviour, Yu Mei immediately called out,

"Chang Zheng, I am here!" Cai saw Chang Zheng coming and ran away. Yu Mei waited until Chang Zheng came near, could not help but lean on his shoulders, and cried, half worried about her father, and half angry about the sexual harassment by Cai. By virtue of the broad shoulders of Chang Zheng, Yu Mei felt a sense of comfort and security. When a woman felt weak, she needed the protection of a man. But suddenly she thought of Zhang Feng, so she wiped her tears and tried to calm down.

"Is that guy bullying you? The bastard! Next time I'll slap him!" Chang Zheng said loudly. "I heard that he had been nothing in the Second Senior Middle School. Now that he is a commander he has become very arrogant." Chang Zheng was indignant. Looking at his tall and strong figure, Yu Mei did feel safe, but he did not make her heart race as Zhang Feng did; for Chang Zheng she only had the feelings of a sister for a brother. Yu Mei knew that her parents and the parents of Chang Zheng all hoped that they would become a couple, but because Zhang Feng was still in her heart, Yu Mei found it even more difficult to accept Chang Zheng, even if it were impossible for her and Zhang Feng to be lovers.

CHAPTER VII

I Want to Accompany My Mother

Dan Dan became more and more concerned, as her mother Wang Hui had become moody after being criticized and denounced in public. Wang Hui lay in bed, silent, for a long time. Dan Dan asked her to eat. However, she did not move, saying that she was not hungry. One morning, Wang Hui was taken away by the hospital's rebel faction to the public condemnation conference again. When Dan Dan was cleaning her mother's room, she felt dizzy all of a sudden. She went to look for some pills in a drawer of her mother's desk. Pulling the drawer open, looking for the pills she had taken when she was dizzy before, she saw a paper bag with a large medicine bottle inside. She took out the bottle and saw it was filled with sleeping pills. Recently, Wang Hui had become nervous and always sleepless, so she often took sleeping pills. Dan Dan was about to put the medicine bottle back in the paper bag when suddenly she felt that something was wrong. Why did Mother prepare such a large bottle of sleeping pills? Was she… Thinking of this, Dan Dan suddenly had a strong ominous feeling. Recently she had heard that many people couldn't endure the criticism, denunciation and personal insults, so they committed suicide in different ways; some of them committed suicide by taking an overdose of sleeping pills. Dan Dan hesitated for a while, took out seven or eight pills and left them in the drawer, and then hid the whole bottle under her own quilt.

At two o'clock in the afternoon, Dan Dan heard someone knocking on the door. When she opened it, she saw that her mother was lying on the ground and had already passed out. She quickly took her mother into the house, laid her gently on the bed, then lifted her up again and gave her a little sugar water. When mother opened her eyes slowly and saw Dan Dan holding her, her eyes brimmed with tears. Dan Dan knew that her mother was a strong woman and rarely shed tears. It must be that these rebel factions had tortured and insulted her again. Poor Mother! Dan Dan couldn't help but have a good cry with her mother. After a few minutes, mother tried to sit up, wiping away her tears. She also wiped the tears off her daughter's face, beckoning for her to sit next to her, before slowly saying,

"Dan Dan, there are some things you should know. I may not get another chance in the future. It is about your father."

Dan Dan asked, "I thought that Dad died when he fell ill on running an errand 10 years ago?" Wang Hui replied,

"No, he died due to political persecution." Then, Mother told a story that shocked Dan Dan.

Wang Hui said that Dad was originally a young teaching assistant at the Normal University. He was handsome and talented, and had graduated from Peking University. However, in

1957, he was labelled a rightist and exiled to the Great Northern Wilderness for labour reform, where life was extremely hard. Along with others, he was beaten and cursed as if a criminal, and constantly starved. He couldn't stand it anymore and fled with two other fellow sufferers. A few weeks later, the police came to our house to search for him. They warned me that if he came back, I must report it to them. A few months later, it was reported that several corpses that had been eaten by wolves were found in the woods over fifty kilometres from the labour camp. Maybe these were the corpses of Dad and his two friends. Wang Hui sighed deeply and said,

"Your father was really wronged as he only gave some genuine suggestions to a leader. No one could imagine that he would finally die an ignominious death." When she finished, her face was streaming with tears. After Dan Dan heard this, her heart was bleeding. She could vaguely remember how her father teased and played with her when she was a child. Mother dried her tears and said,

"I have been dreaming of your father recently. Yesterday I saw a person's shadow near the rockery next to our family home. It was very similar to your father. I thought I saw a ghost. I think that maybe your father's soul is summoning me to reunite with him. Legends say that the souls of those who had not been buried will eternally roam the earth."

When Dan Dan heard this, she shivered. She did not believe that people became ghosts after they died. However, mother said that she was going to meet her father, which made her feel like her heart was being wrenched. She embraced her mother all of a sudden and said,

"No, I don't believe it. We must carry on; find Dad's body and bury him so that his soul can rest in peace."

After mother calmed down a little, she said to Dan Dan that if something really happened to her (the rebel faction was killing people now as easily as killing flies), what made her most uneasy was that there were no relatives nearby to take care of Dan Dan. But she thought of a person who Dan Dan could rely on. Dan Dan asked,

"Who is it?" Mother took Dan Dan's hand and said, "It is your' elder brother Zhang Feng."

Dan Dan suddenly blushed and asked, "Why is he my elder brother? Is he not younger than me? He has always treated me as his elder sister."

With these words, her mother began to reveal the second secret that she had withheld from Dan Dan for so many years; a small secret. She said that in fact, Dan Dan was six months younger than Zhang Feng. When Dad was taken away, it was very difficult for Wang Hui to take care of Dan Dan all by herself. Dan Dan was smarter than other children of her age, and so she reported Dan Dan's birthday one year short so that she could be enrolled in school one year earlier. After she had finished, she looked at Dan Dan and asked,

"Do you like Zhang Feng?"

Dan Dan's face turned red with embarrassment,

"Mom, what are you talking about? A man knows that he can't have a woman older than him. He certainly hasn't thought about it as he always regards me as his elder sister. However, he is really an… outstanding young man."

"How can a daughter conceal anything from her mother? I have known for a long time that you like him."

"He has already had a girlfriend." Dan Dan was stammering shyly. Her mother asked:

"Who is it?"

Dan Dan told her about Zhang Feng and Yu Mei. After hearing the story, she shook her head.

"It is impossible for them to become a couple. The class difference is too great. A high-ranking official of the Communist Party of China won't marry his daughter to the son of a rightist." Dan Dan said that Zhang Feng told her not long ago that his relationship with Yu Mei had come to a close. However, it seemed that he still missed her. Mother said that it was understandable, but not realistic. She also said that she believed that if Zhang Feng knew her true age, he would definitely like her. Her women's intuition told her that long-term marriage relationships are based on having the same family background, same experience, common hobbies and a congeniality of character. Zhang Feng was handsome and cool, whereas Dan Dan was smart and beautiful. Weren't they a perfect match? Dan Dan didn't know what to say, but she could feel her heart pounding.

That night, Dan Dan was sleepless, partially worrying about her mother, and partially as she thought about her true age. In the past, it was only a young girl's dream to fall in love with Zhang Feng. But now it might become a reality.

Over the past few days, Zhang Feng had not seen Dan Dan. He felt a little worried. He had visited her place a few times but nobody ever answered his knocking. When he went again yesterday, he saw a man in black at the street corner facing Dan Dan's house. Zhang Feng was quite familiar with this man's figure, but when he approached, that man left very quickly. Zhang Feng thought this was very strange.

Zhang Feng did not know why he was so uneasy that night. He tossed about in bed and even had a nightmare. At five o'clock the next morning, there suddenly came knocking at the door. Zhang Feng hurriedly got up and opened the door, but he could see no one outside. There was a slip of paper on the floor inside the door. Zhang Feng picked it up and opened it. It was a sheet of yellowed paper with a single line, saying 'Go to Dan Dan's house to see if anything is wrong.' Strange, who would write this? Why wasn't this person going to rescue Dan Dan and her mother directly? But he had no time think about it in that moment, and he had a foreboding feeling that something might happen to Dan Dan's family. He shouted to his younger sister,

"Something has happened to Dan Dan's family; I'm going to have a look!" Then he ran all the way to Dan Dan's house.

Dan Dan's family also lived in a small two-story building built by the Japanese. It was now a dormitory for several faculty members. Dan Dan's family was on the second floor. After Zhang Feng ran up, he knocked on the door with great force, but there was no reply at all inside. 'This isn't right,' Zhang Feng thought to himself. Dan Dan and her mother couldn't have been out at such an early hour. He began to get upset. Kick the door open? He was afraid that might wake up the neighbours. He suddenly remembered that Wang Hai once told him a method used by thieves to break in with a knife. He had a knife on his key chain so he decided to have a go. He tried to insert the knife into the gap of the door lock and pushed the spring bolt to one side. He failed a few times, cursing to himself quietly. After one last attempt he inserted the knife again into the lock, and pushed hard; the door really opened. He ran into the room shouting,

"Auntie! Dan Dan!" Pushing open the door of Dan Dan's room, he found no one inside. He pushed open her mother's door, and was surprised by what he saw. Dan Dan and her mother were lying on the bed, neatly dressed, and Dan Dan was embracing her mother.

"Dan Dan! Dan Dan! Auntie!" Zhang Feng shook them

hard with his hand. But they didn't respond. Zhang Feng began to get anxious. He put his hand on their mouths, and could feel a slight breath; placing a finger on the neck, he could feel a very weak pulse. Still alive! He thought to himself, 'Is artificial respiration needed?' But he didn't know how to perform it, and he was so anxious that he was sweating profusely.

Suddenly he saw two empty medicine bottles on the small table at the head of the bed. He picked them up and saw that they were sleeping pills. They must have taken sleeping pills to commit suicide. Zhang Feng remembered that a relative of his neighbour once took sleeping pills to commit suicide due to a marital problem, and he was sent to hospital to have his stomach pumped before his life was saved. Take them to hospital! Zhang Feng thought to himself how could he take them to hospital? Where to find a car? The university garage was not far from here. Maybe he could try to find a car there. He ran out immediately.

Just as he got out of the door, he saw a Jiefang truck driving over. Without thinking, Zhang Feng jumped into the middle of the road and waved the truck to stop. The driver opened the door and jumped out. Zhang Feng thought that he would be scolded by the driver. Unexpectedly, the driver hurriedly asked him whether Dr. Wang's family lived here. Zhang Feng recognised him as the driver from the university garage. The driver said that he had just received a phone call, saying that something might happen to Dr. Wang, and a truck was needed, so he had hurried over immediately. Dr. Wang was very kind to the school's teaching and supporting staff; everyone knew she was criticised and denounced, and were particularly sympathetic with her. He came just in time. Zhang Feng wondered who had made the telephone call, but it was important to save lives. Zhang Feng asked the driver to open the carriage board. He ran back to the house and took Dan Dan and her mother up to the truck one by one. When holding Dan Dan, Zhang Feng wondered how Dan Dan's soft body could be so heavy in his arms. Looking at her beautiful and pale cheeks, he felt as if his heart were wrenched by a knife. 'Dan Dan, Dan Dan, how could you do such a stupid thing?'

As soon as the truck arrived at the Emergency Department of the Provincial Hospital, Zhang Feng jumped out and ran into the building. It was still outside office hours, so there was only one doctor on duty. Zhang Feng hurriedly told him about what had happened to Dan Dan and her mother. He also showed him the empty bottle and asked him to save them quickly. To his indignation, this doctor only said,

"There are many people who have committed suicide now. They are all Capitalist Roaders and Five Black Categories. The beds here are limited. We must give priority to worker, peasant and soldier patients."

"Then her daughter is innocent! You can't let her die!" Zhang Feng said desperately.

The doctor did not give in, "One class enemy dies, and there will one less class enemy. You should go and find another place."

Zhang Feng wanted to give him a slap. But it was useless arguing with him. He ran outside to discuss the problem with the driver.

Just as he ran outside the emergency room, he saw a middle-aged woman coming in from the hospital gate. Upon closer inspection, Zhang Feng saw that it was Dr Zhang, the classmate of Dan Dan's mother when they had studied medicine in Japan, and also the director of the Medical Department of the Provincial Hospital. Zhang Feng ran up quickly and told her what had happened. He didn't expect Dr Zhang to agree with him so readily.

"My old classmate! Come on, follow me; let's get the stretcher to carry them in."

Zhang Feng thanked her and asked, "Will it not cause trouble for you?" Dr Zhang replied,

"I have nothing to fear. My father is a veteran cadre of the Long March. I'll see who can take advantage of me."

Two nurses helped Zhang Feng to carry Dan Dan and her mother to the medical ward for treatment. After thanking the driver, Zhang Feng sat down on the chair in the corridor and waited. He had butterflies in his stomach. He was anxious and uneasy because Dr Zhang said that if they had taken the pills long before, then they would be in a critical condition as their cerebral nerve centre might have been damaged by the pills. He felt sleepy as he had got up so early, coupled with anxiety and worry. He fell asleep once he leaned against the back of the chair.

He didn't know how long he had slept when suddenly he felt someone gently shaking his shoulder. He opened his eyes and saw it was Dr Zhang.

"How are they?" Zhang Feng asked anxiously. Dr Zhang took off her mask and heaved a sigh of relief, saying,

"Zhang Feng, you are their saviour. If they had come two hours later, they might have died." Dr Zhang said that Dan Dan had been the first to regain consciousness after their stomachs were pumped. It might be that she had taken fewer pills and had taken them later than her mother. Her mother was still not awake, but her life signs were back to normal. Hearing this, Zhang Feng also breathed a sigh of relief, asking,

"Can I go in to see Dan Dan?"

Dr Zhang said, "Wait another half an hour."

Half an hour later, a young nurse led Zhang Feng gently into the ward. Dan Dan was lying on the hospital bed, with her eyes closed. Her face was pale, without the usual peony-like blush. Zhang Feng sat down on the stool next to the bed and said softly,

"Dan Dan, are you awake?" She slowly opened her eyes. When she saw Zhang Feng, her eyes filled with crystal tears. She said in a faint voice,

"Xiao Feng, is it you? How can I be lying here? Wasn't I looking for my father with my mother?" At these words, Zhang Feng held back his tears. He took Dan Dan's hand, which was so soft and cold.

"Dan Dan, how could you act so stupidly? Your mother may be desperate, but your life has not even begun yet. Darkness is only temporary, and light and hope will still be there."

"I thought I could only see you in the afterlife." Dan Dan said. Seeing that no one was around, she suddenly leaned against Zhang Feng's bosom, her tears streaming down. Zhang Feng held her tightly in his arms, for fear that anything else might happen to her again. Looking at Dan Dan's beautiful pale face, Zhang Feng suddenly felt a feeling that transcended that of the brother and sister tie. Yes, Dan Dan was beautiful, intelligent, gentle, and considerate, and had all the external and internal beauty that a woman should have. How preposterous was the idea that a man cannot marry a woman who is one year older than him. To hell with these old ideas. But what about Yu Mei? Why was it that Yu Mei's figure always appeared when Zhang Feng was attracted by Dan Dan's beauty? Cruel reality had completely cut them off, separating them by a river of love. She could only be his dream lover. Dan Dan might as well be his realistic choice, and he could also feel that Dan Dan's feelings for him did not seem to be only that of brother and sister.

"What are you thinking about?" Dan Dan asked the bemused Zhang Feng. He came back from his trance. He let go of Dan Dan and helped her to sit up. He started to ask her about how it had all happened. Dan Dan said that the rebel faction of the hospital criticized and rebuked her mother again last night. After her mother came back from hospital, she was in a stupor and did not eat anything at night. In the middle of the night, Dan Dan suddenly woke up with an ominous feeling, her heart beating fast. She immediately got up and walked into her mother's room. To her surprise, her mother was lying in bed with her clothes dressed neatly and looking calm. Dan Dan ran to her, shouting and shaking her shoulder, but there was no response at all. Dan Dan saw that there was an empty medicine bottle on her mother's bedside table. She took it, and saw it was a sleeping pill bottle! Strange. She remembered that she had hidden the bottle several days ago. There was a piece of paper on the floor. Dan Dan picked it up and looked at it. It was her mother's suicide note. It said that she was sorry for Dan Dan that she had to commit suicide as she wanted to safeguard her dignity and prove her innocence with death. She was going away to find the lonely soul of Dan Dan's father. Maybe she would find it, or maybe not. After she died, she wanted Dan Dan to get help from a particular person. At this point, Dan Dan paused. Zhang Feng eagerly asked,

"Who are you going to ask for help?" Dan Dan's face was flushed and she said,

"Nothing, no-one, she asked me to find a relative." Strange, Zhang Feng thought to himself. He thought that Dan Dan's family had no relatives. But it was not important. What was more important was why Dan Dan, who was always reasonable, had chosen to die with her mother. Dan Dan went on to say that she had felt that everything in her world had collapsed all of a sudden. Her father had long been gone, for so many years, she and her mother huddled together for survival. Mother was everything to her. If her mother was no longer there, the spiritual pillar of her life would collapse. She had cried for a while, holding her mother. She suddenly remembered the sleeping pills that she had hidden a few days ago. Her mother would not find her father in the underworld. People said that the souls of those who died without being buried would roam in the wilderness, with no destination. How awful for her mother. 'No, I would have to accompany my Mom.' Dan Dan could not think straight in the midst of so much grief. She found the sleeping pills, and fetched a glass of water. She gulped down all the pills in a few mouthfuls, and then hugged her mother. Gradually, she lost consciousness.

After listening to Dan Dan's story, Zhang Feng suppressed his tears. He took Dan Dan's hand fondly and said,

"Dan Dan, promise me that you won't do stupid things like that any more. Even if there is a big disaster, please don't do anything like this again. You have cared about me and helped me like a sister for so many years. You are a strong girl. I sometimes feel that you are my spiritual crutch. Don't bow your head before setbacks. I will always support you, help you, and care for you…"

One day later, Dan Dan was completely recovered. Her mother still needed one more day in hospital. Zhang Feng accompanied Dan Dan back home and saw that her house was very messy. Zhang Feng helped Dan Dan sit down in her mother's room and began to clean up. Suddenly he saw a piece of paper on the ground. He picked it up and read it in a low voice without thinking, "Dan Dan, Mom is sorry for you, I am going away. You have to take care of yourself." Oh, it was the will of Dan Dan's mother. He was about to hand it over to Dan Dan when he saw his own name in the next line. He read it curiously, 'Don't forget to tell Xiao Feng the secret…' When he wanted to go on reading, Dan Dan had already rushed over, grabbing the paper from his hand, which shocked him.

"Give it to me! It is my mother's will. I will keep it." Dan Dan said to Zhang Feng, her face flushed.

"Sorry, I should not have looked at it." Zhang Feng couldn't understand why Dan Dan was angry. They were always like a family, and there were no secrets to hide from one other.

"No, it is not that I won't let you see it. It is that it makes me sad every time I see it." Zhang Feng had intended to ask what the secret that Dan Dan's mother wanted Dan Dan to tell him was. It seemed that Dan Dan was very upset, so he didn't dare to ask.

Since then, there was always a question mark in Zhang Feng's mind. What was the secret that Dan Dan was keeping? Was it related to Dan Dan's family, like her father? However, if she and her mother wanted to tell him, they would definitely tell him. If they didn't want to say it, it meant that the situation had changed and they did not want him to know.

A few days later, Dan Dan's mother came home, both her body and spirit recovered a little. Dan Dan kept her company at home every day, for fear that she would do something silly again.

Zhang Feng also came over to keep her company and talked with her. After the hospital's rebel faction knew the news of her attempted suicide, they were no longer hard on her, only asking her to write some self-criticism material at home. Dan Dan, her mother and Zhang Feng guessed that it might be that there was a leader in the rebel faction, who had been a logistical worker in the past, and who had been cared for by Dan Dan's mother when he was ill, so he had persuaded other leaders to deal with Dan Dan's mother leniently.

PART III

The Red Flood

CHAPTER I

Train Encounter

Qing Lian was especially excited these days because news from Beijing said that Chairman Mao was to meet more Red Guards after receiving them on August 18, especially the Red Guards from outside Beijing. This included the revolutionary masses in the rebel faction, that is to say, students who were not Red Guards could also be received by Chairman Mao. Qing Lian and Cai Wenge were busy with counting the number of people going to Beijing, contacting the railway station and other Red Guards' organizations.

Qing Lian had not returned home for more than a month and just lived in the dormitory of the school because she had reported and exposed her father's dissatisfaction with the Cultural Revolution. Her father had been segregated and censored by the rebel faction in the unit. Her mother, brothers and sisters didn't speak to her. She also thought that she had done the right thing and was loyal to Chairman Mao's revolutionary line. No matter who he was, as long as he opposed Chairman Mao, he was our enemy. Hadn't many revolutionary predecessors from the exploiting class also broken with their families?

However, she also had her own worries. At the age of 18, she had begun to notice the changes in her body and her chest had begun to plump up. She wanted to wear a thin shirt to tighten up her chest but it didn't work. At that time, all the girls were unwilling to show their curves, thinking that it was lewd and a bourgeois style. Looking at herself in the mirror, she found that the girlish face had become round and fair plus, with the curved, arched eyebrows, an aura of purity as emanating from her body, like a pink-whitish lotus with dewdrops.

In fact, she did not pay attention to the changes in her body and face at first, but rather, noticed them from the reaction of people around her, especially men. When taking a bus, some men would turn back for a few more looks. Once in the office of the Red Guards, she felt a little hot and took off her yellow uniform, wearing only a white blouse. Suddenly, she noticed Cai Wenge sitting on the opposite table, staring at her chest. With a red face, she asked,

"What are you looking at?"

"You are in really good shape," Cai said, in a somewhat obscene way.

Qing Lian was a little annoyed and said,

"Mind your own business right now."

Qing Lian had always admired Cai since the Cultural Revolution began. She felt that he stood firm in his revolutionary stance and dared to fight against class enemies. However, she also noticed that Cai was sometimes a bit slippery and overly enthusiastic towards girls.

One day, in the dormitory of the school, she couldn't get to sleep in the dead of night, so she got up to light a lamp and read Chairman Mao's works for a while. The moment she picked up the book, she inadvertently looked at the mirror on the wall. Suddenly, she found herself more beautiful in the mirror than during the day. She couldn't help looking carefully at her delicate face in the mirror. 'It's a bit like Xiaoqing in the Legend of the White Snake,' 'Xiaoqing is a beautiful young lady in the story' she said to herself.

For an instant, a girl's fond dream about romance occupied her heart. In a trance, she saw Zhang Feng's handsome face again, 'If I had been as beautiful in the past, he might not have refused me.' But immediately, she remembered Yu Mei and the many people who had said that Zhang Feng and Yu Mei were a perfect match.

Qing Lian looked in the mirror carefully again, 'I am as beautiful as she! And now, since Zhang Feng is the son of the Five Black Categories, they may have long since broken up. No girl is willing to approach him now. If I am kind to him, he might see me in a new light. Well, you might lose your class position." She began to blame herself.

She was a revolutionary Red Guard and Zhang Feng was a member of a social class of the people's enemy. 'Why am I missing him? Moreover, he seemed to have an unusual relationship with Dan Dan, who was one year older than him.' What Qing Lian did not expect was seeing Zhang Feng the next day.

Qing Lian got up early in the morning and went to the school to sort things out in the offices of their red rebel army. Like many Red Guards' organizations in schools, the Red Guards in Second

Senior Middle School were also divided into two groups. Wang Hai and some students formed the Second Senior Middle School Red Rebel Regiment and established the Jili Commune together with several university Red Guards' organizations while Qing Lian and Cai Wenge joined the Second Red Guards' Headquarters, set up by several other universities. Although the two Red Guards' factions were divided on some issues and often held heated debates, they were still revolutionary mass organizations.

Both sides were also expanding their own teams. As long as one was a student or ordinary person, and as long as one was not of the Five Black Categories, then he or she could join the rebel faction organization. Of course, only those from red families could become Red Guards. These days, Qing Lian and her organization were taking advantage of the opportunity of organizing a revolutionary tour to Beijing to exchange revolutionary ideas in order to encourage more ordinary students to join their regiment.

Qing Lian was looking for materials, when, from the open door, she suddenly saw a familiar tall and strong figure coming this way from the corridor. It was him! Qing Lian suddenly felt her heart beating faster. Strangely, she had thought of him last night and he had come today. But another voice in her heart was reminding her that he was no longer the Prince Charming in all girls' hearts. He was the Five Black Categories' son whose presence everyone wanted to shun. However, she stood up involuntarily and adjusted her hair. Then, she walked to the door, and said with a smile to Zhang Feng,

"Hello. You are so early. What can I do for you? Now all students can join rebel groups."

Zhang Feng was startled by the sudden appearance of Qing Lian and instinctively took a step backward. When he saw that it was Qing Lian standing in front of him, she who had been the most active Red Guard since the movement started, dealt the most severe blows, criticized others the most harshly, and even turned her back on her own family and relatives, he took another two steps backward.

"Me? I have no business. Thank you." He did not even dare to look at Qing Lian's expressive face. Seeing that there was no one around, Qing Lian unexpectedly summoned up her courage and said,

"Brother Zhang. You must have some reason to come here. I can help you."

Hearing that Qing Lian had called him her brother, Zhang Feng got gooseflesh all over his body. However, out of courtesy, he stammered,

"I'm here to find Wang Hai. I'm not going to join the rebel organization, I just want to get a letter of introduction for a revolutionary tour to Beijing." Then he turned back to leave.

Unexpectedly, Qing Lian said to him in a very sweet voice,

"I can write it for you, too. You see, I have so many blank sheets."

Zhang Feng was a soft hearted person. Seeing that she was so enthusiastic, it was hard for him to refuse. While he was hesitating, he suddenly heard the crisp voice of an excited young girl.

"Xiao Feng, don't ask her for help. Let's find Wang Hai to write one."

It turned out that Dan Dan was here. Her face was reddened with either agitation or excitement. It seemed that she had already heard what Qing Lian had said. Her woman's intuition made her feel that Qing Lian was trying to seduce Zhang Feng.

* 155 *

The two women looked at each other with hostility. Qing Lian suddenly remembered her revolutionary position. She said arrogantly,

"I will not write you a letter of introduction even if you want. Chairman Mao will receive the Red Guards, not the Black Five Categories' children like you."

Zhang Feng was shocked by her sudden change of attitude, and his self-esteem was hurt. He and Dan Dan said angrily and almost at the same time,

"Whether we can go or not is none of your business. Go, let's go find Wang Hai!"

Having said this, the two left without looking back. Qing Lian returned to her office, thrashing the papers in her hands violently on the table, and had a good cry.

On August 28, when the flood of Red Guards' revolutionary tours began to sweep across the country, trains full of Red Guards and young students rolled out of Jili City and sped across the land of the Northeast. As there were too many people aboard the trains, the carriages were very crowded and even the aisles were crowded with people. In one of the carriages, Zhang Feng, his sister and Dan Dan and a group of university students from Polytechnic University huddled together. As Wang Hai had led a group of students from the Second Senior Middle School Red Rebel Regiment to embark on the revolutionary tour the day before, Zhang Feng, his sister and Dan Dan did not obtain a letter of introduction. They might not be able to find accommodation after arriving in Beijing.

However, time was pressing. If they didn't leave immediately, they would not make it for Chairman Mao's second interview with the Red Guards and the Rebel Faction in Tiananmen Square at the end of August. So Zhang Feng, his sister and Dan

Dan decided to hit the road and postpone their decision until after they arrived in Beijing.

Coincidentally, while waiting for the train at the station, Zhang Feng met a student named Xu Jianguo from Jili Polytechnic University. He knew him because, when they were skating at the provincial sports school in winter, they were the two who skated the fastest in the skating rink, and they often discussed skills together. As they had the same interests and hobbies, they became friends.

At the sight of Zhang Feng, Xu Jianguo jumped up with joy. After shaking hands and exchanging greetings, Zhang Feng told him the trouble he had had. Xu patted Zhang Feng on the shoulder after hearing this and said,

"No problem. Come with us. We are a subordinate university of the Ministry of Machine-Building. The Ministry has arranged accommodation for us in Beijing."

After hearing this, Zhang Feng and the other two were very happy, and they got on the train together with Xu Jianguo. Xu Jianguo's girlfriend, Li Li, was his classmate. She was very beautiful and warm-hearted. She took great care of Zhang Feng, his sister and Dan Dan all the way.

Over 14 hours' ride was actually very tough. There were no sleeping berths and all the seats were hard so one could only sleep sitting upright. It was fortunate to have a seat. Those who did not have seats had to stand all the way and dozed off, leaning on the carriage or on the seat back. Some people simply sat on the floor and even slept under other people's seats. When one was hungry and thirsty, one just ate some biscuits and drank water from a bottle. The most difficult thing was to go to the toilet. One had to carefully walk through the crowded passage and find gaps between legs before one dared to land his feet. Many people drank as little water as possible to reduce the times they went to the toilet. However, none of these difficulties seemed to affect the excitement of these young people as they were heading to Beijing, the capital of the motherland, and would see Chairman Mao, the great leader. This had been the long-cherished dream since their childhood.

Soon, the train drove into the boundless darkness and the Red Guards and students who had been excited all day fell asleep at sixes and sevens. Some people snored like thunder. As the seats were too crowded, Zhang Feng kept standing in the corridor, allowing his sister and Dan Dan to have more room. Dan Dan also asked Zhang Feng to sit down from time to time, but he always insisted on letting them sit.

After a while, Dan Dan and Zhang Lin fell asleep leaning against each other. Zhang Feng looked out of the window at the city lights that flashed past from time to time, thinking about his parents who had stayed at home, and what had happened since the Cultural Revolution. He wanted to go to the toilet and then walk around for a while. He carefully walked past the students lying on the floor and found the toilet. After paying a call to nature, he wanted to stretch his limbs and found a place at the junction of the two carriages where there were few people and stayed for a while. He leaned against the door and the wind stole in from the junction gap of the carriages. It felt very cold but it also sobered him up.

Just as he was closing his eyes and having a reverie, he suddenly smelled a familiar faint, plum blossom-like fragrance. 'Is it her?' He opened his eyes, but saw no one beside him, only two male students who were fast asleep, sitting on the floor. 'Illusion. You still think of her. Worthless,' Zhang Feng thought to himself.

But a few minutes later, he smelled the smell again, and it was stronger than before. Maybe he was too tired, he thought. He felt very sleepy and didn't want to open his eyes. But, strangely, he seemed to hear the familiar sound of breathing. He tried to keep his eyes half open. As a result, he really saw Yu Mei standing in front of him. 'Is it a dream?' He rubbed his eyes and looked with wide eyes. It was indeed Yu Mei, dressed in a new, grass-green military uniform and wearing the Red Guards' armband. Her clear and beautiful eyes were looking at Zhang Feng affectionately.

"Are you okay?"

They both greeted each other almost at the same time. It had been more than two months since the encounter at the train station. Both of them knew that they belonged to two completely different worlds, one red and one black. It was even impossible for them to be ordinary friends. Zhang Feng was in a conflicted mental state as he wanted to talk to Yu Mei, and yet was afraid that others would see and gossip about it. Seeing that there were no acquaintances around, Zhang Feng thought that he would talk to her for just a few minutes, so that this long night could pass faster.

They began to share what had happened to them recently. Zhang Feng found that Yu Mei was not excited about the progress of the Cultural Revolution and what the Red Guards had done. On the contrary, she did not understand why the traditional Chinese culture should be destroyed, and why so many veteran cadres and celebrities in cultural and educational circles had been overthrown and especially, why the class struggle theory was used to divide people into red and black. At this point, she also looked at Zhang Feng plaintively. Zhang Feng certainly understood that it was this that had caused them to break up. They were so lost in the conversation that they forgot the time.

Dan Dan woke up suddenly and felt a little cold. Raising her head up, she saw Zhang Feng was gone. She waited for ten minutes but she still did not see him coming back. Dan Dan was a little worried so she walked past the crowd on the ground, looking for Zhang Feng from one carriage to another.

Suddenly, she saw Zhang Feng's tall figure in front of a door. She was just about to call him happily when she saw Yu Mei standing beside him. They were talking very heartily. How could she be here? Dan Dan's heart sank and she also felt a little peevish. Clearly it was impossible for them to be together. Why did Yu Mei still get in touch with him? Did she mean to hurt Zhang Feng intentionally? Dan Dan was about to walk over and interrupt them. Yet on second thoughts, the two must have met by chance and perhaps it was just a casual talk. So, she quietly returned to her seat.

One hour had passed before Zhang Feng and Yu Mei realized it. Yu Mei suddenly remembered that she had left her seat to wash apples. Chang Zheng had given Yu Mei two apples and asked her to wash them first. Yu Mei had agreed and come out. Seeing Zhang Feng's gaunt face, Yu Mei felt very distressed. She gave Zhang Feng one of the apples in her hand and said,

"Have it and take good care of yourself."

Holding the apple, Zhang Feng didn't know what to say. He feared that Yu Mei would be unhappy if he refused. Just then, a tall boy suddenly ran up and inserted himself between Zhang Feng and Yu Mei and gave Zhang Feng a dirty look. Immediately, Zhang Feng saw it was his old rival, as well as his old rival in love, Chang Zheng.

Zhang Feng instinctively took a step back, thinking that Chang Zheng would fight with him. If they really fought, Zhang

Feng would have no fear of him. Although Chang Zheng was about the same height as Zhang Feng, he was not as strong as Zhang Feng. As the child of a veteran cadre, he lived in comfort and did not have much strength. When he fought with others, he could only put up a showy fight. Obviously, Chang Zheng also knew that Zhang Feng was not to be trifled with but in front of Yu Mei, he still said, with arrogance,

"Behave yourself, OK? If I were you, I would not be so unrealistic as to crave for the swan meat,"(a Chinese saying: a toad wants to eat swan meat, meaning wishful thinking) Obviously, he already knew about Zhang Feng's father's historical problems. Zhang Feng had intended to explain that he had met Yu Mei by chance. But Chang Zheng deprecated him politically, hurting his self-esteem. He retorted to Chang Zheng,

"Birth does not affect one's participation in the revolution. Was Premier Zhou born to a good family? Hasn't he become a revolutionist as well? A good birth does not guarantee that one would not become a traitor, especially those indecent playboys!"

"You, you…" Chang Zheng hadn't expected Zhang Feng to satirize him so much, and he didn't know what to reply for a moment. In front of Yu Mei, he made him feel awkward. In particular, Yu Mei sometimes said that he was like a playboy. Thereupon, he got angry with Yu Mei for his speechlessness.

"I only asked you to wash apples. You've been long enough to dig a well."

Yu Mei had intended to answer back but was afraid that he would tell her father that she had met Zhang Feng again, so she handed the apple in her hand to Chang Zheng and turned to go. Chang Zheng asked,

"Where is your apple?" When he saw sideways the apple in Zhang Feng's hand, he became angry again.

"Why did you give the apple that I gave you to this guy?"

What Yu Mei was annoyed about was Chang Zheng's narrow-mindedness at ordinary times. She said angrily,

"I can give it to whoever I want. It's none of your business!" Having said this, she turned back and went away. Chang Zheng was left in disgrace. As he followed Yu Mei, he turned back and said to Zhang Feng,

"If you can't afford it, don't beg it from others. It might as well be given to a dog."

As soon as Zhang Feng heard this he became furious. He held up his hand and hurled the apple at Chang Zheng. Chang Zheng dodged to one side and the apple hit the carriage wall and smashed into pieces. Seeing Zhang Feng fly into a rage, Chang Zheng slipped away quickly.

A few minutes later, Zhang Feng angrily returned to his carriage. Dan Dan and his sister both stood up to let Zhang Feng sit down. Dan Dan winked at Zhang Lin, who just stood in the aisle and allowed Zhang Feng to sit down. Dan Dan had planned to show her displeasure, as Zhang Feng had said that he would never see Yu Mei again and the class gap between Yu Mei's high ranked family background and his own ignominious family background hurt his self-esteem. But seeing Zhang Feng's anger, her older sister's sympathy came out. She patted Zhang Feng's arm gently and said,

"Why did you quarrel with her?"

Zhang Feng was surprised, knowing that Dan Dan had seen him talking to Yu Mei and did not explain anything. After being silent for a minute, he said slowly,

"I just ran into her by chance and talked for a while. But Chang Zheng talked indecently. I really wanted to teach him a lesson!"

Dan Dan came to realize that Chang Zheng had seen him talking with Yu Mei. Of course, what followed was predictable. Dan Dan knew that Zhang Feng still had a place for Yu Mei in his heart, which made her feel a little sour, but over the years, the 'sister and brother' tie had made her tolerant and magnanimous. She patted Zhang Feng on the shoulder again, took out a tomato from her bag and handed it to Zhang Feng,

"Don't be angry. What happened by chance is not worth getting angry about. The playboy in Chang Zheng is what makes him. Come on, have a tomato."

Dan Dan's gentle persuasion calmed Zhang Feng down. Yes, the conflict with Chang Zheng should not have happened. If Yu Mei were still his girlfriend now, it would be worth fighting for. But they had nothing to do with each other now. Zhang Feng regretted even talking to Yu Mei. However, just as Olivia said in Twelfth Night, 'Nor wit nor reason can my passion hide' (Act Three, Scene I). Although in reality, they were already members of the red and black social classes respectively, yet in Zhang Feng's heart, his love for Yu Mei could not be obliterated. Maybe, she would only be his dream lover forever.

During the ride before dawn, when Zhang Feng went to the toilet several times or went to stretch his limbs, he involuntarily walked slowly to the carriage where he had met Yu Mei in the hope of seeing her again. But his heart was very ambivalent. A voice said to him, 'Don't go, it doesn't make any sense' but another voice said, 'How happy it is to see her fairy-like features, hear her sweet voice. Ah, just for the last time.'

Finally, reason gave way but to his disappointment, he never saw Yu Mei again. Looking at the lights outside the window,

Zhang Feng realized that the social class gap between him and Yu Mei could never be transcended. Forced transcendence could only bring humiliation. He swore secretly that he would never see her again and erased her from his memory.

CHAPTER II

The Crazy Square

On the morning of the next day, Zhang Feng, his sister and Dan Dan arrived in Beijing. It was the first time they had come to the capital. The wide streets, modern high-rise buildings, flowers and trees everywhere, convenient transportation, subways never before seen, all made these young people from outside Beijing feel fresh and excited. Following Xu Jianguo and Li Li, they arrived at the accommodation arranged by the Ministry of the Eighth Machine Building Industry. It was a large conference room with rows of makeshift beds on the floor. Luckily, Beijing was still very hot in late August and a thin blanket would be enough at night.

Although these were humble conditions, for the Red Guards on a revolutionary tour, a place to sleep in, drinking water and eating simple food were enough. Everyone was sleeping with their clothes on as they were too excited to fall asleep for a long time, talking about meeting Chairman Mao tomorrow. At that time, Mao Zedong was as great as a god in the eyes of the Red Guards. Every word he said was the truth and must be strictly followed. In Zhang Feng's mind, Mao Zedong was indeed a great man. Under his leadership, China had become an independent and powerful country, not bullied by foreigners. China was indeed a harmonious society in the 1950s. Since then however, the endless political movements and highly centralized planned economy had brought great social issues to this country.

During the Cultural Revolution, the policy of social class struggle had been used in all aspects of social life, hurting millions of intellectual elites. Democracy within the party had vanished. They were engaged in the cult of personality and turned the Cultural Revolution into a power struggle. Because his father was a patriotic intellectual who sincerely believed in communism, Zhang Feng believed his words, even though at first, he had a sense of disillusionment. During this trip to Beijing, he had no sense of pilgrimage like the other Red Guards and students. What he wanted most was to see what happened in the capital.

Zhang Feng and the others got up very early because they had heard that more than one million Red Guards and students would take part in the reception ceremony in Tiananmen Square today. They could not enter or occupy a good place if they were late. Everything related to the revolutionary tour was free: trains and buses, as long as one was a student, one could move freely.

They got off the bus near Tiananmen Square and walked towards it with Xu Jianguo and his university team, holding up banners. Ah, the sight ahead really stunned them. Thousands of Red Guards were marching to Tiananmen Square, wearing the Red Guards' armbands, holding up the red flags of the rebel faction group, shouting the slogan: 'It is Right to Rebel', singing the song 'Sailing the Seas Depends on the Helmsman', flowing into huge Tiananmen Square like red rivers. The entire huge square turned into a red sea.

His sister and Dan Dan were both very excited as they had never seen such a spectacular scene. As there were many people, Zhang Feng reminded them not to fall behind and not to get lost. He also reminded them that if they were really lost, they should remember how to return to their accommodation. When they were about to enter the square, his sister suddenly shouted excitedly:

"Look! Look! It's Wang Hai!" Zhang Feng looked ahead, and sure enough, he saw a banner printed with: 'Jili City Second Senior Middle School Red Guards.' Wang Hai and Li He walked proudly at the front of the team.

"Brother Wang, why don't you take us with you?" Zhang Lin said to Wang Hai, half-peevishly. Zhang Feng knew that his sister liked Wang Hai who was sturdy and straightforward. However, Wang Hai thought she was still a little girl and always called her that. Wang Hai took no notice of Zhang Lin's greeting. Instead, he greeted Dan Dan warmly:

"Sister Dan Dan, have you ever seen such a big gathering?" Zhang Feng also knew that Wang Hai liked Dan Dan but Dan Dan always felt that Wang Hai was a little rustic, not as masculine and refined as Zhang Feng. Zhang Feng walked to Wang Hai and gently punched him, whispering:

"Hey, guy, you value beauty over friendship. You didn't greet me first." Wang Hai pretended to be hurt, groaning while holding his shoulders with his hand.

"Alright, alright, don't pretend anymore," Zhang Feng said. Wang Hai enthusiastically asked them to join their team. Zhang Feng said that the big brothers of the Polytechnic University were kind to them, so they would follow their team first. Besides, they had not yet gone through the formalities of joining Wang Hai's rebel team.

After they parted from Wang Hai, they followed the team of the Polytechnic University to the central area of the square. Xu Jianguo said that their position was owing to their association with the rebel faction of the Ministry of the Eighth Machine Building Industry.

At noon, the square became very crowded with people. Like devout pilgrims, the passionate one million Red Guards and young students waited for the emergence of their god, Mao Zedong, the red sun in their mind: singing, chanting slogans and brandishing red flags. In late August in Beijing, although the autumn cold could already be felt in the evening, the sun at noon was still hot. Zhang Feng, his sister and Dan Dan were sweating due to the heat and had to drink water from time to time. Zhang Feng took off his outer clothes and covered Dan Dan's head to block out the scorching sun.

When would Chairman Mao come to inspect them? News came constantly, saying that it was 3 o'clock in the afternoon, but when it was almost 3 o'clock, they were told that the inspection was to be at 4 o'clock. Zhang Lin was getting a little impatient. Dan Dan comforted her and said,

"Don't worry. He will definitely come."

The Red Guards and students were anxiously looking in the direction of the Tiananmen Gate Platform, hoping that Chairman Mao would appear on the platform. At this point, Xu Jianguo suddenly squeezed over and told Zhang Feng that the head of the Beijing Red Guards had informed the Red Guards' organizations across the country that Chairman Mao would take a car to inspect the Red Guards on the square first and then ascend the Tiananmen Gate Platform. This news clearly caused a commotion on the square. The Red Guards standing on the periphery wanted to move towards the centre. Zhang Feng, his sister and Dan Dan were pushed forward by the people behind them. The Red Guards, holding megaphones, continually yelled at the crowd, asking them not to push as everyone would be able to see Chairman Mao!

At 6 o'clock in the afternoon, there suddenly came deafening shouts from the east side of the square: "Long live Chairman Mao! Long live Chairman Mao!" Behind more than a dozen motorcycles, several convertible green jeeps slowly drove along. Mao Zedong, who was tall, and Lin Biao, his close comrade, were standing on the first jeep. His fleet drove into the red sea like a giant ship, creating wave upon wave. The Red Guards almost shouted the 'Long-Live Chairman' slogan with their loudest ever voices. Everyone tried to push forward and wanted to see more clearly because in their lifetime, this might be their only chance to witness the great leader in person. All the teams were disorganized because the heads of the Red Guards themselves had no time to heed their own team.

Zhang Feng and his group were about 20 meters away from Mao's fleet so they could see him rather clearly but they had to try hard to prevent their bodies from being pushed down by the people who came up behind. The huge flow of the crowd first pushed from the sides to the middle and then followed the fleet, to surge ahead and there were screams from those being trampled. The ground was scattered with trodden down shoes and schoolbags everywhere. Zhang Feng took his sister with one hand and Dan Dan with the other, sustaining the impact of the crowd with his own body. They had already been squeezed far away from their original location and the Polytechnic University team was nowhere to be seen. Sweat was running down their faces and they were panting for breath. Both Dan Dan and Zhang Lin felt a little dizzy. Zhang Feng said,

"Let's go to the square side and take a rest. Anyway, Chairman Mao is going to ascend Tiananmen after his inspection. We could also see him at the side of the square." So the three of them tried to squeeze through the crowd and headed to the north of the square.

Finally, they squeezed out of the crowd. Dan Dan and his sister almost fell down under a big tree, leaning against the trunk and gasping. Zhang Feng also sat down to cool himself in the shade. Suddenly his sister said,

"Look, what is happening over there?" Zhang Feng and Dan Dan saw that there was a group of people around a student lying on the ground a dozen meters away.

"Maybe a heat stroke," Zhang Feng said, as they had seen several Red Guards being carried away on stretchers. After a few minutes, his sister said,

"It's strange… how come the student is still lying there and isn't being cared for by anyone?" Dan Dan said:

"Both the Red Guards and students have their own organizations and somebody should be there." His sister was curious by nature. She said,

"I will go and see." She got up and walked over. Zhang Feng and Dan Dan were still sitting under the tree, talking.

"You two! Come over quickly, look!" Zhang Lin shouted to Zhang Feng and Dan Dan. It would just be a Red Guard who had passed out with heatstroke, nothing more, Zhang Feng and Dan Dan thought, but they still stood up and walked over. When they approached, they found it was a female Red Guard. Zhang Lin had turned her over with another girl.

"She's one of the First Senior Middle School students and there are small characters on the red armband," Zhang Lin said. "Where are the other people? She's been left alone," she added.

Dan Dan wanted to help Zhang Lin to lift the girl up, but when she saw the girl's face, she cried in surprise:

"Ah, it is her!"

At the same time, she looked at Zhang Feng. Zhang Feng came over immediately. When he saw the familiar face that he had missed day and night, he felt shocked. How could it be her? Yes, lying on the ground was Yu Mei. Her eyes were shut but the pale complexion still couldn't hide her beauty. Instinct urged him to hold Yu Mei up immediately but he suddenly remembered what he had said to Dan Dan on the train. He had vowed never to see Yu Mei again because his personality had been insulted and his self-esteem hurt. But fate was always playing a joke with him and allowed him to meet her again and again.

He looked at Dan Dan helplessly and saw a bitter smile quickly cross her face. Dan Dan was a kind, large-hearted girl after all. She said to Zhang Feng that Yu Mei must have been pushed away from her team and stepped down. Now it was imperative to save her life. Hearing Dan Dan's words, Zhang Feng had no worries any more. It was his nature to save someone he did not know when they were injured. Because Yu Mei was still in a coma, Zhang Feng carried her on his back. He asked Dan Dan and his sister to return to the accommodation after the inspection if they could not find Xu Jianguo. He would stop a car on the road and take Yu Mei to hospital.

Zhang Feng carried Yu Mei to Qianmen Street. It happened that there was a tricycle approaching. An old man was riding it. Zhang Feng went over and explained the situation to the old man, who agreed with the warmth of Beijing citizens. He helped Zhang Feng put Yu Mei onto the tricycle and asked Zhang Feng to sit on it too, and then rode the tricycle with great energy to the nearest hospital.

After 20 minutes, they came to a hospital near Dongdan. After Zhang Feng thanked the old man, he carried Yu Mei to the emergency room. A nurse on duty asked what had happened and placed Yu Mei flat on a rise-and-fall sickbed. Seeing that Yu Mei was still not awake, Zhang Feng anxiously asked the nurse:

"Is her condition serious? Can she be saved?"

The nurse comforted him and said that Yu Mei might have fainted due to the excitement coupled with heatstroke. Today, over a dozen such Red Guards had been admitted into hospital. The hospital dared not neglect Yu Mei as she was a Red Guard. After a few minutes, two doctors came and one of them was the director of the hospital. Yu Mei was pushed into the clinic for first aid.

CHAPTER III

The Quarrel in the Ward

Zhang Feng anxiously waited outside the clinic, not knowing when Yu Mei would wake up. He knew that Yu Mei was weak and hoped there would be no other complications apart from the heat stroke. At the same time, he was also concerned about Dan Dan and his sister, wishing that they would find Xu Jianguo and Li Li. Hey, he thought to himself, how strange it was that every time he met Yu Mei, it always brought him trouble and hurt his feelings. He had vowed not to see Yu Mei again but God had made him meet her repeatedly. He had no way to get away even if he wanted to. He was ambivalent. Sensibility made him look forward to seeing Yu Mei, yet his common sense reminded him not to do anything stupid. Well, he made up his mind that when Yu Mei woke up, he would have the nurse ask where the First Senior Middle School Red Guards lived in Beijing and then call Chang Zheng. He cursed Chang Zheng in his mind. What a jerk! He always saw himself as the protector of Yu Mei yet abandoned her every time.

Over an hour later, a nurse came out of the clinic and said to Zhang Feng,

"Your classmate has woken up but we found that her right arm has been broken, so she will have to stay in hospital for a week. Once her condition is stable, she can be discharged from the hospital with a clamp plate."

Zhang Feng saw that the clinic door open and the nurses had pushed Yu Mei to the ward. Zhang Feng quickly hid himself in a corner. After they had made arrangements for Yu Mei, Zhang Feng quietly asked the nurse he had just talked to outside the ward,

"Excuse me, can you do me a favour by enquiring about her temporary residence in Beijing so that I can call her organization to send someone to take care of her and pick her up?" The little nurse looked at Zhang Feng with a strange look,

"Why? Aren't you classmates? How can you not know where she lives?" Zhang Feng said,

"We… we are from the same city but not the same school. I used to meet her but I am not familiar with her background."

"Aren't you? You are so concerned about her. It doesn't seem like you are not that familiar with her." The nurse smiled mysteriously and said,

"She is the most beautiful Red Guard I have ever seen." Zhang Feng felt a little awkward and had to change his approach:

"My dear elder sister, I beg you!"

"Hey, hey, I am not much older than you! Call me your younger sister!" The little nurse said, a little coquettishly. Obviously, she liked Zhang Feng. Since Zhang Feng's arrival with Yu Mei, the news that, 'one pretty male and one female Red Guard' had arrived at the hospital had been going around among the nurses. Some young nurses also walked past Zhang Feng from time to time and secretly stole a glance at him.

When Yu Mei woke up, she found herself in the hospital ward. Strange… how could she be lying on a hospital bed? And her right forearm was very painful, still fixed with a clamp plate. She only remembered that when Chairman Mao's inspection car came towards Tiananmen Square, everyone was desperately squeezing forward. Those behind pushed her forward. She could barely stand. She hadn't slept well these last few days, making her very weak. She had wanted to follow Chang Zheng who simply took no notice of her, pushing forward with all his might. In the end, Yu Mei felt as if the sky and earth were spinning round and she fell to the ground. She still remembered the feeling of being trampled and then she lost consciousness. It must have been Chang Zheng and the others who had taken her to hospital. Yu Mei thought to herself that, alas, she had been so unlucky. She had been hurt before she could see Chairman Mao clearly.

While Yu Mei was thinking, a young female nurse came in. Yu Mei was about to thank her for their treatment and care when the nurse said to her,

"How do you feel? Your arm still hurts? The male student who brought you here asked where your temporary residence in Beijing is. He wants to call your organization to send someone to look after you."

'What? Was Chang Zheng playing a joke?' Yu Mei thought to herself. She asked,

"Is he tall?"

"Yes, plus, he's very handsome. He said that you both come from the same city, but that he does not know you well. However, he is very concerned about you and he has been waiting for some time in the corridor. Seems to be very sad. Seems to be your…" The nurse had intended to say 'your boyfriend' but she stopped short. Strange, Yu Mei thought. Tall and handsome. Chang Zheng was not handsome. Who was it that did not know her well but also cared about her in particular?

"Can you let him in to talk?" Yu Mei asked the nurse. The nurse said reluctantly:

"It seems that he does not want to see you. He is right here in the corridor but wanted me to come in and ask you." Yu Mei felt even more strange.

"Anyway, he saved me. I have to thank him. Let me go and see him."

The little nurse seemed a bit hesitant but did not stop Yu Mei. Yu Mei got out of the bed and walked to the door. She quietly opened it and saw Zhang Feng sitting, tired, on the bench in the corridor, his eyes closed, having a rest.

Yu Mei was both surprised and happy but immediately her expression dimmed. Her most beloved was unwilling to see her at all. Because the nurse was standing behind her, she couldn't be too emotional and so she patted Zhang Feng on the shoulder, gently. Zhang Feng opened his eyes and suddenly saw Yu Mei. He was also very surprised. He immediately looked around and found there was no one else. He stood up and held Yu Mei by the hand,

"How did you come out? What if you fall again? Go back to the ward now."

He thought, since Yu Mei already knew, it would be better to enter the ward and explain it all to her so he helped Yu Mei into the ward and onto the bed. When the nurse saw that the relationship between the two was very unusual, she said to Zhang Feng,

"It seems that I have completed the task." After that, she knowingly shut the door behind her and left.

This single-person ward was originally intended for senior officials but because many of them were brought down after the Cultural Revolution, it had always been unoccupied. The authorities had told the hospital to try to render its best services to the Red Guards so they had placed Yu Mei here.

The ward was quiet, like a peaceful sanctuary in a political storm. Destiny was so strange. It would be almost impossible to find one particular person in a square where millions of Red Guards gathered yet, they had met once again. At this point, mixed feelings seized them. They were experiencing excitement, melancholy, helplessness and sorrow at the same time. Yu Mei suddenly covered her face as she did not want Zhang Feng to see her crying.

"Please, don't be like this, you will be fine." Zhang Feng deliberately changed the topic.

"Am I so awful to you that you don't want to say anything to me?" Yu Mei began to cry quietly. Zhang Feng was most loath to see women crying, let alone his beloved.

"No, no, you listen to me."

Zhang Feng comforted Yu Mei while taking out his handkerchief to hand it to Yu Mei to wipe her tears. Yu Mei took it and inadvertently saw the plum blossoms embroidered on the handkerchief. She suddenly opened her eyes and said,

"This is the handkerchief that I gave you! Didn't you say that you had thrown it away? You only use the handkerchief that Dan Dan gave you."

Zhang Feng was a bit embarrassed. Actually, from the time he said that he would break up with Yu Mei, he had kept the handkerchief that she had given him.

"You lied! You have never forgotten me! Is it a fabrication that you and Dan Dan are on good terms?" Zhang Feng was struck dumb for a moment, not knowing how to explain. He gently helped Yu Mei to dry her tears and told her how they had found her, passed out in the square earlier today and taken her to hospital. He also complained that Chang Zheng hadn't taken care of Yu Mei.

"But you haven't said why you don't want to see me." Yu Mei was still pressing for an answer. Zhang Feng saw there was no way to avoid this question any longer so he told her the truth. He told Yu Mei that he had been warned against her by her father's secretary and especially by her father, at Yu Mei's home that day, which hurt his self-esteem. Plus, he was provoked by the contempt and ridicule from Chang Zheng and those Red Guards so he had decided to stay away from Yu Mei.

"Yu Mei, I really love you deeply but fate is playing a joke on us. This political storm is destined to separate us. I don't understand why our society has become one where black is confused with white, where good people suffer yet bad people flourish. If we stay together, it will only be a tragic ending. I don't want to bring you any trouble nor do I want to be insulted and mocked by those people."

Yu Mei held Zhang Feng's hand and listened to him silently. After that, she wiped her tears and said slowly, "Brother Feng, I know. Although I don't understand politics, I can still judge good and evil and have a fundamental conscience. I believe that, as a man sows, so shall he reap. The current chaos will not last long. The situation for you and your family will be better. I will wait for you: three years, five years, ten years! I don't care how long it is! Anyway, I won't fall in love with another man in this life again."

Having said this, she gently leaned against Zhang Feng's shoulder and closed her eyes happily. Zhang Feng was shocked. He thought he could persuade Yu Mei and then he would quickly leave the scene while asking Chang Zheng and others to pick her up from the hospital. However, he was trapped here, once more, by Yu Mei. Faced with the tears and warmth of his beloved, it was really difficult for him to hurt her again. Hearing that the corridor was quiet and there was no one there, Zhang Feng allowed Yu Mei to stay close to him with confidence. 'Forget about the red storm around us and forget about the groaning, pain, suffering, persecution and death,' Zhang Feng thought to himself. 'Love is like a ray of sunshine in the long night, warming you heart and melting that strong, spiritual shell you have formed to protect yourself. Life is brief and happiness is fleeting, so get lost in it, like savouring a glass of wine.'

Some unknown interval of time passed before Zhang Feng was suddenly awakened by a gentle knocking at the door. Yu Mei still leaned against his shoulder and had already fallen asleep with a happy smile on her fairy-like face. Zhang Feng quickly laid Yu Mei down on the bed. It turned out that the little nurse came in. From the way she made a face, Zhang Feng knew that she had seen how he and Yu Mei had held each other. While the nurse was checking Yu Mei, he quickly asked if he could use the hospital's telephone to contact Yu Mei's Red Guards' organization to pick her up. The little nurse asked,

"Has she already told you the phone number?" Zhang Feng faltered,

"No, not yet."

When the little nurse walked to the door, she quietly said to Zhang Feng,

"That means she is reluctant to part with you." After that, she made a grimace again and walked off with a smile.

After Yu Mei woke up, Zhang Feng hesitantly said to her, "Yu Mei, we have to face reality. Chang Zheng and others must be looking for you everywhere. You tell me their address and telephone number, I will contact them to pick you up." Yu Mei took Zhang Feng's hand and said, half-coquettishly,

"Brother Feng. Thank Goodness we finally have such an opportunity to be together. Don't drive me away. Besides, the doctor said that I need to be hospitalized for observation for at least one week. Just let Chang Zheng and his guys look for a few days. Why did he leave me alone? Just let him worry about me." Zhang Feng said reluctantly,

"But what if they find out that I stayed with you? I will get in trouble. He might think that I deliberately hid you and did not tell them." Yu Mei thought for a moment and said:

"Brother Feng, just three days. I will contact them after three days. I have been dreaming about you these several months. I will be satisfied and can die without regrets if I can live with you for three days."

After she finished, she threw herself into Zhang Feng's arms and closed her eyes happily. Zhang Feng was shocked and quickly covered up Yu Mei's mouth with his hand.

"Don't say unlucky words. We don't want to be Romeo and Juliet. Our life is still ahead."

Just three days, Zhang Feng thought. His existence would have been worthwhile if he could stay with his darling happily for three days in the haven of this storm. How many days are there in a life after all?

After dinner, the warm-hearted little nurse helped Zhang Feng find an empty duty room which was very close to Yu

Mei's ward, and where he could spend the night. Zhang Feng was afraid that Dan Dan and his sister might be worried. He asked the little nurse for permission to use the hospital telephone and called the guesthouse of the Ministry of the Eighth Machine Building Industry, asking them to tell Xu Jianguo and Dan Dan that he was taking care of Yu Mei at the Dongzhimen Hospital, and would be back in two or three days. He asked them to participate in other activities without him in Beijing. The man on duty said that he would definitely relay the message to them.

When Yu Mei woke up the next morning, she felt much better and the injured arm was less painful. Thinking that Zhang Feng could take care of her and that they could stay together happily for three days, she felt warm in her heart. Suddenly, she heard someone knock at the door.

"Brother Feng, don't play jokes with me. Come on in!" said Yu Mei affectionately. But when the door was opened, Yu Mei was shocked to see who it was. It turned out to be the woman who was closest to her beloved man, Dan Dan. Dan Dan slowly approached the bed and gently asked:

"Are you feeling better?" Yu Mei was taken aback and couldn't say anything until she saw that there was no enmity in Dan Dan's eyes. She said in a low voice,

"A little better."

Dan Dan sat down in the chair next to the bed. The two young and beautiful rivals sat close together for the first time, looking at each other. They both admired the other in their minds at the same time.

'Oh, she is so beautiful. No wonder he…'

'The goddess of the moon has descended to the world…'

'Like the breath-taking beauty, concubine Yang…'

In order to break the ice, Dan Dan described how they first saw how Yu Mei fainted in the square yesterday, and how Zhang Feng had carried her to hospital. Yu Mei also talked about the treatment she had received in the hospital. Dan Dan suddenly seemed to ask, inadvertently,

"Where is he? Was he taking care of you last night?"

Yu Mei's face flushed. "No, no, he slept in the nurse's duty room. Maybe he is not awake yet." Dan Dan was a smart and rational girl. She knew Zhang Feng's emotional entanglement with Yu Mei. She also knew that she could directly interpose between them but she also wanted to remind Yu Mei to face reality, otherwise the result must be that they would both be hurt.

"Li Yumei, I know your love for Zhang Feng but you are destined to be separated due to the class status difference between you. The pressure of society is irresistible."

Yu Mei was silent for a while. Then, as if she had mustered her courage, she said,

"Dan Dan, I know that you are a good girl. You have been looking after and caring for Zhang Feng like his sister for so many years. With a woman's instinct, I also know that you like him, not just in the brother-sister sense. You are not only beautiful but also smart, gentle and virtuous. Well, Zhang Feng and I are destined to be star-crossed lovers. I hope you can take good care of him."

Dan Dan could feel that Yu Mei's concluding words were a little reluctant. She just wanted to comfort Yu Mei a little so she said,

"Yu Mei (she used a cordial address term), no one can predict the future but I really want to be friends with you."

Yu Mei listened, and was very moved. She did not expect Dan Dan to be such an open-minded woman. She took Dan Dan's hand and said,

"Dan Dan, let us be like sisters, okay?"

The two rivals in love turned into friends immediately which was a relief to them both. But neither of them noticed Zhang Feng, who was standing next to them, until they heard the familiar baritone,

"Congratulations to you two sisters!"

The two women who had melted the tension between them naturally threw themselves at the man they both liked.

"You scared me. Why didn't you knock at the door before you came in?" Yu Mei asked.

"You are disturbing us!" Dan Dan also said, half-jokingly.

Seeing that the two women closest to him could get along well, Zhang Feng was naturally very happy, so he said,

"You are both hungry so I am going to buy breakfast, Beijing's deep-fried sticky rice cakes and pancakes with fillings are especially delicious." After that, he turned back and walked out of the ward.

Zhang Feng walked out of the hospital gate to buy breakfast in high spirits. However, he did not notice that a slim figure had been following him for more than ten minutes, all the way from the nurse's duty room to Yu Mei's ward, until he stepped out of the hospital.

Of course, Zhang Feng wouldn't have thought that the woman he hated most would come here. Yes, this woman, who secretly followed Zhang Feng, was Qing Lian. As luck would have it, Qing Lian had caught a bad cold after the Tiananmen Square inspection rally that day. Cai Wenge took care of her assiduously, buying medicine for her and applying a cold towel to her forehead. He even gave her a massage, which annoyed Qing Lian greatly. Finally, the staff of Jili Provincial Office in Beijing suggested that she go to the Dongzhimen Hospital nearby to prevent her condition from worsening. So, early in the morning, she came to the Dongzhimen Hospital. After seeing the doctor, she was given an injection and some medicine. She felt a little better.

When she was about to leave, she suddenly saw a familiar figure in the corridor. Was it Zhang Feng? She felt her heart throbbing. Every time she saw him, her heart throbbed excitedly in spite of herself, even though she kept blaming herself for losing her revolutionary position.

After Zhang Feng entered Yu Mei's ward, Qing Lian had quietly stood at the door and eavesdropped. She got angry while listening. After Zhang Feng went out to buy breakfast, she went back to the ward. She pushed the door open and went in. Regardless of the surprised looks of Yu Mei and Dan Dan, she launched into a loud reproach of Yu Mei.

"Li Yumei! Li Yumei! Shame on you! Now, Chang Zheng and others are looking for you all over the city but you are malingering and hiding in here to meet your lover in private!" She looked at Dan Dan again and said coldly,

"Liu Dan Dan, you are so generous you allow your sweetheart to have a rendezvous with another woman here. Have you learned this from the decadent sexual liberation in the West? Have you discussed this among yourselves? Who would be his wife, and who would be his mistress?"

Dan Dan and Yu Mei were totally provoked by the outrageous accusations of Qing Lian. Yu Mei was so angry that she couldn't utter a single word. Dan Dan calmed down a little and said coldly,

"Liu Qinglian, this is not the place where you can launch excessive criticisms. Put away the trickery of your rebel faction. Chairman Mao said that he who makes no investigation and study, has no right to speak. Yesterday, Yu Mei passed out on the square and her arm was trampled on and broken. We who found her, brought her to hospital. Your rebel faction did not care about her."

Yu Mei also excitedly said, "Yes, if they hadn't got me to hospital in time, I would have been in danger. They also took care of me day and night. Why are you saying these harsh words?"

Qing Lian retorted, "It's weird. The square is so big and there were more than one million people. How could it be that you met each other by chance? Also, it's so close to Jili Provincial Office in Beijing. Why don't you get someone to make a call to inform Chang Zheng or send someone to give him a message? It won't take 20 minutes!"

Hearing this, Yu Mei was really struck dumb as it was she who had not let Zhang Feng send a message. Fortunately, Dan Dan was clever. She said,

"It was already dark when she was brought to the hospital yesterday. The doctor was busy saving her. She woke up in the middle of the night and she was still weak this morning. Everyone was worried and busy as bees. We didn't have time to even think about sending them a message at all. If they are anxious to look for her now, what did they do at the time?"

Yu Mei also helped Dan Dan to reason with Qing Lian. Qing Lian did not show her white feather at all.

"I just heard you three talking and laughing! It seems that there is nothing to worry about and you are not busy at all!"

"You eavesdropped on other people's conversations, really shameless!" Yu Mei and Dan Dan simultaneously rebuked her. The noise was enough to raise the roof.

Zhang Feng bought steaming, deep-fried cakes and Chinese hamburgers at the snack stall outside the hospital and headed back merrily. When he arrived at the hospital, he suddenly heard someone calling him. Looking up, he saw it was Wang Hai and Li He. They had heard from the students who knew Zhang Feng's sister that Zhang Feng and Dan Dan had gone to the hospital. They didn't know what was going on and were worried that something might have happened so they had hurried over too. Zhang Feng knew that Wang Hai was more concerned about Dan Dan and told him what had happened yesterday.

They walked to the ward, saying the Red Guards in Beijing were launching a major campaign as they were besieging and attacking various ministries and commissions, trying to seize capitalist roaders from there. Wang Hai reminded Zhang Feng that if Chang Zheng knew that Yu Mei was here, he would surely be jealous and fly into a rage. Zhang Feng said helplessly that Yu Mei had not told him the address of their temporary residence. Wang Hai said that they were all living in the Jili Provincial Office in Beijing. He could pass on a message. Zhang Feng asked him not to at first. It would be better for Yu Mei to tell them herself.

When they got to the ward, they heard a quarrel taking place inside. They felt very strange. Wang Hai gently pushed the door open. Everyone looked inside and was shocked. They saw that the three beautiful girls were arguing fiercely and excitement and anger had tinted their faces with a rosy colour, making them appear even more beautiful. They hadn't expected that Qing Lian, who was the most annoying to them, would be here. Wang Hai gently closed the door and put a finger on his lips, gesticulating to everyone not to speak. Zhang Feng thought that he had something important to say. However, he said to Zhang Feng and Li He:

"Remember the divination of the old Taoist priest in the north mountain temple to Brother Feng? He said that Brother Feng has a lot of good fortune in love affairs and there would be three females around him. Three flowers on that slip of paper. Look! The plum, the peony and the lotus in the room! The prophecy given by the old Taoist priest is quite accurate!"

Li He also suddenly came to understand, "It really is like this!"

Zhang Feng was annoyed. He was not interested in Wang Hai's words at all.

"How can you tell such a ridiculous story? You see who among them is likely? Nonsense. Help me figure out a way to stop their quarrelling."

Wang Hai said, "Don't worry. See what I do."

The three of them pushed the door open to walk in. Wang Hai was good at being a mediator. He first went to Dan Dan and comforted her.

"Don't be angry. Don't be angry." Then he turned back and said to Qing Lian,

"Commander Liu, (Qing Lian was the deputy commander of their red rebel army.) Nice to meet you. Nice to meet you. We are classmates and come from the same place. We can solve the problem through consultation. It's not worth getting angry."

Qing Lian said with anger, "I'm too busy with the revolutionary rebellion and have no time to poke my nose into their …" She wanted to say, 'dirty affairs', but when she saw Zhang Feng, she stopped short.

Dan Dan said angrily, "A member of the rebellion faction came to the hospital and was so nosy!"

Qing Lian saw that all around her were enemies so she quickly retreated, leaving behind harsh words,

"Wait and see who will settle with you." Then she slammed the door behind her and strode out of the ward.

"Those who refuse to acknowledge their own relatives and friends and poke their noses into others' business are most annoying. Can you tell me whether she has anything to do with this matter?" Zhang Feng asked angrily.

"Jealous!" Wang Hai whispered.

"What? Jealous?" Zhang Feng asked, bewildered.

"It is right, that love letter…" Wang Hai stopped short. Earlier that year, he had secretly put Qing Lian's love letter to Zhang Feng on the wall without telling Zhang Feng, sowing the seed of Qing Lian's grudge against Zhang Feng. Yet Zhang Feng was still in the dark about it. Li He immediately changed the topic. He knew that if Zhang Feng discovered Wang Hai's mischief, he would not spare Wang Hai.

The atmosphere in the room gradually eased. After, they chatted for a while. Zhang Feng asked Wang Hai to send Dan Dan back to their temporary residence. He would be back in the afternoon. When they parted, Wang Hai also pointed to Yu Mei and said to Zhang Feng in a low voice,

"Grasp the forelock of time and get thick with her. That guy (Chang Zheng) may rush over here any minute."

"Get away to your post, commander!" Zhang Feng gave him a punch gently.

Back in the hospital, Yu Mei grabbed Zhang Feng's hand.

"Brother Feng, why is Heaven always acting against us? We don't even get three days." Zhang Feng also sighed and said,

"This might be our fate."

Zhang Feng felt that he had better hit the road as soon as possible. However, Yu Mei wanted him to stay longer, saying that the others would not come so quickly. Finally, Zhang Feng said that he would leave after lunch.

The hospital's meal was not very delicious. Zhang Feng wanted Yu Mei to have a taste of Beijing snacks. He walked out to the street and looked for a restaurant selling Beijing snacks, in the direction of Dongdan. At last, he found one when he had walked quite far. He hurried back in high spirits. Near the hospital, he suddenly remembered that there was a walnut cake that Yu Mei liked in his backpack, so he walked to the duty room first.

While he was opening the door, someone suddenly forced his arms and shoulders behind him. Zhang Feng instinctively used the 'Wild Goose Spreads its Wings' trick that his martial arts master had taught him to break free of the two people behind him. At the same time, he kicked back swiftly at them. He heard the two people behind him screaming and falling to the ground. Zhang Feng turned back and saw the two policemen lying on the ground and standing next to them were Chang Zheng and an official, aged about in his fifties. Zhang Feng thought Chang Zheng would come but he hadn't expected it so soon.

Since Yu Mei had disappeared on the square yesterday, Chang Zheng had been looking for her everywhere. He also regretted that he had been rushing ahead to see Chairman Mao, forgetting to take care of Yu Mei behind him. Yu Mei had not been very well the past few days. However, he had searched various Red Guards' organizations and the local Public Security Bureau and there was no news of Yu Mei. Director Yang of the provincial office in Beijing was the former subordinate of Yu Mei's father and was also very anxious. Near noon, Cai Wenge had suddenly rushed over and said to Chang Zheng,

"There is news! Your GF Li Yumei is not seriously injured and is meeting with her old lover!"

Then he dramatized the situation, telling Chang Zheng that she and Zhang Feng had connived to have a secret meeting at the Dongzhimen Hospital by faking sickness. Qing Lian had seen them when she went to the hospital to see a doctor in the morning. Cai did not tell Chang Zheng that Yu Mei had fainted on the square and that Zhang Feng had taken her to the hospital, as Qing Lian had told him. Instead, he vividly made up dirty things that would anger and provoke Chang Zheng, such as how they were holding each other and kissing.

After Chang Zheng heard this he flew into a rage immediately. He went to find Director Yang right away and they drove to the hospital. He reported the case to the local public security bureau at the same time, saying that someone had kidnapped a woman and brought two policemen to the Dongzhimen Hospital.

"Zhang Feng, you haven't given up your bad intentions and you pester Yu Mei time and again. This time, you dare to kidnap her!" Chang Zheng rebuked Zhang Feng furiously. Zhang Feng helped the two policemen up and said,

"I'm sorry, sir." At the same time, he said to Chang Zheng, "Don't tell a dirty lie. You didn't take care of Li Yumei and she was trampled and injured in the square. It's us who found her and took her to the hospital so that she could recover. Do you still have the face to denounce me?"

The two policemen saw that Zhang Feng was a gentle and handsome young man, very unlike a criminal, so they did not try to control him. The director said to Zhang Feng,

"We can't believe you based only on what you say. We have to investigate to be responsible to Secretary Li." Zhang Feng said,

"Alright. You can just ask Li Yumei." So they went to Yu Mei's ward together. At the door of the ward, Chang Zheng stopped Zhang Feng.

"You can't go in. Yu Mei will not dare to tell the truth in front of you."

"No problem. You can ask her any questions," said Zhang Feng.

Zhang Feng, who stayed outside the door, heard the sound of quarrelling between Yu Mei and Chang Zheng, and Yu Mei seemed to be crying. A few minutes later, Director Yang walked out of the ward and said to Zhang Feng,

"What Li Yumei said is similar to what you said but we have to check with the hospital." Then he went to the director of the Emergency Department.

Zhang Feng sat down on the corridor chair and waited. He heard Yu Mei in the ward who seemed to be clamouring to come out but Chang Zheng and the police advised her not to.

After several minutes, Director Yang returned. He did not speak to Zhang Feng and went straight into the ward. After a few minutes, the door opened and Director Yang and Chang Zheng came out together. He said to Zhang Feng, seriously,

"According to Li Yumei's narrative and our investigation at the hospital, things are basically as you described although there are still many doubts. Anyway, now that Yu Mei has been found, Secretary Li can rest assured. We will not hold you accountable. However, I advise you to keep a good distance from Li Yumei. Don't always harry her like a rogue."

Director Yang's words were really unpleasant and Zhang Feng wanted to argue with him but he thought this was the influence of Chang Zheng. His temper was suppressed. Chang Zheng grew impatient.

"I have already treated you generously. Beat it right now!" Zhang Feng did not want to quarrel with Chang Zheng again. He calmly said to the director,

"Can you allow me to say goodbye to Li Yumei? The doctor told me about some precautions for her recovery."

At this time, Zhang Feng could hear Yu Mei crying in the ward, wanting to talk to Zhang Feng. Director Yang looked at Chang Zheng and seemed to ask for his opinion. However, Chang Zheng pulled a long face and said coldly,

"I don't think it is necessary."

In order to maintain his dignity and not bow his head to Chang Zheng and his party, Zhang Feng turned away and left. He tried hard to repress his tears and wondered why fate was always playing tricks on them. It would have been a luxury for poor Yu Mei to spend a few days in peace with her darling in this political storm.

In front of the guesthouse of the Ministry of the Eighth Machine Building Industry, Wang Hai, Li He and Xu Jianguo and Li Li were bidding farewell to Zhang Feng, Dan Dan and Zhang Lin. Wang Hai chatted with Dan Dan for a while and was reluctant to part with her. He turned back and consoled Zhang Feng,

"Elder brother, this is a good opportunity to travel across the motherland. You can experience both revolution and tourism at the same time. There will be no such opportunity in the future."

Zhang Feng knew that the revolutionary tour of the Red Guards nationwide at this time was organized by Chairman Mao and the Central Cultural Revolution Group, so all localities and organizations would give it the green light. Transportation, accommodation and even eating were free of charge. Wang Hai and his group had already planned to visit Shanghai, Guangzhou,

Xi'an and other large cities in central, southern and western China. For most Chinese, this was a chance to experience luxury which they had never had in their lifetime. In those days, only those who ran errands had the opportunity to travel to other places.

However, Zhang Feng had already been disheartened by this tour and Yu Mei's accident. His personal future and the country's future were both uncertain. He had lost interest in the revolutionary tour. He was concerned about his parents and Dan Dan's mother, so he decided to return to Jili. Dan Dan was certainly willing to accompany him, even though Wang Hai tried to persuade her to continue the revolutionary tour with them. His sister was rather more willing to go with Wang Hai but both Zhang Feng and Wang Hai thought she was too young and had to be taken care of, so she had to go back with Zhang Feng.

Sitting on the bus bound for the train station and looking at the crazy Red Guards' team at the roadside, holding up red flags and shouting slogans to storm schools, universities, organizations, government departments and factories, to seize capitalist roaders and class enemies, Zhang Feng could not help but recall Hitler's Schutzstaffel but he immediately reminded himself that it was too dangerous to think like that. But could all this destruction and persecution in the name of revolution really make society better? From Dan Dan's eyes, he also saw the same confusion. The afterglow of the setting sun shrouded the Forbidden City, reminiscent of the glory of this ancient empire, but no one would know for sure in which direction the current People's Republic would move.

PART IV

January Storm

CHAPTER I

To Find the Biggest Capitalist Roader out

In the blink of an eye, the New Year was over and millions of Red Guards ended their revolutionary tours. They returned to their hometowns and started to attack the local party and government, and even the military, on a large scale, rebelling and taking over power. It was Chairman Mao who called on them to down all capitalist establishments and restore power to the hands of the proletarian revolutionaries.

The rebel faction in Jili City also began to attack the party and government organizations at all levels in the province; they all wanted to share a piece of power after power was regained. Therefore, the rebel organizations slightly relaxed the control of the old rightists such as Zhang Feng's father and the reactionary academic authorities, who were already 'dead tigers' anyway. His parents could return home every night now but during the day, they still had to go to the class opened by the university rebels.

In the low and shabby civic district of North Bank, Zhang Feng was a guest with Li He in Wang Hai's house. They had been there several times before. Wang Hai's father, a man of honesty and kindness, was an old worker in a car factory. His mother worked in a textile factory and she was a kind and virtuous working woman. Whenever Zhang Feng came, they always took out the best things in the house to entertain him.

At that time, the living standards of ordinary Chinese families were unfavorable and the food supply was measured. Every person got only 100 ml of cooking oil and 500 grams of pork per month. Foods, like sugar and milk, were difficult to buy. Northeast China was extremely cold in winter, and the only vegetables were cabbage, radishes and potatoes stored in the autumn. The days were very tough at that time but people seldom complained because they believed in the party and the government, thinking that the future would be better.

Whilst Zhang Feng was sitting and talking with them in a dim room, a nice smell greeted him suddenly. He knew that Wang Hai's mother was cooking. He ran into the kitchen and saw that Wang Hai's mother was making crisp fried pork. The meat must have been the food that they had prepared for the Spring Festival.

"Aunt, you can't take the New Year's things out to entertain me! If so, you will have no meat to eat in the New Year!"

"Just sit down and don't worry. We still have some. Xiao Hai's father bought some in the free market."

Wang Hai's mother persuaded Zhang Feng just as she used to do. After the famine years in the early 1960s, the government relaxed control of the farmers' market so that farmers could sell their own vegetables, poultry and livestock at the farmers' free market in the city but citizens with low incomes still could not afford it.

After eating, Zhang Feng took a bus home. He got off on the South Bank Bridge especially, to see the beauty of the river in winter. The Songhua River flowed down from the bustling dam to the urban area of Jili City, only 10 kilometers away. In winter, it did not freeze and the surging, foggy river flowed through the city. In extreme cold weather, the mist and water vapour condensed in the branches of the trees, making granular ice, also called rime. These crystal and white icicles shook slightly in the wind, presenting a beautiful silver-white world of ice and snow. However, the turbulent political situation prevented people from enjoying such natural beauty so there were very few tourists by the river.

At the thought of the poverty of Wang Hai's family, compared with the luxury of Yu Mei's family, Zhang Feng could understand why some people were dissatisfied with the party and government senior officers and even wanted to rebel. Perhaps Chairman Mao had really witnessed corruption within the party and wanted to mobilize the masses to strike them down or he wanted to clear his political opponents by the power of the Red Guards and the masses, especially these old officers. They had forced him to step down after the failure of the Great Leap Forward, including Liu Shaoqi who had succeeded him. Zhang Feng had overheard this in a private conversation between his father and some of his best friends who were professors. However, what Zhang Feng could not understand was that these downed people were Chairman Mao's former comrades. Just forget it; history would make everything clear eventually.

The snow-white icicles before him reminded him of the crystal-clear eyes of Yu Mei. 'She must be scared every day,'

Zhang Feng thought. Wang Hai and Li He told him that the rebels in the provincial capital had begun planning to find and publicly criticize Yu Mei's father, Li Jianguo, secretary of the provincial party committee. It would be their greatest victory to find him in that he would be the biggest capitalist roader in the province. Although Li Jianguo had broken his relationship with Yu Mei, Zhang Feng still did not want Yu Mei to be sad about that. Since the beginning of the Cultural Revolution, or even since the anti-rightist campaign in 1957, thousands of people had been implicated by their parents. Treading on the thick snow, Zhang Feng slowly walked towards his home.

These days, Li Jianguo always felt uneasy. More and more party and government leaders from central to local government had been downed by the Red Guards and the rebel faction as capitalist roaders, including several of his former leaders in central government. But now, they couldn't protect themselves. He was so nervous that he phoned Zhao Wu, his old comrade-in-arms, and also the provincial military commander, inviting him to his home for tea and a chat.

Commander Zhao, Chang Zheng's father, was Secretary Li's old classmate at Sun Yat-Sen University. After graduation, they had gone to Yanan to participate in the revolution. Li Jianguo had worked politically while Zhao Wu had joined the army and become a commander. Coincidentally, after liberation, they had all been transferred to the Northeast to work. One became the provincial party secretary, and the other, the provincial military commander. Naturally, there was a good connection between the two families. That was why Chang Zheng regarded Yu Mei as his sister and even took it for granted that Yu Mei was his girlfriend. This was also acquiesced to by both of their families. Wasn't it better to turn friends into relatives?

With a tall, burly frame, honest and frank Zhao Wu also retained his military bearing in uniform. He walked into the living room, shaking hands with Li Jianguo and then sitting on the sofa.

"Lao Li, have you been feeling nervous?" He got straight to the point because he knew that Li Jianguo had not just asked him for tea.

"Yeah, Lao Zhao, the current situation is really unpredictable. The revolution has been continuing for so many years, and this time, it is my turn," Li Jianguo replied.

They were both old comrades-in-arms and friends so they could speak their minds to each other.

"I know that Jiang Qing and the Cultural Revolution Group want to down all the old officers and substitute them with people on their side. However, I don't understand why Chairman Mao does not get involved in this," Zhao Wu said.

Li Jianguo pondered for a while and said,

"Lao Zhao, you have been in the army for so long and may be unfamiliar with the factional struggle within the party. After the failure of the Great Leap Forward, Chairman Mao handed over the party and government power to Chairman Liu Shaoqi and has remained in the background. Now the country has two top leaders but a country can only have one top leader. You see that the downed old officers mostly worked in the White Party (the organization established by the Communist Party of China in the area under the control of Kuomintang was called the White Party.) They were the people on Liu Shaoqi's side. So I will be downed sooner or later."

Zhao Wu thought for a moment and said,

"It seems that this is really the case. I am under the leadership of Peng (Peng Dehuai, strategist and politician, Marshal of the People's Republic of China,) so I also need to be careful."

Li Jianguo said again,

"Du Zhong Qing, the special commissioner of the Cultural Revolution Group in the provincial party committee, who we all call 'the man in black', has kept on stirring up trouble and has let the rebel faction continue to dig out the biggest capitalist roader in the province. Is it obvious that they want to down me. There was already a big character poster with this information, which I heard about from my secretary. I assumed that the time was closing in for me being taken out and publicly criticized. However, my conscience is clear."

He added,

"And I have devoted myself to the revolution and never done anything against the party or socialism, as well as anything related to capitalism. If they impose these accusations on me, I will never accept them."

Finally, he said,

"Lao Zhao, if I am downed, you must not contact me anymore and I don't want you to get involved. And, if possible, please take care of my family, especially Yu Mei, who is of great beauty and simplicity."

Zhao Wu took Li Jianguo's hand and said,

"Lao Li, please feel assured that as long as I have not been downed, I will try my best to help you and your family."

On parting, they held each other's hand tightly; it looked like the farewell scene of life and death during the War of Liberation. Strangely, why was it happening in peacetime?

In winter, the sky got dark early in the River City. The road was filled with car horns and the crunching sound of pedestrians on the thick snow. Zhang Feng's family were preparing for dinner and her mother, Hu Yun, had made an extra dish of pork slices with sauerkraut because of Dan Dan's arrival. When everyone was sitting around the dining table, the loudspeaker of the Red Guards' radio car suddenly came from the road.

"The Red Guards' rebel friends and the revolutionary masses! Tonight, there will be a public condemnation conference at People's Square at 7 o'clock, for Li Jianguo, the biggest capitalist roader in our province. This is a great victory for Chairman Mao's revolutionary line. Down the stubborn capitalist roader, Li Jianguo! He will either surrender or be destroyed by us!"

What? Zhang Feng and his father stood up at the same time.

"Is Li Jianguo also downed?" they shouted together.

Zhang Feng put on his coat and cotton hat and was ready to go.

Dan Dan said,

"I will go with Xiao Feng."

His mom told them to come back as soon as possible.

Zhang Feng and Dan Dan soon arrived at People's Square by bus. The square was ablaze with light and was already crowded with people. On the north side of the square, there was an improvised platform on which there were some tables and chairs. Heads of various rebel faction groups sat at the table. Zhang Feng and Dan Dan went to the side of the table so that they could see Cai Wenge, Qing Lian and that man in black were sitting on the side of the Second Headquarters. Chang Zheng did not sit inside while Wang Hai and Xu Jianguo sat on the side of the Jili Commune.

For a while, the melody of a song (Sailing the Seas Depends on the Helmsman) came from the loudspeaker. Then, one of the heads of the provincial party rebel faction groups announced the start of the conference. He said that today was the day when Jili's Cultural Revolution achieved great victories. Under the guidance of Chairman Mao's revolutionary line and the proper leadership of the Central Cultural Revolution Group, Li Jianguo, the biggest capitalist roader in the province, had finally been found out.

"Put up Li Jianguo, the obstinate capitalist roader," he then said.

Cai Wenge and the man in black stood up and took the lead in yelling the slogan: 'Down Li Jianguo'. Then two Red Guards bought Li Jianguo onto the stage. There was a big sign on his chest which said: 'Li Jianguo, traitor, capitalist roader'. The two red guards held his head and let him bend down and plead guilty to the revolutionary masses. However, every time Li Jianguo straightened up, he was pressed and appealed against the accusations imposed on him. At this moment, because of his courage to stand on his dignity, Zhang Feng felt great admiration for Li. Although Zhang Feng did not like these high-ranking officials because they enjoyed their prosperous life, while the workers and peasants who fought for the Communist Party suffered poverty. Moreover, Li had also ruthlessly broken his relationship with Yu Mei.

However, just like the other people with a conscience, Zhang Feng would never accept personal insults against people and violent acts in the name of the Cultural Revolution. People were dignified. If Li really was guilty of something, he would be punished according to party discipline and state laws instead of in such an insulting way.

Special commissioner Du Zhongqing, who was the man in black, walked on stage. He said with a sneer,

"Li Jianguo, although you are so obstinate and have concealed yourself so well, you see that thousands of the revolutionary masses in Jili Province will not let you go. You have practiced for more than a decade in compliance with Liu Shaoqi's bourgeois reactionary line, combined with your traitorous crimes. If you don't bend your head and plead guilty, you will have no choice but to be punished."

Then, the scene was filled with shouts of downing and condemning Li Jianguo. A group of Red Guards came up and hit and kicked Li Jianguo then they held his head and made him kneel on the ground, bowing his head, to plead guilty.

Zhang Feng couldn't stand any more. He said to Dan Dan, "Let's go."

"This is too much," Dan Dan whispered. They left the crowd and walked to the bus stop.

CHAPTER II

On the Edge of the Cliff

When Zhang Feng came home, his father asked in detail about the public condemnation conference. At first, he was very excited but after hearing that Li Jianguo had suffered torture and violence, a sense of sympathy appeared in his eyes. Zhang Feng had never told his parents about him and Yu Mei, as his father always taught him that a man should put his career first. Since Zhang Feng was less than 18 years old, he should not fall in love at such an early age. Therefore, his father didn't know the reason why Zhang Feng was concerned with the fall of Li Jianguo.

That night, Zhang Feng tossed and turned restlessly, constantly thinking about Yu Mei's situation and whether she could bear it or not. To his surprise, Yu Mei was also now the child of a counter-revolutionary family. Their status was equal at this time. He was only in pain for the mental shock suffered by Yu Mei.

The next day, when he got up early in the morning, Zhang Feng made an excuse to his family that he wanted to visit his martial arts master in North Mountain. In fact, he was taking a risk to go to Yu Mei's house to comfort and encourage her.

Along the path of South Bank Park, which he was familiar with, he went past the residential district of senior officials inhabited by provincial and municipal leaders. This road recalled sweet memories of his love for Yu Mei. The pity was, that good times were always brief.

When nearing Yu Mei's house, a noise came to Zhang Feng's ears. A truck had stopped in front of the building and some people, dressed like workers, were unloading some old furniture from a truck. This made Zhang Feng feel quite strange. He came forward and asked a young man,

"Excuse me, is secretary Li still living here?"

The young man stared at him and said,

"Who is secretary Li? He is a capitalist roader right now and has no right to live in such a good house. Now, it is the right of our working class to enjoy it."

Zhang Feng went blank for a time and asked,

"Do you know where they moved?"

The guy wanted to know the relationship between them.

"Why are you asking so much? I don't know where they moved. The head of our organization said that these capitalist roaders should experience the taste of the slums."

After saying that, he continued to move the furniture. Zhang Feng knew that, after the start of the Cultural Revolution, many of the authorities who had fallen from power: the academics and the literary and artistic celebrities, were driven from their houses to a very poor place, as a punishment. But where had Yu Mei moved to?

Zhang Feng left the residential district of senior officials anxiously. He passed the bridge and took a bus to North Mountain. Since protecting the Taoist Temple together with master Hai Jing last time, he hadn't visited for several months. The whole mountain was covered with snow. Those hundred-year-old pines were covered with glittering and translucent rime, shimmering in the sunlight. Zhang Feng met the master in the backyard of the temple. Only a few months had passed but the master seemed to be haggard.

He made some tea for Zhang Feng and asked about the situation of Zhang Feng's family. The master asked about Dan Dan's mother and explained that she used to go to the temple to pray. So, Zhang Feng described her experiences, from the suicide attempt with Dan Dan to being sent to the hospital and finally, being saved. In addition, Zhang Feng said,

"I still don't know who sent me the letter which let me save them."

"It may have been a neighbour," the master replied.

The master changed the topic immediately and began to talk about the present situation of the Cultural Revolution. Zhang Feng told the master that Li Jianguo had been overthrown. The master said,

"He deserves this. In the past, he made many people suffer and made the members of their families disperse and sometimes die. In the Anti-Rightist Movement in 1957, he was the propaganda chief of the Provincial Party Committee and caught thousands of counter-revolutionaries. Many young rightists were sent to the Great Northern Wilderness (in Northeast China) to reform through labour and suffered a lot of inhumane torments. Actually, these so-called rightists were all patriots; what they did was only to give some suggestions to the party and the government."

"Master, since you are a Taoist monk, how can you know so many things?" asked Zhang Feng.

The master faltered,

"I…I hear from others."

After knowing all these things, Zhang Feng finally realized why his father had been so excited when hearing about the fall of Li Jianguo. Maybe there were some links between his father's identity as a rightist and Li Jianguo. Since the master did not show any sympathy towards Li, Zhang Feng did not mention his torture by the Red Guards and the matters related to Yu Mei.

Zhang Feng had lunch with the master. The food in the temple was as simple as that of ordinary citizens, that is, steamed bread of corn and cabbage radish soup. After lunch, Zhang Feng did kung fu with the master for several hours. Since the start of the Cultural Revolution, normal life had been disrupted. Zhang Feng hadn't practised kung fu seriously for several months. Near 4:00 pm, the sun began to sink. Zhang Feng said good-bye to the master and went back home.

The master entreated him to stay and said,

"Just talk for a few minutes. We seldom get a chance to meet."

They walked to the open area behind the temple in which there were thick pines and old trees that reached into the sky. Approaching the pine forest, there was a cliff about 100 meters high with the fast-flowing Songhua River below it. Standing on the edge of the cliff, the whole South Bank District and the distant mountains could be seen. Staring at the pine forest, the master's face became serious. He heaved a sigh and said,

"The landscape is so beautiful but how many people took their own lives in there and died?"

The master told Zhang Feng that since the beginning of the Cultural Revolution, a lot of people had jumped from this spot into the river. The master once saved several suicidal people who were regarded as part of the Five Black Categories (a general designation of the landlord, the rich peasant, counter-revolutionary, bad element and rightist) who tried to commit suicide after the insults and torments they bore. While they were talking, Zhang Feng suddenly saw a slowly moving figure in the woods. Normally, no one would go there to enjoy the scenery on such a cold day. Zhang Feng said to the master,

"Master, is that man intending to commit suicide?"

The master looked for a while and answered,

"It seems that he might commit suicide. Generally, a man who wants to commit suicide would wander back and forth. They will have a fierce struggle in their hearts: to be or not to be."

"Let's go and dissuade him," Zhang Feng said.

They walked quickly into the forest and followed the man secretly. He was almost near the edge of the cliff. He leaned on a tree every few steps, sighing and talking to himself. Zhang Feng and the master couldn't hear clearly what he was saying, but just vaguely heard that he had been treated unjustly. He had been working for the party and did as the party said. It seemed that he had also said some kind of goodbye to his family.

Suddenly, Zhang Feng realized that the voice and the figure of the man were familiar. There was no doubt that this man intended to take his own life. When the man finally reached the edge of the cliff and was ready to jump, with a quick movement, the master acted just like a carp jumping in water. He hugged the man's waist and they rolled down together in the snow. Zhang Feng was about to go and help the master but, unexpectedly,

Zhang Feng saw that after looking at the man's face, the master suddenly stood up and said to the man,

"Go to hell! How many people have you killed! You deserve this!"

The man slowly looked up at the master and murmured,

"Yes, I used to harm other people, but right now, I am harmed by others. I now realize that those who were harmed by me were innocents. I do deserve to die!"

After saying that, the man struggled up to the cliff edge and insisted on jumping down. Zhang Feng felt strange about why the master had changed his attitude. Generally, the master would always tell him that Taoism cherished life, saved lives and would not kill life. As Zhang Feng had been influenced by his father's belief of Confucian Benevolence since he was young, Zhang Feng had been taught to give love to others. Thus, he could not leave somebody in the lurch. At the moment when the man climbed to the edge of the cliff and was going to jump down, with no hesitation and with a quick step, Zhang Feng caught the man's legs. The man struggled as he shouted and tried to get free of Zhang Feng's hands but he had no strength to stop Zhang Feng pulling him back.

After pulling him back more than 10 meters, Zhang Feng thought it was safe and stopped. He was eager to see who the man was and why the master hated him. He said,

"Sorry, did I hurt you?" while turning over the man's body. There was snow on the man's face and body. Zhang Feng cleared the snow from the body of the man with his gloves, and carefully removed the snow from the man's face.

"Oh, it's you! Uncle Li! No… Secretary Li!"

To his surprise, the man who wanted to commit suicide was the father of Yu Mei, Li Jianguo. The man was pale and gaunt and his face was still covered in blood. Li Jianguo seemed to recognize Zhang Feng too, with embarrassment, sadness and despair in his face. At that point, the master went back. He had been calm. He said to Li Jianguo,

"You should thank this young man. It is he who saved your life. I wish you could confess your sins. For your family, you should live. Maybe you are innocent this time. What you did was in accordance with the directives of the leadership. History is the best judge. If you are innocent, your reputation will be cleared one day. Don't forget those who were harmed by you. If it is possible, please prove that they were innocent too."

Li Jianguo nodded powerlessly. Zhang Feng helped Li Jianguo up and said,

"Uncle Li, let me send you back. Yu Mei…"

He was going to say that Yu Mei would be so worried about Li but he never dared to say it at the thought of Li Jianguo's warning. Perhaps, with the thought of his daughter and his family, Li Jianguo gained the courage to live. He walked slowly down the hill with one of his arms supported by Zhang Feng.

On the way down the mountain, Li Jianguo kept thanking Zhang Feng for saving his life and apologized for his past attitude towards Zhang Feng and Yu Mei's relationship. Of course, he couldn't disapprove of them right now because the situation had changed. He was no longer the Secretary of the Provincial Party Committee but the overthrown capitalist roader and Yu Mei was no longer the daughter of a senior official but the daughter of a capitalist roader. In this situation, Zhang Feng just said generously that it was all in the past. As long as he, Yu Mei and his family could live peacefully and get through the difficulty, Zhang Feng would feel relieved.

With tears in his eyes, Li murmured,

"What a nice boy."

Zhang Feng asked Li Jianguo about where he lived now. He had already been to Li's house and knew that they had moved away. Li Jianguo sighed and said that they had been forced to move to a small house in the Erdao River District of the North Bank area yesterday. Zhang Feng knew that was a slum area, no gas, no heating and very poor conditions. He felt heavy hearted when he realized that Yu Mei would be living in such a hard environment. However, what pleased him was that he could now see Yu Mei again. In order not to attract attention, Zhang Feng put his mask on Li Jianguo and they exchanged coats. They took the bus all the way to the North Bank area. Fortunately, they hadn't been noticed by anyone else.

Walking through a section of small, shabby and little houses, they finally came to an adobe house of yellow mud, where the iron smokestack, extending through the inside to the outside of the house, was creating a plume of smoke. Walking closer to the door, they could hear a woman crying inside. Zhang Feng and Li Jianguo pushed the door open.

What they saw was Li's wife, Song Lihua, sitting near the cooking bench, tending the fire and crying. Yu Mei's younger brother, Li Xiaogang, was sitting on the side stool and looked stunned. There was old furniture and simply heated brick beds in the bedrooms on both sides. There was no beautiful villa, no deluxe living room, kitchen or bedroom, no heating system, coal, gas or convenient lavatory, no special supply of rice, wheat flour, fish, meat and eggs, no secretaries, guards and no nannies. Zhang Feng was shocked by the strong contrast between the past situation in his memory and the scene in front of him.

Song Lihua had never seen Zhang Feng before and was trying to ask who Zhang Feng was looking for, when, suddenly, she saw Li Jianguo who was standing behind Zhang Feng. She stood up at once and said,

"Jian Guo! You came back in the end! We were worried about you. Why do you want to take your own life? We have faced a storm of shots and shells and lived till now. What kind of things can't we get over? Since you are innocent, the party will prove it for you."

After that, she hugged Li Jianguo and cried. It was very obvious that they had read Li's last words and knew that Li was going to commit suicide.

Li patted his wife's shoulder and said,

"Well… I would not do such a stupid thing again. I have understood that. The most serious situation is to be in jail. As long as you are all right, there is nothing for me to worry about." Then, he pointed to Zhang Feng and said,

"Thank you for saving me and encouraging me to live." Song Lihua and Li Xiaogang knelt down to Zhang Feng immediately to thank him for saving Li's life but Zhang Feng was a little anxious and asked,

"Where is Yu Mei? Where has she gone?"

Li Jianguo's wife sighed and said,

"She went to find her father. Although we persuaded her that the city was so large it would be too difficult to find him. But Yu Mei insisted on finding her father. We could not stop her because there was no other way to find him; even going to the police was of no use. The death of a capitalist roader who cut himself off from the public… no one would take it seriously."

On hearing this, Zhang Feng immediately said,

"I am going to find her."

Then, he rushed out of the door.

CHAPTER III

I am Politically Blacker than You

Where could he find Yu Mei? Li Jianguo had not mentioned the place where he wanted to commit suicide in his last words. Zhang Feng was burning with anxiety and had a sense of premonition. Yu Mei could not have found her father, so if she had taken things too hard when she felt desperate… What should he do?

It suddenly occurred to Zhang Feng that many people who cared little for their lives since the Cultural Revolution committed suicide by drowning themselves in rivers. Perhaps, Yu Mei had gone to the river to find her father. Zhang Feng thought of this and quickly returned home. He borrowed a bicycle from his neighbors, so he could check the miles of riverside as quickly as possible.

Riding out of the university campus gates, he met Dan Dan who walked into him head-on. She was wearing a white cotton jacket with her face frozen like a blooming peony. Dan Dan asked Zhang Feng where he was going in such a hurry. Zhang Feng briefly told her that Li Jianguo had attempted suicide and Yu Mei couldn't be found. Now, he was going to find her and was worried that something bad had happened to her.

Dan Dan understood and said,

"Go ahead or it will be dark soon."

Zhang Feng rode across the South Bank Bridge quickly and searched along the riverside. At first, he rode towards the east for over 40 minutes but he did not find Yu Mei. Then he turned around and searched the west. Another hour passed. The sky had already got dark but there was still no sign of Yu Mei. Zhang Feng was dripping with sweat through worrying and had to ride back again.

At this point, the street lights of the river embankment were already lit. Lights reflected on the crystal tree icicles, which reflected on the river and were covered with moonlight. This scene was full of dreamy colours. However, it was not the time to recall romantic times with Yu Mei; it might be a moment of life or death.

He had already ridden to the South Bank Bridge. Suddenly, he thought that Yu Mei might be on the riverside where they had dated with each other in the summer. He crossed the bridge quickly and rode along the path, under the bridge to the beach where they had dated.

When he vaguely saw the big poplar tree, there, indeed, was a shadow on the riverside in the moonlight. He wanted to call Yu Mei's name but was afraid of making a mistake. He lay down the bicycle and walked to the shadow. On edging closer, he could see that it might be a girl from the slim figure. Moving much closer, he was quite sure that it was Yu Mei. He was overjoyed and heaved a sigh of relief.

He was about to call her when he suddenly heard Yu Mei crying,

"Dad, why are you so heartless? You committed suicide without thinking about the impact on us and what should we do next? There is no hope and everything has been destroyed, so let me die with you. If so, you will feel no loneliness in the underworld. Mom and my younger brother can support each other. Life is no longer pleasing to me…"

She suddenly stopped and muttered,

"Brother Feng, I still yearn for your love but now it is impossible – I am not the child of a high ranking official but the child of the biggest capitalist roader, and the bitch everyone avoids. I am not worthy of you. If there were an afterlife, I would reincarnate into a Red family (The family, whose members contributed to the Chinese revolutionary cause, was called the Red Family.) and come back to you!"

After she said these words, sobs choked her speech. She took off her coat and walked into the river. Zhang Feng couldn't wait anymore. He rushed over and hugged Yu Mei. Yu Mei shouted while struggling,

"Little demons, let me go! I am going to chase my father!"

She had obviously lost her mind and believed that she had already reached the gates of hell. Zhang Feng hugged her while patting her head gently. Then he whispered,

"Yu Mei, you look at me. I am Zhang Feng!"

Yu Mei tried to open her eyes and muttered,

"Brother Feng, is that you? Why are you here? Are you going to walk me to my doom? Where is my dad? I have to chase him."

Zhang Feng raised his voice and said,

"Yu Mei, you are still alive! So is your father! I have come to bring you back."

"You lie to me! My father is dead, leaving us alone."

Then she held Zhang Feng and burst into tears. Zhang Feng picked up her coat to wrap round her body. He carried her to the big poplar tree, sitting on one thick branch and holding her in his arms. He rocked his body gently and comforted her as if he were hushing a baby to sleep. A few minutes later, she stopped crying and became calm. She slowly opened her eyes and looked at Zhang Feng, saying weakly,

"Brother Feng, is it really you? Am I dreaming? Where am I?"

"No, Yu Mei, this is not a dream. It is real. Your father is still alive and has already gone home. It's me who sent him home."

"Really? Great! Let's go home quickly!" Yu Mei said as she tried to stand up, but she was too weak to do that.

Zhang Feng immediately lifted her up, letting her sit on the back of the bicycle. Then, he pushed the bike towards the bridge.

It was so late that there was no bus. Taking Yu Mei, Zhang Feng rode directly to Yu Mei's house, a dilapidated and shabby hut in the Erdao River District. As soon as they entered the house, Yu Mei's father, mother and younger brother expressed a sense of relief. Yu Mei suddenly threw herself into her father's arms and cried. The whole family cried on each other's shoulders. Zhang Feng didn't want to bother them and wanted to leave quietly. However, he felt the extreme coldness in the room all of a sudden and found no fire in the iron stove. He realized that they did not know how to use the stove and the heated brick beds, which were only used in ordinary, poorer families. Although Zhang Feng's family lived in a house built by the Japanese and there were both heating and gas, he learned how to use them in Wang Hai's family.

He filled the stove with coals and firewood and the fire flamed brightly in the stove after a while. Subsequently, the heated brick beds got warm. Yu Mei's family sat together, speaking to and comforting each other for a while as if there were no Zhang Feng present; he was busy at the side. Instantly, Li Jianguo realized that they seemed to have ignored Zhang Feng, so he spoke to him immediately.

"Xiao Feng, don't bother and come over here," he said to the whole family while patting Zhang Feng's shoulder.

"Thank you Xiao Feng for saving me and Xiao Mei. You are the saviour of our family!"

Zhang Feng said,

"Uncle Li, don't say this. It is a coincidence. Since the beginning of the Cultural Revolution, it has been really miserable and painful to witness so many people die without reason. People's lives are the most valuable things in this earthly world. We can only mourn for those who have died, but those who are still alive should cherish their lives."

Li Jianguo said,

"Xiao Feng is right and we are alive. As to rights and wrongs, just leave them to people and history to make comment."

Zhang Feng was about to say goodbye when he saw the empty pots and bowls on the stove. Might they not have eaten yet? He thought that they probably did not know how to cook without a chef and a kitchen. He asked if Yu Mei's mother had cooked. She was embarrassed to say that she did not know how to light the stove and that there was no food to cook. Zhang Feng fumbled in the small cupboard and found only a small bag of cornmeal and some cabbage. He remembered that, in the famine of 7 or 8 years ago, his mother had often made corn paste for them, so he had learned how to make it. Nowadays, only the poorer people still ate this. Senior officials had a special supply of rice, flour, chicken, fish, meat and eggs, so they never ate such food.

Having lit the stove and found a pot, he began to make corn paste. He asked Yu Mei to wash some cabbage leaves. After 10 minutes, a pot of steaming corn paste was ready. Zhang Feng put some leaves, soy sauce and a few drops of chili oil into it and said,

"Uncle and aunt, you may never have eaten such a plain and unsavoury thing before, but there is no alternative as we have nothing else. We only have this to eat."

Unexpectedly, the whole family almost gorged on the pot of corn paste in a short time and said that it was really delicious. Zhang Feng knew that it was not because the food was really tasty but they were so hungry and might not have eaten for one, or even two days.

Seeing the mess in the house, Zhang Feng helped Yu Mei to tidy up roughly. At this point, an envelope fell from the table and a roll of paper fell out. When Zhang Feng picked it up, the paper roll unfolded. At the sight of it, he was shocked. It turned out that it was the picture of a dancing lady by a river in spring, drawn by him on the day he met Yu Mei on the river bank. Yu Mei also saw it at the same time.

Zhang Feng said,

"It's so strange. I remember that this painting was burned by Cai Wenge and other Red Guards when they searched my house and confiscated it with other books."

"I took it out of the fire," Yu Mei said awkwardly.

Zhang Feng understood. Even though they had broken up then, Yu Mei still loved him.

Zhang Feng said,

"Thanks."

Yu Mei blushed and said,

"Brother Feng, could you please let me keep it?"

"Of course," Zhang Feng replied.

Zhang Feng said goodbye to them all and returned home. When he arrived, it was already midnight. He really felt exhausted when he lay down.

The next morning, Zhang Feng's father asked him the reason why he had come back so late last night. Zhang Feng gave his father a full account of how he had saved Li Jianguo yesterday. His father was surprised at first when he heard it, and then he was silent for a while.

"Is there really such a thing as coincidence?" he asked himself.

Then he said to Zhang Feng slowly and impressively,

"It is reasonable to say that he used to take the extreme-left route and killed many people. Even death will not expiate all his crimes. Especially in the time of anti-rightists in 1957, he was the Provincial Party Committee propaganda minister and in charge of anti-rightist work. He caught more than 10,000 rightists in a short time. Although this campaign was launched by the Party Central Committee and Mao Zedong, he and other local officials are also to blame. You know, I was the big rightist he named. He accused me of attacking the party's policy on literacy education; in fact, I just gave the party and the government some advice."

Having heard his father's words, Zhang Feng was shocked. Li Jianguo was his father's enemy. He had wanted to tell his father about him and Yu Mei.

His father continued,

"Relatively speaking, I just had some minor penalties, including expulsion from teaching, transference to work in the library and lower wages. Nevertheless, many young rightists were sent to the Great Northern Wilderness (in northeast China) for labour-reform. Many people were exhausted and starved to death there. Do you know that Dan Dan's father was sent there and that he was shot dead when he tried to escape? Alas, he was my best postgraduate."

Zhang Feng felt startled again: what? Dan Dan's father was also a rightist? And he was persecuted to death? Dan Dan had never mentioned this before. Zhang Feng felt a bit sad. Yu Mei's father had turned out to be the blood enemy of his relatives. He suddenly realized that Master Hai Jing also seemed to have a grudge against Li Jianguo. Perhaps, he shouldn't have saved him.

His father spoke again,

"Since 1957, no one has dared to advise the Communist Party. China's politics have been dominated by the Communist Party and the people have no democratic rights. The Cultural Revolution seems to be the party's internal cleansing of Stalinist style. Some people have greater rights and even want the country to be their personal possession. There is no democracy within the party. Therefore, Li Jianguo also became a victim of that time. I hope that he can put himself in others' shoes and repent of his past crimes, making himself a clear-minded person politically. Only when he can admit to what is wrong will he find the right way to political development. Kid, you saved him and you did the right thing. Tolerance, love and sympathy are the traditions of our Chinese Confucianism, while hatred and obscenity can only make our society more divided."

After a while, he went on,

"We can't kick a person when they're down or take pleasure in others' misfortune. Instead, we should help them so that they will appreciate us for the rest of their lives. Well, if you see Li Jianguo again, please say hello and send my best wishes to him."

Having heard his father's words, Zhang Feng was relieved otherwise, he would not dare to go to Yu Mei's house again.

The following morning, Zhang Feng went to find Dan Dan first. He always regarded her as his elder sister and was used to talking with her when he had something to resolve. Zhang Feng told her what had happened yesterday and told her about the plight of Yu Mei's family. On hearing this, Dan Dan also sympathized with the suffering of Yu Mei's family so she went to Yu Mei's house with Zhang Feng to see if Yu Mei's family needed any help.

As they edged nearer to Yu Mei's house, they suddenly heard a loud noise. When they came closer, it turned out that a group of teenagers was bullying Yu Mei's younger brother, Li Xiaogang, who had just returned from outside.

The group of children shouted,

"Pup of capitalist roader, the pup of capitalist roader, pup of capitalist roader…" while throwing stones and rubbish at him.

Zhang Feng rushed over and dispelled this group of children. He took the boy and Dan Dan into the house. There was only Yu Mei sitting alone there. On seeing Zhang Feng and Dan Dan coming in together, she got depressed. She managed to stand up and said,

"You have come. Thank you for coming to see me."

Zhang Feng asked why her father and mother were not there. Yu Mei told them that this morning, people from the special group of the Provincial Party Committee rebel faction had taken Li Jianguo away to write a confession and expose other cadres. Her mother had also been taken away to write exposures and report material. She didn't know when they would come back.

Zhang Feng comforted her saying,

"Uncle Li will survive. Don't worry."

The house was in a mess and there were no coals for the stove and the heated brick beds. Zhang Feng left Dan Dan to help with the cleaning while he went to the coal yard to buy coal with Yu Mei's younger brother. Fortunately, Wang Hai's house was not far away so Zhang Feng ran to his house and borrowed a trolley. Then he bought a full load of coals from the nearby coal yard and transported it back to Yu Mei's family.

When he arrived, he only saw Yu Mei. She said that Dan Dan had gone to buy candles because, most nights, there was no electricity. Having finished unloading the coals, Li Xiaogang said that he would return the trolley. Although he was only a teenager, he had already understood the relationship between his sister and Zhang Feng, so he deliberately left them alone for a private conversation. There were only Yu Mei and Zhang Feng in the room. Zhang Feng lit the stove, making the house warm. He suddenly felt very happy in that he could always be together with Yu Mei again. However, when he turned back to talk to Yu Mei, he found that she was frowning and worried, which was something that Zhang Feng had never seen before. He quickly walked into the bedroom and comforted Yu Mei.

"Yu Mei, don't be sad. Life will never be plain sailing. People will always inevitably encounter difficulties. Your father and mother will overcome their difficulties. And I will be with all of you. At least, your father will not be against me being here now."

Zhang Feng thought that Yu Mei would be relieved at his words. Unexpectedly, she looked more depressed. She came down from the heated brick bed and took Zhang Feng's hand and led him out of the door. Zhang Feng assumed that she wanted to go out for a walk, but to his surprise, she said seriously,

"Brother Feng, thank you for saving me and my father. I will remember it in my heart forever and I will repay your kindness. However, you should never come again for fear that your prospects should be damaged. I am already not the daughter of the provincial party secretary anymore, but instead, the daughter of the largest capitalist roader in the province, as well as the meanest person who everyone avoids like the plague. Chang Zheng does not come any longer nor do those cadres who were around me before. I know that you came to see me out of sympathy. I really appreciate this. If there were an afterlife, I would come to you again."

Before she could finish her words, she was already choked with sobs.

Having heard her words, Zhang Feng understood why she had been so indifferent. He gently patted Yu Mei's shoulder and coaxed her into being calm.

He said,

"Yu Mei, what do you think of me? Am I that kind of snob? I like you because of your beauty, cleverness, tenderness and kindness, not because of your high-ranking family. No matter what changes happen in your family, you do not change. My love for you will never change. Besides, when my father was publicly criticized, I became the child of the Black Five. (During the Cultural Revolution, the 'Black Five' referred to the children of the Black Five, namely the children of the landlords, the rich peasants, the counter-revolutionaries, the bad people and the rightists.) Did you leave me alone?"

Yu Mei heard his words and felt better. However, she said, "It is not the same. Now I am blacker than you politically. I am the most disgraced person among the eight categories including traitor, spy, capitalist roader and the Black Five. People, like my father, are the major subjects of the Cultural Revolution cleansing. We can't get rid of this for our whole life. Brother

* 225 *

Feng, I don't want to implicate you, so just leave me. Dan Dan is a good girl! You will be happy if you are with her. Don't tell me that you just regard her as your sister. Feminine intuition tells me that she loves you deeply."

Zhang Feng held Yu Mei in his arms and said with great fondness,

"Stop talking. You are my only love in this life and my love for you will never perish. You are already the other half of my soul. Without you, my life will be in darkness."

Yu Mei looked up at Zhang Feng affectionately.

"Is it real? You will never leave me alone?"

Her beautiful eyes shimmered with tears, and her pink lips trembled as if she were craving something. Zhang Feng couldn't control himself anymore so he hugged her tightly and they kissed warmly. Yu Mei's lips were cold but her heart was warm.

Suddenly, it seemed that someone was outside the door. They quickly separated and then heard Dan Dan's voice.

"Sister and Xiao Feng, are you there?"

Actually, the door was unlocked and Dan Dan slowly pushed it open. Had she heard their conversation? Both Yu Mei and Zhang Feng were thinking this.

"I bought the candles. I had to walk for two streets before I found a small shop."

Dan Dan was very calm. However, she had actually waited outside for five minutes. The door of the small house was not soundproof at all. She had heard the whole conversation. Of course, her heart was aching. In fact, when she heard the news that Li Jianguo had been downed, she had already guessed that Zhang Feng and Yu Mei might get together again. Over the years, Dan Dan had hidden her love for Zhang Feng under the cover of the love between sister and brother, and sometimes, this love even turned into a kind of maternal love. As long as she could love and help him, and see that he was happy, that was enough for her.

"Sister Dan, I am sorry to bother you," Yu Mei said apologetically.

Dan Dan understood that these words had another meaning. Zhang Feng was still thoughtless in this regard as usual and just called Dan Dan in to warm up in front of the stove. Dan Dan put the candles on the small table by the heated brick bed and chatted politely with Yu Mei. A few minutes later, she left with the excuse that there was something to do in her house. Zhang Feng did not think too much of this, just saying,

"See you tomorrow!"

But Yu Mei knew that Dan Dan would never come again because she did not want to interrupt them. Yu Mei's heart was also very contradictory. She actually liked Dan Dan and wanted to regard her as a good sister. Nevertheless, love is selfish, so it was impossible for them to share the god in their heart.

CHAPTER IV

We Can no Longer Regard Friends as the Enemy

In the next few weeks, Zhang Feng went to Yu Mei's home almost every day to see whether they needed some help. However, Dan Dan always made an excuse and avoided going there. Zhang Feng asked Wang Hai to find someone to repair the heated brick bed. In addition, he bought another big stove. The air leak in the window was also plugged up. Since there was no special supply for Li Jianguo, Zhang Feng helped them go to the grain store to buy sorghum rice, corn flour, limited rice and wheat flour. Zhao Wu sent someone secretly to offer them some rice, chicken, meat and eggs.

Whilst the life of Yu Mei's family was no longer as luxurious as before, it gradually became more stable. Li Jianguo still needed to go to the task force to have his identity checked and answer questions every day but he did so more calmly. He finally understood that it was not only him but also hundreds of veteran officials who had been knocked down and that the operation of the party and the country were facing paralysis. Only the military could help. He began to believe that this kind of situation would not last long. Leaders, such as Prime Minister Zhou and others with clear heads, struggled with those ambitious people who had launched the Cultural Revolution.

At the same time, he also reflected on his own mistakes which he had made politically and economically during the period of seizing power by the Communist Party. Especially as part of past political movements, he had punished a lot of people who were innocent. He had treated those friends of the Party as the enemy and hurt a lot of people. He felt sorry for taking part in this political persecution and therefore, he decided to do something, regardless of his status.

One day, Li Jianguo told Zhang Feng,

"Xiao Feng, I have a request. Could you do me a favour?"

"No problem, Uncle Li. Please go on," Zhang Feng answered.

"I want to see your father. In fact, we used to be classmates in Zhong Shan University before liberation. Although we have been in the same city for more than ten years, there has been no opportunity to meet due to political reasons. It's my fault your father was identified as a rightist in 1957. I didn't dare say anything for your father and was worried that if someone knew about the relationship between us, they would regard me as suspicious. In the end, your father and you all suffered from misfortune. I so regret this. It's all my fault and I want to apologize to him face to face."

Li continued,

"But, I don't know whether your father will forgive me or

not. If he doesn't want to meet or is worried about what others will say and that we are bad people who are making an alliance, that's all right."

Zhang Feng was happy to open the way for his father to befriend Li Jianguo again. Thus, he promised to go home and tell his father.

On a cold, windy night, Zhang Feng and his father, who was wearing a large mask, gently knocked on the door of Yu Mei's house. Li Jianguo came out and warmly shook hands with Zhang Feng's father. Li Jianguo took them into the left room; the others were in the right room. Zhang Feng intended to stay out but Li Jianguo signaled for him to come in with his father.

Zhang Feng and his father were shocked by the following behavior of Li Jianguo. At first, Li Jianguo asked Zhang Feng's father to sit down on the chair, then he stepped back a few feet and suddenly knelt down. On seeing this, Zhang Feng's father quickly stood and tried to raise Li Jianguo up.

Li Jianguo said,

"Wen Bo, I would like to make an apology to you, as well as to all the people I hurt. I was influenced by the thought of an extreme left wing and saw our own friends and comrades as the class enemy. It is I who made them and their families suffer greatly and even ruined them. In 1957, you were regarded as a rightist, only because you made some suggestions about the Party's policy of education on literature and art. I knew about you. Though you hadn't joined the Communist Party, you were a patriotic student with advanced thoughts when we were learning together. When I saw your material, I knew you were not going to oppose the Party, instead, you were sincerely going to help it. However, considering my own situation and wanting to avoid being involved, I didn't dare to support you. It is my fault you suffered from it. I'm so sorry."

Before his voice had died away, he was full of tears. Zhang Wenbo stood up again and raised Li Jianguo.

He said,

"Jian Guo, it is in the past. You have figured it out and have had the courage to apologize, which is very valuable. Well, please sit down."

After sitting down, Li Jianguo continued,

"Only when people have suffered themselves can a man understand how they hurt the innocent. Only when I lost my privileged life, did I realize how hard the lives of those ordinary people were. We, those senior officials, cared too much about power, regardless of the fact that our mission was to let the people live a good life."

Since the two men hadn't met for more than 20 years, they had a lot to say. It was not until Yu Mei's mother came into the room to serve the tea, that everyone realized that it was so late. When Zhang Feng and his father were about to leave, Li Jianguo suddenly said,

"Wen Bo, thank your son for saving my life. I used to stop the relationship between your son and my daughter. I am so regretful."

Zhang Wenbo was shocked after hearing this, and said to Zhang Feng,

"You and his daughter? When? Why? I didn't know!"

Zhang Feng said, embarrassed,

"We knew each other through several activities. It wasn't so long. We were still students…"

Noticing that Zhang Feng was quite embarrassed, Li Jianguo said,

"Wen Bo, you are so lucky to have a son so excellent. He is not only handsome but also has abilities in many different ways. If my political career hasn't been ruined, we will become a real family."

Zhang Wenbo thought for a while and said,

"Now, the current situation is unstable, we don't know how the future will go. The relationship of these two children depends on their own fates."

The words of Li Jianguo and Zhang Wenbo indicated permission for the relationship between Zhang Feng and Yu Mei. Therefore, Zhang Feng was secretly very happy.

On the next morning, Dan Dan saw Zhang Feng and his sister building a snowman at the door, singing. Dan Dan came forward and said,

"Xiao Feng, what makes you so happy?"

Zhang Feng drew her aside and said, secretively,

"You guess!"

"Is it about you and Yu Mei?" Dan Dan blurted out.

"Dan Dan, you are a wonder!" Zhang Feng said.

"Yesterday, my father and Yu Mei's father met. The resentment between them was resolved. Besides, when they talked about us, they understood."

Zhang Feng didn't notice the sadness flashing through Dan Dan's eyes. He only heard her say,

"I'm happy for you. Yu Mei is beautiful and kind. You are a natural pairing of talent and beauty. You should get along well with her although there may be a lot of difficulties in the future."

Then, she asked Zhang Feng about preparations for the Spring Festival and the decision to go to the free market.

The rebel faction had seized power at party and government offices at provincial and municipal levels. The revolution in the

River City seemed to be having a brief period of calm. Moreover, the Spring Festival was coming, so the citizens could temporarily forget the anxiety-ridden situation and start preparing. Besides the revolutionary slogans posted by the Red Guards, there were also some couplets displayed. Of course, these couplets were revolutionary.

Since the beginning of the Cultural Revolution, the system of city management had been disrupted. Many small vendors were suffering. There were some free markets selling chicken, fish, meat, eggs, vegetables and fruits along with some groceries, but at a higher price than the state-owned stores. However, people could only buy things that were limited in state-owned stores. For the Spring Festival, that kind of food would not be enough. Zhang Feng went home and asked his mother for some money then, he went to the free market with Dan Dan in Guilin Road.

Surprisingly, the free market was bustling. Nearly all necessities for the New Year were there such as pork, live chickens, eggs and fishes from the Songhua Lake. (At first, people needed to make some holes in the frozen lake then, they put their prepared fishing nets into the holes and just waited for the fishes to be trapped by their nets.) There were vegetables, frozen persimmons and frozen pears, especially for winter, rice cakes made by the Koreans and sticky bean buns from the Northeast. There were even various firecrackers and New Year pictures. The market was full of pedlars' cries, laughter and the sound of bargaining. People seemed to have forgotten the harsh, political atmosphere which surrounded them.

Both Zhang Feng and Dan Dan wanted to buy some pork, so they wandered around to see which meat dealers sold pork with thick fat. At that time, dishes were plain. Therefore, if they could get fatty meat, they could boil it down for oil to cook with. But the fattier the pork, the more expensive it would be. Zhang Feng learned how to bargain from watching others. They could buy pork with a three-finger thickness of fat (about two inches thick) at a cheaper price. The rural pedlar said to him,

"Young man, you are not only handsome but also honey-mouthed. I will sell the pork to you at a low price. Ah, your girlfriend is also beautiful."

Her words made Dan Dan blush. Zhang Feng did not explain anything and just smiled; he had got accustomed to such misunderstanding when he was with Dan Dan.

However, he did not expect that Yu Mei and her younger brother were out shopping at a booth next to them. Yu Mei had clearly heard the words of the seller and had seen their reaction. Yu Mei had wanted to say hello to them but she hesitated when hearing this conversation. She saw Zhang Feng and Dan Dan buying frozen pears and frozen persimmons enthusiastically and Dan Dan seemed to spoil Zhang Feng occasionally. Yu Mei felt heavy-hearted and in no mood to wander round so she bought something quickly and went home with her brother.

The Spring Festival was the time for a family reunion. Even if the children were thousands of miles away, they would go home to see their parents. As people's spiritual fortress and the source of their strength, the family home inspired those who had suffered from hardship and survived bravely. The Spring Festival in this red storm would offer those beaten and persecuted people an opportunity for spiritual healing.

The families of Zhang Feng, Dan Dan and Yu Mei were all looking forward to this opportunity. The afternoon of New Year's Eve was the first time that Zhang Feng had invited Yu Mei to his home. Li Jianguo couldn't go because of his situation but they had asked Zhang Feng to come on the first day of the New Year. Naturally, Dan Dan was the guest invited by Zhang Feng's family. Although this was the first time that Zhang Feng had asked Yu Mei to come to his house, she seemed unexcited. Zhang Feng asked her why. She just said that she was feeling uncomfortable.

In the afternoon of New Year's Eve, Zhang Feng and Yu Mei walked into the family area of the university. They could hear the whispers of neighbours all the way.

"Zhang Feng brings a fairy-like girlfriend!"

"The old Zhang's son is really blessed!"

When she walked into Zhang Feng's house, all his family, including his father, mother and sister, greeted her zealously. They were making dumplings which were not only necessities for New Year's Eve, but more importantly, created a family reunion atmosphere. Everyone sat around. They talked and laughed while making the dumplings. Yu Mei was encouraged by such a happy atmosphere and joined them.

A few minutes later, Dan Dan also arrived and she greeted Yu Mei enthusiastically. She sat next to Yu Mei and taught her how to make dumplings. Dan Dan was not only smart and able, but also capable of cooking, doing housework and knitting sweaters. There had been chefs and nannies in Yu Mei's family since she was a child, so Yu Mei knew nothing about all these things. Compared with Dan Dan, Yu Mei felt a little embarrassed, especially when Zhang Feng's mother praised Dan Dan for her ability. His mother also showed everyone Zhang Feng's sweater that Dan Dan had just knitted. Without noticing the subtle changes of expression on Yu Mei's face, Zhang Feng also praised Dan Dan and said that if Dan Dan opened a dumpling house in the future, he would give her a hand. Everyone laughed… except Yu Mei.

Since Yu Mei had to go home and be with her family, they

cooked some dumplings in advance and made a special salad with sheet potato jelly, a favourite food of Northeasterners. Zhang Feng's father even took out the famous Northeastern spirit called Yushu Daqu (Daqu: yeast for making hard liquor). Everyone sat together, ate and drank. Yu Mei couldn't resist their persuasion, so she also drank two small mouthfuls of spirit. Dan Dan had a capacity for liquor, so she drank two glasses. As a result, their faces turned red. Hu Yun, Zhang Feng's mother, said to herself that Yu Mei was slender and pretty, while Dan Dan was brilliant, like a beautiful peony, and elegant. Unfortunately, she knew that her son was not blessed to be with them because of custom and the current political situation.

On the way to Yu Mei's house, Zhang Feng walked along the riverside with her. Lights on both sides of the bank reflected in the river, and the weeping willows, with icicles under the moonlight, gently swayed in the wind, shaking off some crystal ice. There were very few pedestrians, so Zhang Feng could enjoy this wonderful, two-person world. He got very excited because of the alcohol and talked so much that he did not notice the silence of Yu Mei. Suddenly he heard Yu Mei's voice,

"Dan Dan is both smart and beautiful."

"Yeah," Zhang Feng replied casually.

"And she is able, so she will be a virtuous wife and good mother."

"Yeah," Zhang Feng replied again, carelessly.

"Did you feel very happy when you walked with her and heard others compliment her beauty? Did you feel warm when you wore the sweater made by her?"

"What?" Zhang Feng was confused. Why had she mentioned Dan Dan in such a lovely moment? A cold wind blew up and Zhang Feng woke up from the wine.

"What happened to you? You seem to be jealous! Oh, did you see us in the free market a few days ago?"

"You seemed like a pair of lovers who were shopping intimately," Yu Mei murmured.

"Oh," Zhang Feng held Yu Mei's hand. "How can I explain so that you will believe me? Since the first time we met, I told you that Dan Dan and I are like brother and sister and that she has taken care of me from being very young. We are really like family. But it is not that kind of a relationship. When your family forced me to break up with you, I said that I would be with Dan Dan. I just wanted you to give up."

Yu Mei seemed unpersuaded.

She said again,

"Men are unable to perceive the subtle psychology of women. Women's intuition is accurate. It is impossible that Dan Dan merely regards you as her younger brother. When I was hospitalized in Beijing, I told her to take care of you. All women would know what I meant. At the time, she did not refuse. This time, did you tell her that our parents have agreed for us to be with each other?"

"Yes, I did. She also blessed us!"

"Brother Feng, I am not petty, although I also have some feminine weaknesses. In fact, I like Dan Dan and regard her as my sister because she is smart, beautiful, mature and capable. A few days ago, I thought that she would be more suitable for you and you would be happy if you are with her."

"Oh, my little fairy, why are you so single-minded? To tell you the truth, according to Wang Hai's words, there is a 'spell' between me and Dan Dan – age. The old saying goes that a man cannot marry a woman who is older than him. Although I am not superstitious and do not believe these old feudal traditions,

I still believe the words of my parents. A few years ago, I told my parents that I was interested in Dan Dan. Unexpectedly, my parents told me very seriously that men must marry women who are younger than themselves because women's youth is very short. If a man marries an older woman, the woman begins to age while the man is still young and vigorous. This kind of marriage would not be stable."

Here Zhang Feng looked at Yu Mei and found that she was listening carefully. He continued,

"Because my parents are open-minded intellectuals who were influenced by Western culture, I trust them. Therefore, I've never thought about it since. The funny thing was that Wang Hai was very happy after hearing that because he liked Dan Dan. However, Dan Dan thought that he was not elegant enough and she did not like his approach. For this reason, Wang Hai always asks me to say some good words for him and also warns me not to break this 'spell'."

On hearing this, Yu Mei remembered that Wang Hai had tried to flatter Dan Dan in the Beijing hospital, and she couldn't help laughing. Seeing that Yu Mei was happy, Zhang Feng breathed a sigh of relief.

At this point, Yu Mei said pettishly,

"Bother Feng, I am a bit cold."

Zhang Feng looked around; no one there. He untied his cotton coat and held Yu Mei in his arms. Yu Mei curled up in Zhang Feng's generous and strong chest and closed her eyes happily. Although the weather was cold, their hearts were warm and they were intoxicated with love.

After a long time, Yu Mei suddenly turned back and said to Zhang Feng,

"Brother Feng, will you love me forever?"

"My love for you will last far longer than forever and is deeply rooted in my soul. No one can replace you, my little fairy."

Yu Mei smiled sweetly. Her face leaned close to Zhang Feng's and she closed her eyes with her lips trembling slightly. Zhang Feng understood her meaning. He hugged Yu Mei and kissed her warmly.

After a while, Yu Mei suddenly changed her expression. She said to Zhang Feng,

"Brother Feng, although we can be together now, I am still worried. We don't know how long this political disturbance will last and where we will be carried to. Will we embrace happiness together?"

Zhang Feng comforted her,

"Don't worry, no matter what difficulties we face, I will be with you. I believe that the sober and conscientious people both within and outside the party will try to end this turmoil. It is impossible for a country to develop without education. In the future, the school will return to normal. I am still learning by myself, and I will try to finish all the high school courses. If the university still does not enroll students in one or two years' time, I will study the university course by myself."

Yu Mei said feelingly,

"Brother Feng, I really admire you. You have promising prospects and I trust you."

To Zhang Feng's surprise, the turmoil would last for a full decade and his university dream would only be realized ten years later.

PART V

A Bloody Storm Sweeps the Divine Land

CHAPTER I

Finding the Capitalist Roader Hiding Behind the Army

As time went by, the spring came. The weeping willow on both sides of the Songhua River had already bloomed light yellow in the warm spring breeze. After the rebel factions had seized power at the provincial and municipal party and government offices, the situation didn't calm down totally. Like other places in the country, the rebel factions were divided into two opposing factions. They all claimed that they adhered to the revolutionary line of Mao Zedong, and the other side was trying to implement the revisionist or even counter-revolutionary line. Both sides had their own political backstage supporters. The backstage supporter of the Second Headquarters of Red Guards where Chang Zheng, Cai Wenge, Qing Lian, and Hei Tou were was the provincial military command, the major general, Zhao Wu, while the backstage supporter of Jili Commune where Wang Hai, Li He, and Xu Jianguo were was the Central Cultural Revolution Group led by Jiang Qing, the wife of Mao Zedong. The representative in Jili City was the special commissioner, the man in black, Du Zhongqing. Jiang Qing and her associates were anxious about the huge military system. They doubted that many generals truly followed the line proposed by Mao Zedong and they would have liked to knock them down by using the power of the Red Guards. Due to the different leaders in the party and the government administration, this was not easy. The generals had armies themselves. Therefore, a bloody 'civil war' began.

One day in April, there were thousands of Red Guards and the rebel factions from the Jili Commune (the rebel organisations in many factories and government units also took part in the two groups, so there were more than just students in the rebel factions). They were holding the banner of the commune and the slogans of fighting against capitalist roaders, shouting,

"Beat down capitalist roaders in the military region in Jili." "If Zhao Wu doesn't surrender, we will overthrow him." They requested Zhao Wu to account for his own crime in front of the rebel factions. The guards in the courtyard blocked them and said that they would only be allowed in with a commanding order. Wang Hai, Li He, Xu Jianguo and other leaders of the commune had a dispute with the guards. They said in a threatening tone that if the guards still did not allow them to go in, they would rush the door. After receiving a phone call from the guards, Mr. Lin, the secretary of the military area, as well as the secretary of Zhao Wu, quickly dispatched a reinforced platoon to guard the gate and set up barricades and temporary fortification. On seeing this, the rebel factions became angrier, were going to rush the door, and sing the song We are not afraid of sacrifice for the revolution. For a while, the two sides were at loggerheads.

In the military command Headquarters, the commander Zhao Wu, political commissar Zhang Qiang, and the chief of staff Liu Jianqiang were taking part in an emergency meeting to discuss counter-measures. Zhao Wu said angrily,

"Shit, I have been in the revolution for nearly 40 years. I have experienced a hail of bullets and I'm still alive. Do you think I would be afraid of a few thieves? Tell the guards, if they dare to rush in, shoot."

Zhang Qiang said, "Lao Zhao, that won't work. The leaders are about to find the representatives of repression of the rebel factions. Just calm down. As our Marshal Peng Dehuai has already been criticised by Red Guards, instead of resisting directly, we should waste their time first. At the same time, we should dispatch staff officer Lin and your son Chang Zheng to contact the Second Headquarters of Red Guards to help us. Then we can get out of this trouble, as the conflict between them is nothing to do with us."

Zhao Wu and Liu Jianqiang both agreed with this suggestion. Therefore, Zhao Wu hurriedly called back home to tell Chang Zheng to wait for staff officer Lin and then go together to the Second Headquarters to ask for help. Chang Zheng told his father that it would be easy for him to deploy about ten thousand of his men.

The situation became even worse in the courtyard of the military region. The rebel army of Polytechnic University, which was loyal to Xu Jianguo, had taken some bullet-proof steel plates for possible rush in action. In addition, Wang Hai was yelling to the soldiers in the courtyard with a bullhorn, saying that if Zhao Wu didn't come out in ten minutes, they would rush inside. In the Headquarters, Zhao Wu and the others were very anxious. As the reinforcements of the Second Headquarters still hadn't come, what should they do? Liu Jianqiang said that the Red Guards didn't know him, so he could go out to negotiate with them and tell that Commander Zhao Wu was absent and had gone to the greater military region for a meeting and he wouldn't be back for a few days. He said this way they could buy some time. Zhao Wu and Zhang Qiang said then try it. Liu Jianqiang went to the door and yelled to the people of the commune,

"I am sorry, the guards haven't contacted the Headquarters in time. They don't know Commander Zhao Wu has gone to the greater military region for a meeting. It will take several days for him to come back. Please go home right now, and I will inform you as soon as he comes back."

On hearing this, Wang Hai and others were rather in doubt. Xu Jianguo said,

"This must be their measure to stave off the attack. We can't be fooled." As a result, Wang Hai yelled to the courtyard and said,

"You are liars. Zhao Wu is in the courtyard. This morning our detector saw his car in the courtyard."

In fact, Wang Hai was lying. Liu Jianqiang didn't know what to say for a moment. Noticing there was no response inside the courtyard, Wang Hai and the others realised that they had been deceived. This inflamed them even more. Then, Wang Hai turned back to the crowd behind him and said,

"You see, they are liars. What they want is only to delay. Revolutionaries would not dare to die. When I say one, two, three, everybody rush the door!" Then, Wang Hai started to yell,

"One, two…" When he was ready to yell "three", a shout of came from the back. Wang Hai turned back and saw the Second

Headquarters flag, followed by several hundred people. The leader of this army was a man with a moustache, Chang Zheng. They were running and shouting,

"Do not ruin my impregnable bulwark!"

"Oh, shit! The Second Headquarters is coming." Li He said to Wang Hai.

Wang Hai hastened to command the team to turn over and lay out the battle array against the Second Headquarters. Knowing that Chang Zheng had only brought several hundred people, Wang Hai and the others were relieved. The two armies maintained their ground. On the one side, there was Wang Hai, Li He, and Xu Jianguo; on the other, Chang Zheng, Liu Ming (the commander of the rebel army of the Normal University), and He Qiang (the general director of the general Headquarters of the workers' revolutionary rebellion). Wang Hai said to Chang Zheng and his men contemptuously,

"You, these royalists are very fast. Well, to save your dad?"

His words aroused a loud laugh in the commune. After hearing these words, Chang Zheng was red with anger and said stutteringly,

"You – you, you dare to resist the People's Liberation Army with a disorderly crowd. You are too audacious in the extreme, right? Chairman Mao asks the whole nation should learn from PLA. You dare to disobey his order!" Xu Jianguo said,

"Can your dad alone represent the whole PLA? It is he who disobeys the order of the Central Committee of the Cultural Revolution. He suppresses rebel organisations and there is really a small group of capitalist roaders in our army. We just want to pull him out and overthrow him!"

Soon, the two parties changed from debate to mutual abuse. Li He patted Wang Hai's arm, and whispered,

"We are wasting time. They are few, we can leave only half of our men to fight against them, while the remaining half goes on to the military area." Wang Hai said,

"Right. Good idea." Wang Hai turned back to consult Xu Jianguo, and then decided to ask Xu Jianguo and Li He to continue to attack the military area, while Wang Hai himself took another part of the men to fight against the Second Headquarters.

The tension in the courtyard of the military region had gone. The political commissar Zhang Qiang and the staff officer Liu Jianqiang were commending Zhao Wu for having such a good son. Suddenly, the staff officer Lin reported,

"It's bad. The rebel faction leads off an attack again! What's going on?" The three men were all muddled. Staff officer Lin said that it seemed that there were not many people in the Second Headquarters, and they could not stop the men of the commune. Zhao Wu complained,

"Why doesn't Chang Zheng bring more people?" Zhang Qiang comforted him and said that maybe there were a few people on Chang Zheng's hands. He heard that the Second Headquarters had several different activities today. Chang Zheng must have already informed the other leaders. There would be more reinforcements soon. At this moment, yelling could be heard from the courtyard. It was Xu Jianguo's voice. Xu Jianguo wanted Zhao Wu to come out immediately and confess his guilt. Liu Jianqiang said,

"Let me handle it." Liu Jianqiang went to the door again to address the crowd with a speaking trumpet. Liu Jianqiang still made the excuse that Zhao Wu had gone to the greater military region for a meeting. On hearing this, Xu Jianguo and others were angry and threatened again that if Zhao Wu still did not come in five minutes, they would rush the door immediately. In addition, they selected more than ten strong men with heavy bullet-proof steel plates to prepare for the charge. One, two, three minutes had gone… Zhao Wu, hiding in the building, was sweating with tension. Although Zhao Wu had already sent more soldiers to guard the courtyard, Zhao Wu and the political commissar were still worried that the consequences would be unthinkable if they fired. Zhao Wu clenched his fist and scolded,

"I have experienced a hail of bullets and hundreds of fierce battles, but never be annoyed like this." Just after ten seconds, suddenly, shouting came from the west of the courtyard. With a walkie-talkie, Liu Jianqiang excitedly reported that there were several thousand people arriving from the Second Headquarters. This time, the leaders were members of the standing committee, Cai Wenge and Qing Lian. Therefore, Xu Jianguo had to tell his men to stop attacking the courtyard of the military region and to see whether Wang Hai's men could resist the forces of the Second Headquarters. When Xu Jianguo, Wang Hai, and Li He were discussing counter-measures, they suddenly heard shouting from the east of the courtyard. It turned out to be the men of the pickets of the Second Headquarters, which were more than one thousand, and led by Hei Tou. They were not only aggressive, but also attacking with wooden sticks, whips, double-joined cudgels and other weapons. The weapon in Hei Tou's hand was a seven-section iron whip. This was his favourite tool. The Cultural Revolution had given Hei Tou, the hooligan, an opportunity to release his natural inclinations. Now, he could hit people in the name of revolution. Rushing to the front of the commune faction, Hei Tou directly swung his whip and several people were instantly beaten down. The hatchet men led by Hei

Tou were also waving all kinds of weapons and rushing into the commune troops. A tangled warfare had begun.

Realising that the situation was bad – their side was empty-handed and would suffer losses when fighting – Wang Hai and the others decided to retreat. Next, Xu Jianguo yelled to the courtyard with a speaking trumpet:

"You try to suppress us by using the Second Headquarters, but that won't end well. Just wait and see, we will come back."

Then Xu Jianguo ordered the commune to withdraw. People supported the wounded and withdrew to the west. There was a sound of mocking from the Second Headquarters behind them.

Two days after, in the Headquarters of the rebel army of Polytechnic University (one of the main forces of the commune faction), the members of the standing committee of the Headquarters of the Jili Commune were holding an emergency conference because after the failure of the rebels against the military region, the men of the Second Headquarters had smashed an office of the commune. Xu Jianguo was saying angrily,

"We should no longer be lenient. The commissioner conveyed the will of Jiang Qing that we should attack with the pen and defend with the sword, and we should be armed to defend the revolutionary line of Chairman Mao."

"Can we believe him?" Wang Hai said. "I still think that he is unreliable and always changes his mind."

"Whatever, we should arm to protect ourselves and establish our own pickets," Xu Jianguo replied. "Our Polytechnic University has its own mechanical processing plant. We can make full use of everything and make some knifes and spears. Other available weapons, like cudgels, three-section and seven-section iron whips and so on, can also be used." He went on,

"Right, what's your opinion about the candidates of the captain of the pickets?"

Wang Hai answered, "There is a ready-made person. You know him too. What about Zhang Feng? He is highly skilled in fighting. Besides, he is our close friend."

Thinking for a while, Xu Jianguo said:

"That's right. But on the one hand, maybe he doesn't want to do this. On the other hand, he comes from a black family. Would this make us an object of ridicule for the Second Headquarters?"

Wang Hai said, "Now we should unite all the people that can be united. He can be the captain as long as he is loyal to the revolutionary line of Chairman Mao."

This decision was adopted unanimously. Then Li He was dispatched to seek Zhang Feng's opinion.

When Li He got to Zhang Feng's home, Zhang Feng was reading a book. On the table, there were lots of books, including English, Russian, high school mathematics, physics and chemistry. Li He said with a smile,

"You are really a carefree guy. The situation outside is so tense and the two parts have already been fighting. But you are still doing your own business while ignoring what is going on outside. Since the colleges and universities are all closed, what's the point of preparing for the university entrance examination"

"As both parts are rebel factions, why are they fighting against each other?" Zhang Feng said. "I know there is no way to go to university now. I just don't want to waste my youth and I want to try to learn something."

Li He looked like a scholar; he was gentle and refined in manner and got high scores in liberal arts in class. Li He was very impressed by Zhang Feng's versatility. Because of his good family background, Li He had joined the Red Guards with

Wang Hai and acted as a leader. Li He told Zhang Feng that Wang Hai and the others wanted Zhang Feng to hold the post of captain of the pickets. Hearing this, Zhang Feng frowned and said that it would be kind of difficult. For Zhang Feng, the purpose of practicing Kungfu was only to build body strength and self-defence, rather than hit or hurt others. Furthermore, Zhang Feng's master would never allow him to do so. As a child from the family of Five Black Categories, it would bring Zhang Feng trouble in the future. Li He knew that Zhang Feng was a man of special righteousness, so he told Zhang Feng how Hei Tou and the others had used violence against the commune faction. Zhang Feng was very angry when he heard this.

"How could the Cultural Revolution let these scums of society make trouble? Hei Tou is a total bully. You can tell Wang Hai that I won't be the captain of the pickets, but I will give my hand if you are in danger." Knowing that it was very difficult to convince Zhang Feng, Li He had to go back.

There was another reason why Zhang Feng didn't want to get involved in the fights of Wang Hai and the others. He had recently met four smart and knowledgeable university students. They were all friends. Usually they would get together and talk about everything in the world. All of these men had a wide range of hobbies and interests, just like Zhang Feng. They showed no interest in participating in the Cultural Revolution and all belonged to the typical carefree people. They were known as the 'Four Talents of the River City.' One Sunday, Zhang Feng had met them, through the introduction of a friend, in the house of Liu Tian, the eldest of the 'Four Talents.' They all felt like old friends at the first meeting and got along well with each other. They liked Zhang Feng and had heard from their friends that he was a remarkable talent of the Second Senior Middle School.

Liu Tian was a talented student in Beijing University, while the next eldest of the four, Wang Yang, was a talented student of Tsinghua University. Tsinghua and Beijing University were the two best universities in China at that time.

Liu Tian said to Zhang Feng,

"Xiao Zhang, you can go to Beijing University in the future and study physics to be a scientist." Seeing this, Wang Yang said immediately,

"You should go to Tsinghua University in the future and major in electronic engineering, which has a practical contribution to society."

The third of the 'Four Talents,' Li Yue, and the youngest of the four, Chen Xing said with smile,

"What are you two arguing about? The universities have all closed. Whether they will open or not is still a problem." Liu Tian and Wang Yang sighed and said,

"Yes. What a pity. A large number of talented young people like Zhang Feng are influenced by this." Liu Tian said,

"Well, it's hard to think about the situation. Let's talk about something else."

Then they began to talk about Chinese and foreign literature. Although the Four Talents of The River City were all students of science and technology, they also showed great interest in literature. When they debated whether there was a dramatist who could compare with Shakespeare in China, Li Yue said that Guan Hanqing's tragedy can be compared to Shakespeare. But Wang Yang showed the opposite opinion; he believed that Tang Xianzu had lived in the same era as Shakespeare, and his work the Peony Pavilion had the same charm as Romeo and Juliet. Zhang Feng very much enjoyed their discussion. When he found out that Liu Tian had the complete works of Shakespeare translated by Zhu Shenghao in the house, he was very excited, because his father only had a few Shakespeare comedies. Zhang Feng asked Liu Tian whether he could borrow several copies of Shakespeare drama for short time, Liu Tian agreed without hesitation. This made Zhang Feng as happy as a lark. Shakespeare was his favourite dramatist. Since then, every time he went to visit his four friends, Zhang Feng would return and borrow a few Shakespeare plays.

Since Yu Mei's father had gone to the May Seventh Officials Schools (where officials were supervised carrying out physical labour and ideological reform), Yu Mei had calmed down a lot. Anyway, her father's downfall was complete. According to the statement of the time, her father was a dead tiger (a man who has lost his power and influence) and would no longer suffer the same fierce struggle and torture as before. Besides, Yu Mei could often meet Zhang Feng now. Both of them were carefree persons who were not involve in the factional struggles of the Cultural Revolution. They avoided political storms and enjoyed their love even if it was only for a short time. Today, it was a fine sunny day. According to their arrangement, Yu Mei was on her way to Zhang Feng's home. She took a bus and got off a few stops early, on the riverside, because she wanted to take a walk and enjoy the beauty of the riverside. When approaching the bridge, she suddenly saw a large crowd of people surrounding a tall man who was speaking. When she got closer, Yu Mei saw that the man was Chang Zheng, who she hadn't seen for a long time. Chang Zheng wore a green uniform, armed with a Sam Browne belt, and he had a moustache, just like a commander. Around him was a group of Red Guards of First Senior Middle School. There were several beautiful female Red Guards, including Wu Xiaoli, who made a deep impression on Yu Mei. Wu Xiaoli had always been interested in Chang Zheng when they were at school, but she had had to restrain herself, considering the relationship between Yu Mei and Chang Zheng. However, Wu Xiaoli could be with Chang Zheng without consideration now. Seeing this, Yu Mei felt disgust and turned away. Just a dozen steps away, Yu Mei heard someone calling her name. Looking back, she saw it was Chang Zheng.

"Yu Mei, I'm sorry," he said guiltily. "I've been too busy recently to visit you and your father."

Yu Mei said coldly,

"You'd better care about your own revolutionary career. Having a relationship with a capitalist roader and the daughter of a capitalist roader would affect your loyalty to the revolution." Chang Zheng was very embarrassed and tried to explain while Wu Xiaoli came up and snapped at Yu Mei,

"Li Yumei, remember what you are. You are no longer the child of a senior official. You are only the child of Five Black Categories. You have to stay away from Chang Zheng, or you will influence his future. He is the deputy commander of the Second Headquarters of the Red Guards and has a lot of things to do." Chang Zheng said immediately,

"Yes, I am too busy. The commune wants to fight against the PLA, they even want to beat down my father. This is sheer daydreaming. We have military support, shall we be afraid of them? There are several staff officers giving support to us."

"Right." Wu Xiaoli said, "Chang Zheng has said that there will be a big battle here and we will attack their stronghold."

Chang Zheng immediately made a gesture to remind Wu Xiaoli to keep it down and said,

"This is a military secret. Don't let the commune know about it." Chang Zheng turned back to Yu Mei and said, "Well, you are one of us. Yu Mei, I will go to see you when I have finished the business." Yu Mei still said coldly:

"I have no interest in your business. You'd better act as the commander, which is what you want to be." Then, Yu Mei turned back and spoke to Wu Xiaoli, "Take care of your Chang Zheng and don't let him run away." After saying so, Yu Mei walked away.

When she got to Zhang Feng's house, only Zhang Feng himself was at home. knowing that Yu Mei was coming (Yu Mei usually came on Tuesdays and Thursdays, and Zhang Feng went to Yu Mei's house each Wednesday and Friday), Zhang Feng's father, mother and sister all left the house in order to create a world for Zhang Feng and Yu Mei. Seeing Zhang Feng, all Yu Mei's anger, caused by Chang Zheng, was gone. Zhang Feng and Yu Mei together had endless words to say. They talked about dreams, the future, even building a new family. Zhang Feng said that he liked children and would like to have three or four. Hearing this, Yu Mei always tapped Zhang Feng's shoulders shyly.

"You are a rogue. You think so far ahead but I haven't said that I'll marry you." When she said this, Zhang Feng always took Yu Mei in his arms and asked,

"So who do you want to marry? Tell me, and I will go and beat him up." Sometimes, Zhang Feng would play the violin, and Yu Mei would dance the Chinese classical dance. The two were immersed in a strong sense of love.

By five o'clock in the afternoon, Yu Mei had to go home. When they were saying goodbye, suddenly the words what Chang Zheng and the others had said came into Yu Mei's mind. She knew that Zhang Feng's friends Wang Hai and Li He were the leaders of the Jili Commune, therefore she told Zhang Feng that the Second Headquarters were preparing to attack the Jili Commune. Hearing this, Zhang Feng looked worried and said:

"Why didn't you tell me earlier? Wang Hai and Li He will be in danger. No, I have to go to the general Headquarters of the Polytechnic University so that they can make preparations."

"Be careful!" Yu Mei said anxiously. "I've heard that there were a lot of ferocious hatchet men and the leader was Hei Tou who made life difficult for me that year."

"Don't worry. I will come back as soon as I give Wang Hai the message. Hei Tou will always be a warrior vanquished by my hand."

They came out of the house together. When they walked to the corner of the street, they happened to meet Dan Dan. Yu Mei told Dan Dan that Zhang Feng was going to send a message immediately. Dan Dan looked worried too. She said,

"Xiao Feng, don't get yourself involved in the conflicts between the two parts. It's too dangerous. One day if they make an alliance, you would be regarded as the backstage supporter." Zhang Feng said:

"Dan Dan, it won't be so serious. I just worry about the security of Wang Hai and Li He. I will come back as soon as I've sent the message. Don't worry."

After this, Zhang Feng rented a bicycle and sped off to the Polytechnic University. Looking at his receding shadow, Dan Dan said to Yu Mei:

"Zhang Feng is too loyal to his friends, and always helps them without any hesitation. Only men like him would show filial respect for his parents and show his loyalty to his beloved. How rare is that!" After that, she looked at Yu Mei with a meaningful look, and Yu Mei blushed.

CHAPTER 11

Back to the Ancient Battlefield

Zhang Feng rode to Polytechnic University as fast as he could. The gate was heavily defended; dozens of Red Guards armed with spears and clubs guarded the gate and were interrogating everyone who went in and out. Zhang Feng told them his name and said that he was looking for Wang Hai. Hearing his words one man, who seemed to be their leader, said:

"Ah, you are the pickets captain recommended by the Standing Committee Wang. Just as expected, you are very different. Welcome!" Hearing this, the other people made way for Zhang Feng at once. Zhang Feng replied politely,

"No, I am not come to be the captain, but to tell Wang Hai something urgently." Having heard his words, the leader immediately arranged for a person to take Zhang Feng directly to the main building where the rebel army headquarters was located. The atmosphere here was very tense. Patrols armed with knives, spears and clubs were going in and out. The door on the first floor had been sealed with brick and cement, leaving only a small door. The windows on the first floor were also nailed with wooden boards. It seemed that they were ready to guard this place to the death. Zhang Feng looked at the scene and felt very uneasy. How did a Cultural Revolution turn into armed fighting? They were young students and ordinary people, why did they want to kill each other? Meanwhile, he felt relieved that at least Wang Hai and the other people were in a state of preparedness.

When he entered the headquarters, he saw that Wang Hai, Li He, and Xu Jianguo were all there. At the sight of Zhang Feng, Wang Hai jumped up happily.

"Elder brother, you have finally come. Our pickets have been waiting for you for so long!" Zhang Feng shook his head and said,

"I am not here to join you, but to tell you something urgent." Wang Hai sat down disappointedly. Then Zhang Feng told them the news that the Second Headquarters would besiege the commune base camp tomorrow. Xu Jianguo said,

"This is something we expected. We just didn't expect it to happen so quickly. We have three strongholds. I reckon that they will attack the Polytechnic University primarily, so we need to discuss counter-attack now." When Zhang Feng was about to leave, Wang Hai stopped him.

"Don't be in such a hurry. It's so tiring to be with Yu Mei every day. You just stay here for one night and teach us the basic skills of picket fighting." Then, ignoring Zhang Feng's willingness, Wang Hai dragged him to a hall in which there were over fifty selected robust young men. Wang Hai announced that

Zhang Feng was their pickets captain and was going to teach them the basic skills of fighting and self-defence on the spot. Zhang Feng had no choice but to promise to stay for one night and leave tomorrow morning.

At night, Wang Hai and he slept in the same room. They chatted excitedly until midnight. At about six o'clock in the morning, when they were sleeping soundly, a piercing alarm woke them up. They quickly got up and ran to the platform on the roof of the building. They saw thousands of people fully armed with knives, spears and clubs from the Second Headquarters. They held banners and had already broken the warning line at the gate. Now they were pushing onwards to the main building along the main road on the campus. Wang Hai immediately rushed to the command post, leaving Zhang Feng alone on the platform. Zhang Feng regretted not leaving yesterday, but it was the way it was now. If he slipped away now and left Wang Hai and the other people in danger, he would hardly be a real friend. Therefore he braced himself to stay and improvised according to the situation.

A few minutes later, Zhang Feng saw a team of hundreds of people from this university rushing out of the building. They had a home-made tank made by the teachers and students of the mechanical department, which opened the way in front and faced the enemy. The two parties encountered each other a few hundred metres outside the building and began to fight. Zhang Feng was about to run to the command, hearing the alarm ringing again. He could hear the sounds of fighting coming from the back, left and right sides of the building. Zhang Feng ran to the rear of the platform and started in surprise. The scene was just like an ancient battlefield on which a dense mass of the Second Headquarters with spears and clubs closed in from the back, left and right sides as if they were a movable forest. There must have been tens of thousands of people. 'It is indeed a well-planned battle.' Zhang Feng thought. No wonder Yu Mei had mentioned that the army staff would help them. Zhang Feng rushed down the platform at the top of the building to the command. It was in chaos. The telephone line used for connecting to the outside world had been cut off. Wang Hai and the others couldn't contact other strongholds of the commune to mobilise the reinforcements. Looking out of the window, they could see the hundreds of people who had been sent out were being driven back. Many people were injured and the tanks were broken and burned. Xu Jianguo told them to retreat immediately to the building and block the door. Then the people of the Second Headquarters surrounded the building. In the building, the commander ordered,

"We will go down with the headquarters of the rebel army of Polytechnic University!"

Each detachment was responsible for guarding its own part, especially the windows on the second floor because the windows on the first floor had been sealed. Without thinking of his own situation. Zhang Feng led over fifty pickets to protect the standing committee members. Last night he had taught them some fighting skills and also demonstrated some other things, such as the bare hand snatch sabre, which made all of them admire him.

Just then, the people of the Second Headquarters outside the building began to shout at people in the building. It was the voice of Chang Zheng:

"Listen, people of the commune. You have been surrounded by our army of tens of thousands of people, and it's impossible for you to escape. So you'd better open the door and surrender quickly, and we will be nice to captives and promise not to kill you." Li Li, the female broadcaster in the building, was Xu Jianguo's girlfriend. While playing the song whose lyric was "Revolution fears no death, and if you fear, do not participate in", Li Li replied passionately,

"It's a fantasy, and you think that you can sew things up with the support of Zhao Wu. In order to safeguard Chairman Mao's revolutionary line, we will fight with you to the last drop of our blood today." Chang Zheng was so angry that he didn't know what to say. Hei Tou next to him grabbed the loudspeaker and said,

"Little bitch, even now as you draw your last breath, you still pretend to be brave. If you don't surrender, we will fuck you when we storm in!" Then he commanded his pickets to attack. They had carefully prepared for this; they had already scouted the defensive situation of the commune, and they had prepared a long ladder for climbing and a big hammer for smashing the window. When the attack command was given, dozens of ladders were put against the walls to reach the windows on the second floor on all sides of the building. With a hammer at his waist and a sabre in his hand, Hei Tou climbed up the ladder first to start the attack. The commune people guarded the windows on the second floor. They threw stones and heavy objects down to prevent the invaders coming up, or used spears or clubs to push the ladder away, making those already on the ladder fall. The sounds of fighting, cursing and shouting and the screaming and the moaning of the wounded were truly terrible. Wang Hai knew that Zhang Feng did not want to hurt people, so he told his pickets to concentrate on protecting people of the command.

It was already noon, but the people of the Second

Headquarters were still being held back. The people of the commune had been defending perseveringly. Moreover, Polytechnic University had its own machine-processing factory and they had already prepared many iron and steel bars. More than half of the windows on the second floor had been sealed with iron and steel bars at intervals from the inside. Therefore, even if the people from the Second Headquarters managed to climb up and smash the windows, they wouldn't be able to get in. Additionally, the people inside could fend them off with spears and clubs. The cheers, screams and bawls of tens of thousands of people around the building were fading. Hei Tou put his hands to his injured bottom, which had been caused by his fall from a ladder, and he groaned painfully. Li Li, the broadcaster of the rebel faction of Polytechnic University, one moment laughed at them and the next she shouted the slogan of being ready to die in defence of Chairman Mao.

Some time later and the attack still had not made any progress. The standing committees of the Second Headquarters gathered to find a solution. Hei Tou advocated a hard attack, but Commander Liu of the rebel faction army of Normal University disagreed with him. Cai Wenge said,

"I have an idea, but we need the cooperation of the standing committee member Chang Zheng." Chang Zheng asked him what it was. Cai said that if you could get explosives, they could blast the door on the first floor. Was it feasible to use explosives? The other committee members all thought this would be too much. Cai said,

"How can you be so conservative? People used guns and cannons in the fight in Wuhan, so it's nothing serious for us to use some explosives. Besides, we will not use them to blast the people." Chang Zheng thought for a while and said,

"I will contact Staff Officer Lin and Staff Officer Deng to see if they can provide me with the explosives." Hei Tou said,

"There are several demobilised soldiers in our pickets. As long as you can get the explosives, we can go ahead and blast the door."

At about three 3 o'clock in the afternoon, the sun was beating down. Looking down from the platform of the main building of Polytechnic University, they could see that more than 10,000 people of the Second Headquarters were resting under the shade of the trees.

"The hard attack will not work. It seems that they are determined to besiege us. Fortunately, we have no need to fear since we have enough prepared foods and supplies for us to live for over a month. People of the commune in other strongholds will come to save us." Wang Hai said to Zhang Feng,

"What if they use explosives to blast the door, what should we do?" Zhang Feng said. Wang Hai thought for a moment and said,

"It is possible. They have the support of the military region, so they can get anything they want. If they really break in, we can't resist them." Finding no one around, he whispered to Zhang Feng,

"We have no choice. Xu Jianguo told me that in this building, there is a secret underground passage leading to a small yard of the school's logistics office hundreds of meters away for combat readiness. In case we can't keep this place, we can escape through that passage. Especially at night, no one will be able to see us. However, only I and other standing committees know this secret." Then he said laughingly:

"Do not worry. Your little fairy will be back in your arms again in a few days." Zhang Feng gave him a gentle punch.

"We are facing our enemies and now you mention this so light-heartedly. It is good to protect yourself." Wang Hai asked,

"Has Dan Dan often mentioned me recently? I am now a standing committee member of the Jili Commune, the commander of hundreds of thousands of rebel factions. Can I be considered a hero?" Zhang Feng said with some impatience,

"What hero? You really are dreaming! Dan Dan said that you always deliberately try to find trouble for yourself and now you really are in trouble."

Just then, a Red Guard ran over to say that Xu Jianguo wanted Wang Hai and Zhang Feng to attend the emergency standing committee meeting. Zhang Feng said:

"Are you kidding? I am just an outsider. How can I attend your standing committee meeting?" Wang Hai turned to him,

"Come on, you are the pickets captain. Of course, you have to attend." Zhang Feng had to follow him, saying,

"I have not accepted your appointment yet."

At about five o'clock in the afternoon, when the people of the commune in the building were preparing to have dinner, they suddenly heard a loud noise followed by the shouts of the people of the Second Headquarters.

"No, they've blasted the door!" An urgent shout came from the first floor. Each detachment leader took their own team to guard each floor in accordance with the orders of the headquarters. If they couldn't resist, they just needed to close the two doors.

"Go down with the building!" the soldiers of the commune roared. There were sounds of knives and screaming everywhere. Some wounded people fell to the ground, groaning in pain, and blood was flowing everywhere. Zhang Feng and the command were on the third floor. Over more than an hour, the two doors in the corridor on the third floor were broken down. Chang Zheng, with his tall and strong body, took the lead in storming in. Xu Jianguo rushed over with a spear and fought against Chang Zheng. Both of them were very strong athletes. Chang Zheng had learned some hand-to-hand fighting skills in military training, so he had the advantage. Seeing that Xu Jianguo was being defeated, Zhang Feng ran over and shouted to Chang Zheng:

"Stop! Put down your weapon!" Chang Zheng saw with immense surprise that it was Zhang Feng.

"Why are you here?" he cried. "Aren't you a carefree person?"

"Yes, I belong to no faction," Zhang Feng replied. "But I don't want to see the people of the two factions killing each other." Chang Zheng said again:

"You speak in an arrogant manner. I know that you have a command of martial arts, but I am not afraid of you. Get out of the way quickly!"

Zhang Feng protected Xu Jianguo and told him to retreat while keeping on the right side of Chang Zheng. Zhang Feng was unarmed, but Chang Zheng attacked him with a spear without scruple. Zhang Feng first parried left and right, so that Chang Zheng's aim missed him. Then Chang Zheng tried his best to stab Zhang Feng's chest. Zhang Feng dodged swiftly to one side, grabbed his spear and kicked Chang Zheng down to the ground with a leg sweep. Then he aimed the spear at Chang Zheng's chest. Chang Zheng thought that he really wanted to kill him.

"Brother, please let me go," he said, terrified. "I am sorry for the things I did to you. I will give up pursuing Yu Mei." Zhang Feng did not want to really stab him, he just wanted to intimidate him.

"Stop talking nonsense! I have no grudge against you. Just tell your people not to hurt my friends." Then he threw down the spear and ran off. Having seen that Chang Zheng was so terrified, the people of the Second Headquarters behind Chang Zheng did not dare to chase him.

Meanwhile, Li Li was still carrying out her duties, passionately shouting slogans to inspire the people of the commune to resist the attack of the Second Headquarters. Suddenly the door was kicked, and Hei Tou rushed in with two pickets.

"Hah, you little slut, I found you. I want to enjoy you today." Then he dived at Li Li. She picked up a short stick from behind her.

"Hooligan, how dare you! I'm going to kill you!" But she couldn't fight back. Hei Tou grabbed her stick and pressed her onto the table. His two subjects thought that he was really carry out his threat and quickly intervened, saying,

"Captain, do not do this. If you do, the people of the commune will get a subject of ridicule." Just then, Cai Wenge came in. Seeing Hei Tou holding Li Li down, he saw immediately what was happening.

"Captain Yu (Hei Tou's family name is Yu), you can't do this. Although we belong to the rebel faction, we are still revolutionaries." He saw that Li Li was a beautiful girl with a plump figure, which also made his mouth water. Then he said,

"You cannot act indecently against her, but you can punish her for her boldness." Hei Tou immediately replied,

"Right, I should give her a lesson and she will dare not to be progressive later." He had played so many girls before, who, however, were all from the poorer level of the society. In the face of such a beautiful female university student, he certainly did not want to let her go. He grabbed Li Li's collar with both hands and pulled it by force. He pulled off the buttons of both her top and underwear, revealing a pair of white plump breasts. At this time, the men in the house could not help but be excited and especially Cai Wenge, who applauded. Li Li was furious. She covered herself with one hand and gave Hei Tou a loud slap with the other. Hei Tou retaliated and grabbed Li Li's neck with one hand while he was about to touch her breast with the other.

At this moment, the door was kicked in. Wang Hai rushed in with three people. Seeing Hei Tou insulting Li Li, Wang Hai screamed,

"Stop! You are not rebels, but a group of hooligans!" Hei Tou looked around and picked up the seven-section whip on the ground. Then he started to fight with Wang Hai. Wang Hai was also a strong athlete. He fought back with a spear. Their subjects also began fighting each other. Cai Wenge was a villain. He never did dangerous things, so he did not directly go to fight. He saw Li Li in the corner, wrapped tightly in her shirt, looking in horror at the fighting, and he went quietly round to her back. He suddenly held her neck with one hand and aimed at her chest with a short knife with the other. He shouted to Wang Hai,

"Wang Hai, put down your arms and surrender! Otherwise, I will kill her!" Wang Hai was stunned and then he was hit by Hei Tou's seven-section whip on his right shoulder, which tore into his flesh and started the blood flowing. He screamed angrily,

"Cai Wenge, you are a rascal!" While fighting of Hei Tou's attack, he was moving towards Li Li, trying to save her. At this dangerous moment, the door was pushed open violently and a man rushed in. At the sight of this person, everything stopped. It was Zhang Feng, the rescuer Wang Hai was expecting. He had a long stick in his hand. Firstly, he didn't want to hurt people. Secondly, his master had taught him Shaolin cudgel so he would be able to use it freely. Hei Tou had been defeated by him a few years ago, and he was worried when he saw him. Cai Wenge was also afraid of him and immediately let Li Li go. Zhang Feng saw that Wang Hai's arm was bleeding, knowing that it had been lashed by the seven-section whip. It made him very angry.

"Hei Tou, you are nothing but a violent thug. Why are you here with the rebel faction? I will teach you! Wang Hai, you retreat with Li Li now, and I'll cover you."

Then he began to attack Hei Tou with his stick. Hei Tou was frightened out of his wits, and his seven-section whip suddenly seemed useless. Zhang Feng found an opportunity and directly struck his chest with his stick. He fell to the ground and screamed. Seeing this, his two subjects did not dare to come near for fear of Zhang Feng. Cai Wenge had already hidden under the table. Knowing that Wang Hai and the other people had left safely, Zhang Feng was unwilling to continue fighting and he left.

An hour later, the sky was dim. The commune had been unable to withstand the attack of the Second Headquarters. The command issued the order to retreat. Zhang Feng guarded the injured Wang Hai, Xu Jianguo, Li Li and Li He and they all went into a storage room off the dark corridor. They locked the door from the inside because they were the people who had retreated last. Then they moved away a wooden cabinet and found a small secret passage. They bent down to enter the narrow passage one by one. Zhang Feng was the last to leave. He slowly moved the cabinet back to its original position to block the entrance, and then retreated with Wang Hai from the building.

CHAPTER III

In the Rain of Bullets

Under the cover of night, the people of the commune faction withdrew from Polytechnic University. Xu Jianguo took some people to the Jili Hotel, another camp of the commune faction. Wang Hai was injured. After consultation, all the people agreed that was not safe to send him home so they decided to send him to Dan Dan's house to recover. Dan Dan's mother was a doctor, so she could help Wang Hai to nurse and dress his wounds. At the same time, they also sympathised with the commune faction, because the Second Headquarters suppressed and bullied the commune with the support of the army. Wang Hai was delighted. He said to Zhang Feng that his wounds had already recovered partially even on the way to Dan Dan's house.

When they arrived at Dan Dan's house, Dan and her mother were still awake and were listening to the radio. They were very distressed at the sight of Wang Hai's wounds, which Dan Dan's mother immediately bandaged. Then Zhang Feng told them about today's battle. After hearing his story, Dan Dan told him off him for being involved in the fight, while admiring his spirit of being a friend in need. Wang Hai must show his masculinity when facing Dan Dan. Therefore, when Dan Dan's mother sterilized his wounds with alcohol, he tried his best to endure the pain without making any sound. Dan Dan felt distressed when she saw this, so she said to Wang Hai that if he felt pain, he should shout out.

"It's nothing." Wang Hai said, sweating. "It's nothing and I feel no pain." After that, they told Wang Hai to stay inside the room and have a good rest. Zhang Feng saw that there was nothing for him to do, so he went home.

In the next few days, Dan Dan and her mother carefully took care of Wang Hai, so his wounds recovered quickly. Zhang Feng came to see him with Yu Mei and heard him talk about the fierce battle of that day. Wang Hai deliberately described himself as an extraordinarily brave guy before two beauties. Zhang Feng could not help giving a cough, and Wang Hai knew it was a reminder that he should stop bragging. Therefore, he stopped and said,

"Of course, if hadn't been for Brother Feng's help, we would have been in more danger."

After Zhang Feng and Yu Mei left, Wang Hai sat on the bed. He straightened himself and said to Dan Dan mysteriously:

"Sister Dan, do you know that Brother Feng and Yu Mei are with each other now?"

"I know and I am happy for them."

"So what do you do?"

"What do you mean by what do you do?" Wang Hai was frank. Since there was nobody else in the room, he said directly:

"Sister Dan, I know that you like Brother Feng, but now he has a girlfriend. Do you have someone else to think about?"

Dan Dan knew what Wang Hai meant. A clever girl is always sensitive to a man's attitude. Although Wang Hai was a bit shorter than Zhang Feng, he was also a masculine and robust man with bushy eyebrows and big eyes. However, there was no gentility in his masculinity, which was a fly in the ointment for Dan Dan, this beautiful and intelligent girl. She did not want to hurt Wang Hai, so she said half-jokingly,

"Wang Hai, you are a leader of hundreds of thousands of rebel factions and a man who does big things. You can't be immersed in love at such a critical moment of the revolution." Dan Dan avoided his question intentionally, so he was embarrassed to ask again. Then he said:

"Sister Dan, you must find a man who can protect you in the future."

Two days later, the command of the commune asked Li He to visit Wang Hai to see how he was. Li He told Wang Hai the shocking news that the fight had already escalated to modern warfare. Both groups were using guns and ammunition and they were casualties on both sides. The commune faction had more casualties because the weapons they were using were old rifles from local militias, while the Second Headquarters used new weapons. However, the provincial military region did not admit that they had given these weapons to the Second Headquarters. Dan Dan was very worried after hearing this, but Wang Hai was excited.

Zhang Feng came over. After hearing Li He's words, Zhang Feng finally realised why there had been shooting sounds in the city in the last few days and why some buses had stopped. Dan Dan was anxious to ask Zhang Feng to persuade Wang Hai not to go back to fight. Zhang Feng thought that the two factions were all used by different political forces, and both of them were political victims. Therefore, he urged Wang Hai not to get involved again. Nevertheless, Wang Hai was born with great bravery. He said that he must share weal and woe with his rebel brothers, and wouldn't leave them to face the enemy alone. He told Li He that he would go home to see his parents tomorrow because his mother had been not in the best of health for some time. After that, he would go to the Jili Hotel, the base camp of the commune. He was so determined that Zhang Feng and Dan Dan could see it was useless to try to talk him out of it.

The next morning, Wang Hai was reluctant to say goodbye to Dan Dan. He came out and met Li He and Mr. Yang of the automobile factory rebel faction, who was driving a Jie-fang truck with five or six people in the car. Mr. Yang told Wang Hai that the command of the commune had already contacted the commune faction organisation in the automobile factory and told them that they were going to go to the arms department of the car factory to get a batch of better guns. Since the militia organisation of the automobile factory had often won prizes in past militia contests, their superiors offered them relatively new weapons. Wang Hai's father had a good relationship with Director Chen of the militia department, so the command asked Wang Hai to do this.

Li He told Wang Hai that he had been to his house yesterday and his mother was much better now, so there was no need for him to worry. His father had already gone to the factory this morning and was waiting for them there. Wang Hai was delighted. For one thing, he would see his father soon. For another, he could bring good weapons to the commune to fight against the attack from the Second Headquarters.

In the afternoon, Wang Hai and the others drove the Jiefang truck loaded with rifles, pistols, and grenades, along the way out of sight of the Second Headquarters, and sneaked into the city. Wang Hai was so eager to see his comrades that he asked the driver to drive directly to the Jili Hotel. However, Li He and Mr. Yang argued that the Second Headquarters had blockaded the main access to the hotel with dense firing in the building opposite, the Fifth Department Store. Several commune people had already been killed. Even a hawker who sold roast chicken nearby was injured accidentally. Therefore, they did not drive the truck to the gate of the hotel until dark. Xu Jianguo greeted them at the door. Wang Hai hugged him warmly, and both of them were moved to tears. At the sight of the unloaded weapons, Xu Jianguo said happily to Wang Hai,

"Well, now we dare to fight with them. A few days ago, we only had a few dozen broken guns and a few bullets, so we had no choice but to bear their bullets. Now, things will be different and we can fight with them with firepower." After that, he took out a Type 54 pistol and handed it to Wang Hai.

"Take it. Every member of the standing committee has one pistol." He then asked the demobilised soldiers from the automobile factory to teach everyone how to use the new guns while he took Wang Hai to the provisional command.

The River City was now in midsummer. One day at noon, Zhang Feng and Yu Mei met again under the big poplar tree by the river. Yu Mei closed her eyes and leaned on Zhang Feng's shoulder, listening quietly to the cicadas chirping from the tree. Zhang Feng was preoccupied and looked down in silence. After ten minutes, Yu Mei opened her eyes and looked at Zhang Feng. She asked,

"Brother Feng, what's the matter with you?" Zhang Feng held Yu Mei's hand gently and said,

"Nothing. To be with you is my biggest happiness. However, as a man, I have to think about my responsibilities and my future, as well as the future of the country. Nowadays, our society is so chaotic and the fighting between two factions keeps escalating. Social life had been interrupted. Factories have stopped work and schools are closed, which represents a disordered society. Nevertheless, everything is in the name of revolution in accordance with the supreme instructions of our great leader, I…"

Yu Mei looked around and covered Zhang Feng's mouth with her hand.

"Brother, please lower your voice. Don't let anyone hear you. It's dangerous to say and even think so. I am apolitical. Before my father went to the May Seventh Officials School, he warned my brother and me that we'd better keep far away from politics. Anyway, no matter what happens outside, I will always feel steadfast as long as you are here." Zhang Feng gently caressed Yu Mei's fine slim hand and tried to reassure her.

"Don't worry, I will not tell anyone else." Zhang Feng knew that Yu Mei was naïve in politics, while Dan Dan was much more mature and rational in this respect. This was related to their family background and personal experience. Yu Mei asked Zhang Feng not to get involved in the fight. Now the fight had already entered the bullet stage, so his safety could not be guaranteed, even if he had learned martial arts. Zhang Feng said that he knew this. Wang Hai had once sent someone to look for him, but he refused. He was not afraid of death. Instead, he believed that it was in vain to sacrifice himself for factional fighting. Yu Mei said that her father had come back from the May Seventh Officials School a few days ago, saying that the struggle between the two factions was closely related to the instigation of the man in black, Du Zhongqing, the commissioner of the Cultural Revolution Group. He had instigated the commune faction to attack the army, while the army sent the Second Headquarters, supported by them, to fight with the commune faction. In the end, the victims were ordinary people in the rebel factions. Those who died in the fight were all victims of political struggle. Zhang Feng echoed that people sympathised with the weak. In fact, there was no fundamental conflict of interests between the two factions. The Second Headquarters had the support of the army and a good source of weapons and supplies, so they always bullied the commune faction. That's why a lot of people sympathised with the commune faction. Yu Mei thought for a moment and said that she had heard from an official's son, who had heard Chang Zheng's brag that the arsenal of the military region was just like Chang Zheng's house and he could take anything he wanted. Zhang Feng said that that was why he was worried about the safety of Wang Hai, Li He, and Xu Jianguo. If the fight continued to escalate, they would face greater danger. At the same time, he was also worried about the condition of Wang Hai's mother. A few days ago, Dan Dan's mother had been to see her, and she said Wang Hai's mother might have gastric cancer.

The area of the Jili Hotel and the Fifth Department Store in the city centre had been almost deserted for more than a month. Every day, people could hear shots and loud shouts from both sides. The two factions occupying the two places kept firing at each other. The walls of the two buildings were covered with bullet holes. People could hear the mournful music every day. At such a moment, the citizens would lament that another young man had lost his precious life. The Second Headquarters had better weapons and even some snipers who had transferred from other sections. Therefore, the commune faction had more casualties.

One morning, on the top floor of the department store of the Second Headquarters, Hei Tou, with a pistol in his belt and the latest rifle on his shoulder, said to the shooters standing by each window,

"You must keep your eyes firmly on the commune faction. They will run out of ammunition and foods soon, so they may ask someone to deliver supplies and ammunition for them. Blockade their entrance with gunfire."

A gunman asked, "What if there are peddlers and pedestrians near their buildings?"

"They are the people of the commune in disguise," Hei Tou retorted. "What kind of people can wander in their territory? Kill all of them!"

As Hei Tou finished speaking, Qing Lian came over and said to the gunmen,

"Attention please, the command orders that you try not to kill ordinary citizens. Otherwise, the commune faction will bring us before the central committee accusing us of killing innocent people."

After hearing this, Hei Tou whispered, "What a shit command this is!"

At four o'clock in the afternoon, both sides stopped shooting. They had probably got tired. Cai Wenge and Qing Lian were patrolling the floors. When they reached the top, they heard a gunman muttering:

"Does this guy not want to live? Why is he always strolling around?" Cai went over and asked him what was going on. The gunman said that a tall young man was trying to get into the Jili Hotel. He didn't seem to be a person of the commune because he had no weapons. He might be a roast chicken hawker who wanted to sell his chicken inside. After hearing the words of the gunman, Cai and Qing Lian raised their telescopes and observed the hotel. "Ah…" Qing Lian's heart suddenly trembled, because she saw clearly that the person was Zhang Feng.

"Well, why is he here? Is he tired of being alive?" Qing Lian still had a love-hate relationship with Zhang Feng, her former love. Although he had hurt her, she still couldn't forget him.

"It is the man who injured several of our people when we attacked Polytechnic University. Kill him!" Cai said to the gunman. Qing Lian was shocked. She quickly said to Cai,

"Lao Cai, don't do that. He is our classmate! Besides, he is just a carefree and neutral person. I heard that he had gone to Polytechnic University just wanted to see Wang Hai last time."

"Yeah, you are right," Cai said with a reluctant smile. "We are classmates and I can't do too much."

Qing Lian walked a dozen paces and heard Cai say something to the gunman. Then he left. She was still worried, so she looked again at the door of the distant hotel with the telescope. She saw that Zhang Feng was ready to rush to the hotel door again. Then she looked back at the gunman, who had already aimed at Zhang Feng. Without thinking, she flew a few steps and hit the gunman's shoulder. The bullet shot out with a popping sound. The gunman looked at Qing Lian and said,

"Committee member Liu, what's wrong with you? I missed. Committee member Cai will blame me for that. He told me that that person is the black background of the commune, so I must kill him."

"Don't believe him. That person is my classmate with a poor family background and he is just a neutral person." After that, she lifted her telescope and checked again. She saw with relief that there was no one lying on the ground in front of the hotel.

Eventually Zhang Feng managed to get into the Jili Hotel. The people inside were all worried about him. He ventured to come in because Wang Hai's mother had been diagnosed with gastric cancer. She wanted to see Wang Hai because the doctor said that she only had six months or less to live. All the hospitals had been disrupted, and patients couldn't get immediate treatment. The main hospitals in the city had become strongholds of the Second Headquarters, and the external telephone line of the Jili Hotel had been cut off. Therefore, Zhang Feng had to risk getting in to find Wang Hai. With luxurious decoration and excellent service, the Jili Hotel was the largest in the whole province and had a very high charge. There were different restaurants with different styles of foods, including Kanton, Sichuan, Jiangsu, Zhejiang cuisine, and so on. The eight big cuisines were all here. Zhang Feng's favourite was the north-eastern cuisine. A few years ago, when his father was dining with some old friends, Zhang Feng went with him. However, there was no time for Zhang Feng to notice the changes here now, so he found Wang Hai quickly with the help of Li He. Wang Hai had just attended the funeral of two comrades who had died yesterday. His eyes were red and swollen. Zhang Feng took Wang Hai to a small room and told him about his mother's condition. Wang Hai sobbed with his head on his crossed arms. Zhang Feng patted his shoulder to comfort him and asked him if he would go home to see his mother. Wang Hai was silent for a long time and whispered,

"It's so hard. Now the situation is very tense. The Second Headquarters has kept attacking, sometimes even at night. The people in our command are very nervous and do not dare to relax even for a moment. Well, I'll write a short message to my parents. After a week or two, when the situation has turned back in our favour, I'll go back to see my mother."

Zhang Feng had wanted to persuade Wang Hai not to make unnecessary sacrifices in these power struggles, but he was embarrassed to say anything at the sight of his determination. Wang Hai asked Zhang Feng not to leave until dark and said that the chef who made north-eastern dishes was still there. He could already taste the crisp fried pork. Zhang Feng told him that he didn't want to wait to have dinner. His relatives and friends were all in distress, so he was in no mood to enjoy delicious food.

CHAPTER IV

A Tall Figure in the Smoke

The armed confrontation between the Second Headquarters and the Jili Commune had lasted for more than two months, and both sides had casualties. The weapons the commune used were not as good as those of the Second Headquarters, so the commune had more casualties. The factional struggles throughout the country were also in a standoff. The Central Cultural Revolution Group (Mao Zedong was its political backstage supporter) wanted to suppress all the disobedient generals in the military. However, the rebel faction supported by these generals were confronted by those supported by the Cultural Revolution Group, so both sides were involved in a 'civil war' in what was supposed to be peacetime. In Jili City, people from all walks of life were involved in this life-and-death struggle; students, Red Guards, workers, officials, staff, citizens, and even peasants. Some of them joined the war directly, some of them giving support and help, and some of them showing their sympathy. They had already divided the whole city into two factions.

One day at the standing committee meeting of the Second Headquarters, Hei Tou and Cai Wenge both proposed upgrading their weapons because the latest news had reported that there were heavy weapons, including cannons, tanks, and rockets in the battles in Sichuan province. Qing Lian argued that there were so many arsenals in Sichuan, it was easy for them to get these weapons. Chang Zheng said that we could also get those heavy weapons easily in that the head of the military artillery regiment had been his father's subordinate, but he didn't know if he dared give them the weapons. Additionally, did anyone even know how to operate cannons? Cai said that it was easy, and also, he could say that the rebel faction had stolen the cannons, so he would not be responsible for that. "As to operation," he went on, "We have so many demobilised soldiers in our organisation, some of them must have been in artilleries."

Early the next morning, Zhao Wu's phone rang. He picked it up to hear the hurried tones of the Regiment Commander Zhang. He said that he had made a big mistake and that he might be sent to the military court. Zhao Wu asked him what had happened. Regiment Commander Zhang said that a group of rebel factions from the Second Headquarters had run into their encampment last night saying that they wanted to borrow some artillery. He had told them that he couldn't lend them the weapons without an order from above. They took the guns anyway and left Commander Zhang tied up. Then they snatched five or six pieces of artillery and some shells. Zhao Wu murmured:

"There is going to be a fierce drama"

"Commander, what did you say? Am I in a lot of trouble?" Zhang said.

Zhao Wu said, "We have no option. We can't afford to offend them, because they have the imperial carte blanche given by the great leader. Well, what is done is done. I will ask the logistics department if they can supply us with some pieces of artillery." after hearing this Regiment Commander Zhang repeatedly thanked him.

Yesterday Yu Mei's father had returned home again from the May Seventh Officials School. Since the whole country was involved in the fighting between factions, they had relaxed control of the capitalist roaders and allowed them to go home once a month. Zhao Wu had lent them a quiet hand, so the logistics department of the Provincial Party Committeearranged a better residence for Yu Mei's family, which was close to both the university district and the provincial military region. It was a Japanese-built unit with two bedrooms. There was a kitchen, toilet, gas and heating in the house. Although it was not as good as the big house they used to live in, it was much better than the dilapidated slum where they were living now. The whole family felt very happy. Therefore, Yu Mei's father had wanted to go to see Zhao Wu today in secret and express his thanks in person. He came back late at night, his face flushed and very excited, which apparently was the sign of alcohol. He told the whole family to sit down and they listened to the news he had heard from Zhao Wu.

According to Zhao Wu, there was now a deadlock between the two fighting factions. The Cultural Revolution Group could not continue its plan to weed out all the disobedient generals in the army. Therefore, Mao Zedong would have to reconcile the contradictions between the two factions soon so that the situation could improve. Yu Mei's younger brother asked when the militant fighting of the two factions would end in this city. Li Jianguo lowered his voice and said that he had heard something from Chang Zheng. He had said that the commune group would be defeated soon because the Second Headquarters had acquired cannons. Li Jianguo knew that Chang Zheng was always exaggerating, so he looked carefully at Zhao Wu. Zhao Wu, however, immediately changed the subject.

Yu Mei didn't sleep well that night. She knew all about the relationship between Zhang Feng and his friends from the commune faction. So if the Second Headquarters really used artillery against the building of the commune faction, his friends would face even greater danger. Should she tell this news to Zhang Feng? If she told him, what if he went to inform them personally as he had done last time and got into trouble again? She got up very early in the morning while the rest of the family was still sleeping. She put on her sports suit and sneaked out. She ran along the road by the river and wondered if she would go to Zhang Feng's house. Unconsciously, she ran across the river bridge, which was close to Zhang Feng's house. Yes, she was ready to tell Zhang Feng the news, but she would ask him not to deliver the message on his own. Instead, he should find someone else to go.

She knocked on the door of Zhang Feng's house, and Zhang Lin opened the door. She said that her brother had not yet got up. She led Yu Mei into the house.

"Hurry up! Get up now and see who has come." She said as she lifted up Zhang Feng's quilt. Zhang Feng blinked his eyes and sat up, muttering,

"Who is here so early, stopping me sleeping little longer?" But when he saw that the person standing by the bed was Yu Mei, he immediately jumped up.

"Not early, not early, welcome, welcome." Both Yu Mei and Zhang Lin laughed. After Zhang Feng put on his clothes, Yu Mei said to him,

"Brother Feng, I have an important thing to tell you. But you must promise me one thing."

"What is it?" Zhang Feng asked.

"You must find someone else to do this." Yu Mei said.

"OK. What is the important thing?" Yu Mei told Zhang Feng the news which she had heard from her father that the Second Headquarters would use artillery to attack the commune faction's stronghold,. Zhang Feng frowned and said,

"If so, Wang Hai and other people will face a great danger. No, I should tell them immediately so that they can prepare in advance. Ah, no, I have to find someone to inform them right away." Then he stood up and was ready to go. Yu Mei took his hand and said,

"Brother Feng, you must not risk yourself to go"

"Don't worry. I will be back soon and you'll be waiting here for me." Yu Mei worriedly sent him off to go out.

Zhang Feng ran to the bus stop and took a bus to the station near the city centre. The traffic ahead had already been interrupted because of the fighting. He hoped to find someone of the commune faction near the Jili Hotel and ask them to go to deliver the news. However, when he got near the hotel, he saw no one but he could hear non-stop shots. What should he do? He saw a truck slowly coming towards him. One side of the truck was welded with thick steel plates. He assumed that it must be the truck which delivered supplies for the commune. He waved to the driver. The driver stopped the truck and asked him what was wrong. Zhang Feng asked the driver if he was going to the hotel to deliver something. The driver said yes. Then Zhang

Feng asked if he could give a letter to the headquarters of the building. The driver looked at his watch and said,

"if it was important, you should go in and say it to them personally. Now, the gunmen of the Second Headquarters were taking a short break, you got on the truck quickly and we rushed over."

Zhang Feng had no choice, but jumped into the truck and went with the driver. When they were halfway, they were spotted by the gunmen on the opposite building. A bullet connected and banged the side of the steel plates loudly. Fortunately, no bullets hit the tyres. The truck arrived at the front of the hotel. Zhang Feng jumped out of the truck swiftly and ran into the hotel. The atmosphere inside the building seemed to be very tense, and fully armed commune soldiers ran up and down the stairs. Zhang Feng came to the command, where they were holding an emergency meeting. The guard at the gate let him in after he told him that he had something urgent to say. When Xu Jianguo, Wang Hai, and Li He saw that Zhang Feng was coming, they greeted him warmly and showed him to a set. He did not want Yu Mei and his family to worry about him, so he told them that he had something urgent to tell them and he would then leave. He said that the Second Headquarters was about to use artillery to attack the stronghold of the commune faction. Xu Jianguo said,

"We have already foreseen that they will attack us with more aggressive methods. We didn't expect that they would use cannons. We have to discuss how to resist them,"

One of the members of the standing committee was a demobilised soldier. He said that if it was a mortar, it could only break doors and windows. However, if it was a plat trajectory gun or a howitzer, it might destroy the building. Then everyone began to talk about how to cope with various situations. When Zhang Feng was ready to go, Wang Hai asked him to wait for 20 minutes because he wanted to know something related to his mother's condition.

Zhang Feng waited for more than an hour, but Wang Hai didn't show up. Zhang Feng was very anxious because he knew that if he was trapped here this time, the result would be much more serious than being trapped in Polytechnic University last time.

When Zhang Feng was thinking about going to the command to find Wang Hai, he heard a loud noise all of a sudden. The whole building trembled and the glass of many windows shattered.

"No, the Second Headquarters has already begun to attack." Zhang Feng said to himself. At this moment, the loudspeaker of the Second Headquarters began to broadcast,

"People of the commune faction, listen to me. We have begun firing artillery, and the small cannon was just a warning for you just now. The powerful cannons are still to come. If you disarm and surrender within half an hour, we promise to ensure your personal safety. If you do not, you will be engulfed in a sea of flames."

There was panic now in the building because they had no weapon to fight back. They could only bear the attack passively. Zhang Feng heard the order of the command from the corridor.

"Go down with the building. If there is anyone who fears death, he can retreat first." No one rushed to escape, and it seemed that all of them were ready to devote themselves to defending Chairman Mao's revolutionary line.

Wang Hai rushed over and urged Zhang Feng to leave quickly. He said that it would be too late if he did not go now. Zhang Feng asked, "What are you doing?"

Wang Hai said that they would rather die than surrender. But if there was no hope, they would leave the building. Zhang Feng found that it seemed that there were not enough people to carry the injured away with stretchers. He then said,

"Wait. Although I am unwilling to participate in the fight, I can help you take care of the wounded. I will help them carry the stretchers and retreat with the wounded."

Half an hour later, Zhang Feng and several wounded people lying on the stretchers were waiting in the foyer of the hotel for a car to pick up them. Suddenly they heard several continuous loud noises, the entire building shaking fiercely. Thick smoke was coming from the stairs on the second and third floors. "Oh my god," Zhang Feng thought. It seemed that the Second Headquarters had begun to attack with heavy artillery. Then there came several louder noises followed by the sound of the building collapsing. At this time, a man with a gun flew upstairs shouting,

"Oh no, Commander Xu is injured!"

Zhang Feng asked quickly: "Where is he?"

"He is in the command post on the 3rd floor" Zhang Feng ran to the third floor under heavy smoke and flames. There was a man lying on the ground outside the command post, and two people kneeling beside him, calling him. The person lying on the ground was Xu Jianguo. He was covered in blood and his right arm was still twitching.

"Jian Guo! Jian Guo!" Zhang Feng leaned down and shouted. Xu Jianguo slowly opened his eyes and looked at Zhang Feng. He said hoarsely:

"Zhang Feng, is that you?" Then he reached into his inside pocket and took out a blue jade bracelet, which had been stained with his blood. He handed the bracelet to Zhang Feng and said,

"Li Li went back to her home to see her father. This… this bracelet is from my grandmother and she would like me to give this bracelet to her future granddaughter-in-law. I intended to give it to her when I proposed. But now, it's too late. You…you replace me to give it to her. Let…let her find another man who deserves her entire life!"

Then his head went down. He was dead. Zhang Feng felt pain as if his heart had been run through with a knife. He helped put Xu Jianguo on the stretcher, and told them to hurry to find a doctor to see if they could do something to save his life, even though the pulse of Xu Jianguo had already stopped.

"Wang Hai!" Zhang Feng suddenly thought that since the command had been blown up, Wang Hai must also be in danger. Then he ran to the other side of the corridor disregarding his own safety under the smoke, the raging fire, the bricks and wooden beams collapsing from the roof continuously. Zhang Feng saw that half of the third floor facing the Second Headquarters had completely collapsed. The shelling was still going on, and it seemed that they really wanted to kill the commune faction. Zhang Feng suddenly saw a body crawling under a broken wall. He rushed over and found that it was Wang Hai. His legs were bleeding and he could not stand up.

"Wang Hai, hold on, I will save you." Wang Hai looked up at Zhang Feng and said,

"Elder brother, it is too dangerous here. Just leave me and run. The roof is collapsing. If you do not run now, you will be hit."

Zhang Feng pulled a big cloth from his shirt, bandaged the wound on Wang Hai's leg, and then lifted him up. The ceiling was falling down all around them. Wang Hai squatted on the ground after only two steps, because his thigh was injured very badly. "Elder brother, don't bother and just run quickly." Then he pushed Zhang Feng with his hand.

"No, I can't leave you alone. Come and I will take you away." Then he knelt down and told Wang Hai to hold his shoulder. Wang Hai was so strong that average people couldn't carry him. Fortunately, Zhang Feng was robust and had learned martial arts. He tried twice before he was succeeded in lifting Wang Hai.

"Come on!" Zhang Feng said and then slowly walked into the hallway. The roof above collapsed as soon as they had left the broken room.

On the top floor of the department store opposite, Chang Zheng was observing the shelled hotel with a telescope. When his vision turned to the collapsed part of the third floor of the hotel, he suddenly saw a slowly moving figure in the fire and smoke. It seemed that it was one person carrying another, and both of them might be his acquaintances.

'Is it him?' Chang Zheng thought of Zhang Feng. Was this guy involved again? He really did not want to live, Chang Zheng thought. He knew that Zhang Feng did not participate in the commune faction; he was only worried about Wang Hai and other people's safety like last time in Polytechnic University. Chang Zheng couldn't help admiring him. 'This guy is a man who helps his friends at any cost,' he mused at heart.

Zhang Feng carried Wang Hai down, and saw many people in the corridor waiting to get out of the building. To avoid further sacrifices, the rest of the standing committees of the headquarters decided to evacuate the building to the other commune strongholds in the suburbs. Since the Second Headquarters had already strengthened the fire blockade of the clearing at the entrance of the building, they could rely on two home-made ballistic vehicles to move people out slowly. The wounded had priority. When Wang

Hai was put in the vehicle, there were still several other casualties needing to be removed as soon as possible. Although Wang Hai talked with them about letting Zhang Feng go first and they did agree, Zhang Feng gave his opportunity to the wounded and told Wang Hai to see the doctor as soon as possible.

Again and again Zhang Feng let other people take their places in the evacuation vehicles. By the time he left, almost all the people in the building had been evacuated. But unexpectedly, the truck had just turned onto the road when it was hit by a burst of intense fire, and the tyre was blown off so that it could not move anymore.

"Lay down your arms and we'll spare your lives!" The gunmen of the Second Headquarters surrounded the truck, shouting. The people inside were logistical personnel and had no weapons; they had to get out and surrender. They were now captives, including Zhang Feng.

They were taken to the department store by the people of the Second Headquarters. The minute they went in, they heard the loud voice of Hei Tou. He called,

"The hated commune! Now it is over!" Zhang Feng knew that he would be in trouble when he met Hei Tou, so he bowed his head and turned his face to one side. However, when Hei Tou heard that there were some captives, he immediately came over, wanting to crack his whip at them.

"Ha, guys, where are you going to flee? Today, I will let you know the power of my whip." Then he gave every captive two lashes of the whip. Hei Tou had just lifted the whip when he suddenly recognised Zhang Feng. He put down the whip.

"Ha," he said grimly. "Every dog has its day. Today is the day of reckoning for you!" Zhang Feng had no fear at all. He straightened up and said,

"Hei Tou, you are a little rascal. Although you are now the head of rebel factions, you still do not look like a revolutionary."

"You…you!" Hei Tou turned red with anger because he was insulted by Zhang Feng before so many people. He was so angry that he took out his pistol and said to Zhang Feng,

"I… I must kill you today." The vice-captain, standing next to Hei Tou held down his pistol and said,

"Captain, we are red rebel faction, not the Kuomintang, so we can't shoot captives." Hei Tou was not convinced and said,

"Am I the head, or you? I should at least make him disabled, if not kill him." He still wanted to shoot Zhang Feng.

"What are you quarrelling about here?" A tall head of the Second Headquarters came down from upstairs followed by many attendants,

"Commander Zhao, you need to control this. Captain Hei Tou wants to kill a captive." A low level team leader who couldn't bear the bandit operating style of Hei Tou said,

"No. How can we shoot a captive randomly?" Zhang Feng knew it was Chang Zheng when he heard his voice. He breathed a sigh of relief inwardly because he knew that Chang Zheng would not treat him like Hei Tou, though they had once been rivals. Additionally, Zhang Feng had let him go last time in Polytechnic University.

"It's really you!" Chang Zheng said in surprise. "I saw you through the telescope walking with a person on your back. I thought you were hit by the roof. You must lead a charmed life." Zhang Feng said,

"I just saved my friend. I couldn't let him die." Chang Zheng wanted to say something, but it was hard for him to say in front of so many people. So he said,

"We do not know whether you got involved in the fighting, so we need to investigate." He said to his attendants,

"Take them away and lock them up first. We need to investigate further."

In fact, he saved Zhang Feng. Hei Tou dared not argue with Chang Zheng but he stamped his feet in anger.

Somehow, Zhang Feng was confined to a small room in the basement alone. After a while, the door opened and a man appeared that Zhang Feng was most reluctant to see. It was Cai Wenge.

"Ah, my old classmate, we meet again. No offense, but you should stay away from the campaign if you have no good family background. Just be a free man and don't get yourself in any trouble." He said in a strange voice. Zhang Feng did not reply. Cai Wenge added:

"We are old classmates. I will try to save you. But you have to cooperate." Then he took out a few sheets of paper and a pen and said that as long as Zhang Feng wrote something to admit that he had participated in the fighting and helped the Jili Commune fight against the Second Headquarters, and opposed Chairman Mao's revolutionary line, he would let him go. Then he said with a smirk,

"Be released early and your little fairy will be waiting for you." Zhang Feng knew that Cai was a sinister and cunning villain. He envied everything about Zhang Feng. It was impossible that he would do anything to help Zhang Feng. So he said firmly:

"I did not participate in the fighting, just like the last time in Polytechnic University. It was only that Wang Hai's mother was seriously ill, so I came to him. And he was injured, so I helped him." Zhang Feng kept a watchful eye so that he didn't mention anything about his purpose for coming here. Cai listened and blinked. Then he said,

"Is there such a coincidence? Every time you get into the fight… You need to think about it. If you don't write the confession, you will not be released any time soon!" Then he walked away angrily.

To Zhang Feng's surprise, the people he hated came one after another. When the door opened again, Qing Lian came in, followed by two people who seemed to be bodyguards, with whips in their hands. Zhang Feng thought that he was going to be whipped. Qing Lian took a whip from one of the attendants and then told them to go out. After the door closed, there were only two of them in the room. Zhang Feng thought that although he was a captive now, he couldn't lose spiritually to this self-proclaimed most revolutionary madwoman. Therefore, he looked her up and down boldly. Strangely, Qing Lian was not so fierce as usual. She was dressed in smart military uniform and her hair was neatly combed in her cap. There seemed to be a bit of vanishing cream on her white face.

"Do you acknowledge your crime, Zhang Feng?" Then she raised the whip and shook it with a crackling sound, but the whip did not lash Zhang Feng. Then she raised her voice and said,

"It's a serious crime to help the people of the commune on the side of revisionism to fight against our revolutionaries!" Zhang Feng felt that these words seemed to be said to the people outside the door. Then she waved two whips. After a few minutes of silence, her face suddenly turned red and angry. She held her whip high, and seemed that she was really going to lash Zhang Feng, but she put it down at once. Strangely, her eyes were filled with tears.

"Zhang Feng, I really want to lash you, not for your political opposition to us, but for the wrong thing you did to me. Why did you humiliate me in public? Tell me the reason!" Her voice was hoarse with anger.

"What?" Zhang Feng was puzzled. "I have never done anything wrong to you."

"You still quibble. Ah, maybe you, the playboy, have hurt so many girls that you can't even remember all of them now."

Zhang Feng said very seriously,

"Please, firstly, I am not a playboy; secondly, I really haven't done anything wrong to you."

Qing Lian began to get impatient.

"Stop pretending! You put my letter on the wall and made me a laughing stock in front of the whole class and the whole grade. You didn't do it?" Zhang Feng was surprised.

"I have a good memory. If I really did this thing, I would never forget it. Besides, I never received your letter, nor do I play tricks like this. How did you send me the letter?"

"During the break, I put it on your desk so you could see it." After a moment's thought, Zhang Feng suddenly realised,

"It was those two guys!" So he explained that Wang Hai and Li He had often searched his desk to see if there were cookies and candy. It must have been the two boys who had seen the letter and put it on the wall when he had asked for sick leave one day. Zhang Feng then said,

"No wonder that whenever we mentioned you before, Wang Hai began to talk about something else, like 'Dear Brother Feng, you are my Prince Charming,' and Li He always grinned and winked. But whenever I asked them what they were talking about, they kept silent."

Qing Lian said dubiously,

"Was it really those two who did this? I must fix them if there is an opportunity! They are also my opponents now. Hum!" Qing Lian seemed to calm down. Then she said,

"You shouldn't waste your time on two unsuitable women. Song Dan Dan is older than you and Li Yu Mei's father has been a capitalist roader. You should find a girl who has a good family background to make up for your political deficiencies." Then she pushed back her hair and looked at Zhang Feng gently, which was a rare thing. Zhang Feng found her irritating, but he still said politely,

"Thank you for your advice. It's my own business. I'll take care of it." Qing Lian saw that he was unwilling to talk to her and then she left reluctantly.

The standing committee of the Second Headquarters held a victory meeting. After the main stronghold of the commune was removed, the city centre was completely under the control of the Second Headquarters. At the end of the meeting, someone asked how to treat the captives. Hei Tou and Cai Wenge both agreed that the core members, like Zhang Feng, must be severely punished. However, Qing Lian and Chang Zheng argued that Zhang Feng had been visiting friends these two times and did not participate in the fighting.

"Although he hurt our people last time at Polytechnic University, he just wanted to protect his friends," they argued. Hei Tou turned red with rage and quarrelled with them. Finally, Commander Liu, Chang Zheng's friend, said,

"Then we will take a few days to investigate, and if he is not a core member, we can release him."

Zhang Feng didn't go home for two days, and all his family were worried. Both Yu Mei and Dan Dan came to his house. Yu Mei talked about the thing she had told to Zhang Feng and said that she shouldn't have told him the news that the Second Headquarters was going to attack the strongholds of the commune with artillery. Now she heard that the Jili Hotel had been blown up and the commune faction had suffered heavy casualties. Zhang Feng's whereabouts were unknown. Yu Mei cried and cried. Dan Dan was calmer. She said that Zhang Feng was very smart and he would be okay. Then someone knocked on the door. It was Li He. Everyone rushed over. Li He narrated the story of how Zhang Feng had saved Wang Hai. But Zhang Feng and the last group of people had not reached the strongholds of the commune in the suburbs, and they must have been captured. Since there was not any punishment for captives in the two factions so far, Zhang Feng was safe for a short period. Yu Mei was glad to hear it. She immediately stood up and said that she would go to find someone at the Second Headquarters to ask about Zhang Feng's situation. Dan Dan also said that she would find someone to inquire.

Dan Dan thought for a long time. Cai Wenge and Qing Lian were her only two acquaintances among the heads of the Second Headquarters. Qing Lian was jealous of her relationship with Zhang Feng, so she wouldn't help her. Then she had to find Cai, though it was disgusting to see his indecent face. It was not easy for her to find Cai Wenge in the command of the Second Headquarters in the department store. At the sight of Dan Dan, Cai beamed happily. He had been drooling over Dan Dan for years because not only was she Zhang Feng's girl but she was also beautiful and wise. She was mature, plump, and brilliant as a beautiful peony.

He took Dan Dan to a small house and prepared tea for her. He thought about how all the beautiful girls surrounded Zhang Feng and didn't even glance at him. 'How about now? I am the leader of the rebel faction, and the day is coming that beautiful women are coming to me.' He knew that Dan Dan was looking for Zhang Feng, but he pretended to know nothing and started chatting about other things. But Dan Dan was in no mood to chat and asked him about Zhang Feng directly. Cai said seriously,

"Dan Dan, you don't know how serious his problem is. He has a bad family background and also he got involved in the fighting. We are going to punish him as the black background of the commune faction." Dan Dan was anxious when she heard this, and argued in favour of Zhang Feng. Cai gave her a sympathetic look. He said,

"Well, we are old classmates. Besides, you, our campus belle, have pleaded for him. So I have to help him. Have another cup of tea." Then he stood up and poured another cup of tea for Dan Dan, sitting on the chair beside her. He said lewdly,

"No problem. I will certainly help him. So how are you going to repay me?" The stench in his mouth almost sprayed onto Dan Dan's face. Dan Dan felt disgusted and stood up quickly. Cai also stood up with his eyes staring at Dan Dan's plump breasts greedily. A girl with a poor family background was just like a lamb to the slaughter for him, a high-ranking rebel faction leader. He could not control his desire.

"At least let me kiss you for once." He suddenly held Dan Dan and kissed her lips. At the same time, he grabbed her breast with one hand. A loud slap hit on the face of Cai.

"You are a hooligan!" Dan Dan broke away from Cai's arm and shouted, "I am going to sue you!"

Cai covered his face and said impudently, "You can go to sue me, but everyone will say that you, the child of the Black Five Categories seduced the leader of the rebel faction in order to save her lover."

"You are shameless!" Dan Dan held back her tears and ran out of the room.

Yu Mei was luckier than Dan Dan. She went to Chang Zheng's house and found him at home. Chang Zheng had recently felt guilty when facing Yu Mei because Chang Zheng had drawn a demarcation line with Yu Mei's family after Li Jnguo had been toppled down, for fear that they would be implicated by them. He was a very realistic person. He knew that if he wanted to advance politically, he must find a girl with a favourable political background. What's more, there were many beautiful girls around him in the military compound, so he had lost interest in Yu Mei, and now he only regarded her as his sister. That was why he had changed his attitude towards Zhang Feng. In addition, Zhang Feng had not hurt him in the last encirclement and suppression in Polytechnic University. Zhang Feng was a loyal friend, true and an honest person, which made Chang Zheng really admire him. Therefore, before Yu Mei explained why she was here, he said directly,

"You've come here for your Brother Feng? I am also trying to get him out as soon as possible." Then he told her all about the fact that Zhang Feng had risked himself saving Wang Hai, as well as about the disagreement among the heads of the Second Headquarters about his punishment. Yu Mei did not expect that Chang Zheng to be so straightforward. He had used to be Zhang Feng's mortal enemy. Yu Mei kept thanking him. Then she proposed a hard request for Chang Zheng – that she wanted to visit Zhang Feng. Chang Zheng thought for a moment and said,

"No problem, but you can't stay for too long." Then he hesitated and said, "There are several storerooms on one side of the basement corridor. Sometimes the workers who send things will forget to close the door. But you can't let him escape."

Chang Zheng actually implied that they could escape. In fact, Commander Liu had already said that if there was still no result after a few days of investigation, Zhang Feng could leave. So he just did a good turn.

Before dark, Chang Zheng took Yu Mei into the basement of the department store. There were two guards with guns at the entrance. Chang Zheng told them that it was a family visit and it should last for an hour. The two guards saw that Yu Mei was a beautiful girl without weapons, so they let her in. Chang Zheng also left. Yu Mei pushed open the door of the room where Zhang Feng was confined and saw him doing fitness exercises. Zhang Feng looked back at Yu Mei and jumped up in surprise. They hugged each other tightly. Yu Mei shed tears and touched Zhang Feng's face with her hand. She asked,

"Did you suffer? Are you injured? Did they beat you?" Zhang Feng tried to comfort her,

"Nothing, you can see that I am fine."

"I was so scared. I heard that the Jili Hotel was destroyed by artillery and many people died." Zhang Feng's face hardened suddenly.

"Yes, Xu Jianguo, my good friend, died. Wang Hai was also seriously injured."

"Li He told us that you saved Wang Hai. He is now out of danger and is recovering in a suburban stronghold of the commune. Now everyone is worried about you." Zhang Feng's brow cleared after hearing that Wang Hai was fine. He heaved a sigh and said,

"Hey, this is a meaningless sacrifice." They talked for about ten minutes. Then Yu Mei looked around the small, cold, dank room and said,

"Brother Feng, we can escape from here. A long delay means

trouble. Chang Zheng told me that Hei Tou and Cai Wenge want to harm you and don't want to let you go."

"There are guards with guns outside, and how can we escape from here?" Zhang Feng asked. Yu Mei then told Zhang Feng about the secret of the basement that she had heard from Chang Zheng.

"Well, let's have a try," Zhang Feng said.

He checked the things he was carrying and walked stealthily out of the door with Yu Mei. There were several doors leading to the corridor on the other side of the basement. They passed the first door smoothly. After passing the second door, they suddenly saw a few people standing in front. One of them was Cai Wenge. smirking, with four big men carrying rods standing behind him.

"Old classmate, we never expected to meet here. A fairy accompanies you. You are so blessed." Cai said to Zhang Feng while looking Yu Mei up and down with a lustful look.

"What do you want to do? You have been investigating me for a few days. Have you found any evidence? Why don't you let me go?" Zhang Feng said.

"Take it easy." Cai said in a strange voice, "Since there is a fairy, you can stay for a few more days." Then he signalled to the big men to take Zhang Feng back to his confined room. Zhang Feng knew that he couldn't fight with them, so he had to go back to the small cell with Yu Mei. Cai Wenge said something to a big man at the door and left. Then the big men forced Zhang Feng to sit on the bed and suddenly held his head down on the bed. Yu Mei screamed:

"What are you doing?" The leading big man said,

"You dared to try to escape from here, shouldn't you be punished? I will hit you 50 times with my rod to smash your courage." Then he lifted the rods aimed at Zhang Feng's legs and started to hit him hard. Zhang Feng concentrated all his energy on the muscles of his legs and back with the internal energy exercise method taught by his master. As a result, when the rod hit his leg, it bounced, which made the big man's hand go numb. He stamped his feet with anger and said,

"Fuck you! You have learned martial arts. Well, I have an iron rod and it's impossible that your legs are harder than iron!" Then he took a thick iron rod from the hand of his accomplices. Yu Mei shouted,

"What are you doing?"

"Our head said that we should break his leg and make him disabled before you, the little fairy, to see if he will still be so proud!"

Zhang Feng was shocked and thought that Cai was really brutal. If now he was pushed around, he would definitely suffer. Therefore, he had no choice but to fight with them. Although these four men were big and powerful, it seemed that they had not learned martial arts so that would not be so difficult to fight against them. So he concentrated on his strength and broke free from the hands of the two big men. He jumped up from the bed and flew to the big man with an iron bar. In a twinkling, his lightning boxing had already hit the chest of the big man. Although he only used half of his strength, the big man had already fallen to the ground.

"Great!" Yu Mei screamed excitedly. The other three big men with rods surrounded Zhang Feng and began to fight with him. Although he was outnumbered, Zhang Feng was not afraid of them because his master had taught him 'Hands of Lightning' and 'Legs of Lightning,' which was especially useful when one was attacked by more than one person. In less than a minute, two of the three great men had been knocked down.

At this moment, something unexpected happened. The leading big man stood up stumblingly from the ground, and suddenly grabbed Yu Mei's neck from behind. He shouted to Zhang Feng,

"Stop and surrender! Otherwise, I will kill her!" Zhang Feng was stunned. He wanted to save Yu Mei, but another big man waved his rod to attack him. Then the door suddenly opened and a man in black, wearing a mask, rushed in. When everyone was still recovering from the surprise, he kicked down the big man who was holding Yu Mei's neck with a flying kick and knocked down the last person who had fought with Zhang Feng. He quickly tapped on the four big men's vital Meridian point, so they wouldn't be able move for a few hours. He grabbed Zhang Feng and Yu Mei, and said in a low voice,

"Follow me!" Zhang Feng didn't have time to think, and he followed the black man out of the room with Yu Mei. They quickly ran to the other side of the corridor. When they came to the storeroom area with many small rooms, the black men led them into a small room and went confidently to open the door to the outside, but he couldn't open it. He whispered,

"Oops, what's happened?" Zhang Feng thought his voice was a bit familiar, but there was no time for questions. Obviously, their escape had been discovered. The man took them to try to open the other door to the outside, but none of them could be opened. They could hear footsteps coming towards them. The black man pushed the door to the outside, but the door was still closed. When he was about to push it for the second time, the door suddenly opened from the outside. There stood a slender figure, whose hat was pressed very low. They could not see the face clearly. This person pointed a finger at the small alley in the dark, which signalled them to run quickly. Three of them rushed to the small alley at the corner. A few gunshots came from behind. Zhang Feng took Yu Mei's hand for fear that she would fall. They ran until they were far away, and they could no longer hear the sounds of the chase. They stopped, gasping for breath. Zhang Feng was going to thank the man in black and ask him about the vital Meridian point of attack. He had heard about this legendary martial art skill, but he had never seen it. Today, he had seen it with his own eyes. He was very curious and wanted to know all about it today. However, when he turned back to talk to the black man, the man had disappeared completely. There was only the rustling sound of the weeping willow blown by the night wind and the heavy breathing of Yu Mei beside him.

PART VI

Sweep Away All Monsters and Demons

CHAPTER I

Clean Up the Ranks of the Class – the Horrifying Red Terror

Spring 1968. The River City was once again shrouded in a soft pale green. The situation of the civil strife in Jili province was the same as that in the whole country. Neither faction could eliminate the other completely. Although the Second Headquarters occupied the downtown area, the commune faction had started guerrilla warfare in the suburbs against the Second Headquarters. According to Wang Hai, the commune faction's plan was to implement Chairman Mao's strategic idea of 'Encircling the cities from the countryside'. The Cultural Revolution Group, controlled by the Gang of Four, did not expect the Cultural Revolution to develop into such a situation. They had to compromise with the generals of the PLA and created various levels of revolutionary committees – a temporary regime. The original party and government organs had completely lost their position. The Revolutionary Committee consisted of three types of people: revolutionary officails, representatives of the revolutionary masses, and representatives of the PLA. This was called the 'Triple Combination'. Zhao Wu, the commander of the provincial military command in Jili province, had rightly become a representative of the People's Liberation Army of the revolutionary committee. Zhao Wu was fortunate enough to escape the elimination of the Central Cultural Revolution Group, although he was attacked by the rebel faction, and he was also a former subordinate of marshal Peng Dehuai. The representative of the revolutionary officials, surnamed Yang, was a former deputy minister of the Organisation Department of the Provincial Party Committee. He was a former subordinate of Li Jianguo. Because he had disassociated himself from Li Jianguo in time, and also took the initiative to have a good relationship with Du Zhongqing, the special commissioner of the Central Cultural Revolution Group, Yang became the deputy director of the Revolutionary Committee. Du Zhongqing, the commissioner in black, did not return to Beijing and was appointed the deputy director of the Revolutionary Committee. Although Zhao Wu strongly opposed the appointment, he was defeated by stronger voices in the central government. The representatives of the revolutionary masses were composed of different rebels. The Second Headquarters got a position as deputy director because of the strong backstage. Cai Wenge, Qing Lian, Chang Zheng and Hei Tou were members of the Revolutionary Committee. As a result of the exclusion, the commune faction had only a few members on the Revolutionary Committee, including Wang Hai, Li He and others.

As the civil strife was almost over, Zhang Feng continued his unfettered life. In addition to reading and playing the violin every day, he would go to Yu Mei's home twice a week. Occasionally Zhang Feng and Yu Mei went to the cinema together to see the old movies — the ones about the communists defeating the Kuomintang during the Revolutionary War. During the period of Cultural Revolution, most of the films and literary books were labelled as feudalist, capitalist, and revisionist. There were very few legitimate films and books that people could watch and read. Zhang Feng was disgusted with the revolutionary model operas promoted by Jiang Qing, Chairman Mao's wife. He often slipped away without seeing half of them. Dan Dan often came to Zhang Feng's home to help with the housework. Dan Dan also discussed with Zhang Feng some foreign literature books they had read before, or techniques of painting and calligraphy. However, if Zhang Feng went to Yu Mei's house, or Yu Mei came to Zhang Feng's, Dan Dan would definitely avoid them. Zhang Feng's mother had always regarded Dan Dan as her daughter, and she seemed to be more fond of her than she was of Yu Mei.

A few days ago, Zhang Feng's mother unexpectedly said to Dan Dan that "A woman who is one year older than a man can't be the man's wife" was the idea of feudal superstition. This topic made Dan Dan blush shyly, and she quickly moved to other topics.

On the day of the first anniversary of Xu Jianguo's death, Zhang Feng, Wang Hai and Li He went to clean the grave. It was in a woodland near the river. The members of the commune faction who had died in the civil strife were also buried there. When they walked into the woodland of the graveyard, they saw a bunch of people around the grave of Xu Jianguo. Upon approaching, it was clear that it was Li Li and the 'Four Talents of the River City'. Zhang Feng had not seen the 'Four Talents' for a long time, and he quickly stepped forward to greet them, introducing them to Wang Hai and Li He. Everyone was disposed to be friendly because they were all friends of Xu Jianguo. Li Li said hello to Zhang Feng, Wang Hai and Li He with tears in her eyes. Zhang Feng noticed that Li Li wore a bracelet on her wrist. This bracelet was entrusted to him by Xu Jianguo when he was dying.

After the memorial ceremony for Xu Jianguo was completed, the crowd prepared to leave. At this time, Liu Tian, the eldest brother of the Four Talents, said to Zhang Feng,

"Drop in at our house if you have time. Our salon of literature and art has resumed its activities." Zhang Feng was glad to hear that. The Four Talents were all versatile. They knew everything from ancient and modern times as well as techniques about music, chess, calligraphy and painting. Zhang Feng could learn a lot from them. At the beginning of the civil strife, Zhang Feng felt that time had passed too fast every time he went to their house. The Four Talents also appreciated Zhang Feng's capability.

One weekend, Zhang Feng asked his friends to attend the salon of the Four Talents. Wang Hai was unable to participate because of a prior engagement. In the end, Zhang Feng went with Li He. The location of the salon was still in the old-style black brick house of the eldest brother, Liu Tian. Zhang Feng liked it very much. Poplars and weeping willows were scattered in the quiet and quaint courtyard. Compared with the turbulent situation outside, here was like a land of idyllic beauty. All Four Talents belonged to the 'neutral people' and were not interested in the Cultural Revolution. From the beginning of the Cultural Revolution, Liu Tian and Wang Yang, the eldest and second eldest of the Four Talents, did not participate in the Red

Guards of Beijing University and Qinghua University. Due to his unacceptable family background, Li Yue, the third brother, did not participate in the Red Guards of Jili University. Chen Xing, the youngest brother, was an alumnus of Xu Jianguo at Jili Polytechnic University , but he was not interested in the Cultural Revolution. He had repeatedly tried to persuade Xu Jianguo to quit the rebel faction organisation. After Xu Jianguo's death, he regretted that he had not been able to prevent Xu Jianguo from continuing to participate in the civil strife.

Entering Liu Tian's home, Zhang Feng saw that the Four Talents had gathered there and were discussing whether a painting of Wang Yang's collection was genuine or fake. It was a Chinese brush painting by a famous painter of the Ming Dynasty. The painting had been brought to northeast China by Wang Yang's grandfather from his hometown. Liu Tian and Wang Yang believed the painting was genuine, while Li Yue questioned the authenticity of the seal on the painting. Zhang Feng knew something about engraving. He also believed the painting was genuine. Wang Yang was happy with the result, so he called out to everyone,

"OK, let's have some tea. I've brought high-class Longjing tea. Let's have a drink." Everyone sat down to have tea and a chat. Suddenly, Liu Tian gave a long sigh.

"'On war-torn land, streams flow and mountains stand. In vernal town grass and weeds are overgrown.' Beautiful China has become such a mess of dilapidation, and we are loafing around and indulging in empty talk."

"Yes, factories are shut down, schools are closed, and all walks of life are not working properly. I don't understand what benefits this revolution can bring to our country," Wang Yang agreed.

"There is no cultural learning, no entertainment, and all culture and art are labelled feudal, capitalist and revisionist," Li Yue added. Chen Xing took a sip of tea and said angrily,

"When personality worship dominates the whole society, the people become fools. This society has become a society where good and evil are turned upside down. Bad people, crafty people and whistle-blowers have become the mainstream of society. Good people and educated people are persecuted." Zhang Feng listened attentively, but Li He seemed nervous. Although Li He was a moderate in the Red Guards and was not willing to use violence against the Five Black Categories (landlord, rich peasant, counter-revolutionary, bad element and rightist), he still believed that Chairman Mao's revolutionary line could create a new world and that the current chaos was only temporary. Since the people who participated in the salon were friends of Zhang Feng, he could not say anything against them. When the Four Talents talked about whether Liu Shaoqi, the state president, should be attacked or not, Li He frowned with displeasure, because they were talking about a very sensitive political topic. Li He stood up and said,

"Sorry, there are guests coming to my house in the afternoon. I have to leave now. " Then he said goodbye to everyone and left. Liu Tian asked Zhang Feng,

"Is Li He a trusted friend?"

"Don't worry, although he is very active in the Cultural Revolution, he is still very loyal to his friends," Zhang Feng said.

At noon, Liu Tian's mother cooked lunch for everyone. Because she was Sichuanese, she could make authentic Sichuan cuisine, especially Mapo tofu and kung pao chicken. Everyone said it was delicious. In the afternoon, the friends gathered to talk about literature, art and poetry. They talked until the evening, when everyone reluctantly said goodbye. Zhang Feng borrowed two books from Liu Tian, two Shakespeare drama books translated by Zhu Shenghao. He had read all of Shakespeare's tragedy works and part of the comedy works. At the time, all literary works were banned from being published and read therefore these literary books could only be circulated secretly among friends. Zhang Feng believed that Shakespeare opened a door to a beautiful and wonderful world, where there was intoxicating poetry along with colourful and kaleidoscope-like humanity.

When Zhang Feng returned home, both his parents and his younger sister were sitting around the radio listening to the news report – this was the political weathervane of China at the time. Mao Zedong's highest instructions and the new policy of the Central Cultural Revolution Group on the Cultural Revolution were broadcast nationwide in the news report.

The voice of the announcer this night was particularly excited. 'Something serious is definitely going to happen,' Zhang Feng thought. He sat down with his family to listen to the radio. The announcer on the radio said that it was necessary to carry out a nationwide purifying movement for the class ranks, and to 'launch a 12-scale red storm that will sweep away all monsters and demons.' Seeing his father's expression, Zhang Feng guessed that something serious was going to happen. After the news report ended, Zhang Feng's father shut down the radio and said to the whole family,

"A larger movement to eradicate class enemies is about to begin. This time it will definitely be bigger than the beginning of the Cultural Revolution. Everywhere in China is still in chaos, and the central government wants to create a climate of political coercion and terror to control the situation. I don't know how many people will have their families broken. We must be prepared and not be afraid. The darkness will always pass, and the light will come. My son, your mom and I are very worried about you. Because of me, you are burdened with an unacceptable family background, and you have participated in the civil strife before, so you must speak and behave with caution."

"Don't worry, I haven't done anything against the party or against socialism," Zhang Feng reassured his parents. "I participated in the civil strife only to protect my friends' safety. It will be all right." But Zhang Feng did not expect that a serious disaster would happen to him.

The trouble came faster than expected. One morning, a few days later, someone knocked urgently on Zhang Feng's door. Zhang Lin opened the door and saw Dan Dan. She was flushed and short of breath.

"Where is Zhang Feng?" she asked. Zhang Feng had walked out of the room. "Something awful has happened, Wang Hai has been arrested, Li He was also detained for introspection," Dan Dan said.

"What? Is the Second Headquarters going to retaliate?" Zhang Feng asked. Dan Dan told Zhang Feng it seemed that the new movement was not just a struggle between factions. All traitors, spies, capitalists, and Five Black Categories would be detained and re-investigated. At the same time, everyone would be mobilised to find more class enemies. Revolutionary Committees at all levels had established specialised organisations called Mass Dictatorship Headquarters to review and detain class enemies. The Mass Dictatorship Headquarters of the hospital of the Normal University had told Dan Dan's mother to register. Zhang Feng's cousin, who worked at the Fengman Hydropower Station, wrote to say that their father had been detained as a Japanese spy because he had studied in Japan. 'Dad was right,' Zhang Feng said to himself. 'A twelfth storm of terror is really coming.'

The words soon became a reality. In the afternoon, two people dressed like workers came to Zhang Feng's house to inform father he had to register at the Mass Dictatorship Headquarters of the Normal University the next morning. Father agreed calmly. The whole family was very worried about father, but he said,

"I have experienced many movements, and now I am like a dead tiger, no longer worried about being tortured." Because of the fear of going through such a difficult period, mother wanted to make some preparations, that is, to hoard some daily necessities. She asked Zhang Feng and his younger sister to go to the grain store to buy several months' quota of grain, and then went to the grocery store to buy the whole family's quota of meat, eggs and sugar. Both the grain store and the grocery store were on the same street. Zhang Feng and his younger sister bought dozens of pounds of cornflour and sorghum in the grain store. At that time, living conditions in northeast China were very tough. Rice and refined flour could only be bought and eaten during the spring festival. On their way to the grocery store, Zhang Feng and his sister suddenly heard the noise of car engines, shouts and loudspeakers. They saw a dozen large trucks moving slowly; each one had a big banner with a different slogan, 'Sweep away all monsters and demons!' 'Leniency to those who confess, severity to those who resist!'

The people standing on the truck were bent down with lowered heads, and there were big boards around their necks, on which were written their crimes, such as 'Active counter-revolutionary', 'Pre-liberation counter-revolutionary', 'Rightist', 'US spy', 'Traitor' and so on. Each man's head was held from behind by a Red Guard or militiaman. The loudspeakers of the broadcast truck were shouting murderous slogans, which sent chills down the spines of the onlookers. Seeing his younger sister's frightened expression, Zhang Feng said to her,

"Xiao Lin, you should go home first. I can go to the grocery store by myself." Zhang was disgusted with this kind of behaviour that creates terror by degrading the dignity of a person. But in order to understand the situation fully, he had to continue to watch with a forbearance of disgust. Zhang Feng quickly figured out that it was a public punishment assembly parade launched by the Revolutionary Committee of the Provincial Cultural Education Sector. Among the people who were being public punished, Zhang Feng recognised writers, actors, composers and musicians who were famous at the provincial and municipal levels. Suddenly, Zhang Feng saw someone familiar on one of the trucks, although he could only see half face of the person's face. 'Representatives of the revisionist educational line' had been written on the big board hanging around the neck of this person. "My old principal!" Zhang Feng screamed, just as he started forward to comfort the old principal Chang Jingyu, there was a person behind him holding him back. He looked around and saw Dan Dan. She put two fingers to her lips, gesturing to Zhang Feng not to make a sound. She led Zhang Feng out of the crowd.

"You're crazy!" said Dan Dan. "Anyone who shows sympathy for these people will be arrested. Just now, an old lady saw a person who was being publicly punished, a 70-year-old man who fell down on the truck and was picked up by the red guards. She said only three words, 'what a pity.' She was arrested on the spot. Those who sympathise with the counter-revolutionaries are also treated as the member of anti-revolutionaries."

Wiping tears from his eyes, Zhang Feng mumbled,

"I wonder if the old principal will survive this time." Dan Dan didn't want Zhang Feng to get into any more trouble so she took him home. On the way, they saw many more horrible scenes. At the gates of many buildings, the big sign saying of 'Mass Dictatorship Headquarters' was hanging. A group of people with boards hanging around their necks were detained in these Mass Dictatorship Headquarters under the escort of the militia. Moreover, the screams and shouts of the people who were being beaten and tortured within the high walls could be heard continually. Dan Dan held onto Zhang Feng's arm, frightened, and said,

"Xiao Feng, we can't hide this time." Zhang Feng comforted her, and told her that she must take care of her mother. Dan Dan said sadly,

"Xiao Feng, the person I am most worried about is you. In the past two days, our Second Senior Middle-school set up a Mass Dictatorship Headquarter, and began to arrest people. Many teachers and workers with historical problems have been arrested. Now the Military's Propaganda Team and the Workers' Propaganda Team have all been stationed in various places, and together they have set up revolutionary committees at all levels to jointly launch a movement to purify the class ranks. A few days ago, that wicked guy Cai Wenge came back from downtown. He spread the news at the mobilisation assembly of the movement about purifying the class ranks. He said the class struggle in the Second Senior Middle School was like deep water. Class enemies are mixed with students like big fish. Are these words that he said against you? Some time ago, he always wanted to find opportunities to frame you."

"Don't worry," Zhang Feng reassured Dan Dan. "I didn't do any about beating, smashing, looting, or saying anything against the party and socialism. He won't be able find evidence to frame me." Then he smiled at Dan Dan and pretended to be confident.

However, two days later, in a quiet place on the bank of the river, Yu Mei met Zhang Feng. Yu Mei was intoxicated by the beautiful scenery in front of her eyes. The tranquil river was in bright sunshine, with gentle ripples, quietly flowing into the distance. The green mountains seem to want to kiss the sapphire skyline. The weeping willows on the bank fluttered in the breeze, like a beautiful girl showing her long hair to her boyfriend. It was noon, and there were few pedestrians by the river. Yu Mei laid her head on Zhang Feng's shoulder and held his hand in the hope that he would feel more relaxed. But Zhang Feng remained silent and was frowning

"What's the matter, Brother Feng? Aren't you glad to see me?" said Yu Mei softly. Zhang Feng sighed heavily and said to Yu Mei,

"Yu Mei, do you know? The movement to purify the class ranks recently has been much more serious than the beginning of the Cultural Revolution. I don't know how many people will have their families broken."

"I know that the people in the Provincial Party Committee and the municipal party committee said that they have arrested and tortured a lot of people," Yu Mei said. "Fortunately, my father is already a dead tiger. They have been detained in the May Seventh Cadre Schools and are not allowed to go home."

After pondering for a while, Zhang Feng said,

"Yu Mei, please don't come to me for the time being. I foresee that someone wants to frame me, although I belong to 'politically neutral persons' and I have not participated in the movement. However, in order to save my friends, I fought in the civil strife.

Cai Wenge, Chang Zheng and Hei Tou all saw this. Along with my black family status, they can tell people that I am an evil backstage manipulator. But don't worry, I will survive this storm."

Yu Mei clutched Zhang Feng's hand and said,

"Brother Feng, you will be alright. Your kindness will come back to you. God will bless us." Seeing no-one around, Zhang Feng hugged Yu Mei tightly. He thought, 'I will fight with them for the sake of my beloved Yu Mei.'

The next day, Zhang Feng strolled to the school. The loudspeaker of the radio station was broadcasting a critique of the old principal and his bourgeois education line, as well as a list of pre-liberation counter-revolutionaries that had just been discovered. These people were also old teachers who had taught students for decades. After a while, there was a new and exciting slogan in the broadcast: 'Uncover the cover of the class struggle in the Second Senior Middle-school! Dig out all hidden class enemies!' Zhang Feng left the campus in disgust.

Two days later, at noon, a knock on the door woke Zhang Feng and his younger sister from their nap. Neither of their parents was at home. Father had been detained in the Mass Dictatorship Headquarters of the Normal Universities, and mother was on the way to take father some clothes and daily necessities. Zhang Feng opened the door. Three people stood there; they were the backbone of Cai Wenge's team at the Rebel Faction.

"You must come with us. The school is in the process of inspecting class enemies. You need to cooperate with the investigation." Zhang Feng could sense their murderous intentions. He knew that there was no way to escape this time. He calmly said to his younger sister,

"Xiao Lin, I need to go to the school for a while, and I will come back soon." His younger sister said with a look of fear,

"Brother, you will be fine, right? Then come back quickly, please " Zhang Feng reassured her,

"It will be fine. I have done nothing wrong. Tell mom where I am going when she comes back."

Zhang Feng followed the three to the campus. He was surprised that the campus was so quiet; there was no sound at all, not even from the big speakers at the radio station. But Zhang Feng felt that there was a vaguely sinister atmosphere surrounding him. The three men took him to the gate of the school's grand auditorium. One of them asked Zhang Feng to wait outside the gate and then walked into the auditorium. After a minute, the gate opened. When Zhang Feng walked in, he was surrounded by the deafening slogans 'Down with Zhang Feng the active counter-revolutionary!' 'If Zhang Feng does not admit his guilt, we will completely destroy him!' 'Leniency to those who confess, severity to those who resist.'

Wherever he looked, the entire auditorium was filled with people. Two rows of tables were placed on the rostrum; there sat the leaders of the Revolutionary Committee, the Military's Propaganda Team and the Workers' Propaganda Team. Cai Wenge sat in the middle of the rostrum and looked like the highest official sent by the Revolutionary Committee of the Province. Zhang Feng was surprised, but calmed down immediately, because he knew that this day had to come sooner or later. Two people behind him seized his arms and led him up to the rostrum as a prisoner. Zhang Feng stood proudly in the middle of the rostrum and looked at Cai Wenge without fear.

Someone named Wang, a former worker of Zhang Feng's school and a mainstay of Cai Wenge's team during the period of civil strife, was the managing captain of the Mass Dictatorship Headquarters. He pounded the table and yelled at Zhang Feng,

"Zhang Feng, you must behave yourself! You have attacked the revolutionary line of Chairman Mao, attacked the Cultural Revolution, provoked the revolutionary masses, and you are the evil backstage manipulator behind the civil strife. You must bow your head and admit your crimes honestly."

People in the auditorium began shouting slogans again to put pressure on Zhang Feng. After the people were quiet again, Zhang Feng said serenely,

"You have accused me of a lot of crimes. Do you have any evidence?"

Cai Wenge stood up with a sneer and pointed at a large stack of documents on the table.

"Your crimes are so numerous that it would take more than an hour to list them." he said, "Now your fate depends on your attitude to confession. If you confess your crime honestly, you get a reduced prison sentence. If your crimes are revealed by others, that means you have resisted the movement to purify the class ranks and you will be dealt with severely."

Cai Wenge motioned to his men with a wink to hang a big board around Zhang Feng's neck. On the board was written 'Zhang Feng, active counter-revolutionary.' Zhang Feng was so angry he tried to break away from the two men holding his arms. As he knew kung fu, of course the two men could not control him. At this time, several people approached him and were also knocked down by Zhang Feng. At this time, the captain of the Mass Dictatorship Headquarters shouted,

"You dare to resist!"

Zhang Feng felt someone behind him hit him hard on his head and then he lost consciousness.

CHAPTER II

In the Dark Jail

When he woke, Zhang Feng found himself lying on a cold concrete floor. He was cold and had a terrible headache.' Where is this? How can I be here' He suddenly remembered that he had just been denounced. In that case, this place must be a prison in the Mass Dictatorship Headquarters. Zhang Feng struggled to stand up, but found his arm tied with a rope. Suddenly the door opened. Four vicious thugs came in. Without saying a word, they dragged Zhang Feng up off the ground.

"Follow us!" One of them said angrily to Zhang Feng.

"Where are we going?" Zhang Feng asked.

"Where else can an active counter-revolutionary like you go? A public conference in front of the whole school to condemn you monsters and demons!"

Soon they were back in the school auditorium. It was full of people, and there were seven or eight people being publicly criticised on the rostrum. They were all teachers and staff of the school. The old principal was among them. Everyone had a big board around their neck with accusations written on them. Zhang Feng was taken to the rostrum and placed next to the old principal. He also had a board around his neck; on it was written 'active counter-revolutionary'. He was the only student to be publicly criticised. The fanaticism of the public condemnation conference reached its peak when Zhang Feng was taken to the rostrum. "Leniency to those who confess, severity to those who resist! Strike down and destroy Zhang Feng the active counter-revolutionary!" The sounds of the slogan were growing louder.

The captain of the Mass Dictatorship Headquarters walked to the front of the podium and began to read the main ten crimes of Zhang Feng, including inciting the masses to struggle against each other, acting as the evil backstage manipulator of the violent civil strife, viciously attacking the Cultural Revolution, speaking out against socialism and the leadership of CCP, and so on. They did not allow Zhang Feng to defend himself, saying that every crime was exposed by people along with the irrefutable evidence. 'They can distort the facts about the violent civil strife,' Zhang thought, 'But how did they get evidence that I have attacked the Cultural Revolution and socialism?' He suddenly remembered that he had discussed the social chaos caused by the Cultural Revolution with several well-connected classmates, 'Did they expose me?' Zhang Feng thought. In this era of whistle-blowing and betrayal, son could betray father, friends could betray friendship, and there was no trust between people. Moreover, in order to frame a person as a class enemy, others could fabricate an unwarranted crime against him.

Just then, a crowd of thugs from the Mass Dictatorship Headquarters rushed to the rostrum. In pairs, they held the shoulders and grabbed the hair of the accused to force them down, bending them to ninety degrees, bowing their heads to the revolutionary masses. This was the so-called 'jet plane' posture that was invented during the Cultural Revolution and used to torture class enemies. The two thugs assigned to Zhang Feng were tall and strong. In addition, the board around his neck was heavier than the others because Cai Wenge had ordered the thugs to fill it with sand.

The public condemnation conference lasted more than two hours. Several of the accused fell on the rostrum because their bodies were so weakened. Instead of helping them, the thugs kicked and punched them, pulling them up onto their feet so they could continue to be tortured. Zhang Feng was strong enough to stand up to the ordeal. However, he was very worried about the old principal next to him, so he quietly held onto one leg of the old principal. The boards around their necks blocked the sight of the people under the rostrum, so Zhang Feng's actions could not be seen.

After the end of the public condemnation conference, the accused people were escorted back to the jail in the Mass Dictatorship Headquarters. At this time, Cai Wenge whispered a few words to his men. Four thugs took Zhang Feng away alone. They escorted him all the way to the gate of the school.

"Where are you taking me?" Zhang Feng asked them.

"To let you meet the revolutionary masses," the most ferocious captain said with a sneer. "Weren't you an influential man of the Second Senior Middle School? Now we want to let everyone know that you are a hidden class enemy."

Zhang Feng understood that Cai Wenge wanted to use this method to humiliate him. It was not only to torture him and corrupt his reputation within the school, but also to let the whole city know that he was no longer the handsome talent that everyone used to admire, but a public enemy. Zhang Feng was full of rage, but he knew that resistance was useless. In this brutal political movement, once you were accused of being a class enemy, you could be destroyed as easily as a fly. There was no defence, no trial. No one even dared to say a word of support for you.

Zhang Feng was escorted to the school gate. The thugs ordered him to stand facing the road, to be visible to the largest number of pedestrians. They twisted Zhang Feng's hands behind his back and tied them tightly, and then hung another board around his neck, on which was written 'Zhang Feng active counter-revolutionary.' Immediately, a group of pedestrians were attracted by the sight. Some of the bystanders were silent and some cursed, "damn the counter-revolutionary!" One person said,

"This man was the respected president of the Second Senior Middle-school student union. How did he become a counter-revolutionary?"

"Men cannot be judged by their looks. Some people look good, but think evil." Another person said.

A few teenagers threw stones at Zhang Feng. Zhang Feng closed his eyes and tried to calm his heart. Suddenly, he heard a familiar scream,

"Hah, serves you right!" Then, he was hit by a heavy punch to his chest and almost fell to the ground. Zhang Feng opened his eyes and saw that the man who had hit him was Hei Tou. He was removing his favourite whip from his belt. Zhang Feng glared at Hei Tou and roared,

"You dare!" Hei Tou hesitated for a moment, and then he saw the board around Zhang Feng's neck. Hei Tou laughed and said,

"You are an active counter-revolutionary now, do you dare to fight back?" With that, Hei Tou swung his whip at Zhang Feng. Zhang Feng dodged aside and avoided the hit of the whip. Zhang Feng was preparing to avoid the second attack, but the two people behind him who were watching him held his shoulders from both sides, making him unable to move. The whip made contact with his face and the blood started flowing. Zhang Feng had never been defeated by Hei Tou. It was only because Zhang Feng was in a bad situation that Hei Tou was able to get the better of him. Zhang Feng was furious and was ready to risk his life in resistance of Hei Tou. Just then, two Red Guards, who had been admiring Zhang Feng before, came over and pulled Hei Tou away.

"Captain Hei, just leave him to us. Just do your own work."

Hei Tou was concerned that Zhang Feng would risk his life to fight back, so he walked away, continuing to curse.

Zhang Feng had been standing in the hot sun for over an hour. The autumn sunshine was still very hot. He was sweating, and the sweat mixed with blood ran down his face. He tried to wipe it with his hand, but he could not because his hands were still tied behind his back. He was dizzy and thirsty. But he was still enduring the ordeal because he didn't want to plead with the two thugs sitting under the tree. He closed his eyes and muttered, "Water, water."

Suddenly he felt something cool touch his lips, and there was cool water on it. He thought it was an illusion. When he opened eyes, Zhang Feng saw Dan Dan standing in front of him, standing on tiptoe to feed him with water. Zhang Feng drank thirstily. Dan Dan took out her handkerchief and wiped the sweat and blood from his face. He could see the tears in her eyes. Just as Zhang Feng was about to speak to Dan Dan, the two thugs ran over and asked Dan Dan,

"What are you doing? Are you a counter-revolutionary sympathiser?"

"Even if he were a prisoner, should he have the right to eat and drink?" Dan Dan replied without fear. "He is almost fainting from heat and thirst. You have to have some humanity."

"Humane with a counter-revolutionary?!" One of the thugs said ferociously. The other said,

"Man, time is almost up, the captain said it would be enough for him to bow his head and plead guilty. It's been more than two hours, and it's time to get it done." So they pushed Zhang Feng back to the campus and sent him back to the jail of the Mass Dictatorship Headquarters.

Zhang Feng was awake the whole night. He was thinking about his family and wanted to know what his parents and sister were doing. They must be worried about him. He also thought about Yu Mei, worried that she would not accept such fact that he was denounced and put into the Mass Dictatorship Headquarters. There were eight bunk beds in the room where he slept, and sixteen 'Monsters and Demons' were held. The building used to be a dormitory for students, and now the entire ground floor was being used by the Mass Dictatorship Headquarters to hold people who had been tortured. It was actually a temporary prison. The door was surrounded by guards.

Zhang Feng was escorted to the interrogation room by two men after eating a breakfast of salted vegetables and steamed corn breads. Several people, who were members of the school's Revolutionary Committee responsible for investigating and interrogating class enemies, took out a large stack of documents about Zhang Feng's crimes. Zhang Feng was very clear that some of his crimes were to do with bourgeois ideology, such as wanting to be famous and getting married, etc. Even if he confessed, there would be no serious consequences. But such serious problems such as anti-party, anti-socialism and anti-Cultural Revolution acts must not be admitted. Many of these crimes were invented by Cai Wenge's men. Although they intimidated and inveigled Zhang Feng with statements such as 'Leniency to those who confess, severity to those who resist,' Zhang Feng only admitted a few crimes in the hour-long trial. This situation made the guys very angry.

Just then, the door opened and Qing Lian came in. As she was a member of the provincial Revolutionary Committee, the men stood up very respectfully. She glanced at Zhang Feng standing in the corner and asked,

"Does he confess?" The captain of the Mass Dictatorship Headquarters said angrily,

"This guy is quite stubborn and has only admitted a few crimes."

"You guys better go out," said Qing Lian. "I'll persuade him to confess." The men were losing patience with the trial and were eager to go out and relax.

Qing Lian looked smart and capable in her new military uniform and her bobbed hair. She sat down and said in a soft voice,

"Zhang Feng, a wise man should submit to fate, you must understand the situation. You are in serious trouble. If you plead guilty, you can get leniency, otherwise… " Zhang Feng interrupted her.

"You don't have to worry about me. I am innocent. Those charges are made by others. How can I confess?" Qing Lian was anxious,

"You have so many charges, are they all false accusations? Is it true that you were involved in violent civil strife? If I hadn't saved you, would you still be here today? Why do you always have to make people worry about you?" Zhang Feng couldn't understand why Qing Lian said she had saved him. He said coldly,

"According to what you said, I should thank you? You'd better think more about yourself and do less harm to others."

"What! How unreasonable you are!" Qing Lian was so angry that she stood up and picked up the whip left by the captain of the Mass Dictatorship Headquarters and lashed it towards Zhang Feng. Zhang Feng did not show weakness. He squared his shoulders, ready to suffer the beating. But before the whip hit Zhang Feng, Qing Lian dropped it on the ground and ran away crying. Ten minutes later, the interrogators returned with four tall strong thugs. They tied Zhang Feng's arms behind his back without giving any reason.

"Will you plead guilty or not?" the captain of the Mass Dictatorship Headquarters said angrily.

"You want me to confess under torture to false charges?" Zhang Feng said.

"That is, the class enemy who is so stubborn will be punished mercilessly." The captain said. He then ordered several thugs to beat Zhang Feng. Punching and kicking mixed with whip and sticks, and Zhang Feng was beaten to the ground. He couldn't resist because his arms were tied. He also knew that he could be killed if he fought back. These days he had seen many bodies being lifted out of cells, people who had been beaten to death or who had committed suicide. Those who died were said to have died because they were guilty of great crimes, or to have committed suicide because they were ashamed. Even their families were afraid to claim the bodies.

The thugs yelled as they hit, "You said you knew kung fu? Today, we will abolish your capability of kung fu." Zhang Feng knew that his skin and muscles would definitely be damaged, but he must protect his internal organs. So he used the Shaolin QiGong, which his master had taught him, to send Qi (vital energy) to his abdomen, back and limbs to avoid internal injuries. Ten minutes later, the thugs were tired and pulled Zhang Feng up from the ground. Zhang Feng's head and face were covered with blood and his body was black and blue. But he tried to straighten himself up and glared at the thugs. The captain of the Mass Dictatorship Headquarters looked at Zhang Feng,

"Well, I didn't know you were a tough guy. Good, I have more powerful things for you. Let's see if you will beg for mercy! Commissioner Cai told us that we should take special care of you." With that, he dragged Zhang Feng into another room with the other thugs.

Zhang Feng saw that the room was full of crude homemade instruments of torture. These instruments were used to torture and interrogate detainees and force them to admit their 'crimes'. In one corner of the room stood a piece of torture that looked like a bed. This was what the history books called the Creepy Tiger Bench.

The captain sneered and said,

"No matter how tough a man is, he will get a layer of skin peeled off here. If you confess, you won't have to suffer." Zhang Feng knew what would happen if he did not admit to the 'crimes'. But he also remembered that his father had said that leniency was a trick. Even if you confessed, they would still convict you of a felony. The captain was impatient.

"Come, torture him!" The thugs pushed Zhang Feng down onto the Tiger Bench and tied his hands and feet. Then they put bricks under his knees. One brick, two bricks. By the time they placed the third brick, Zhang Feng was already feeling pain in his thighs, legs and knees. He gritted his teeth and sent Qi to his legs and squeezed the rope. Ordinary people couldn't endure the pain when the third brick was placed under the knees.

The captain saw that three bricks did not help him achieve his goal.

"Well, you know Qi Gong. I would like to see if the bricks are hard enough or if your legs are harder. Add a brick!"." Add one more brick!" The thugs tried to push the fourth brick under Zhang Feng's leg, but there was no space for the brick. So they took a sledgehammer and hammered the fourth brick bit by bit into the gap between Zhang Feng's leg and the other three bricks. The captain saw that Zhang Feng was still defending himself with Qi. He took a wooden stick and hit Zhang Feng on the head while the hammers hit the brick. Zhang Feng felt great pain in his knee and then fainted.

When Zhang Feng woke up, he didn't know how much time had passed. He opened his eyes and saw that he was lying in a cell in the Mass Dictatorship Headquarters' jail. The old principal, with tears in his eyes, was wiping the blood from Zhang Feng's face. Seeing Zhang Feng wake up, the old principal hurriedly gave him some water, and said in a low voice:

"They are so cruel." Zhang Feng wanted to sit up, but he lay down again when he felt the great pain in his leg.

Seeing no one close to them, the old principal whispered. "They tortured you? They are so cruel to do that to young people." He rubbed Zhang Feng's leg and told him to take good care of himself. The old principal also told him that if the thugs of the Mass Dictatorship Headquarters asked, he should tell them he could not stand up. Then they would let him off for a few days. As for food and water, his fellow inmates would help him.

These days, Yu Mei was as anxious as a cat on hot bricks. After learning from Zhang Feng's family that he had been put in the jail of the Mass Dictatorship Headquarters, she tried to go and see him. But they would not let her pass the gate of the Mass Dictatorship Headquarters. The guards at the door refused to let her in, saying that the inmates were all class enemies and were not allowed to have contact with the outside world. Yu Mei had no choice but to stay at the corner of the building not far from the gate of the Mass Dictatorship Headquarters, hoping to see Zhang Feng when the prisoners came out to eat. However, Yu Mei did not see Zhang Feng when they were escorted by guards to the dining hall at noon and at night. Yu Mei was even more worried so she ventured to walk toward a very old person in the group of prisoners and asked if he knew where Zhang Feng was. This elderly man was just the old principal. He whispered Yu Mei that Zhang Feng was recovering after being tortured. When Yu Mei was about to ask the old principal to send a message to Zhang Feng, the thug supervising the prisoners turned around and saw her. He immediately yelled and drove Yu Mei away.

Yu Mei was not willing to let things end this way, and returned the next day, hoping to see Zhang Feng. When it was nearly lunchtime, Yu Mei suddenly saw an awe-inspiring person surrounded by a group of people, coming from afar. She took a closer look and saw the person in the centre of the crows was Cai Wenge. Yu Mei knew he was the sworn enemy of Zhang Feng.

However, she was determined to find out how Zhang Feng was so she went to Cai Wenge and tried to say to him in a soft voice,

"Excuse me, can you tell me how Zhang Feng is now?" Cai Wenge did not expect to meet Yu Mei here, his face immediately took on a dirty smile,

"Ha, it is you, the little fairy. I advise you to stay away from him now. He is now an active counter-revolutionary and this is a very serious crime."

"What are you going to do with him?" Yu Mei asked anxiously.

"He is very stubborn and refuses to plead guilty," said Cai with a smirk. "If he confessed, he might get more lenient treatment. If he continues to resist, he will be punished mercilessly. If he is taken away by the people of the Public Security Bureau, then he will stay in jail for at least eight years."

Yu Mei's face blanched with fear. But Cai Wenge continued, with obscene smile,

"You better hurry to find another boyfriend, or you can consider being my girlfriend, and you could end up being the commissioner's wife." Cai Wenge's men all laughed. Yu Mei was blushed with anger and scolded,

"Rogues!" Then she ran away, wiping her tears.

The development of the situation was much more serious than Zhang Feng and the people who cared about him had expected. Two weeks later, the whole school was asked to attend an important conference. Several police cars were parked outside the school gate, one of them a prison van. The conference place was in the school playground. The atmosphere was solemn. Everyone had the presentiment that something important was going to happen. When Zhang Feng and more than thirty other 'evil counter-revolutionary elements' were escorted into the conference, the entire playground erupted in an earth-shattering chant: 'Leniency to those who confess, severity to those who resist. The enemy will either surrender or be destroyed by us!'

At the front of the playground, Zhang Feng saw Cai Wenge sitting at the middle of the table with a look of solemn triumph. Next to him sat an official of the municipal Public Security Bureau, flanked by members of the school Revolutionary Committee.

Once the conference got underway, the deputy director of the school Revolutionary Committee announced,

"In accordance with the supreme instructions of Chairman Mao, the great leader, to purify the ranks of the classes, we are exposing and excavating all the class enemies hidden in the revolutionary ranks. We'll strike them down and stomp on them to subjugate them forever." He continued, "Today, we will grant leniency to those who have confessed their crimes. But those who resist the revolutionary masses and refuse to confess their crimes must be punished mercilessly."

The playground again filled with the sound of chants. Then he announced that a worker named Chen had originally had a good family background because he came from a family of poor and lower-middle peasants. But he had forgotten his class attitude. He once said that Chairman Mao had white hair. These words violated the desire of hundreds of millions of the revolutionary masses to bless Chairman Mao's longevity. Chen's wife had denounced him, so he was punished. But he admitted to his crimes and repented, so he got leniency. From today he was released and could go home to repent further. Then, the worker named Chen was allowed to leave after he had knelt down and kowtowed to the portrait of Chairman Mao to show gratitude for the leniency he had received.

Then the deputy director announced in a very stern voice,

"Zhang Feng, the active counter-revolutionary, comes from a landlord class. He adhered to the reactionary position, viciously attacked the Cultural Revolution and socialism, as well as incited the masses to struggle against each other. He also refused to plead guilty. Recently he was discovered to have participated in the activities of a counter-revolutionary group. Zhang Feng has committed the most serious crimes and only a merciless punishment can calm the anger of the masses. Following an internal discussion of the Revolutionary Committee and approval from the higher authorities, the Public Security Bureau has now formally arrested and dealt with Zhang Feng in accordance with the law."

When the deputy director finished speaking, the chant of 'Down with Zhang Feng the counter-revolutionary' rang out again, and two police officers stepped forward and handcuffed Zhang Feng. Zhang Feng seemed to be arguing loudly, but no one cared what he said. He was taken to a police car and away from the campus. Dan Dan was in the crowd, she was very pale and would have fallen down without her friend's help. At this time, the sarcastic voice of Cai Wenge was heard over the big speaker.

"Zhang Feng is the best-hidden class enemy. In the past, he was the man of the school, so he charmed many people. But after all, evil can't be hidden forever, and his disguise will be recognised in the end. He will certainly be punished mercilessly by the Dictatorship of the Proletariat."

In the interrogation room of the 1st municipal prison, the police told Zhang Feng that his criminal charges, such as involvement in the violent civil strife and the speech against the Cultural Revolution, had been decided by the Mass

Dictatorship Headquarters. What he needed to confess now was his relationship with the 'Four Talents of the River City'. The four had been arrested on charges of counter-revolutionary activity. This was a very serious crime.

"My relationship with them is just friends," Zhang Feng said. "The reason we are together is because of the art salon." A police officer asked,

"Is it a Petofi Circle?" Zhang Feng certainly knew that the Petofi Circle of Hungary was a political organisation so he did not admit to participating in political activities in the salon of the Four Talents. Seeing that Zhang Feng refused to confess, the three policemen handed him a piece of paper. This was a copy of a document.

"Look, isn't it familiar? Because you were involved in drafting the document," one of the policemen said. Zhang Feng opened the paper. The title was 'The Declaration of the River City: A Letter to the People of the Whole Country'. Zhang Feng was shocked and then thought, 'Is this written by Liu Tian?' He went on to read the article. The general idea of the article was that the Chinese nation had reached a crisis moment. Several ambitious politicians had promoted personal worship on a large scale, deceiving and inciting young students and the masses in the name of revolution. This movement was destroying our party, society, economy and culture. They were madly persecuting our veteran cadres, and even the president of the country had not been spared. They also persecuted intellectuals and ordinary people. They had turned the socialist new China, which had been created through the death of millions of revolutionary martyrs, into a lawless hell… Zhang Feng couldn't think straight in the excruciating tension. But he thought to himself that the article was well written and profound. He was also acutely aware that the writer of this article had committed a capital crime. He looked up and said,

"I have never read this article and I don't know who wrote it." One of the three policemen, who seemed to be the leader, slammed the table and screamed,

"You are still lying. Liu Tian and his companions have admitted they wrote it and said you were involved in the drafting." Zhang Feng knew that they were trapping him. Liu Tian and the other talents were righteous gentlemen. They would not betray their friends. The policeman said: "You may think they will unite and speak with one voice? But there is another person who can prove that you were involved in the drafting of this document."

'Is it true?' Zhang Feng thought to himself. 'Is someone else who knows?' The three policemen were impatient. They began to slap Zhang Feng in the face in turn and shouted,

"Do you admit your guilt?" Zhang Feng stayed silent, so they continued slapping him. Zhang Feng soon felt the blood flowing from the corner of his mouth. After a while, the policemen began to tire of this. Seeing Zhang Feng still not confessing, the policemen said maliciously,

"You don't confess, it doesn't matter. We have a witness, we can convict you, and you only need to wait to be shot!" Then Zhang Feng was sent back to the cell.

When Yu Mei heard from Zhang Feng's family and from Dan Dan that he had been formally arrested and put in prison, she felt like the whole world was crashing down around her. Just like Dan Dan and the others, she did not understand why Zhang Feng was in prison, since surely the police would only intervene if someone had committed a particularly serious crime. The usual problems were handled by the local Revolutionary Committee.

A former deputy director of the Public Security Bureau, named Huo, was the former subordinate of Yu Mei's father. Now Huo was the deputy director of the Revolutionary Committee of the public security system. Yu Mei tracked him down and begged him to allow her to visit Zhang Feng in prison. After overcoming some obstacles, Yu Mei was finally allowed to visit Zhang Feng at the 2nd municipal prison. The prisoners in the 2nd municipal prison had all committed serious crimes, murder and arson, or they were political criminals. Through the heavily-guarded dark corridor, Yu Mei was taken to a row of cells with small windows. The prison officer opened one of the windows and said,

"That's it. You've only got five minutes. Don't waste time." Yu Mei looked into the room and saw a man sitting on a low bed.

"Brother Feng, it's me." Yu Mei said in a soft voice. The man immediately got up from his bed and went to the window. In the dim light, Yu Mei saw her beloved looking gaunt. His face was black and blue, his hair was long and his chin was covered with whiskers. Yu Mei felt her heart had been wrenched.

"Is it you? Yu Mei, why are you here?" Zhang Feng reached out his hand; Yu Mei took it in hers, shaking with agitation. His usually warm and powerful hands were so cold now.

"Brother Feng, you have suffered…" Yu Mei couldn't stop crying. Zhang Feng stretched out his other hand and held the lily-fingered hands of Yu Mei tightly to calm her and said,

"Yu Mei, don't cry. I am fine. Don't worry, I can hold on." Yu Mei suddenly remembered the words that Dan Dan and Zhang Feng's parents had told her before she went to visit Zhang Feng. She must find out what charges they had imposed on Zhang Feng, what evidence they had and who the witnesses were. That way they could find the falsified evidence and the people behind it all. Thus, Zhang Feng's innocence could be proved. Thinking of this, Yu Mei stopped crying and asked in a low voice,

"Brother Feng, what charges have they imposed on you? Why should they mercilessly punish you? Tell me quickly, we only have a few minutes." Zhang Feng calmed himself down and whispered to Yu Mei that he was accused of being a member of the Four Talents counter-revolutionary group and of participating in the drafting of the 'Declaration of the River City'. In fact, he knew nothing about these activities. They said that someone could prove his crime.

Zhang Feng had repeatedly recalled these days. He believed that the Four Talents could not frame him. The only possibility was Li He. The last time he attended the salon was with Li He, when Li He has acted strangely. However, Zhang Feng believed that Li He was just like Wang Hai, who had been his faithful pal for many years. Would he give false evidence to frame Zhang Feng? Yu Mei was about to ask Zhang Feng in more detail but the prison officer came over and said,

"Time is up. I have tried my best and given you ten minutes. You should leave now." Yu Mei had to take leave of Zhang Feng reluctantly.

After leaving the prison, Yu Mei hurried to find Dan Dan. By this time, the two girls were not considering who would become Zhang Feng's wife in the future. They both wished the same thing – to rescue Zhang Feng as soon as possible. Dan Dan was a smart girl. After listening to Yu Mei's news of her visit to the prison and to Zhang Feng's parents' analysis, she said,

"It seems that the most likely possibility is that Li He betrayed Xiao Feng. Although he is one of Zhang Feng's best friends, he is sometimes a little weak. Wang Hai was rougher, but manlier. When Wang Hai was detained for investigation,

I saw that Cai Wenge also continually investigated Li He. Cai Wenge is Xiao Feng's sworn enemy. He has been trying to get even with him for years. It is likely that he took advantage of Li He's weakness and forced him to give false testimony."

Zhang Feng's father replied, "If Li He was there when Xiao Feng last met the Four Talents, and he was behaved strangely, he must have been disturbed to hear them discussing some sensitive political topics. Then he would not be able to bear the pressure and would drop Xiao Feng into it."

Dan Dan stood up. "Time is running out," she said. "I am going to find Li He now and ask him if he betrayed Xiao Feng." Then she left.

Since Wang Hai had been quarantined and investigated, Li He was also questioned by Cai Wenge for a long time. Then he disappeared. Someone said he was staying at home and writing a self-criticism letter. But Dan Dan couldn't find him at his house. Eventually, she found him at his relatives' house in the suburbs. Li He looked surprised when he saw her. Dan Dan told him straight out about Zhang Feng's arrest. Li He said he didn't know anything about it and asked for details with great concern. When Dan Dan said that Zhang Feng had been involved in the case of the Four Talents, and may be sentenced to a felony, Li He said at once, "It won't happen, Zhang Feng is only a student. He will be fine as long as he has written self-criticism letter."

"How did you know that?" Dan Dan asked.

"I'm just guessing," Li He said with hesitation. Dan Dan also mentioned that someone had proved that Zhang Feng and the Four Talents drafted the 'Declaration of the River City'. But Zhang Feng was actually not involved.

"It must be some one of the four who testified against him." said Li He eagerly.

"Zhang Feng said it was impossible. First, he believed in the character of the Four Talents. Second, someone of the Public Security Bureau said there was another witness."

"It's not me!" Li He said immediately. "I've only been there once with brother Feng. And they talk about calligraphy and poetry and things like that. Besides, brother Feng and I have been friends for years. How could I sell him out?" Dan Dan noticed that when Li He said these words, he dared not look Dan Dan in the eye. She wondered. But Li He refused to admit anything, and there was nothing else she could do. Maybe Li He really didn't betray Zhang Feng? Dan Dan left with a heavy heart.

In the building of the provincial revolutionary committee, Zhao Wu was hosting a meeting to discuss the recent situation about the purification of the class ranks and the measures to strike at class enemies quickly and severely, especially the treatment of several counter-revolutionary groups. After reading the report about the 'Four Talents of the River City: an anti-party group' provided by the Public Security Bureau, all the members were indignant and agreed that the 'Declaration of the River City' was a counter-revolutionary document that comprehensively denied the Cultural Revolution and maliciously attacked the great leader Chairman Mao, along with inciting the masses to resist Chairman Mao's revolutionary line. The members of the Four Talents of the River City had to be executed to assuage the people's anger. Zhao Wu thought for a while and slowly said,

"Their crimes are serious indeed. However, we should treat them differently. These kids are all young university students and are the talents for the future construction of the country. For some of them, especially those with good family backgrounds, if they have been brainwashed by bad guys, then they can be dealt with leniently."

In fact, Zhao Wu's own innermost views on the chaos caused by the Cultural Revolution were the same as the content of the declaration. However, in those days, such an idea could only be hidden in the heart. Those who said these words in public would be executed. Then the meeting began to discuss the case of Zhang Feng.

"According to the investigation, Zhang Feng was not one of the Four Talents," said one of men from the Public Security Bureau. "But sometimes he took part in their activities. He has also been proved to be involved in discussions about the declaration. Zhang Feng's family background is the exploiting class, so he is probably a reactionary. In addition, his father is known as the great rightist."

"What's his name?" Zhao Wu asked.

"Zhang Wenbo." This name shocked Zhao Wu. 'Zhang Wenbo? Isn't that my classmate from Sun Yat-sen University? Li Jianguo had mentioned him a few years ago. But he advised me not to go to visit Zhang Wenbo. Zhang Feng is his son?' Zhao Wu quickly read Zhang Feng's materials, then looked up and said,

"Zhang Feng is only a high school student."

Du Zhongqing, the special commissioner dressed in black who sat nearby and never spoke, said indifferently,

"High school students are already adults, so they have to take legal responsibility." Cai Wenge wanted to speak. Qing lian, who was sitting next to him, touched him with her hand, indicating that he should stay silent. However, Cai Wenge quickly stood up and said,

"Although Zhang Feng is only 20 years old, he is the most reactionary and the most hidden class enemy. I am his classmate, so I know him best. Because of the influence of his reactionary family, Zhang Feng is a playboy, essentially, who insisted on the white special road (to do his own professional work well, but not to care for politics) and was morally corrupt." Saying this, Cai Wenge looked around the meeting room, hoping to get Chang Zheng to stand up to tell everyone how Zhang Feng seduced other people's girlfriends. However, Chang Zheng had not come to the meeting so Cai Wenge began to list how Zhang Feng's ideas were reactionary. He said that Zhang Feng had been very active in the violent civil strife of the Cultural Revolution and had incited the masses to fight against each other. Thus Zhang Feng was the evil backstage manipulator of the violent civil strife. He looked at Zhao Wu and said,

"Director Zhao, didn't Chang Zheng tell you that he was almost stabbed to death by Zhang Feng with a spear?"

This made several of the military representatives angry because they remembered the events of the provincial military compound surrounded by the Jili Commune and other events of the violent civil strife. Because almost all the people of the commune faction had been removed from the Revolutionary Committee, the views of the committee members were overwhelmingly in favour of the merciless punishment of Zhang Feng.

In truth the violent civil strife had been incited by Du Zhongqing, the special commissioner dressed in black, but now he was telling everyone that a class enemy like Zhang Feng had incited the masses to fight against each other. Zhao Wu was also very angry when he remembered the attack initiated by the Central Cultural Revolution Group to 'Uncover a small number of reactionaries in the army'. Zhao Wu thought, 'Zhang Feng, you are committing suicide. Since your family background is unacceptable, you should keep a low profile. But you still took part in the violent civil strife to attack me.' Therefore, Zhao Wu originally wanted to say some words in Zhang Feng's defence, but now he gave up. The final decision of the meeting was that the Public Security Bureau was responsible for making judgments on these people and then reporting to the Revolutionary Committee for final approval.

Zhang Feng's family and friends spent the next few weeks in a state of high tension, worry and anxiety. But there was a glimmer of hope. They hoped that Zhang Feng, who was just 20 years old, could be treated as a juvenile and therefore receive a light sentence. However, in those days, justice in law did not exist. As long as your words and behaviour seemed to violate the principles of the 'revolution', you were a criminal. The standards of 'revolution' and 'counter-revolution' were completely defined by Mao Zedong and his followers. In the red horror times, no-one knew when they might be accused of being counter-revolutionary, or even executed, just like the witches who were burned to death in medieval Europe.

One day, Yu Mei and her brother were on their way to the grocery store. After walking along two streets, Yu Mei suddenly saw a notice on the wall, surrounded by a group of people reading it. Yu Mei and her younger brother rushed into the crowd to get a closer look. This was a judgment notice from the Jili Provincial Court: 'In the movement to purify the class ranks, in order to strike and eliminate class enemies, the court has decided to punish a number of counter-revolutionary criminals quickly and severely.' Then there were the names of the criminal, each with a red 'X' and an overview of their crimes. The first one was Liu Tian. He was accused of being the prime criminal of the 'Four Talents of the River City' Anti-Party Group. His family background was the landlord class, and he had organised the counter-revolutionary group, issued a counter-revolutionary declaration to attack the great leader Chairman Mao and the Cultural Revolution. Thus, Li Tian had to be executed to assuage the people's anger.

When Yu Mei saw this, her heart began to beat so hard that she could hardly look any further. The next to be sentenced to death was Li Yue, the third elder of the Four Talents, who was also born into a family of historical counter-revolutionaries. After Li Yue's name was Zhang Feng. It said that he was a counter-revolutionary, born into a rightist family and was reactionary in thought. He was active in the Cultural Revolution to provoke the masses to fight against each other. He had also participated in the anti-party activities of the 'Four Talents of the River City' Anti-Party Group. He had committed the most heinous crimes and therefore was sentenced to death. Seeing this, Yu Mei felt the whole world collapse. She fainted away into the dark.

CHAPTER III

On the Way to the Execution Ground

When Yu Mei woke up, she was already in bed at home, and her brother and mother were anxiously sitting around her. Yu Mei's mother said to her with tears in her eyes,

"Xiao Mei, you have to accept reality. Xiao Feng is a good boy, and we know he is wronged. But they have so much evidence that we can't help him.

Yu Mei sat up and said,

"I can't give up. I must save him."

Regardless of her mother and brother's attempts to dissuade her, Yu Mei took a bus to Zhang Feng's house. Knocking on the door, Yu Mei could hear a cry inside. It seemed to come from three women; the one who was crying the most was Zhang Lin. It was Zhang Feng's father who opened the door. He looked very sad. Seeing Yu Mei's eyes red with crying, Zhang Feng's father asked in a low voice,

"Do you already know?"

Yu Mei nodded. Walking into the house, Yu Mei saw that Dan Dan was comforting Zhang Lin and her mother Hu Yun, along with wiping her own tears from her eyes. Seeing their sad looks, Yu Mei could not hold back her tears. Men are much stronger than women.

"Don't cry anymore," Zhang Feng's father said in a low voice. "Don't cry anymore, we need to think about ways to save Zhang Feng."

Dan Dan also advised everyone to calm down. She said she believed the most important charge was Zhang Feng's involvement with the Four Talents. Without this charge, Zhang Feng would not have been sentenced to death. The testimony of Li He was perhaps the most important key. The last time Dan Dan saw Li He, he had hesitated to speak, indicating that he had concealed the truth. However, how could they make Li He tell the truth?

Just when everyone seemed to be at a loss, someone knocked at the door. The person who walked in surprised everyone. It was Wang Hai. Zhang Lin stopped crying. She jumped up from her chair and took Wang Hai by the arm,

"Brother Wang, why are you here? They didn't hurt you, did they?" Wang Hai looked gaunt and had lost a lot of weight. He told them that he had been put in isolation for more than a month, and they had asked him to account for the beating, smashing and looting during the violent civil strife. But in the end, they let him go because they did not find he had done anything seriously wrong, but they removed him from all his posts on the Revolutionary Committee and ordered him back to school to write a self-criticism letter.

Wang Hai had just read the court notice about Zhang Feng's and rushed to find Dan Dan and Zhang Feng's family.

After listening to Dan Dan's description of Zhang Feng's experience from being publicly criticised and detained by the Mass Dictatorship Headquarters to being arrested and sentenced, Wang Hai said he had expected Zhang Feng to be in serious trouble. Wang Hai said that during his detention, Cai Wenge repeatedly asked him about Zhang Feng, especially the relationship between Zhang Feng and the Four Talents. But he did not expect that they would really sentence Zhang Feng to death for this crime. Yu Mei was desperate to tell Wang Hai that Li He was now suspected of betraying Zhang Feng. The last time Dan Dan had asked him about Zhang Feng, he clearly hiding something. Wang Hai listened to these words, his brow wrinkled and said:

"He is a real coward! It must be that bastard Cai Wenge threatening him. It's not good. Time is running out. Usually after the notice is posted, the prisoner will be sent to the execution ground within a few days. We should find Li He immediately, and make him tell the truth." Finally, they decided that Wang Hai and Dan Dan would go and find Li He. Zhang Lin was also clamouring to go with them, but was stopped by her mother.

They took the bus together to Li He's relatives house in the suburbs. When the door opened, a man told them that Li He was not at home. He had gone out in the morning without saying where he was going. Wang Hai and Dan Dan had no idea what to do. In his anxiety, Wang Hai kept punching the small trees along the road. Dan Dan thought for a moment said calmly,

"It's three o 'clock in the afternoon and it's only three hours before dark. From what I have just observed, his relative looks a little flustered. I guess Li He must have hidden somewhere. We hide quietly and watch his house from a distance. Li He will be back for dinner soon." Wang Hai agreed to Dan Dan's suggestion. They hid behind a big tree and stared at the house. Wang Hai looked at Dan Dan with a loving look and wanted to say something to comfort and care for her. But when he saw how worried Dan Dan was, Wang Hai was afraid to say anything. Now that their best friend's life was at stake, there was no mood for romance. Wang Hai felt sleepy because he hadn't slept well last night. Suddenly Dan Dan touched him.

"Look, that man is coming out." Wang Hai saw the man coming creeping out of the door. He looked around to make sure no one was watching. Then he walked quietly towards the river.

"Come on, let's follow him." Wang Hai whispered to Dan Dan. After five or six minutes, they saw a man in a straw hat sitting by the river and fishing. Wang Hai said to Dan Dan,

"Look! That's Li He. He always goes fishing when he is in a bad mood." When Li He's relative went to talk to the fisherman, Wang Hai darted up and shouted,

"Li He, I've finally found you!" The fisherman was so frightened that he almost fell into the river and his straw hat tumbled off. Dan Dan saw that the man was indeed Li He. He shivered with fear and said,

"Not… Not me." Dan Dan was clever enough to say to the relative,

"We are his classmates. There's something important we need to ask him. You can go back to the house. We won't hurt him."

After the relative left, Wang Hai said angrily to Li He,

"Tell us how you set up Brother Feng with false testimony!" Li He was ready to make some repudiation at first but when he saw that Wang Hai was going to beat him, he was so frightened that he knelt on the ground and kowtowed to Wang Hai.

"I am guilty, I am guilty, Brother Feng was framed by me," said Li He repeatedly. Dan Dan told him to get up and tell the truth. Li He said that since Wang Hai had been detained, Cai Wenge interrogated him every day. He was asked to expose Zhang Feng's crimes, especially the relationship with the Four Talents. Li He said at first that he had only been there once with Zhang Feng a few weeks ago. He heard them talking about the Cultural Revolution, but nothing illegal. Cai Wenge was not satisfied and kept asking if they had discussed the contents of the Declaration of The River City. Li refused to cooperate with him at first, Hence, Cai Wenge threatened Li He and accused him of having a relationship with a gang of hooligan. Cai Wenge was prepared to use this against him to convict him. In fact, Li He had been seduced by a girl from the gang and had not participated in any criminal activities. But in that period of time, hooliganism was a serious crime. So Li He was a little scared. The worst thing was that Cai had tortured him for confessions. Li He's body was weak, he couldn't withstand torture, and finally succumbed to the Tiger Bench. Thus, under the threats of Cai Wenge, Li He wrote a letter to disclose Zhang Feng's involvement in the anti-revolutionary activities of the Four Talents. Li He was worried that his disclosure would lead to Zhang Feng's arrest and death sentence. But Cai Wenge tricked him into saying that Zhang Feng was still a young student. He would only be let off lightly and would not be sentenced to death. It was not until yesterday that Li He had heard the shocking truth about Zhang Feng's punishment.

Wang Hai was red with rage. He gave Li He a resounding slap in the face,

"You are a scum of a friend who sells a friend! Brother Feng would do anything for his friends, but you put him to death."

Dan Dan stopped Wang Hai.

"Zhang Feng's life is in danger now," she told Li He. "Can you deny your previous confession in order to save him?" Li He stammered,

"Yes, yes, in order to save Brother Feng, I would rather stay in prison for years." Dan Dan quickly took out paper and pen. and together they wrote Li He's letter of repentance. It said that Li He had committed perjury and could prove beyond a doubt that Zhang Feng was innocent. At the end of the letter, in addition to signing, Li He's fingerprint was needed but they had no red inkpad. Without another word, Wang Hai took out his knife and cut his finger, and the blood flowed out. He put his bleeding finger in front of Li He. Li He was so frightened that he touched the blood of Wang Hai with his fingers and pressed a blood finger-mark on the letter of repentance.

Wang Hai and Dan Dan went back to Zhang Feng's house when it was getting dark. Zhang Feng's family and Yu Mei were still waiting for their message. Everyone was relieved to see the Li He's letter. But Zhang Feng's father said,

"It is too early to celebrate. The police and the courts will not easily believe Li He's testimony. Moreover, if someone really wants to frame Zhang Feng, they will find other excuses. However, we should at least, and we had better talk directly with the person in charge of the Public Security Bureau and the court."

Yu Mei volunteered to say that she knew the deputy Director of the Revolutionary Committee of the Public Security Bureau. She would go to find this person at the next morning.

With her heart hammering and butterflies in her stomach, Yu Mei found Deputy Director Huo in the Provincial Public Security building the next morning.

The Deputy Director asked brusquely,

"Are you here for Zhang Feng's case again? You should not try again. He has already been sentenced to death." Yu Mei took out Li He's letter and showed it to Director Huo, asking whether there was any chance of a retrial of Zhang Feng's case. After reading the letter, Director Huo shook his head and said,

"It's too late. It's not the same as before. In the past we had a full procedure of court hearing, sentencing, appeal and retrial. Now the entire system of public security, procurators and people's courts has been disrupted after the Cultural Revolution, and there are no legal provisions. Now, the Revolutionary Committee of the Public Security Bureau has convicted the prisoners according to the 'Six Provisions of Public Security' and then reported them to the Provincial Revolutionary Committee for approval. After being approved, the suspects with less serious crimes were put in prison and those with more serious crimes were immediately killed. They did not even have an opportunity to appeal. If you only have this letter, they will not reconsider Zhang Feng's case. Moreover, Zhang Feng will be executed the day after tomorrow."

When Yu Mei heard these words, her tears immediately flowed.

"Or you can go to Director Fan for help, because he has more power," Director Huo said sympathetically. Director Fan was only a section chief before but because he followed the special commissioner in the Cultural Revolution in rebelling against the system of public security, procurators and people's courts, he was recommended by the special commissioner to become the director of the Revolutionary Committee of the new system.

After wiping away her tears, Yu Mei reluctantly went to Director Fan. In order to save her beloved she would do absolutely anything.

Waiting until noon at the Director's office, Yu Mei was shown in by the secretary. She saw a man in his forties wearing a green military uniform, sitting behind the big desk, smoking, with his legs crossed. Seeing Yu Mei, who was as beautiful as a fairy, the man stood up and said lustfully,

"Oh, it's the daughter of Secretary Li, please sit down. What can I do for you? Your father is being reformed in the May Seventh Cadre School. You know that I can't help him."

Instead of sitting down, Yu Mei spoke eagerly to Director Fan about Zhang Feng's death sentence and showed him the letter.

"It's hard for me to help you," Director Fan frowned and said, "This case has already been sentenced. It is difficult to change the judgment. Moreover, such a letter cannot prove that Zhang Feng has no relationship with the counter-revolutionary group. The notices have been publicly announced, and the death penalty will be executed the day after tomorrow. Oh, what is his relationship with you? Why do you care about him so much? Is he your boyfriend?"

While Yu Mei knelt down, crying,

"Director Fan, please save him! He is only 20 years old, he is wronged!" Director Fan got up from his chair and went up to Yu Mei. He took her hands and said:

"Don't cry, my little fairy. let me think about other ways, I am too busy during the day, there are many meetings waiting for me. Come to me at six o 'clock after I finish work." As he spoke, he stroked Yu Mei's hands, which were as white as marble.

Yu Mei immediately thanked him profusely. She did not notice that Director Fan's lustful eyes were staring at her chest.

Unable to get in touch with Wang Hai and Dan Dan, and also worried that Director Fan would change his mind, Yu Mei stayed in the building until closing time. During this time, she only left for a few minutes to buy some rice cake to alleviate her hunger.

At last it was six o'clock, and all the workers poured out of the building. Yu Mei knocked on the door of Director Fan's office nervously. He opened the door with a lustful smile and let Yu Mei in, then locked the door from the inside. He asked Yu Mei to sit on the sofa and he sat down next to her. Yu Mei felt uncomfortable and moved sideways, but Director Fan moved closer. Yu Mei could not think of anything else now. She asked anxiously,

"Director Fan, is there any hope for Zhang Feng?"

"I can hardly help you," Fan said, looking helpless. "The sentence has been approved by the provincial Revolutionary Committee." When Yu Mei heard these words, she burst into tears.

"Then he must die?" Fan took out a tissue and wiped her tears, taking the opportunity to touch Yu Mei's face.

"Don't cry, don't cry, little beauty, there's still some hope." Yu Mei stopped crying at once when she heard these words.

Fan continued, "I can ask them to suspend execution and conduct an investigation first." Yu Mei immediately expressed gratitude to him. Fan said again, "I can help you if you promise me one thing."

"I can promise anything if you can save him." Yu Mei said.

Fan had a dirty smile on his face, "It's easy, as long as you make me happy." Yu Mei did not understand his words, and then asked,

"How can I make you happy? I can buy you a present."

"No, no, just bring pleasure to me." By this time, Fan's face had turned red with lust. He seized Yu Mei's hands.

"Little fairy, I want to be intimate with you." Then he put his arms around Yu Mei and tried to kiss her. Yu Mei was frightened out of her wits. She instinctively tried to break away from him. Fan began to fondle Yu Mei's body, trying to kiss her lips.

"Director Fan, don't do this, don't do this." Yu Mei was still trying to break away from him. Fan had almost lost his mind with desire.

"Do you want to save him? He will be fine if you agree to be intimate with me."

'That's right,' Yu Mei suddenly remembered. 'I should sacrifice myself in order to save brother Feng.' With this in mind, Yu Mei's resistance weakened. Fan began to unbutton her clothes. But Yu Mei suddenly realised that she would be Zhang Feng's wife in the future. If she allowed someone else to touch her, she would lose her chance to marry Zhang Feng.

She didn't know what to do. On the one hand she thought that she must sacrifice herself to save Zhang Feng, but on the other she could not betray her and Zhang Feng's love.

Fan could no longer control himself, and began to tear at Yu Mei's clothes. He untied her coat and tore at her shirt, murmuring words of lasciviousness:

"Little fairy, I love you so much, I will give you pleasure soon…"

At this moment, there was a sharp knock on the door. Both Yu Mei and Fan were startled. Yu Mei quickly broke away from Director Fan and stood up to sort out her clothes. Fan got up quickly and went to the door, gently releasing the lock. He cleared his throat and asked in an impatient voice,

"Who is there?"

"It's me, Director Fan. I have something urgent to ask you." It was Fan's secretary.

Fan motioned to Yu Mei to sit on the sofa. When the door opened, the secretary saw at first glance the flustered and dishevelled Yu Mei sitting on the sofa.

"I'm sorry to disturb you, Director Fan," he said at once.

"It's OK," Fan said, looking as if nothing had happened. "I am investigating a situation with the relatives of a prisoner."

He asked Yu Mei to step out of the office for a moment. He told her to wait in the reception room across the hall and come back to his office after ten minutes. Obviously, he thought that Yu Mei would resign herself to him in order to save Zhang Feng. Yu Mei ran down the stairs quickly and towards the gate. All she wanted was to get away from the devil. But as she approached the gate, she suddenly seemed to see Zhang Feng's handsome, haggard face.

"My Brother Feng!" She stopped and squatted on the ground, covering her eyes with her hands, crying bitterly.

'I can't leave,' she thought. 'I must sacrifice myself for my Brother Feng. If he can survive, even if I can't marry him, Dan Dan can be his wife. I can still be his friend. I shall never marry in my life.'

Thinking of this, Yu Mei stood up again and walked back reluctantly. This time she knew she was walking towards hell.

Back at the door of Director Fan's office, Yu Mei wanted to know if the secretary had left, so she listened at the door to hear if there were voices inside. As she listened, she was shocked by the conversation coming from inside the room.

She heard the secretary say,

"Director Fan, will the death penalty still be executed the day after tomorrow on schedule?"

"I said so. It's on schedule!" Fan's voice was impatient.

"What about Zhang Feng the middle school student?"

"Shoot him.",

"But his girlfriend has just come to beg for leniency," the secretary said hesitantly.

"She's just a currish daughter of an insignificant capitalist roader, who cares about her? Ha-ha!"

Hearing this, Yu Mei felt the whole world collapse. Meanwhile, flames of anger were burning on her cheeks. She returned to the reception room. When the secretary left, Yu Mei went over and knocked on the door of the office. Director Fan opened the door, smirked and said to her,

"Ah, sweetheart, can't wait? Look at your red face." Yu Mei refrained from voicing her anger and asked,

"If I have satisfied your desire, can you let Zhang Feng survive?" Fan hurriedly grabbed Yu Mei's hand.

"No problem, I just told my secretary. We will review Zhang Feng's case. Don't worry, come on in, my sweetheart, I can't wait." Yu Mei gave Fan a resounding slap in the face,

"Rogue! Scoundrel! Not only will you destroy me, but you will also take his life. You are a demon!" She ran away, wiping her tears.

When Yu Mei got home, her mother saw her red eyes and knew that things were not going well, so she tried to comfort her. At this time, the door opened and Li Jianguo entered. Yu Mei jumped up with a cry of surprise. She hugged her father and began to cry. This was that Yu Mei's mother had anticipated about the situation, so she had urgently contacted Li Jianguo and asked him to come back to try to save Zhang Feng.

Yu Mei told him that Zhang Feng would be executed the day after tomorrow, and told him all about Li He's evidence letters obtained by Dan Dan and Wang Hai, and how the people of the Public Security Bureau refused to help her. (She did not mention the matter of Director Fan's indecency, fearing that his father would be angry and it would affect the rescue of Zhang Feng.) Li Jianguo had experienced many political movements, so he was very familiar with the internal operations of the party, the government and the military. He thought for a moment and said,

"Xiao Feng is the saviour of me and our family. We must find a way to get him out. Although I am losing power now, interpersonal relationships still exist."

Yu Mei immediately said,

"Look for uncle Zhao. He is now the head of the Revolutionary Committee."

"You read my mind," Li Jianguo said. "I can't waste any more time. I'll go and see him now."

Li Jianguo spent some time and effort in the provincial military command compound of before meeting Zhao Wu. The guard in the reception room had recognised him and refused to let him in. Finally, Li Jianguo called Zhao Wu, and the guards were ordered to let him in, and they even sent two guards to accompany him because of worrying his status.

The first thing out of Li Jianguo's mouth when he saw Zhao Wu was,

"It's changed, I can't move around in the compound at will." Zhao Wu was still an enthusiastic old friend and asked him how he had been at the May Seventh Cadre School. After a few pleasantries, Li Jianguo stated the purpose of his visit and took out Li He's letter. Zhao Wu read it and said:

"So that's how matters stand, great! I didn't know Zhang Feng was Zhang Wenbo's son until the meeting to discuss the verdict. I wanted to propose that he should be punished lightly, but most of the people at the meeting advocated something much more severe, especially the special commissioner of the Cultural Revolution Working Group. I guess he was trying to blame someone like Zhang Feng for provoking a confrontation between the two factions during the violent civil strife. I can't say anything because they have evidence, especially that Zhang Feng was involved in the activities of the Four Talents counter-revolutionary group. Nowadays, no one dare to say Chairman Mao is at fault, because that is the crime of death!"

"Lao Zhao, if you can save him, I thank you on behalf of me and my family. To tell you the truth, when he was in love with Yu Mei, I strongly opposed it. But he saved my life regardless of the past. Not only is he handsome, charming and intelligent, but he is also a man of righteousness, responsibility and loyalty.

Zhao Wu said jokingly,

"No wonder he can steal my daughter-in-law. But it's also my shiftless son's fault. When you are in trouble, he avoids Yu Mei. I have scolded him many times for this. History is a good magician. How did it mingle our sons and daughters up with each other?"

It was midnight when Li Jianguo left. Zhao Wu had promised to deal with Zhang Feng's case tomorrow and avoid the special commissioner as much as possible. At least he would try to put Zhang Feng's execution on hold in order to buy time to investigate the case. In this way, Zhang Feng's innocence could be proved. As expected, Zhao Wu sent someone to tell Li Jianguo at noon the next day that he had directly intervened in the case. Someone in the public security system promised to suspend Zhang Feng's execution and there would be a retrial. Besides, Zhao Wu had just been told to attend an emergency meeting on combat readiness in the major military command. The meeting would take a day or two. He would continue to follow Zhang Feng's case when he returned until his sentence was annulled. The staff officer Lin, who was the messenger, also wrote down Li He's address and told them to hide him carefully. Everyone was glad to hear the message. Li Jianguo had to go back to the May Seventh Cadre Schools immediately, because he was an overthrown capitalist roader, and people like him are strictly watched by the school.

Yu Mei wanted to visit Zhang Feng immediately to tell him the good news. Just at the moment Dan Dan and Wang Hai came to her house. Hearing that Zhang Feng had a chance to be saved, they all jumped for joy. They all wanted to visit Zhang Feng and tell him this good new. But Wang Hai was worried that he was too conspicuous because many in the interim government knew him. In the end, Yu Mei and Dan Dan went together. They found Director Huo. He had also heard that a high-level person was interfering in Zhang Feng's case. But he did not look optimistic. Dan Dan and Yu Mei met Zhang Feng through the coordination of Director Huo. They couldn't wait to tell him the good news. But Zhang Feng did not look happy

"The public security system is now controlled by the special commissioner, Director Fan and Cai Wenge," he said. "They won't let me escape so easily. I was interrogated this morning, and they pursued the matter about Li He maliciously."

Dan Dan and Yu Mei tried to reassured him by saying that Zhao Wu was the head of the provincial Revolutionary Committee and should have more power to handle his case, so he should not worry. When they were about to separate, Zhang Feng stopped Yu Mei alone and whispered to her,

"Yu Mei, if I can't survive this time, you can bury my ashes under the poplars by the river, so that I can see you every day."

"You'll be fine, Brother Feng… If, if so, I will stay with you." She held Zhang Feng's hand tightly. The sadness of parting for ever tortured the two young people who loved each other.

Dan Dan and Wang Hai gathered at Zhang Feng's house by noon the next day, and waited anxiously for news. Zhang Lin suddenly came running in breathlessly.

"Oh, no, one of my classmates told me that this morning there was a public verdict conference in the people's square. The prisoners condemned a few days ago will be shot today. She said… She said… She saw brother Feng amongst the prisoners who will be shot."

"What?!" Everyone was stunned. Mother collapsed on the bed, unable to stand.

"It's impossible." Maybe she recognised the wrong person?" said Wang Hai. Zhang Feng's father calmed down and said,

"Will it be an accompanied condemnation? Some of the reprieved prisoners will be paraded through the streets following the prisoners that are going to be executed."

"Director Zhao is not here today," Wang Hai said anxiously.

"Maybe the bad guys in the Revolutionary Committee want to take the opportunity to murder Brother Feng." Dan Dan said. "All the prisoners on the way to the execution will be paraded through the crowded streets. Let's go and find out."

Dan Dan advised Zhang Feng's father to take care of Zhang Feng's mother. Dan Dan went out with Wang Hai and Zhang Lin.

Just after six o 'clock in the morning, Zhang Feng was awakened by a noise in the corridor. He saw Liu Tian and Li Yue being escorted away by fully armed police along with a few other prisoners sentenced to death. Zhang Feng understood that today was the day of execution. These last few days, Zhang Feng had philosophised death. 'Death befalls all men alike, as long as one keeps a loyal heart to truth and faith, it would be a worthy death and he will be honoured for his whole life.' Although he had not participated in the activities of the Four Talents, he agreed with their political views. When hundreds of millions of people lost their minds to a fanatical cult of personality, and in the name of revolution destroyed their own society by their own hands, along with destroying the economy, culture, education and moral tradition, as well as persecuting innocent people, only a few minds like the Four Talents could look through it all. It would be justice and heroism to go with them to die. History would correct its wrong course sooner or later and give innocence back to the wronged people.

The corridor was quiet again. No-one came to escort Zhang Feng. Maybe Zhao Wu's intervention had really worked, he thought. Just then he heard a group of people coming towards him. Then the door opened and a policeman called him out. Zhang Feng was surprised to see Du Zhongqing the special commissioner, Director Fan, Cai Wenge and Hei Tou all standing in the corridor. Cai Wenge smiled smugly and said,

"Zhang Feng, now is the time for you. You might think that it is Director Zhao come to release you? Yes, we'll send you to a good place, a place that others are not qualified to go even if they want to."

"We will send you to heaven," said Hei Tou viciously.

"According to our investigation, Li He was forced to make an inauthentic confession by your friends," Fan said, "You are a member of the Four Talents counter-revolutionary group, so your sentence remains unchanged. Today, you and the Four Talents will be executed together by shooting. Take him away!" Four prison guards tied Zhang Feng tightly and led him away. Zhang Feng cried out,

"I am wronged. You guys tried everything you could to murder me. You are all bastards. I curse you all!" He was dragged into the police car.

At that time, the government held public trial conferences and paraded prisoners through the crowded streets to intimidate people and create an atmosphere of terror. Zhang Feng and five other political prisoners sentenced to death were taken to the People's Square. There were tens of thousands of people there.

Then the prisoners were taken in a truck and paraded through the crowded streets of the city. There was a police car at the front of the convoy and a broadcasting truck following, shouting the slogans about suppressing anti-revolutionaries. Behind them were six Jiefang trucks, each carrying a prisoner, all tied up and with a long and narrow board on their back, with the name of the prisoner and a big red X. Zhang Feng was the third, the first truck was Liu Tian, then Li Yue. Wang Yang and Chen Xing were exempted from death and sentenced to 20 years in prison because they came from good families.

The case of the Four Talents, which caught the attention of the central government, was identified as flagrant opposition to Chairman Mao the great leader, and an overall slander of the Cultural Revolution. The people involved were given heavy sentences for these serious crimes.

At the beginning of the parade, Zhang Feng had feelings of humiliation and sadness. Then he saw that Liu Tian and Li Yue in front both held their heads high and faced death undaunted. He also raised his head up and looked straight ahead. He thought that they were not criminals, and history would prove that they were heroes of their time, just like the Six Gentlemen of the Hundred Days' Reform who were killed in 1898.

When the parade convoy arrived at a place not far from Zhang Feng's home, Zhang Feng heard someone calling him,

"Brother Feng!" "Xiao Feng!" "Brother!" He looked down at the side of the truck. It was Wang Hai, Dan Dan and Zhang Lin. Wang Hai shouted and punched the willows at the side of the street in despair. Dan Dan and Zhang Lin were crying and running desperately after the truck. It was probably approaching the time for the execution, so the convoy suddenly sped up. Zhang Feng wanted to say farewell to them, but his hoarse throat made him almost speechless. He seemed to hear Dan Dan's shouting through all the noise,

"Don't be afraid, Xiao Feng. I'll be with you."

Tears blurred Zhang Feng's eyes. As the convoy drove past the Second Senior Middle School, he saw many familiar faces. He saw the people who had been detained with him in the Mass Dictatorship Headquarters prison. They were standing by the roadside with an escort of thugs. The old principle was among them, wiping his tears mournfully. Zhang Feng turned his face away. He could not stand seeing their faces. Qing Lian stood by a window in a school building at the side of the street. Her heart was filled with contradictions as she watched Zhang Feng go by, tied up, standing on the back of the truck. Her girlish tenderness was torn to shreds by the thought that the handsome talent she had loved so passionately was about to disappear from the world. But her revolutionary beliefs as a Red Guard made her hate the counter-revolutionary elements that attacked the great leader and slandered the Cultural Revolution. Her heart was torn between love and hate. At last she looked at the far-away convoy, shedding tears and shouting "Go to hell!"

More than an hour later, the convoy was back on the river side, ready to take the main road out of the city. On the surface of the Songhua River in autumn, the yellow weeping willows were flowing in the autumn wind, and reflecting the waves of the passing water, as if singing a sad song of farewell to the life of these dying people. 'Take one more glance around. Tomorrow when the sun rises, I will not be in this world,' Zhang Feng thought. 'But my life has just begun. I still have countless ideals that have not been realised. I am in love with life, my family, my friends and my girl. But all this will be taken away by this brutal regime.'

Zhang Feng seemed to see Yu Mei's clear eyes in the river; he could almost hear her sweet voice. 'Oh no, how did that sound become so sad?' Zhang Feng listened carefully, as if Yu Mei was really calling him. He looked to the side of the road. She was waving at him desperately under a willow.

Yu Mei was too late to get the news that Zhang Feng was to be sent to the execution ground. By the time she arrived, the convoy was about to leave the downtown.

"Brother Feng, Brother Feng, wait for me! Wait for me!" She screamed at the top of her voice. Zhang Feng did not understand what she meant, but just shouted to her,

"Yu Mei, don't forget to bury my ashes… by the river…" But the police who were watching him suddenly put a hand over his mouth, for they thought he was going to call out a reactionary cry. Liu Tian and Li Yue shouted slogans several times on the road of parade and had had their mouths taped over.

The convoy began to speed up towards the execution ground. Zhang Feng could only watch Yu Mei run desperately with the convoy for a while, then she fell down on the road side.

The execution ground was more than 10 kilometres from downtown. By the time the convoy was halfway there, the two sides of the road were lined with suburban vegetable fields. At this time, the truck escorting Zhang Feng suddenly bumped and stopped. Zhang Feng looked to the roadside and saw a man dressed in black rushing from behind a big tree and instantly disappear into the cornfield.

'Is that him?' Zhang Feng remembered the familiar figure that had saved him before.

"Somebody's going to save the prisoners!" Shouted one of the prisoners escorts. The armed police in the last escort truck all got out and searched both sides of the road. Finally, they found that someone had punctured the tyres of Zhang Feng's truck with a throwing dagger. The whole convoy stopped, and the police were began preparing to face a formidable enemy. After more than ten minutes and seeing no movement, they began to replace the punctured tyre. After this incident, there was a total delay of more than twenty minutes. It was about four o 'clock in the afternoon when they arrived at the execution ground. The prisoners were escorted off the trucks one by one into the heavily guarded execution ground.

The sky was overcast and light rain began to fall, as if the clouds were weeping for them. Liu tian walked in front, followed by Li Yue. For some reason, Zhang Feng was the last. On his way to the earthen wall where the prisoners were to be shot, Liu Tian turned back and waved to Li Yue and Zhang Feng. His eyes were saying,

"Brothers, see you in heaven." Then he walked with dignity to the wall and refused to kneel down. He wanted to die like a dignified man. The gun went off and he fell in a pool of blood, ending his brief life at the age of 24.

"My brother!" Tears flowed from Zhang Feng's eyes.

Then, Li Yue ended his young life in the same way. In the next ten minutes, three other political prisoners were shot one by one.

"Big brother, I'm following you," Zhang Feng said to Liu

Tian in his heart, who had just died.

"Farewell, my family and friends. Yu Mei, please don't forget to let me see you at the riverside every day."

Just as he was walking towards the earthen wall, suddenly the clouds began to drift away and a ray of bright sunlight shone onto the execution ground.

Ah, heaven has opened the gate for me. I am going to be reunited with Teacher Sun, Xu Jianguo and Brother Liu and Li.'

He stepped up to the earthen wall and also refused to kneel down. He seemed to hear someone arguing. But this had nothing to do with him. He took a deep breath and closed his eyes. Then he heard the order for the firing squad to raise their guns, and then the gun went off. He lost consciousness for an instant, could not see anything, and could not hear anything.

CHAPTER IV

At the Gates of Hell

A gust of cold wind blew Zhang Feng back to consciousness. He thought in a trance, 'Has my soul left my body? So why do I feel my hands cool and my feet soft, almost untenable?' Suddenly he felt someone holding him. 'How peculiar it is,' he thought,' 'that the goblin of hell in charge of should be so friendly.'

"Are you all right?" the 'goblin' spoke. Zhang Feng's eyes widened in shocked. In front of him was a PLA officer. Zhang Feng was still stood in front of the execution wall. Looking beyond the PLA officer he was even more shocked. The policeman in charge of his execution stood dumbfounded and his gun fell to the ground. The police chief and his subordinates were surrounded and disarmed by a group of armed PLA soldiers.

"Zhang Feng, you are saved," The PLA officer said to him very kindly. "Director Zhao saved you. I was his Staff Officer and Confidential Secretary, I'm Lin." Zhang Feng felt as if he had seen the officer somewhere. He suddenly remembered. He was the PLA officer who Chang Zheng had ordered to drive Zhang Feng away from the banquet for distinguished North Korean guests in the hotel. The PLA officer had been very polite to Zhang Feng.

Lin gave a brief description of the rescue of Zhang Feng. Before going to the meeting, Director Zhao told Secretary Lin to pay attention to the special commissioner and closely protect the witness Li He. Unsurprisingly, Director Fan and Cai Wenge wanted to kill the witness. They kidnapped Li He this morning. Just as they tried to throw him into the river in order to make it look like he was committing suicide, the men arranged by Lin's secretary saved Li He and caught the murderer at the same time. The would-be murderer confessed to everything. On the other side, the special commissioner and Director Fan mistakenly believed that Li He had been killed so they hastily decided to execute Zhang Feng. Thus, by the time Director Zhao returned, Zhang Feng's death had become an unchangeable fact.

It was noon when Secretary Lin got these messages. He quickly called Director Zhao who was in the Shenyang Military Region to tell him hurry back to Jili City. It was about three o' clock in the afternoon when Director Zhao returned to the provincial military command. Coincidentally, Chang Zheng also arrived at the same time. Secretary Lin gave a brief report to Director Zhao in the office and concluded that Zhang Feng was not involved in the activities of the Four Talents at all. In addition, he hadn't participate in the violent civil strife. All he did was save his friends. Wang Hai's testimony together with the circumstantial evidence of Chang Zheng could prove it. Chang Zheng also said repeatedly that although Zhang Feng was his former rival, he admired Zhang Feng as a man who would do anything for his friends. Director Zhao also appreciated people like Zhang Feng. He believed that Zhang Wenbo's son must be a good man. Secretary Lin reminded Director Zhao that the scheduled execution time was 4 p.m. It was already half past three. Zhao Wu pounded the table and said,

"I need to show them my power this time. How dare they hide the truth and build a false case? This is wronging a good man!" He asked Secretary Lin, with his handwritten order file and a fully armed guard platoon, to rush to the execution ground as quickly as possible to save Zhang Feng. When they were five minutes away, they heard the first gunshot. Secretary Lin told the driver to speed up. The jeep sped to the execution ground at top speed. Then they heard a succession of gunshots. At the gate of the execution ground, the armed police guard tried to stop their car. Secretary Lin was a former special force solider. He angrily took out his pistol, pointed it at the police guard and shouted,

"Order from Director Zhao of the Revolutionary Committee – stop the execution immediately! Anyone who dares to disobey will be killed with lawful authority."

Terrified at the sight of the machine guns and the fully armed PLA soldiers on the two trucks behind the jeep, the police let them sweep past. When the jeep came to the execution wall, Secretary Lin saw that the police had raised his gun and aimed it at Zhang Feng. He shouted,

"Hold your fire!"

He jumped out of the jeep and reached the policeman in a few lunges. Just as the policeman was about to pull the trigger, Secretary Lin lifted his gun. The bullet whizzed over the earthen wall and disappeared into the distant woods.

Secretary Lin was soaked in cold sweat. Zhang Feng would have been sent to the world beyond the grave if he had acted one second later.

After listening to this story, Zhang Feng expressed his sincere gratitude promptly to Secretary Lin and Zhao Wu for saving his life. Secretary Lin said that Zhao Wu had ordered them to take Zhang Feng to a safe place in the provincial military command for protection. The next day, the public security and the court system would officially confirm that Zhang Feng's case was a miscarriage of justice, then Zhang Feng would be released and he could go home. Zhang Feng suddenly remembered that his family was worried about him.

"Let's get on," said secretary Lin. "they must be at the gate of the execution ground. The prisoners' families are all there and preparing to identify the bodies."

Zhang Feng looked back at Liu Tian and Li Yue, who were still lying in a pool of blood, and got into Secretary Lin's jeep with tears in his eyes. Just beyond the gate of the execution ground, Zhang Feng saw his father sitting on the ground with his hands over his face. Wang Hai was standing beside him comforting him. Nearby were many of the prisoners' families, including those of Liu Tian and Li Yue. Zhang Feng told Secretary Lin to stop. He jumped out of the jeep and ran to his father and Wang Hai. Wang Hai suddenly looked up and saw that Zhang Feng was running to him. He was shocked because he was superstitious and believed that someone was wrongly executed, then his soul would return to the world seeking vengeance. He looked pale.

"Elder Brother…" he stammered. "Elder Brother, why did your soul come back so soon?"

"What are you talking about? I'm not dead!"

Wang Hai was trembling. He touched Zhang Feng to make sure that the person in front of him was not a soul without a body. He touched Zhang Feng's strong arm and shoulder.

"Oh, it's not a ghost!" He hurriedly turned back to Zhang Feng's father,

"Uncle Zhang, Zhang Feng is not dead!" Zhang Feng's father was still crying. He just waved and said.

"Please don't try to comfort me." Zhang Feng rushed to his father. He put his hand on his father's shoulder and said,

"Dad, it's me. I'm not dead."

"What?" His father jumped up at once. They hugged tightly and cried.

Secretary Lin came over. Knowing that Zhang Feng's father was a former classmate of Zhao Wu, he explained Zhao Wu's intervention and Zhang Feng's rescue. Secretary Lin said he had to go back and report to Director Zhao as soon as possible. Then he left together with Zhang Feng.

Zhang Feng's father and Wang Hai then remembered that they should notify Zhang Feng's family and friends that he had been rescued. But in those days, most people didn't have a phone at home, so they had to hurry back. Wang Hai was smart enough to save a lot of time by asking the driver of a vegetable delivery truck from the vegetable commune to take them downtown.

After passing the bridge over the river, Wang Hai separated from Zhang Wenbo because he had been thinking about Dan Dan and was worried about her depression. Wang Hai hurried to Dan Dan's home and told her mother the good news that Zhang Feng had been rescued. But he didn't see Dan Dan. He had an ominous presentiment because he remembered Dan Dan words when they were chasing the prisoner's truck: "Xiao Feng, I'll be with you."

He asked Dan Dan's mother urgently where she had gone. She said that Dan Dan had left home half an hour ago saying she felt sad and wanted to go to the riverside to relax. When Wang Hai heard this, he ran towards the riverside immediately. 'The giant poplar, she must be under the giant poplar,' Wang Hai thought. Because he had told Dan Dan that Zhang Feng and Yu Mei had fallen in love under the giant poplar, Dan Dan must have believed that she could see Zhang Feng's soul there.

Wang Hai ran as hard as he could, through the woods in South Bank Park and then towards the giant poplar tree. He saw a man in black in the water, holding a figure in his arms, walking step by step from the water to the riverbank. The figure looked like a woman in blue. This must be Dan Dan! She wore the blue dress only on important days.

"Dan Dan! Dan Dan!" cried Wang Hai. When the man in black saw Wang Hai, he laid the woman on the riverbank and waved at Wang Hai, meaning that she was handed over to you. Then he ran away. Wang Hai rushed to the woman. She was Dan Dan indeed. He held her as she choked out the water from her stomach and then let her lie down to rest. A few minutes later, Dan Dan stirred, looked at Wang Hai and burst into tears.

"Wang Hai, why can't you let me die with Xiao Feng? He will be lonely in the other world."

Wang Hai helped Dan Dan sit up and said to her,

"I must tell you that Brother Feng is not dead. He was saved."

"You lie! We all saw that he had been sent to the execution ground. Who could save him? No, I have to go with him." Then she stood up and started walked back to the river. Wang Hai quickly put his arms around her. He was moved to tears by Dan Dan's undying love for Zhang Feng.

"It's true," he sobbed. "I wouldn't lie to you. It was Zhao Wu and his men saved Brother Feng at the last moment."

He told her about the rescue. Dan Dan listened doubtfully and asked,

"When will Xiao Feng be able to go home?"

"He will be back the day after tomorrow," Wang Hai said. "Don't worry."

"Wang Hai, I feel cold," said Dan Dan, trembling. Wang Hai quickly picked up his coat from the ground and wrapped it around Dan Dan. Then he helped her walk home slowly.

At noon the next day, after having lunch in the dining hall of the provincial military command, Zhang Feng returned to a room guarded by soldiers. Secretary Lin came in, along with Director Huo, who was the Deputy Director of the Revolutionary Committee for public security and the people's courts. They announced the conclusion of the re-examination of Zhang Feng. According to detailed investigation and evidence collection, it was confirmed that Zhang Feng was not involved in the political activities of the Four Talents nor directly involved in the violent civil strife between the two factions. Although Zhang Feng was somewhat dissatisfied with the Cultural Revolution, this was simply a matter of youthful ideological misunderstanding but not a counterrevolutionary action. Therefore, Zhang Feng's behaviour should not treated as criminal, so he was freed. Zhang Feng was asked to go back to school and reflect on his past behaviour to improve the level of his ideological understanding. Zhang Feng thanked Secretary Lin and Director Huo for the result of handling. But he was also worried about the possibility of reprisals from Cai Wenge and his men.

"Don't worry," said Secretary Lin. "Director Fan has been removed from his post and investigated on suspicion of murder.

Now Director Huo is in charge of public security organs and the people's courts. He is the former subordinate of Li Jianguo." Zhang Feng quickly expressed his gratitude to Director Huo. He remembered what Yu Mei had said that when she came to visit him in the prison, that it was Director Huo who had helped her.

Zhang Feng missed his family, Dan Dan and Yu Mei. He was anxious to go home. After saying goodbye to Secretary Lin and Director Huo, he immediately departed for home. At the gate of the compound, he met Wang Hai, who had come to pick him up, and some of his former classmates who had good relations with him. They all shook hands and hugged him, saying they thought they would never see him again. Then they got on a truck that Wang Hai had borrowed and drove to Zhang Feng's house. In the vehicle, Wang Hai wanted to tell Zhang Feng about Dan Dan's attempted suicide but he remembered Dan Dan had told him not to tell anyone about it. In addition, Zhang Feng had just escaped from death; he would not want to hear such sad news. So Wang Hai took back all the words he wanted to say.

When he returned home with Wang Hai, Zhang Feng saw a table of delicious food prepared by his mother to celebrate that he escaped from death. Zhang Feng's mother and father came up and hugged him, tears flowing from their aged eyes. Then Zhang Lin hugged her brother, in tears.

Dan Dan came in. Ignoring all the people around her, she rushed into Zhang Feng's arms and burst into tears. Zhang Feng and Wang Hai tried to calm down her, but she couldn't stop crying. At last, Zhang Feng's father invited everyone to sit down to dinner together, and Dan Dan calmed down eventually. Zhang Feng's father took out the vintage wine that had been preserved for many years. He invited everyone to have a drink to celebrate that Zhang Feng escaped from death. The atmosphere in the room had just changed from grief to joy when there was a sharp knock on the door. The door opened and in came Li Xiaogang, Yu Mei's younger brother. He said to Zhang Feng in horror,

"My god, my sister took poison yesterday and was taken to hospital. I didn't hear the message that you weren't dead until noon today. She is unconscious. Please go to see her now!"

"What!?" Zhang Feng stood up at once. Then he left with Li Xiaogang without saying another word.

Yu Mei was lying in a hospital bed in one of the wards of the First Municipal Hospital. Her face was pale. Her mother was sitting at the bedside, sobbing helplessly. Zhang Feng ran in, knelt on the ground and held Yu Mei's hand with a sorrowful cry.

"Yu Mei, Yu Mei, why are you doing this?"

On the way to the hospital, he had remembered the words that Yu Mei had shouted while chasing the prisoner truck. "Brother Feng, wait for me!" He now knew what it meant. She wanted to commit suicide for Zhang Feng. He was extremely grieved and was eager to die with her. Yu Mei's mother patted Zhang Feng on the back. With tears in her eyes, she told him about Yu Mei's attempted suicide. Yesterday, after returning home, Yu Mei told her family that Zhang Feng had been sent to the execution ground. Then she locked herself in her room. Since she hadn't come out this morning, they broke into her room and found her lying in bed in her new clothes, with a picture of the riverside landscape. Under the bed was an empty bottle of highly toxic pesticides. They knew then that she had tried to commit suicide by taking poison. They took her to the hospital immediately.

Although she had had her stomach pumped, the poison had already infiltrated the blood. The doctor had tried bloodletting and detoxification but she also needed a blood transfusion. But the hospital did not have enough blood in its own blood bank. They were contacting other hospitals now. However, this was during the movement period, when the management of the hospitals was in a mess, and many doctors had been sent to jail.

Zhang Feng immediately said,

"Take my blood, I am type O blood." He found a doctor and said he wanted to donate blood to Yu Mei. The doctor looked at Zhang Feng and said,

"You look very strong, but you also look gaunt. The patient needs at least 1000 millilitres of blood. An average person can draw only 400 millilitres of blood at a time. Otherwise, it would harm your own health."

"It doesn't matter. I used to be an athlete. I am strong enough. I will recover soon." By coaxing and pestering the doctor unceasingly, Zhang Feng persuaded them to draw 800 millilitres of blood from him to give to Yu Mei. He felt a little faint and lay down on the porch chair. After a few days of torture and anxiety, plus the blood donation just now, Zhang Feng soon fell asleep. After about an hour, Zhang Feng was awakened by voices. He opened his eyes and saw several people around him, including Wang Hai, Dan Dan, Zhang Lin, Li Xiaogang, and Li Jianguo, who had come after hearing what had happened. Zhang Feng sat up quickly. Li Jianguo said,

"Xiao Feng, you've just donated a lot of blood. You'd better lie down and rest."

"I'm sorry, uncle Li," Zhang Feng said apologetically to Li Jianguo. "It is all because of me that your family has so much trouble."

"Don't say that," said Li Jianguo magnanimously. "You did your best to help us when we were in trouble."

Everyone began to discuss how to save Yu Mei. Yu Mei's mother told them that the doctor in charge of saving her said because Zhang Feng had given his blood to Yu Mei, her life would not be in danger for a day or two. But the poison had begun to damage her liver and kidneys, so an antidote medication had to be found soon. Traditional Chinese medicine could help the detoxification, but the most experienced TCM doctor in the hospital, Doctor Zou, was doing forced labour under supervision because of his historical problems. He had to clean the toilets every day. Wang Hai went to find this old TCM doctor and took him to the ward to examine Yu Mei. Doctor Zou made a prescription of traditional Chinese detoxifying medicine from his ancestral secret recipe. But he said that the prescription contained a rare herbal medicine called 'resurrection herb', which was not available at regular pharmacies. This herb was only be found in the primeval forests of the Changbai Mountains. Only this herb could save Yu Mei's life. Without it, there would be no complete detoxification. Within three days, she would still be close to death. Doctor Zou also drew up a sketch of the herb; it looked like leeks with wide leaves. He said that it took at least five leaves to have a curative effect, and seven leaves were better.

Everyone was trying to figure out how to get the resurrection herb as soon as possible. Li Jianguo said that his school was not far from the Changbai Mountains. He could go back immediately and try to visit the local villagers to see if they could get the herb. Wang Hai said that his family had relatives living in the Changbai Mountains and that he would contact them immediately. Zhang Feng suddenly remembered that his martial arts master once said that someone in the Taoist temple of North Mountain had made a resurrection pill. The most important source material was the resurrection herb. Ignoring Dan Dan's worry, he immediately went to the Taoist temple of North Mountain to find his master.

He had been able to run up the mountain in the past, but now just walking made him out of breath. Zhang Feng was eager to see his master because they hadn't seen each other for a long time. But to his disappointment, his master had gone out early that day, leaving a message that he was going to visit some relatives. No one knew how many days later he would be back. Zhang Feng had to go home despondently. He felt exhausted and needed a good sleep.

When Zhang Feng woke up the next morning, it was after nine o 'clock. He had slept for twelve hours. After eating a little, he felt energised and rushed back to the hospital. In the ward, Yu Mei's mother was bent over the bedside, fast asleep. Zhang Feng woke her up and told her to go home to rest. He would stay and take care of Yu Mei.

Yu Mei's mother said that Doctor Zou had come back again last night and treated Yu Mei with acupuncture. This treatment could delay the further spread of the toxin. He also told her to press the Yu Mei´s two acupuncture points, often called the 'Four Gates,' to increase the circulation of Qi and blood and to help the immune function.

After Yu Mei's mother left, Zhang Feng began to knead Yu Mei's acupuncture points. He gently took up her hand. Her little hands used to be warm, but now they were getting cold. He kneaded her points as gently as he could. Zhang Feng's master had taught him some important acupuncture points while he was teaching him Qigong. Martial arts and Qigong were followed the system of human body meridians. Zhang

Feng wanted to use Qigong to treat Yu Mei, but he remembered that his master had told him that poisoned people could not be treated with Qigong. Then he just continued kneading Yu Mei's 'Four Gates' points, whispering to her,

"You must wake up, Yu Mei. Open your eyes and take a look. I was pulled back from the gates of hell, so you will be alright too. You must hold on. Why did you do such a stupid thing? Why did you want to die together with me? Without you, one of the most beautiful things is missing in this world. I know your beauty and kindness, but I did not expect you to have such stubbornness in your character. I'm not worth it… "

It was said that real men didn't cry easily. Zhang Feng had no tears in the face of suffering, torture and death. But thinking about Yu Mei's undying love for him, Zhang Feng, a man as strong as steel, could not help shedding tears.

Two days passed. There was no message from anyone who was looking for the resurrection herb. Everyone was very anxious. A message came from Li Jianguo saying it was difficult to find this miraculous herb in autumn. It was only possible to find the resurrection herb in a place with a waterfall in the mountains. He had asked more people to go into the mountains to find the herb. He hoped that Doctor Zou could help to delay the further spread of the toxin. The people who were not out searching were getting more anxious with every hour that passed. Yu Mei's mother, Zhang Feng and Dan Dan took turns to take care for Yu Mei. Doctor Zou asked them to boil up the other herbal medicines so that the antidote would be ready for the addition of the resurrection herb and it would only need to be boiled for another five minutes.

During the night of the third day, Zhang Feng was at Yu Mei's bedside. He looked at his watch every few minutes, waiting anxiously for any messages about the resurrection herb. If the resurrection herb was not be found before dawn, Yu Mei would be in extreme danger. Looking at the skin on Yu Mei's face begin to blacken, Zhang Feng felt the tension in his body tighten even further. He thought, 'if Yu Mei really can't live, I won't either. Such a delicate girl like her was willing to die for me. I am a man, and I should have the courage to die for her. I have experienced death. God has given me a few more days to live, so that I can see with my own eyes the true love of my beloved girl. It is worth dying with her and loving each other in eternity. 'Thinking of this, he looked at the electrician's knife at his waist, which he used to defend himself. 'That's it,' he thought. 'Cut my wrists to kill myself, start to hurt and pass out in five minutes, then it's all over.' He looked at the electric stove on the little table, on which was a pot with the boiled herbal medicine in it, waiting for the resurrection herb. 'My lord,' Zhang Feng prayed in his mind, 'bless my Yu Mei, and let the resurrection herb appear quickly.'

It was four o 'clock in the morning, and Zhang Feng was very sleepy. But he did not dare to sleep. He found that Yu Mei's face was getting darker and her body was getting colder. His heart began to beat violently. 'as there really no hope of her being saved?' God had pulled him out of the jaws of hell at the last second. 'If you really want us to be together, please save Yu Mei too.' Zhang Feng thought. After a while, Zhang Feng looked at his watch anxiously. It was now five o 'clock. A faint morning light appeared outside the window. He pulled out his electrician's knife and pointed it at his wrist. 'In another hour I'll die with Yu Mei if the resurrection herb hasn't arrived yet.' He thought.

Suddenly he heard a cry of surprise.

"You can't do that, Xiao Feng!"

Dan Dan and Yu Mei's mother had come. Dan Dan didn't want to wake the people in the room, so she had opened the door quietly. She saw Zhang Feng pointing the knife at his wrist..

"Xiao Feng, you can't just give up like this. It is not morning yet, and there is still hope for Yu Mei." Dan Dan said.

Zhang Feng didn't want to frighten Dan Dan. So he said,

"it's not what you think. I'm just playing with the knife."

Yu Mei's mother came in behind Dan Dan and didn't see Zhang Feng holding the knife. She rushed to the bedside and seized Yu Mei's cold hand, crying.

"Wake up, my daughter. You can't die like that! How can we live without you?" As the electronic clock on the wall moved forward minute by minute, all of them were wondering whether they should prepare the Yu Mei's funeral. But no one wanted to be the first to mention it.

Time moved inexorably towards six o'clock. The sky was already beginning to light up. They looked at Yu Mei, who was breathing faintly. They were all in a state of great anxiety and utter despair. Just as the hour hand was pointing to six o 'clock, there was a gentle knock on the door.

"Who is it?" Zhang Feng asked. He rushed to the door and opened it, but the corridor was empty.

CHAPTER V

The Magical Herb

Zhang Feng thought someone had arrived with the resurrection herb. But when he saw no one outside, he was very disappointed. Just as he was about to close the door, he saw a small bamboo basket on the floor at his feet. He picked it up and saw something that looked like leeks inside it. There was also a small piece of paper, on which was written 'resurrection herb' in the Song-Dynasty imitation style.

"There's a chance to save Yu Mei!" Zhang Feng cried excitedly. Dan Dan and Song Lihua both came to see it. Zhang Feng took it out of the basket. There were two herbs, each with seven leaves.

"Great!" said Song Lihua. "Doctor Zou said that the resurrection herb with seven leaves has the best effect."

"Be quick," Zhang Feng said. "Mix it with the other herbs and boil for five minutes."

They had no time to think about who had sent the resurrection herb. They quickly used the electric stove to boil the medicine. Then they sat Yu Mei up against her pillow to feed the medicine to her. But her mouth was tightly shut and could not be opened. Song Lihua had to prise open her mouth with a small spoon, and then Dan Dan poured the medicine into her mouth little by little.

Doctor Zou quietly walked in while this was happening. If the men of the Rebel Faction knew he was still treating people, especially a daughter of a capitalist roader, he would be in big trouble. The old doctor was very happy to see that the resurrection herb had been found. He took Yu Mei's pulse, and said that the medicine was beginning to take effect. Her pulse was not so weak as before. He told them to let Yu Mei rest for ten more minutes before feeding her the rest of the medicine. When her face began to turn red, he would perform another acupuncture treatment for her. Everyone was relieved to see that Yu Mei's face began to turn red slowly. At this time, Zhang Feng began to wonder out loud about who had sent the resurrection herb. Dan Dan said it was probably from someone dispatched by Li Jianguo.

"That's impossible," Song Lihua said. "Why didn't whoever sent the herb come in and talk to everyone?" Zhang Feng said he would talk to the nurse on duty at the gate. The night nurse was already off duty when Zhang Feng walked to the gate. The young day nurse saw that Zhang Feng was a handsome young man and was willing to talk with him. She said the night nurse had told her something strange. It was at about six o'clock, a man in black, with a hat shielding his face, said he had something urgent and needed to visit a patient. But then he had left in less than a minute.

'Is it the mysterious man in black?' Zhanh Feng thought, 'He has helped me several times now. Last time I would be dead if he hadn't delayed my prisoner truck by puncturing the tire. This time he sent the resurrection herb in time and saved Yu Mei. But why does he always help us secretly and never show up? It must be that this man has some unspeakable secret and cannot reveal his identity.'

By noon, Yu Mei's face had become rosier, her body was warmer, and her pulse was stronger. Everyone was relieved. Doctor Zou had conducted acupuncture but he said that while her body would gradually recover, she would not wake up right away because the poison had damaged her brain. She could only wake herself up with her own will. She needed more kneading and talking to stimulate her central nervous system. They decided to take care of Yu Mei in turns. Song Lihua sent someone to make a long-distance call to Li Jianguo to tell him that Yu Mei was out of danger. Dan Dan took the message to Zhang Feng's family and Wang Hai to reassure them. Zhang Feng volunteered to take care of Yu Mei this night because everyone else was so exhausted. From eight o'clock in the evening, Zhang Feng was constantly kneading Yu Mei's acupuncture points, talking to her softly, especially about the past, when they fell in love. But by twelve o'clock at midnight, he was completely exhausted. He took Yu Mei's hand and fell asleep. Time was passing by quietly. In his dream, Zhang Feng was holding hands with Yu Mei and watching the beautiful scenery along the river. After a while, he was afraid that Yu Mei might catch cold, so he said let's go back. But Yu Mei held his hand tightly. Zhang Feng suddenly woke up from his dream. He was surprised to see that Yu Mei was holding his hand. He remembered that he had been holding her hand before he fell asleep. When he looked carefully, he found that Yu Mei's fingers were moving slightly.

"Yu Mei, are you awake?"

Zhang Feng cried happily. He leaned over and looked at Yu Mei's face. It was pink and soft. Her lips moved slightly as if she wanted to speak. Her eyes were also moving as if she was making an effort to open eyes.

"Yu Mei, Yu Mei, wake up!" Zhang Feng cried, gently shaking her shoulder. A few minutes later, a miracle happened. Yu Mei slowly opened her eyes, which were as clear as the stream in autumn. Zhang Feng hugged her excitedly.

'Thank God, thank the mysterious friend!' Zhang Feng thought.' My beloved Yu Mei is back from the land of death.'

Yu Mei slowly raised her head and looked at Zhang Feng. Suddenly, she trembled all over and asked in an incredulous tone,

"Brother Feng, is that you? Why am I seeing you after walking for such a long time? Why does it look like a ward? Why is there a ward in hell?" She suddenly hugged Zhang Feng tightly. "Brother Feng, will the goblin come to torture me? You must protect me." It was obvious that Yu Mei was not fully awakened. She thought she was in hell. Zhang Feng said to her,

"Yu Mei, you didn't die, neither did I. This is a ward in the municipal hospital. You've been here for three days."

Yu Mei opened her eyes and said, "No, you are deceiving me. I saw them taking you to the execution ground." Zhang Feng told her the brief story of his rescue. It was not until a night duty nurse came in for the ward round that Yu Mei finally believed she was not dead, but in hospital. After the nurse left, the two young people held each other tightly as if afraid of losing each other again. Both of them had put one foot through the gate of hell, and then returned to the upper world. They couldn't be separated by anything, even death.

The news that Yu Mei had woken up was joyous for her family, relatives and friends. In the next few days, Doctor Zou gave Yu Mei several prescriptions of more powerful Chinese medicine to stimulate Qi and nourish the blood. To speed her recovery even more he even gave her the feral ginseng of the Changbai Mountains, which he had treasured for years. After three or four days, Yu Mei was almost completely recovered. Wang Hai borrowed a jeep and drove her home. Hearing the news that Yu Mei had died for Zhang Feng's martyrdom and had come back from the dead, Zhao Wu was deeply moved. He said to Chang Zheng,

"You are not blessed. You won't have the opportunity to have a beautiful and faithful girlfriend like Yu Mei."

"My girlfriend, Xiao Li, is a fine woman too." said Chang Zheng. a little embarrassed.

"How could she be comparable to Yu Mei?" Zhao Wu said. Chang Zheng's girlfriend was also a descendant of military cadres who had grown up with Chang Zheng in the military compound. She had loved Chang Zheng since childhood but because of her plain appearance, Chang Zheng had not paid much attention to her before. After graduating from junior high school, Xiao Li became more and more beautiful, although not as beautiful as Yu Mei. Then Chang Zheng alienated Yu Mei after Li Jianguo had been overthrown. Xiao Li took the opportunity and had been courting Chang Zheng enthusiastically. Then they fell in love. However, Chang Zheng felt a sense of guilt towards Yu Mei. Thus, he had wanted to bury the past and gave evidence in favour of Zhang Feng to save him from execution.

A week later, Zhang Feng returned to school. His teachers and classmates, who knew that he had survived, greeted him enthusiastically because they knew that he had been wronged.

Those who did not know his story, especially those who had been particularly active when Zhang Feng had been publicly criticised, were frightened into hiding, thinking that his ghost had returned for revenge.

In front of the main school building, Zhang Feng came face-to-face with Cai Wenge. Zhang Feng held his head high, went up and said to him in a loud voice,

"Thanks for sending me to the Palace of Hell, Commissioner Cai. But their quota is already full, so they sent me back, sorry to disappoint you."

"I know you found your backer who saved your life," Cai Wenge said and looked embarrassed. "But don't get too excited. Although your actions were not enough to make you be sentenced by law, your disaffected speech about the Cultural Revolution is enough for you to be punished." He turned to the thugs behind him and said, "Come on, send him back to the Mass Dictatorship Headquarters for a few days, and wait till we have a conclusion for his case." Zhang Feng already knew that he would have to be re-examined about his other problems when he returned to school. But those were not serious problems; he had said that the Cultural Revolution caused inconvenience for people's life, and so on. Ordinary people were also voicing such complaints so he wasn't really worried about Cai Wenge's words.

"I don't care. I've been almost dead once, so I'm not afraid of anything else you might try." Zhang Feng said.

With that, he followed the men to the Mass Dictatorship Headquarters cells. The detained people were overjoyed to see Zhang Feng. They all thought Zhang Feng had been shot, but he was still alive! The old principal hugged him, weeping. He stroked the scars on Zhang Feng's face over and over again. After everyone had calmed down, Zhang Feng told them the story about his escape from the dead. Of course he didn't mention that the man in black had punctured the tyres on the prisoner truck because he didn't want anyone to know that there was such a mysterious man. The police who escorted the prisoners did not know the special relationship between the man in black and himself.

What Zhang Feng did not expect was that the conspiracy of Cai Wenge was shattered so quickly. At noon the next day, Wang Hai and his father, Master Wang, came to the Mass Dictatorship Headquarters to announce the decision of the Revolutionary Committee of the school about Zhang Feng's case. With them were several worker-like men, as well as the representative of the school-stationed Military's Propaganda Team. They believed that Zhang Feng's problem was an insufficient level of ideological understanding to do with the internal contradictions among the people, not the contradictions between ourselves and the enemy. So Zhang Feng was released from the detention. He could return to his class and join in 'The resumption of study goes with the revolution' with other students. Zhang Feng, of course, was very happy and said goodbye to the old principal and other detainees.

Wang Hai's father was the new captain of the Workers' Propaganda Team. When the Revolutionary Committee had discussed Zhang Feng that morning, Master Wang had demanded resolutely that Zhang Feng's case should be treated as an internal contradiction among the people and that Zhang Feng should be released from detention, regardless of the opposition of Cai Wenge and his men. Fortunately, the military representative also supported his opinion, so Zhang Feng was released. Zhang Feng thanked Master Wang for his help.

"It is a good man who will do anything to help his friends," said Master Wang. "You have saved Wang Hai several times before."

However, to everyone's surprise, Cai Wenge, a despicable and insidious man, secretly asked his man who was in charge of personnel files to add a dozen exaggerated 'reactionary speeches' into Zhang Feng's files. This could seriously affect Zhang Feng's future. In those days, everyone had a political personnel file, which mainly recorded your family background, historical issues, political attitudes and degree of loyalty to the Chinese Communist Party. If you had any 'stains' on your personnel file, it would affect your future development, including education, party membership, military service, overseas study and promotion opportunities. Thus, you would become an unacceptable person, a second-class citizen.

Time passed quickly, and the tumultuous year of 1968 ended. On the eve of the Spring Festival in 1969, factional fighting was temporarily suspended under the dual effect of the political balance of the Triple Combination and the Red Terror of purifying the class ranks. The Red Guards returned to school and started the so-called "resumption of study goes with the revolution.' They were now restrained by the Military's Propaganda Team and the Workers' Propaganda Team. Society seemed to be returning to a state of calm. In the Mass Dictatorship Headquarters, where 'Monsters and Demons' were detained, the exhortation of confessions by torture also temporarily stopped. The prisoners were simply forced to do physical labour, along with pleading guilty to Chairman Mao and writing confession statements.

Zhang Feng with his family and friends looked forward joyfully to the Spring Festival during the brief period when the storm had subsided. When the River City was dressed up as a world of ice and snow in winter, people began to celebrate the arrival of the Spring Festival. On the first day of the lunar New

Year, Zhang Feng's family invited Yu Mei's whole family and Dan Dan to dinner. Everyone wanted to have a happy reunion after so much suffering. Zhang Wenbo asked his wife to buy all the rationed pork, eggs and refined flour that belonged to his family. She also bought some high-priced pork at the free market. After two days of intense preparation, their family had a complete and abundant feast of North-eastern Chinese cuisine. The dishes included Zhang Wenbo's famous stewed pork with soy sauce, sour pickled cabbage vermicelli with plain boiled pork and fried aubergine. Dan Dan's mother cooked stewed chicken with mushroom, and Song Lihua made crisp fried pork and glutinous rice cake. They first made dumplings together when all the people arrived. Then everyone sat down around the table. They ate the dumplings first, followed by the other dishes. For the average family, such an abundant dinner could only happen once a year. Li Jianguo used to be a senior official who enjoyed special treatment. After being demoted to civilian and subjected to the ordeal of reformation through labour, he felt that the meal was almost too delicious. Li Jianguo brought the 'Yushu Daqu,' a famous local white spirit. He let everyone enjoy the drink until thoroughly drunk. Zhang Wenbo picked up his glass and looked at Li Jianguo, Zhang Feng, Yu Mei, Dan Dan and Wang Hui (Dan Dan's mother). Then he said,

"I propose a toast to our lucky survival from disaster and fortunate escape from death!" Everyone held up their glasses together, each with tears in their eyes. Li Jianguo said to Zhang Wenbo,

"Wenbo, let me, as a capitalist roader, give a toast to you, the stubborn rightist. It would be great if Zhao Wu were here, so that our three classmates could reunite for the thirtieth anniversary of our graduation." Before he had finished speaking, there was a knock at the door. Everyone looked nervously at each other.

"We are all political losers," Li Jianguo said calmly, "What else can we be afraid of? Is it illegal for us to get together with our classmates for dinner?" The words were very reasonable, but everyone was surprised when they saw the man coming in. This man was burly, wearing a black woollen coat, along with a black leather hat and a mouth muffle. Li Jianguo thought of the special commissioner in black, Zhang Feng thought of the mysterious man in black who had saved him several times. To everyone's surprise, this person was exactly Zhao Wu, whom Li Jianguo just talked about. The first to shake hands with Zhao Wu was Zhang Wenbo, and then Li Jianguo. The three university classmates were reunited after more than 30 years. They are all emotional and tearful. Zhang Wenbo said,

"You, the Director of the Revolutionary Committee and the Commander of the Military Area Command, mustn't get involved with us, a stubborn rightist and a capitalist roader," Zhang Wenbo said.

"Don't worry," said Zhao Wu. "It is not against the law to meet my old classmates. Moreover, I am dressed as an underground agent." His words made everyone laugh.

After Zhao Wu had sat down, Li Jianguo proposed a toast to everyone for the reunion of the three old friends and for their sons and daughters who had also become friends. Zhao Wu said that Chang Zheng had expressly asked him to convey his greetings to Zhang Feng and Yu Mei, as well as to apologise to Zhang Feng for his past unjust treatment of. They would be good friends in the future. Zhang Wenbo gave Zhao Wu heartfelt thanks for saving Zhang Feng's life. Zhao Wu said,

"Don't mention it. Xiao Feng is a good young man. He was wronged. It's just that the process of the rescue was so alarmingly dangerous and scared you all."

How much laughter, gratitude and tears there were at the feast. In this political storm full of ignorance, madness, persecution and killing, there were countless good people who had died in injustice, and there were also countless unyielding people who persevered bravely and helped each other out of the storm.

The unusual Spring Festival family party proceeded from afternoon to evening. Hu Yun took out the frozen pears and frozen persimmon after dinner for everyone to eat. These were the favourite desserts of the natives of Northeast China. Then Zhang Lin grabbed her elder brother to go outside to set off the firecrackers with Dan Dan and Yu Mei. The parents stood outside the building to admire the fireworks and firecrackers that were burning everywhere, though they knew it was only a momentary pleasure. They still didn't know where they would be blown by the storm that had not ended yet.

After the family party, the guests all said goodbye to the host and went home. Everyone suggested Zhang Feng accompany Yu Mei for a walk along the riverside before taking her home. They walked slowly along the bank of the river. There were hardly any people here on the eve of lunar New Year. The silvery moonlight enveloped the glittering world of ice and snow. The segment of the river was not frozen during the winter in Jili City. The fog met the weeping willows on the banks and then formed white crystals, hanging like a group of girls wrapped in white gauze dancing in the breeze. Two young people in love, who had just escaped from death, were deeply absorbed in the beauty of the scene. Zhang Feng broke the silence,

"Yu Mei, I feel how beautiful the world is after I have experienced the threat of death." Yu Mei leaned against Zhang Feng and held his waist tightly.

"Brother Feng," she murmured. "I will never lose you again. Now I feel that I am still in an unfinished dream. I don't know why I can still hold you. My heart died inside me when I saw the prisoner truck driving away." Zhang Feng hugged Yu Mei to him and said,

"Promise me you won't do anything stupid again." Yu Mei looked up at Zhang Feng and nodded. Her face was as smooth as white jade in the bright moonlight. Under her willow leaf eyebrows, her eyes were as clear as a rippling autumn stream, now shining like ice and snow. The white frost hung on her eyelashes because the weather was so cold. She looked like the Snow White. She closed her eyes in happiness, delicate lips trembling slightly. Zhang Feng understood what she wanted. He lowered his head and kissed her passionately.

PART VII

In the Days of Exile

CHAPTER I
_____

In the Backcountry

In 1969, three years after the Cultural Revolution started, Mao Zedong achieved total political victory at the Ninth National Congress of the Chinese Communist Party. Liu Shaoqi, and a large number of old revolutionary leaders, were slandered as the potentates who upheld the capitalist roaders and were overthrown as a result. However, the price China paid for the Cultural Revolution was also disastrous. The national economy went backwards, culture and education were completely destroyed. The constitution and the law were broken. The talents and elites, most needed for building the country, were identified as bourgeois intellectuals. In the early days of the movement, millions of Red Guards were mobilized to rebel. They destroyed party and government organisations at all levels in order to seize power.

The situation stabilized. The Cultural Revolution Group, controlled by the Gang of Four, no longer needed these enthusiastic and impulsive young people. If they were left in the city, there would not be enough work for them and the young people who had been idle for a long time would cause social instability. Therefore, the central government decided to give them a place to vent their youthful energy: China's vast and remote countryside. They took Chairman Mao's firmest instructions to encourage these Red Guards and the rebel faction to go to the countryside:

"It is necessary for the educated youth to go to the countryside to receive re-education from the poor and lower-middle peasants."

"The countryside is a vast world where there is a lot to do."

Thus, in a few years, nearly 10 million young students aged 16 to 22, in their most receptive years of education, left their parents, their families, their homes and the city they lived in. They went to the countryside with inconvenient transportation, a harsh environment and a hard life. They performed inefficient and unproductive farm work every day. They spent their youth in vain.

One day in the spring of this year, the banks of the Songhua River re-emerged with green willows. The railway station in Jili City was crowded. They were sending off the first batch of middle school students from the city. These students would be settled in the countryside as members of agricultural production brigades. Students from the Second Senior Middle School were assigned to Huadan County, a mountainous area more than 500 kilometers away from the city. Because a large number of students of the First Senior Middle School were the children of military cadres and of those officials who had not yet been overthrown, they were assigned to rural communes, not too far from the city. Among the people who sent their children off were the families of Zhang Feng, Wang Hai, Li He and Dan Dan, who were reluctant to say goodbye.

Three boys were assigned to a collective household for educated youth, to the first production team of the first production brigade in the Henghe Commune. The three good friends were together and could help each other. Dan Dan was assigned to the third production brigade of the same commune, a dozen miles from Zhang Feng. Wang Hai told Zhang Feng that Qing Lian was in the second team of the first production brigade, only a few miles away from them. He added,

"Fortunately, this disgusting 'Marxist-Leninist old woman' isn't in our collective household."

Just then, the announcer's voice came over the platform's loudspeaker,

"Classmates, parents, attention please. Mr.Cai Wenge, Deputy Director of the Culture and Education System of the Provincial Revolutionary Committee, is now invited to give a send-off speech."

Then, on the radio, came the pretentious and feigned voice that Zhang Feng and others were familiar with. In his speech, Cai Wenge encouraged these educated youths to respond to Chairman Mao's call to settle in the countryside as members of agricultural production brigades, to fight against the harsh natural environment and build a new countryside.

"This guy is good at politics," said Zhang Feng. "The worse the things he does, the higher his official position becomes." Wang Hai was also indignant and said,

"Now in this world, the bad guys have become high ranking officials and the good guys are bullied. A man who can snitch and flatter will be able to take a higher position on the pretext of being revolutionary. People who are honest, kind, unassuming and truthful are marginalized and framed." He added, "You know that, elder brother, this guy passed the buck to Hei Tou for all the beating, smashing, looting and killing during the violent civil strife. As a result, Hei Tou was put in prison and he was promoted. He is flattering the Special Commissioner Du of the Central Cultural Revolution Group devoutly. So even though Zhao Wu hates him, there is nothing Zhao Wu can do about him. He was involved in all the business of that last time when you had been sentenced to death and were to be executed in advance without telling Zhao Wu, as well as silencing Li He, the witness, by committing murder. But in the end, he put the blame on director Fan and hid himself perfectly."

Zhang Feng said,

"This despicable, shameless guy used to oppose me on everything because he was jealous of me. Now the political movement has given him a chance for a position. Thus, he's trying to do everything to kill me."

Just then, a familiar girl's voice suddenly came from the speaker. It was Qing Lian expressing her determination on behalf of the educated youth who were going to the countryside.

"We will not disappoint Chairman Mao's earnest hope for us," she said in an impassioned voice. "We will root in the countryside and accept the re-education of the poor and lower-middle class peasants."

Zhang Feng asked Wang Hai,

"Why didn't Qing Lian become an official?"

"She's the kind of person who thinks she's a real revolutionary," Li He immediately answered the question. "She will foolishly charge towards the bullets. Cai Wenge is a man who fights for his own interests in the name of revolution. He hides behind the battle line and won't push forward. Then he declares that the victory is the result of his efforts."

Since betraying Zhang Feng and then repenting, Li He had become respectful and cautious when he was with Zhang Feng. Zhang Feng was a magnanimous person. Although Li He's betrayal almost killed him, he still regarded Li He as his friend as long as Li He didn't do anything else to betray him.

"Brother Feng!" A sweet voice called out.

It was Yu Mei who had come to see them off. She would go to the countryside with her classmates in a few days. She looked all the more beautiful in her dark blue coat. She said hello to Wang Hai, Li He and Dan Dan, one by one, then told them to take good care of themselves. She also deliberately took Dan Dan's hand and asked Zhang Feng to take good care of her. Dan Dan knew what she meant and said with a smile,

"Don't worry, I'll take care of your Brother Feng. I will help him to dismantle his cotton coat and quilt and then wash them."

At this moment, everyone suddenly heard the raucous and deep voice of a man,

"Why don't you wait for me to send you?"

They looked back and saw that the person was Chang Zheng. He was wearing a new uniform and he had joined the PLA. Next to him was Wu Xiaoli, his girlfriend. Because Chang Zheng had played an important role in the rescue of Zhang Feng, everyone was very grateful to him. The past antagonism between them had disappeared with their smiles. Chang Zheng also said repeatedly that he was guilty of causing harm to the Commune Faction during the violent civil strife as he had been incited by others. Because they were all Red Guards and the rebels, the goal of the revolution should be the same.

These young and childish students did not know what was waiting for them in the years to come. Many people were still excited, thinking that there were plenty of opportunities waiting for them in the countryside. But parents, especially level-headed intellectuals like Zhang Wenbo, knew that these young people would be in exile. What awaited them was suffering and torment, as well as a meaningless and wasted youth. Cries were heard everywhere on the platform as the train moved away. Zhang Feng saw his younger sister was struggling to wave at him, with tears in her eyes. She and her peers would go to the countryside next year.

Yu Mei ran and followed the train with tears in her eyes.

"Don't forget to write to me!" she cried to Zhang Feng who was on the train. Zhang Feng turned his head because he didn't want Wang Hai to see his tears. These two young people in love had been separated by the political storm, once again.

The train moved sluggishly through the night. The next morning, the train arrived in Huadan County. The small county, surrounded by mountains, had only a few streets. On both sides of the streets were dark, two-storey buildings. After getting off the train, more than one hundred students who were going to the Henghe Commune, got on some old buses. It took another two hours for the bus to reach the Henghe Commune.

It was a very small town with only one street. Several small bungalows made up the administrative departments of the commune. There were several small shops, restaurants, hotels and barbers. The educated youths were surprised at how old and backward the countryside was. They thought they were getting close to the location of their agricultural collective household. To their surprise, however, the lead teacher said it would take another two hours to send them to the production brigade by horse carts.

After a simple lunch, they got on a dozen carts. These carts would take them to different brigades. The carts plodded along the rough dirt road, through green valleys, streams and fields. Even after a night's bumpy journey, these young people still felt fresh and even excited about what they saw. They didn't know that, if you were a tourist, it was a pleasant journey to see the countryside but when you needed to live and work there, you would be bored, tired and find it hard.

Qing Lian was still as passionate as when she had been a Red Guard. She sang revolutionary songs with the people in her cart, including praise for Chairman Mao's 'Ship cannot sail without a helmsman' and praise to the people's commune 'All the commune members are sun flowers' and so on. Wang Hai was leaning against Zhang Feng's shoulder, napping. He said contemptuously,

"Humph, she always seeks the limelight everywhere she goes!"

After an hour's bumpy ride along the rugged mountain road, Dan Dan and the others who had been assigned to the third production brigade, headed for another fork in the road. Dan Dan waved goodbye to Zhang Feng from a distance. They moved on for another half hour. When they came to a stream with a canoe bridge, the dirt road split into two forks. The owner of the cart said to the educated youths,

"Let's go to the left side of the road. This is the way to the first team. The one on the right is to the second team." Pointing to another road that was used by local people, leading to the road into the woods on the hillside, he added,

"This path leads directly to Xinglong village. That is the location of the first team. It's a short cut."

When the cart carrying Zhang Feng and the other nine educated youths separated from the cart carrying Qing Lian, Wang Hai breathed a sigh of relief. He said,

"The 'Marxist-Leninist old woman' has finally got off. Now we can be quiet."

Everyone in the wagon laughed. In this agricultural collective household to which Zhang Feng was assigned, there were ten educated youths, five boys and five girls. They were all from the same school. Except for Wang Hai and Li He, the other students were very honest and kind. When Zhang Feng had been publicly criticized, they all chose to remain silent and did not follow the others so everyone felt very relaxed together.

As the cart began to go downhill, a girl shouted,

"Look at that!"

Looking ahead, they could see dozens of thatched houses scattered in a small valley. Thin smoke rose from the chimneys of each house. The sound of dogs barking could be heard faintly. The owner of the cart said,

"This is Xinglong village. You will be settled down here."

The cart stopped at the threshing ground of the village. Zhang Feng and the others got off the cart. As they unloaded their luggage, a group came up to them. Wang Hai used to be the leader of the rebels so he was good at dealing with officials at all levels. Because of his good family background, the school had appointed him to be the leader of the ten students of this collective household. He hurried over to meet the group. At the head of the group was a man in his fifties with a face full of stubble. He introduced himself,

"I'm Pan, the leader of the production team." Then he pointed to a man in his forties behind him, who had a wrinkled face with a smile and said, "This is Li, the secretary of the village party branch."

He then introduced the other three people, one by one: Accountant Song, who was in his thirties, Lieutenant Wang of the militiaman platoon, who was in his twenties and Leader He Hua of the women's production team, who was wearing her hair in braids. Wang Hai also introduced his classmates to them, one by one. When Zhang Feng was introduced, they all looked at him a little longer for some unknown reason, especially He Hua. Leader Pan said to the rest of the students,

"I am uneducated and cannot make nice speeches. You are all learned people and we will learn from you in the future."

Wang Hai immediately continued,

"Please don't say that. We come here in order to receive the re-education of the poor and lower-middle peasants."

Secretary Li said,

"Our living conditions are not good and can't compare with the city. You need to get used to it gradually. If you need anything, just tell us."

Then, Accountant Song led the educated youths to the house where the agricultural collective household was located. Through the village, chickens, ducks, pigs and dogs barked, clucked and quacked together, until they came to an adobe thatched cottage with a small yard in front. There was a stack of firewood made up of dry branches in the yard. The educated youths, who were used to living in city buildings, were shocked by the house. Could such a shabby house be lived in? But when they entered the room, they were even more disappointed. It was very dark.

Accountant Song walked to the cooking hearth and lit a kerosene lamp. He turned to the educated youths and said, regretfully,

"Our village is located in a remote mountain area with no electricity. Now the electricity supply has just been extended to the production brigade. Next year, we will have electricity in our village. By that time, you will be able to read books and newspapers at night."

With the light of the kerosene lamp, they could see the layout of the house. The hallway contained the cooking hearth, like a kitchen but the device in the room was simple and crude. There was only a cooking hearth and on it was a large iron pan. Next to it was a shabby table with a dirty chopping board. In the corner of the room was a large water jar. There was no tap water here so people had to go to the well in the village for water. On either side of the kitchen were two rooms, each with a large, heated, brick and earth bed (very popular in Northeast China with cold winters) which was connected to the chimney on one side and the cooking hearth on the other. When cooking on the hearth, the fire in the stove heated the bed. This was how rural areas in northeast China heated their homes in winter.

The young people slept in their own beds at home in the city. Seeing that they were going to sleep on one, big, heated bed with no private space, they all felt uncomfortable. Finally, Wang Hai broke the awkward silence.

"Well, it doesn't matter. It's just a place to sleep. Come on, put your luggage down."

The boys were in one room and the girls were in the other. They all put their luggage in their rooms.

Next, Accountant Song told Wang Hai how to cook on the cooking hearth. There were two rice jars next to the water jar containing sorghum and corn flour, and some cabbage and potatoes on the chopping board. Wang Hai thought Accountant Song was a bit verbose and told him there was no problem, they knew how to cook. Then he sent Accountant Song away. Wang Hai thought that among the five girls, there must be someone who could cook. He shouted to the girls' room,

"Who can cook?"

Two pretty girls came into the kitchen, one named Li Yulan, the other, Wang Xiaohong. They once had a secret love for Zhang Feng. The two girls were very happy because this time, they had been assigned to the same agricultural collective household as Zhang Feng.

"I can cook. I always cook at home," Li Yulan said confidently to Wang Hai and Zhang Feng.

Wang Xiaohong also hastily said,

"I can cook too. My father is a chef at the Jili Grand Hotel. I learned cooking from him. I can cook not only Northeast dishes, but also Sichuan dishes."

After hearing this, Wang Hai was very happy and said, "That's great! You two will be responsible for the cooking in the days ahead," but when the two girls saw the food in the kitchen, they didn't know what to do.

Wang Xiaohong asked Wang Hai,

"Is that all? What can I cook with these?"

Li He said jokingly nearby,

"Even the cleverest housewife cannot cook a meal without rice, right?"

Zhang Feng looked at the food and said they could only cook sorghum or corn batter. The dish could only be stewed potato with cabbage.

Wang Hai said,

"Ok, boys are responsible for making the fire and the girls are ready to wash rice and vegetables."

Zhang Feng and the other students had never used firewood to cook because they used gas to cook with in the city, and there, even the poorest families had coal to burn. They believed they could make fire by putting the firewood in the cooking hearth and then lighting it. However, the boys spent more than half an hour on it and did not succeed. It also made smoke everywhere in the house and made everyone choke and cough.

He Hua, the leader of the women's production team, came in when everyone was at a loss what to do. When she saw the room full of smoke, she knew that the students didn't know how to make a fire so she taught Zhang Feng and Wang Hai how to do it. She told them not to stuff the firewood into the hearth too full and to pour kerosene over the old newspaper to start the fire. A few minutes later, the fire was blazing inside the cooking hearth. The students cheered with joy because everyone's stomach was already empty. He Hua also wanted to help them cook. The girls were afraid of being looked down upon by the boys, so they refused.

After more than one hour's endeavour, a pot of sorghum and a pot of stewed potato with cabbage were cooked. Everyone sat on the beds and ate their first meal in the village under the dim kerosene lamp. Looking at the vegetable soup without even a drop of cooking oil, Li He sighed and said,

"It looks like a meal which recalls past sufferings. It's so hard to eat."

Wang Hai stared at him and said,

"Be contented. We couldn't even eat a full meal during the famine years."

Zhang Feng continued,

"That's right. We went through three years of famine when we were in primary school. I was so hungry every day that I couldn't even concentrate in class. The greatest wish then was to have a full meal."

After listening to Zhang Feng's words, they began to recall those hard years in various ways then they felt the food in the bowl could be eaten.

Most people didn't sleep well that night because it was the first time they had all slept in one, big bed. They were not used to it. A lot of them were disappointed. How could they go through such hardship in the years ahead? But they didn't yet know that more hard jobs awaited them.

Zhang Feng couldn't sleep either. He thought of Dan Dan and was afraid that she would not be able to stand such a disgusting living environment. He thought more of Yu Mei and wondered if the conditions in the place where she had settled were as tough as this.

When he was finally about to fall asleep, Wang Hai, who was sleeping next to him, began to snore loudly. Zhang Feng could also hear Li He muttering about Wang Hai's snoring. Zhang Feng tapped Wang Hai on his shoulder. Wang Hai had told Zhang Feng before he went to bed that he had the habit of snoring but it could be stopped if Zhang Feng hit him when he was snoring.

After Zhang Feng tapped him, his snoring actually stopped but just as Zhang Feng was about to fall asleep again, Wang Hai's snore returned. It was Li He who tapped Wang Hai this time but the effect only lasted for half an hour. As a result, Zhang Feng and Li He were tortured by Wang Hai's snoring until midnight before they fell asleep.

When Zhang Feng got up the next morning, he saw that Yu Lan had been cooking. Zhang Feng asked her how she had slept last night. She said, with a wry smile, that she did not sleep well. It was uncomfortable to sleep on the bed. Zhang Feng consoled her by saying that she would get used to it gradually. Seeing that everyone else was still sleeping, Yu Lan told Zhang Feng that they were all sympathetic to Zhang Feng's experience during the period of purifying the class ranks. Yulan said that Zhang Feng's experience was the result of Cai Wenge's personal revenge.

"He is just jealous that you are better than him in everything. He is a real villain, and he is proud of himself all day long. In fact, no girls are willing to pay attention to him."

Then she looked at Zhang Feng with gentle eyes and said,

"Zhang Feng, if your clothes and quilt need mending and stitching, I can help you."

Zhang Feng knew that his handsome appearance attracted the attention of girls but he was not a philanderer. Even when he had been popular in the past, he could control himself, even more so now when he was a second-class citizen. With his political problems, coupled with his love for Yu Mei, he was completely unresponsive to expressions of love from other girls. So he said politely,

"Thank you."

When the day was completely bright, team leader Pan came to the house of the educated youths. He told everyone that they didn't have to go to work that day. They could take a day off and settle down. When he asked them what they wanted, the girls all said that they needed another toilet. There was only one toilet in the backyard, which was inconvenient for the girls. Pan said it was no problem. He took the boys with him to bring back a lot of corn straw to build the toilet. Toilets in rural areas were very primitive. The villagers dug a pit in the ground and then surrounded it with straw. In the winter, the frozen faeces in the pit would be dug out and used as fertilizer for crops. They completed the building of the toilet in no time so they had two toilets, which were used separately by the boys and the girls.

They cleaned the whole house on this day off. Zhang Feng and Wang Hai also went to fetch water and filled the water jar. Their house was more than 100 meters from the village well. The weight of two buckets of water was more than 40 kilograms.

Even the average boy could not carry it, not to mention girls. Everyone said it was lucky to be living with two strong men like Zhang Feng and Wang Hai. Even drinking water was a big problem.

After dinner, they sat together and chatted. They all said they had never thought that since the new China had been established for twenty years, the countryside would still be so poor and backward. These uneducated, plain and hardworking peasants seemed to have been forgotten by society. They were so silent and were struggling to survive. However, Zhang Feng and Wang Hai and the other students did not yet know how hard and unbearable rural work could be.

CHAPTER 11

Peasants Weeding at Noon,
Sweat Down the Field Soon
(From an Ancient Chinese Poem)

The next morning, team leader Pan arrived just after the students had finished their breakfast. He was accompanied by a thin, dark man in his forties. Pan introduced the man to the young people. His name was Hou and he was the working leader of the production team: the foreman who led the villagers in their farm work. If there was anything the educated youths didn't understand, they could ask him. Lao Hou had a strong Shandong accent when he spoke. He told everyone that the work to be done today was to weed and shovel the ground. He said,

"You are all learned people, and you can learn this simple job quickly."

Then he led them to the administrative department of the production team and gave each one a hoe. Wang Hai tried the weight of the hoe and said,

"It's so light. Today's job is just shovelling grass. It's a piece of cake."

But Li He took his hoe and said,

"It's not light. You and Brother Feng may think it's light, but we think it's a bit heavy."

The other two boys and the girls also said the hoes were heavy. Wang Hai consoled them, saying,

"Don't be afraid, just watch what I do. I have a relative who lives in the country. I used to help them with the farm work."

Zhang Feng didn't say anything. He understood that the purpose of their being sent to the countryside was in fact forced reformation through labour and it was impossible to refuse to work. Lao Hou put ten students and a dozen male and female members of the production team to work together. He Hua, the leader of the women's production team, and Lieutenant Wang, the leader of the militia platoon, were also there. He Hua greeted Zhang Feng and Wang Hai warmly but Lieutenant Wang did not say anything to them at all.

Lao Hou led them through the hills, ravines and streams and they walked five or six miles until they arrived at a wide plain. The fields were planted with maize seedlings, about a dozen centimeters high. Lao Hou told the educated youths that today's work was to remove the weeds next to the corn seedlings, and to use the shovel to loosen the hard surface of the soil at the same time. This would keep the moisture in the soil from evaporating. He also showed the students how to do it. Then he put everyone in charge of a piece of strip-shaped land, shovelling from top to bottom. Zhang Feng estimated the length of the strip of land at about 200 meters.

After Lao Hou had finished, the young people thought that the work was very simple. However, what they did not expect was that the farm work required speed. After Lao Hou shouted at them, everyone started working. At the beginning of the task, the speed of the villagers was not fast, so the students could keep up with them. Perhaps Lao Hou heard Wang Hai mutter,

"This is too easy."

So Lao Hou suddenly sped up, and all the villagers around him sped up together. All of a sudden, the students were at a loss. They were more than 20 meters behind the villagers in just five minutes, and only Wang Hai and Zhang Feng could just about keep up with the villagers. Yu Lan and Xiao Hong were in a hurry, desperately waving shovels to speed up the weeding, sometimes, accidentally, maize seedlings were also cut down.

As the sun rose, the weather got hotter and hotter and everyone became hot and sweaty. Yu Lan and the others had only completed half of the weeding when Lao Hou and the villagers had finished. Lao Hou wanted the villagers to help the students but Lieutenant Wang and several male villagers said,

"We have the same points every day. More work won't get more points, so why should we help them? We're going to take a break." They all sat down to rest and smoke.

Zhang Feng complained to Wang Hai,

"It's all because you said it was too easy. You didn't hear the rural people say that they are not afraid of their hair turning grey, but they are afraid of the foreman being angry. When the foreman speeds up, those behind him are in big trouble because they cannot keep up with him."

Wang Hai scratched his head and said,

"What shall we do then? All right, let's help them to shovel the land from bottom to top."

So Zhang Feng and Wang Hai began weeding in that direction, from the bottom to the top of the strip-shaped land which the girls were responsible for. When He Hua saw this, she asked several female villagers to shovel from the bottom to the top to help the youths who were behind in their work.

About 15 minutes later, the land that the students were responsible for was also completed. Li He and the other two boys, along with the girls, all sat on the ground panting and wiping away their sweat. Lao Hou came to them and said,

"It is harder to read than to farm, but it is not so easy to farm. You have to get used to it."

At this point, they suddenly saw that Lieutenant Wang was beckoning everyone to the place that had been weeded and shovelled by the students. Lao Hou, He Hua, Zhang Feng and Wang Hai went up to him and asked him what was wrong. He pointed to some maize seedlings that had been cut down on the ground and said,

"Look, what they did! The seedlings were cut down."

Lao Hou was a little unhappy to see the cut down seedlings. He immediately waved his hand to call all the students over and said,

"Our purpose is weeding the grass, not the seedlings! We are peasants and we are fed by growing grain. You have cut down the seedlings so the grain will not grow. It will starve us to death!"

The educated youths were petrified. They had just tried to catch up to the speed of the villagers but they hadn't made clear the difference between the grass and the seedlings. He Hua came to ease the tension and said,

"They are all students who have never done farm work before so they won't know how to do it to start with. They will improve in the future after doing more farm work."

Lao Hou turned around and left angrily. Wang Hai saw that there might be trouble so he hurried to follow Lao Hou to explain. Wang Hai also gave Lao Hou a cigarette. Wang Hai convened the educated youths for a meeting when Lao Hou was no longer angry.

The students all complained that it was not easy to do farm work as they had to be careful and fast, and the hoes were heavy. These villagers had been working on the farm for many years so of course, the students could not compete with them. Then Wang Hai discussed an idea with Lao Hou to make two students responsible for the maize seedlings in a strip. The first person would shovel ten meters of land in front, while the second person started to shovel ten meters of land behind. The two people would move forward alternately, like a relay race. This would help the educated youths keep up with the villagers. Lao Hou thought for a while and said,

"Let's try this for a few days. However, when evaluating the working points, it is difficult to give you enough points. For those who work too slowly, they will earn fewer points so they won't earn much money by the end of the year."

Wang Hai didn't know much about the points but at least the students could cope with the current farm work. He discussed the plan with Zhang Feng and Li He. They decided to adopt this method first.

In the afternoon, when weeding the second piece of land, Zhang Feng and Wang Hai were responsible for one strip-shaped piece of land each while all the others were in pairs. This was just enough for them to keep up with the villagers. In fact, even though Zhang Feng and Wang Hai had good physical strength, they also felt very tired after doing such difficult farm work for the first time. But in order to maintain the honour of the students, they gritted their teeth and persevered. They finally stopped when the sun went down. Lao Hou announced that they could stop work.

The young people were all relieved. At this point, everyone was sweaty and panting. When they thought about having to walk forty minutes to get home, they all felt that their legs were weak and would not move. Sure enough, they were soon left behind by the villagers ahead. It was the warm-hearted He Hua who stopped to wait for them. He Hua said that they were not familiar with the environment and might get lost so she wanted to show them the way home. Wang Hai said gratefully,

"Elder sister He Hua, thank you so much. You are so warm-hearted."

He Hua's face turned red. She spoke to Wang Hai but looked at Zhang Feng,

"Do I look very old? I'm only 19 years old."

Wang Hai immediately replied,

"Ah, then we should call you He Hua, the younger sister. We're all almost twenty-one years old."

He Hua smiled like a pink lotus. As she was walking, she told everyone the situation about the production team. She also told everyone to call on her if they were in trouble.

Everyone felt exhausted when they arrived back at the house. They didn't want to move an inch when they lay down on the heated brick bed. Those who had stayed at home to cook had to drag them out, one by one, to eat their supper. After the meal, some of them fell asleep without even washing their faces. After discussing how to improve things tomorrow with the others, Zhang Feng felt exhausted and drowsy. Then he lay down and fell asleep.

The next morning, Zhang Feng felt strange when he got up. He felt that he had slept so soundly last night that he had not heard Wang Hai's snoring. He touched Wang Hai, who had just opened his eyes.

"Hey, why didn't you snore last night?"

Wang Hai said with a smile,

"You were all exhausted and sleeping like logs. How could you hear my snoring?"

"It seems that the best cure for insomnia is to let him work in the countryside," said Li He, who had just woken up. Then Leader Pan knocked on the door. He said they were to get going earlier today to take advantage of the cool weather in the morning, avoiding the uncomfortable midday heat. The students quickly got up and ate their breakfast in a hurry. Then they took up their hoes and went out to work.

While they were walking on the road, Wang Hai told everyone that he and Zhang Feng had thought about the right way of weeding and shovelling the land: not to waste energy blindly, but to pull the hoe backwards in the direction of force and not to bend too low. This not only saved energy, but also, would help them to work quickly. Everyone was very happy to hear that and said that they would try this method.

Today, they would go to a hillside, farther away than yesterday. Wang Hai asked Lao Hou about the possibility of three students taking charge of two pieces of strip-shaped land today. In this way, they could work more efficiently than yesterday. Lao Hou agreed without any consideration. He said to Wang Hai,

"I'm an illiterate person who doesn't know how to speak euphemistically. Don't be upset at what I say. For you guys, there's no difference between doing more and doing less. We have no shortage of labour in this place because there are a lot of people here and very little farmland. It is the government that asked us to accept urban students like you guys to settle here."

Wang Hai felt a little uncomfortable hearing Lao Hou's words. After starting work, he quietly told Zhang Feng what Lao Hou had said. Zhang Feng said in a low voice,

"You didn't know why until now? To accept the re-education of the poor and lower-middle class peasants is an absolute cover. The basic reason is that there are not enough jobs for us in the city and we are cannot go to university because the university is closed. The government says that university education was revisionist for the previous seventeen years. So now, only the countryside can accommodate us, the once troublesome Red Guards and students. The farmers are simple and honest and they will do whatever the government wants them to do. See?"

Wang Hai also whispered jokingly,

"You are so reactionary. That's why you almost got shot!"

Zhang Feng gave him a gentle thump. Zhang Feng had a friend like Wang Hai, a friend like Damon and Pythias, who could tell him anything without fear of being betrayed.

Following Wang Hai's suggestion, the educated youths improved the method of weeding so the progress of work accelerated and the quality of the weeding also improved but they were still tired and sore. Most painful of all, almost everyone had bleeding blisters on their hands after work. Touching these bleeding blisters was very painful. Lao Hou did not say anything until the end of the work, indicating that he felt the work of the students was good enough or that he did not care about their work at all.

Everyone was too tired to talk back at the house. They did not even respond to Wang Hai's jokes. Zhang Feng said to Wang Hai,

"We are almost dead with exhaustion. Who is in the mood to listen to your jokes?"

Just then, He Hua came in. She knew the students had bleeding blisters on their hands and she brought disinfectant and adhesive tape. She told everyone to sterilize the bleeding blister first and then put tape on it. He Hua walked up to Zhang Feng intentionally and said to him,

"Brother Zhang Feng, let me see your hands."

She did not wait for him to answer but took one of Zhang Feng's hands and said,

"Oh my god! You have several blisters."

Then, without getting Zhang Feng's consent, she began to clean the bleeding blisters with disinfectant and said,

"It will hurt a bit, you will have to bear it."

She gently treated Zhang Feng's wounds and asked him if he had any clothes to wash. She said that she could help Zhang Feng with washing. Wang Hai came up immediately and said,

"He Hua, younger sister, I also have blisters on my hands. Can you help me to treat them? I'm the last person to do laundry. Will you wash it for me when you have time?" Zhang Feng said to him,

"Go away, don't mess around. You deal with your own wounds. He Hua is so busy, don't bother her."

Wang Hai pretended to be dissatisfied and said,

"Why? Is it only you who can enjoy being treated like a senior official?"

Before he fell asleep at night, Wang Hai quietly said to Zhang Feng,

"Elder brother, why do you get the favour of girls anywhere? I know you are handsome, but I'm not much worse than you. You know that when He Hua looks at you, her eyes are full of tenderness. You must pay attention to this matter. You already have two or three girlfriends so don't add any more."

Zhang Feng replied impatiently,

"Why can't you stop this lustful way of talking? That's why Dan Dan doesn't like you."

Wang Hai said in a hurt tone,

"I am just saying that, but in my heart, I am still a principled man."

Wang Hai's words triggered Zhang Feng's nostalgia for Yu Mei. Turning his back on Wang Hai and ignoring his nagging, Zhang Feng quietly took out the photo of Yu Mei from his backpack and looked at it silently.

For the next few days, they did the same simple, boring farm work every day. They were all exhausted after work. Their backs were so sore they could hardly straighten up after a whole day of bending down.

One day, when they were resting at noon, they saw a group of people working in a nearby field. Besides the peasants, there seemed to be a dozen students. When they moved closer, Lao Hou greeted some of them. Wang Hai also recognized that these were his classmates in the second team.

After several days of separation, everyone greeted each other warmly. Wang Hai and Zhang Feng sat together and also said hello to the educated youths of the second production team. Suddenly, a girl in a straw hat came up to them. Wang Hai had good eyesight and immediately recognized the girl was Qing Lian. Wang Hai said to Zhang Feng in a low voice,

"Oh no, the 'Marxist-Leninist old woman' is here. I need to avoid her."

Just as he was about to get up and leave, Qing Lian said hello to him,

"Hi, Wang Hai, don't go. It's hard to see you. We are both the heads of our collective households. We should swop work experience notes and discuss how to do the ideological work well."

Wang Hai hurriedly answered her in a perfunctory way,

"Commissioner Liu, my ideological level is too low to compare with you, the honorable one. If you have any instructions, I am all ears."

When Qing Lian saw that Wang Hai did not want to talk to her, she said seriously,

"Wang Hai, now the two factions have been united, the time of fighting has passed. Why are you still holding on? The Cultural Revolution has entered a new stage. You must keep up with the times."

"I'm a man with bound feet so I can't keep up," Wang Hai said. Then he left immediately.

Zhang Feng thought that Qing Lian should also leave immediately. Unexpectedly, she sat next to Zhang Feng, which made him embarrassed. Zhang Feng pretended not to see her but he could hear the tones of apology, comfort and pity in her words,

"Zhang Feng, I'm sorry, I know you still hate me but when they wronged you earlier, I didn't know they were trying to frame you. I was trying to save you by letting you know your mistakes."

"According to what you said, I still have to thank you?" said Zhang Feng coldly.

Qing Lian said apologetically,

"No matter what, you finally survived, I am still happy for you."

Zhang Feng really did not want to talk to her, so he said,

"Hmm, that is because it was not my time to die. Those who want to kill me will not easily fulfill their wishes."

Qing Lian felt that Zhang Feng was being cold to her so she said a few words to end the talk,

"In fact, I also do not agree with some words and deeds of Cai Wenge. Anyway, we came to the countryside to settle down. It is a good opportunity for you to promote yourself. Do your job well and you will still have a good future." Then she hurried away.

A few days later, the students had an afternoon off at home. The girls were doing the laundry. Zhang Feng and Wang Hai looked at their already stinking clothes and were worried about how to wash them. Zhang Feng stopped Wang Hai from asking Xiao Hong and Yu Lan to help them wash their clothes. Just then, Dan Dan came in. Wang Hai looked overjoyed. He knew that Dan Dan often washed clothes for Zhang Feng and would also help him in passing. Zhang Feng was very happy to see Dan Dan because he had been thinking of her and was worried that she might not become acclimatized to the hard farm work.

They led Dan Dan into the room. Dan Dan saw that the girls were doing their laundry, while Zhang Feng's and Wang Hai's dirty clothes, which they had taken off, were lying on the bed. She knew what was going on immediately.

"Xiao Feng, bring your clothes here and I will help you with the washing."

Hearing this, Wang Hai came over immediately with his dirty clothes. Just at this moment, Yu Lan and Xiao Hong went to the water jar to scoop up water. When they saw that Dan Dan was preparing to wash clothes for the boys, they quickly said,

"Dan Dan, elder sister, please stop being so busy. You take a break. We will help Zhang Feng and the other boys wash their clothes."

All the students in Zhang Feng's class knew Dan Dan. They also knew that she was a talented girl as well as being Zhang Feng's 'elder sister' although the girls had questions about the real relationship between them. So Dan Dan sat down with the other girls and helped the boys wash their clothes. Zhang Feng and Wang Hai sat next to Dan Dan and asked her to tell them the conditions in her collective household.

The conditions in Dan Dan's collective household were similar to Zhang Feng's. Because there were few girls in Dan Dan's collective household, the girls didn't do farm work in the first week but they cooked at home instead and did some chores in the small vegetable plots owned by the collective household. Seeing Zhang Feng's hands covered with medical tape, Dan Dan picked up his hands immediately and stroked them sadly. Just then, He Hua came to help Zhang Feng and Wang Hai with their washing and cleaning. Seeing that Dan Dan cared very much about Zhang Feng, as well as washing his clothes and examining the wounds on his hand, He Hua hid and did not approach Zhang Feng.

From then on, He Hua avoided Zhang Feng and did not talk to him until one day, during a break from work, she quietly asked Wang Hai,

"Brother Wang, the beautiful girl who came to visit you that day is Brother Zhang's girlfriend?"

Wang Hai replied immediately,

"No, no, she is Brother Zhang's elder sister."

When He Hua heard this, she became much happier. She began to get close to Zhang Feng again and talked with him happily.

Two weeks passed in a twinkling. One day, the work ended earlier. Lao Hou told Wang Hai that Leader Pan said there was something important and asked everyone to go to a meeting. On the way back to the village, Wang Hai asked Zhang Feng,

"Lao Hou looks a little different. What's the important thing he has to say?"

Zhang Feng thought for a moment and said,

"It's probably the evaluation of the working points. It's an important thing in the countryside because it determines how much money you can make in a year."

The students returned to the village's threshing floor with the villagers. Leader Pan and Accountant Song were already there, waiting for them. When they had all sat down, Leader Pan said,

"We have an important matter to discuss today – the evaluation of working points. We need to evaluate how many working points each person can earn each day. So by the end of the year, you can figure out how much food you will get and how much money you can make. It's a bit like worker ratings in your city." He turned to the educated youths.

"You are rated as level 1, level 2 or level 3, depending on your skill level." He added, "The criteria are as follows: the fastest and the best, like Lao Hou, get ten points a day. The good get seven or eight points a day. The mediocre get five or six points. Those who work poorly get only three or four points. Because most of the commune members are the same as in previous years, only two more vagrants have been added. So the evaluation today is mainly for the students from the city."

Everyone began to talk to each other after Leader Pan finished. Leader Pan asked Lao Hou to speak first. Although Lao Hou was clear in his mind, he did not want to offend anyone.

"These kids from the city have never done farm work before, so they didn't do well at the beginning," he said, "but now they have done a good job. However, how many points each student should get needs to be decided by everyone."

The villagers looked at each other and no one wanted to speak on their own initiative. At last, Lieutenant Wang said,

"If you are afraid of offending people, I will speak first. The students have not done farm work before and were not physically strong. I think the boys should be given six points and the girls should be given five points, that's enough."

Unexpectedly, He Hua opposed him immediately,

"It is wrong. Brother Zhang and Brother Wang have done very well. They should be evaluated as robust labourers of our village. I think they should get nine points or ten points."

Lieutenant Wang stared at He Hua and then said in low voice,

"Why are you partial to them?"

At this point, the villagers began to talk to each other again. Some said that nine points was very high and eight points would be fine. Leader Pan asked Lao Hou to make a decision.

"Eight points, nine points or ten points are all fine," said Lao Hou somewhat awkwardly.

Zhang Feng knew that the villagers didn't want the students' working points to be set too highly because it meant that they would take more food and money that should belong to the villagers. He stood up and said,

"My friends, we have come here to learn from you. We've just started farm work and we're still the fresh hands. Wang Hai and I would be satisfied if we could get eight points."

He Hua stood up and said,

"They are showing humility. We can't bully people who come from far away and work hard for us. My advice is to give nine points or ten points."

Seeing He Hua was taking the side of Zhang Feng, Lieutenant Wang became redder and more angry. He stood up and said,

"If they want to get the points of the most robust labourer, they must have the strength of the most robust labourer. It's no use just being big. You have to be strong. Let's make a bet."

Pointing to the sacks of fertilizer piled on the threshing floor, he said, "If you two can carry a sack and take a turn along the threshing floor, we'll give you ten points. If you can't, you can only have eight points. To be fair, I'll go first."

The villagers all knew that a sack weighed more than one hundred kilograms and an ordinary person was not able to carry it. So they agreed to the bet for a bit of fun. Zhang Feng and Wang Hai did not want to compete for high working points. However, after being provoked by the platoon leader, both of them felt that if they admitted defeat, they would damage the dignity of the students. In addition, their friends were cheering for them so they accepted the challenge.

Lieutenant Wang was very strong though he was not tall. He crouched down and had two commune members put a sack on his shoulders, and then he stood up, trembling. He walked a turn around the threshing floor. Throwing down the sack, he looked at Zhang Feng and Wang Hai with a complacent expression on his face. Wang Hai said to Zhang Feng,

"I'll go first."

He also crouched down and had the two commune members put the sack on his back, and then stood up, vigorously. As he neared the end of the round, Wang Hai's foot slipped. It was probably because of his eagerness to win. The sack fell to the ground. Lieutenant Wang shouted immediately,

"This is not a success!"

But the villagers and the educated youths applauded him. Leader Pan nodded.

"That's good enough," he said.

Zhang Feng knew it was not easy to carry such heavy sacks. He distributed the weight onto his legs, shoulders and back beforehand. His body was already strong enough, so when the sack was put onto his back, he was still able to stand up steadily.

The students and some commune members began to applaud him. He grabbed the sack hard and seemed to finish one round easily. When He Hua jumped up and applauded, he started the second round. The students clapped him hard. Lieutenant Wang left the meeting because he was so angry.

Finally, everyone agreed to give ten points to Zhang Feng and to give Wang Hai nine points. Zhang Feng won honour for the educated youth. He did not know, however, that this triumph would cause trouble in the future as there were sinister people among the unsophisticated peasants.

In the scorching summer, Zhang Feng, Wang Hai and their classmates worked in the fields under the hot sun every day. The crops in the fields started to grow taller from tiny seedlings, day by day. They included corn, sorghum and sunflowers. In the end, they all grew tall and bushy, like sheets of green folding screens.

The students' faces were tanned and their hands were full of calluses. There was no entertainment, no television, no radio. There were no weekends and no holidays. They worked from dawn to dusk every day. What did they get out of this hard work? Only the harvest days in the autumn would tell them.

CHAPTER III

In the Harvest Season

The students watched the crops in the field turn from green to yellow, day by day. Time passed quickly and autumn arrived. This was the harvest season. A year's hard work would bring them a bumper harvest but the labour of the harvest season was as hard as other seasons.

They worked from morning till night. They needed to cut off the stalks of corn or sorghum which were nearly two meters tall. They used sickles and then the stalks were transferred from the field to the threshing floors by carriages. The corncobs and the ears of the sorghum then had to be detached. It was a laborious job and the educated youths, with their skinny bodies, worked strenuously. Even Zhang Feng and Wang Hai felt very tired. The hardest part was that the leaves of corn and sorghum were so sharp, tearing their sleeves and leaving bloody marks on their arms. The girls would cry in pain. Reaping soy was even more difficult. Not only did they have to bend down very low but their hands would also be torn by the pods and bled.

Yu Lan and Xiao Hong could not stand the pain. They told Leader Pan that they wanted to give up earning working points for soy reaping. Leader Pan had to assign them to the yard to detach the corncobs. This job was not too tiring but it earned low working points.

Wang Hai took out a pair of old gloves and put them on to make him feel better at work. He Hua found that Zhang Feng had no gloves so she gave him her own gloves. Zhang Feng wanted to refuse her but He Hua said that she had more gloves at home. Lieutenant Wang saw this in the distance and his face became sullen at once.

While working in the fields, Zhang Feng noticed a young commune member who was limping and working hard. Wang Hai told Zhang Feng that the young man was named Liu Wen, the son of a previous landlord. At the beginning of the Cultural Revolution, his father had hanged himself as he couldn't stand being publicly criticized by the poor and lower-middle peasants. He went to argue with the leader of the production brigade. Consequently, he was beaten so severely that his leg was broken.

Wang Hai said to Zhang Feng in a low voice,

"I heard that the one who hit him was Lieutenant Wang. Lieutenant Wang is a ruthless villain. He is always lazy at work but he talks about class struggle every day and does nothing but persecute others. You should stay away from him. I heard that he is pursuing He Hua now but He Hua dislikes him. He Hua is interested in you, obviously. You'd better not give yourself another love rival."

Zhang Feng replied,

"I thought the people in the countryside were all so unsophisticated… I didn't expect that there would still be some despicable individuals among them."

"The political movement has provided a breeding ground for these despicable individuals' success," Wang Hai said quietly. "Our classmate Cai Wenge, you know, is a typical character."

One day after the autumn harvest, the whole of the first production team gathered at the threshing floor. This was the most important day of the year. The production team would distribute food and money, according to the working points earned by each person. After a year of hard work, everyone hoped to exchange their hard work for a satisfactory reward. The students were especially looking forward to it as this was their first time participating in the year-end distribution. Everyone was excited.

Only Zhang Feng had been prepared mentally because He Hua had told him that there was very little money to be distributed with the food every year. The slogans about letting educated young people go to the countryside were very stirring: 'To construct the new countryside' and 'To accept the re-education of the poor and lower-middle class peasants'. The sober-minded person understood that it was the city which could not accommodate these young students so they had been banished to remote villages. Hence, Zhang Feng wasn't interested in how much money he could get.

First was team leader Pan's speech. He said that everyone had been working hard this year, including the students who came from the city. This year's climate had also been very good. There had been no serious natural disasters apart from the sorghum, which had suffered from insect damage so that harvest was not very good but the harvest of the other crops was not bad.

Then Accountant Song looked at his ledger and read out the names of people and told them how many working points they had earned this year, how much of the gross grain (the grain with the shell) and cash would be distributed to them, according to their working points. Accountant Song first announced the income of the commune members. The educated youths were all shocked when they heard the income of the commune members. Even a first-class, robust labourer like Lao Hou, who had earned more than 3000 working points, was given no more than 250 kilograms of gross grain and 100 Yuan in cash. In contrast, a low-skilled worker in a city typically earned more than 500 Yuan a year. Female commune members earned much less.

Then Accountant Song announced the working points earned by the students. Because they had arrived later, the total number of their working points was lower. Both Zhang Feng and Wang Hai had more than 2000 points. Each of them was given more than 250 kilograms of grain (including the government's subsidies for the first year) and only 60 Yuan in cash.

Wang Hai said in a low voice,

"There's not enough money. Is it enough to buy a bottle of wine after buying all the necessities?"

Zhang Feng stabbed him and said,

"You still want to buy wine? Go and drink the water from the well every day."

Other students received a smaller share. Apart from the grain, each person got only 30 Yuan in cash. Everyone was disappointed but Wang Hai still had to express his appreciation to the poor and lower-middle class peasants for their care on behalf of the educated youths.

After returning to the house, everyone was so disappointed that they hung their heads and didn't even want to eat dinner.

Li He said,

"We have only got this small amount of money after a year of hard work. I had heard that the countryside was poor but I didn't expect it to be so poor."

In order to encourage the others, Wang Hai said,

"You should be content. Some production teams are even poorer than we are. Their members cannot get any money. They have to pay to buy the grain for their own food."

"I don't think I'll have enough money to buy skin care products," Yu Lan said. "My face is getting tanned. How will I…"

Wang Hai jokingly continued,

"How will you find a boyfriend in the future? Don't worry. You and Xiao Hong both belong to me!"

Both girls were embarrassed and chased Wang Hai around the house to beat him.

"Please stop the chasing and romping. I know everyone is disappointed," Zhang Feng said. "But now that we have come to this place, we must keep on living. We must pull together to get over the difficulties. Anyway, at least we have food to eat. Can you still remember the famine period eight years ago?"

Although Zhang Feng was not the head of the collective household, his prestige was the highest. He always helped the others like an elder brother, so everyone was willing to follow his words.

"Brother Zhang is right," said Xiao Hong. "Let's cheer up and not be intimidated by the difficulties."

"We should do something to celebrate. After a year's hard work, we should eat something delicious," suggested Wang Hai.

"Where are we going to get something delicious? Li He said. "In this poor place, people only kill pigs and eat meat once a year during the Spring Festival."

"I'll go out and look for some meat," said Wang Hai. Everyone thought he was joking. Unexpectedly, he came back a moment later with a big hen. Everyone was surprised.

Zhang Feng said,

"You are not allowed to be a sly dog."

"The hen came to our vegetable field by itself," Wang Hai said. "I didn't steal it from someone else and no one would even know if we ate it."

Many hungry eyes looked at the chicken. Everyone's mouth watered when they thought of delicious stewed chicken with potatoes. They didn't want to think about it too much. They decided to satisfy their desires for delicious chicken before thinking about other things; so Wang Hai killed the hen by the side of the cooking hearth and then cleaned it. Yu Lan and Xiao Hong cooked up a pot of stewed chicken nuggets with mushrooms and potatoes. Ten people wolfed down the pot of chicken and even the chicken bones were chewed up and eaten by them. They all said it was the most delicious meal of their lives.

Just as everyone was sharing the last drop of chicken soup left in the pot, someone pushed open the door and walked in (people in the countryside do not knock). It was Lao Suntou, their neighbour, nicknamed Lao Shandong.

"Have you seen my old hen?" he asked.

Wang Hai immediately answered,

"No, we didn't go out when we came back from the threshing floor."

Lao Suntou sniffed and said, "How come you have the smell of stewed chicken in your house?"

"It's sausages we brought from home and it's also the smell of meat," Wang Hai said.

Lao Suntou looked at the floor of the kitchen and went out, full of doubt. While Wang Hai was breathing a sigh of relief, he suddenly heard two men who were talking outside the door. They sounded like Lao Suntou and Lieutenant Wang. Then they pushed the door open and stepped in. Lieutenant Wang looked at Zhang Feng and Wang Hai coldly, and then he said,

"You are all educated people and should not do wicked things. Lao Suntou is a single old man. It was not easy for him to raise a chicken for eggs. How can you steal his chicken to eat?"

Just as Wang Hai was preparing to explain, Lieutenant Wang went to the cooking hearth and uncovered the pile of chicken feathers after removing the garbage. He asked Lao Suntou what colour his chicken was. Lao Suntou said it was dark brown. Sure enough, the feathers on the hearth were dark brown. When Wang Hai saw the truth was out, he had to say,

"Sorry, this chicken came into our backyard. I thought it was a pheasant."

"You are all knowledgeable," Lieutenant Wang said. "Can't you even tell a domestic chicken from a pheasant?"

Zhang Feng knew that Wang Hai was in trouble. He also sympathized with Lao Suntou. Lao Suntou was so poor that he didn't even have a chair at home. His life was really difficult. Zhang Feng said to Lao Suntou,

"Sorry, grand elder, we killed your chicken by mistake, and we'll pay for it." Then he asked Lao Suntou how much his chicken was worth.

"At the farmer's market, a chicken costs one Yuan," Lieutenant Wang said. "This is an old hen that can lay eggs. It is worth two Yuan."

"Two Yuan is too much. One Yuan is enough," Lao Suntou said.

Zhang Feng took out two Yuan and gave it to Lao Suntou, who kept nodding his head to thank Zhang Feng.

After Lao Suntou had left with Lieutenant Wang, Wang Hai stuck out his tongue and said,

"It's bad luck to meet this officious Lieutenant Wang."

Zhang Feng glared at him and said,

"Don't do such a selfish thing again."

Everyone was ready to give Zhang Feng the money because they didn't want him to pay for the chicken by himself. Zhang Feng said liberally,

"Don't mention it. It's my treat. But in the future, we should be careful not to do anything to harm relations between us and the villagers. It's really not easy for them to constantly live this hard life."

The happiest thing to happen in the dull and simple lives of the students was to receive a letter from their families. So every week or two, Zhang Feng would go to the administration office of the production brigade to collect the letters. He had not heard from Yu Mei for two weeks, so early this morning, he went to the office, together with Wang Hai and Li He, to see if there were some letters for them, as well as to buy some daily necessities from the supply and marketing co-operative.

When they arrived, they found their team's mailbox. Zhang Feng was glad to see a letter from his parents but he was disappointed immediately because Yu Mei had not written to him.

At this point, Wang Hai said hello to two middle-aged people who had just entered. Wang Hai told Zhang Feng they were Brigadier Zhang and Secretary Chen. Then Wang Hai introduced Zhang Feng and Li He to the Brigadier and Secretary. They seemed to look at Zhang Feng with special attention. Secretary Chen said to Zhang Feng,

"You should improve yourself and learn from the poor and lower-middle class peasants."

Wang Hai said immediately,

"Zhang Feng is very good at his job. He got the full working points in our production team."

Brigadier Zhang and Secretary Chen said,

"That's good, that's good."

After getting the mail, Zhang Feng and the others went to the supply and marketing co-operative to do some shopping. The supply and marketing co-operative was a small shop where you could buy only the most common household items such as toothpaste, towels, soap, thermos bottles and so on. They saw a girl looking at the face cream on the counter as they walked in. Zhang Feng and the others recognized that it was Qing Lian when she turned around. Her appearance had changed so much after a few months' separation. Her face, full of ruddy youth and vigour, was gone. She had become dark, thin and listless. Wang Hai still made fun of her.

"Commissioner Liu, you should buy a few more bottles of face cream, otherwise you will become a female Li Kui (a famous dark and brawny warrior from an ancient Chinese novel) in a few days."

Qing Lian glared at Wang Hai and said,

"Do you want to buy it for me? I can't afford it."

"I heard that you have been promoted to the leader of the women's team and joined the party," Wang Hai said. "Congratulations. You must get the high-level working points. How come you still can't afford to buy the face cream?"

"Our team had a bad harvest this year," said Qing Lian. Then she was ready to leave. She didn't seem to have the energy to argue with Wang Hai.

Zhang Feng asked, for the sake of politeness,

"Are you here to collect a letter?"

"Yes."

After she left, Li He said with a smile,

"She is lying, no one will write to her. Her parents had already cut off their relationship with her because she disclosed them during the Cultural Revolution. She's a loner now, with no friends or relatives. Only ghosts will write to her."

His words made Zhang Feng and Wang Hai laugh. They met Xiao Li, a classmate of theirs, outside the supply and marketing cooperative. He and Qing Lian were in the same collective household. Wang Hai asked him why Qing Lian had changed so much. Xiao Li looked around and whispered,

"In order to make herself stand out. Qing Lian always says she wants to put down roots in the countryside. If she really wanted to root, she would marry a farmer. So the leader of our production team wants Qing Lian to marry his mentally retarded son. But our Excellency, Commissioner Liu is a very high-minded person who just wants to marry a handsome guy like Brother Feng. So she turned the leader down. Can anyone who offends a local dignitary have a happy ending? As a result, her application for party membership was rejected and her title of the leader of the women's team was removed. In addition, she's working so hard on the farm that now she is in really low spirits."

"It sounds so pathetic," Li He said.

"This is evil which will be rewarded with evil. Do you still remember that she flogged teachers and principals during the Cultural Revolution and was so aggressive in the violent civil strife? She is not worthy of pity," said Wang Hai.

"I wish she could reflect on her actions and stop using the excuse of the revolution for being immoral," Zhang Feng said.

The most unbearable thing for the young people was life in the countryside without culture and entertainment. In the city, although all the Chinese and foreign literary works had been criticized and banned after the beginning of the Cultural Revolution, people could still borrow some science and technology books from the library, or secretly borrow some Chinese and foreign masterpieces from their relatives and friends. In the countryside, most people were illiterate and few could read. Reading books, watching movies and listening to concerts were extravagant dreams for the students. Zhang Feng still had his high school maths and physics textbooks that he had been carrying with him since he left the city. Sometimes, he would read and calculate under the kerosene lamp at night. Wang Hai always said to him,

"Elder brother, is it useful to read these books? All the universities have been shut down. Chairman Mao has said that education has been revisionist for the past 17 years. Do you still expect to go to university in the future?"

Zhang Feng said, "Without knowledge, how can we build a modern country? It is better to learn more knowledge than to waste our youth."

Li He said, "Brother Feng is right. We do farm work with a hoe every day. If we don't learn something, our minds will rust away as time goes on." Then he took out a book of traditional Chinese medicine and began to read.

Wang Hai muttered,

"I think I'll have to find something to read too."

Coincidentally, Dan Dan came to see Zhang Feng a week later and secretly brought the translation of four great tragedies of Shakespeare and A Tale of Two Cities by Dickens. Wang Hai snatched the Dickens and said he did not want to read sad works. Dan Dan laughed and said,

"A Tale of Two Cities is not only sad, but also full of terror."

Wang Hai quickly covered up his embarrassment and said he had confronted the bullets during the violent civil strife, so he was brave and not afraid of terror.

Dan Dan said,

"OK, talk about your feelings after reading it."

Wang Hai said to Zhang Feng in a low voice after Dan Dan left,

"Elder brother, you are so selfish. You already have Yu Mei, you can't own Dan Dan any more. Do you want her to be your backup girlfriend?"

"How can you blame me for your poor performance? Dan Dan is a talented girl. You have to improve your educational level if you want to win her love. You should not always act like someone who hasn't been educated."

"OK, OK, I will improve myself immediately," Wang Hai said repeatedly and he began to read A Tale of Two Cities.

The students managed to find joy amid hardship. Once, when Zhang Lin came to visit Zhang Feng, she brought him a guitar and a collection of songs called Two Hundred Foreign Folk Songs. Inside, were world-famous folk songs. Because there were no informants among them, the students often let Zhang Feng sing while playing the guitar. Sometimes, they would ask him to teach them some famous foreign songs, such as the Katyusha of the Soviet Union, or the folk songs of England and Scotland. When everyone had learned, they liked to sing together. This brought pleasure to their dull and dreary lives. Sometimes, the villagers were attracted by the singing. They opened the door, walked in and sat down on the bed and listened to their songs.

People in the countryside liked to drop round. They would often push open the door and walk in without asking the host.

They also did not consider whether the host would welcome them but sat down immediately and stayed for a long time. Sometimes it was very late and the host was falling asleep but they still did not want to leave. The students were not used to it at first. If it was time to go to sleep and some villagers still didn't want to leave, the students would start to yawn loudly. However, the villagers remained. Finally, Wang Hai couldn't stand it anymore, so he deliberately put out the oil lamp, saying that the kerosene had run out. Only in this way would the villagers leave. Zhang Feng, however, understood the villagers because dropping round and chatting was probably their only entertainment.

But this happy time did not last long. A few weeks later, Secretary Li and Lieutenant Wang arrived suddenly. In the kitchen, they told Li He and Xiao Hong seriously,

"Someone reported that you were singing obscene songs and reading yellow (obscene) books."

Wang Hai heard this in his room and quickly stuffed A Tale of Two Cities into the quilt. Then he went to the kitchen and said with a smile on his face,

"Ah, Secretary Li, Lieutenant Wang, sit down, please. Xiao Hong, hurry to make tea for the leaders. The boiling water is in the thermos and the first-class Longjing tea is in my small bag."

Wang Hai's enthusiastic behaviour quickly softened Secretary Li's serious face.

"We just want to remind you. You know whether it is true or not. Just be cautious."

Lieutenant Wang did not want to give up. He said,

"I heard that your classmate Zhang Feng has been playing a somewhat foreign musical instrument. It sounds like decadent music."

Zhang Feng came out and said,

"The foreign musical instrument that I have been playing is a guitar. The villagers have never heard any musical instrument before except the erhu and flute. Guitars are very popular in Cuba and Albania, which are our socialist brother countries. So you can't say that the music played on the guitar is decadent music."

Li He also took out the traditional Chinese medicine book with the yellow cover from the room.

"Might the villagers have made a mistake? My book is a traditional Chinese medicine book with the yellow cover. They might have thought it was a yellow (obscene) book."

Lieutenant Wang said with a wink,

"Is it just this book? You might have other books."

Wang Hai knew that his book was already hidden, so he said,

"Why don't you go in and search the room?"

Secretary Li eased the deadlock immediately.

"Well, well, they are all young people and like a lively atmosphere, singing is not a mistake. You should sing more revolutionary songs in the future."

"Secretary Li, you can stay for tea. I have something else to do. I'll go first," said Lieutenant Wang, displeased.

The students got together after Secretary Li had left and discussed who the informant might be.

"Lieutenant Wang is hostile to us," Zhang Feng said. "Will he send his men to spy on us?"

"I suspect it is Er Laizi. He is a gluttonous and lazy guy. He's been coming to us lately and stays all night," said Yu Lan.

Wang Hai sighed and said,

"I didn't expect there to be informants among these unsophisticated peasants. It looks like there are people everywhere who love to engage in class struggle."

"We should be careful in the future. Lower the singing. Don't read banned books when the villagers visit us," said Li He.

When Er Laizi came the next day, everyone deliberately sang the songs of Chairman Mao, such as The East is Red and The Ship Cannot Sail without a Helmsman. The volume was so loud that the ears of Er Laizi couldn't stand it and he left after a short while. After he left, the students began to sing Red River Village.

Sanitation in rural areas was particularly poor. There were no public bathhouses so it was difficult to take a bath during the year. The students' skin became very rough. In addition, as many people slept together on one big bed, everyone had parasitic lice. They often felt itchy and strangled the lice, one by one.

It happened that He Hua also came to see Zhang Feng. Seeing that Dan Dan was helping Zhang Feng with hygiene, she came over to help Dan Dan. Dan Dan quite liked this beautiful and pure country girl. At the same time, her woman's intuition also made her sense that He Hua secretly loved Zhang Feng. For years, Dan Dan had protected Zhang Feng like a sister. She knew that many girls liked Zhang Feng, the handsome and charming boy but she was not in the least jealous of them. She knew what kind of girl Zhang Feng liked. Yu Mei, who had ethereal beauty and was refined and polite, was his favourite. Dan Dan blessed them sincerely, like their mother and sister. But whether Zhang Feng and Yu Mei would be able to continue their love in the future was far from certain, as the red political storm had blown them apart, again and again. They might be in love but they could never marry. Therefore, under the appearance of intellect, Dan Dan still had a secret desire for happiness. Dan Dan and He Hua chatted while washing clothes.

He Hua said with envy,

"Sister Dan Dan, how lucky you are. You are very beautiful and so knowledgeable. I am not as lucky as you."

Then He Hua told Dan Dan the story about her childhood. Her father died when she was very young. Her mother had a hard time raising her and her young brother. He Hua dropped out of primary school in the third year because her family was so poor. She had to do farm work and help to support her family. The memory made He Hua sad, with tears in her eyes,

"Sister Dan Dan, I really want to study. I want to be a capable person in the future, not a woman who can only take care of the children and do housework."

Dan Dan consoled her by saying,

"You are still young, you will have a chance. If you can find primary school textbooks, I and Brother Zhang can teach you."

He Hua jumped up with joy at Dan Dan's words. She came more often after that. Not only Zhang Feng, but everyone in the house was willing to help this innocent and lively rural girl to learn. He Hua had almost become a member of the collective household. Of course, Lieutenant Wang looked more and more angry.

CHAPTER IV

In the Blizzard and Chilliness

The ground was fully covered with the endless snow as autumn turned to winter. Yu Mei and her classmates were sorting vegetables in the underground vegetable cellar of the Hongqi Commune, more than 50 kilometers from Jili City. Compared with the heavy labour in spring, summer and autumn, there was less farm work in the winter in northeast China. The villagers called this the 'cat winter' (meaning to stay indoors like a cat to avoid the cold). When people came to working outdoors, the cold weather was still unbearable. When Yu Mei and the other young people transported fertilizer to the fields or repaired vegetable greenhouses, they still shivered from the cold, even with thick, cotton-padded clothes, trousers, cotton caps, masks and gloves.

Fortunately, Yu Mei also had the military cotton-padded overcoat that Zhao Wu left for his father when he was transferred to another provincial military command. Yu Mei felt much better after putting on the overcoat but she still had chilblains on her hands and feet like her classmates. Later, the leader of the production team offered her special work to keep her from being outside. The chilblains began to improve after she was allowed to work in the cellar and warehouse.

Ever since Yu Mei and her classmates had come to settle in the countryside, the villagers had spread the story of 'a fairy from the city' who had joined their production team. Many farmers, especially young men, often wandered around the house of Yu Mei in their spare time. In fact, they had come to see how beautiful Yu Mei was.

The leader and other members of the production team also took good care of her. Only the secretary of the production brigade knew that Yu Mei was the daughter of a capitalist roader. Fortunately, he did not tell the others about this.

Today, Yu Mei and her friends were sorting out the cabbages in a vast, underground cellar. In winter in Northeast China, people could only eat three kinds of stored vegetables: Chinese cabbage, radish and potatoes. The vegetables stored in the cellar needed to be cleaned every once in a while. With Chinese cabbage, in particular, it was necessary to remove the rotten leaves from the outer layers so as not to cause the whole cabbage to rot. Yu Mei was sitting on the bench and picking off the cabbage leaves. Sitting next to her was Xiao Fang, who was her good friend. She was also the daughter of an official. Her father had been publicly criticized during the Cultural Revolution and now worked in the May Seventh Cadre Schools.

Xiao Fang whispered to Yu Mei,

"Has he written to you recently?" Xiao Fang knew about the relationship between Yu Mei and Zhang Feng.

Yu Mei bowed her head and said,

"Maybe the heavy snow delayed it. There has been no letter for two weeks."

Like Zhang Feng, through the arduous and boring work, the happiest event for Yu Mei was to receive a letter from Zhang Feng and to confide in each other. They wrote to each other almost every week. They talked about the joys and sorrows of their lives and how they missed each other. Yu Mei knew that Dan Dan was very close to Zhang Feng and that he was also cared for by Dan Dan. But deep down inside, she was also a little worried that the distance would alienate them. Yu Mei still believed that Dan Dan would only be his sister as long as Yu Mei was Zhang Feng's girlfriend.

"A few days ago, when the officials of the culture and education systems came to inspect our work and life, I saw that the young Director Cai was very pleased with you. Why do you ignore him? You know, a lot of girls want to marry him. That way, they would be able to go back to the city right away, without having to suffer any longer in the countryside," said Xiao Feng.

"You don't know him," said Yu Mei. "He is Zhang Feng's sworn enemy. In the past, he was jealous of Zhang Feng so he did everything possible to frame him during the Cultural Revolution. He has no real talent and will only get promoted by fawning on his superiors. So he's a snake in the grass."

After hearing this, Xiao Fang said,

"People's faults are not written on their foreheads. He looks like a gentleman."

At the same time, Zhang Feng and his classmates, who were thousands of miles away, were cutting wood in the mountain forests. The snow there was more than 30cm thick. The production team had less work in the winter so the students had time to do their own household chores.

Firewood was an important thing. The students needed to collect firewood for next year's cooking and heating. Every winter, the villagers would go up the hill to collect firewood and store it in the firewood stack in the house yard. They were running out of firewood in their house and had to go up the hill to collect it by themselves and then pull the collected firewood back by oxcart. They borrowed the oxcart from the production team and then they went up the hill with sickles. He Hua was worried about them. She worried that they could not drive the oxcart so she asked if they needed her to go with them.

"No problem," said Wang Hai. "I can drive the oxcart."

When they reached the hill a few miles from the village, they all went in separate directions to cut wood. The boys used sickles to chop down dry, small branches, the girls searched and picked up the dry branches that had fallen on the ground, then they put the branches on the oxcart. For much of the time, they struggled to walk through knee-deep snow. When they were hungry, they ate a bite of cold corn bread, and when they were thirsty, they grabbed a handful of snow and put it in their mouths.

It took almost a day to collect enough firewood. Everyone was cold and tired. The old ox suddenly went 'on strike' just as they were struggling to drive the cart home. No matter how Wang Hai tried, the old ox would not move. At last, the ox overturned the cart in a ditch by the side of the road which frustrated them. Several girls were so worried that they began to cry.

Zhang Feng and the boys pulled the cart out of the ditch. He told them to pick the firewood up and put it in the cart and then he raced back to the village and to the house of He Hua. He Hua was cooking. After hearing what Zhang Feng told her, she said nothing but picked up a bundle of hay and then left with Zhang Feng. She said,

"The old ox refused to go because it was hungry. I thought that you would be back at noon, but I didn't expect you to be back so late."

Everyone was overjoyed to see He Hua and Zhang Feng return. He Hua gave the old ox hay to eat, then took the whip to drive it on. As expected, the old ox went on his way obediently. The girls sat in the cart and the boys followed. Everyone thanked He Hua who looked at Zhang Feng and said,

"That is as it should be. Brother Zhang has spent a lot of time helping me to learn."

It was dark when they returned to the village. Everyone was too tired to eat dinner and they fell asleep on the bed.

"Whoever wants to put down roots in the countryside, let him stay," Li He complained. "Anyway, I don't want to stay in the countryside. There is gas in the city for cooking, central heating for warmth. In contrast, it is too hard to live here. I have to cut firewood myself."

He waited for Wang Hai's response but Wang Hai lay on the bed and had already started snoring loudly.

When they woke up the next day, Wang Hai said,

"Last night, I had a bad dream about a group of wolves surrounding and attacking me."

"I thought I heard the wolf barking when we were collecting firewood yesterday," Zang Feng replied.

"You should be careful," Li He said. "Dreams sometimes become reality."

Wang Hai said to Zhang Feng,

"Do you remember? Dan Dan will come to pick up the book at 4:00 this afternoon. I have to prepare well to discuss it with her."

Zhang Feng said with a smile,

"Well, you should talk properly to Dan Dan and show that you are a learned person."

Wang Hai sat on the bed all morning, concentrating on reading A Tale of Two Cities. He discussed the characters of the novel with Zhang Feng over and over again. Dan Dan planned to come and stay in the girls' room for the night, so she would arrive later. By noon, Wang Hai had read more than half of the novel.

"The Great French Revolution was horrible," he told Zhang Feng. "It's a bit like our Cultural Revolution. A man who was alive one day would be guillotined the next. And even the revolutionaries were killing each other."

Zhang Feng replied,

"You have made the wrong comparison. Dickens' position was humanitarian. He sympathized with the poor who were oppressed by the aristocracy, but he was critical of the cruel and extreme methods adopted by the revolutionaries, as well as their indiscriminate killing of innocent people."

Wang Hai said,

"Yes, yes, this is very important. I will discuss this with Dan Dan later. Thanks, elder brother." He jotted it down in his notebook.

It was four o'clock in the afternoon and Dan Dan hadn't arrived yet. Then it began to snow. Zhang Feng was a little worried. He said to Wang Hai,

"We can't wait any longer. We will have to go and pick up Dan Dan. It's getting a little dark and I'm afraid she'll get lost. And I'm afraid the dream you had last night will come true."

"How can such a clever atheist like you believe such superstitions? Well, let's go and get her." Wang Hai replied.

They went out, carrying sickles, and walked to a small hill, more than a mile from the village. Thick snow had accumulated in the woods. There was a forked road in the woods. In the summer, the road from Dan Dan's production team to Zhang Feng's production team was easy to identify but after snow, it was easy to get lost. Zhang Feng recognized the footprints on the snow at the fork in the road.

"Uh-oh!" he said to Wang Hai, "Dan Dan has gone the wrong way. She went the way to the fourth team."

Wang Hai was also in a hurry and said,

"Let's catch up with her as soon as possible."

They trotted along the road to the fourth team to catch up with Dan Dan. The farther they went, the thicker the trees grew on both sides. Suddenly, they heard a woman's voice shouting,

"Somebody, help!"

"No, it's Dan Dan! Hurry up!" Zhang Feng said to Wang Hai. Then Zhang Feng ran forward at full speed and Wang Hai followed. After a distance of 100 meters, Zhang Feng saw that Dan Dan was hiding behind a big tree and two wolves, 10 meters away, were preparing to attack her. It seemed that they had followed Dan Dan for some time.

"Dan Dan, here I am!" Zhang Feng shouted at the top of his voice and dashed to her at the speed of a 100-meter sprinter. Fortunately, Zhang Feng had been a 100-meter sprint athlete. Wang Hai was left far behind by Zhang Feng.

Seeing Zhang Feng rushing towards them, the two wolves did not retreat at all. Instead, they seemed happy to have more prey so that they did not have to share the flesh of Dan Dan.

One of the wolves dashed towards Zhang Feng, and the other rushed towards Dan Dan, who was hiding behind the tree.

Zhang Feng's kung Fu came in handy at this moment. Just as the wolf was about to pounce on his chest, he ducked and kicked the wolf hard in the stomach. The wolf howled and fell to the ground. Then Zhang Feng rushed towards the other wolf. The wolf had brought Dan Dan down to the ground. At this critical moment, Zhang Feng used his sickle to chop into the wolf's buttock fiercely. The wolf howled and fell over on the snow. The blood reddened the snow. At that moment, Zhang Feng heard the shouting of Wang Hai, who had just arrived,

"Watch out, elder brother!" He looked back and saw that the wolf he had kicked down, was jumping up on him again. Zhang Feng was more unruffled this time. He even threw away his sickle and struck the wolf's head from the side with the Thunderbolt Fist the master had taught him. At the same time, he kicked the wolf in its belly. Zhang Feng used 100% of his strength this time (his master had warned him to use only half of his strength when fighting with others), so the wolf fell to the ground, completely motionless and probably unconscious. Then Wang Hai arrived.

Dan Dan was still in shock, looking at the two wolves lying on the ground. Knowing that she was safe, Dan Dan cried in Zhang Feng's arms. Zhang Feng could not stop being vigilant and looked at the two wolves on the ground. A few minutes later, they struggled up and slowly escaped into the woods. Drops of blood were left on the snow. Wang Hai still wanted to pursue the wolves with his sickle. Zhang Feng said,

"Don't. Let them go. I don't think they'll live much longer."

Zhang Feng was comforting Dan Dan who was in his arms. Dan Dan stopped crying but still hugged Zhang Feng tightly.

For years she had seldom had the chance to be cuddled by her beloved so she wanted Zhang Feng to continue to hug her for a while. She murmured,

"Thank you, Xiao Feng. You saved me once again."

Wang Hai looked at them, a little envious and jealous. He said, "Elder brother, can I take your place for a while if you are tired? You saved Dan Dan again, but she's really worth it. She used to… "

He just wanted to say that Dan Dan had nearly committed suicide for Zhang Feng but he suddenly remembered that Dan Dan had told him it was a secret and never to tell Zhang Feng. Thus, Wang Hai swallowed his tongue. After a few minutes, Dan Dan finally calmed down. Wang Hai wanted to help Dan Dan back, but she still leaned on Zhang Feng's shoulder and walked with his help.

Wang Hai said to himself,

"It seems that today's reading has been done for nothing."

It was dark when they returned to the village.

Two weeks later, something happened which made Zhang Feng feel mortified. The Armed Forces Department of the commune arranged for the educated youths and young peasants to participate in military training by making the production brigade a training unit. Trainees would be trained in alignment and shooting. While handing out rifles, Lieutenant Wang said,

"Listen, not everyone is qualified to hold a gun. He who comes from an unacceptable family gets only a stick. Because the rifle is used to protect the Dictatorship of the Proletariat, it can only be given to the sons and daughters of the poor and lower-middle class peasants."

When he came to Zhang Feng, he took out a stick that was used to practise bayonet drill. He lifted it up deliberately so everyone could see it, and then handed it over to Zhang Feng. Zhang Feng refrained from getting angry. He was not interested in military training at all. He Hua, who was standing nearby, was angry about his unfair treatment.

"Wang Congjun, why don't you give Brother Zhang the gun?"

"Let him tell you about his family background," said Lieutenant Wang, complacently.

Zhang Feng waved to He Hua, meaning not to bother about the words of Lieutenant Wang. Zhang Feng, Dan Dan and several other students with unacceptable family backgrounds could only watch nearby during the training of shooting. In fact, Zhang Feng was a born sharpshooter. His eyesight was particularly good and coupled with the stability brought by practising Qi Gong, this enabled him to hit the target with every shot. After the educated youths finished shooting, Lieutenant Wang said in a dismissive tone,

"Each one shoots three rounds, and the score for hitting the bull's eye is 10. Wang Hai is the best of you guys. He is only 18. So I don't think you guys can do anything more than read a few books."

Wang Hai was unconvinced and said,

"Lieutenant Wang, can you show us what score you can get?"

Lieutenant Wang took the gun and shot three rounds. The marker reported that the score was 24. Lieutenant Wang stood up complacently.

Wang Hai said,

"You have been a soldier, so it is not unusual to get such a score. Although we have not been soldiers, there is a sharpshooter among us. He is sure to get a higher score than you." Then he pointed at Zhang Feng.

Hearing this, Zhang Feng waved his hands to show he had no interest in shooting. But the students and He Hua all wanted Zhang Feng to make a good showing on their behalf. They all encouraged him to have a competition with Lieutenant Wang. Captain Zhang of the militia company who was at the scene, also wanted to see Zhang Feng's ability so he allowed Zhang Feng to take part in the target shooting.

Lieutenant Wang deliberately gave him an obsolete and tattered rifle. Zhang Feng checked the rifle and its front sight. He took the prone position to shoot three rounds. The marker waved his flag excitedly when Zhang Feng had finished, indicating that the score was 29. The students and He Hua all jumped up and down and applauded. Captain Zhang knew that Zhang Feng hadn't given his best effort intentionally in order to save Lieutenant Wang from embarrassment otherwise, he would easily have got the full score. Captain Zhang was an enlightened veteran. He said that he would let Zhang Feng participate in the military competition of the commune and the county on behalf of their production brigade. Lieutenant Wang's face was distorted with anger.

After returning home, Li He said to Zhang Feng and Wang Hai,

"I know why Lieutenant Wang made it so difficult on brother Feng today and why Qing Lian is swaggering again. According to reliable information, Director Cai, who we both know recently came to the county to inspect our work, told the local officials that there are some reactionary students here. He let them pay more attention to these students. The students who want to settle in the countryside should be cultivated more. I heard that Qing Lian will become the captain of the women's team once again. Moreover, the commune is considering her application for party membership. Doesn't what happened today just verify what they have said?"

Both Zhang Feng and Wang Hai agreed with Li He's analysis.

Two days later, He Hua asked Zhang Feng secretly what was wrong with his family background. Knowing He Hua was a reliable girl, Zhang Feng told her that his father had been classified as a rightist because he had given the leaders some advice in 1957.

"Your father was wronged," said He Hua. "You're a good man, and your father must have been a good man too." She also asked Zhang Feng to ignore Lieutenant Wang and the others. She would do her best to help him. Zhang Feng felt very grateful to this kind girl.

The Chinese Spring Festival was approaching in the coldest February of northeast China. The educated youths finally had a chance to go home. One day before the Spring Festival, Zhang Feng, Wang Hai, Li He and Dan Dan made their way home, carrying local specialties for their families. Zhang Feng had to go to where his parents had settled in the countryside. The intellectuals who had lived in the city were driven to rural areas after the students had been sent to the countryside. This was given the pleasant sounding name of "Taking the Road of May 7th" (it meant receiving the re-education of the poor and lower-middle class peasants to reform their bourgeois world view).

They went first to the commune to take the bus but there were so many people waiting that they didn't get on it all day. It looked hopeless for the next day, too.

Wang Hai said,

"We can't just wait and do nothing. I think we should hitch a ride on the highway. There are lots of trucks going to the country. I've heard that some kind drivers are willing to take students there."

They all agreed to try it so they went to the roadside and waited. They waved to show they wanted to hitchhike when a truck passed by, however, four or five trucks had passed and none of them stopped.

"We have too many people so the drivers don't want to stop," Wang Hai said. "We can try to get one person to stop the truck and the others could hide. When the truck stops, the others can come out."

Zhang Feng said he was willing to be in charge of stopping the truck. Wang Hai rolled his eyes.

"It's not the best choice," he said. "We should let Dan Dan stop the truck. The drivers are all men and when they see a beautiful girl, they will definitely be willing to stop."

"What do you want to do? To seduce others by beauty?" said Li He.

Dan Dan standing next to him said,

"It's OK. I am willing to try. You are all nearby so I am not worried."

Finally, a truck actually stopped next to Dan Dan who was waving. The middle-aged male driver agreed to give Dan Dan a lift and let her get on the truck. Just then, Zhang Feng and the others jumped out from behind the tree. Wang Hai said,

"Uncle, we are all her classmates. Please take us as well."

Seeing the driver was not so happy, Wang Hai quickly gave the driver a pack of cigarettes and then the driver agreed to let them get on the truck.

They boarded the train at the railway station without buying tickets. Like many educated youths, most of the money they had earned by working had been spent on buying daily necessities so they had little money left. A few years ago, when the Red Guards launched the revolutionary tours, they all took trains for free. Perhaps, because of their influence, the railway staff also turned a blind eye to the fact that students caught trains without paying.

After the train had passed several stops, the conductor began to check tickets. Zhang Feng and Dan Dan had a lot of self-respect and were embarrassed to tell the conductor that they did not buy tickets so they pretended to go to the toilet to avoid the ticket check. Wang Hai was thick-skinned and didn't care about any criticism. When the middle-aged, female conductor asked them to show their tickets, Wang Hai said,

"Dear Auntie, we are educated youths settled in the countryside. We do not even have enough food to eat because of the natural disasters in the village this year and there is no money left to buy train tickets. You know, it's almost the Spring Festival and we have to go home to see our parents." Then he pretended to wipe his eyes.

The conductor relented after listening to his words. She said,

"Yes, you have a tough time indeed. My child is an educated youth, too. All right, forget it" and she let them go.

"You are a good actor indeed," Li He said.

"I did not lie. We really didn't make any money this year."

More than two hours later, the train arrived in Jiu An county. Zhang Feng got off the train to visit his parents and sister who had settled here. Dan Dan and Wang Hai went on to the provincial capital. Wang Hai promised Zhang Feng to take good care of Dan Dan.

After more than two hours on the bus, Zhang Feng arrived at the production team where his parents had settled. Upon entering the village, Zhang Feng saw his parents were sitting with a group of commune members and picking out corn kernels on the threshing ground. They looked very old. His father had grown a long beard. Zhang Feng felt very sad. They were university professors who were supposed to be teaching and researching at the university, but who were now forced to work on the land. In a country short of intellectual elites, they were supposed to be valued and important. However, they were distrusted and even treated as enemies of the people, having to take reformation through labour.

Zhang Wenbo and Hu Yun were overjoyed to see their son. They asked for leave hurriedly and returned to their thatched, earthen house together with Zhang Feng. It was similar to Zhang Feng's house in the countryside but with only one bedroom. Zhang Lin was making pancakes on the cooking hearth. She came over immediately when she saw her elder brother. She hugged Zhang Feng and cried and laughed at the same time.

In the evening, they killed a chicken they had raised, and together with the vegetables they had grown, they cooked a hearty, farmhouse dinner. Everyone sat around the small table on the heated earth bed, eating and talking. They had not been so happy for a long time. Zhang Feng felt that only kinship, friendship and love could give him courage, strength and hope in this harsh and repressive era. It was the torch that guided him in the darkness.

His parents told him about their situation. They said that although the officials told the peasants that Zhang Wenbo was a rightist, the unsophisticated peasants still respected knowledgeable people. The villagers took good care of them and let them do light work. They grew their own vegetables and raised chickens, and thus led a pastoral life. In Zhang Wenbo's words, he was now a modern Tao Yuanming (a famous scholar living in a reclusive village in ancient China). Compared to being criticized and censored in the city, this place was like a political haven. It was regrettable that they couldn't contribute to society with their knowledge.

Zhang Feng stayed at home for a few days. He really wanted to spend a few more days with his family but in his heart, he missed his beloved more because he and Yu Mei had made an appointment to meet in the provincial capital.

Three days before the Spring Festival, keeping the appointment with Yu Mei, Zhang Feng arrived at the poplar tree on the riverside at noon, where they had previously dated. Yu Mei hadn't arrived yet, or maybe the train was late. Leaning against the poplar tree and watching the mist of the river and the white and crystal rimed trees on both sides, Zhang Feng was looking forward to seeing his Snow White princess. In a trance, he saw Yu Mei dancing like a fairy to the melody of A Night of Flowers and Moonlight by the Spring River, against a beautiful and intoxicating fairyland.

Suddenly, someone hugged him from behind. Looking at the two slender, white hands, Zhang Feng knew they belonged to Yu Mei. He quickly turned around and hugged her. The missing and heartache caused by the separation became excited hug and tears in this moment. They were touching each other's cheeks, wiping each other's tears and asking questions. Forgetting the cold weather, they spent more than two hours by the riverside.

They came to the house of one of Zhang Feng's uncles in Jili City because neither of them had a home here. Zhang Feng's uncle was a young member of staff at the Polytechnic University. He had not settled in the countryside. He had gone back to his hometown during the Spring Festival. He agreed to let Zhang Feng stay at his house for a few days.

Zhang Feng and Yu Mei entered the house after taking the key from the neighbour. The house was a staff property and had only two small rooms. Zhang Feng had bought some food so he and Yu Mei could spend a happy time here, like a married couple. In the evening however, they slept separately in two rooms because in those days, people still followed the traditional idea that couples couldn't have sex before they got married. Cuddling and kissing were the baseline of people in love. But on the night of the third day, also the last night, Yu Mei went into Zhang Feng's room after Zhang Feng had lain down for a while. She sat by Zhang Feng's bed and said, "Brother Feng, I can't sleep. We will be separated tomorrow, and I feel so sad."

Zhang Feng held her hand and replied,

"Don't be upset. We will still have a chance to meet." After a while, Yu Mei said,

"Feng, I feel cold. Can I lie down with you for a while?"

Zhang Feng hesitated for a moment, then lifted the quilt and let Yu Mei lie down. Yu Mei hugged Zhang Feng tightly. Zhang Feng could feel her cold body. He hugged Yu Mei tightly and warmed her with his body. After a while, Yu Mei's body began to warm up but her face was burning hot.

Zhang Feng asked her with concern,

"Yu Mei, have you got a fever?"

"No, I… "Yu Mei murmured, then she hugged Zhang Feng more tightly. Although both of them were wearing cotton clothes, Zhang Feng could still feel Yu Mei's soft breasts pressing against him. As a vigorous young man, Zhang Feng had a normal, sexual reaction. He immediately released Yu Mei who looked surprised and then asked,

"Don't you love me, Feng? You don't think I'm a slut, do you?"

Zhang Feng cuddled Yu Mei again and said tenderly,

"How could I? You are the purest girl in the world." He gave her a kiss lovingly and said, "We will have a lot of time together in the future. I must give you a good life in the future but I have nothing now. No degree, no job, no income. I can't give you a happy life yet. But I will. I will marry you fair and square."

Yu Mei cried and said,

"Feng, I believe in you."

They just cuddled and slept together for the night.

At noon the next day, they separated at the railway station. Zhang Feng would see off Yu Mei to the May Seventh Cadre Schools where her father stayed. She would spend the Spring Festival with her father. Zhang Feng accompanied Yu Mei to the train and stayed until it was about to leave. The music of A Night of Flowers and Moonlight by the Spring River was heard from the loudspeakers of the platform when the train began to move off. Yu Mei waved desperately to Zhang Feng and he waved back as he ran with the train until it left the platform.

Zhang Feng's tears blurred his vision. The image of dancing Yu Mei gradually floated into the distance.

PART VIII

'Escape to Victory'

CHAPTER I

A Political Event that Shocked the Whole Country

It had been almost three years since the students came to the countryside. At the age when they should have been learning knowledge and being educated to become the talent needed by the country, they had to spend their youth and their best years doing arduous and inefficient farm work and living a simple, boring and empty life. They couldn't see their future or feel any hope. Their bodies and minds were severely damaged. They felt helpless. They had always missed their parents and their loved ones who lived in the city. Their parents and loved ones also missed them, living in the countryside hundreds of miles away. But the chaos caused by the Cultural Revolution prevented them from any family reunions.

As the victims of the Cultural Revolution and the sacrificial objects of the class struggle, the students were like a group of people abandoned by society. They could only continue their suffering in misery. Many young people, like Zhang Feng, Wang Hai and their classmates, thought: 'Do we have no chance to change our fate? Shall we be forgotten forever in this obscure village?'

However, what the educated youth and all those who suffered in the Cultural Revolution did not expect was the occurrence of a political event that shocked the whole country and was like a thunderbolt, blowing up the atmosphere of political oppression. Marshal Lin Biao, the Defense Minister of PRC and the successor and close comrade of Mao Zedong, fled, by air, and crashed into the desert of Mongolia. Although the state media immediately explained that Chairman Mao had recognized Lin Biao's ambition to seize power early, anyone with a bit of political savvy understood that the official explanation was far-fetched.

When Zhao Wu completed his official travels and returned from other provinces, he visited Li Jianguo, who was still doing physical labour at the May Seventh Official School. They discussed this political event in private. They all felt that Chairman Mao had not won the full victory of the Cultural Revolution yet and that he still needed the support of Lin Biao, so it was a mystery as to how Lin Biao had died.

According to Zhao Wu's analysis, it was probably Premier Zhou, who had been trying to maintain political balance during the Cultural Revolution. He had launched a campaign to 'clean up those treacherous people around the emperor' by joining up with the old marshals and generals who were still in power in the armed forces, as well as other old senior leaders who were dissatisfied with the Cultural Revolution. He launched a surprise attack on Lin Biao and it was also an 'act first and report afterwards' operation for Chairman Mao.

When Chairman Mao got to know, there was nothing he could do and Chairman Mao himself was not a hundred percent sure of Lin Biao's loyalty. Considering the fact that Chairman Mao had rapidly aged after the political incident, he had to hand over some of his power to the anti-Cultural Revolution high-level leaders so the analysis of Zhao Wu made sense. When Zhang Feng visited his parents, Zhang Wenbo also believed that the death of Lin Biao would curb the severely leftist route of the Cultural Revolution and bring the country's operation back to normal. His words made Zhang Feng feel very excited.

Deng Xiaoping, who was identified by Mao Zedong as the second greatest capitalist roader, was re-appointed after the strong recommendation of Premier Zhou, just six months after the incident with Lin Biao. This cheered up all the politically minded and the persecuted in the Cultural Revolution because they saw a chance to right the wrongs.

Deng Xiaoping began to make great efforts to rectify the chaotic political and economic order, as expected, after he came to power again. He tried to solve many thorny social problems caused by the Cultural Revolution. Among them was gradually solving the problem of more than 10 million students who had been trapped in the countryside and could not come back to the city.

Economic activity in the city was gradually returning to normal. Factories and enterprises began to recruit student workers. The army also began to recruit from the educated youth. What was more exciting to excellent high school students like Zhang Feng and Dan Dan who were eager to go to university, was that universities had also resumed recruitment. However, what disappointed them was that, because the Cultural Revolution had negated education for the past seventeen years since the founding of the People's Republic of China, the universities had not dared to admit students through examinations. Students needed to be admitted through recommendation and selection. That meant that young workers, peasants and soldiers, with good political backgrounds, were recommended for university by the basic units and organizations, regardless of their levels of education. Even a person with just primary school education could be recommended. This approach seemed to be very ridiculous but in an era when the concept of class struggle determined everything, such an approach was considered correct.

In the collective households of the students, Wang Hai held a stack of application forms and said excitedly to everyone,

"Changxia Machinery Factory is recruiting workers! Everyone can apply!"

There were many advantages to being a worker in the city, including a good salary, working eight hours a day, weekends and holidays and the chance to learn skills with a much lower intensity than farm work. The social status of urban workers was much higher than that of farmers. People living in poor villages envied those with urban household registration because the wealth gap between urban and rural areas was very large. Changxia City was the second largest city in Jili province. It was located in the plain area with convenient transportation. It was enviable to be a worker there.

At that time, Zhang Feng dreamed of going to university one day and becoming a scholar or a scientist like his father; being a worker was not his goal. Of course, the living conditions and cultural life as a worker in the city would be much better than in the countryside but when he viewed the application, he was discouraged immediately. It was clearly stated on the form that the applicant must have the acceptable family background and must have behaved well in politics. There was also the 'family background' column on the form. The theory of class struggle, which prevailed during the Cultural Revolution, artificially divided the Chinese people into different classes. Workers, the poor and lower-middle class peasants, revolutionary leaders and soldiers were the classes on which the CCP depended. Landlords, rich peasants, capitalists and subsequently, traitors, spies, counter-revolutionaries and rightists were all enemies of the CCP. People born into the families of the first category were called 'Red Children'. They had priority in applying for jobs, getting an education, joining the army, joining the CCP and getting promoted. Those who came from the families of the latter category were regarded as the children of 'Five Black Categories'. They were second-class citizens. All their rights and opportunities were denied and they became people of humble origin. The theory of class struggle was carried out to the extreme in the Cultural Revolution. Therefore, people like Zhang Feng and Dan Dan, who were called 'those with unacceptable family backgrounds', would instinctively feel depressed and uncomfortable as soon as they saw the 'family background' column on various forms.

So, Zhang Feng returned the application form to Wang Hai and said,

"I don't want it. Each production brigade has only one quota. Wang Hai, you are the most qualified for this recruitment. You have to work hard for this quota, and for the honour of our collective household."

Li He was in poor health. The girls knew that the machinery factory wanted male workers so they didn't want to apply either. Only Wang Hai and another boy finally signed up.

A few weeks later, the commune posted up a notice. Wang Hai and two other boys from other production brigades had been admitted. Zhang Feng and the other classmates were very happy. Everyone asked Wang Hai to give them a treat. Wang Hai bought a chicken from a villager, then let Xiao Hong and Xiao Fang cook a hearty dinner. Dishes for dinner included Kung Pao Chicken and Stewed Chicken with Mushroom. Wang Hai repeatedly claimed that he had bought the chicken, not stolen it. Everyone joked,

"You'll be hundreds of miles away by the time the villagers come looking for you."

Zhang Feng was very happy that his good friend could get away from this abyss of misery and return to the city. He bought the local sorghum liquor specially. Everyone ate and drank. Wang Hai told everyone that although he was the only one leaving this time, the door to return to the city had been opened for all of them. In the future, there would be more factories, organizations and schools to recruit workers and students.

"Elder brother," he said to Zhang Feng, "You will definitely have the chance to study at Tsinghua or Peking University." Everyone was a little drunk that day. Half the reason for getting drunk was to feel happy for Wang Hai, and the other half was to feel sad for themselves, continuing to suffer there. Wang Hai was drunk. He pulled Zhang Feng's arm and said,

"Elder brother, I feel bad about leaving you. You are my good brother and my lifesaver. Because you saved me in the violent civil strife, you became implicated. Otherwise, Cai Wenge would not have framed you. I am worried that Lieutenant Wang wants to frame you after I leave. My family background is good so I'm not afraid of anyone and can protect you. But soon, I won't be here anymore…"

He suddenly said to Li He,

"Li He, you will have to guard our elder brother after I leave. You must protect him. If you betray him again, I will not forgive you."

Wang Hai had publicly announced Li He's secret which he did not want people to know. This made Li He feel embarrassed.

Then Li He hurriedly said,

"No problem, you need not worry about it. Brother Feng's business is my business."

The next day, Zhang Feng and the others sent Wang Hai to the commune's gathering place. Then they said goodbye, reluctantly.

Yu Mei had been very excited. She had received a call from her mother. Her mother said that since Deng Xiaoping had come to power, he had begun to liberate the old senior leaders who had been overthrown during the Cultural Revolution. Li Jianguo's political problems had been defined as 'the people's internal contradiction' which was the problem of cognition. He was not the capitalist roader any more. The authorities had allowed him to return to Jili City, the provincial capital, and had assigned him a place to live. Although the assigned residence was not a large villa as before, it was an independent, small building in good condition. Because Li Jianguo had been doing a lot of physical labour in the May Seventh Official School for a long time, together with the harsh living conditions, he had developed gastric and liver disease. Therefore, the authorities let him recuperate for a period of time. He would be assigned to work again when his health was improved.

A few days later, Yu Mei took a leave of absence to return to Jili City and her new home. Her new home was also in the senior governmental staff residence area on the South Bank of the river. As she walked into the familiar street, memories of the past suddenly came to her, and all sorts of feelings welled up. She felt her heart beating violently as she would see her parents soon. Walking to the door of her new house, she saw a car parked there. There seemed to be a visitor. Yu Mei's mother opened the door for Yu Mei. They hugged each other excitedly. Yu Mei asked her mother,

"Are there any guests in the house?"

Her mother replied,

"It is the Deputy Director Cai of the Culture and Education System."

"Deputy Director Cai?" Yu Mei was startled. Was it Cai Wenge, the man she hated most? She followed her mother into the living room hesitantly.

In the living room, Li Jianguo was talking to a man sitting on the sofa with his back to the door. Li Jianguo looked much older than before. Half of his hair was turned to grey. On the table were two bottles of the famous Maotai spirit and several packages of Ginseng cigarettes. It looked like gifts from the guest.

Li Jianguo stood up happily when he saw Yu Mei come in. The guest had also risen with him. Yu Mei almost threw up when she saw the smirk on his face which disgusted her. The guest was Cai Wenge but unlike before, he was dressed neatly in a Chinese tunic suit and his hair was neatly combed. It made him look like a gentleman.

Yu Mei left the living room immediately without looking back, even though her father asked her to say hello to Cai Wenge. Song Lihua hurried to catch up with Yu Mei and asked her what the matter was. Yu Mei told her mother that Cai Wenge was a villain who had been promoted by framing good people. He became an official and had relied on the rebellion since the beginning of the Cultural Revolution. He was Zhang Feng's sworn enemy. He had been trying to persecute Zhang Feng in order to put him to death. Hearing Yu Mei's words, Song Lihua said,

"Well, I can see he's a slippery guy but your father has just been rehabilitated. He hasn't been given a position yet so he must show respect to all the visiting leaders. Just for the sake of your father, you should say hello to Cai Wenge anyway and show him your courtesy."

Yu Mei returned to the living room, unwillingly, with her mother. Cai Wenge stood up immediately when he saw Yu Mei come back in. He gave Yu Mei a respectful bow, as if to a queen, and then said humbly,

"Miss Li Yumei, how do you do? It's been a long time. You must have suffered in the countryside. Physical labour should not have been done by a noble lady like you."

Seeing that Yu Mei did not answer him, he bowed to her again and said in a very reverent tone,

"I'm sorry, we misunderstood each other before. I apologize to you if I have done anything that harmed you and your friends."

Seeing that Yu Mei had begun to look at him, Cai Wenge immediately said,

"We were all so impulsive during the violent civil strife in previous years and we could not avoid hurting good people. In retrospect, we all share the same revolutionary purpose so we should not kill each other. I really regret thinking like that now."

Li Jianguo and Song Lihua were actually moved by his words. They believed that he had the intention of confessing so they persuaded Yu Mei to sit down and kept talking.

Cai Wenge was secretly pleased to see that his acting had worked. He calmed himself down then raised his voice and said,

"I have two purposes for this visit. The first is to visit Elder Li. I congratulate Elder Li who has been rehabilitated from the unjust situation and returned to a leadership position." (He flattered Li Jianguo intentionally who was still waiting for a job assignment.)

"The second purpose is to bring good news for Li Yumei. The History Department of Jili Normal University has two quotas allocation for student admission in the suburbs of the city. I have the ability to admit her into the university so your family can be reunited. Moreover, I can help Li Yu Mei to work in the provincial and municipal education bureau after she graduates. Thus, she can become a governmental member of staff. In this way, you two can rest easy."

Hearing these words, Li Jianguo and Song Lihua were very pleased. If Cai Wenge could really let their daughter come back to the city and could also let her go to university and in the future, became a governmental member of staff, their greatest wish would be realized. They paid great respect to Cai Wenge immediately and invited him to drink tea and eat fruit.

Yu Mei did not expect that Cai Wenge would be able to solve so many problems for her but she was reluctant to show her gratitude and she was not sure if Cai Wenge was bragging or really had such power. She said, imperturbably,

"Many educated youths want to come back to the city and go to university. Moreover, if you want to go to university, you must obtain the recommendation of the masses and the approval of the leaders. There are a lot of excellent, well-educated youths in our production brigade. I'm just an ordinary girl who's not as good as everyone else at work. How can I get the quota allocation of enrolment?"

Cai Wenge smiled confidently and said,

"Elder Li is a senior leader and should understand the truth. All the other procedures are the completion of the established process. Only the leadership approval is the most critical. I happen to be in charge of admissions for the education system. The directors of the Revolutionary Committees of several universities and I have a very trusting relationship so I can totally decide which student should be admitted."

With that, he picked up his cup complacently and took a sip. Both Li Jianguo and Song Lihua had been senior leaders who had maintained the revolutionary tradition. They had followed the right principles and refused to rely on personal relationships. But, for the sake of their daughter, they could no longer follow the right principles. Moreover, from the beginning of the Cultural Revolution, the ethos of the whole of society had become worse. In order to handle affairs for themselves and their families, such as transferring household registration, entering a school, joining the army, finding a job, and so on, people needed to rely on effective, interpersonal relationships. It was called 'going through the back door.' What's more, who could refuse the offer of unsolicited help from someone like Cai Wenge?

After leaving Li Jianguo's house, Cai Wenge got into his car and headed back to his office for a meeting. He whistled complacently all the way.

'This move of mine really killed two birds with one stone,' he thought. 'Not only will I be able to curry favour with Li Jianguo so that I will have another official backer in the future, as well as more opportunities for promotion, but also, perhaps, I might be able to get the beautiful girl who I've been coveting for years.'

He knew that Yu Mei hated him and that she and Zhang Feng were faithful lovers until death. But times had changed. Zhang Feng had an unacceptable family background and political defects. His future was sure to be stuck in the countryside. At most, he might be recruited as a worker. Compared with him, a departmental level leader, Zhang Feng's social status was much lower. When Yu Mei graduated from university and became a governmental member of staff, her social status would be very different from that of Zhang Feng. Then Cai Wenge would have the chance to really pursue Yu Mei. At that time, Li Jianguo and his wife would be positively inclined towards him. When he thought that one day, he would have the chance to hold Yu Mei in his arms, Cai Wenge salivated.

Yu Mei returned to the countryside with some small hope of going to university, though she was dubious about Cai Wenge's promise because firstly, he was a villain who forgot honour at the sight of money, and secondly, he was a braggart. But in order to curry favour with Li Jianguo, maybe he could indeed help her.

Two weeks after Yu Mei had returned to the countryside, the commune sent a notice to each production brigade as expected, saying that several universities in the city of Jili were coming to the countryside to recruit students. Among them, Jili Normal University had two quotas of enrolment, so qualified educated students would be allowed to apply. As it was a normal university, the proportion of female students in enrolment was greater. Almost all the girls had applied, except those who had unacceptable family backgrounds. Xiao Fang said to Yu Mei excitedly,

"Yu Mei, in this recruitment of students you have a very good chance of success. Your father has been rehabilitated so your family background is that of revolutionary governmental staff. The leaders of the commune and the brigade now know that the little fairy's father is a senior leader. I heard the leaders of the brigade come back from the meeting saying that the admission officers have accepted you. If you become a university student, you must have a treat to celebrate."

Yu Mei was certainly glad to hear that. She thought Cai Wenge had really tried to help her.

Then, Xiao Fang said mysteriously,

"I heard that this recruitment quota is not allocated in proportion to the production brigade of the commune. So as long as the requirements are met, the same one collective household can get two or three quotas. My dad has made effective relationships at the provincial admissions office. It would be great if we could go to university together."

Xiao Fang was the best friend of Yu Mei. If she could also enter normal university, then she and Yu Mei could take care of each other in school which would be great.

There were no exams and no interviews in the admission process. Then there were several weeks of waiting after the application materials were submitted and the medical examination was completed. Yu Mei and Xiao Fang received the matriculation letter of the History Department of Jili Normal University. Both of them were very excited. They were finally preparing to leave the harsh countryside and return to the city and they would have a great future. After graduating from university, they would become governmental staff with stable incomes and higher social status.

When the tram drove them home from the railway station, along the wide road with bustling crowds and high buildings, Yu Mei felt as if she were dreaming. Her life and youth seemed to begin anew. At the same time, she also fantasized that if Zhang

Feng could also go to university, he would definitely become a social elite. In that case, they could get married, raise a happy family and have their own children. She felt her face flush hot with shame at the thought.

Yu Mei was surprised to find that Cai Wenge was sitting on the podium at the opening ceremony. He also made a speech on behalf of the Revolutionary Committee of the Provincial Cultural and Educational System. He talked a lot about the need for universities to cultivate proletarian successors rather than those who follow the road of the bourgeois white special (do one's own professional work well but do not care for politics).

Yu Mei was going to the History Department with Xiao Fang after the ceremony. She suddenly saw that Cai Wenge was walking towards her with a group of university leaders and then he shook hands with her enthusiastically. Yu Mei had to cope with talking to him. Cai Wenge told the leaders of the university that Yu Mei was the daughter of Li Jianguo, the Secretary, and asked them to take good care of her. As a result, Yu Mei and Xiao Fang were assigned to a dormitory with better conditions that had originally been for young teachers. The room was spacious with only Yu Mei and Xiao Fang living in it. The other students were crammed into an eight-person room with four bunk beds.

"I gain the benefit along with you," said Xiao Fang. Then she asked about the relationship between Cai Wenge and Yu Mei. Yu Mei told her what had happened in the past.

Xiao Fang thought for a moment and said,

"It seems that he is interested in you. You have to pay attention to him. He's not as good-looking as your handsome Zhang Feng but now he is a senior leader who has power. If your handsome Zhang Feng can go to university, there's hope for both of you. If he stays in the countryside forever, your future will be a question mark."

"Even if he is a peasant all his life, I will still be with him," said Yu Mei. Of course it would be better if he could go to university.

Xiao Fang was a clever girl. She said,

"Why not use the power of Cai Wenge to recruit Zhang Feng to university? Although they are political enemies, and they may be rivals in love now, Cai Wenge would probably do this to please you. Zhang Feng's social status cannot be compared with Cai Wenge's, even if he goes to university."

Xiao Fang's words made Yu Mei reconsider. She finally accepted the invitation of Cai Wenge after he had invited her to dinner repeatedly.

One night, Cai Wenge came to pick Yu Mei up in a car and took her to a luxury restaurant. There was a sumptuous dinner, as well as candlelight, wine, music and flowers. But Yu Mei was not in the mood to appreciate these. Cai Wenge sincerely expressed his love to Yu Mei during the dinner. He said that he had fallen in love with Yu Mei when she first danced at the cultural and artistic performance but at that time, his social status was low, so he could only secretly love her. In fact, he hated Zhang Feng because he was jealous that he loved Yu Mei too much. Yu Mei felt goose bumps all over her when she heard his words but she had to keep listening reluctantly because she needed his help.

At the end, Yu Mei timidly asked Cai Wenge if he could help Zhang Feng to go to university. The expression of displeasure was evident on Cai Wenge's face but he was pretending to be magnanimous and immediately said,

"As long as it is your request, I will certainly meet it. Of course you know it's a little hard. Although Zhang Feng is a student with excellent academic performance, university recruitment is now mainly based on political conditions rather than academic performance. Zhang Feng has an unacceptable family background and he had political problems during the Cultural Revolution. Perhaps even the leader of his commune was afraid to recommend him. I will tell the admissions officers to try to recruit him to the university."

Yu Mei was very happy to hear these words and thanked Cai Wenge repeatedly. What she did not expect was that Cai Wenge, the sinister and cunning villain, would not help her; he would put a bigger obstacle in Zhang Feng's way.

CHAPTER II

Why Can't He Go to University?

Zhang Feng received a letter from Yu Mei. In her letter, she excitedly told Zhang Feng that she had been enrolled by the History Department of Jili Normal University. She had been reunited with her family and her father had been rehabilitated. He was currently at home recuperating and waiting for the organization to assign him to a role. Her younger brother, Li Xiaogang, had joined the army a few days ago. The officer in charge of conscription happened to be Chang Zheng. He was now a regimental commander.

Yu Mei said her greatest hope now was that Zhang Feng would be able to go to university so that their hopes for the future could be fulfilled. Yu Mei didn't dare mention in her letter that Cai Wenge helped her get into university. She also told Zhang Feng that, hopefully, she had made useful relationships which would help him leave the countryside and attend university. Of course, she didn't mention who she was talking about.

Zhang Feng was very happy after reading the letter but he only told Li He and Dan Dan about it. Dan Dan felt both happy and worried after listening to Zhang Feng. She was happy that such an excellent young man might have the opportunity to enter higher education. The worry was that she would feel lonely if Zhang Feng left.

News came from the commune after a few weeks. The Physics Department of Jili University was going to recruit a group of students in Huadan County. The Henghe Commune was assigned two quotas. The students of Zhang Feng's collective household were very excited. Everyone thought Zhang Feng was the most qualified applicant. He always ranked first in mathematics, physics and chemistry exams. He had been repeatedly awarded the first prize in several provincial mathematics and physics competitions. All believed that he would become a mathematician or physicist, like Hua Luogeng and Qian Xuesen, in the future. Jili University was a national, key university with many well-known scientists, scholars and professors. Zhang Feng would have a bright future if he could study there. Of course, Zhang Feng knew that his family background and political conditions were not favourable in an age when everything was about political conditions and class. Yu Mei said she had found some useful relationships to help him so he had to make every effort to take this chance.

Li He was now the leader of the collective household. He was particularly enthusiastic about recommending Zhang Feng. Not only did he work with the leaders of the production brigade to write a good appraisal for Zhang Feng, he also went to the commune to develop interpersonal relationships to help. Zhang

Feng knew that Li He was trying to atone for the past betrayal of his friends.

Although He Hua was reluctant to see Zhang Feng leave, she also believed that he was very talented. It would be a pity if he was trapped in the countryside. So He Hua also went to the brigade and the commune to ask her relatives and friends, who were leaders, to help Zhang Feng.

Zhang Feng also received a letter from the former Principal Chang unexpectedly. In his letter, Principal Chang said that he had ended his labour reform. Although he was not the Principal now, he could still teach some lessons. He told Zhang Feng that an important point was that Teacher Li, who was in charge of recruiting students for Jili University in Huadan County, was his university classmate. Teacher Li used to hear Principal Chang say that Zhang Feng was a very excellent student so when he heard that Zhang Feng had settled in Huadan County, Teacher Li was very happy and said he would try his best to recruit Zhang Feng. Having read the old Principal's letter, Zhang Feng felt more hopeful because the people in charge of enrolment at the university usually had the power to make a final decision.

Two weeks later, all the materials to apply for Jili University had been sent to the educated youth office of the commune. One night, Teacher Li, who was sent by Jili University to recruit students, was staying in the hostel and looking at the forms of the recommended applicants. He looked for Zhang Feng's application particularly. He was glad to see that the commune had written a good evaluation of Zhang Feng. According to the application, although Zhang Feng's family background was unacceptable, he had done well in the countryside.

Just then, someone knocked at the door. A middle-aged man with a frosty look came in. He introduced himself as Xie, the Deputy Director of the Provincial Admissions Office. The purpose of his visit was to check the admissions work. Deputy Director Xie left after he finished speaking. Teacher Li suddenly felt a sense of foreboding because the Provincial Admissions Office always paid special attention to the political conditions of enrolment.

As expected, a heated argument broke out the next day at the meeting to discuss the admission of new students. In the morning meeting, the people in the conference room included the leaders of the commune, Teacher Li and another teacher of Jili University who was responsible for enrolment, and Deputy Director Xie who arrived yesterday. The secretary of the commune, who was in charge of recruiting students and workers, first introduced the applications of the eight students who had been recommended. Three of them had been high school students before coming to the countryside, including Zhang Feng. The other three were junior high school students. Two others had only received an elementary education. Because these two people were fine examples of progressive, educated youth, and were also CCP party members, they got the recommendation.

Teacher Li went on with his speech. He said all the young people who had been recommended were those who had done well in the 'Going to the Countryside' initiative so they were all politically reliable. Therefore, Jili University should consider the educational level of the applicants when selecting students. The Physics Department needed to train students who were both socialist-minded and professionally competent. Several professors in the Physics Department were nationally known scientists. If students were undereducated, they would have difficulty in learning. Then he picked up Zhang Feng's application and said,

"Although this applicant has an unacceptable family background, he has good academic performance. He has been a champion of maths and physics competitions for many years and his academic performance has always been the highest in the year. He was the president of the school's student union. As students can be educated politically, as long as they perform well, we should encourage and train them."

Several leaders of the commune nodded in agreement after listening to his speech but the expression of Director Xie became more and more gloomy. He cleared his throat and said,

"I want to remind you folks not to go back to the old days of bourgeois education of the last 17 years before the Cultural Revolution. People like Zhang Feng are typical of the white special roader of the past. No matter how good his academic performance has been, as long as he does not support the revolutionary line of the proletariat, or is opposed and hostile to the the Cultural Revolution, he is not the right person to be trained by our new university. You may not know, Zhang Feng was once sentenced to death for his involvement in an anti-revolutionary group. He was treated with leniency later because of his sincere confession. Still, he is a reactionary student."

The words of Director Xie surprised everyone present. Apparently, he had already made a detailed investigation of Zhang Feng's background. Teacher Li was also surprised. It seemed that Director Xie had specifically come to prevent Zhang Feng from going to university. But Teacher Li didn't want to give up on Zhang Feng – such an excellent student. Fortunately, he had learned about Zhang Feng's experience in the Cultural Revolution from Principal Chang.

"What Director Xie said may be different from the truth. As far as I know, Zhang Feng was sentenced for being framed. His ideological problems are just his views on some of the chaos in the Cultural Revolution."

Director Xie replied immediately,

"That is not a generally recognised problem. I read his personal file in the county, which contained ten charges of attacking the socialist system and the Cultural Revolution."

Teacher Li didn't know how to answer him for a moment. These crimes had been exaggerated, or even fabricated, by Cai Wenge and secretly inserted into Zhang Feng's personal file. Most people inside and outside the school didn't know it.

Director Xie said complacently,

"More than that, according to my investigation, Zhang Feng's performance is also not so good after coming to the countryside."

Then he spoke to a deputy director of the commune sitting in the corner (a relative of Lieutenant Wang).

"Tell us what you know, Director Zou."

"Zhang Feng had many problems during his settlement in the countryside, according to the report of the masses. He sang obscene songs and read obscene books. He stole chickens from the villagers. What is more serious is that he still has a behaviour problem with women. He seduced local young women and was a very bad influence."

Teacher Li did not believe that Zhang Feng had done these things so he asked,

"Have you investigated these reports?"

"There has been no investigation," said Director Zou. "I have heard these things from the masses."

Teacher Li said,

"We should be responsible for the future of our young people. We cannot easily draw conclusions without investigation and verification. I suggest the commune makes a survey of Zhang

Feng's performance before the next meeting and then draws a conclusion."

Director Xie snorted disdainfully and agreed.

"Zhang Feng can be disqualified from admission as long as his family background is unacceptable."

He had been sent by Cai Wenge to prevent Zhang Feng from being admitted to the university. Yu Mei was so naive. A fox may turn grey but never kind. How could it be possible for Cai Wenge to allow Zhang Feng to gain access to the upper class by going to university? Yu Mei's behaviour had actually been more of a hindrance than a help.

A week later, the admissions office of the commune met again to decide on the candidate for admission. Teacher Li had given up hope of recruiting Zhang Feng. He had received a phone call from the director of the university's admissions office a few days ago. The director warned him over the phone that he must strictly follow the principles of political suitability first. Applicants with unsuitable political conditions could not be admitted, no matter how good their academic performance was. It was obvious that Director Xie had contacted the leaders of Jili University. He wanted the university to put pressure on Teacher Li. Teacher Li knew that, even if he accepted Zhang Feng, the university would disqualify him.

Even so, Teacher Li insisted on listening to the results of the investigation into Zhang Feng's behaviour which would have a great impact on Zhang Feng's future. Fortunately, the leaders sent to investigate were more impartial. The result of the investigation was that the rumour about Zhang Feng was completely untrue, especially the problem of his behaviour with women. The rumour-monger had said that Zhang Feng and He Hua had had intimate contact because Zhang Feng couldn't release his hands to wipe the sweat away when tying the cornstalks so He Hua had wiped away the sweat for him. Apparently, these rumours were started by Lieutenant Wang.

As a result of Director Xie's persistence, one of the two students admitted to the university was a junior high school graduate; the other had only graduated from primary school. They were admitted because they were from red families and were party members of the CCP. At the same time, they were also active in learning the 'Selected Works of Mao Zedong'.

Back at the hostel, Teacher Li's mind was weighed down with anxiety. Universities rejected excellent high school students liked Zhang Feng, preferring to recruit people with extremely low educational levels. Could such universities produce useful talents for the country? It may be that the rulers believed that it was easier to rule a compliant fool than an excellent talent. Would there be any hope for the country if it continued like this? It was destroying China.

Knowing that he had not been admitted, Zhang Feng was disappointed even though he was mentally prepared. He knew he was the child of a Five Black Categories family so he had little chance of going to university. It seemed that neither Principal Chang nor Yu Mei had found the people who could help. Zhang Feng, who had been healthy and strong, fell ill because of the anxiety. His friends were all concerned about him and came to see him, one after another. Dan Dan asked the production team for leave and took care of Zhang Feng for several days. He Hua came to see him every day. She even killed her own chicken to make braised chicken soup for him. They sat together to comfort him and they felt the unfairness.

"Don't worry, there will be opportunities in the future," Li He said.

He Hua said indignantly,

"What kind of world is this? They don't choose talent like Brother Zhang, but choose those fools. It's virtually a waste of the country's money."

"You can't just expect to go to university," said Dan Dan. "Don't ignore the opportunity with the recruiting of workers. As long as you can get out of this obscure village, you will not only improve your living conditions, but also have better conditions for self-study."

A few weeks later, Yu Mei received a letter from Zhang Feng and knowing that he had not been able to enrol, she felt very sad. However, he comforted Yu Mei, saying that it did not matter and he would continue to look for opportunities in the future. Yu Mei felt very disappointed. It seemed that Cai Wenge had not helped her. Maybe he had never wanted to help her at all.

Yu Mei went to the office of the Provincial Party Committee to find Cai Wenge and asked him, angrily, why he had not admitted Zhang Feng. Cai Wenge seized the chance and took Yu Mei to a high-end restaurant and ordered expensive seafood and famous wine. He said that he had been busy with his work recently and hadn't been able to tell Yu Mei about the recruitment.

"The man I sent did his best," he said, pretending to look sorrowful as he gave Yu Mei food with chopsticks. "But the leaders of the counties and communes insisted that political conditions come first. Many of their applicants are party members, role models of educated youth and activists, learning the 'Selected Works of Mao Zedong'. Zhang Feng's family background is unacceptable. He made mistakes during the Cultural Revolution… and, he has other problems."

Having said that, he stopped. Yu Mei asked him to explain what he had said. When Yu Mei asked him again, he told her about the theft of the chickens, singing obscene songs and reading obscene books. Seeing that Yu Mei didn't care too much about these, Cai Wenge said rudely,

"The worst thing is that he also has a problem with women. The masses said he was having an affair with a beautiful female leader."

Hearing this, Yu Mei stood up suddenly.

"Impossible! Zhang Feng is not a man like that."

Cai Wenge also stood up and took Yu Mei's hand to make her sit down. He readily seized the chance to touch her smooth and white delicate hands.

"Don't be angry! Don't be angry!"

He pretended to comfort Yu Mei. "I can understand him. A man likes to be surrounded by women, especially men as handsome as he is. You may not know it yet. In the past, almost all the girls in our school openly pursued or secretly loved him."

Yu Mei sat down in a disturbed mood and whispered,

"It must be all rumours and speculation."

Cai Wenge also whispered,

"It's not a rumour. Someone saw that they were hugging in the corn fields… and kissing. He also… "

With that, Cai Wenge glanced over at Yu Mei's chest.

"He also touched the woman's breasts with one of his hands and put the other hand into her pants… "

"Enough! Don't go on!" Yu Mei's face was red with anger. She got up and ran out of the restaurant.

'What a silly woman – so easily deceived,' Cai Wenge thought triumphantly while eating his seafood. 'I am really killing two birds with one stone. Not only have I alienated them but also, I have enjoyed sexually fantasising about her.'

Yu Mei couldn't concentrate on her studies for days after going back to university. Lying in bed at night, her mind was filled with images of Zhang Feng cuddling with the village girl. Although she was dubious about what Cai Wenge had said, she worried that a long-time separation could create problems. She had often heard that husbands and wives who were living apart from each other, had extramarital affairs and she knew about Zhang Feng's attraction to young girls. Yu Mei had not written to Zhang Feng for several months. She wanted to know if Zhang Feng was still sentimentally attached to her. Zhang Feng thought Yu Mei was too busy studying and didn't take it too seriously.

A year went by in a flash and it was 1974. One day in the winter of that year, Zhang Feng walked back to his collective household in the commune with more than one foot of snow under his feet. His mind was weighed down with anxiety. By going to university, being recruited as workers and joining the army, more than half of the educated youths in his and the surrounding collective households had left the countryside but people with unacceptable family backgrounds, like him, were rejected, time and time again. Li He went to the provincial Institute of Traditional Chinese Medicine. Xiao Hong and Xiao Fang returned to the city, recruited as workers. Dan Dan would soon be working as a salesclerk in the supply and marketing co-operatives of Shijing County nearby. Although Dan Dan's family background was unacceptable, the commune approved her application because no other student wanted to work as a county salesclerk.

In his letter to Zhang Feng, Wang Hai told him again and again that he should not be so dull and should give gifts to local officials. Many people did that now or they would stay in obscure villages forever.

This time, the provincial chemical factory in Shijing County wanted to recruit a dozen workers. Although the chemical factory was located in a remote valley, it was a large factory. The workers in the factory had a salary, stayed in dormitories and had home leave. It was much better than the conditions in the countryside. Besides, the chemical factory was not far from the county where Dan Dan was located. So many students, who were still in the countryside, wanted to be recruited.

This time, Zhang Feng did not want to just stay in the collective household, waiting. He asked others to buy high-class cigarettes and wine in the city, then he gave these as gifts to the secretary of the production brigade. He also gave a bolt of cloth to an official of the commune who was a relative of He Hua. He had just returned when he heard from the man that this time, more than a hundred students had applied to work in the chemical factory and the competition was fierce. Zhang Feng was still worried that he might not be able to leave the countryside this time.

It was getting dark when he came to the fork in the road towards the first production brigade. Zhang Feng suddenly saw a figure, shaking in the woods on the hillside beside the road. He felt very weird because nobody would be gathering firewood at this time. Had someone lost their way? Zhang Feng was a warm-hearted man and he walked over, hurriedly, but there was no one to be found. He heard the sound of sighing and crying as he was looking around. He walked in that direction at once.

As he approached a large tree, he was stunned by what he saw: a woman was hanging from the branch of the tree, her legs still kicking hard in the air. She was going to kill herself! Zhang Feng ran over before he could think of anything. It was incumbent on him to save her life. He hugged the woman from behind, and, with one hand, quickly untied the rope around her neck. Zhang Feng put her on the ground. She was gasping for breath.

It was several minutes before she struggled to sit up from the snowy ground. Zhang Feng could not see her face clearly before because of her cotton hat and untidy hair but when she took off her hat and brushed her tangled hair and opened her eyes to look at Zhang Feng, she and Zhang Feng both exclaimed,

"It's you!"

The woman who wanted to commit suicide turned out to be Qing Lian. Zhang Feng took two steps back in surprise: the woman he most disliked and who was once the most active Red Guard in the Cultural Revolution. She had flogged her teacher, accused her parents, been involved in the violent civil strife and went to the countryside without hesitation. This crazy woman, who had sown hatred and destroyed society, was unexpectedly, prepared to end her own life.

"Why did you save me? Let me die!" Qing Lian shouted at Zhang Feng, "I believe it would make you happy to watch me die."

Then she stood up unsteadily and walked to the branch where she had been hanging.

Suddenly, she turned to Zhang Feng and said,

"I know you hate me but I still want to ask you to do something for me. Please bury me under this big tree after I die."

Then she began to hang the rope on the branch.

'The division and destruction of our society since the Cultural Revolution was caused by political maniacs like her', Zhang Feng thought. 'To remove a person like her would reduce the damage to society.'

The memory of her flogging him during the purifying of the class ranks came back to Zhang Feng's mind. Thinking of this, Zhang Feng prepared to walk away but after a few steps, he remembered that his father had told him to treat others with Confucian kindness. His martial arts master, the Taoist Priest, Hai Jing, had also taught him that one of the Taoist principles was compassion. He looked back at Qing Lian, who was trying to put the rope around her neck and thought to himself, 'Anyway, this is a young and fresh life.' Thinking of this, he ran quickly back to Qing Lian. He released her once again and made her sit on a stump. She burst into tears and beat Zhang Feng's chest with her fists. She said,

"Why are you so nosy? It's hard for me to carry on living. I never thought it would be so hard to die."

Zhang Feng held her shoulder to calm her down and asked her in a soft voice,

"Why do you want to commit suicide? Are you in any trouble? You are red and upstanding and also, a model example of educated youth. Whether you stay in the countryside or want to return to the city, it should all be easy."

Qing Lian looked at Zhang Feng with a brooding eye and then lowered her head without speaking. She began to speak after Zhang Feng's repeated persuasion,

"You all think it was roses all on my way, in fact, I was feeling miserable every day." Then she slowly explained the reasons for her attempted suicide.

Qing Lian became a model of educated youth who was prepared to settle in the countryside. That was to say, she planned to stay in the countryside all her life. Usually, such an educated youth would marry a local villager so the leader of her production team wanted her to marry his son. As Qing Lian did not want to, the leader began to persecute her in revenge. Later, by relying on the commune officials, Cai Wenge re-established Qing Lian as the benchmark but later, Qing Lian thought that the students had nothing meaningful to do in the countryside. Moreover, her physical condition was getting worse due to the heavy work. She began to regret what she had said about setting down roots in the countryside.

As students had begun to return to the city by going to university or into factories, Qing Lian wanted to do the same but the leaders of the team, or the brigade, refused to let her leave the countryside. Their reason was that she was the model student who was prepared to settle in the countryside. Qing Lian only understood their evil purpose later.

The leader always behaved lewdly when he saw her. Head Zhang of the brigade seemed to be unsophisticated, but every time Qing Lian went to him about personal affairs, he always hinted that he wanted to be repaid by her. There was nothing else that Qing Lian could do but to give him gifts but he still refused her request.

This time, Qing Lian heard that the chemical factory was recruiting workers and she had to reluctantly go and ask for Head Zhang's help. When his wife went to her parents' home, Head Zhang asked Qing Lian to talk to him in his house. He also said that he could offer help with the recruitment but Qing Lian had to repay him. Qing Lian took out the cigarettes and wine immediately but Head Zhang said that she needed to repay him in some other way. With that, he looked at her breasts obscenely.

"The way a woman repays a man is simple: just have sex with him," he said. Then he hugged Qing Lian and kissed her and fondled her body as well. Qing Lian was so angry that she slapped him and ran out.

She heard Head Zhang say bitterly,

"You will never leave the countryside without having sex with me."

Returning to her collective household, Qing Lian collapsed on the bed in despair. She felt nothing but hopelessness. No family, no friends, no way out. She thought she had devoted everything to the revolutionary line of Chairman Mao but in the end, she was a victim of abandonment. What was the point of being alive? So she had decided to end her life…

After listening to Qing Lian's story, from a rational point of view, Zhang Feng thought that she had suffered as a result of her own actions. On a human level, he began to sympathize with this pitiful, feminine girl, even if she used to be a revolutionary maniac so he persuaded Qing Lian to give up the idea of suicide because she was still so young and had a long life ahead of her. She needed to have the courage to face adversity.

Qing Lian sighed and said,

"I also think I should be a bit stronger but I have no other way to leave this dangerous place."

Seeing that it was getting dark and snowing at the same time, Zhang Feng said,

"I suggest you come to our house for tonight. There are two other girls in our house. You can sleep with them. Wait until tomorrow and we'll figure it out together."

Qing Lian, who had escaped death, was so weak that she could hardly walk. Zhang Feng helped her waddle through the snow and walked her back to the collective household.

Zhang Feng didn't sleep well all night. He had been thinking about how to help Qing Lian. He knew that if Qing Lian could not leave the countryside, she would try to commit suicide again.

The next morning, Zhang Feng got up quietly while Qing Lian and the others were still sleeping. He took the 'Tianjin' watch, which his parents had just bought for him, and went to the administrative department of the production brigade. Walking to the front of Head Zhang's house, he looked around and picked up a thick stick in the yard. He knocked on the door. Head Zhang opened it with eyes fogged by sleep. He was stunned when he saw Zhang Feng, then, seeing the stick that Zhang Feng was holding, he was scared and took a few steps back immediately.

He stammered,

"What…what are you going to do? The production brigade has approved your application. I did not object this time."

Zhang Feng looked fierce and said,

"I'm not talking about my affairs. It's about Liu Qing Lian of the second team. What did you do to her that forced her to attempt suicide?"

Hearing Zhang Feng's words, Head Zhang was startled and then hesitated, saying,

"I… I didn't do anything. Why should you care about her?"

"She is my girlfriend now and I have to care about her," Zhang Feng said.

Head Zhang had heard that Zhang Feng knew powerful kung fu so he was sweating with fear.

Zhang Feng said to him,

"Now you have two choices: one is to let me punch you. Then I go to the commune to report that you wanted to rape a female educated youth. The government strictly punishes those who persecute students. Xinjiang Production and Construction Corps have already executed several heads and captains. The second option is that you take this 'Tianjin' watch as a gift and give her a job quota at the chemical factory. Now, make your own choice."

With that, Zhang Feng put one end of the stick on the cooking hearth and then used his palm as an axe. With a snap, he cut the thick stick into two parts.

With a shudder, Head Zhang quickly said,

"OK, OK, I have one last application form. Give it to Liu Qing Lian. I don't want your watch either."

Zhang Feng took the form and left the watch on the hearth before he left. Head Zhang collapsed on the ground immediately.

Back at the collective household, Zhang Feng watched as other people went out; only Qing Lian was left sitting at the side of the cooking hearth, alone. Seeing Zhang Feng had returned, she looked at him sadly,

"You are back."

Zhang Feng called her to the back room. He gave the form to Qing Lian and said,

"This is the application form for the chemical factory. You need to fill it out quickly and take it to the administrative department of the brigade to stamp it and then just send it to the educated youth office of the commune. Well, cheer up! You'll have a new life soon!"

Qing Lian took the form and looked over it skeptically. She suddenly knelt down to Zhang Feng and said, with tears streaming down her face,

"Thank you, Zhang Feng. You not only saved my life, but also saved me from suffering. I used to treat you so maliciously but you repay good for evil and forgive the evil I have done to you. You are the embodiment of great love. I've been thinking a lot these days. I used to believe that I was a real revolutionary and was fighting with the class enemies bravely. But what have I done? I persecuted good people, destroyed precious, traditional culture, sowed hatred, destroyed society and betrayed friends and family. In the end, I myself became a victim of the movement. I'm so regretful. I apologize to you and to everyone I've hurt."

Zhang Feng helped her up and said,

"I'm glad you have admitted your mistakes. Remember, love is the cement of a harmonious society. Hatred is the poison that divides and destroys society. Our society will be happy and harmonious if all of us can spread some love."

Two weeks later, a carriage carrying Zhang Feng, Dan Dan and Qing Lian left the village where they had worked and lived for five years and took them to the chemical factory and the supply and marketing co-operatives in Shijing County to start their new lives.

The day before leaving, He Hua said goodbye to Zhang Feng with tears in her eyes. Shyly, she handed Zhang Feng a pair of her own, handmade cloth shoes and a pair of cotton gloves. Zhang Feng knew that this beautiful and kind country girl loved him but he did not want to hurt her, so he received the shoes and gloves. He also encouraged He Hua to keep studying. He told her the countryside would improve in the future with proper policies. He Hua wrote down Zhang Feng's address at the chemical factory and said she would write to him as well as visit him when she got a chance.

CHAPTER III

Life in the Chemical Factory

After their separation from Dan Dan in Shijing County, Zhang Feng and Qing Lian took a bus and drove along the bumpy road for an hour and a half to the Shijing Ravine United Chemical Factory which was surrounded by mountains. The distant towering chimneys puffed different coloured smoke. Huge pipelines surrounded the plant. This was a chemical factory with over a thousand workers, producing many different chemical products. One was polyformaldehyde, an engineering plastic that could be used in the military. As a result, this chemical factory was highly valued at that time.

Outside the production area was the living area, where there were houses for workers' families, dormitories for single workers, the staff dining hall and the auditorium where films could be shown. It also had a public bathhouse, canteen, restaurants and so on. The living conditions and cultural life here were much better than in the countryside. The two-storey dormitory had heating and toilets. It was both comfortable and convenient. Each room had bunk beds for eight people to live. Male workers lived downstairs and female workers upstairs.

Zhang Feng and Qing Lian were very excited in the first few weeks. Living conditions had improved. They had salaries, weekends and family leave. Zhang Feng had more time to read and study on his own in addition to working eight hours a day. Zhang Feng also got to know a group of young music enthusiasts. They would gather together to play and sing.

When they were assigned to work in the workshop after three weeks of training, they realized that the working conditions in the factory were very hard. Zhang Feng also perceived that, due to the influence of the Cultural Revolution, the factory put class struggle first and production, second.

Both he and Qing Lian were assigned to work as operators in the most important polyformaldehyde workshop. Zhang Feng felt some pressure because the products were related to military uses and the operators were generally required to have good family and political backgrounds. Moreover, there was a strong atmosphere of class struggle here. It was said that there had been an accident a few years ago which resulted in a criminal sentence for the worker on duty. He was convicted of deliberately sabotaging military production.

Qing Lian said to Zhang Feng,

"Don't worry, just be careful. I'll help you if you need anything."

Their eyes stung and produced tears with the strong, pungent chemical gas when they first entered the workshop.

"It's the smell of formalin, the raw material we use," said Chen Hao, the director of the workshop who led the group of new workers. "You can't stand it when you first come here but you'll get used to it soon."

Zhang Feng was startled to hear that. He knew that formalin was a chemical liquid used to keep bodies from rotting. It must be harmful to the health of humans. They saw some workers wearing gas masks when visiting the workshop.

"Sometimes, chemical materials leak out and you need to wear gas masks to protect yourself," Director Chen said.

When they got to the operational stage of polymerization, Director Chen walked up to a worker in his 40s with a slight figure and then said to him,

"Master Wang, here are two apprentices for you."

Then he introduced Zhang Feng and Qing Lian to him, and said,

"They are both high school students, well-educated and quick to learn. Please teach them well."

Zhang Feng was startled again to hear that because he had heard that the operating stage of polymerization was the most important in the whole workshop. The man who had been sentenced for the production accident worked at the operating stage of polymerization. However, Zhang Feng had to comply as he was a newcomer. Zhang Feng had to stay here and learn the operation procedure from Master Wang.

Since the production of polyoxymethylene was uninterrupted for 24 hours, the workers worked round the clock in three shifts. Zhang Feng learned from Master Wang, the production team leader. Qing Lian learned from Master Jia, the deputy team leader. They worked between morning shift, afternoon shift or night shift every week and had a day off on Sunday. After a time,

Zhang Feng thought the morning shift and the afternoon shift were bearable but he was uncomfortable with the night shift. The main reason was that during the day, the dormitory was too noisy to sleep well. He didn't dare take a nap on the night shift for fear of a production accident.

Zhang Feng was so clever that he learned quickly about operational techniques. Soon, he was able to operate independently. Master Wang was an unsophisticated old worker who was very kind to Zhang Feng. He often invited Zhang Feng to his home for dinner. This made Zhang Feng feel very warm.

Qing Lian had taken good care of Zhang Feng since coming to the factory. She often came to help him with his washing and quilting. She worked on Zhang Feng's next shift. She always brought food for him every time she was on the shift, like boiled eggs, stewed chicken and even dumplings she had made herself. Although everyone's staple foods, edible oil and non-staple foods were limited at that time, the food in the factory was still much better than in the countryside because the factory was surrounded by agricultural communes. Peasants often sold their own poultry and eggs at the small street market in the factory. Zhang Feng and the others used to buy eggs with food coupons. Seeing that Zhang Feng was sometimes choked by the chemical gases in the workshop, Qing Lian gave him a handkerchief, embroidered with lotus, to wipe away his tears. Zhang Feng wanted to refuse because he already had two handkerchiefs given to him by Yu Mei and Dan Dan but he found it difficult to say no because he knew that Qing Lian's care for him was sincere.

Qing Lian's care of Zhang Feng soon attracted the attention of people around them. Many young workers asked Zhang Feng if Qing Lian was his girlfriend. Even Master Wang and Master

Jia asked him the same question. Zhang Feng had to explain that they had a good relationship because they were classmates and had been in the same place in the countryside but their relationship was not that of boyfriend and girlfriend.

Qing Lian had been in a better mood ever since she came to the factory. With good nutrition, her face had returned to the ruddy complexion of the past; her body had become plumper and her hair had become more black and shiny. More importantly, her personality seemed to have changed completely. She became gentle, kind and helpful; not the crazy and murderous Red Guard she used to be.

One day, when she came to help Zhang Feng wash clothes in his dormitory, he suddenly found that she was wearing a blue working suit, just allocated, with two braids tied into a knot behind her head, making her look slim and graceful. Along with her pink face, she looked like a lotus flower blooming in the water, just like her name. Zhang Feng wanted to say,

"You are so beautiful."

But he suddenly remembered that Qing Lian had written him a love letter at school. As his heart had been belonged to Yu Mei, he didn't want Qing Lian to misunderstand his intentions. So he said,

"You look smart in your new suit."

A shy blush flickered across Qing Lian's face. Zhang Feng remembered that he should clarify the relationship between them, in order to avoid misunderstandings in the future so he said, seriously,

"Qing Lian, thank you for taking care of me all this time but don't waste too much of your time. I know you want to thank me for saving you and helping you get out of the countryside but I helped others without expecting anything in return. Dan

Dan will help me with housework like quilting when she comes to visit me."

Qing Lian understood the meaning of Zhang Feng's words. She blushed and said,

"Zhang Feng, you may have misunderstood me. I just want to repay your kindness. I have no other intentions. I know your heart belongs to Li Yu Mei and Dan Dan. You are a man dedicated to love. I know I am not worthy to love you and I will never love anyone else in my life. I want to be your maid. To serve you is to redeem my sin and it is also my greatest joy."

Then she ran out with tears in her eyes. Zhang Feng felt he was in an awkward position but one thing made him wonder…

He had joined the factory's basketball team recently and had become the lead player. His tall figure and handsome appearance attracted the admiration of the young girls. They kept cheering him on. Of course, Qing Lian would come to cheer for Zhang Feng every time. However, when she saw the girls all cheering enthusiastically for Zhang Feng, she would ignore him for a few days. 'Was she jealous?' Zhang Feng thought. Her explanation may not have been exactly what she meant.

A few months after coming to the polyformaldehyde workshop, Zhang Feng had become a popular man among the young workers. He was responsible for writing the blackboard newspaper, organizing the art performances and participating in the sports competitions. Director Chen, Secretary Wang, the workers and several technicians who had graduated from the university all liked him.

Only a committee member of the branch, Mao Hongxin, always looked at him with sombre eyes. Qing Lian told Zhang Feng that she had heard other workers say that this man was a former member of the Rebel Faction. He was not interested in production but was preoccupied with class struggle and interested in framing others. Qing Lian asked Zhang Feng to pay careful attention to this man.

On the eve of National Day on October 1st, the factory asked the workshop to improve the output and the quality of the product, in order to present it as their gift for National Day. But somehow, there were three consecutive 'clear soup' accidents (that is, the process of aggregation failed and the polymer chain was not formed). These occurred during Zhang Feng's independent operation. This caused an uproar in the factory and in the workshop. The factory sent an investigation team to the workshop. At the meeting to analyze the accident, Zhang Feng said he had worked completely in accordance with the operational specifications so he could not understand the cause of the accident.

Then, Mao Hongxin said,

"I'm afraid this is not a simple accident. The class enemies are now running wild and trying to undermine our military production. I suggest that this incident should be investigated as if someone was deliberately sabotaging production."

Although Director Chen and Master Wang both believed that this was a production accident, not damage caused by class enemies, the investigation team from the factory still demanded that Zhang Feng's work should be suspended until the incident was cleared up.

After Zhang Feng had left the meeting, Mao Hongxin told everyone about his family background and political problems. He said such people should not be allowed to work in important positions.

Zhang Feng didn't expect the situation to get worse. The next morning, two people from the security department of the factory came and placed Zhang Feng in temporary confinement. Zhang Feng felt nervous. He wondered if he would be sentenced for sabotage as a counter-revolutionary; the man who'd had an accident in the past was sentenced because of his unacceptable family background.

Qing Lian was also very nervous. She was constantly meeting with the leaders of the workshop and factory. She told them that although Zhang Feng was from an unacceptable family, he had a very good political background and he would never do anything to undermine production. Moreover, she took responsibility for the accident herself. She said that the sample she handed to Zhang Feng during her shift had been mixed with moisture because of her mistake during sampling which led to inaccurate test results. Finally, this had caused Zhang Feng to make a mistake in calculating the amount of catalyst needed. Director Chen and several technicians had investigated Qing Lian's words and believed that her explanation was reasonable.

Because Qing Lian's family background was good and she was also a party member, she was only punished with a delay of half a year before becoming a formal worker. The factory had planned to let her serve as deputy secretary of the youth league committee; this was cancelled because of the accident. Mao Hongxin refused to accept this. He felt that Qing Lian was protecting Zhang Feng deliberately. She had taken responsibility. Others, in favour of Zhang Feng, agreed with the punishment because this was the best way to save Zhang Feng.

Two days later, Director Chen arrived at the department to release Zhang Feng and told him that the incident had been resolved. He said it had been Qing Lian's fault that caused the accident. Zhang Feng knew immediately that it was Qing Lian who had saved him.

On Sunday, Zhang Feng invited Qing Lian to dinner in the county town in order to thank her for rescuing him.

"Don't forget you are my saviour," said Qing Lian. "I'm glad that I could do something to help you. What's so great about being the deputy secretary of the youth league committee anyway?"

Zhang Feng agreed to Qing Lian's request after dinner to go shopping together. As they walked side by side, many young people, especially young girls, looked at them with envy. Qing Lian felt extremely happy though she knew Zhang Feng was not her boyfriend. She would be satisfied if she could see him every day and do things for him. What's more, she could spend time with him, like a real couple.

Qing Lian's dreamlike happiness was suddenly interrupted by Zhang Feng's words. He said he was going to visit Dan Dan to see how she was and if she had encountered any difficulties. Qing Lian came to her senses. She knew her place in Zhang Feng's affections was still far behind Yu Mei and Dan Dan. She sighed in her heart and said, sensibly,

"Then I won't go."

Zhang Feng was now always nervous at work in his operational post since the 'accident' for fear of another 'accident'. His nervous tension increased with each operation. Whenever the pressure meter of the polymerization reactor was raised, he was so nervous that he felt his heart actually beating in his throat. He was afraid that the rising pressure would cause an explosion. Gasoline was used as the solvent in producing polyformaldehyde so there was often a leak of gasoline at the operating stage. Any careless operation of gasoline might cause an explosion. This also made Zhang Feng nervous.

Once, an iron plate caused a spark when it fell onto the the work table which terrified Zhang Feng. Sometimes, the chemical gas leakage would occur in the workshop and people could not breathe. Even wearing a gas mask didn't help; the workers had to run to the roof. Zhang Feng was often holding his breath as he ran up the stairs to the roof where he would lie down, breathing heavily. It would take him a long time to calm down.

The hardest part was not the leak of gasoline. When the polymer dried in clumps, the workers had to take a gas mask into the reactor and use tools to break up the clumps. The one who went into the reactor would be burning and itchy within minutes because there was still gasoline left in the reactor. The workers could only hold out for ten minutes at most. It was said that this would cause infertility in young men and women but Zhang Feng always held out for fifteen minutes at a time. He wanted the other workers to suffer less.

Sometimes, Zhang Feng would sit on the roof of his workshop when spring was coming and look at the green mountains in the distance. He began to miss being in the countryside. Although the life there was hard, you could still breathe the fresh air. There were no chemical gases harmful to health. There was also less political pressure. But at the chemical factory, Zhang Feng was always terrified of being called a counter-revolutionary.

Of course, there was some joy in the pain. One day, Zhang Feng saw a woman who looked like a technician when he was passing another workshop. She was slim and pretty and looked familiar to Zhang Feng. The woman also stopped to look at Zhang Feng. Suddenly, they recognized each other at the same time. She was Li Li, the girlfriend of Xu Jianguo before his death. She still treated Zhang Feng as her little brother and after recognizing him, hugged him and started to cry. Apparently, it was Zhang Feng who reminded her of the painful past. Zhang Feng hurried to comfort her.

Li Li told Zhang Feng, after she calmed down, that she had been assigned to the chemical factory after graduating from the Polytechnic University because she had majored in chemical engineering. Recently, she had been transferred to the Shijing Ravine United Chemical Factory to work on a new product. She said she also lived in the single staff dormitory. She was so happy to meet Zhang Feng again and would now not feel lonely here. Zhang Feng wanted to ask her if she was married and had a family but he knew she was still single as soon as he heard she was living in the single staff dormitory. Maybe she could not forget Xu Jianguo and therefore, she could not think of other men. Although Li Li was nearly 30 years old, she still looked very young: 24 or 25. From then on, Zhang Feng had three women who would care for him.

On a Sunday, in the early summer month of May, Zhang Feng's dormitory was full of happiness and joy. Dan Dan came to the factory to visit Zhang Feng, bringing fresh pork mince and leeks. Li Li and Qing Lian also stopped by to help him with his sewing and washing.

"Let's make dumplings together," said Dan Dan.

She had met Li Li in Beijing during the revolutionary tours and had a good impression of her. Meanwhile, she knew that Li Li was three years older than Zhang Feng so she was not worried about their relationship. Qing Lian always paid attention to Li Li and Zhang Feng. Sometimes, Li Li would touch Zhang Feng's head or lean on his shoulder. These behaviours would make Qing Lian uncomfortable. Li Li suggested that everyone should go to the mountains near the factory to pick some herbs and come back to eat them with dumplings.

"The weather is so good," said Dan Dan, "how nice it will be to go out and climb the mountains, pick edible wild herbs and relieve our boredom."

Then the four of them, together with a young worker Xiao Sun who adored Zhang Feng, went up the mountain happily. Xiao Sun also brought an old-fashioned camera. He said he would take some pictures for the good-looking boys and girls. They were talking and laughing, picking herbs in the woods and enjoying the scenery.

By the top of the hill, the girls were out of breath and their red cheeks made them look even more pretty.

Xiao Sun said,

"Well, it's beautiful to look down from here. Let me take a picture of you."

Li Li pulled Zhang Feng over and said,

"Come on, the charming boy should stand in the centre."

She stood next to Zhang Feng. Dan Dan stood on his other side and Qing Lian consciously stood next to Dan Dan.

"Everyone should smile," Xiao Sun said as he operated the camera.

Everyone posed in a relaxed manner because they were in such a pleasant and cheerful mood. Li Li and Dan Dan leaned on Zhang Feng's shoulders. Qing Lian smiled and waved at the lens. Xiao Sun took several pictures in succession.

"I'll give one to each of you when the picture is developed."

Li Li said,

"I want two, I will pay you."

Dan Dan and Qing Lian also said they wanted two pictures. Zhang Feng suddenly felt sad while looking at these three, pretty, young girls because Yu Mei – his favourite fairy girl – wasn't there. The number of times Yu Mei had written to him had become less and less. As Zhang Feng's chances of going to university had slipped away, the difference in social status between him and Yu Mei had grown larger and larger. Zhang Feng began to worry that, one day, he would lose her. He just didn't expect the day to come so soon.

CHAPTER IV

A Tear-Shedding Wedding

In the blink of an eye, another two years had passed and it was now 1976. Yu Mei was about to graduate. She spent every day in nervousness and anxiety. She did not worry about her future because Cai Wenge had already arranged everything for her but she worried about her marriage: she was almost 28 years old. However, she was in a dilemma about who she should choose: Zhang Feng or Cai Wenge. There was now no hope of Zhang Feng going to university nor of being transferred to Jili City. The household registration management in big cities was very strict.

Li Jianguo felt well sometimes but bad at others. His high level status temporarily gave him a job without power. The original rebel faction was in charge of personnel and household registration management and he couldn't use any personal connections. Moreover, Cai Wenge's political control was powerful and he wouldn't allow Zhang Feng to return to work in Jili City. Cai Wenge kept flattering Li Jianguo and Song Lihua so that they were less disgusted with him and he pursued Yu Mei relentlessly. He sent her flowers, invited her to dinner and gave her gifts continuously. Yu Mei disliked him so she just dealt with it in most cases. However, there was something different about him which did not disgust Yu Mei as much. She just regarded him as an ordinary man. Sometimes, Yu Mei even thought that he could help Zhang Feng change his destiny.

Yu Mei had once sought the advice of Xiao Fang, her confidante, and she had said that, emotionally speaking, women liked handsome men, not just because they were talented. However, Zhang Feng had a lower social status than Cai Wenge. In the long term, everything would be ok if the man's social status was higher than the woman's but if it was the other way around, the marriage would be unstable. For instance, if you were a government official and your husband was just a worker, you would feel ashamed, while he would feel more inferior. The blazing love between you would be extinguished gradually. Xiao Fang's words made Yu Mei even more upset.

At this time, Zhang Feng's parents had been transferred back to the city. Zhang Wenbo was one of the last elderly teachers transferred back to the city by the university because of his political problems. Zhang Feng and Zhang Lin felt very happy that they could visit their parents frequently after their return.

What made Zhang Feng even happier was that he could see Yu Mei again. He was very happy writing to Yu Mei to tell her that he would go to the normal university to see her when he visited his parents. Zhang Feng wanted to talk with Yu Mei because he had already realized that the relationship between them was in crisis. He told Yu Mei that he would see her in two weeks.

However, the date for his parents' return was suddenly advanced. Zhang Feng asked for the day off from the workshop and rushed to his parents' village to help them move. Zhang Lin also came back from the Changxia Textile Factory and brought Wang Hai's regards. It seemed that they often contacted each other. The university sent a big truck and Zhang Feng spent a whole night loading luggage and furniture onto the truck. He escorted the truck and drove back to Jili City while his parents and sister took the train back.

When he returned to the university, it was already Saturday. The university had arranged shabby, tube-shaped apartments for teachers who had come back from the countryside. These apartments had formerly been student dormitories. Every family had only one room and five or six families shared one kitchen. Zhang Feng's original home was occupied by support staff and workers who had not been sent to the countryside. Despite this, Zhang Feng was still very excited because they were back in the city. His parents and sisters soon arrived and he hurried to help them move in and then eagerly rushed to the other campus to see Yu Mei.

He found her dormitory at the address Yu Mei gave him. As he approached, he felt his heart pounding. Suddenly, he saw a small car parked outside which was a special car, only available for senior officials. Just as he was about to move forwards, the door of the dormitory opened and two people came out. One was a young woman with a slender figure, wearing a red sweater. Zhang Feng recognized Yu Mei at once; he missed her day and night. The other person was a middle-aged man in a tunic suit, holding a bouquet of flowers. Zhang Feng quickly hid behind the tree.

The man led Yu Mei to the car. Zhang Feng could only see his profile but he felt that this person was very familiar to him. However, when this person turned back and opened the door for Yu Mei, Zhang Feng was shocked to see Cai Wenge, his deadly enemy for many years. He couldn't imagine how the fairy Yu Mei could be with the evil Cai Wenge. Looking at the car driving away, Zhang Feng almost fell to the ground.

When he turned to go back home, his excited younger sister Zhang Lin and his parents were tidying up the room. Seeing Zhang Feng's unhappy face, Zhang Lin asked him whether he'd had a row with Yu Mei. Zhang Feng didn't want his family to worry about him because things were not clear so, in order to avoid his family's upset, he lied and said he just felt tired with the move.

On the train back to the factory, the scene of Yu Mei with Cai Wenge was continuously flashing through Zhang Feng's mind. Had Yu Mei really betrayed him? She so loved him that she would have died for him. Had she thrown herself into the arms of Cai Wenge, who once disgusted her, because he was only a worker now? Was it only because Cai Wenge was a senior official who had both power and authority now? But Yu Mei was not the kind of girl who disliked the poor and cherished the rich.

During the first few days following his return to the factory, everyone saw that Zhang Feng was preoccupied with troubles. Of course, Qing Lian and Li Li were the people who cared most about him. However, Zhang Feng didn't want to talk about Yu Mei with them.

As Zhang Feng couldn't stop thinking about it, he went to town and told Dan Dan everything one weekend. Dan Dan was a magnanimous girl. Although this message was good news for her, she still saw Zhang Feng's happiness as the most important thing. Dan Dan reasoned that Yu Mei hadn't given up Zhang Feng. Maybe, Yu Mei had become entangled with Cai Wenge. Yu Mei was in a dilemma now. Dan Dan suggested that Zhang Feng should write a letter to Yu Mei and explain that he was in a bad situation and needed to re-consider their relationship in order to test her.

Zhang Feng wrote the letter and said that he still loved her but right now, he was only a worker in another county and had an uncertain future while Yu Mei was going to graduate from university and would become a state official in the big city. The difference in social status was too great. He didn't want to be a burden to Yu Mei and didn't want her to be disappointed and to regret the second half of life. Thus, he would like to end their relationship. Before sending the letter, Zhang Feng wandered around outside the post office for ten minutes. He could feel his heart bleeding. The letter in his hand was just like a suicide bomb but his pride finally made him throw it into the post box.

After receiving the letter, Yu Mei cried all night. She thought the reason why Zhang Feng hadn't come to find her was that he wanted to break up with her but had felt too embarrassed to say it face to face. She also wondered whether Zhang Feng had heard something about the relationship between her and Cai Wenge but why hadn't Zhang Feng asked directly? Thinking of Zhang Feng's love for her and how he had disregarded many dangers, saving her several times, Yu Mei made a decision to stay with Zhang Feng even if he remained a worker all his life.

Yu Mei wrote three letters to Zhang Feng showing her unfailing love for him but nevertheless, Zhang Feng didn't reply. This disappointed Yu Mei. Li Jianguo and Song Lihua had noticed that Yu Mei was preoccupied with some troubles. One night, they sat together talking about Yu Mei's marriage.

Song Lihua said,

"Xiao Mei, you can't wait. You are 28 years old! If you don't marry, you will be an old maid. It seems that you will have to choose between Zhang Feng and Cai Wenge. What do you think?"

Yu Mei was confused and therefore, she had to tell her parents about what was happening.

Li Jianguo said,

"In my mind, I like Zhang Feng. He was endowed with both good looks and talent as well as integrity and kindness. He was trapped in this situation and we could not get him out. He was a gentleman and always considered others first. He wrote this 'Dear John' letter because he didn't want to delay you."

Song Lihua hesitated for a while and took out a photo, then said,

"Xiao Mei, I have heard that Zhang Feng already has a girlfriend in the factory. It is understandable. Zhang Feng is also almost 28 years old. A man needs a partner more than a woman. Look at this picture. There are quite a lot of girls around him."

Hearing this, Yu Mei was anxious and picked up the photo. She stared at the picture and her face gradually turned pale.

It turned out to be the picture of Zhang Feng, Dan Dan, Qing Lian and Li Li on the mountain. It was acquired by Cai Wenge through his indirect relationship with the factory. Cai Wenge was delighted and showed the picture to Li Jianguo and his wife immediately in order to make Yu Mei forget Zhang Feng forever.

Yu Mei whispered,

"It can't be the truth. This is faded. Alright, let me look again."

So saying, Yu Mei ran into her room with the picture. Lying on the bed, her heart was thumping. Yu Mei thought it looked like Dan Dan wanted to be more than Zhang Feng's sister but what could she do? After all, they were far away from each other. While the grass grows, the steed starves. How did Qing Lian get involved with Zhang Feng? Hadn't Zhang Feng bothered her most? Yu Mei didn't know the third woman who was so beautiful and mature looking. It seemed Yu Mei had no hope but she still couldn't believe in Zhang Feng's betrayal. It was sick society that had ruined their happiness.

Since the April Fifth Movement in May 1976, Deng Xiaoping had been overthrown by the Gang of Four again. As Premier Zhou Enlai died at the beginning of the year, Deng Xiaoping could rely on nobody. The faction supporting the Cultural Revolution was starting to revolt. The veteran cadres and officials who had been liberated for only a short time, just like Li Jianguo, were suffering. The rebel faction in the provincial revolutionary committee forced Li Jianguo to retire on the excuse of his poor health and the atmosphere in his family became tense.

Unexpectedly, instead of observing a clear distance from Li Jianguo, Cai Wenge still visited the family frequently. This made Song Lihua very grateful to him and she believed that Cai Wenge was a young man with a sense of justice. In fact, Cai's plan was to have Yu Mei. He couldn't hide his greed for the beauty of Yu Mei and couldn't wait to get her. Song Lihua persuaded Yu Mei to marry Cai Wenge quickly; since she couldn't marry Zhang Feng, Cai Wenge would be the best choice.

Cai Wenge had already been the director of culture and education, equivalent to the Bureau-Director level. As Cai Wenge was barely 30 years old, he belonged to the young officials. Young officials were promoted and selected by the leaders more quickly and therefore, Cai Wenge had boundless prospects. Besides, Li Jianguo had lost his position and was in poor health. The family needed political backing. Yu Mei's close friend, Xiao Fang, also persuaded Yu Mei to marry Cai Wenge. In her view, Cai was sincere in his love for Yu Mei.

Under the pursuit of Cai Wenge, Yu Mei agreed to marry him hesitantly and the wedding was arranged at the re-decorated Jili Hotel. The afternoon before the wedding, Cai Wenge asked Yu Mei to go to the luxurious provincial hotel and showed her the booked room. Cai Wenge said they would stay here for three days after the wedding and then he would take her to the south for the honeymoon. Yu Mei followed Cai Wenge absently. There was no sense of excitement in Yu Mei's heart. After looking at the room, Yu Mei said she wanted to return.

Cai Wenge said affably,

"Don't be so worried. I have already ordered a sumptuous dinner with sea cucumber, lobster and French red wine. These things are not available usually."

Soon after, the waiter brought many dishes which filled the entire table and Cai Wenge kept selecting the food for Yu Mei and persuading her to drink. Even the rare seafood that wasn't usually available tasted insipid in Yu Mei's mouth. Suddenly, Zhang Feng appeared in Yu Mei's mind. She was so uncomfortable that she drank too much and tried to numb herself.

In a little while, Yu Mei began to feel dizzy and blurry. Actually, even if she had drunk only a little wine, she would have become unconscious because Cai Wenge had drugged it. Cai couldn't wait to have Yu Mei and was worried that she might change her mind. She was so beautiful with her face flushed with red contrasting with her black hair and snow-white skin. Cai

Wenge drooled. He couldn't wait to lie Yu Mei on the bed and take off her clothes. Seeing Yu Mei's naked body, Cai Wenge was filled with lust and put her under his body.

Half-conscious, Yu Mei thought that it was Zhang Feng who embraced her and she clung to him and murmured,

"Brother Feng, you are here finally. Feng, Feng…"

Next morning, Yu Mei woke up very late. When she opened her eyes and found herself lying on the bed, she got up quickly.

"Why am I here? What happened?" she wondered.

She only remembered that Cai Wenge had brought her to look at the house last night. Noticing the pillow next to her had been slept on she cried,

"Oh no! Cai Wenge must have…"

She pushed back the covers and saw the blood stains on the mattress. Then she felt some pain in her private parts.

"It's over. I was raped by this man."

Yu Mei cried sorrowfully.

"He could not wait for the wedding. It seems that he was afraid that I would change my mind."

Yu Mei lay down despairingly, covered herself with the quilt and cried bitterly. In that era, a woman who had lost her virginity meant that no other man would want to marry her anymore. She could only follow Cai Wenge.

"Brother Feng, I am sorry. It is impossible."

Yu Mei thought sadly that she would spend her whole life with a man she did not like.

At noon of the next day, the bridal car drove up to Yu Mei's house. With her mother's persuasion, Yu Mei got ready. In her face, there was no joy. Yu Mei seemed to be numb. Li Jianguo was not enthusiastic about this marriage so he refused to attend the wedding with the excuse of poor health. Song Lihua went alone to the Jili Hotel by car. The car drove away from Yu Mei's home gradually.

Crossing Southbank Bridge, Yu Mei looked at the rolling river and the big poplar tree on the bank. She was heartbroken remembering the days spent there with Zhang Feng.

As the car drove into the centre of the city, suddenly, there were a lot of people on both sides not far from the Jili Hotel. Yu Mei asked Cai's secretary what had happened. The secretary said they might have been attracted by the flowers and the firecrackers which had been set off outside the hotel. Actually, the secretary hadn't told Yu Mei that people were wondering what the former secretary Li Jianguo's beautiful daughter looked like, knowing she would be getting married.

Suddenly, Yu Mei saw a tall man standing at the corner. She thought he was familiar. Was that him? Yu Mei thought: it's impossible. He was so far away from here. How could he be here? But when the car pulled up to the man, she saw his face clearly, like an electric shock. This young man was Zhang Feng, the lover she missed day and night.

"Stop!" roared Yu Mei. The driver didn't know what was happening. He stopped immediately. Yu Mei opened the door and rushed to Zhang Feng and wanted to throw herself into his arms but she saw he was staring at her coldly.

Yu Mei stopped.

"Wish you a happy wedding," Zhang Feng said, without emotion.

Several days before, Zhang Feng had received an anonymous letter that told him Yu Mei and Cai Wenge would get married today. Zhang Feng was familiar with the handwriting in the letter but he could not remember whose it was. He felt near to collapse. Yu Mei hadn't replied to his letter and this made

Zhang Feng uneasy. But Zhang Feng hadn't expected that things would develop so fast. It seemed that what he had seen when Cai Wenge picked up Yu Mei had just confirmed his suspicions. He wanted to forget Yu Mei, but at last, he had decided to have a look. Seeing Yu Mei crying with tears rolling down her face, Zhang Feng softened and asked,

"Do you really love him?"

Yu Mei shook her head.

"Why didn't you reply to my letter?" Zhang Feng asked. "Even if you have decided to break up with me, you should have at least told me."

"I wrote three letters to you because I didn't want to lose you but you didn't reply and besides, I heard that you already have a girlfriend. I have seen the picture of you and three of them so I despaired. My family persuaded me to marry. So I …"

Zhang Feng suddenly realized that Cai Wenge must have been playing tricks to separate him and Yu Mei. Seeing Cai Wenge's secretary coming from the car and walking towards him fiercely, Zhang Feng asked Yu Mei,

"Would you still like to be with me?"

Yu Mei nodded while crying and said,

"I do. I do."

She was about to rush into Zhang Feng's arms but stopped suddenly and cried bitterly,

"Brother Feng, I can't… it's too late. I am not…"

Yu Mei was struggling to tell the truth that she was no longer a virgin, when a cold voice rang out behind them.

"She is already my woman."

Zhang Feng and Yu Mei looked back and there stood Cai Wenge in a handsome groom's outfit. He said to Zhang Feng, bitterly,

"Zhang Feng, how dare you! How can you seduce a nearly married woman? In order not to delay my wedding, I will tell you clearly. It was me who intercepted Li Yumei's letters, took your photos and said that you already had a girlfriend. I wanted to make both of you forget each other forever. You were always more powerful than me and attracted great attention so I vowed that one day, I would take revenge. I will have everything. Fortunately, you are just a little worker, but I…I have everything including power, money and now, beauty. I want to tell you how easy it is to play with the little fairy. What will make you even sadder is that she still called your name during orgasm. However, she can only be your dream lover now. Ha ha ha!"

Yu Mei was in floods of tears and Zhang Feng clenched his fists angrily. He wanted to beat up Cai Wenge. His secretary and his followers came forward hurriedly. Cai Wenge said to Zhang Feng,

"If you are sensible, you should go quickly or I will call the police to arrest you."

After that, he said to his secretary and followers,

"Put her back in the car, the wedding will be held as scheduled."

Then he got into the car and drove away. Zhang Feng desperately slammed his fist against the big poplar tree on the side of the road and blood flowed out from between his fingers.

After he returned to the factory, Zhang Feng was seriously ill. All his friends were anxious to see him and someone also brought him the ancestral secret recipes of Chinese medicine. Zhang Feng did not tell them why he was sick. Qing Lian and Li Li could tell that he might be suffering from a disappointment in love, but it was hard for them to ask him directly. Only Dan Dan knew the truth.

Dan Dan came to see him one day when there was no one else in the dormitory. Zhang Feng told her all about the wedding. At the sight of him sobbing, Dan Dan also cried. Zhang Feng was so sad that he couldn't sit still. Dan Dan held him in her arms to comfort him and said,

"Xiao Feng, you must let it go and be rational. In fact, this unhappy ending was inevitable. She is from a high-ranking official's family and grew up in favourable conditions. Although your father is a senior intellectual, his social status is equal to a civilian's because he was labelled as a rightist. If there had been no Cultural Revolution, you would also have been in the upper class through your own talent and hard work. However, this disastrous political movement has made us forever second-class citizens and we can only struggle at the bottom of society. Even if you and Yu Mei had been able to live together, the difference in social status would have led your marriage gradually to the brink of breaking."

After hearing Dan Dan's words, Zhang Feng wiped his tears and sat up. He thought for a moment in silence. Then, he said to Dan Dan,

"Well, it seems that we have no chance. Dan Dan, I am a little hungry."

Dan Dan knew that he had not eaten for several days. She was just about to go to the restaurant to buy something for him to eat when Qing Lian brought over the braised pork that was only available once a month in the cafeteria. She was always reluctant to eat it and brought it to Zhang Feng. Li Li also brought her own barbecued eggs. When they saw that Zhang Feng was in relatively good spirits, everyone was happy. Dan Dan remembered that there were spiced, canned anchovies and a bottle of Changbai Mountain wine in the basket. Everyone was eating and talking and Zhang Feng smiled for the first time in weeks.

A few weeks later, Wang Hai and Zhang Lin came together to see Zhang Feng. They already knew about Zhang Feng and Yu Mei. One day, they walked together along the waterfront near the factory. When Zhang Lin went into the woods to pick up mushrooms, Wang Hai said,

"Elder brother, I think you should completely forget Yu Mei. She can only ever be your dream lover. You must be realistic and find a girl who is equal to you. That's the right choice for you."

"Is there a suitable match for me?"

"Yeah, she is just beside you!" Wang Hai replied.

"She is by my side? Are you kidding? You mean Dan Dan?"

"Yes, Dan Dan! She has been in love with you for more than ten years. However, you don't know that so you really are a fool!"

"It's impossible. I have thought of her as my sister from being very young. I also asked her once whether she was in love with somebody and she said that she already had her own sweetheart. She was looking for an opportunity to confess to him. I advised her to be with you and she did not object."

Wang Hai laughed and said,

"You are a fool with a high IQ but why is your EQ so low? She dislikes me because she has you in her heart. I am not as good as you. Well, I do not want to waste time anymore. I will tell you two secrets. After that, you will see things more clearly."

Then, Wang Hai told Zhang Feng that Dan Dan was Zhang Feng's own age; actually, she was six months younger. Since she had been born with great intelligence, her mother had wanted her to go to school earlier so she had changed Dan Dan's date of birth to make her one year older. A few days ago, Wang Hai had met Dan Dan's mother and she had told him this. She also thought that Zhang Feng already knew this secret because she had written a will for Dan Dan, confessing this secret when she had tried to commit suicide during the Cultural Revolution.

Having heard Wang Hai's words, Zhang Feng suddenly recalled that he had not finished reading the will before it had been grabbed by Dan Dan. She hadn't wanted him to know about this secret.

The second secret shocked Zhang Feng. Wang Hai said that when Zhang Feng had been taken to the execution ground, Dan Dan tried to take her own life because of her love for him. When a mysterious person had saved her, Wang Hai had also arrived. Later, she knew that Zhang Feng had been freed and Yu Mei also did the same thing for him. Therefore, she had asked Wang Hai to keep this secret for her. Since Yu Mei had already married someone else, Wang Hai thought that there was no need to keep this secret. He wanted Zhang Feng to know how much Dan Dan loved him.

Wang Hai was a warm-hearted person. Besides, he was already with Zhang Lin now and he did not need to think about Dan Dan anymore. He wanted to see Zhang Feng and Dan Dan together with each other.

Under Wang Hai's arrangement, Zhang Feng and Dan Dan met at the riverside near the factory on a sunny Sunday. Zhang Feng had arrived first. He sat on a large rock on the riverside and looked at the turbulent river. He had not realized that in the past, Dan Dan was prepared to die for him because she loved him – like a lover, not a sibling. All Dan Dan's hints had been ignored by him. At the thought of this, Zhang Feng felt so sorry for Dan Dan. In fact, Wang Hai had said the right things; Dan Dan was more suitable for him in all aspects, the same social status, family background and hobbies. In the environment at the time, most of the clever, well-learned girls did not look good, while the pretty girls were probably not so good at learning. There were barely any girls like Dan Dan who were intelligent and beautiful. After putting aside their relationship of younger brother and older sister, Zhang Feng suddenly found that there had been a pearl by his side for so many years. However, he had been blind to its light.

While Zhang Feng was still thinking, there was a rustling sound in the bushes behind him. He looked back and saw Dan Dan walking lightly towards him. She wore an azure lapel coat with a white shirt and her pale face was particularly beautiful against the pink wildflowers. Such a scene reminded Zhang Feng of the verse: "A rosy face reflects the peony." Zhang Feng was surprised to find that when he used to regard Dan Dan as his sister, he had seen her beauty but he had never appreciated it. Now, from the perspective of a man looking at a woman, he realized that Dan Dan was also drop-dead gorgeous. She was plumper than Yu Mei and had the grace and beauty of the ancient concubine, Yang Gui Fei. Yu Mei looked more like an ethereal fairy in the sky. Zhang Feng and Dan Dan had grown up together for so many years but it was the first time that Zhang Feng had seen Dan Dan sit beside him shyly. They had talked about a world of things before but they suddenly had nothing to talk about today.

After five minutes, Zhang Feng said,

"Dan Dan... Sister."

Dan Dan suddenly covered her face and cried,

"Don't call me sister!"

She obviously knew that Wang Hai had told Zhang Feng the secret of her birthday.

"For so many years, I was tired of being your sister because

I couldn't spoil things and tell you what was in my heart. Xiao Feng, no…Brother Feng, I will call you Brother Feng from now on. I was so envious when I heard Yu Mei calling you Brother Feng. Brother Feng, I will tell you the secret that has been hidden in my heart for more than ten years. I have been in love with you for all these years. I couldn't tell you the secret of my age so I could only approach you as an older sister. Nevertheless, do you know how painful it has been? Especially when you and Yu Mei were together. I even thought of committing suicide but then I let it go because I knew that if I really loved you, I must take your happiness into consideration. At that time, I thought that I would love no one else for the rest of my life. Even if I could only be your sister, I would be content as long as I could stand by you and you were happy."

After hearing Dan Dan's words, Zhang Feng felt very shocked. He had not expected Dan Dan to make such a big sacrifice for him. He grabbed Dan Dan's shoulder and said affectionately,

"Dan Dan, I am sorry for torturing your heart. Why didn't you tell me earlier that you are the same age as me? If I had known, we would have been together. No, you did nothing wrong. I believed the old saying: 'if a woman is one year older than you, she can never be your wife'. It is an outdated thing. For two people who really love each other, the difference in age should not be a problem at all."

Dan Dan for the first time behaved like a lady. She fell down in his arms with shyness and said pettishly,

"Brother Feng, you should spoil and protect me in the future as I am not the sister who protects you anymore."

Zhang Feng said again and again,

"Right, I will love and protect you my whole life."

Dan Dan closed her eyes happily, her lips twitching slightly as if she was longing for something. Zhang Feng understood. He hugged Dan Dan tightly and bowed his head to kiss her lips which were as smooth and moist as peony petals. She trembled and shed tears of happiness.

While they were intoxicated with their love, this happy scene was watched by two women in the bush. They were Qing Lian and Li Li who were now friends. Qing Lian reflected thoroughly on what she had done during the Cultural Revolution and realized that both parties were victims of this political struggle. She apologized for Xu Jianguo's death so Li Li forgave her. However, Li Li did not understand why Qing Lian, who had also been the head of the rebel faction, did not get anything but Cai Wenge had become a high-ranking official. Qing Lian told her that she had been so stupid that she had only thought of revolution but Cai had speculated and thought about personal gain. He had climbed up the ranks by betraying others. Currently, this kind of person was popular in official circles.

They had wanted to find Zhang Feng to pick wild vegetables with them this morning. However, they had found no sign of him in the dormitory so they had gone to the river to look for him as they knew that Zhang Feng used to doing morning exercises there. However, they did not know that Dan Dan had a date with Zhang Feng today. Therefore, when they saw Zhang Feng and Dan Dan hugging together, they were astounded. They left smartly. Of course, they had different psychological reactions.

Li Li felt a little uncomfortable because when she had first met Zhang Feng with Xu Jianguo, she liked him. After Xu Jianguo's death, she felt disheartened and had no interest in men. However, after meeting Zhang Feng in the factory, she felt the desire for love rekindle in her heart. She thought that she had the same opportunity as Dan Dan and Qing Lian. Qing Lian perceived Li Li's disappointment and told her about Zhang Feng and Yu Mei.

Qing Lian already knew about the marriage of Yu Mei and Cai Wenge, therefore, she had expected Dan Dan to be Zhang Feng's next girlfriend. Qing Lian was even quite happy because she had got one step closer to Zhang Feng. When Yu Mei had been Zhang Feng's girlfriend, Dan Dan was his 'sister' and Qing Lian only a maid. Now, Yu Mei had walked away and Dan Dan was the girlfriend. She could be promoted to his 'sister'.

Qing Lian and Li Li decided to prepare a celebratory meal for them. Li Li thought that it would be nice to treat Zhang Feng as her younger brother. She smiled again and went to prepare dumplings with Qing Lian.

PART IX

Finally the Storm has Passed

CHAPTER I

Dawn on the Horizon

The year of 1976 was the most unusual year in contemporary Chinese history. The Cultural Revolution that had swept China for ten years in total had finally come to an end. People who had struggled to survive in darkness and suffering would finally see the dawn of hope. The destiny of our leading characters would finally embrace a turning point.

One day in May, Zhang Feng and Dan Dan were sitting in the dormitory listening to the broadcast of the Central Radio Station. On hearing the report of Beijing's Tiananmen Square incident, they knitted their brows. On May 4th, tens of thousands of people voluntarily gathered in Tiananmen Square to mourn Premier Zhou who had just passed away in January. They also wanted to demonstrate their discontent with the Cultural Revolution that had caused such social disaster but instead, they were brutally repressed. The Gang of Four had taken this opportunity to go against Deng Xiaoping again. They feared that Deng Xiaoping would expose and condemn the disastrous policies of the Cultural Revolution and would reverse the crimes of the Cultural Revolution.

Zhang Feng said with a heavy heart,

"It looks like the storm will go on but the discontent of the public and rebel forces are becoming stronger and stronger. It is always darkest just before the dawn."

Even with the companionship of Dan Dan and Qing Lian and Li Li's care, Zhang Feng was still depressed. The reason was because Zhang Feng had made many friends during his years living in the factory and one was a university graduate whose family name was Li; Zhang Feng called him 'big brother Li'. The other friend was Master Wen, the model worker in the factory. Master Wen and Zhang Feng were friends from different generations but these two friends had both committed suicide recently.

Big brother Li was a university graduate from Tianjin University and because he was good with words, he was assigned to the Publicity Division and became an effective writer on the revolutionary committee. He knew that Zhang Feng was clever and loved learning so he always encouraged Zhang Feng to self-study. Whenever Zhang Feng had problems while studying advanced mathematics in the factory's spare-time school, he always consulted big brother Li. But just recently, brother Li had been found to have an overseas relation and he hid it from the organization. He was then regarded as politically unreliable from that point on and was given the toughest job of carrying heavy material bags as a punishment. His girlfriend even broke up with him for this. This treatment was too much for him to bear so he drowned himself in the river one quiet night.

Hearing this, Zhang Feng didn't sleep well for many nights. His heart became very heavy and he thought to himself that receiving unfair treatment, just because of one's family and relations, was not what an equal society should be like. He himself had also lost many rights just because of his family background and thinking of this, he could only feel sadness in his heart.

But Master Wen's suicide shocked him even more. Wen was an old worker from a red family and he was the model worker in the factory. He was the man most trusted by the Communist Party. However, for a long time, he had been separated from his family which made him feel depressed. The registered residents' system was very strict during that time, and people could not simply move from city to city which meant that many couples and families had to live in two different places. Sometimes, Wen could only see his family who lived in another city, once a year. He was the model worker and whenever there was a holiday, he was expected to take the lead and stay in position and not go back home. He was a humble man and did not dare to say anything about it, even though he felt reluctant.

For a long time, his pain grew more and more hard to bear, and finally, one night, he chose to kill himself in a public wash room. Wen liked Zhang Feng very much and always asked him to have a drink with him and he also encouraged Zhang Feng never to give up his dream of going to university. Wen's death made Zhang Feng feel even sadder.

When there was no hope for the citizens and the nation, Nature gave some strange signs. According to traditional Chinese astrology, these signs predicted big social changes in China. The first was in the city of Jili in Jili province where Zhang Feng lived. A huge rock that weighed 1770kg, the biggest in history, had fallen from the sky. Zhang Feng and the others were just chatting when they suddenly heard loud thunder booming and even the earth was shaking; everyone thought it was an earthquake. The next day, people learned it was a meteor. Liu Shan, a technician very close to Zhang Feng, secretly said it was a sign, according to superstition, that someone important would pass away. In ancient times, such astronomical phenomena usually happened when the Emperor died.

A short time after, two earthquakes occurred in Yunnan and caused many deaths. The most astounding natural disaster was the Tangshan earthquake in July in which the whole city was razed to the ground. 240,000 people lost their lives and 150,000 people were injured. Huge natural disasters usually spell disaster for people. The three most important national leaders passed away in one year. First was Primer Zhou, then Zhu De, the supreme commander, and the last was Mao Zedong, the great leader who had launched the Cultural Revolution. For educated people like Zhang Feng, who never believed in superstitions, it felt very strange.

Mao Zedong's death was the biggest political shock of all. In the mythmaking movement during the Cultural Revolution, he had become the God of the Chinese. Every word he said was the truth; every word he said was an imperial edict and no one dared doubt it. Now he had passed away and the Cultural Revolution he had launched would be reviewed by history.

During the national mourning, normal people, especially workers, farmers and soldiers, shed sincere tears for him. They hadn't received much education and had no idea what was going on around the world. They did not understand what had gone on behind the struggle for power. But the intellectuals, the politically minded and the elderly, high ranking officials who were struck down, as well as the victims of the Cultural Revolution, all knew that his death meant the era of the personality cult was about to end.

During the Cultural Revolution, even democracy had ceased to exist within the Communist Party. Lin Biao and the Gang of Four could easily have exposed former party leaders and the comrades-in-arms to mortal danger, such as President Liu Shaoqi. But senior officials of the party all kept silent about the crimes of the Cultural Revolution out of fear. But now, people and their families who had suffered during the Cultural Revolution felt that the red storm, which had lasted for ten years, was about to end.

On one afternoon in early October, a string of rapid knocks awoke Zhang Feng as he was sleeping following the night shift. It was Dan Dan who had come in a rush from the county. A few minutes later, Li Li and Qing Lian all arrived, out of breath, and they told Zhang Feng that the Chinese national radio station would broadcast important news to the whole nation shortly.

Li Li whispered,

"Something big has happened in Beijing!"

"Is it good or bad news?" Zhang Feng asked quickly.

"It should be good news," Dan Dan said.

Just then, some good friends of Zhang Feng also arrived to listen to the radio. This was because he had a seven-tube, semiconductor radio so he could listen to the central and local stations and even, the voices of American radio, very clearly. (Zhang Feng often listened to English 900 to learn English, of course, he had to listen in secret or he would have been reported!)

Twenty minutes before the news broadcast began, the radio announcer spoke in an extraordinarily loud, clear and serious voice,

"This is China Central Radio Station! This is China Central Radio Station! Important news for tonight! Please listen with attention! Please listen with attention!"

From his voice, audiences could feel that a major political incident had already taken place. After the music, The East is Red, the news broadcast began. Everyone held their breath and listened to the voice coming from the radio:

"Under the leadership of the party central committee, led by Chairman Hua Guofeng, the conspiracy of the Gang of Four, usurping party and state power, has been smashed…"

Hearing this, Zhang Feng and his friends jumped up and clapped their hands for joy. The Gang of Four included Mao's wife, Jiang Qing, and three other members of the Central Cultural Revolution Group who were mainly responsible for Mao launching the Cultural Revolution. During the Cultural Revolution, they had been very powerful and overrode all the leading sectors of the Communist Party of China. Before Mao passed away, he handed his primary powers to Hua Guofeng who had a relatively neutral stance. This made the Gang of Four unhappy. Hua Guofeng also feared that his power was not stable, so he united a group of senior marshals, particularly Marshal Ye Jianying who still held military power during that period, and some senior cadres who were still in position, and arrested the Gang of Four. They were all dissatisfied with the Cultural Revolution and now Mao was gone, they had nothing to be afraid of. Though no one dared to reverse the doctrine of the Cultural Revolution at that time, it was already clear that they would soon begin to expose and criticize it.

While the whole country rejoiced in parades, people like Zhang Feng, Dan Dan and Zhang Wenbo who were persecuted in the Cultural Revolution, felt extraordinarily excited. This unprecedented havoc would be gone. The destiny of the country and its people would be changed.

In the next few months, until the spring of 1977, almost every day, the political situation changed for the better. The return of Deng Xiaoping to the centre of power for the third time, miraculously inspired those who expected to bring order out of chaos.

Zhang Feng's dormitory had become a 'political salon' for the politically minded to talk about the current situation. They all hoped China would recover from this calamity although Mao still had influence even after he was gone. The mistakes he had made and the wrong things he had said were still regarded as great causes and the truth. Deng Xiaoping had to use flanking tactics, and very cautiously, tried to maintain Mao Zedong's image on the one hand, and tried to clear up the pernicious influence of the Cultural Revolution gradually on the other. In order to theoretically break the political curse of the Cultural Revolution, Deng Xiaoping and his aides launched a big discussion called: 'Practice is the Sole Criterion for testing Truth'; it rocked the whole country. A heated discussion was held between the counter-Cultural Revolution group who supported Deng Xiaoping and the extreme leftists who stuck to the philosophy of Mao.

In the conference hall of the Provincial Revolutionary Committee, Li Jianguo and his former old subordinates who were newly liberated, were talking about the political changes with excitement. Ten days ago, he had been assigned as the deputy director of the Revolutionary Committee of Jili Province by the Central Organization Department which supported Deng Xiaoping. This assignment had greatly enhanced the counter-Cultural Revolution force in the Revolutionary Committee. At the thought of facing Du Zhongqing, the special commissioner who had struck him down during the Cultural Revolution, and Cai Wenge who made him sick, the flame of anger and hatred grew in his heart.

Last year, after Yu Mei and Cai Wenge's marriage, Yu Mei had hidden from Cai and refused to live with him. At first, Cai went to Yu Mei's house to persuade her to change her mind but after the events of Tiananmen Square, Deng Xiaoping was thrown out of office and a group of old officials, including Li Jianguo, were dismissed again.

After that, Cai stopped coming to look for Yu Mei. Yu Mei told her parents how Cai had tried to alienate her from Zhang Feng and her parents became very angry and regretted letting her marry Cai. But just at that time, Yu Mei found she was pregnant which put them in a dilemma. Then, Cai Wenge's secretary sent over the divorce agreement. Song Lihua was very worried and she invited Cai over to talk. Cai was quite different this time to the person he was in the past and he looked very cold. When Song Lihua told Cai that Yu Mei was pregnant and that this child could not be born without a father, he replied with contempt,

"Who knows whose this bastard is. She fornicated with Zhang Feng behind my back long ago."

"Yu Mei isn't like that!" Song Lihua said.

Just then, Li Jianguo walked into the living room.

"You try to dump my daughter because you know that now I have no power, right? Cai, you used tricks to marry Yu Mei and now you try to claim ties of kinship with a new big wig. You have planned all this already, haven't you? I heard that you seduced the special commissioner's daughter after you dumped Yu Mei and you will marry her, that's your plan, right?"

Cai was speechless at Li Jianguo's words and explained hesitantly,

"It's your daughter who cheated on me. I have to divorce her."

Hearing this, Li Jianguo's anger grew beyond his endurance. He pointed at the door.

"Get out! You are a double degenerate in politics and morality!"

Cai Wenge fled away in dejection.

After he had left, Yu Mei said that she would rather raise the child alone than live with that bastard Cai and she resolutely signed the divorce agreement.

As Li Jianguo recalled this, the door of the meeting room opened and a familiar figure who had often appeared in Li Jianguo's nightmares walked in, all dressed in black and wearing a very low hat. This was Du Zhongqing, former special commissioner of the central Cultural Revolution group, the current deputy director of the Provincial Cultural Committee. He was the greatest evildoer who had brought the storm of the Cultural Revolution to Jili Province for ten years and ruined their society. Behind him, following closely, were his helpers and among them, Cai Wenge stood, proud as a peacock.

Du Zhongqing, Cai Wenge and the others were sitting on the other side of the long meeting table. The former old officials from before the Cultural Revolution, headed by Li Jianguo, were sitting on one side. They were going to restore order to society and return it to the simple and peaceful life of the 1950s once again. On the other side of the table were the extreme leftists of the Cultural Revolution, headed by Du Zhongqing. They still wanted to stick to Mao's doctrine of creating groundless struggles between the proletariat and capitalism, restraining people's creativity and turning the whole country into a society of slavery with political oppression and economic depression.

The meeting room was filled with the smell of gun powder. Both sides were silent, looking at each other sternly. They all wanted to intimidate the other side but, at last, it was the chairperson of the meeting, the secretary general of the Provincial Revolutionary Committee who broke the silence. He represented the middle ground and offended no one.

"Relax everyone. Today, we'll talk about the standard of truth and everyone can express their opinions."

Du Zhongqing stood up after looking at Li Jianguo coldly and said,

"I think someone sitting here has been expecting this day for a long time. They think it's time for change and will try to use the theory of 'Practice is the Sole Criterion for testing Truth' to overthrow Mao Zedong Thought, and then to review the case for the Cultural Revolution. But they are wrong. President Hua Guofeng has clearly stated that we should firmly stick to all decisions made by Chairman Mao and follow, unswervingly, all his instructions. That means, Mao Zedong Thought is the only truth. Do we need anything more than that? Anyone who tries to use other rubbish to replace Mao Zedong Thought has evil intentions."

Finishing these words, he sat down with pride. Li Jianguo was just about to refute this but Director Liu, sitting next to him, who had just been liberated, stood up with agitation, and said to Du Zhongqing,

"Some people just want to carry out counter-revolutionary activities in the name of the revolution. The purpose of the revolution is to create an equal society with happiness, instead of a society filled with poverty, discrimination and oppression.

That's why we need to test our policies with practice, to see if they were right or wrong, or if they need to be modified. Deng Xiaoping once said, Mao Zedong Thought was an ideology instead of individual words. He said, to seek truth from facts was the essence of Mao Zedong Thought."

Before he had finished speaking, Cai Wenge stood up and scolded Director Liu severely, saying that he meant to cut down the 'flag' of Mao Zedong Thought. Obviously, he just wanted to make himself look like he was sticking to his stance at this critical time. He thought Mao's prestige still enjoyed boundless power and the pro-Culture Revolution Group would prevail. Thus, the two parties started to debate heatedly.

Just then, loud noises came from outside and Director Liu stood up and looked out of the window. He saw many policemen gathering in the yard outside and felt that something bad was going to happen. Could it be a sudden attack started by Du Zhongqing? He walked to Li Jianguo and whispered to him. Li Jianguo spoke quietly,

"Stay calm, we've been struck down twice already, we won't be afraid the third time."

Suddenly, Du Zhongqing stood up, pounded the desk very hard and pointed at Li Jianguo.

"Enough! Anyone who tries to pull down the 'flag' of Mao Zedong Thought and reviews the case of the Cultural Revolution is counter-revolutionary. I arrest you in the name of the Provincial Revolutionary Committee!"

As he finished, he shouted to the door,

"Come in, please!"

The door of the meeting room opened and Director Fan from the Revolutionary Committee of the Provincial Police Security Bureau, rushed in with a group of fully armed policemen. He was the running dog for Du Zhongqing and the ringleader who had tried to put Zhang Feng to death. He was later removed from position by Zhao Wu but was then restored with the help of Du Zhongqing.

Fan commanded the armed police to besiege the meeting room, with muzzles pointing directly at Li Jianguo and the other old officials.

Li Jianguo stood up calmly and said,

"What is this? You privately deploy armed police behind the back of the Party Central Committee and start a coup with the remnants of the Gang of Four?"

Du Zhongqing also stood up and said,

"Anyone who opposes Chairman Mao is our enemy! We will defend Chairman Mao's revolutionary line to the death. Take them away!"

"Listen clearly! The world does not belong to your Gang of Four remnants. Vice Chairman Deng and Marshal Ye are already in command of military power and are in control of the situation. You are just kicking against the pricks and putting up your deathbed struggle," Li Jianguo shouted to Du and his accomplice.

Then they heard the roar of the traffic and noise coming from the yard. Du Zhongqing and Director Fan were struck dumb. A few minutes later, a group of fully armed soldiers of the People's Liberation Army burst into the meeting room and disarmed all the police. A resonant voice came from the corridor with which Li Jianguo was very familiar,

"Old Li, I startled you!"

A stalwart army officer walked towards Li Jianguo. It was Zhao Wu who was now deputy commander of some major military commands.

"Old Zhao!"

Li Jianguo gave his old comrade in arms a big hug. In fact, the Central Government and Military Commission had already learned that the remnants of the Gang of Four were trying to hold armed rebellions everywhere in their last desperate struggles. Last night, as soon as Zhao Wu received Marshal Ye's order, he took his reinforced regiment and rushed there overnight, arriving just before Du Zhongqing caught these old officials.

The rebellion of Du Zhongqing and the others was brought to an end and Li Jianguo and the old officials were saved. The vice minister of the Central Organization Department, who arrived with Zhao Wu, announced the dismissal of all inner party duties of Du Zhongqing and the other remnants of the Gang of Four on the spot. They would be arrested and brought to justice or be isolated for censorship. He also announced the appointment of Li Jianguo as the Director of Jili Provincial Revolutionary Committee and Political Commissar of the Provincial Military Command to take charge of the daily work in the Party, Government and Army. Du Zhongqing, Cai Wenge and the others were taken away, hanging their heads in dejection. The old officials clapped their hands together warmly and firmly supported the Party Central Committee's decisions.

Li Jianguo tapped Zhao Wu's shoulder and said,

"Ten years this storm has lasted… the world is finally at peace."

"Yeah, all is at peace," Zhao Wu said with emotion.

CHAPTER II

Walking Out of the Underclass

The rebellion launched by the extreme leftists of the Cultural Revolutionary Group in Jili Province was put down and news that Li Jianguo and other officials had been returned to power soon spread across the whole of China. Some technicians and engineers who were close to Zhang Feng, gathered together in the workshop and excitedly talked about the developing situation.

Liu Shan said,

"The extreme leftists were cleared which means that what they claimed happened during the Cultural Revolution will all be stopped. Politics, economy, culture and education will all return to normal. We intellectuals will be valued again and will no longer be labelled as 'Stinking Number Nine.'" (Intellectuals were 'No 9' on the list of the people's enemies during the Cultural Revolution).

Just then, Chen Hao, director of the workshop, walked by and jokingly said,

"I know you intellectuals will be liberated soon but remember, don't get too excited and be careful not to be caught as rightists again."

Everyone laughed. Chen Hao had been very unhappy that the factory had to focus on class struggles instead of production during the Cultural Revolution and that bonuses for the workers had been cancelled so he was happy that the Gang of Four was struck down.

"Work hard everyone! If our productivity goes up, everyone will get a bonus!"

During the Cultural Revolution, various incentives for encouraging workers had all been cancelled so there was no productivity at all.

Hearing that Du Zhongqing, Cai Wenge and other remnants of the Gang of Four had been caught, Zhang Feng cheered up and he was no longer troubled by desperation and repression. The storm gradually faded on the horizon. The nation had hope and he had a future. He and Dan Dan took some days off and went back to the provincial capital to see their parents and also to find out more about the current situation.

On the way home, they were very happy to see the changes that had taken place in the city. Everything was lively which was quite different from the lifeless scene during the Cultural Revolution. Long-lost smiles appeared on people's faces again. When they walked past a store, they heard beautiful music called 'Billowing Waves on Honghu Lake' coming from the loudspeaker and both Zhang Feng and Dan Dan's eyes filled with tears as they listened. This widely known song had disappeared from people's lives for ten years because all art work, like novels, operas, movies and music, were prohibited during the Cultural Revolution. They were all criticized as being toxic. Cultural life in the Cultural Revolution was like a desert. People could only watch Jiang Qing's 'Eight Model Plays'.

Walking across to the Xinhua Bookstore, they found people were waiting in a long queue outside so, curious, they went up to the line and asked what books were on sale inside. Two student-type boys said with excitement,

"Come and line up quickly, brother! They are selling world-famous masterpieces and Chinese classics! They were sold out in an hour after the store opened yesterday but they soon purchased a large number of books for today and if you don't line up, you can't buy anything. "

Hearing this, Zhang Feng and Dan Dan soon joined the queue. They noticed that everyone was carrying a bunch of books as they came out of the bookstore. Zhang Feng asked a middle-aged man what books he had bought,

"See! *A Tale of Two Cities*, *'David Copperfield'*, *Shakespeare's Four Great Tragedies*, *'Les Misérables'* and *'Notre Dame de Paris'*. They are selling different books every day! If you want to buy all the world-famous masterpieces, then you have to come here every day!"

Zhang Feng and Dan Dan were very excited. These books had been forbidden during the Cultural Revolution. People could only pass copies around for reading secretly among friends and relatives. They waited in the queue for an hour and bought dozens of world-famous masterpieces which cost Zhang Feng almost one month's salary.

The next afternoon, the family got together happily in Zhang Wenbo's simple, tube-shaped apartment and listened to him analyzing the political situation. Hu Yun was peeling apples and gave them to everyone. She gave the biggest one to Dan Dan. She was extraordinarily happy to know that Dan Dan and Zhang Feng had got together at last because they were the same age so she felt more assured. Zhang Wenbo still believed in the old tradition that a woman who is one year older than the man is not a suitable wife. To Hu Yun, Dan Dan complemented Zhang Feng more than Yu Mei.

Just as everyone was talking about what kind of measures Deng Xiaoping would take to bring order out of chaos, the sound of car horns came from outside. Zhang Feng looked outside and saw a car and a military vehicle parked outside the building. He felt strange. Usually, only teachers who had been transferred from rural areas lived here; no leaders or cadres had ever visited this place so how come high-ranking officials were visiting?

Only five minutes later, someone knocked on the door. When Hu Yun opened the door, she was startled and couldn't help but cry out. Everyone looked to the door and saw Li Jianguo walk in and whilst his face looked withered, he was in high spirits. A stalwart army officer followed him. To everyone's surprise, it was Zhao Wu whom they had not seen for almost ten years.

Zhang Wenbo was overjoyed and he hugged his two old classmates. The three men were all weeping. Another soldier was standing behind Zhao Wu and Zhang Feng recognized him immediately; he was secretary Lin who had saved him from execution. He held Lin's hands firmly and said,

"I am so grateful that you saved me from death that year."

"That's not worth mentioning. It was Commander Zhao who came just in time. And you were also very lucky – only seconds later and you would have gone to see the King of Hell," Lin replied, and everyone laughed.

The room was very crowded so Dan Dan and the others stood up and left the sofa to Li Jianguo, Zhao Wu and Secretary Lin.

"My humble flat has made you feel uncomfortable – please forgive us," Zhang Wenbo jokingly said.

"It is because of the Cultural Revolution that many well-known intellectuals in China, like Wenbo, live in such humble houses," replied Li Jianguo.

Zhang Wenbo answered,

"Compared to the thatched cottages in the country, this is much better. I am really happy for you to be reinstated. I heard you almost got framed by Du Zhongqing."

"Yeah, luckily, Zhao Wu came just in time with his soldiers," Li Jianguo replied.

"It's fortunate that we received the intelligence in time, otherwise Lao Li would have been in trouble," said Zhao Wu.

Li Jianguo then said to Zhang Wenbo,

"I know you are a man of letters and want to stay in your ivory tower. I knew you wouldn't come to see me when I regained my position so I have come to see you with Zhao Wu. The Provincial Government has approved construction funds for your university and not very long from now, you will have your own nice house. But that is not the most important thing."

He lowered his voice and continued,

"The most important thing is about you and Xiao Feng's future. According to the news coming from above, comrade Deng Xiaoping is determined to rehabilitate all those wrongfully convicted in the Cultural Revolution, including President Liu Shaoqi, who was supposed to be the biggest capitalist roader. Our party has realized we were influenced by the extreme leftist line in every political decision and many good people were wrongfully captured. So Wenbo, your rightist problem of 1957 will be rehabilitated very soon."

Hearing these words, Zhang Wenbo grasped Li Jianguo's hands firmly with excitement.

Zhao Wu, who was nearby, said,

"Lao Li has good news for Xiao Feng too!"

Li Jianguo then said,

"Right, Xiao Feng has been oppressed and left at the bottom of society due to his family background. He has not been able to go to university and could only be a worker. Now it's different. According to my comrade-in-arms who is now in the Education Department, Deng Xiaoping has asked for expert opinions in the educational world and has been instructed to reinstate National University Entrance Examinations by the end of this year. Students will be enrolled according to their exam scores instead of their political performances. In this case, good students like Xiao Feng and Dan Dan will be able to go to university through their own abilities and become the much needed talent for the nation."

Zhang Feng jumped up in excitement when he heard this and grasped Li Jianguo's hands, saying,

"That's great Uncle Li! I've been waiting for this day for ten years."

But Li Jianguo suddenly sighed,

"Oh Xiao Feng, you were once my life saver. I thought you could become my son-in-law, Wenbo and I will become relatives by this marriage, but Xiao Mei didn't have this blessing. We should be blamed too. We didn't resist the marriage. We believed that liar Cai Wenge and were fooled by him."

Zhang Feng tapped Li Jianguo's shoulder,

"Don't be so sad Uncle Li, it was Cai Wenge who ruined Yu Mei."

He wanted to ask how Yu Mei was but then he realized Dan Dan was nearby so he stopped.

Hu Yun said,

"I'll cook some dishes, crisp fried pork, braised meat and tossed, clear noodles with sauce and everyone can stay and have some wine. Let's talk about the old days."

"Domestic Northeastern cuisine is great, Secretary Lin and I have a bottle of Mao-tai in my car, let's all get drunk today!" said Zhao Wu.

The humble house was filled with the air of liberation, easiness and joy after ten years' suffering and hardship. In the pleasant aroma of good wine and food, the older generations recalled their friendship and the past, and the younger generations longed for the future.

It was very late when Li Jianguo got home. Yu Mei was waiting for him in the sitting room. She wanted to know Zhang Feng's current situation although she already knew it was impossible to be with him. After hearing Li Jianguo's words, Yu Mei felt both happy and heart broken. She was happy that Zhang Feng could finally get away from the mountains. Yu Mei knew Zhang Feng would be admitted to a good university and become an elite in society but she also felt sad that she had not waited for him. She had not only been dumped by that evil man, but she was also pregnant with his child. Lost and distracted, Yu Mei fell down the stairs and miscarried.

One month after Zhang Feng had returned to the factory, the Education Department officially announced the restoration of University Entrance Examinations to the whole country. Since all the universities in China had been closed ten years ago, this was the first official enrolment and the first exam in ten years to select students by their abilities. Everyone was equal, regardless of family and political background. People like Zhang Feng and Dan Dan, who were children of the Five Black Categories, would have an opportunity to go to university.

The years lost in the Cultural Revolution were considered and they also loosened the restrictions on age so that students like Zhang Feng and Dan Dan, who were senior middle school students before the Cultural Revolution, could be admitted at 30 years of age. Over 5.7 million middle school students over the ten year period would take this exam together. This unprecedented phenomenon was caused by the terrible Cultural Revolution. However, youths who wanted to change their social status were at least offered a chance. Over one hundred youths in Zhang Feng's factory wanted to try. In fact, only very few of them would pass and be admitted to university but the opportunity was once in a blue moon and everyone wanted to try their luck.

It was said that only five percent of the students could be admitted to university but the opportunity was there for those students who were prepared, like Zhang Feng and Dan Dan, who had continued to self-study, even during the ten year Cultural Revolution.

With only two months before the exam, Zhang Feng and his friends were taking their time to revise. Although they knew they were very likely to be admitted, they didn't dare to underestimate their opponents. Zhang Feng's dormitory had become a place where everyone studied together and discussed questions. If anyone had study materials sent from their relatives or friends, they would share them with each other. Leaders and master workers in the workshop also supported them a great deal and arranged less work for them and gave them more holidays. Former university students also came to share their experiences of the exam. Technician Liu Shan even gave them practice examination questions he had remembered.

Every weekend, Dan Dan would come and study with the others. Qing Lian knew she hadn't read any books during the Cultural Revolution so she was a little discouraged and wanted to give up but Zhang Feng encouraged her. This was the chance that could change one's destiny! At the thought of following Zhang Feng, she was encouraged to study with the others. Zhang Feng also helped her very patiently when she was stuck.

Soon, the application forms were sent to the examinees to fill in and apply for the major university of their choice. Ten years ago, Zhang Feng and Dan Dan had wanted to study science and engineering, but now they were entering their thirties and thought it might not be helpful to choose those subjects again. Many colleagues in Zhang Wenbo's university suggested that Zhang Feng should apply to the Chinese Department at Jili University. At that time, Jili University was ranked third among the national key universities, behind Peking University and Tsinghua University. There would be many different careers to choose from after graduating from the Department of Chinese Language and Literature, such as scholars, professors, news reporters, editors of magazine and working in newspaper offices. It was also possible to become a government official.

After the Cultural Revolution, Zhang Feng felt that both Chinese society and the Chinese people needed to learn a lesson from it. Why could this disaster not have been stopped from happening? Why had this disaster lasted for ten years in total and almost ruined the country and the party? Perhaps studying Chinese literature and culture could help to influence and change society for the better, like the famous Chinese writer Lu Xun, who abandoned medicine for literature many years ago.

Zhang Feng and Dan Dan's parents were aged so studying at a local university also meant that they could take care of their parents.

At last, Zhang Feng decided to apply to study Chinese Language and Literature at Jili University and Dan Dan applied to study Economics there too. She said that the Chinese people were still very poor and she was interested in studying how to develop the economy. Qing Lian knew she had not studied in the past ten years, so she only applied to the local Teachers' College of Jili City.

The end of November 1977 was icy and snowing. Several trucks drove away from the factory taking over a hundred youths to the examination hall in Shi Jing County. Everyone had hopes of moving into higher society but only five or six of them would realize their dreams.

When they arrived at the examination hall organized by the county middle school, their hats and masks were covered with a thick layer of white frost. Dan Dan was waiting with Zhang Feng and the others at the entrance. She poured two cups of hot soybean milk for Zhang Feng and Qing Lian from her thermos bottle to warm them up. She also told them to wear more clothes because she had heard it was very cold inside the examination rooms.

When they entered, there was only one small stove as expected. Their fingers were too cold to move and they could only hold their pens by rubbing their hands. When the bell rang, all the examinees opened their examination papers with trembling hands and jumping hearts. This was the moment that would determine their destinies!

Once admitted to university, it was possible to become a national talent or an elite of society. Not going to university meant staying at the bottom of society forever, as an ordinary worker or farmer. Zhang Feng and Dan Dan were already the best students from the best middle school and they had also continued their self-study during the Cultural Revolution so they were more confident.

Influenced by his father since he was young, Zhang Feng had a very good foundation in literature and wrote beautiful articles so he did very well in the Chinese examination; his composition was smooth and filled with passion. He was also the top student in mathematics, physics and chemistry and probably scored maximum marks in mathematics. He had read a lot of historical and geographical books during the Cultural Revolution so history and geography examinations were not difficult for him either. Only a few questions in the political examination made him feel very dogmatic and his answers may not have been the same as the standard answer.

The three-day examination soon passed and then it was anxious waiting. Everyone guessed that Zhang Feng and Dan Dan would pass the exam. Qing Lian felt she had not performed very well but the Teachers' College usually had a low admission threshold so she would probably pass too. Zhang Feng was a little worried about his political background check because his comments on the Cultural Revolution were still kept on his record although Li Jianguo had once said that this exam was very relaxed about political checks. The Cultural Revolution had not been denied totally at that time and some officers still believed that criticisms of the Cultural Revolution were reactionary. As expected, what he worried about did happen.

A month later, Dan Dan, Qing Lian and the other two received their admission letters and were all admitted by the universities they applied to. Strangely, Zhang Feng hadn't received his admission letter yet and those who envied him started to mock him.

Mao Hongxin, who always enjoyed class struggles, started to yell loudly in the workshop,

"He thought he could easily go to Qing Hua and Peking University. So what? He failed. It's easy to talk big. With his family background of the The Five Black Categories and his previous convictions in the Cultural Revolution, no university dares to admit him. Our universities are going to raise the successors of the proletariat!"

Just then, director Chen of the workshop and Technician Liu Shan walked in and became angry after hearing Mao Hongxin's words.

Liu Shan said,

"Mao, have you got nothing else to do except say bad things about Zhang Feng? How do you know Zhang Feng has failed the exam? The admission letters haven't all arrived yet. Xiao Zhang has always been a good, high school student, if he can't be admitted to university, you think they will let a pig head like you in?"

Chen Hao also gave Mao Hongxin a lesson.

Noticing Zhang Feng was not in a good mood these days, Qing Lian and Li Li came to see him and gave him delicious food. They suggested Zhang Feng's father should go and talk with Li Jianguo and ask for his help. They assumed it must be the political check that had affected his application because Zhang Feng should have had no problem being admitted to university based just on his scores. He said his father never sought advantage through connections so he would follow the will of Heaven.

Li Jianguo had been very excited recently. Under the leadership of Deng Xiaoping, the whole country was rapidly being restored to order and rehabilitating those who had been wrongfully convicted. Social life was also gradually getting back to normal. Party organizations at each level started to recover normal operations. Li Jianguo was re-appointed as the First Secretary of the Provincial Committee. Although he was already 60 years old, he felt rejuvenated.

Every day, he was busy guiding staff members of the Provincial Committee in their work. With the lessons of history in mind, he listened to people's ideas and thoughts more carefully and worked on improving people's lives. He told the cadres that they should not treat themselves as special and regard themselves as bureaucrats. But just recently, he had not been feeling good digestively and sometimes, he felt very tired with a vague pain in his lower right belly. Song Lihua told him to see a doctor but he always said he was too busy to see a doctor and put it off.

One morning, he received a phone call from Director Zhang of the Provincial Education Department who said he needed Li Jianguo's advice on some answers he had read in the university entrance examination. The Admissions Office and the people in charge of enrolment of each university would discuss this issue together and he wanted to invite Li Jianguo. When he hung up the phone, he suddenly thought of Zhang Feng and didn't know if he had passed the exam or not.

At 10 o'clock, Li Jianguo showed up on time in the meeting room of the Provincial Education Bureau which was already full of working personnel in charge of university enrolment. The environment was very serious; it seemed like there were divergences on some big issues. First of all, Director Zhang introduced the admission conditions of the universities in Jili Province. He said generally, it had gone well. However, people had different opinions on admitting some students with high scores but with political problems. He took a typical student as an example.

Director Zhang's words soon captured Li Jianguo's attention because that typical student was Zhang Feng. Director Zhang said this examinee, called Zhang Feng, had been a good student in the key Second Senior Middle School and in this exam, he ranked first in the liberal arts. It stood to reason that he should be given priority for admission. Not only Jili University, where he applied, wanted him, but also Peking University and Renmin University of China where he didn't apply; they wanted to admit him too. He was found to have a bad family background during the political review: his grandpa was a landlord and his father was a famous rightist in the Province but they had loosened the restrictions on family background plus, he performed well both in rural areas and in the factory so the family background was not a big problem.

The thing was, he had a serious problem during the Cultural Revolution. He used to relate to an anti-revolutionary group and almost suffered the death penalty because of this. He had also made reactionary comments about the Cultural Revolution.

After hearing Director Zhang's words, Li Jianguo thought to himself that it was lucky he had come otherwise, Zhang Feng might not be admitted but he didn't rush to express his opinions; he wanted to listen to other people's opinions first.

Most of the people there wanted to admit him because they believed it was not easy to find such talents but others in the Provincial Education Bureau insisted that they needed to be strict on political problems. Section Chief Shen still insisted that Chairman Mao launched the Cultural Revolution so anyone who opposed the Cultural Revolution also opposed Chairman Mao. As he made his speech, Director Zhang said in low voice to Li Jianguo that this Section Chief was the sworn follower of Cai Wenge and he was now a big leftist.

At last, everyone looked to Li Jianguo and wanted to know how he was going to react. His attitude would determine Zhang Feng's destiny.

He drank some water and said slowly,

"The Gang of Four has brought calamity to the country and the people. Our education has been neglected for ten years. Now we are undergoing full scale reconstruction under the leadership of Deng Xiaoping. The country needs all kinds of talents urgently. We need to use people because of their merits and forget the class struggles of the past. I have heard of Zhang Feng's case in the Cultural Revolution from a colleague in the Public Security System; Zhang Feng was wronged. As to his comments attacking the Cultural Revolution, I think anyone who cares about the situation should know the current trend of the central government. The theory of 'Chairman Mao only' has been put aside. To seek truth from facts and liberate the minds are the mainstream ideas of the present and people with extreme leftist thoughts in their mind really should wake up."

Li Jianguo had clearly indicated his support for Zhang Feng. Everyone applauded warmly. Some who strongly supported Zhang Feng, even shed excited tears.

Section Chief Shen was still not reconciled and he asked with displeasure,

"Do you want to repeat the 17-year bourgeois education line?"

Li Jianguo became angry at his words and pounding the desk said,

"It's not up to you to decide the nature of the line of 17 years. The central committee of CCP will have a conclusion by the end of the year. Anyone who tries to stop the wheel of history will be smashed."

He left the meeting room as he finished these words. Director Zhang gave Section Chief Shen a stare and he left too, leaving the working personnel heatedly scrambling for Zhang Feng's record.

When Li Jianguo returned home, he couldn't help feeling excited and he told his wife what had happened during the day in a low voice. They were all trying to avoid mentioning Zhang Feng in front of Yu Mei but she heard everything. She was happy at first and then felt sad. She was happy that Zhang Feng could finally see some light in the future but sad that she could no longer be with him. She thought Zhang Feng must be very anxious waiting for the admission letter so she made an excuse of going out to the nearby post office and sent Zhang Feng an anonymous telegram.

The next day, Zhang Feng was off duty. Dan Dan had resigned from the shop and was getting ready to go back to the city. She came to see Zhang Feng in the early morning to accompany him because she was worried that he might not be in a good mood but she didn't expect Qing Lian, Li Li and Xiao Sun to be there too! They said there were other students receiving admission letters today but Zhang Feng knew that they were trying to console him and he said nothing and just smiled.

Soon it was time for lunch and the girls tried to cook delicious food for Zhang Feng but he had no appetite. As the girls were wondering how to console Zhang Feng, the noise of a motorbike came from outside. It was the postman with the telegram. A few minutes later, Mr. Liu from the reception office came knocking at the door,

"Xiao Zhang, here's a telegram."

Everyone in the room stood up and thought the news had come. Zhang Feng opened the envelope, took out the telegram and read it. First he looked excited but then he became doubtful.

"Tell us! What is it?"

Everyone was anxious to know. Zhang Feng passed the telegram to Dan Dan and when she had checked that there were no outsiders nearby, she started to read it out loud,

"Don't worry, you have been admitted, the admission letter will soon be sent to you. You're the top scorer among all the candidates in liberal arts. Congratulations to you."

Everyone in the room cheered, Dan Dan hugged Zhang Feng in tears. She then noticed that there were other people nearby and she let go of him shyly,

"I'm too excited."

"What's the big deal?" Li Li said. "This is such good news, I also want to…"

She then looked at Dan Dan, wanting to know if she would be allowed to hug Zhang Feng. Dan Dan nodded her head and smiled.

Li Li held Zhang Feng tightly and said, in tears,

"I'm so very happy for you, my little brother."

Qing Lian also wanted to hug Zhang Feng but she looked at Dan Dan and only shook Zhang Feng's hand. Zhang Feng still felt a little strange about this telegram. He wondered why this person who had sent it didn't leave his or her name. Friends or relatives would definitely do that. If this was from the government, there would also be a name.

Li Li said,

"He/she must be related to a senior official to know such inside information and they must also be closely related to you and don't want you to know them."

Who could it be? Zhang Feng still had no clue. The three girls all thought it might be Yu Mei but they didn't want to remind him about her.

The next morning, Xiao Sun loudly announced in the workshop that Zhang Feng had been admitted by Jili University and that he was also the top scorer in the liberal arts in the province. The workers all cheered and were happy for Zhang Feng and his brighter future.

Only Mao Hongxin doubted the news. He asked Xiao Sun,

"Did he receive the formal admission letter? Otherwise, this grapevine news doesn't count."

Master worker Wang and master worker Jia were angry with Mao Hongxin.

"You are just jealous. Xiao Zhang is very smart and an excellent man. It's not a surprise that he is the top scorer."

Other workers criticized Mao Hongxin too. They said he had no real business every day except for giving other people a hard time. As Mao Hongxin continued to insist that Zhang Feng's telegram was not real, director Chen Hao excitedly walked into the workshop and said loudly to the workers,

"Let me tell you some good news! I have just received a phone call from the factory headquarters who said they had been told our Xiao Zhang has been admitted by Jili University. The admission letter will be sent to him tomorrow. He is the top scorer in the liberal arts of the province."

The entire workshop cheered at his words. They felt that their golden phoenix could finally fly out of the valley! Mao Hongxin was criticized by everyone so he hid in the wash room.

Zhang Feng did receive the admission letter from the Chinese Department of Jili University the next day. His friends helped him pack up happily. Those who had deprecated and bullied Zhang Feng and regarded him as a child of the The Five Black Categories were stunned. They didn't expect that this ugly duckling would suddenly turn into a flying swan.

In his last days at the factory, Zhang Feng busily said all his goodbyes to the workers, engineers, technicians and to the leaders of the workshop and the factory who had treated him well. They arranged a truck to carry Zhang Feng and Qing Lian back to the city and to the university.

One night, Li Li came to Zhang Feng and wanted to have a walk with him. They walked slowly along the banks of a small river behind the dormitory. Li Li encouraged Zhang Feng to study hard at the university and to cherish this hard-earned opportunity. Zhang Feng told her to take good care of herself and find a nice guy to marry.

Li Li sighed and said,

"I'm already over 30 years old – an older, leftover woman, where on earth will I find a good man? Since Jianguo left, I have felt so disheartened. I don't think I will find another man like him, and I don't think I will fall in love with someone again."

She paused for a moment.

"Actually, there was one man who touched me but we cannot be together for various reasons. I am older than him and he has got a girlfriend too."

Zhang Feng replied without thinking too much,

"It is regretful but sister Li, you're a university graduate, you are smart and beautiful. There must be a lot of other guys chasing you."

Li Li didn't reply and they were both silent for a while and soon, they returned to the dormitory. Li Li looked up at Zhang Feng, as if she were trying to remember his face.

Her face turned red in the twilight and she muttered,

"Xiao Feng, after you leave, will you remember me?"

"Of course," Zhang Feng replied without hesitation.

To his surprise, Li Li suddenly grabbed his arm, raised herself on tiptoe and kissed Zhang Feng. She then ran away in tears. Zhang Feng was stunned, and in that moment, he remembered what Li Li had just said: she liked someone who was younger than her and who had a girlfriend already.

'She meant me?' Zhang Feng thought to himself. He then remembered that she used to say he and Xu Jianguo looked like brothers, tall and handsome. 'She must have thought of me like Jianguo. It's really a pity that he died.' Zhang Feng sighed and he sympathized with Li Li very much and understood her pain.

Before he left, he went to visit brother Li and Master Wen's graves. He put some fruit in front of their graves and also poured liquor on their graves and knelt on the ground, sobbing,

"Brother Li, Master Wen, thank you for your encouragement, I did not let you down and finally got admitted to university. Although we can't celebrate it together, I still want to share this good news with you. I miss you and wonder how you have been over there?"

A gentle breeze blew and the woods echoed with Zhang Feng's mournful voice.

On the morning he was ready to leave the factory, Zhang Feng was soundly asleep when Xiao Sun woke him up.

"Brother Zhang, it's time to go."

Zhang Feng opened his eyes; it was already half past six.

"Gosh! I overslept! My luggage hasn't been packed onto the truck yet."

"Don't worry. We have already done that for you."

Qing Lian walked in and urged Zhang Feng to get on the truck quickly because it took over eight hours to drive to the city.

When Zhang Feng walked out of the dormitory, he was surprised by what he saw in front of him. Outside was full of people, standing in the morning mist, to see him off: workshop leaders, master workers, friends among the youth workers, even his female fans. Zhang Feng was speechless but time did not allow him to shake hands with everyone and say goodbye.

He stood on the truck and said to everyone,

"Thank you for coming to see me off and thank you for your help and encouragement for all these years. You have been there for me in my most difficult times in life and if not for you, I would not have held on. I won't let you down. I will study hard and become the country's much needed talent. Someday, I will come back to see you. Please also come to see me too if you have time. Farewell my friends!"

As the truck moved off, Zhang Feng waved to the crowd in tears. He then saw a beautiful shadow behind a big tree. It was the lonely and heartbroken Li Li.

The truck drove through the mountains. Northeast in March was still chilly in early spring. Qing Lian didn't want to sit in the cab with the driver so she sat with Zhang Feng on the truck, side-by-side, near the luggage. She gently took out a blanket and shared it with him. She also kept taking out biscuits and canned meat to give to Zhang Feng. She was very happy to have this eight hour journey alone with Zhang Feng. When Dan Dan was with Zhang Feng, she could only be his servant girl. Zhang Feng was in a good mood today and he talked easily with Qing Lian.

Qing Lian felt courageous and said to him,

" I have a little request, Zhang Feng."

"Why are you so serious? What is it?"

"Can I call you Brother Feng? I know Yu Mei used to call you that and now it's Dan Dan's right. Am I asking too much?"

"Yeah you can. Many friends call me Brother Feng and I'm several months older than you, so I can be your elder brother."

Qing Lian grabbed Zhang Feng's arms with joy and said in a childish way,

"Great! And you can call me Qing Lian. Of course, I will never call you Brother Feng in front of Dan Dan, don't you worry about that."

"Dan Dan is not narrow-minded, it's ok."

Zhang Feng smiled.

He turned his head and looked at Qing Lian and found that she looked very pretty today. She had probably put on some cream to protect her face from the chill. Her face looked white, touched with red, and with her willow-leaf eyebrows, she looked very girlish and pretty. Noticing Zhang Feng was watching her, she was a little shy,

"What are you looking at? I'm not as pretty as Dan Dan."

Because Zhang Feng was in a good mood, he jokingly said,

"And you're not worse than Dan Dan either. I was wondering how come you have changed so much. Before, you were a bustling, ruthless and merciless Red Guard, feared by all. Now suddenly, you have turned into an amiable, gentle, kind-hearted and thoughtful, sweet girl. If my words have offended you, please accept my apologies first."

"You're right," Qing Lian said. "In the past, I was a female tiger like Wang Hai described me. But you have changed me. You saved me when I was most desperate. You made me examine myself and regret the wrongs I had done in the past. Those so called revolutionary activities not only harm society, but also harm us. And you have melted the wild ice in my heart and made me regain my kind nature."

Zhang Feng said,

"Yeah, this political storm really made countless people mad and made them lose their kindness."

Because they had woken up early and with the truck jolting along, they soon felt sleepy. Qing Lian leaned on Zhang Feng's shoulder and fell asleep. When the noon sunlight shone on her face, she woke up. She found Zhang Feng was also asleep. She watched his handsome and mature face carefully. She could not help thinking about kissing him as she leaned on his broad and strong shoulder. When she tried to get closer to his face, Zhang Feng woke up and she hurriedly said,

"Just now there was a fly on your face and I drove it away."

"I didn't know I had fallen asleep."

They began to talk about things that had happened during the Cultural Revolution.

Qing Lian hesitated a while and said,

"Brother Feng, I've have two secrets. I don't know if I should tell you. I'm also afraid that you'll misunderstand me and assume that I want you to thank me."

"What is it?" Zhang Feng said, "If you have helped me then I should thank you."

Qing Lian then told the story of the sniper who had tried to shoot Zhang Feng in the department store during the violent civil strife. Qing Lian had nudged the sniper and made him miss his shot.

Zhang Feng was very surprised to hear this and said,

"I remember... I rushed into Jili restaurant to send a message to Wang Hai – his mother was very sick. Sniper shots were constantly coming from the department store. I tried several times to get through and although I got through the last time, a sniper almost shot me in the head. So if not for you, I would be a victim of the violent civil strife already. But how did you know it was me from such a far distance?"

"Cai Wenge was excitedly gesticulating. It seemed like he had found important targets. I looked into the telescope and I saw you. You were in a white t-shirt. You know that all these years he has regarded you as his enemy because he can't compare with you. The Cultural Revolution gave him an opportunity to climb up the social ladder. It also gave him a chance to take revenge on you. He issued the death sentence and let the sniper shoot at you."

"He is an evil villain, cruel and sinister. Now he will pay the price. I heard he will be judged soon," Zhang Feng said angrily.

After a while he calmed down and looked at Qing Lian,

"Then why did you save me? Didn't you hate me at that time?"

"You want me to tell the truth?" Qing Lian flushed.

"Of course."

Qing Lian told him that she'd had a crush on Zhang Feng at that time, like other girls in school, but the love letter she wrote to him had been pasted on the wall and she thought it was Zhang Feng who did it deliberately to humiliate her and so she had started to hate him.

When the Cultural Revolution began, Zhang Feng became one of the Five Black Categories and lost his halo. She felt conflicted. She loved Zhang Feng but also hated him. As a Red Guard, she hated him and regarded him as a class enemy. But being a girl, she still had tender feelings in her heart and she wanted to care for Zhang Feng and didn't want to see him suffer. When she talked about the day she saw Zhang Feng being taken away to the execution ground in a prison van, her heart was bleeding. Then she blamed herself for not sticking to her class stance at the same time. Tears ran down her face as she spoke.

Zhang Feng hurried to console her,

"It's all right, everything has now passed. It seems that I was very lucky to escape death several times. So you're my saviour and I'm also yours. We're even, right?"

Qing Lian smiled through her tears and she punched Zhang Feng's shoulder lightly, in a childish way. Zhang Feng thought, if Wang Hai had been here, he wouldn't believe that this was the crazy Red Guard who used to hit people with a whip who had turned into a shy and lovable little woman…

Qing Lian continued with her story. After that violent civil strife, Zhang Feng was put in prison. Yu Mei later went to see him and when they tried to escape, she had opened the door for them from outside.

Zhang Feng said,

"I remember! A man in black came to rescue me but could not open the door, then the door was opened from outside by a woman. So it was you!"

On this trip to the city, Zhang Feng and Qing Lian became heart-to-heart friends. Of course, Zhang Feng was a moral man so he would never get too close to Qing Lian emotionally. He regarded her more like a little sister.

CHAPTER III

History Has Proved You Are Innocent

As Zhang Feng and Dan Dan walked into Jili University, many new students were taking pictures at the gate. Everyone was overflowing with happiness and the joy of success. Older high school students like Zhang Feng and Dan Dan, who had been delayed for ten years, were very emotional. They were supposed to go to university at eighteen or nineteen but because of the red, political storm, they were going to university almost in their thirties. Luckily, they had caught this 'last bus'.

What's more, they were liberated politically too and became free citizens. They were no longer the discriminated children of the Five Black Categories and they could enjoy the same rights as other people in education, join the Party, join the army, get promotion and even go abroad. The theory of the evil class struggle that tore apart the whole country, society and families during the Cultural

Revolution had been thoroughly buried. Love, friendship and trust started to reunite the scarred country. So, going to university was a turning point for their destinies. It opened the door for them to the upper reaches of society and the country's elite.

Like in his middle school days over a decade ago, Zhang Feng became a star in the university very quickly. He was the main member of the track and field team, the backbone of the University Art Group and he was also chosen as the President of the University Students' Union. With his handsome looks, fine figure and his engaging attitude, he once again became Prince Charming for many girls.

After going through the trials of the political storm, he had become more mature and persistent. He cherished friendship even more and he always politely turned down the girls who came to show their affections. When he went to the library, he always chose a place in the corner to avoid attention but there were still many girls trying to sit beside him. Although they were studying different majors, they always found questions on literature to ask him. When he practiced track and field events in the afternoon, there were always many girls crowding around him. Every time he jumped the bar, girls would cheer for him.

One day, Wang Hai and Li He came to see him. Wang Hai had been transferred to the city and was now working in an automobile factory. He was also studying at the Open University. Li He had graduated from medical college and was now pursuing his graduate study. When they saw Zhang Feng surrounded by a group of girls, they both laughed.

After the training, Wang Hai pulled him away from the crowd and pretending to be very serious, said,

"You just came out of hell and now you are entering heaven! Remember, don't go beyond yourself. Being surrounded by beauties every day will be envied by other people, you know that?"

Zhang Feng said worriedly,

"I am also very troubled. You can't just drive them away or shout at them."

Wang Hai came up with an idea and whispered it to Zhang Feng.

A few days later, those who admired Zhang Feng so much found a beautiful and dignified girl always sitting beside him in the library. They also always ate together in the student canteen. Soon, news of this 'lucky girl' spread among the female students.

"I hear that she is Liu Dan Dan, studying Economics and she is a 'blue-stocking' – the childhood sweetheart and middle school classmate of Zhang Feng. Their experiences of being together would fill a book."

The girls stopped chasing Zhang Feng after that though they still looked at him with affection.

The Teachers' College, where Qing Lian studied, was not far from Jili University. She also studied Chinese so she often came to see Zhang Feng. To avoid displeasing Dan Dan, she would come to visit her first and tell her that she intended to see Zhang Feng and ask him some questions. Zhang Feng had inherited an understanding of ancient Chinese and classical literature from his family so he could explain things more clearly to Qing Lian than her teacher could.

After Qing Lian had returned to the city, she had reflected on the way she had disclosed her parents with 'reactionary words and deeds.' Her parents understood. She also went to apologize to the teachers of the Second Senior Middle School who she used to criticize and torture during the Cultural Revolution. They too forgave her. Free from ideological burdens, she was in good spirits every day, running here and there like a twenty-year old girl but she was already 30 years old.

Her parents were very worried about her and wanted to find a boyfriend for her. Zhang Feng sometimes wanted to introduce a potential boyfriend to her too. Li He was still single so both Zhang Feng and Wang Hai wanted to bring them together but she refused. She still loved Zhang Feng and she couldn't possibly fall in love with any man who was not as good as Zhang Feng.

After all the political troubles, Zhang Feng still remembered Master Hai Jing and his care over the years. Not long after he went to university, he went to visit him in his North Mountain Taoist temple. Zhang Feng was happy to see him looking so well.

Master Hai Jing said,

"It is very fortunate that we, especially you, were not destroyed by everything which has happened."

He seemed to know the political situation very well.

He asked Zhang Feng whether he still remembered Kungfu after all these years and Zhang Feng said he practised whenever he had time. Master Hai Jing was in a very good mood and he practised the Thunderbolt Fist together with Zhang Feng on the backyard lawn for a while. Before Zhang Feng left, Master Hai Jing said,

"I will go back home very soon."

"Where is your home? Are you resuming secular life?" Zhang Feng asked with surprise.

Master Hai Jing smiled and said,

"Don't worry, my home is very close to yours and I can always come to see you."

Zhang Feng left the temple, confused. There is a Chinese saying: 'A teacher for a day, a father for a lifetime' and Zhang Feng really regarded Master Hai Jing as a father. He was afraid that Master Hai Jing would be too far away and that he wouldn't see him again.

People had realized the Cultural Revolution was not a political movement that had brought progress to society, but rather, a calamity that had caused huge damage to Chinese social politics, economy, culture, education and morality. Leaders, headed by Deng Xiaoping, started to clear away the damage caused by the Cultural Revolution in every way. The first step was to bring order out of chaos and rehabilitate those who were persecuted with all kinds of charges, including officials, cadres, intellectuals and common people. Former President Liu Shaoqi and many senior officials who fell with Mao Zedong, and were persecuted to death by the Gang of Four, were also included. Jili University also rehabilitated Zhang Wenbo and others who were known as 'the reactionary academic authorities of the bourgeois.'

To Zhang Feng's surprise, one day, the Secretary General of the Branch asked him to go to his office and declared that his so called 'reactionary speeches' in the Cultural Revolution were invalid. The files added to his record by Cai Wenge were destroyed. The Secretary even praised him for realizing that the Cultural Revolution had been wrong at such a young age. Finally, he encouraged Zhang Feng to join the party and said that the more good people joined the party, the better, and the more promising the party would be.

One day, Zhang Feng was reading in his dormitory when Dan Dan suddenly came in and gave him a newspaper, the 'River City Daily', published that day.

"Look! The people in the case of 'Four Talents of the River City' have been rehabilitated and they were even praised as heroes for fighting against the Gang of Four!"

"Really?"

Zhang Feng stood up and started to read. He trembled with excitement; his eyes filled with tears. He finished reading the report quickly, turned around and held Dan Dan firmly in his arms and said,

"We have waited for this day!" Dan Dan enjoyed being held by her lover but she heard footsteps from the corridor and reminded Zhang Feng,

"Ah, don't let other people see us."

"What's the matter? I am holding my girlfriend," Zhang Feng said.

Then he kissed Dan Dan's face. Dan Dan said nothing and closed her eyes, enjoying this happy moment.

One sunny day, Zhang Feng, Wang Hai and Li He, together with Dan Dan, Qing Lian, second brother Wang Yang and fourth brother Chen Xing of the 'Four Talents', held a memorial ceremony for Liu Tian and Li Yue at their graves. Wang Yang and Chen Xing had just got out of jail recently. Qing Lian had nothing to do with this at first but she wanted to attend any activities organized by Zhang Feng.

As they walked to the woods near the river, they saw that Liu Tian and Li Yue's graves had been restored. They had still been counter-revolutionaries when their parents buried them so their names could only be written on a small headstone. Now they were rehabilitated, people had added a bigger headstone and a line beneath their names: 'You have awakened the nation's conscience with your blood.'

A few minutes later, Liu Tian and Li Yue's relatives, as well as Wang Yang and Chen Xing, arrived. Liu Tian's mother hugged Zhang Feng in tears and Zhang Feng also hugged and shook hands with Wang Yang and Chen Xing. They looked thin but in good spirits. They put some flowers on Liu Tian and Li Yue's grave.

Everyone spoke some words of condolence and remembrance. When it was Zhang Feng's turn to speak, images of Liu Tian and Li Yue falling down in blood came into his mind and he couldn't help crying before their graves. Dan Dan and Qing Lian hurried forward to tap his shoulder and console him. After a while, he stopped crying and said in a hoarse voice,

"Brother Liu, Brother Li, you really died tragically. You were brutally killed when you were in your prime. You cared for the fate of the nation and the people and you went to your deaths like heroes. You used your life to defend against this evil storm bravely and History has proved that you are not only innocent, but also, national heroes. Now you can rest in peace."

His words made everyone shed tears and Liu Tian's mother was so moved that she nearly fainted and Dan Dan and Qing Lian hurried to support her.

After the memorial ceremony, Zhang Feng held Wang Yang and Chen Xing's hands and asked about their situations. Knowing that they were gradually recovering from the torments of the labour camp, he was very happy. The Government had arranged jobs for them according to their former majors and after resting for some days, they would go to work.

Xu Jianguo's grave was not far away so Zhang Feng and his friends decided to hold a memorial ceremony for him too. Earlier, Dan Dan had bought some flowers and because Chen Xing and Xu Jianguo were university classmates, he also came along.

After walking for over ten minutes, they saw a vague, small grave mound deep in the woods. Strangely, they saw a slim woman in black mourning before the grave. When they walked closer, Zhang Feng and his friends were surprised to find that it was Li Li, Xu Jianguo's ex-girlfriend. Seeing Zhang Feng, she wanted to hug him but then she saw Dan Dan was nearby so she only shook hands instead.

She said she had been admitted to the Polytechnic University to do a master degree and that was why she had also come to the city. Zhang Feng wanted to say that she could get together with them sometimes but then he remembered how Li Li had kissed him on the day before he left the factory, so he kept quiet. It was Dan Dan and Qing Lian who finally asked for her contact information.

After mourning Xu Jianguo for a while, Zhang Feng recalled their friendship. Wang Hai and Li He recounted the days when they fought together. Qing Lian surprisingly knelt down before the grave… perhaps she felt she had had something to do with his death. He died in the violent civil strife launched by the Second Headquarters to attack the Commune Faction.

Li Li held her up and said,

"Never mind, we are all victims of this so called revolution. We were fooled and were being used and we became insane. We wasted our youth in vain but at last, we have woken up."

More than ten days later, beautiful music was coming from the riverside as people walked in the South Bank Park. They saw a tall, young man playing the violin in front of a grave and beside him, was a middle aged woman. It was Zhang Feng playing Teacher Sun's favourite violin piece from when he was alive. The Academy of Arts had just rehabilitated Teacher Sun a few days ago and cleared him of the charges brought during the Cultural Revolution. They even praised him as an outstanding teacher. Zhang Feng was both happy and sad to hear this news so he played the violin in front of his grave as a way to remember him and to give him this message through the beautiful melody which also consoled his anxious soul. His former vocal music teacher, Ms. Ye, also came along. Teacher Ye was already over forty years old and she was still single. She still couldn't forget Teacher Sun after all these years.

Zhang Feng did not forget to visit the old principal who had suffered with him during the cultural revolution. One day, he travelled to the Second Senior Middle School during the lunch break. The corridor leading to the office of the principal was very quiet and Zhang Feng walked up to the door quietly. Gently pushing it open, Zhang Feng saw the old principal sitting in the chair, having a nap, with his eyes closed. Seeing his grey hair fully covering his head, Zhang Feng felt very sad. While hesitating about whether he should go in or not, he heard the old principal say,

"Xiao Feng! Please come in!"

Zhang Feng walked into the room and asked,

"How did you know I was coming?"

"As a teacher, student and inmate, the sound of your steps are very familiar to me."

He stood up from the chair and embraced Zhang Feng warmly, tears flowing from his aged eyes. With tears in his own eyes, Zhang Feng knew that the old principal was remembering the common ordeal and suffering they had shared during the Cultural Revolution.

Zhang Feng tried to comfort the old principal and said,

"It is all over. We have survived."

After they had both sat down, the principal told Zhang Feng that although he would retire in a few years' time, he was still working very hard. He wanted to put everything in the school back to normal. Zhang Feng tried to persuade him to think about his health but he said,

"I have to make up for wasted time. The Cultural Revolution has totally destroyed our education system. The future of our country depends on our educated young people so I must work even harder to train our youngsters."

Suddenly, there was a knock at the door and a cleaner came in and asked the principal whether his office needed cleaning. Strangely, he looked very fearful when he saw Zhang Feng was there. Zhang Feng had also recognized this person; it was the previous teaching director who had persecuted him and the principal so severely during the Cultural Revolution. He quickly ran away after seeing Zhang Feng begin to stand up.

"People say 'good will be rewarded with good, and evil with evil'. He has been removed from his post and has undergone labour reform to atone for his crime," explained the principal.

"He was so aggressive during the political storm. Our society nearly became totally chaotic and innocent people suffered because of evil people like him," Zhang Feng replied.

Before Zhang Feng left, the old principal invited him to dinner at the weekend and asked him to bring Dan Dan. Zhang Feng accepted the invitation happily.

Zhang Wenbo felt restless these days. Though he was no longer called the 'reactionary academic' and the authorities and the university had also agreed that he could return to work in the Institute of Literature, he still had a problem with his rightist identity. Professors of the university were discussing this privately. Injustices were being rehabilitated but the Anti-Rightist movement started before the Cultural Revolution which was in 1957.

At that time, Mao Zedong and the Communist Party wanted everyone to make suggestions to the party and the government. They didn't expect leaders of the Communist Party to become anxious when they heard some strong opinions so they launched a political movement and labelled over 500,000 people who had made suggestions as 'Rightist'. Most of them were intellectuals. As a result, many people, like Zhang Wenbo, were degraded or dismissed. Many young rightists were sent to the labour camps in the Great Northern Wilderness and, like Dan Dan's father, a lot of people died there. The rightists' families were affected too, like Zhang Feng, who became a child of the Five Black Categories.

Zhang Wenbo told his friends that Li Jianguo had once said that some top leaders in the party had already suggested rehabilitating the rightists but he assumed there would still be resistance because it would affect the Communist Party's prestige and image. Zhang Wenbo said that the Communist Party could actually win more support if they rehabilitated the rightists. People would think that the party was daring to acknowledge and correct its own mistakes and would be trusted and supported even more.

The situation developed even faster than Zhang Wenbo had expected. The Central Government soon released notification of rehabilitating over 500,000 rightists. Zhang Wenbo and his rightist friends were very excited and the children of the rightists were elated too. They knew it meant another political barrier would be removed from the path to their future.

A week later, the meeting room of Jili University was full of people. This was a general meeting for rehabilitating over two hundred teachers and students labelled as rightists that year. Over 20 primary 'major rightists' of the university were invited. Zhang Wenbo and other rightist professors were invited to sit in the front rows and the rest were seated in their own departments. Dan Dan's father would have been in the department section since he was a teaching assistant at that time. Leaders of the university and principals of the Organization Department of the Provincial Committee were all seated at the front.

When the meeting began, the minister of the Provincial Committee read out the decision of the Central Committee and rehabilitated over 200 Rightists' reputations and reinstated their positions. He expressed apologies for their suffering. The meeting room was filled with applause but there were also people who didn't applaud and perhaps they thought one apology wasn't enough to make up for the suffering they had received over 20 years. When the meeting was half way through, a secretary brought an official into the meeting room. Zhang Wenbo looked up – it was Li Jianguo. The minister of the Organization Department stood up and said,

"Secretary Li, why have you come here when you are ill?" Li Jianguo did not look well.

"I must attend this meeting. My secretary concealed it from me so I only just found out it was being held today. That is why I am late. I'm sorry."

After these words, he waved to Zhang Wenbo and sat down.

Before the meeting was closed, Li Jianguo stood up and wanted to share some words with everyone. He said, over 20 years ago when he was a minister of the Propaganda Department of the Provincial Committee, he participated in the Anti-Rightist movement himself. Affected by Leftist thought inside the Party, he wrongly regarded comrades and friends who had sincerely made suggestions to the Party, as enemies and caused them huge damage and psychological trauma. He felt deeply sorry for them. He bowed to Zhang Wenbo and others. The meeting room again filled with warm applause.

At last, Li Jianguo said,

"We need to keep in mind these historical lessons and stop the class struggles of the extreme Leftists. We need to carry forward democracy, inside and outside the party, listen to people's voices and stop personality cults. Our party, our nation would then have hope."

People again applauded warmly at his words as he left to attend other meetings.

Zhang Feng and Dan Dan were at home when Zhang Wenbo returned home so he told them about the meeting that day. Zhang Feng and Dan Dan were happy that his rightist problem was resolved which meant Zhang Feng could now join the party and even enter into political circles but when Zhang Wenbo saw Dan Dan, a shadow crossed his face.

"It's really a pity that your father can't see this day."

Dan Dan replied,

"It's true. My mother is so sad these days. The Chinese Department of the Normal University invited her to attend the rehabilitation meeting tomorrow but she didn't dare… she is afraid that she will find it too much."

"Why not attend?" Zhang Feng said. "Now the justice of history has finally arrived, let's go with her."

The next day, in the meeting room of the Chinese Department of Normal University, many people who had been downed as rightists had come. When Wang Hui, Dan Dan and Zhang Feng came in, colleagues of Dan Dan's father all stood up and greeted them. Wang Hui took out a black and white picture from her handbag and put it on the desk.

She said, with tears in her eyes,

"Oh, Zhong Guo, you see, you have finally been rehabilitated."

Zhang Feng looked at the picture and saw a young man, aged around 30, with bright, piercing eyes. He felt as if he had seen him somewhere before. 'This is impossible,' he thought to himself.

When he was little, Dan Dan's father had been sent to the labour camp but he felt he had seen this man just recently. Zhang Feng was trying hard to recall where when the General Branch Secretary of the Department suggested they should hold a minute's silence for comrade Liu Zhongguo.

As everybody got ready to stand up, the door suddenly opened and a low voice said,

"There is no need, he is here."

People turned around and saw a man of around 50 in black. Zhang Feng remembered the man in black who had saved him several times. His figure, motion and voice were very familiar. He then looked carefully at his face. Gosh! He was his Kungfu Master, Hai Jing! He had shaved off his long beard and looked very different.

His appearance caused panic. Wang Hui went up close to him and touched his hand and arm; she wanted to see whether he was a human or a ghost. Then she felt his body temperature and was assured he was human because a ghost isn't warm to the touch. Several old colleagues recognized his face too and exclaimed,

"It's him! Yeah right! He has grown old but it is still him."

Wang Hui held him and cried,

"You're alive, Zhong Guo! Where have you been all these years? Why didn't you come home and see us earlier? You have suffered a lot, haven't you?"

"You have suffered a lot too," Liu Zhongguo said in tears.

Zhang Feng was eager to ask more but he said with a smile,

"I'll explain to you when we go home. We have plenty of time to talk."

Then he said to everyone,

"I know you may have a lot of questions. Let me explain simply. When I was in the labour camp, I couldn't bear the torture so I escaped in the middle of the night with two other friends but later, we got separated. I came to a fellow villager's home. They were kind hearted and helped me bind up my wounds and gave me food. They feared the labour camp would send people to search for me so they sent me to a temple, deep in the mountains where I became a Taoist priest. They even taught me Kungfu. Six years later, because I missed my family, I returned to Jili City secretly and became a Taoist priest in the North Mountain Taoist temple. I kept my hair long to avoid being recognized. I was an escaped prisoner so I couldn't involve my family and I could only take care of them in a secret way. Until today, I was a ghost. I have dared to walk out of the darkness and live under the sunlight again."

As he finished, people applauded warmly. His colleagues hugged him, one by one.

The Department leader said,

"Zhong Guo, you are still dead on your cancelled residential registration but don't worry, we will recover your residential registration tomorrow and in a week's time, you can come back to work. You don't need to go back to your Taoist temple and be a priest again."

People laughed at his words. Tears filled Dan Dan's eyes. She grabbed Liu Zhongguo's arm and said,

"Let's go home, father. We are together at last."

Zhang Feng also came up and said,

"Master, oh no, Uncle! Your experiences could fill a book!"

Liu Zhongguo tapped his shoulder and said,

"I didn't lie to you, right? I did leave the temple but I will be very close to you. And we will become family soon, right?"

Dan Dan was a little shy, she said,

"We are not there yet, we need to wait."

When they returned home, Zhang Wenbo came over in a hurry. He hugged his former best student, tears flowing from both their aged eyes. When everyone had calmed down, they couldn't wait to hear all the mysterious things which had happened during the Cultural Revolution from Liu Zhongguo, especially Zhang Feng. He wanted to know if Liu Zhongguo was the man in black who had tried to save him several times.

Liu Zhongguo drank some tea and said slowly that after he had secretly stayed in the North Mountain Taoist temple under the identity of Hai Jing, Taoist priest, he would often go out to ask about Dan Dan and her mother's situation. After knowing Zhang Feng, he asked for more news about them when teaching him Kungfu. When the Cultural Revolution began, he worried about Wang Hui and Dan Dan's safety. He always went out to observe and inquire. He was almost recognized by Wang Hui one time. When he felt that Wang Hui may have wanted to commit suicide, he gave Zhang Feng a note and asked him to see them. He also made a phone call to the garage and asked them to send a vehicle so Dan Dan and Wang Hui's lives were saved. During the violent civil strife, it was also he who rescued Zhang Feng from imprisonment.

When the political clearance began, he was even more worried by the Red Terror because there were more people he needed to take care of. First, he stabbed the tyres of the prison van taking Zhang Feng to his execution which gave Secretary Lin time to arrive. Then he thought of Dan Dan and returned to the riverside and saved her from the water. When he saw Wang Hai, he then put Dan Dan on the beach and watched Wang Hai take Dan Dan away.

Everyone listened with amazement.

Zhang Feng said,

"You really were the man in black! You are the saviour of us all. It feels like Captain Nemo who secretly saved five people in trouble on the mysterious island and who always showed up at the most critical times."

Everyone laughed at his words. Zhang Feng remembered one thing and asked Liu Zhongguo,

"Did you get the resurrection herb that saved Yu Mei?"

"Yes. After I heard the news, I hurried to Chang Bai Mountain overnight. I used to live in the mountains for several years after I escaped from the labour camp. I had seen this herb several times but my Taoist priest who taught me Kungfu, wouldn't let me pick it. He told me to pick it only when needed because it is most effective when it's fresh. So I looked for it for a total of two days and nights. Luckily, I found several plants and saved Li Yumei's life."

Zhang Feng suddenly remembered Master Hai Jing's strange actions when Li Jianguo committed suicide. Now he could understand. He remembered Li Jianguo had led the Anti-Rightist movement so he hated him but why had he taken so much effort to find the herb which saved Yu Mei since he knew she was Li Jianguo's daughter?

Zhang Feng asked Liu Zhongguo about it.

"Hatred shouldn't be carried on from generation to generation. It's love that will make our society more harmonious. Taoists cherish life and Yu Mei is a good girl. She is not arrogant like other children of the senior leaders. And what's more, she was your girlfriend. Xiao Feng, do you know that I liked you very much when I taught you Kungfu? After knowing your relationship with Teacher Wenbo and Dan Dan, I treated you as my own son."

Zhang Wenbo said with pleasure,

"It seems that our two families are destined to become relatives as teachers and students."

Hearing this, Dan Dan flushed out of shyness.

Zhang Wenbo said,

"Zhong Guo, how about we start an optional course on Taoist and classical Chinese literature? Do you agree?"

"Sure, sure," Liu Zhongguo said, with a smile.

CHAPTER IV

At the Funeral

In those sunny days after the storm, Zhang Feng, along with his family and friends, absorbed the good news of victims being rehabilitated every day. But what about those bad guys who had added fuel to the fire and who did whatever they wanted in this political storm to destroy society and culture and to injure all the kind-hearted people? Would they be judged by history and the people?

One night, Zhang Feng's family, Dan Dan, Liu Zhongguo and Wang Hui were all crowded in the living room of Zhang Feng's house, watching the ballet: 'Swan Lake' on their newly bought, black and white television.

When the show finished and Dan Dan and her family were about to leave, a picture of the trial hall of the Provincial High Court of Justice appeared on the screen. The chief judge announced that the public trial of Du Zhongqing and other sworn followers of the Gang of Four had begun. They watched as the special commissioner Du Zhongqing and his fellow party members who had dominated the Cultural Revolution in Jili province, were escorted by policemen to the hall. Zhang Feng recognized Director Fan who had wanted to sentence him to death.

Dan Dan cried,

"Look! It's Cai Wenge!"

Cai Wenge was the last one to enter the room and looked crestfallen. His sallow, triangular face looked even paler and he had grown a longer beard.

"Today, you will be judged!" Zhang Feng said with anger and clenched his fists; how he wish to beat him hard! This man, who had profited and benefited during the troubled times of the Red Storm by informing against and injuring other people, had committed numerous, evil deeds in the name of the fake revolution. He used to be jealous of Zhang Feng and wanted to destroy him and his future and he stole his lover.

After enumerating the crimes of Du Zhongqing and his fellow party members, the chief judge announced Du Zhongqing's sentence of fifteen years' imprisonment. He would also be deprived of his political rights for life. Others were sentenced to imprisonments of between ten to fifteen years too. Cai Wenge was sentenced to twelve years. Zhang Feng and Dan Dan's family all applauded.

At the same time, Li Jianguo's family was also watching the television and he and Song Lihua vented their anger after watching his mortal enemy, the special commissioner in black, being sentenced. Seeing Cai Wenge escorted by the policemen, Yu Mei covered her face with her hands. She ran back to her room and started to cry. This evil man had ruined her happiness and her future. She was worried her parents might hear her crying so she buried her head in the quilt. She hated Cai Wenge. She also hated her own foolishness and weakness. Why had she chosen the ugly and obscene Cai Wenge instead of Zhang Feng, who was like a god? Why had she made such a foolish decision?

Song Lihua wanted to go upstairs and console Yu Mei but Li Jianguo said,

"Let her be alone and cry for a while. Such pain is not bearable for anyone."

A few days later, Wang Hai went to Zhang Feng's home and discussed his marriage to Zhang Lin. He tried to present himself as courteous and cultured in front of Zhang Wenbo and Hu Yun because Zhang Lin was a university student of the Engineering Institute while he was only a workshop director. He was also studying at the Open University but it was not the same standard of university so he felt a little inferior.

Zhang Lin complimented Wang Hai's merits in front of her parents; he was sincere and reliable and he cherished friendship and worked hard.

Zhang Wenbo and Hu Yun were not very happy with Wang Hai but their daughter liked him and he was also a loyal friend to Zhang Feng. He had gone through the testing and stormy times of the Cultural Revolution which should prove that he was a loyal and reliable man. Therefore, they could rest assured that their daughter would be happy with him and they agreed to the marriage.

He said to Zhang Feng, as he wiped away his sweat afterwards,

"Ah, finally it's over Elder brother, no! My future brother-in-law! How was I today?"

Zhang Feng smiled,

"You barely passed but I warn you in advance. If you do not treat my sister well from now on, I will serve you with my thunderbolt fist!"

Wang Hai hurriedly replied,

"No! No! I wouldn't dare to do that. My love for her will never be enough. How would I dare to treat her badly?"

He continued,

"Now that Master Hai Jing is going to be your father-in-law, you don't need to go to the mountain to learn Kungfu from him anymore. If time allows, can I learn Kungfu from him too?"

Zhang Feng replied,

"He is very busy making up for the last twenty years he missed with his family and he won't have time to teach you but you are already good enough to learn a little more from me!"

They walked to the street along the campus dependents' area, talking and laughing.

Wang Hai said he was thirsty and wanted to buy an ice-lolly. There was a vendor's stall selling ice-lollies nearby. Zhang Feng said he wanted one too, milk flavoured. The vendor became nervous when he saw Wang Hai walking towards him and even lowered his hat. Wang Hai took out a coin and handed it to the vendor and asked for two milk flavoured ice-lollies. The vendor received the money and opened the box beside him, looking for milk ice-lollies but his hands trembled too much to find one.

Zhang Feng noticed this and said,

"Sir, are you not feeling well?"

The vendor replied in panic,

"No…No…" He wanted to hide but his hat dropped to the ground.

Zhang Feng and Wang Hai both cried,

"Hei Tou! It's you!"

Yes. This man was the hooligan who had bullied them in the past, and also, the ruthless Red Guard who beat and killed people in the Cultural Revolution and violent civil strife. After being in prison and a labour camp for over ten years, he had become blackened and thin. He was no longer strong.

He knelt down to Zhang Feng and Wang Hai quickly and mumbled,

"My two lords, I'm sorry. I have done terrible things to you in the past and I beg your forgiveness. It was not all my fault – it was the revolution! Violent civil strife was instigated by Jiang Qing and Du Zhongqing and I was made to do many things by Cai Wenge but he blamed me for all the bad things. He became an official and I ended up in jail."

At the thought of all the bad deeds he had done in the past, such as beating, smashing and looting, killing Teacher Sun, and at the thought of his evil appearance and the satisfied way he had looked as he sent Zhang Feng to his execution, Zhang Feng really wanted to thump him but he controlled himself.

He said coldly to him,

"Hei Tou, on the day you sent me to be executed, you told me that you would send me to my death, do you remember? You didn't expect that I would still be alive today and able to see you end up like this, did you?"

Hei Tou was terrified and hurriedly bowed his head. He stuttered,

"Lord Zhang, Lord Wang, you are great men with generous hearts. I used to be a fool and I have hurt you; I deserve to go to hell. I haven't slept well for the past ten years and I have nightmares every night. In my dreams, the people I killed all come after me. Now I believe in Buddhism and I have prayed for the people I murdered every day and I beg their forgiveness. I have been kept in prison for over ten years and couldn't find a job when I came out. It's really not so easy to borrow money from relatives and live on selling ice-lollies so I beg your forgiveness. You can have the ice-lollies for free! For free!"

"You don't deserve forgiveness," Wang Hai said, angrily.

Zhang Feng thought. Taoists cherished charity and Buddhists believed in the afterlife and becoming a Buddha. If he could give up evil and return to goodness, perhaps he could be forgiven this time so he said,

"Never do evil things again, run your business and be an honest and a kind man."

"Yes, I will, I will," Hei Tou said hurriedly as he bowed his head.

One day, as Zhang Feng finished his lesson, a student came to deliver him a note. It was a message from his father which said: 'Uncle Li is seriously ill in hospital, let's go to see him in the afternoon.' He remembered Li Jianguo had not been in good health recently and he felt very worried.

In the afternoon, he went to see Li Jianguo with Zhang Wenbo in the ward for high-ranking officials at the Provincial Hospital. When they went in, they saw Zhao Wu was talking with Li Jianguo at his bedside. The three old classmates held hands together. Zhao Wu and Zhang Wenbo asked Li Jianguo to rest properly and regain his health as soon as possible.

The Chinese are not used to telling patients the bad news of having cancer to avoid their anxiety. Zhang Wenbo and Zhao Wu already knew that Li Jianguo had later-stage hepatoma. According to the doctor, long-term mental depression could lead to cancer which is why lots of old officials who were downed in the Cultural Revolution and people who were persecuted in public condemnation conferences, finally died of cancer.

When Zhao Wu and Zhang Wenbo were about to leave, Li Jianguo said,

"Lao Zhao, Wen Bo, I know I don't have much time. Happily, Wen Bo's rightist problem was rehabilitated and Lao Zhao has also been promoted as a Commander in Chief. Now the Cultural Revolution has been thoroughly renounced and our party and our country will have hope again. But I may not be able to see that day… If one day, China becomes a society of democracy and prosperity, don't forget to tell me when you come to tidy up my grave."

Zhang Wenbo and Zhao Wu agreed to do this with tears in their eyes. Zhang Feng stood up and began to say goodbye and leave with his father and Zhao Wu, but Li Jianguo said in a weak voice,

"Xiao Feng, can you stay for a little while? Uncle wants to say something to you."

Li Jianguo asked Zhang Feng to sit by his bedside and held his hands.

"Xiao Feng, you are a good son, honest, smart, kindhearted and politically minded. You have a bright future. Uncle wasn't blessed and can't be your father-in-law but I really regard you as my own son."

"Uncle Li, I also regard you as my father," Zhang Feng replied.

Li Jianguo continued,

"Xiao Feng, I have some advice for your future. I know you will be like your father and become an excellent scholar. But you see, from the lessons of the Cultural Revolution and each political movement, our party and our nation lack elite citizens who are well educated, open-minded and who think of the people first. If talented people like you can enter the political field, our party and our nation will have a future. Think about this, if our young officials are deceitful and self-seeking, like Cai Wenge, will our nation have any chance?"

Zhang Feng thought about this.

"You are right, Uncle Li."

As Zhang Feng was about to say goodbye and finally leave, he asked carefully, "How is Yu Mei?"

Li Jianguo said she had been assigned to the Provincial Education Bureau but she was in low spirits.

"Xiao Feng, I am worried about Yu Mei most of all. Promise you will take care of her for me if possible. You are my foster son now and she is your younger sister. You are a man who values friendship. Could you look after her like a sister without it affecting your relationship with Dan Dan?"

Zhang Feng agreed to his request in tears. As he was about to leave, the door opened and in came Yu Mei. She was wearing a sky blue uniform but still looked delicate and attractive although her face looked worn.

Her face turned pale when she saw Zhang Feng and she said, awkwardly,

"You keep talking."

Then she turned around and went out; the bag of fruit she had brought fell to the ground. Zhang Feng did not know what to do. Li Jianguo gestured to him, indicating that he should go after Yu Mei. Zhang Feng said goodbye to Li Jianguo and hurriedly ran out.

When he got to the corridor, he looked up and down but he couldn't find Yu Mei. He ran downstairs to the first floor but still couldn't find her. At last, he disappointedly left the hospital. Just at the same time, Yu Mei was hiding in the wash room, crying.

Li Jianguo's illness got suddenly worse and he passed away in less than two months. The memorial service was held in the auditorium of the Provincial Committee. Two ministers from the Central Government also attended the funeral along with many old army and official comrades.

That noon, Zhang Wenbo and Zhang Feng wore black clothes with white flowers as they entered the yard of the Provincial Committee. Dan Dan said she would come too but she might be a little late because her lecture that afternoon ended late. They could see many people walking towards the auditorium.

Zhang Feng saw a familiar figure – a tall, young officer. Zhang Feng walked up to him in a hurry and when the officer turned his head, they were both surprised and said simultaneously,

"It's you!"

This young man turned out to be Chang Zheng whom Zhang Feng hadn't seen in years. He was in a smart colonel's uniform. The two former rivals in love were now tapping each other's shoulders with their fists like old friends. Chang Zheng said he was now a regimental commander of a reinforced regiment in the Northeast area. He was married and had two children.

He said to Zhang Feng,

"I heard you are doing quite well and will join the Party soon and will also become the Secretary of the University Youth League Committee. After graduation, you will soon be promoted to a party or government office. The country needs educated young officials like you very urgently."

Zhang Feng said he hadn't decided yet whether he would be a scholar or enter the political field.

Chang Zheng replied,

"Don't think about it too much! After ten years, you will be the Mayor and I will change my job and be your Municipal Committee Secretary, like my father and Uncle Li, two old partners!"

Zhang Feng smiled.

"I have no idea about official circles. How could I be promoted so quickly?"

Because they knew each other through Yu Mei, it was impossible not to talk about her.

Chang Zheng sighed and said,

"It's that damned Cai Wenge who ruined both you and Yu Mei. When I was in the Second Headquarters, I knew he was not a good guy but it was this political storm that separated you after all."

After a while, he continued,

"I went to see her a few days ago. She is really in a pitiful state. You know how in our society, women, once divorced and pregnant, are treated like they are second hand. No man will want to marry her again, even if she is a beauty. I wanted to introduce her to a vice captain whose wife had died but she scolded me and said she never wants to marry again."

Then he sighed. Zhang Feng's heart became heavy after hearing Chang Zheng's words.

The funeral was held at two o'clock in the afternoon. A Chinese Communist Party flag covered Li Jianguo's remains and white flowers surrounded his body. On two sides of the auditorium, there were funeral wreaths and elegiac couplets. On one side of the coffin, Zhang Feng saw Yu Mei and her younger brother standing there, supporting Song Lihua. The representative sent from Central Government highly commended Li Jianguo's life.

He said Li Jianguo had been a loyal Proletarian Revolutionary Fighter, a good officer of the party and a good son of the people. Representatives of the Provincial Committee and Provincial Government also made speeches. Then, with solemn funeral music, the farewell ceremony began.

Starting with the leaders of the Central Government and the Provincial and Municipal Government, everyone went to the front of Li Jianguo's remains and bowed three times, and then went to Song Lihua and the other relatives to condole with them and to share their grief.

Zhang Feng expected to talk to Yu Mei and console her but there were so many people attending the funeral, that when the time came for Zhang Feng and Zhang Wenbo to bid farewell to Li Jianguo, it was already one hour later. Zhang Feng's eyes filled with tears. He bowed three times to Li Jianguo's remains and said in his heart, 'Uncle Li, you can rest in peace. I will keep your request in mind. I will do it.'

As he passed close to Song Lihua, he wondered how he would console Yu Mei but he only saw Song Lihua and Yu Mei's younger brother, Li Xiaogang. After condoling with them, he asked Yu Mei's younger brother in a low voice,

"Xiao Gang, where's your sister?"

"She was here just now and then she said she was not feeling well and wanted to get some fresh air outside."

Zhang Feng understood immediately; Yu Mei was hiding from him again. He could understand. The passing away of her father had already made her sad and if she saw Zhang Feng again, she would only be more uncomfortable. But he had promised Li Jianguo to take care of Yu Mei. He at least needed to console her. At the thought of this, Zhang Feng walked out of the auditorium quickly. He saw a little wood on the right and thought Yu Mei might be hiding in there so he walked over, quietly.

It was high summer and the sunlight shone through the branches and cast mottled shadows on the grass. The sounds of cicadas made people sleepy. Zhang Feng looked around but he couldn't find Yu Mei. Suddenly, he heard someone sobbing from behind a big poplar tree and he hurried over. He saw Yu Mei, sitting there with her back against the tree, crying with her face buried in her hands.

Zhang Feng lowered his voice and said,

"Yu Mei, you need to be strong. Uncle Li has lived a glorious life and he will rest in peace in Heaven."

Yu Mei heard Zhang Feng's footsteps approaching. She kept her face buried in her hands and said heartbrokenly,

"Why are you here? It is making me suffer more."

Zhang Feng said tenderly,

"Don't be so sad, Yu Mei. Though we can't be together, you are still young, your life has just begun. You will find someone who will love and cherish you."

Yu Mei shook her head,

"No. It's too late. My weakness and my shallowness have ruined our ten-year relationship."

Zhang Feng hurried to console her.

"Don't blame yourself too much. This was all caused by that evil Cai Wenge, his dirty tricks and by this evil political storm. If I had not been trapped at the bottom of society after we were sent to the countryside… if my family background hadn't blocked my future… we wouldn't have ended up like this!"

Yu Mei lowered her hands. She looked at Zhang Feng sadly. Tears still remained in her beautiful eyes.

"Brother Feng, I'm about to collapse. Can I rest on your shoulder for a while?"

Zhang Feng was bleeding inside and he folded Yu Mei into his arms without thinking too much. Yu Mei was crying hard in his arms.

Zhang Feng held her tenderly and said,

"It's alright to cry, you will feel better afterwards."

So they hugged each other and it was like they had returned to the old times when they were both passionately in love. How they wished time would stand still in that moment forever!

Holding the girl he loved most, scenes from when they were in love flew into his mind, one after the other: the chance encounter on the bus, the rescue of the damsel from the hooligan's harassment, the pledge of love on the riverside, their break up by force during the Cultural Revolution, the rescue of Yu Mei on Tiananmen Square, his rescue by Yu Mei during the violent civil strife, the visit in the dark prison, the death of love before he was sent to be executed…thinking of all these unforgettable scenes of life and death and love, he suddenly had a great impulse. He didn't care about the fact that Yu Mei had been ruined by an evil man. If he could persuade Dan Dan to give him up, he could be with Yu Mei forever.

He then said, with a trembling voice,

"Yu Mei, would you like to be together again? I haven't got married yet…"

Yu Mei was stunned.

"What are you saying? Can we be with each other again?"

A light of happiness quickly appeared in her eyes but it only lasted a few seconds before she looked sad again. She pushed Zhang Feng away and said resolutely,

"No, you will be sorry for Dan Dan who has also loved you for many years and it will kill her if we get together again. I'm a woman so I know a woman's heart. I am no longer as pure as before. I was fouled by the man you hated most and this will cast a shadow on your heart forever. I'm going to attend the cremation ceremony for my father now. Please leave and never come back for me again."

Then she ran away, rubbing her tears away, leaving Zhang Feng there alone and stunned. This scene and the conversation were accidentally seen and heard by Dan Dan as she arrived late for the funeral but she didn't interrupt them.

That night, Zhang Feng went to see Dan Dan with ambivalence and guilt. In the sitting room, Wang Hui and Liu Zhongguo were watching their newly bought, 14-inch black and white TV.

"Aunt? Master? Oh no! Uncle!"

Liu Zhongguo smiled and said,

"It's alright, you can call me whatever you like but soon, you will call me by a new name."

He meant that if Zhang Feng and Dan Dan married, he would become Zhang Feng's father-in-law so Zhang Feng would call him 'father'.

"Stop teasing him. Dan Dan is in her room, go and see her," Wang Hui said.

Zhang Feng went to Dan Dan's room where she was reading books on western economics. He knew Dan Dan had also gone to Li Jianguo's funeral that day but he was afraid she already knew he had been alone with Yu Mei. He watched Dan Dan's face carefully and didn't find any differences so he felt relieved.

Sitting next to her, he asked carefully,

"You went to the funeral too?"

"Yes."

"Who did you see?"

"Some acquaintances and Uncle Li's family."

Then she looked at Zhang Feng and said,

"It's strange that Yu Mei was late. She only showed up when the funeral was almost finished."

"Maybe she was too heartbroken and went out to get some air."

Dan Dan was a sensible and generous girl and she didn't blame Zhang Feng for talking with Yu Mei directly. She didn't want to embarrass him.

"I really pity Yu Mei. She had an unhappy marriage and she lost her father as well. But when I shook hands with her and started to console her, she didn't forget to wish me well and I felt strange."

Zhang Feng didn't know what to say so he kept silent.

Seeing Zhang Feng didn't want to continue, Dan Dan started to 'attack'.

"Did you see her too?"

"Ah…"

Zhang Feng didn't want to talk much so Dan Dan continued.

"You are still in love with her?"

"I … No…"

Dan Dan suddenly started to speak like the older sister she had been before.

"Xiao Feng, I know you are a man who values feelings and friendship, otherwise, I would not have loved you for so many years. You and Yu Mei have been lovers in life and death for ten years. It's impossible for you to forget her. I can understand it. If you really can't let her go, if you don't mind she has been divorced, I could… let go of you."

The last three words were too softly spoken to be heard. But Zhang Feng heard them clearly.

He held her hands with emotion and said,

"No, no, Dan Dan, I can't let you go. I will be responsible for you for your entire life. I will love you a hundred percent."

Dan Dan changed her tone and she fell into Zhang Feng's arms like a little bird and said childishly,

"Brother Feng, stop it. That's not true. I am satisfied as long as you share half of your love with me and give the other half to her."

Zhang Feng held her closely and kissed her passionately without saying anything. He was no longer feeling ambivalent. He remembered what Yu Mei had told him that day; if a man's beloved woman was sexually abused by another man, especially by his foe, it would cast a shadow on his soul forever. In that era, no man in China could overcome this psychological barrier.

Two months after Li Jianguo's funeral, Yu Mei disappeared. She left a letter for her family saying that she was going to a distant place to mend her broken heart. She asked them not to look for her; she would take care of herself. She said that maybe she would be back after a little while.

Zhang Feng felt guilty after hearing this. Li Jianguo had asked him to look after Yu Mei before he died but he hadn't taken good care of her. He became depressed about this for a long time. Dan Dan tried to cheer him up and Liu Zhongguo tried to practise Kungfu with him every day to help him forget. Qing Lian often came to visit him too and always brought some specialties from her hometown. After a period of time, his father and Liu Zhongguo invited him to do some research for a task and he became even busier in the Students' Union. Gradually, he slowly forgot that Yu Mei had disappeared.

EPILOGUE

In the spring of 1980, the Water City was once again painted green by nature's marvelous brush. In the genial sunshine, the boundless mountains in the distance contrasted with the blue sky. Willows on the riverside were dancing in the warm, spring breeze. The rippling river slowly flowed into the distance and the occasional, gentle ripples told people stories of the past. After being torn by the wind and the rain of the Red Storm, the beautiful Water City regained its peace and harmony.

Zhang Feng had been in a good mood recently. He was doing very well in his studies and he had already published several influential theses in provincial and national academic publications. Some famous universities were eager to offer opportunities for him to go to their graduate schools.

At the same time, the door to an official career opened for him too. First, Li Jianguo had wanted him to become a government official before he passed away. Second, he was influenced by his father's Confucianism, who had cared for the fate of the nation and wanted him to enter politics and change society.

His father said,

"Learning the lessons of the past will change society, with better justice, better democracy, better freedom, better legal systems and better harmony. This new society will be free from social hierarchy and political persecution. This will be a much bigger contribution than publishing several academic books."

Because his father's rightist problem had been thoroughly rehabilitated and with Zhang Feng doing so well in social works, he entered the party very smoothly.

The party secretary of the university also hoped Zhang Feng would be the Secretary of the Youth League Committee after he graduated. This position was usually filled by a preferred candidate for young officer promotion. Just as Chang Zheng told him, it meant that he would enter politics successfully. He and Dan Dan's marriage was settled too and they decided to marry after they both graduated.

On a sunny Sunday, Dan Dan organized a spring outing to North Mountain. It was also a classmates' reunion. Several old classmates from the Second Senior Middle School were also invited. Qing Lian was very happy about this spring outing as she said it was just the right time for picking wild vegetables and they could also dig wild garlic and pick truffles.

After gathering at Zhang Feng's house, they went to the riverside together by bus. Dan Dan proposed going across the river and arriving at North Mountain by ferry boat. Actually, the ferry would be dismantled soon and people would only be able to travel by motor boat. When the bridge was widened, the ferry operation would stop forever. They started off early so there were not many people waiting. The boatman was no longer the old man of the past; he was the son of the former boatman!

Sitting on the ferry boat, they could see the water rippling as it sailed along. They enjoyed the gentle breeze and listened to the rhythm-like sound of rope and tight wire, rubbing together.

Watching the beautiful scenery pass before their eyes, Zhang Feng said,

"Time is passing, like the river."

Everyone felt time flying by as Confucius once said. This Red Storm that had raged for ten years had passed so quickly. But for those who had been persecuted and still suffered, time had passed by so slowly.

"Look! Look!" Wang Hai pointed at a big poplar tree covered in blossom.

"It is still blooming!"

Zhang Feng noticed it was the poplar tree behind which he and Yu Mei had pledged their love for each other. Li He also knew about the story behind this tree. Dan Dan also remembered the time when she was about to jump in the river near this tree and die for Zhang Feng. Everyone seemed to have memories about this tree. It reminded them of their happy or miserable experiences but no one wanted to mention those experiences again. Wang Hai noticed his friends' reactions and he became silent.

When they arrived at the foot of North Mountain, tourists were already gathering at the entrance. Among them, were many middle school students in groups.

As they were about to start climbing the mountain, Wang Hai suddenly said,

"Look over there! Are those people digging the drainage trenches convicts doing labour reform? They are all in labour camp outfits and there is also a correction officer watching them."

"Looks like they have no weekends," said Li He.

Wang Hai had sharp eyes and could always notice something the others missed. As everyone started to move on, Wang Hai pointed at the convicts again and said,

"Look!"

Qing Lian was a little impatient as she was ready to climb the mountain.

"Why are you so interested in those convicts, Wang Hai? Do you want to work in the jail?"

"Hey! What are you talking about? Look! That guy sitting there smoking looks like Cai Wenge!"

Hearing this, they all looked in the direction he pointed and saw a shaven headed convict, sitting on a rock, smoking. The dark yellow, triangular face really looked like Cai Wenge's.

"Let's go and take a look!"

Wang Hai grabbed Zhang Feng and Li He and went up to him. Dan Dan and Qing Lian didn't want to see the man who had made them so unhappy again. Later, Qing Lian remembered how Cai Wenge used to try and seduce her with obscure sexual advances. She was very young then and was also, totally immersed in the revolutionary fever of the Red Guards so she didn't understand what he meant.

As Zhang Feng and his friends went up to him. They saw clearly that it was Cai Wenge; the man who used to arrogantly swagger around. At that moment, he suddenly looked up too and saw them. He looked a little panicked and stood up immediately, as if he wanted to run.

Wang Hai coughed,

"Director Cai! How have you been since the last time we said goodbye?"

Cai thought these three men he had persecuted wanted to get back at him. He pretended to be calm and said,

"What do you want? It's illegal to beat prisoners."

"I didn't think you knew anything about the law," Zhang Feng said.

"You were really lawless when you commited those crimes. All these years you wanted to put me to death, suppressed me and kept me at the bottom of society… and you even took away my girl. Today, you didn't expect to see that I am not only alive, but also, I have been to university and now I have a bright future, did you? But you will stay in the dark jail, with hard labour as your companion, and live the latter half of your life in misery. I wonder, will your demonic soul ever repent with such punishment?"

Cai Wenge was silent for a while and then he sneered, "As if the dead pig fears no boiling water. Life is full of ups and downs. It's only been twelve years, hasn't it? I will be a hero again after I get out of jail."

Just then, a prison officer came up to them. Cai was feeling more courageous as he knew the officer would not allow Zhang Feng and his friends to beat him so he spoke provocatively,

"Yes, you have a bright future. But I have already tasted your beauty and she will be second hand if you take her back. Ha, ha, ha!"

Wang Hai got so angry he tried to thump him with his fist. The prison officer shouted,

"Hey! Stop! You can't hit the prisoner. You and him are enemies, right? The government has already punished him so you can't beat him again. He can't work if he gets hurt."

Then he said to Cai Wenge,

"Get back to work. Why are you always so lazy and always stopping for a smoke?"

He took Cai Wenge back to work.

Seeing Zhang Feng and Wang Hai's faces turn red with anger, Li He tried to persuade them to calm down.

"He is just a loathsome creature. Let's stay away from him. Come on, let's go. Don't let him ruin our good mood."

Dan Dan and Qing Lian saw they were angry and figured that they must have argued with Cai Wenge. They persuaded them to forget about it because the bad guy had received his punishment and he would suffer. Zhang Feng and Wang Hai slowly calmed down.

They walked to the top of the mountain and Dan Dan asked Zhang Feng to take her to the Taoist Temple where her father had lived and where they had practised Kungfu together. Qing Lian said she wanted to come along too. Wang Hai and Li He went to check the stone lion which had been damaged by Hei Tou and Cai Wenge during the Cultural Revolution when Red Guards destroyed the 'Four Olds'.

Over ten minutes later, Zhang Feng returned to the gate of the temple by himself and said that Dan Dan and Qing Lian had found many wild vegetables at the back of the temple and were picking them. Looking at the wall of the temple, Wang Hai seemed to remember something important.

He looked at Zhang Feng and Li He and said secretly,

"Elder brother, oh no! Brother-in-law and Li He, do you remember that we invited a Taoist to tell our fortunes for us when we three came here on a spring outing many years ago?"

Zhang Feng thought for a while.

"Yes but I don't think what he said was quite true at that time and I didn't take it seriously."

"I remember the old Taoist gave brother Feng a picture. It looked like a painting of mountains and water," Li He said.

Wang Hai tapped his head.

"Yeah, I remember that too. Our elder brother didn't want to keep the picture and wanted to throw it away but I thought it was a pity to discard it, so I kept it. And I wanted to see if the fortune telling was true or not in the future. But where did I hide the picture?"

Li He looked around and when he saw the wall he said,

"Right, I remember you hid it in the bricks."

"Yeah, I remember it too! I hid it in the bricks. But I can't remember which brick. I need to find it."

Wang Hai walked to the wall and started to check the bricks, one by one, but he still couldn't find the picture after searching for over ten minutes.

Zhang Feng said,

"Never mind. It's all superstition and it isn't serious."

Wang Hai rubbed his head.

"I remember it's a loose brick which can be taken out. Let me check again."

As Zhang Feng and Li He were leaving to look for Dan Dan and Qing Lian, Wang Hai suddenly exclaimed,

"I've found it!"

He took out a yellowing paper from a crack in a darker brick. Then they walked out of the yard quickly, sat on a step and started to study it.

Wang Hai began to explain.

"You see, this mountain in the middle is Brother Feng, the two lower mountains on either side are your brothers, Li He and me. But this mountain on the right, tilted a little outwards, means it used to turn its back on the main peak. Li

He, this is the record of you betraying Brother Feng before. Do you admit it?"

"Yes, yes, I admit it," Li He said, a little awkwardly.

Zhang Feng looked at something rope-like which was wound around the main peak. He remembered it used to entwine the entire mountain at that time but now, only a little was left round the bottom of the main peak, like a tail. The rest of it had all fallen to the foot of the mountain. He used to think it was a huge vine but Wang Hai said it was a snake.

Zhang Feng thought for a while and said,

"Wang Hai, you are right. This is a terrible, poisonous snake which has threatened me; it's like my enemy. In the past, I thought it was Hei Tou and then I thought it was Chang Zheng. Finally, now I understand."

"It's Cai Wenge!" both Li He and Wang Hai said at the same time.

Wang Hai said,

"It's amazing! Didn't we just see this same snake at the foot of the mountain?"

"Unbelievable! The old Taoist priest was like a god. Let's see if we can find anything else hidden in this picture," Li He said.

Wang Hai replied,

"Keep looking... I remember there were three flowers at the bottom of the picture. Ha, here they are! That year, we said our elder brother had good fortune with women but he didn't admit it. Now you see!"

They all looked at the three flowers carefully.

Wang Hai suddenly exclaimed,

"Ah, this is really amazing! Look! On the left we can see a lotus flower – Qing Lian, the peony – Dan Dan – is in the middle, on the right it is like a winter sweet – Yu Mei – but the winter sweet's colour is a little dark. The brightest is the peony and the lotus flower is the usual colour. Brother Feng, you are a very smart man, I think you see it now, right?"

Seeing Zhang Feng looked amazed, Wang Hai said,

"Our elder brother just joined the party and the communists are atheists so don't make it hard for him… I'll speak for him."

"Go on. Brother Feng can understand even if you don't say anything," Li He said with a smile.

Wang Hai was a man who couldn't keep what he wanted to say inside.

"Elder brother and Yu Mei were life and death lovers for ten years, but in the end, they cannot be together so the winter sweet is dark. His childhood sweetheart, Dan Dan, waited for him over a decade, and at last, the god was touched and let them be together so the peony is a brilliant red. As for Liu Qing Lian, she was a maniacal Red Guard before, but she had a crush on our elder brother early on so their relationship continued. Later, she was saved by him when she decided to commit suicide and after that, she regretted what she had done in the past and regained her kind nature. But looking at this picture, she still has the ambition of winning his heart so you need to be more alert, our rising political star!"

Zhang Feng smiled and thumped Wang Hai's shoulder.

"Wang Hai, it's really a waste of talent if you don't go into storytelling."

"If I can't find a job in the future," Wang Hai said, "I will open a storytelling library."

Zhang Feng continued,

"I am a man who values feelings. Since I am with Dan Dan now, I will be with her forever. I won't have anything to do with Qing Lian. Now, I only regard her as a younger sister. It is also a kind of redemption for her to take care of me so putting her in this picture was a mistake by the old Taoist."

Wang Hai said,

"Don't be so absolute. Dan Dan was you older sister before, you remember? Human relationships change with time."

Li He interrupted quickly.

"Look! There is a number on the picture… what does it mean?"

They looked closely. Li He thought it was the number 13 but Zhang Feng and Wang Hai thought it looked like 15.

Wang Hai was enjoying this. He asked,

"Do you remember what year it was last time we went to see the old Taoist fortuneteller?"

Zhang Feng and Li He thought for a while and said it must have been the year before the Cultural Revolution – 1965.

Wang Hai laughed.

"That's it! We have the answer! This is 1980 and it happens to be 15 years ago!"

Both Zhang Feng and Li He were quite amazed. How did the old Taoist know they would come back to visit the old place 15 years later?

Wang Hai said,

"Let's all believe in Taoism and then learn to tell fortunes for other people! We could make a lot of money doing this!"

Zhang Feng said,

"If you believe in religion, you have to be faithful and forget about utilitarianism. If you believe in religion for the purpose of making money, you will surely tell incorrect fortunes."

He continued,

"There is one thing that the old Taoist didn't get right. If everyone in this picture should be here today, then where is Yu

Mei? No one knows where she went. She must have gone to a place very far away… maybe she went to Chang Bai Mountain."

As the three men were having this heated conversation, Dan Dan and Qing Lian ran over very happily. They held their fully laden bags up and said,

"Look! These wild vegetables are so big and there are fiddleheads too. We can have delicious food tonight."

Wang Hai hid the picture quickly because he believed this was a 'men only' topic.

Dan Dan looked at them and asked,

"How come you three look so strange? I saw you were talking together rather warmly just now but why did you stop when we arrived?"

Wang Hai said,

"It's nothing… we were just talking about how to repair the damage caused by destroying the 'Four Olds'."

Qing Lian said,

"Zhang Feng, you must be very familiar with this temple. Wasn't this Taoist Temple only for Taoist priests? How come Dan Dan and I just saw a Taoist nun? She is very slim and was just watering the vegetable plot in the back yard. When she saw us, she hid herself. Does she regret becoming a nun after seeing us?"

A Taoist nun? Zhang Feng thought this was strange. He had come here many times over the years but never seen a Taoist nun before.

Suddenly, he thought of that picture. Everyone in the picture seemed to be here today. He then stood up quickly. Was it her?

"I may have dropped my library card when I did Kungfu with the Master for the last time. I haven't found it anywhere else so I'm going to try and find it here again."

Then he ran to the back yard quickly. Wang Hai and Dan Dan were taking a rest in front of the temple.

Zhang Feng searched for a long time but he didn't see anyone. He felt strange. If this was not Yu Mei, she wouldn't be hiding. Then he looked over to the far woods on the cliff side... had she hidden in the woods? Zhang Feng was very familiar with the woods. It was the cliff where Li Jianguo had decided to jump off and kill himself.

He walked very quietly and looked for the Taoist nun everywhere. Suddenly, he saw there was someone in Taoist style clothes standing at the end of the woods, near the cliff. 'This is not good,' Zhang Feng thought, 'She may want to commit suicide. A woman who chooses to be a Taoist nun must have a great deal of psychological trauma. No, I am going to save her, whether she is Yu Mei or isn't.'

So Zhang Feng walked stealthily towards her and when he was about ten steps away, he became a hundred percent sure that it was Yu Mei. They were both so familiar with each other that they could even feel each other spiritually. As he was deciding if he needed to get closer or not, a familiar and beautiful voice came to his ear.

"Don't come any closer, or I will jump!"

Obviously, Yu Mei had already recognized him by his footsteps although they had been very light.

"Yu Mei, don't take things too hard," Zhang Feng said, worriedly.

"Didn't my father jump from here? I would be happy to die in such a beautiful place," Yu Mei said.

"But your father survived and he lived on strongly. You need to be strong too."

Yu Mei took a few steps back.

"Don't worry. It's not the end for me yet. I just wanted to ease my broken heart with the beautiful scenery in front of me. When I saw Dan Dan and Qing Lian, I knew you would try to find me so I hid here."

Knowing that Yu Mei wasn't intending to commit suicide, Zhang Feng was relieved and he leaned against a tree and asked her carefully,

"Why did you choose to be a Taoist nun? You are still young and your life has just begun."

Yu Mei sighed,

"My heart is already as cold as ice and I can't even see my future. Life is like a dream. I've seen through everything and I can truly understand how Lin Daiyu in 'Dream in the Red Mansion' felt when she buried those flowers. But I have loved passionately once and I am satisfied. It's this terrible Red Storm which blew us apart every time. You have bravely got through the storm and acquired an education, a career and a lover while I became its victim because of my weakness. Brother Feng, if there is an afterlife, I think I will come to you then."

Zhang Feng heard her sobbing very quietly and just as he was about to say something to make her feel better, Yu Mei stopped crying and said, in a calm voice,

"Don't come here for me again and don't tell anyone that I was here. Otherwise, I really will jump… I'm going to read Scripture now."

"Yu Mei, can you turn around and let me take one last look at you?"

"No," Yu Mei said resolutely. "It's not easy for me to calm down and I don't want to return to all my earthly troubles again. Close your eyes and don't look at me."

Zhang Feng had no choice but to do as she said. He heard light footsteps pass him and when he opened his eyes again, Yu Mei had gone, leaving only the picturesque scenery and the echo of sobbing, like a duet of the sound of waves and the soughing of the wind in the pines. In a trance, 'Moonlight of Spring River' was playing in his heart and he said to himself, 'Our love was like a dream and she can only be my lover in my dreams forever."

When he returned to the temple, Wang Hai hurried up to him and asked quietly,

"Have you found that Taoist nun? Is she Yu Mei?"

Zhang Feng shook his head.

Wang Hai said disappointedly,

"It seems that even the best Taoists can't predict the future a hundred percent accurately."

Zhang Feng thought this was really a miraculous fortune-telling picture. Was it all coincidence? There are indeed many mysterious things in this world that cannot be explained with common sense.

"So how are we going to deal with this picture? Will you keep it or throw it away?" Wang Hai asked.

Zhang Feng thought for a while and said,

"Put it back behind the brick. We will come back one day in the future and see if it can still tell my future then."

Because Wang Hai knew this picture could not be seen by the girls, he walked towards Li He, Dan Dan and Qing Lian and said,

"Li He, I hear you are now the graduate student of the famous Doctor Zhou who saved Yu Mei's life. How about you check the pulses of these two ladies and see if they are healthy?"

"No problem! I'd be happy to do that! Come on! It's free for volunteers!"

As Li He was checking the pulses of the two girls, Wang Hai put the picture back behind the brick.

After Li He had finished checking their pulses, he told Dan Dan and Qing Lian that there were some small problems with their health deliberately. Zhang Feng came over and he asked Dan Dan and Qing Lian if Li He had made a good diagnosis. They said he was very accurate and he deserved to be a graduate student of the Traditional Chinese Medicine Institute.

"I heard that Li He will be promoted to the post of Deputy Director of the Internal Medicine Department after he graduates. If we have anything wrong with us, we can go to see him."

Li He looked at Qing Lian and nodded.

"Sure, no problem."

He had become fond of Qing Lian and even courted her sometimes.

When Zhang Feng returned from the back of the Taoist Temple, Dan Dan had looked over at him from time to time. After discussing the relationship between traditional Chinese medicine and Yin-Yang and the five elements of Taoism, Dan Dan said to Wang Hai,

"There is a small market selling keepsakes of Buddhism and Taoism at the foot of the mountain. Don't you want to buy something for Lin Lin? You can go and have a look first. Brother Feng and I will join you later."

Wang Hai and Li He soon understood what she meant; she just wanted to be alone with Zhang Feng and enjoy their 'two-person world'. Wang Hai dragged Li He down the mountain and Qing Lian followed them.

Noticing that nobody was around, Dan Dan held Zhang Feng's arms and leaned on his shoulder as they walked slowly to the distant pinewoods where they could gaze at the river and distant mountains. They sat on a big rock. Zhang Feng was a little distracted because of Yu Mei but Dan Dan was a smart girl and she already knew what had just happened. But she never doubted Zhang Feng. She looked at him cheekily and asked,

"Don't you want to say something to me?"

Zhang Feng said hesitantly,

"The scenery is so beautiful."

Dan Dan pretended to be unhappy.

"Don't make excuses to me. You saw her."

Zhang Feng was surprised.

"How do you know that?"

Dan Dan smiled.

"It's all written on your face. I could read your face when I was little and I know what you are thinking and what has happened from your face."

Zhang Feng was relieved to know Dan Dan was not really angry.

"You're incredible! I think you should be a psychology professor in the future. Yes, I've just seen her. She has become a Taoist nun but she told me not to tell anyone."

Dan Dan pretended to be angry again and said,

"Not even your most intimate friend?"

Zhang Feng hurriedly explained,

"I promised Li Jianguo. He regarded me as his adopted son and wanted me to take care of Yu Mei like a big brother. Just now, Yu Mei said she has seen through this world and doesn't want to be bothered by earthly troubles so I have to keep the secret for her and help her to be free from the interference of her relatives and friends."

Dan Dan said with a smile,

"Alright, alright. I know you are a good man who values feelings."

After a little while, she added,

"She is really to be pitied. Her father was regarded as the biggest capitalist roader in the Cultural Revolution. When he finally survived it, he passed away. I can really understand the pain of not having a father's love. Although Yu Mei looks fragile, she has a strong heart. You may not see it from her appearance alone. Maybe, it's a good choice for her to be a Taoist nun. The Taoist philosophy of inaction is good for helping people with deep psychological trauma like hers. I believe she will return to society very soon."

Zhang Feng was happy to hear this.

"Is it?" he said. "Then I will be relieved."

Dan Dan asked him pettishly again,

"After you saw her today, will you love me less? Like from fifty percent to thirty percent less?"

Zhang Feng held her closely.

"I still love you a hundred percent. For over ten years, you have always been like an older sister to me. How come I didn't know you could be so childish? Before it's always been you being kind to me but from now on, I am going to be kind to you."

Dan Dan laughed.

"What girl doesn't want to be taken care of by their lover? Before, I was seen as the older sister every day and I got used to looking after my younger brother. I fell into the role too much. Now, I am free from this burden at last. Will you be kind to me and take care of me from now on?"

Zhang Feng stopped her from talking by kissing her passionately.

"No problem, you naughty girl."

They both enjoyed this happy moment of being in love and didn't know how long they had stayed there. A gentle breeze woke them and as Dan Dan sat up, she stared at the beautiful scenery in front of her. She looked like the goddess of wisdom again.

Zhang Feng asked,

"What are you thinking, Dan Dan?"

"I was thinking that this past Red Storm has been like a nightmare. It almost ruined our society and us. We survived with courage, determination and self-reliance. We would all have been defeated if not for kindness, love and friendship."

Zhang Feng also became emotional at this and said,

"Yes, it has been the nightmare of our nation and our people. A dark page in our history."

Dan Dan thought for a while.

"Brother Feng, do you think we will ever return to the simple and peaceful society of the fifties?"

"I've thought about that recently. Now that everything is going back to normal and full-scale reconstruction is under way, the Communist Party has regained people's support. But the lessons of this ten-year period of havoc have made many people with vision inside the party realize the weakness of the soviet-style socialist model. The party lacks democracy and there are also bureaucratic problems. Our centrally planned economy was fossilized and efficiency was low. When we were working in the rural areas, our poverty was caused by a lack of incentive in the production teams where everyone 'eats the same portion from the same big pot'. Everyone got the same, regardless of how much work they did so there was no productivity. When I was in the factory, I also noticed that the factory kept making the same product due to a lack of stimulation in the market and because there was no research and no pressure of making profit, our productivity has lagged far behind Western countries."

Dan Dan asked,

"Does this mean there is no way back for us?"

"Deng Xiaoping is a politician with vision. He has already started to consider a new movement for reform which will thoroughly abandon the wrong practices of class struggle and which will concentrate on economic construction for a strong nation and people's prosperity."

"Looks like you are more and more interested in politics," said Dan Dan.

"Like my father, caring for the fate of the nation is in my blood. If I become a politician, I will be like Fan Zhongyan in the Song Dynasty, and be the first to worry about troubles across the land and the last to enjoy universal happiness. Getting promotion and being rich will not be my ultimate goals."

Dan Dan said jokingly,

"And I don't want to be an official's wife either!"

"If not for this storm, I would have wanted to be a scientist or a scholar but after going through this upheaval, I have realized that in order to avoid such a tragedy from happening again, we must reform all our political systems. We must make sure that we can provide full democracy to our party and the people and be able to supervise and restrict power, prevent personality cults and dictatorships. We need educated and dedicated young people who have revolutionary ideals to take part in this reform. I am willing to be committed to this reform for the sake of tens of thousands of people who were persecuted and killed during the Cultural Revolution. I believe it would be more meaningful to be a politician than a scientist. Li Jianguo also wanted me to enter the political arena before he passed away."

"Alright. Whatever choice you make, I will support you. I will study economics in the future and that will probably be a help to you. Well, I think we have stayed here for too long. Wang Hai and the others must be impatient of waiting for us by now. They probably think that we are too dependent on each other."

Zhang Feng held her hands and stood up.

"Let's take one more look at the beautiful scenery and the magnificent mountains and rivers. Let's complete our studies, gather our strength and experiences and become the elite of society. Let's embrace reform and the wave of time."

Dan Dan looked at him affectionately.

"I will always be there, standing by your side and fighting with you."

The bright sunlight shone on this couple who had gone through the storm together. The ancient Taoist Temple, the surging river and the distant mountains watched them leaving to embrace the fresh air of reform and the surging wave of the future.

Matador

For exclusive discounts on Matador titles,
sign up to our occasional newsletter at
troubador.co.uk/bookshop